The Chrysalis of Oc
Innocent and the Innocents

Their time had come,
when night had passed.
They knew the dawn would be their last.
Yet their faith was strong,
they would not yield.
And with joy in their hearts,
they would burn in the field.
Mother and child, old and young,
They had no fear of what was to come.
For their souls were pure,
they could not burn.
And when the laurel greens again,
they shall return.

PETER V. WRIGHT

Copyright © 2015 Peter V. Wright.

All rights reserved. No part of this book may be reproduced, stored, or transmitted by any means—whether auditory, graphic, mechanical, or electronic—without written permission of both publisher and author, except in the case of brief excerpts used in critical articles and reviews. Unauthorized reproduction of any part of this work is illegal and is punishable by law.

ISBN: 978-1-4834-3775-0 (sc)
ISBN: 978-1-4834-3773-6 (hc)
ISBN: 978-1-4834-3774-3 (e)

Library of Congress Control Number: 2015914500

Because of the dynamic nature of the Internet, any web addresses or links contained in this book may have changed since publication and may no longer be valid. The views expressed in this work are solely those of the author and do not necessarily reflect the views of the publisher, and the publisher hereby disclaims any responsibility for them.

Any people depicted in stock imagery provided by Thinkstock are models, and such images are being used for illustrative purposes only.
Certain stock imagery © Thinkstock.

Lulu Publishing Services rev. date: 09/24/2015

The first crime is when the innocents are slaughtered.
The second is when they are forgotten.

Blessed are the meek
For they shall suffer the persecution of the self-righteous.

Contents

Acknowledgments ix
Preface xi
South Central France xii
A Last Act xiii

Chapter 1	Past and Present 1
Chapter 2	The Long Road North 5
Chapter 3	Unwelcome Guests 11
Chapter 4	The Gathering Storm 19
Chapter 5	An End and a Beginning 30
Chapter 6	A Collision Course 38
Chapter 7	Hide and Seek 47
Chapter 8	A Day to Remember 57
Chapter 9	Flight 72
Chapter 10	Refocus 80
Chapter 11	Pilgrimage to the Sky 92
Chapter 12	The Fortress of France 110
Chapter 13	Settling In 125
Chapter 14	To Catch a Mouse 132
Chapter 15	Sweet Albi 144
Chapter 16	The Black Mountain 160
Chapter 17	Into the Land of the Cathars 171
Chapter 18	To Another World 181
Chapter 19	The Fallen Hero 191
Chapter 20	Rebirth 193
Chapter 21	Metamorphosis 204
Chapter 22	The Tale Begins 215
Chapter 23	The Problem of the Heresy 230
Chapter 24	The Growing Threat of Conflict 241
Chapter 25	A Woman Loved and a Man Despised 256
Chapter 26	Disaccord 269
Chapter 27	The Die Is Cast 279

Chapter 28	Penance and Treachery	294
Chapter 29	The Crusading Horde Assembles	305
Chapter 30	At the Gates of Béziers	315
Chapter 31	In the Name of God	332
Chapter 32	An Ignoble Death	339
Chapter 33	The Blind Will Follow	356
Chapter 34	The Safe Mountain	368
Chapter 35	The Present Intrudes	379
Chapter 36	Aragón and Rome Divide	392
Chapter 37	Chivalry Forgotten	408
Chapter 38	A Tragic Loss	417
Chapter 39	Intolerance Enshrined	431
Chapter 40	An Unwelcome Visit	448
Chapter 41	Uprising	454
Chapter 42	David and Goliath	460
Chapter 43	Blanche de Castile	473
Chapter 44	False Hope	485
Chapter 45	On the Bridge of Avignon	497
Chapter 46	Death of a Nation	514
Chapter 47	Montségur Becomes a Sanctuary	529
Chapter 48	To Rile the Beast	539
Chapter 49	The Vice Tightens	549
Chapter 50	Blessed Are the Meek, for They Will Be Burned	562
Chapter 51	Revelation	589
Chapter 52	A New Resolve	596
Chapter 53	Resurrection	609

Principal towns and fortresses of Occitania	627
Timeline of the Feudal Oligarchy	628
Family Tree – Mirepoix	629
Family Tree – Foix	630
Family Tree – de Montfort	631
Epilogue	633

Acknowledgments

I would like to thank my wife Judith and David Cutler for careful proofreading of the manuscript and encouraging me to complete the work.

I would also like to thank my daughter Erica for her wonderful cover design.

Preface

These pages will take you back in time to events that transpired in contemporary and medieval France. Most of the people whose worlds you will share in this story, and the events that befell them, are as faithful to the historical record as I could make them. I created only the lead character and a few of his contemporaries as literary tools to tie the tale together.

Great injustices can result from error and misunderstanding, or more insidiously by deliberate manipulation of the populace by those in power who fear losing their privilege and wealth. All change, all social upheaval is inevitably viewed as a threat by those who benefit most from the current order. However, it is only through change that human civilization has advanced and improved the lives of most of humanity. When the powerful few succeed in crushing the aspirations for hope and freedom of the many, they draw the very lifeblood from human progress and can set it back centuries.

It is our duty to remember those who strove before us to create a better world and to continue their struggle.

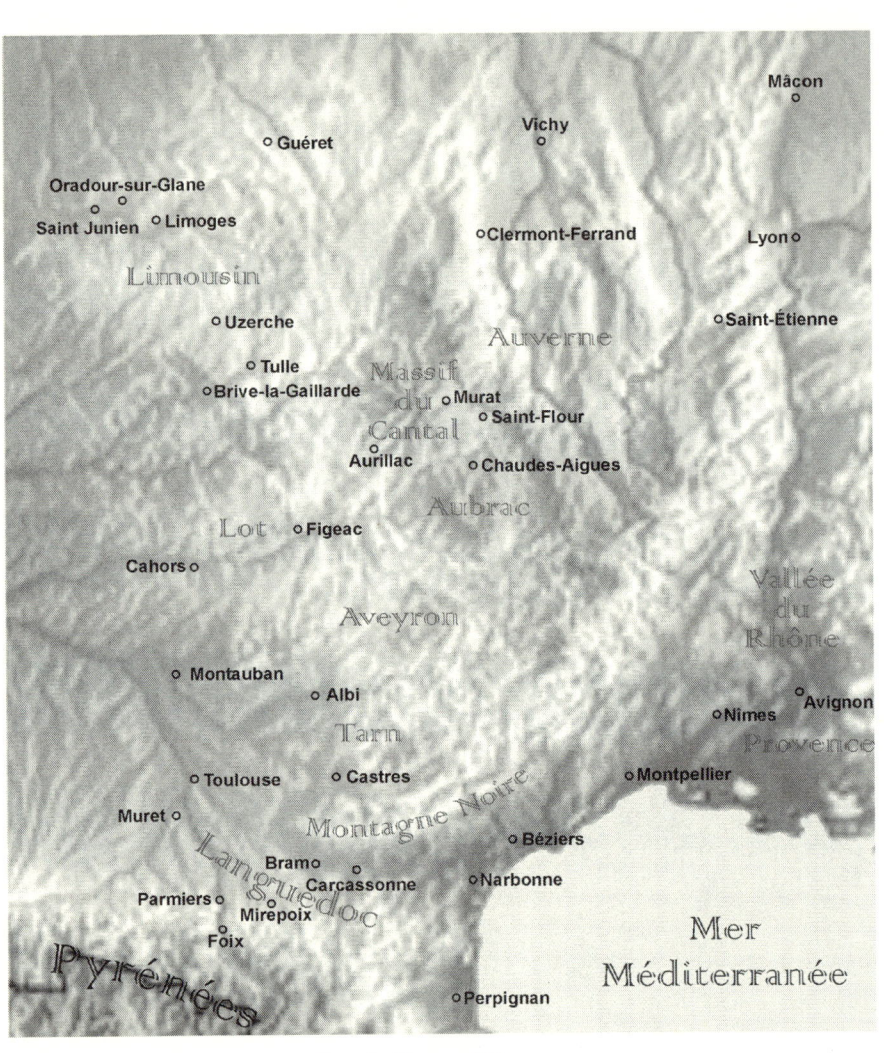

South Central France

A Last Act

It had been a long, hard climb up the mountainside; the years were telling on him. He was tired but determined to complete one last task. The memories of those he had given his word to pressed on him. He could see each of their faces as clearly as if they were standing beside him, but he knew that could never be again, not in this life. It had been exactly three months since they had walked away from him smiling and singing, and each time the memory of that terrible day returned, he fought back tears; the memory was too painful. It would have been easier if he had gone with them, but he had given his word. His only solace was the knowledge that he would not have to endure the pain much longer.

He was a heavyset man with a heavy frame and a short, graying beard. He was not wearing his customary tunic and mantle embellished with fine gold thread and the family coat of arms, nor did his belt carry the sword he had always had by his side. It had saved his life on many occasions, but those things were behind him. He wore only a cloak of coarsely woven cloth made of jute and flax dyed a dark-blue. Despite his attire, he was still a proud man; it was written in the lines of his face. No amount of humility could erase it.

His life had been one of privilege. He had been born into a wealthy family and commanded vassals and peasants alike with a firm but fair hand; he had earned the respect and loyalty of those who called him lord. He had been fortunate enough to have married well, and his wife had borne him five children. Life could not have been better for him and his people until the darkness descended upon them from the north. That way of life was gone, and he feared what the future held for them. The past month had been especially painful for him. Stripped of his power, for the first time in his life, he felt impotent.

Very carefully, he took some articles out of the case he was carrying. They were wrapped in several layers of oilskin to protect them. It was important they came to no harm, for the future of humanity depended on them, and many had willingly sacrificed their lives to protect them. He lifted the lid of a heavy chest that bore his family's coat of arms and was made of stout oak and heavy, metal bands. The inside was lined with copper. It was a safe repository for the items for as long as they remained there. He set the articles in the chest and closed the lid with a sigh of relief.

He sat at the heavy, wooden desk he had seen many times used as an altar and unrolled a sheet of parchment. He looked at it and wondered where to start. He was facing a daunting task but one he had committed to fulfilling. The disaster that had befallen the people of the region and himself had not begun on a single day; it had been gradual, unforeseen. It had been the result of the avarice, duplicity, savagery, and hatred of those who claimed to be divinely superior. It was clear the god they served was not the Good God he worshipped.

The darkness that had consumed them would not pass soon. They had fought against it for more than thirty years, but the evildoers had been too strong. Those who had stood against them had paid a terrible price. The last chance to right the wrongs that had been done and set humanity back on the divine path was in his hands; it was his task to prepare the world for the day when the darkness would pass and the world would be open to enlightenment once again. So it had been prophesied.

His mind ready for the task, he dipped his quill in the ink and began to write.

"In the sixth month of the year of our Lord, June 1244 ..."

CHAPTER 1

Past and Present

Wednesday, June 7, 1944— St. Junien, France

St. Junien lay on the Vienne River, about twenty-six kilometers west of Limoges and in the bosom of France. After the German invasion and the armistice in 1940, it became a part of Free France ruled by the Vichy regime. A bustling market town with a historic Gallo-Roman center, it had been fortunate enough to have seen little action for most of the war. Neither side deemed the leather industry for which it was renowned as strategic.

But on June 7, 1944, that changed.

The resistance, which had learned of the allied invasion in Normandy only the day before, had been mobilized by Free France radio broadcasts from across the Channel. Their orders were to do everything possible to harass the Germans and to impede their ability—at all costs—to send troops and equipment north to reinforce the front.

After four long years, it was the news Emile Garnier had been waiting for. Finally, the tables were turning. He and his men could come out of hiding and do their part to liberate their motherland from the Nazis and their sympathizers. Emile and his group were members of the Francs-Tireurs et Partisans, the FTP, the largest leftist resistance organization in France. They had received information the Germans were sending tanks and other equipment by train on the line from Limoges that crossed the

River Vienne in St. Junien. Their orders were simple: destroy the line and cause as much disruption as possible.

"Quiet!" said Emile, as they lay in the long grass. "Do you want the German army or the Milice to come down on us? They have spies everywhere."

"Let them come so I can kill them," boasted Jean-Paul, trying to show off to the other boys with him.

Stupid boy, thought Emile. *They'll be no match for the SS if they're discovered with their bicycles and poorly maintained Sten guns. Their only hope would to be to run.* But there was no point saying that to his men. It would just make them more nervous.

"Keep quiet. Stay down. Watch the road," commanded Emile. "We were given a task, we will fail at if we get into a fight"

"And fail to see the end of this war," Philippe said sarcastically.

"Okay. Philippe, Marcel. Come with me. The rest of you stay down and signal to us if you see anyone," Emile ordered. "No one is to begin shooting without my order. Understood?"

A few heads nodded reluctantly.

Philippe, Marcel, and Emile picked up sticks of explosives and quietly crept through long grass to the concrete footings of the railway bridge across the Vienne. Fortunately, the bright moon was obscured by heavy clouds.

They climbed a footing and walked gingerly along the steel girders. Emile placed the charges at the center of one of the spans, where the bridge was the weakest. They taped them on and led the detonator wire away. Marcel jumped down to the field, and Emile threw the reel to him.

Emile and Philippe jumped from the bridge and joined Marcel in the field. The three walked slowly away from the bridge, trailing the detonator wire across behind them until they were a safe distance from the bridge. Philippe attached the wires to the detonator.

There was nothing to do but wait for a train to cross the bridge. Emile saw that the boys at the roadside were becoming restless. He sent Marcel to calm them down.

They lay in the field for nearly thirty minutes. Mosquitoes were taking advantage of the fresh food supply. At last, they heard a train and Philippe's heart began to pound. He pulled the plunger up in readiness. Suddenly, he saw Emile frantically waving his hands. "Stop! Passenger train! Women and children! We must wait for the supply train."

Philippe sighed and reluctantly took his hands off the plunger. "Collaborators! All of them! We should blow them up anyway. They wouldn't be on the train if they didn't sympathize with the Nazis. Bastards, all of them!" he hissed.

"That may be, but we are here to destroy German armaments headed north. We must remember our objective. We can deal with all the traitors as soon as the Germans have left," Emile said. "Now get down."

They lay back in the long grass and resumed their wait.

After about ten minutes, a black Citroën with its lights off came down the road. Emile and Philippe crouched in the grass. To Emile's horror, Jean-Paul started running toward the road. Marcel grabbed his leg. Jean-Paul fell on his face. But it was too late.

The car stopped. A spotlight shone in their direction. The doors opened. Two men got out. Emile recognized them. Yves Durand and François Bousquet, members of Darnand's hated secret police, the Milice.

"Come out with your hands up or you'll be shot!" Yves shouted. He and François started toward the boys' hiding spot and raised their machine guns.

Emile nodded at Philippe. Short bursts spat from their Sten guns. Yves and François fell before they had a chance to shoot their compatriots.

Marcel and a couple of the boys dragged their bodies into the field. Marcel drove the car down a small alley out of sight of the road.

Emile looked at his watch and prayed the train would come before the two Milice were reported missing. He did not have to wait long.

A train was approaching slowly, laboring with its cargo. As it got closer, Emile could see the tanks and half-tracks with their machine guns on the flatcars. He felt a rush of excitement and signaled to Philippe. Emile would let the train get onto the bridge section with the explosives before they blew it up. He wanted to make sure the tanks were destroyed and could not be sent by another route.

When the train was where he wanted it, he jerked his fist down to instruct Philippe to push the detonator.

The explosion tore the steel girders as if they were strips of mere balsa wood. Other explosions followed as the munitions on the train were ignited. The flashes lit up the water as the train plunged into it. Emile saw German soldiers swimming. Others were floating.

Marcel and the other boys cheered. Emile and Philippe joined them.

"Let's go. The Milice will be here quickly. We've done what we came to do. Go home all of you. France will be proud of you."

Smiling with a sense of accomplishment, the French resistance fighters pulled their bikes from the bushes and rode off.

Emile was well satisfied with the night's work. His commander would be pleased. He hated the Germans for killing some of his closest friends and all the others who had simply disappeared. The nightmare, though, would soon be over, and France would be free again.

Emile arrived home shortly before midnight and crept quietly up the stairs. He looked in on his daughters, Sophie and Beatrice, who were sleeping soundly. He loved them dearly. Sophie, nineteen, would not be with them much longer; she was going to be married soon. The thought saddened Emile, but he was happy for her. She was not going far. She would join her fiancé in Oradour-sur-Glane, a small town only thirteen kilometers away, so they would be able to visit her often. On Saturday, they were to visit his family to make wedding arrangements.

CHAPTER 2

The Long Road North

Thursday, June 8, 1944

Major Adolf Diekmann looked in the mirror and adjusted his black collar bearing a pair of bright-yellow Sig runes of the SS and the extra flash to show he was a member of the signal corps. He was proud of the uniform and always attentive to his appearance. It was good for morale and discipline. He turned sideways to assure himself he still maintained a slim stature. He straightened his back to increase his height and air of command. He had shaved his fair hair from the sides of his head and was well pleased with the way it accentuated his Nordic features.

Major Diekmann looked older than his thirty-two years, but he had experienced more in his short life than most people did in a long one. He had been close to death many times in Russia, where the conditions had been appalling. He had been badly injured and had lost part of a lung. For his gallantry, he had received the Iron Cross twice. He wore his medals with honor over his heart. Recently, on Hitler's birthday, April 20, he had been promoted to Sturmbannführer of the Third Company of the First Battalion of the "Der Führer" Regiment, a unit of the SS Second SS Panzer Division, known as "Das Reich."

Das Reich had been wintering in the south of France at Montauban, just north of Toulouse. It had been strengthened and reequipped after its return from the Eastern Front. They were not yet at full strength but had received orders from General Lammerding to move north with all due haste to aid in repulsing the allied invasion.

Major Diekmann and his fellow officers anticipated a difficult journey. The division had over 15,000 men and 1,400 vehicles, including 209 tanks and other armored vehicles. The logistics of moving that many soldiers and matériel would have been challenging in peace time alone, but they were at war, and the Allies had air superiority over much of the route they were to take. They had also learned that the heavy armor and personnel would have to travel by road to Normandy, seven hundred kilometers north. They had been planning to transport it by rail, but the resistance had sabotaged the trains; a saboteur had put Carborundum paste in the axle bearings, which had ground them down. It would be trying on men and equipment.

The Der Führer Regiment left Montauban early in the morning with the Fifteenth Motorcycle Company. They were to take a westerly route north, while the rest of Das Reich with the heavy armor would travel on a more easterly route. The two routes would converge at Uzerche, and the division would reassemble near Limoges before moving up to the front.

Adolf did not anticipate much difficulty on the route until they were north of Limoges; before that point, they would be in Free France, a fortunate member of the Third Reich. Marshal Pétain and his government in Vichy had signed an armistice with Germany and had become their ally in 1940. They were in debt to the Germans for having liberated them from the Socialist government in Paris that had oppressed them for centuries. They were part of an empire that would finally unite all Europe again, as it had been under the Holy Roman Empire, the First Reich.

The journey started out well. They were cheered by German garrisons in towns they passed through, but by late afternoon, signs were becoming ominous. The roads and towns were deserted. The major put his troops on alert. He did not have to wait long for his apprehensions to be justified.

As they approached a bridge over the Dordogne at Groléjac, they were fired on by a group of *maquis*, cowardly resistance fighters who hid in the woods. They were poorly equipped with single-shot rifles and shotguns. Diekmann's Panzergrenadiers made short work of them; half were killed. The rest fled. But that was only the beginning of what would prove to be a long night for the major and his regiment.

They were attacked several more times along the road before arriving at Rouffilac in the evening. A roadblock across the main street of the town impeded their progress. As the lead motorcycles approached it, shots rang out. One rider flew across the road on his bike. Someone fired a rocket at an armored car. Diekmann ordered half-tracks to the front. "Destroy that barricade and anyone in the vicinity!"

The cars' heavy guns boomed, and the barricade was blown to pieces. They opened up with their machine guns, strafing all the buildings on the road. Some people who ran from the buildings were mowed down. In less than fifteen minutes, the way was clear. Major Diekmann ordered the column to proceed.

"We cannot afford any more delays," Diekmann told Captain Gerlach, who was on the lead motorcycle. "The men will not sleep until we get to Limoges."

"Yes, Major, but it will be difficult if the *maquisards* continue attacking us en route."

"Captain, they are not soldiers. They are saboteurs, spies, common criminals. They deserve to be treated as such. Show them no mercy. If you see anyone in the road who appears to pose a threat, shoot him. Understood? We have no time for prisoners."

"Yes, Major," said the captain with a quick salute. He roared off on his motorcycle.

The attacks continued along the route. They were no more than nuisances, but they were delaying his progress, and the regiment was needed at the front, where the real soldiering was to take place. He did not want to be fighting peasants with rusty rifles; there was no glory in that. He thought of his friends dying in Normandy for the Führer, for the Fatherland. He desperately wanted to be with them. The maquis were mere ants to be crushed. Diekmann took a sip of vodka to calm his frustration. It was a habit he had acquired during the long, cold winters in Russia. He had confidence that Captain Gerlach would obey his orders and shoot anyone along their route.

When Diekmann arrived at Brive-la-Gaillarde, he met up with Colonel Städler and other parts of the regiment that had come by a different route. It was about the halfway point, and he gave his men a short break to eat and refuel before proceeding to Limoges. Städler had taken over a hotel in the middle of town, and Diekmann reported to him.

"Rough going?" asked Städler.

"Nothing we couldn't handle," replied Diekmann defensively.

"Quite, Major, but you've lost several men, and I lost a dozen or more in Cressenac and Noailles, just eight kilometers south. Came close to being killed myself."

"I am glad you survived, Colonel."

"I was at the front of the column when we were ambushed entering Cressenac. They had us pinned down for a while. There was quite a few of them in buildings and in the forest. Quite a few of our men were hit. I had to call in some armor to blast them away. I ended up blowing the steeple off the church."

"You should have flattened the whole town," Diekmann replied.

"That would have been a diversion we don't have time for, exactly what the resistance is trying to provoke us into doing. However, we need to make them understand that such attacks will not be tolerated and that they will pay a high price for them. The high command has issued orders to 'immediately pass to the counteroffensive, to strike with the utmost power and rigor, without hesitation.'"

"It's about time," Diekmann said. "We have been too soft on the resistance in France. We should have treated them more as we did the Russians. Just because they are Europeans, we have treated them as civilized, but they are no more civilized than the Russian Bolsheviks. Are the orders any more specific?"

"Yes. They state, 'It is necessary to use intimidating measures against the inhabitants and break the spirit of the population by making examples. It is essential to deprive them of all will to assist the maquis and meet their needs,'" Colonel Städler read.

"Very good, Colonel. The orders are very clear. We are to demonstrate that any act of insurrection against our troops will be met by strong reprisals."

"Exactly. This insurrection must be stopped in its tracks."

Colonel Städler was suddenly distracted. He looked past Major Diekmann and called out, "Major Wulf, come here. I need you immediately."

Major Wulf commanded the Pioneer Platoon of the SS Panzer Aufklarungs Abteilung Zwei. He joined them with the obligatory Nazi salute.

"Major Wulf, you are to take your platoon immediately to Tulle, about twenty kilometers east of here, to relieve the garrison."

"Yes, Colonel. How serious is the situation?"

"Very, I am told. The town has been almost overrun by the maquis. There is only one position still holding. The reports are that most of the garrison has been killed."

Major Wulf stiffened and clicked his heels. "We will leave immediately, Colonel." He took his orders and headed out of the hotel, shouting orders to his officers on the way.

"If you will excuse me, I must go too, Major Diekmann," the Colonel said. "Have a safe trip. I hope to see you in Limoges."

"Have a safe trip yourself, Colonel."

Diekmann scanned the room and saw an old friend. "Helmut!"

"Adolf!"

"Major Kämpfe. How are you looking after the Third Battalion?"

"Very well. We will win this war," he said, glowing with self-confidence. "The British and the Americans cannot sustain their losses much longer. When the Second Panzer Division gets there, we will finish them off quickly."

"Confident as ever," Diekmann said. "I trust you are right. Our first problem, however, is to get there with all our men and equipment intact."

Helmut smiled. "You are talking about the maquisards, but they are no more than old men and boys sharing a few old rifles. We will finish them off quickly. They have just been stirred up by the propaganda the British are broadcasting, telling them they are about to be liberated. It's all lies. As soon as they realize the invasion will be defeated, they will crawl back into their holes."

"It's always good talking to you, Helmut." Diekmann patted his friend on the back. "How are your wife and children?"

"Fine, thanks. It's tough in Germany right now, though, with the bombing, but they assure me they are safe. How's your family?"

"They are well, thank you," Adolf said. "Are you still fraternizing with the enemy? I see you've lost none of your charm," Adolf asked, wanting to change the subject.

"There are some pretty girls over here," Helmut said. "No harm in trying to improve Franco-German relations."

Someone across the room waved at him.

"Well, it looks like I must go. The battalion is ready to head out."

"See you in Limoges then," Adolf said.

"Have a safe journey," replied Helmut.

Around ten that night, Major Diekmann and the First Battalion left Brive-la-Gaillarde for Limoges, seventy kilometers north. However, they did not arrive there until midmorning the next day. All along the route, they were harassed by the maquis, and their progress was slowed by roadblocks. Diekmann lost twelve men, and others had been wounded. He was tired and angry when they arrived in Limoges. He reported to Colonel Städler at headquarters. The colonel sent him and his men to bivouac in St. Junien.

CHAPTER 3

Unwelcome Guests

Friday, June 9, 1944

"No, no, stop!" Emile cried out. All he could see were flames leaping high into the air all around him. He could feel searing heat and looked desperately for water to douse the fire. He was drenched from sweating, yet instead of running from the flames, he felt drawn to them. There was something he had to do, something in the flames he had to get to.

"No, put out the fire!" he cried out.

He felt a sharp slap on his face. He looked around. He was in his bedroom. The flames had disappeared. The room was dark.

Monique, his wife, was sitting beside him. "Emile? You were having a nightmare. What was it about?"

"I don't know. The same as before, only they seem to be getting more vivid. All I can see are flames, and I am drawn to them, but I don't know why. I feel as though there is something in the flames I have to get to."

Monique's brown eyes calmed his fear. "Darling, you have been doing too much with the resistance lately. You are not a soldier. You are a teacher."

"I have no choice. I hate this war. All the lies, the hatred, the killing. I wish it had never happened, but it did. People are dying for us in Normandy, dying to free France from the Nazis. We have to do our part to help them."

"I think you've done too much. What time did you get to bed this morning?"

"About two. Our group was ordered to cut phone lines the Germans were using."

"Did you have any problems? I hope you didn't take too many risks. The children need you, and so do I," she said, hugging him tightly.

"No, don't worry. We almost ran into a couple of Milice, but we managed to go around them. I hate them more than I do the Germans. They have betrayed us all, cooperating with the Nazis and sending our friends to concentration camps."

"Father François says God will punish them after the war."

"Well, we could do with some of God's help right now. It's fine for your brother-in-law, tucked away in sleepy, little Oradour, but his God hasn't done much to help us so far."

"Emile, you shouldn't talk like that. You and your Communist ideas. We must keep the faith if just for the children. Don't you feel there's a spiritual side to life too?"

"Sometimes, I wonder if there could be more to our existence, but I can't believe in Father François' 'all powerful God.' Not after all the horrors I've seen. We have to look after ourselves in this life."

"I will pray he will reveal himself to you."

"You're a wonderful woman, and I love you very much. I don't know what I'd do without you."

"I love you too." Monique kissed his cheek. "Now try to sleep. There are still a couple of hours before you need to get up."

Only an hour later, however, they were awakened by the loud roar of motorcycles sputtering and backfiring as they sped down their normally quiet street. Emile recognized the sound. They were Zundapp KS600 motorcycles, used by the German Panzer units. His heart pounded. All he could think of was that they were coming for him, but to his relief, they continued down the street. He dressed hurriedly.

On his way to school, Emile stopped at the bar in the square to find out what was going on. Apparently, officers of the Second Panzer Division were being billeted in the town for a few days as they regrouped for their journey to Normandy. The Devil was among them.

Meanwhile, in Tulle, about seventy kilometers southeast of Limoges, Major Wulf had driven the maquis from the town within a few hours of his arrival the evening before. Das Reich had lost three men, nine wounded, but the toll for the Ninety-Fifth Security Regiment had been much higher.

"Heinrich, the reports I am getting are horrific," said Major Kowatsch. "Many of the garrison were murdered and tortured by the Communist gangs, and their bodies were mutilated. We cannot allow this!"

"I agree," said Major Wulf, shaking his head in disgust. "One hundred thirty-nine of our soldiers were killed and forty wounded, according to the latest reports. Indications are that at least forty were murdered after they had surrendered, and they were brutalized in the most horrific manner. Their genitalia were cut off, and their bodies were dragged behind vehicles. These are not acts of war. They are acts of savagery."

"Indeed. They demand we set a firm example to demonstrate such acts of barbarity will not be tolerated. We must show them if they want to behave like animals, we will treat them as such. We must exact reprisals."

"What do you suggest?" asked Wulf.

"I'm afraid that most of the FTP scum responsible fled town last night."

"Regrettably, that is probably so, but there are many sympathizers in town we can round up to make an example of."

"Very good. I will discuss the matter with General Lammerding. In the meantime, talk to the local commander and start identifying some of these sympathizers."

"Very good, Major," Major Kowatsch said. He left to undertake the task.

Later that morning, the major had his orders. "Major Kowatsch, we are to round up one hundred and twenty men, three for each of our soldiers who were executed. They are to be hanged, and their bodies are to be thrown in the river. We will also issue a warning that next time, three maquisards or their accomplices will be hanged for each German soldier wounded and ten for each German soldier killed."

"That should set an example they will not forget," said Major Kowatsch. "I will take care of it myself."

"Very good," Wulf responded, only too glad to hand off the assignment. "We can then hand this town back to the garrison and go north, where we have a real war to fight."

Adolf Diekmann awoke after a short nap. He was exhausted but too tired to sleep. He had too much to do, too much to think about. Sleep would have to wait until nightfall, which was late that time of year. His staff had prepared reports for him about activities in the area, which was apparently a hotbed of resistance. Attacks and acts of sabotage were continuously being perpetrated against the forces of the Reich and its sympathizers.

The maquis weren't intimidated by their presence. If anything, they were becoming more brazen. Diekmann read the report from Major Wulf in Tulle and was particularly disturbed. The atrocities were horrific. They made his blood boil, but the nearly successful takeover of the town by the resistance was potentially even more worrisome. One success could encourage others, and if that happened, they could be bogged down for weeks chasing the shadowy maquisards from one town to another.

Major Diekmann's fears were confirmed when he read another report on the events in Guéret, a small town thirty-six kilometers northeast of Limoges. The town had been taken over by the maquis on Wednesday, and the German garrison had been captured. He shuddered to think what atrocities might have been committed there. The Communists were barbarians. An attempt to retake the town by the regular army the previous day had failed, so Major Kämpfe had been dispatched with his Panzer division to retake the town. Adolf had every confidence Helmut would prevail. They had been through a lot together in Russia and somehow always managed to get the upper hand.

He glanced through the other reports and noticed one about St. Junien, where he was billeted. The railway bridge over the Vienne had been blown up a couple of nights before, destroying a troop train. He decided to start by making an example in St. Junien. "Fritz! Get my car! I want to visit the mayor."

When he arrived at the town hall, the mayor was not there, so he was "sent for." He arrived in one of the Panzer sidecars. He was disheveled, shaken up, clearly very nervous about being summoned by an SS officer.

"Mayor, two nights ago, a German transport train was blown up on your bridge. German soldiers died. Have you apprehended the terrorists who perpetrated this atrocity?"

The mayor shook his head and threw open his hands apologetically. "Monsieur, we are trying, but it is very difficult. You must understand. They have much support in the town. We have made inquiries, but as usual, no one saw anything. Two of the Milice were even killed."

"That is not good enough! I am sure you have suspicions as to who was involved. Arrest them and execute them. Even if you are wrong, it will serve as a warning to those who were responsible. Such things cannot go unpunished. It is essential we maintain order!" "But Major," said the mayor frantically, "that would make things only worse. My office has been attacked many times. We are already hated by the resistance. If we execute innocent people, the resistance will gain more support."

"And we will crush every one of them mercilessly," Diekmann rebuked him. "What do you estimate is the strength of the resistance in St. Junien?"

The mayor rubbed his chin. He did not want executions in his town, not in his name. The maquis were especially brutal with those who helped the Germans. They did not forget or forgive. Once the Germans left, he would be in fear for his life. To try to escape his predicament, he decided to exaggerate the strength of the FTP in the town in hopes it would deter any hasty action by the SS. "Monsieur, I believe that there could be as many as eighteen hundred members of the resistance in St. Junien."

"Eighteen hundred?" Diekmann was surprised.

"That is what I am told. Of course, we have no way of knowing exactly."

Diekmann looked at his guards and sighed. "That is a very large number for a town this size. You should have been doing a better job. It will obviously take more force to clean it up than I had anticipated. I will talk to the local commander of the Milice."

"Please do, Major. I am sure he will be able to help you."

"Good day, Mayor." Diekmann rose from his chair.

"Good day, monsieur," the mayor said, much relieved.

Diekmann left, followed by his guards. The mayor rubbed sweat from his brow and hoped never to see him again. It was a fine line he had to walk between the Germans and the resistance. Whoever won, he wanted to survive.

Emile cycled home from school and saw Germans everywhere in town. Cars and motorcycles, many with sidecars, were speeding down the narrow streets with no heed for the inhabitants. He hated to see them in the town he had grown up in, the town he loved. They did not belong there. Emile wanted them to leave, but he knew the longer they were delayed anywhere, the longer it would take them to get to the front, and the chance of allied success in Normandy would be greater. He chided himself for being so selfish. *If we have to tolerate the Germans being in town for a few days, that's a small sacrifice to make for those who are risking their lives.* He decided to stay out of their way. There were too many questions they might ask, and he worried for his family's safety.

The evening was warm. Monique had closed the shutters to keep the heat out of their old but well-built house. Its thick stone walls and tile roof helped keep it cool. That night, though, Emile found the house claustrophobic. Too many matters were on his mind. "Let's picnic at the river," he told his wife. "It's cool there, and we can plan for tomorrow."

"Fine. I'll pack wine and cheese, and we can pick up bread and cakes at the bakery."

The river was flowing swiftly; it had rained recently. Emile was soothed by the sight of the water carrying along branches and reeds. He looked at his daughter Sophie with sadness and happiness. She would be leaving soon to marry Pascal, the baker's son, in Oradour. He was a fine lad, and she would not be far away, but it would not be the same without her around. As they walked along the river, Emile squeezed his daughter's hand.

"I remember when you were born," he said. "I remember laying you in your crib for the first time, happy you had come into our lives and happy you would be with us for a long time. Inside, I knew one day you would leave us, but that moment seemed so distant that I tried not to worry about it. Now, though, that moment has arrived."

"Oh Papa," she said with a smile, pulling his hand. "I'm not going far, only to Oradour. You can come see me whenever you like. Don't think of it as losing a daughter but as gaining a son. Pascal can help you in the house. He's very good with his hands. And he can bake the best chocolate croissants, just the way you like them."

Emile tried to return her smile. "I hope you will both be very happy," he said.

Sophie put her arm around him and kissed his cheek. "We will, Papa. We love each other very much."

"Well, that is all that's important. I suppose we'd better prepare to visit Pascal's family with you tomorrow and finalize the wedding plans. Father François will be coming to go over the arrangements."

Just then, Emile noticed a body floating in the middle of the river. He hugged his daughter to keep her from seeing it. The war was never far away.

It was almost 11:00 p.m. and Diekmann was preparing to turn in. He was exhausted from the lack of sleep and the pressure he had been under from the constant attacks on their journey. What he had expected to be an uneventful trip had become a challenge, an ordeal that had cost him men and equipment sorely needed at the front.

He fumed as he thought of the cursed maquis and the infernal radio broadcasts from England that incited them. The resistance fighters were fools who were simply being exploited by the enemy. Germany had brought order to France, and the Allies would bring only chaos. *If we could only jam the radio transmissions!* He knew that was not possible. He had to exterminate the maquis whenever he encountered them. His patience was exhausted.

Adolf looked over the latest reports of continuing attacks and sabotage in the area by the maquisards; two of his men had been killed. He wished they could just go after the resistance as aggressively as they had done in Russia. Resistance fighters were cowards who hid in civilian clothing; they did not deserve to be treated like soldiers. He despised them.

After locking his papers in his dispatch box, Adolf climbed into bed and reached to turn off the light when he heard a loud pounding on the door.

"Major Diekmann, we have an urgent report from headquarters." He recognized the voice of Corporal Droffilc, his communications officer.

"Come in, Gerhardt."

The corporal entered the bedroom, clearly flustered. "Major, we received a report from Colonel Städler in Limoges. Major Kämpfe has been kidnapped by the resistance."

"No!" Adolf banged his fist angrily on the bedside table. "If those animals do anything to harm Helmut, I will kill every one of them myself!

If there is any further news on the subject during the night, wake me. That's an order!"

"Yes, Major."

"Now get out!" he yelled, barely able to control his rage.

CHAPTER 4

The Gathering Storm

Saturday, June 10, 1944

Saturday morning was pretty much like any other for Emile and his family. He left early on his bicycle to pedal the short distance to the Lycée Victor Hugo. Emile taught Latin and Spanish there, and he enjoyed his job. Languages had always brought him pleasure; he had a natural gift for them. For Emile, each language carried along with it a unique culture and way of thinking. In his mind, language was the gateway to other worlds.

In the teachers' room, Emile quietly conferred with some resistance colleagues. They had to be careful as they were never certain who could be trusted.

"The mayor has asked us," whispered one, "to lie low for a couple of days until the Germans have left. He is worried the SS might retaliate against the town if the attacks do not stop. Rumors are they have hanged people in Tulle."

"I think the mayor is worried only about his own hide," said Maurice, sucking hard on his pipe. Maurice was close to retirement; he had a bulbous face, red cheeks, and an impressive moustache. "I don't trust him. He works for the Germans yet pretends to be one of us. I think he's a collaborator. When we finally get rid of the Germans, we should get rid of him too."

"And who would you replace him with?" asked Emile. "You would probably get someone worse, like André Dubois."

Maurice pulled his pipe from his mouth and spat. "André Dubois and the Milice? I curse them both! They are traitors to France. I will kill them with my bare hands when this war is over."

"Let's hope you are around to do that!" Emile smiled. "No, I don't think the mayor is a collaborator. I think he's a coward. He's looking out only for his own skin, like most people in this war. However, this time, his advice might be sound. We don't have enough men to take on a full Panzer division, and the Germans I have seen are very jumpy, nervous about going to the front. Maybe we should not provoke them."

"I heard we captured one of their officers last night, so it's probably a bit late for that. I hear they want to exchange him for some of our captured resistance fighters."

Emile glanced around. He looked at Maurice. "That's a very dangerous game."

Emile's enthusiasm for teaching and languages made him popular with his students. Normally, he had few problems getting them involved with what he was teaching. However, since the arrival of the Das Reich unit in the town, the children had become distracted. Many of them had soldiers billeted in their homes, and they had been forced to give their beds up to them. Others were scared of what the Germans might do to them or their parents. Buried in the heartland of France, St. Junien had never been a cosmopolitan town, and now it had been overrun by thousands of foreigners speaking a language none of them understood.

Emile was trying to distract his students with some Latin poetry when he noticed some students looking behind him at the classroom door. They were fidgeting and talking among themselves. He turned around and saw the Gestapo just outside, looking in the classroom. Emile suspected a couple of his students were Jewish but had managed to hide their identity from the Milice. If the Gestapo had come for them, it was too late for them. The last thing he wanted the children to do was panic and betray themselves. He decided to distract the children. "Okay, children, put away your books. Marc, please get my guitar."

A murmur of excitement spread across the classroom as the children put their books in their desks. Marc brought him his guitar, and he dusted it off and tuned it. The children had always liked his singing and playing. He had not done it enough recently; the war had made him feel they had no right to be singing while others were dying, but that day, he and the children needed to sing. "We will all sing some of the Spanish songs you learned last year. Ready? On three."

Emile began the song, and the children joined in. He was no Segovia, but by most standards, he was very good. Emile had picked up the guitar when he had spent a year in Spain after university to improve his Spanish. He had fallen in love with the instrument; he had taken to it as if it had been made for him. He had even written a few songs of his own, most of them dedicated to his wife. She had cried the first time he had sung one to her.

As Emile and the children sang, two Gestapo officers accompanied by André Dubois entered the classroom. André looked at Emile with pure hatred but said nothing. The two had been playing cat and mouse for some time. André was convinced Emile was with the FTP but had never been able to prove it. Emile, for his part, despised André, whom he held responsible for the deaths and deportations of several of his friends in the resistance. There were few people he wanted dead as much as André.

The Gestapo officers moved through the classroom, opening desks and slamming them shut. Emile encouraged the children to sing louder to drown out the noise. Finding nothing in the desks, the two black-uniformed officers went to the back of the room and began searching the cupboards. They cursed in German and threw many items to the floor. They found nothing. They gave a Nazi salute to Emile and the children, who did not return it. The officers stormed out, leaving the mess.

The door slammed behind them. Emile breathed a sigh of relief. They had not come to look for children, as they hadn't taken the time to ask for identity cards. Emile considered that a great blessing, but he wondered what they had been looking for. He remembered Maurice's comment about a captured German officer and wondered if that was the reason for their visit. They were probably looking for arms, papers, anything to implicate someone in the kidnapping. His fears had been justified. They had stirred up a hornets' nest.

Adolf Diekmann had risen early and had been on the radio since five that morning, talking to headquarters in Limoges. He was hoping for news of Helmut, but there was none. Earlier in the evening, Major

Kämpfe and his troops had recaptured Guéret and had executed twenty-nine maquisards in retribution for the uprising. At around nine, he had driven off alone to Limoges and had not been heard from since.

"We don't know why the major drove off alone," the information officer informed him from headquarters.

"You don't know Helmut," said Adolf. "He never had much patience, and he is completely without fear. Patience was a luxury none of us could afford in Russia, if you wanted to stay alive."

"The troops found his Talbot car abandoned at around nine thirty last night. It was assumed he'd been kidnapped. Colonel Städler ordered an immediate search. One of our motorcycle patrols found some of his papers in the streets of Limoges. We believe he may have thrown them out of a car or truck to help us find him."

"Have you received any ransom demands?"

"No. We have had no contact with the resistance, but Colonel Städler is expecting them to contact us soon."

"How can we be sure they have not killed him already?"

"There was no sign of a struggle at the car. If they'd wanted to kill him, they would have done it there. Colonel Städler is confident the resistance will want to trade him for some their own."

"I trust he is right, but these gangs are not soldiers. They are unorganized thugs and they do not always realize what is in their best interests."

"Well, the colonel is trying to arrange an exchange."

"Tell Sylvester I will come in this morning to see what I can do. I owe Helmut my life. We kept each other alive on the Eastern Front on many occasions."

"The colonel will not be in until after nine. He left only a few hours ago."

"I'll wait till then," Adolf said.

"Oh, one more thing you should probably know, Major. We believe another officer may also have been kidnapped. Lieutenant Karl Gerlach, an orderly officer for the assault gun battery, and his driver have been missing since late morning yesterday. We have a search out for them also."

"This is getting out of control! If we do not show these criminals a firm hand, we shall all be kidnapped."

Adolf was worried. Eight hours had passed without contact, which was not a good sign. They should have heard something by then. They had to find Helmut quickly.

A little after 8:00 a.m., Corporal Droffilc knocked on the door.

"Enter."

"Major Diekmann, there are two members of the Milice to see you."

"What do they want? I'm too busy right now to get involved with their petty affairs. I have to go into headquarters in an hour."

"They say it is about Major Kämpfe."

"Major Kämpfe?" Adolf jumped out of his chair.

"Yes sir."

"Show them in immediately. Send for Captain Richert to translate."

Droffilc saluted and left.

Adolf paced the room, anxious for any news of his friend and fellow officer. After a short wait, two Milice policemen and Captain Richert entered. The policemen were wearing baggy trousers tucked into high, black leather boots, the same French uniforms Adolf had fought against at the beginning of the war, which made it difficult to see them as allies. They wore berets precariously perched on nearly shaven heads. They appeared to be making every effort to look as Germanic as possible; they even gave him a Nazi salute to complete the illusion.

Adolf viewed them with contempt. *They will never be German. No matter how hard they try, they will always be French.* Adolf was sure the French had destroyed Germany after the First World War with their onerous reparations mandated by the Treaty of Versailles and were largely to blame for this war. As members of a defeated people, some had joined the Milice and claimed to be friends of Germany and as such expected to be treated as equals. They would never be equals in his mind. He was not even sure where the allegiances of the many Alsatian troops in his own Panzer division lay, let alone those who were wholly French.

"Heil Hitler," said one policeman. "Major Diekmann, I am Eugene Patry, and this is Léon Pitrud."

"Heil Hitler," Adolf said halfheartedly.

"We may have some information that could help you find your missing officer, Major Kämpfe."

Adolf eyed them with suspicion. "What do you know? If you have information that leads to us finding the major alive, you will be well rewarded."

"It is our duty to find him," Eugene said, feigning insult at the offer of a reward. "Our people report lots of activity last night by the resistance along the N141 between here and Limoges. They believe a German officer was seen in a truck with maquisard terrorists driving from Oradour-sur-Glane. When we went to investigate this morning, we found a burned-out German ambulance. In the back were the remains of four soldiers who appeared to have been burned alive. In the front were the charred bodies of the driver and a passenger who had been chained to the steering wheel before the ambulance was set on fire."

Adolf stood. "Where exactly was this? Show me on the map!"

They moved over to a table with a large map of the area. Léon pointed to a spot on the map. "Right here, Major. Just about four kilometers south of Oradour."

"Did any of your men see Major Kämpfe?"

"No, I'm afraid not."

"And your men last night, they did nothing?" Adolf asked accusingly. "They just let these criminal gangs drive around freely?"

Eugene and Léon looked affronted. "Major, the maquis are very strong here in St. Junien," protested Eugene. "We do not always have enough men to fight them. Last night, our men were outnumbered. When we went back this morning, they had gone."

"If Major Kämpfe is killed by these Communists, they will all pay dearly," Adolf said, banging his fist on the table. "Do you have any idea where they took the major?"

Eugene and Léon looked hesitantly at each other. "Well …"

"Out with it! Do you or do you not know where they have taken him?"

Eugene looked at Léon nervously. Léon nodded. "We have a report from an informer that Major Kämpfe is being held in Oradour-sur-Glane. He executed twenty-nine of their men in Guéret yesterday. The rumor is they plan to kill him in reprisal."

Adolf's face registered hatred and anger. "When?"

"Our informer tells us that the maquis plan to burn him alive this evening as they did the soldiers in the ambulance."

"Captain, get my car!" Adolf screamed at Captain Richert. "I'm going to headquarters."

On the short drive to Limoges, Adolf's anger boiled over. They had come to this backward country to liberate the French from themselves. The corrupt, ineffective Socialist French government had led only to disorder and stagnation in the country. Germany had come to reshape their chaotic society according to the Nazi ideals of order and efficiency. The French should have embraced this gift from the German people with open arms. They were being offered the chance to transform their nation into one in which the strong would lead and the weak would be eliminated. No one could question that was the natural order, and yet incredibly, many of the French supported the resistance fighters.

Under the Third Reich, France was to be incorporated in a new united Europe just as it had been under the Romans two thousand years earlier. Berlin would be the new Rome. The few maquisards, the terrorists, the Communist gangs were no better than the barbarians of old who had refused to embrace civilization. There had always been those who would oppose progress and stand in the way of the greater good. Like the barbarians, they would have to be rooted out and annihilated.

Headquarters was a beehive of activity. Diekmann stormed into Colonel Städler's office. "Colonel, is there any news of the search for Major Kämpfe?"

Colonel Städler glanced up from his papers. "None yet, but we have every man out looking for him. The Milice and the Gestapo are assisting. At least we got Lieutenant Gerlach back alive."

"When was that? Did we free him? Has he any news of Helmut?"

The colonel shook his head. "We didn't free him, and by his account, he is very lucky to be alive. He walked in by himself this morning, in his underwear of all things. He says he and his driver were taken into the forest to be shot by the Communists, but he managed to escape while his driver was fighting them. He saw them shoot his driver."

"And Helmut?"

"He had no news of Helmut. He did not see him or hear any talk of him."

Adolf paced the room. "Colonel, we have to do something about these terrorists. They must be taught a lesson."

"I agree, but let's get the major back first."

"Does Lieutenant Gerlach know where they were taken?"

"He says they were driven around in a truck. He managed to see several of the road signs. He claims they were held in the village of Oradour-sur-Glane for more than an hour before being driven away to be shot."

"Oradour-sur-Glane? Two Milice came to me this morning with a report that Major Kämpfe might be being held there. May I speak to the lieutenant?"

"Certainly. He is still being debriefed."

Major Diekmann left the room to find Gerlach. He did not have to look far. He was in a room a few doors down. Dispensing with formalities, Adolf walked straight in and ordered everyone else out. "Lieutenant Gerlach, I am trying to locate Major Kämpfe. It is critical we find him without delay. Show me exactly where you and your driver were taken."

"Certainly, Major."

They moved over to a large map on the wall. "After being captured in Nieul, we were driven in a truck to Oradour-sur-Glane." He traced their route on the map.

"Are you sure it was Oradour? You could not have been mistaken?"

"I am sure, Major. I saw the sign as we entered the village."

"Did you see any sign of Major Kämpfe or hear anyone mention his name?"

"I'm afraid we didn't understand much of what was going on. They spoke only in French, and neither my driver nor I speak it. The leader of the group was a tall, thin man, seemingly in his early thirties, who appeared to speak some English. 'No SS! SS finished!' he shouted at us. It was obvious he wanted to kill us. I tried to befriend a young Alsatian in the group. He translated a few things for me to their leader, but that didn't help."

"It may have kept you alive. When they were talking, did you hear Major Kämpfe's name mentioned?"

"No, I'm afraid I didn't."

"How were they dressed? These resistance fighters."

"Many of them were in blue uniforms with helmets. That is why we thought they were on our side at first. Otherwise, we would have resisted."

"Very interesting. Please continue."

"We were bound and left in the street in Oradour for about an hour, and it was getting nasty. Two civilians came by on a tandem, and we followed them in the truck toward Bellac. We stopped once, where they fed us, and then we continued north. About six kilometers from Bellac, they drove off the road into the forest. It was obvious they planned to shoot us. I managed to escape while my driver struggled with them. Unfortunately, as I ran, I saw them shoot him. I can only assume he is dead."

"I am sorry to hear that. Your information has been most helpful. I commend you on your fortunate escape and hope that Major Kämpfe will have the same good fortune."

"I hope so too," the lieutenant said. "I have heard he is a very good officer."

"The best."

Major Diekmann headed to Colonel Städler's office. On his way, he bumped into Major Kowatsch, the interpreter, who was leaving an interrogation room in a hurry. "Major Kowatsch, I hear you and Major Wulf dealt severely with the Communists in Tulle yesterday."

"We did. We had no choice. They had butchered our troops and behaved like animals, so we treated them accordingly."

"I commend you," said Adolf. "It is time we showed greater resolve. The army has been too soft on these rebels. They must be taught the SS will not be so tolerant."

"I am not known for my tolerance, Major."

"No," said Adolf, looking past the major into the interrogation room he had just left. Inside was a young woman who seemed to be in her early twenties. Her appearance was somewhat attractive; she had dark, wavy hair and soft, caring eyes. "I see your task today is a little more pleasant, however," Adolf said with a slight smile.

"It is no more pleasant," Kowatsch protested. "She is a spy. We picked her up this morning. I am sending her to Ravensbrück for further interrogation. Their methods are more thorough than ours," he said with clear satisfaction.

"What is her nationality?"

"She claims to be English and admits to parachuting into France four days ago. We believe her mission was to incite the resistance and keep our troops busy so they would not be able to join the fight in Normandy. She was captured about thirty kilometers south of here on her way to Tulle. She put up quite a fight by all accounts."

"It's a pity she's not fighting on our side. Did you learn anything useful about the resistance? Names, local contact points, anything that might help me find Major Kämpfe?"

"No. I'm afraid she won't talk, but all that will change in Ravensbrück."

"I can't wait that long," Diekmann said.

"I'm afraid all she has told us so far is her name, Violette Szabo."

"I doubt if that will be of much help to me. Thank you anyway, Major. If you do learn anything that might help me find Major Kämpfe, please inform me at once."

"You will be informed immediately," Kowatsch said, saluting.

Major Diekmann found the colonel busy giving orders to several subordinates, but Adolf was not intimidated by their presence.

"Colonel, I would like permission to take a search party to Oradour-sur-Glane," he asked. "I believe Helmut might be held there."

The colonel glared at him for his interruption. After a pause, however, he relented. "All right, you have my permission. Take Captain Kahn and the Third Company."

"Thank you, Colonel."

"But mind that you act with restraint until we have the major back alive. If you are not able to find Helmut in Oradour, arrest all the resistance leaders you can identify and bring them back alive. I will try to negotiate an exchange I may need them if you fail."

"I understand, Colonel, but how do you propose to contact his captors?"

"I have already spoken with Lieutenant Colonel Meier. He has agreed to release his highest-ranking resistance prisoner to deliver a message to his superiors in Limoges. I will offer to release thirty members of the resistance we are holding and pay thirty-five thousand marks for the safe return of Major Kämpfe."

Adolf was shocked. "Colonel, has this been approved by General Lammerding?"

"No, not yet, but I will worry about that later."

"He may not approve the payment of a ransom."

"He may not, but Helmut is one of my best officers. My only concern right now is to get him back alive. I would do the same for you."

"I am flattered, Colonel."

The colonel waved him out. "Go. We have no time to lose, and remember to act with restraint. Our primary objective is to get Major Kämpfe back alive. We can wait to punish those responsible after that is accomplished."

"Yes, Colonel." He saluted and left.

"St. Junien," he shouted to his driver. "Quickly. I have work to do."

On the trip to St. Junien, Adolf radioed ahead to request that the two Milice policemen be there when he arrived. He contacted the Gestapo for help in planning the raid. When he entered his makeshift office, the Milice and Sergeant Joachim Kleist, a Gestapo officer from Limoges, were waiting for him.

Around midday, Emile cycled home from school. It had been a trying morning, but he had survived it, and it was a beautiful day. He was looking forward to the trip to Oradour with his wife and daughters that afternoon. It was a sleepy hamlet; nothing exciting ever happened there. It seemed too isolated from the world for anyone to care about the war. The only concern the townsfolk seemed to have was simply getting on with their humble lives. That attitude had frustrated Emile. He had argued animatedly many times in the bar that people in the town should take an active part in the resistance. He had urged them to help fight the German occupation but had always been rebuffed. That day, however, he was glad the town seemed to be isolated from the war, an oasis of calm. They would plan their daughter's future, and he did not want the war to be a part of it.

CHAPTER 5

An End and a Beginning

June, 1244

The oil lamp was starting to flicker and paint dancing patterns on the walls that seemed to take on a life of their own. It was running low on oil, but there would be no need to refill it, nor would he need more ink. His task was almost complete. He had been there for nearly two weeks and had eaten nothing. In the past few days, he had stopped drinking the water he had brought with him. As a result, he was becoming weak. But the more his body weakened, the stronger his resolve became to fulfill the commitment he had made. He had vowed to all those who trusted him, and who loved him, that he would end his current physical being through the endura, or starvation. The endura would free his ethereal soul from the flesh in which it was currently imprisoned, and which he no longer needed. Once free, it would be able to continue its journey, complete its purpose, and hopefully return at last to heaven.

Those he loved had gone on ahead; he was confident their souls had reunited with their spirits at the side of the Almighty. They had been prepared for the journey, but he had not been ready. His soul would have to take a longer journey to attain worldly perfection before it gained release. The evil God, had many names, whether the Devil, Jehovah, or Satan, he had brought ruinous times upon the Friends of God and all good souls. He had been too strong for them to resist, and he had brought darkness upon the land. Though the darkness could last many generations, Bertrand

Marty had promised him that eventually it would pass. The Good God would triumph in the end, and when he did, his soul would be ready. The Friends of God would be reborn, and lightness would return to the world.

He loved this land and its people. A land with fertile and verdant valleys enriched by the waters brought down from the snow-covered mountains in fast-flowing rivers. The vineyards on the warm, south slopes that had first been planted in Roman times and yielded a sweet harvest every autumn. A land of stark contrasts; pinnacles of limestone, many hundreds of meters high, pierced the sky like daggers. Steep escarpments rising abruptly from the river valleys defining the frontiers of another world; a world of high plateaus where rain was scarce and the wind blew without relief. All the plants, desperate to guard their water against the sun and wind, were rich in aromatic oils such as lavender, sarriette, rosemary, and thyme that perfume the air when they were brushed against.

Formed from an ancient seabed, the limestone had been pushed up eons ago by primordial forces deep in the earth. The passing of the seasons and the relentless probing of water to shorten its path down had sculptured a honeycomb of caves. The Good God had given them these caves for their churches.

At the edge of this blessed land was an ocean of the deepest blue, a major source of their wealth from trade. It also brought them cool breezes in the summer and warm breezes in the winter, protection against the icy blasts from the high mountains to the south. Many a time, he had been hypnotized by the moon casting its reflection on the dark, rippling surface of the ocean and appearing as a giant, golden orb, only to be replaced in the morning by the fierce reflection of the sun, which turned its surface into a glistening mirror.

Beyond the land, though, what he had loved most about the country were its people. Theirs had been a culture of freedom, tolerance, equality, enlightenment, and poetry and music shared and enjoyed not just by the nobility but also by the common people. Their troubadours had spread their culture like a lantern for humanity across all the great courts of Europe. Their language was the lingua franca of diplomacy. Openness to outsiders and their ideas had rewarded them with one of the wealthiest economies in all Christendom. In the end, that had ironically been their downfall.

Instead of looking for enlightenment, those outside had looked on with greed and envy for what they had achieved. They had not seen what they might have learned but rather what they might have pillaged and plundered. Their example to the world of an alternative to the feudal system had been seen by those in power as a threat that had to be annihilated.

So they had come with their war machines in the name of the false God and had sought to destroy everything they were too ignorant to understand. A wave of terrible sadness swept over him as he remembered some of the heinous deeds and the suffering caused by the forces of darkness. He quickly blotted a tear. It was no time for him to be weak. He had to keep the faith, confident that in the end, their ideas and their vision of a more righteous existence on earth would be triumphant. Their teachings of the true meaning of humanity's existence and its path to salvation could be suppressed, but only for a time. When the time was right, their message would be heard again, and all humanity would embrace it. He had been told that for most of his life but had never believed it. However, the last ten months in the citadel with the pure ones had revealed the truth of this to him, and he was their messenger.

With a flourish, he signed his name to the parchment with his customary scroll,

Raymond de Péreille.

He was proud of his signature, which had appeared at the bottom of many important documents. This would be the last but the most important to bear it. He blotted the ink. He rolled the parchment up carefully and wrapped it with a ribbon, which he sealed with red wax that dripped from a candle. While the wax was still soft, he pushed his ring into it, leaving the impression of his family crest. He rose with much effort and walked to the chest. He put the sealed parchment carefully inside. He closed the lid for the last time.

With his earthly duties completed, Raymond walked over to his makeshift bed on the floor. He was very weak; it was painful to walk, but he was thankful there would be no need to do so again. With some effort, he lay down and folded his arms across his chest. He waited only for the oil lamp and his current existence to be extinguished.

Saturday Afternoon, June 10, 1944

When Emile arrived home, his wife was in the front garden cutting flowers. "I thought I'd take some roses to Pascal's parents," she said. "We have so many, and they smell wonderful."

"Good idea. I'll pull some leeks from the garden as well. I'm sure they could use them. It's hard finding fresh vegetables with the war on," Emile said, quickly dismounting his bike.

"Please be quick. Sophie doesn't want us to be late. They're planning dinner for us at one, so we'll need to catch the twelve-thirty train."

"It will take only a moment." He gave her a quick kiss before running around the side of the house.

By the time he reappeared with his leeks, Sophie and Beatrice were outside with their mother, clearly anxious to leave. "How are my precious daughters today?" he asked, kissing them. "Pascal is a very lucky boy."

"Oh, Papa," grinned Sophie, turning a little red.

"We'd better get going," Emile said.

"I'm hungry. Let's see what wonderful pastries your baker's boy has dreamed up for us," said Monique.

The four set out to the train station, a short distance away. They held hands, and Emile sang songs he'd taught them as children. Sophie and Beatrice joined in.

The train ride to Oradour took about twenty minutes. The tram station on the rue Émile-Desourteaux was tiny and packed with people gossiping and greeting loved ones.

"Sophie!" a voice cried out. A young man was frantically waving at them above the crowd. Sophie ran to Pascal, and they embraced. Emile fought his way through the throng with Monique and Beatrice.

"Welcome to Oradour," said Pascal excitedly. He kissed Monique on both cheeks, kissed Beatrice, and hugged Emile. "I am so happy you're here. My family is so looking forward to meeting you."

"I never realized Oradour was such a busy place," Monique said.

"Oh it's not normally, but today, all the children are in town for medical exams, and the tobacco rations are being distributed. We also get a lot of fishermen here on the weekends from Limoges."

"I hadn't realized the fishing was that good here! Maybe I can go later with your father?"

"Yes! He'd probably like that," Pascal said.

"Now Emile. That's not what we came for," Monique said. "We're here for Sophie and Pascal. I'm not having you two run off before we've sorted out the wedding plans."

"I wouldn't have it any other way, my love," Emile said with a glance at Pascal.

"Let's get going. I'm sure your mother is waiting for us," said Monique.

Pascal led them out of the small tram house. "The bakery is just a little ways down the street. Come with me."

Pascal grabbed Sophie's hand and led them through the crowd. The streets of the town were narrow and cobbled, and the buildings were of a warm granite. The town was much smaller and poorer than St. Junien. It was a farming town, and the smells of the countryside—animals, straw, fresh manure in the middle of the street—pervaded the air. There was none of the bustle of St. Junien; life in Oradour ran at a slower pace. Emile thought it would be a good place to retire. Maybe they could live close to Pascal, Sophie, and the grandchildren when he retired. He could spend his time fishing and playing *pétanque*.

As they walked past the open windows of the small houses, Monique breathed deeply to savor the rich odors of the Saturday dinners cooking. She could identify the mouth-watering aromas of roast chicken, pork, garlic, and spices. There was obviously no shortage of good meat and vegetables here with all the surrounding farms, and she looked forward with great anticipation to the dinner Pascal's mother was preparing.

Away from the tram station, the town was quiet. The shops were closed for the midday break and would not open until three, after people had eaten and had had their afternoon repose. Wafts of warm, sooty smoke came drifting from the blacksmith's shop as they passed it, testifying to the hot embers still glowing inside, awaiting the artisan's return. It was an earthy, reassuring smell.

Before long, they reached the Compain bakery. The shop had one small window with a display of delicious-looking pastries. Emile saw no bread on the shelves, which was only normal for that time of day. Emile was confident Mr. Compain was busy baking to restock the shelves when the shop would reopen later.

As Pascal opened the locked front door of the bakery, Emile's expectations were confirmed. The warm, sweet smell of baking bread hit them immediately. They all inhaled deeply, and Pascal bade them continue to the back of the shop from where the aroma was emanating. As they walked past the display cases filled with pastries, Beatrice asked her mother if they could have one.

"Maybe later, my dear. I'm sure Mr. and Mrs. Compain have a lovely meal prepared for us. You wouldn't want to spoil your appetite, would you?"

"Oh, Mama!"

After walking through a tasseled curtain at the back of the shop, they found themselves before the ovens. A narrow staircase led up to the family living quarters. They climbed the stairs and entered a bright living room overlooking the street. Mr. and Mrs. Compain were waiting to welcome them.

Mr. Compain was a small man with thin, grey hair and red-veined cheeks. He smiled broadly at his guests. Emile imagined he looked older than he was. He didn't envy the baker's life, having to get up in the middle of the night so everyone could have fresh bread for breakfast. Fortunately, life looked as though it had been easier on Mrs. Compain. Her complexion was much less weathered, and her hair had only tinges of gray, making her look several years younger than her husband. Emile was glad for Sophie's sake since she was destined to become a baker's wife. Mrs. Compain looked kind, and he imagined she would teach Sophie all she needed to know about running a bakery and helping with the pastries.

Monique stepped forward to hand Mrs. Compain the roses, and Emile gave her the leeks.

"Thank you. Those both look wonderful," she said with a smile. "We are so glad to meet you. Pascal has told us all about you. I am Nadine."

"And I am Pierre. It is wonderful to have you come. You have a beautiful daughter, though I don't need to tell Pascal that, eh?" he joked, looking proudly at his son.

"Oh pardon me! I see you have two beautiful daughters," he said, smiling at Beatrice. "It is too bad I have only one son."

Beatrice blushed and looked at her mother.

After ten minutes of mutual hugging and kissing, they all sat on large sofas. Mr. Compain offered champagne to celebrate the betrothal of the two lovebirds. After toasting the couple, Mrs. Compain brought out some pâté as an hors d'oeuvre.

"This is a wonderful foie gras," declared Pierre enthusiastically. "I get it from Mr. Duverne, one of the local farmers. He raises the geese and grows the herbs that go into it. His wife actually makes the foie gras, and I give him bread in exchange. It is a mutually beneficial arrangement. We are having one of his geese for dinner."

"You don't seem to be suffering too much here with the war, Mr. Compain."

"Oh, please, call me Pierre. After all, we will be family soon. No, we are lucky. Oradour is too small and unimportant to be of interest to the Germans or Marshal Pétain for that matter. It is just as well. People here like to keep to themselves."

"If only everyone could do that, but then we wouldn't be at war, would we?" asked Emile somewhat critically.

Monique scowled before turning to Pierre. "Pierre, I would love some foie gras."

Pierre spread pâté on a slice of bread with the care of an artist. Monique took it carefully in deference to his masterpiece. She tasted it, and her eyes lit up. "Ah, this is really wonderful. It is the best I've ever tasted."

Pierre glowed. "I will give you some to take back with you. We can always get more."

The dining table was set with the finest Limoges porcelain. "We don't usually use this," explained Nadine. "It was my mother's, but today is special. It's not every day your son gets engaged."

Nadine had prepared a splendid meal that Pascal helped serve. He was particularly attentive to Sophie's needs, which Monique was glad to see. *He'll make a great husband for Sophie,* she thought.

Emile marveled at the main dish. "This goose is exquisite, madam," he said. "If you spoil my daughter with such cooking, I fear we will never see her again."

Pierre brought three of his best bottles of wine from his cellar, each perfectly complementing one of the courses. For dessert, Nadine had cooked an exquisite tart with apples from the garden. To round out the meal, Pierre served a plate of cheeses. His own preference, which he was not shy to tell them, was a goat cheese covered in a green furry mold.

"It will be hard to match this food for the wedding in St. Junien," Monique said. "We have a market that used to be very good. You could find anything there, but since this terrible war began, most of the produce goes to the soldiers. It's impossible to find good, fresh ingredients unless you live in the country."

"Then just let us know what you need, and we will bring it from Oradour," Nadine said. "Pierre, of course, will bake all the bread, and I will make the pastries."

"You are too kind. Maybe I will ask you for a few things, but Sophie is our daughter, and we will try as hard as we can to give her the best wedding. I'm sure you will be doing enough for her when she comes to Oradour. We can't ask you to take care of the wedding as well. Can we, Emile?"

Emile shook his head. "Of course not. We have many friends in St. Junien, and many of them have gardens. Some even keep a few keep animals. I am sure they will help us out. With the recent news from Normandy, I am even hoping the war might be over before the wedding. That would make life much easier."

"I'll drink to that," exclaimed Pierre, holding his glass in the air.

CHAPTER 6

A Collision Course

Adolf stormed back into the house he had commandeered in St. Junien. He was a man obsessed, a machine with only one purpose—to rescue Helmut. Colonel Städler could sit around at headquarters in Limoges waiting for news, but that was not for him; he was a man of action, a thoroughbred raised for the chase, and the hunt had been called. He had been given the scent, and it came from Oradour-sur-Glane.

"Captain Richert!" he shouted. "Come with me. I need you to translate what those fools of Milice have to say again." He threw open the doors to the room, hardly slowing his pace, and walked toward the occupants clustered around a map. The two Milice officers, Eugene Patry and Léon Pitrud, were arguing over something with Sergeant Joachim Kleist of the Gestapo. However, Adolf's brusque entry ended their discussion abruptly.

"Heil Hitler," snapped Sergeant Kleist, raising his arm and clicking his heels.

"Heil Hitler," responded Major Diekmann perfunctorily, raising his arm slightly. *We do not have time for such nonsense.* "Gentlemen, time is of the essence if we are to save Major Kämpfe. He was kidnapped last night by a gang of terrorists the law enforcement seems to have been completely unable to contain—"

"Major Diekmann, I must protest," objected Eugene Patry. "The Milice has done everything possible to eliminate the maquis, but we do not get the resources we need from the government in Vichy, and they have many local sympathizers."

"Then arrest the sympathizers," Adolf said impatiently. "Line them up and shoot them. Without sympathizers, the terrorists cannot function effectively."

Patry attempted to respond, but Adolf raised his hand. "Save your objections. We will discuss them after we have recovered Major Kämpfe. In the meantime, if you are unable to 'eliminate' these terrorists by yourselves, the SS can help you. I think you will find our methods most effective. Sergeant Kleist, give them any assistance they require."

"Certainly, Major," the sergeant said happily, cocking his head menacingly at Patry, who looked at his colleague Léon. His expression confirmed he too was intimidated by this offer of assistance, exactly as Major Diekmann had intended.

"What is the latest news we have on the kidnapping?" asked Sergeant Kleist.

"Nothing has been heard of the major since his disappearance. We have had no contact with the kidnappers. Colonel Städler is hopeful they will call with a ransom demand. However, we have had other reports indicating the Communists may be preparing to kill the major in retribution for his execution of some of their members in Guéret. Is that not correct?" he asked, looking for confirmation from the two Milice.

"Yes, that is correct," replied Pitrud nervously.

"Very well. Do your contacts also tell you he is being held in Oradour-sur-Glane?"

Léon looked at Eugene for approval. After a pause, he replied somewhat hesitatingly, "We cannot be sure, but we think that is where he was last seen."

Adolf pounced on that. "Then that is where we shall go. Colonel Städler has authorized me to take a force to search for the major under Captain Otto Kahn into Oradour-sur-Glane this afternoon. Our actions must be quick and decisive. Helmut's life may depend upon it."

"Where is Oradour-sur-Glane?" asked the sergeant.

"It is a small town between here and Limoges," replied Patry. "We believe it is a hotbed of maquis activity."

"Do you have evidence of that?" asked Kleist.

"Nothing concrete, but the inhabitants have been very uncooperative with the Milice."

"That's no proof they are maquisards," the sergeant said.

"Enough!" shouted Adolf. "I am uninterested in such details. Let us focus on the mission. Sergeant Kleist, you will be responsible for questioning any partisans we find. I want answers, and I don't care how you get them. Understood?"

"perfectly, Major. You will get what you need. I will have your answers. You will find my methods to be most persuasive."

"I am depending on it. Gentlemen, the goal is to get Helmut back alive. Nothing else matters. I will take whatever risks are required. Helmut would do the same for me."

"What is the plan, Major?" asked Patry.

"We are to meet up with Captain Kahn just south of Oradour. He will be accompanied by a force of Waffen SS troops in armored personnel carriers."

"And if there is any resistance?" Pitrud asked.

"It will be crushed without mercy," responded Adolf.

Léon smiled at Eugene, who likewise seemed pleased with the rules of engagement. "Showing a firm hand to the residents of Oradour will teach them to show more respect to the Milice," said Eugene.

Adolf looked annoyed at their gloating. "We are not going to Oradour to settle a vendetta between the townsfolk and the Milice. We are going there to rescue Major Kämpfe! Do I make myself clear?"

"perfectly, Major," stammered Eugene.

"Yes, Major," added Léon.

"We will leave immediately. Our first objective will be to surround the town. Then, we round up everyone for questioning."

Adolf picked up his cap bearing the outspread eagle emblem of the Wehrmacht. He carefully and proudly positioned it on the short stubble on his head. He removed his P38 Walther from its holster at his waist. He extracted the magazine and examined it. It was full. Satisfied, he snapped it back into place and returned the gun to his side.

His car was waiting. Joachim Kleist joined him for the ride to Oradour, and the two Milice officers followed in their Citroën Deux Chevaux. Its two round bulbous headlights reminded the major of the eyes of a frog, the symbol of this miserable country.

It did not take long for the entourage to reach the outskirts of Oradour. All around was rich farming country, outwardly peaceful and unthreatening, but Major Diekmann had learned from experience on the Eastern Front that such tranquility could belie a dangerous reality. Many times, they had been ambushed in just such bucolic surroundings.

Captain Kahn was there with a motorized column of armored tanks, half-tracks, and trucks camouflaged with foliage. The column comprised around 180 SS Panzers of the Third Company Der Führer of the Second Division of the Waffen SS Das Reich. Most of the soldiers were between eighteen and twenty-five.

Adolf looked into their faces and lamented how the division had deteriorated over the last few years. At the beginning of the war, Das Reich had been an all-volunteer force from Germany and Austria, a well-disciplined and well-trained force. Most of those men had been lost in Russia and had been replaced by inexperienced youth from countries all over Europe. Many were conscripts, and many were from Alsace-Lorraine, which had been part of France until 1940. Adolf had no confidence in their allegiance to the Third Reich.

Otto Kahn came over as Adolf jumped out of the car. "Captain Kahn, I want everyone in the town rounded up for questioning. No exceptions. Is that understood?"

"Absolutely, Major." He saluted.

"This operation is to be conducted with the utmost efficiency. Use whatever force is necessary. If anyone resists, shoot them. The high command has directed us to go on the counteroffensive and take strong reprisals against all acts of insurrection. Kidnapping an officer of the SS is the highest form of insurrection and warrants the sternest retribution. I am determined that when we leave today, there will be no more armed resistance in this town. I mean to make an example of it."

"Understood, Major." Captain Kahn nodded sharply. "My men will be glad to comply. They have no time for civilians who shoot at us from behind haystacks."

"Excellent. Remember that our primary objective is to find Major Kämpfe and those who kidnapped him. They must not be allowed to escape and take him with them. I suggest therefore, that you begin by setting up checkpoints on all the roads into town."

"Very good, Major. We shall make that our priority."

Adolf took out a map to show the captain. "I shall drive into town to tell the mayor we are conducting an identity check and need all the town to assemble in the marketplace, or fairground, as they call it. You will follow me with most of the troops. The convoy is to assemble here, in the square outside the church," said Adolf, pointing to the map. "I want your men to begin a sweep of the town immediately."

"With what instructions?" asked Captain Kahn.

"They are to look for Major Kämpfe and round up everyone they find. I want every house searched for evidence of involvement with the Communists. If they suspect any building is being used by the maquisards, they are to burn it. These terrorists will learn they are not dealing with the local garrison or the Milice. They will think better next time of kidnapping an SS officer."

"Heil Hitler." The captain saluted before returning to his officers and to relay the instructions. After a brief discussion, they remounted their vehicles. A couple of half-tracks split off and headed to Peyrilhac and St. Junien, to the east and west. Another detachment headed in the direction of neighboring farms.

Adolf gave the command to move out. The column followed him. They crossed the bridge over the River Glane and drove into town. Major Diekmann's car continued into the fairground while most of the vehicles pulled up outside the church. A few of the trucks continued up the main road toward Javerdat, which went north through Oradour.

Major Diekmann got out of his car. It was around 1:30 p.m., and the fairground was deserted. There were few people on the streets; most of the town's residents were enjoying their midday meal. Adolf ordered the two Milice officers to fetch the mayor. As he waited, he looked around, wondering if his friend Helmut was close by.

Eugene and Léon returned shortly, accompanied by an elderly man with a white goatee. "Good day, sir," said the man in a firm but annoyed tone. "I am the mayor, Dr. Paul Desourteaux. You asked to see me?"

Adolf stood stiffly. He observed the mayor studying the SS lightning flashes on his collar, but he did not seem to be intimidated. Despite his years, he seemed sharp and energetic. His expression remained impassive.

"Mr. Mayor, there have been attacks against our forces by armed criminals in this region, so we are here to conduct identity checks. We require everyone in town to assemble here in the marketplace so it can be conducted as quickly and efficiently as possible."

"But Major, we are a quiet town of farmers and shopkeepers. There are no maquis in the town. No one from Oradour has attacked your soldiers, I assure you. We had a theft of tobacco a few weeks ago, but there have been no attacks in this town against the occupation forces or the Milice. We are one of the most peaceful areas of the Haute-Vienne. That is why they send refugees here. We even have Gestapo officers come here to get out of Limoges."

Major Diekmann was unbending. "Then you will have nothing to worry about. I expect your full cooperation. If you cannot get your townsfolk to assemble voluntarily, my troops will help you."

"I will have to summon the town council to organize everyone."

"Do so immediately. What is the population of the town?"

The mayor looked troubled by the question. "Normally, we are fifteen hundred and seventy-four, but with the refugees and the children who have joined us from Paris, Alsace-Lorraine, and other areas, the population is around sixteen hundred and eighty. Today is also the day of the meat distribution and tobacco rations, and there are medical checks and vaccinations for the children, so we are surely even more than that."

Four members of the town council arrived to consult with the mayor. He explained the major's demands. Despite their objections, they had no choice but to comply. Dr. Desourteaux turned to Major Diekmann.

"Mr. Jean Depierrefiche, our blacksmith, is our town crier. We will send him with his drum to let all know they must come here to have their identity cards checked."

"Good. I will have one of my troopers accompany him. Everyone must assemble for the check. There are to be no exceptions."

"But what if somebody is sick, or too old to walk?" the mayor asked.

"Then someone must bring them. No one is to remain in his house. Women, children, babies, the sick—I want them all here."

The mayor looked very troubled, but he clearly decided it was not worth objecting further given the resolve in Adolf's voice.

Panzers dressed in combat uniforms, wearing helmets, and armed with machine guns swarmed from the trucks in front of the church. They were running in all directions, with Otto Kahn screaming orders. The mayor and the townsfolk who had already gathered could understand little of what he was saying. However, they could clearly see the Germans were setting up machine-gun posts at all crossroads. Some of the troops set up machine guns on tripods at the entrances to the fairground.

"It is only a precaution," the mayor reassured those who could hear him. "There is nothing to worry about." His words offered little assurance, as further conversation was drowned out by the loud noise of tanks driving up the main street, rue Émile-Desourteaux, named after the mayor's grandfather.

In the Compain house, the meal was over. Nadine and Monique had adjourned to the kitchen to make coffee. It was a little after 2:00 p.m., and Mr. Compain and the others had returned to the comfort of the sofas in the sitting room. Pascal sat close to Sophie and wound his arm around her. Beatrice invited the family cat to sit on her lap.

"Would you like a cigarette?" Pierre asked Emile.

"Thank you, I would love one."

"Then I will just nip down to the tobacconist. I'm all out of tobacco, and today is ration distribution day."

Emile stood. "Oh I can't let you do that, not after that wonderful meal and all the bread you baked for us. I will go. I insist," declared Emile.

"Very well," agreed Pierre without much of a fight. "I was up extra early today, and I will use the time to put the dough in the ovens while you are away. It's not far to the tobacconist. Tell Mr. Dufour he is to give you my ration."

"I will be glad to. The walk will do me good after such a fine meal."

Pierre and Emile walked down the stairs and through the shop to the front door. Pierre opened it. "Go down the street that way," he pointed. "The tobacconist is on the left just after the road turns sharply to the right. You can't miss it. It will be crowded today."

"No problem. I will find it," said Emile. "I'll be back before you know it."

Pierre closed the door and returned to load his ovens. Emile walked away briskly down the street. He looked up at the sky, happy to feel the warmth of the sun on his face. It had rained in the morning, but the sky was clear and the air was fresh. Even in the middle of the horrible war, life still had its pleasures. He thought of Sophie sitting next to her fiancé and was happy they were in love. He recalled the happiness he and Monique had felt when they fell in love. They had both outgrown their youthful infatuation, but they still loved each other as much as ever.

A gust of wind caused the leaves to quiver on a tree as Emile was passing. The dancing patterns of the silvery undersides of the leaves reminded Emile of confetti. Hopefully, by the time it fell on the newlyweds, the war would be over and life would begin to return to normal.

Suddenly, a bicycle came flying around the corner. The man on it was pedaling frantically. "Run, run!" he screamed. "The Germans are coming!"

Emile stopped. "What's he talking about? Why's he fleeing?" Emile had seen no Germans in town when he had arrived. *Maybe he's attacked some of the garrison and they're chasing him.* Emile felt sorry for him but knew there was not much he could do to help. He could not risk getting involved, not in broad daylight, unarmed, and without his men. He stared pitifully at the man as he sped by, his face distorted as if in a terrifying nightmare.

"Go hide or the Germans will kill you!" the man screamed at Emile as he passed.

A few seconds later, Emile heard shots ring out from the direction the man had come. He looked down the street and saw two Germans running toward him, stopping intermittently to shoot at the man on the bicycle. Emile shuddered with the realization they were not merely soldiers from the garrison. They were SS, Panzers in full-combat uniform. *What are they doing in Oradour?*

He turned to the man on the bicycle and saw him hit in his back by a bullet. His body convulsed. His hands leaped from the handlebars. His head was thrown backward, and his body followed as the bicycle wobbled forward. The man's head struck the cobblestones in the street hard. Blood poured from it. It had all happened in just a few seconds, but Emile had seen it all in what had seemed to be slow-motion horror.

Without thinking, Emile ran to help him. He heard more shots. The Panzers were shooting at him. He felt a searing pain in his arm. His jacket started to turn red. He heard more bullets ricocheting around him. He ran in panic down an alley faster than he had ever run in all his life.

CHAPTER 7

Hide and Seek

Emile was nauseous, light headed from the loss of blood and the trauma of being shot. A rush of adrenaline helped him fight off the urge to lie down. He knew his life depended on his staying conscious. The soldiers would soon be upon him if he remained where he was. He had to run. But where?

Another wave of pain shot down his arm, and he squeezed it tightly to stem the bleeding. He looked at his bloodied hand and saw he could move his fingers. A good sign under the circumstances. Maybe just a flesh wound.

He heard the pounding of combat boots on cobblestones growing louder. Near panic, he ran as fast as he could. He exited the alley and spontaneously turned right. He had no knowledge of the town, no idea of where to go, no guess as to where he could hide. The doors to all the houses were shut; they seemed ominously empty. Some windows were broken. Emile had never felt so alone and so helpless.

He knew if he stayed in the open, he would be caught and almost certainly shot. He could not hope to outrun a division of Panzers. He had to hide quickly. He looked around for any opportunity. The soldiers would be exiting the alley at any moment and use him for target practice. Just as he was losing hope, a door across the street opened just a crack. He thought he was imagining it, but it opened wider. He ran toward it, not knowing what he might find in the darkness behind it.

"Mister! Over here," a voice cried out from inside. "Come in. I will hide you!"

It was a young, accented voice. Emile had no idea to whom it belonged or whether it was a trap, but it seemed his only chance to stay alive. He would have to take the risk. Drawing on his last reserves of energy, desperate to get off the street before the Panzers emerged from the alley, he ran to the open door. He felt his legs tiring. The cobblestones were slippery from the morning rain. He mounted the curb but lost his footing and fell on the uneven pavement, banging his head painfully against the stones. He tried to pick himself up. His vision turned red as a gash on his forehead bled freely. He began to despair. He felt a firm grip on his arm. Someone was pulling him into the darkness. He heard the door close behind them and bolts being pushed into their holes. They descended some steps.

Emile sat exhausted on a cold, stone floor. He caught his breath. A sweet, fresh smell permeated the air. For a second, he thought he had been transported into a lush field in the countryside. Maybe everything had just been a terrible dream. Maybe he had just fallen asleep on one of the picnics he and Monique liked to go on. He opened his eyes. He saw he was in a greengrocer's shop. The fresh smells were from vegetables and fruits all around him.

"Good day, Mister," he heard someone say. "My name is Julien Franqueville. You looked like you needed help. Are you hurt badly?"

Emile squinted through his bloodied eyes. The voice belonged to a blond and muscular teenage boy. "Not too much, I think. Thanks to you. My name is Emile Garnier. I owe you my life. You saved me from two SS Panzers."

"What did you do?"

"That's the strange part. I don't know! I was walking to the tobacco shop when they came running down the street shooting at a cyclist who was coming toward me. They hit him, and when I went to help, they shot at me. I have no idea why."

"That is awful! Let me get you some water and bandages. Come to the back of the shop. Those Panzers will be looking for you."

He grabbed Emile's arm and helped him walk past the baskets of fresh cherries, strawberries, and lettuce. His eyes were becoming accustomed to the dim light in the shop, which was below street level; its few windows did not let in much light, and the blind was drawn on the door. Emile saw rough stone walls covered in multicolored salts and mold in places. It was a good place for vegetables, he reflected, isolated from the summer heat.

Julien ran up some stairs midway along one of the side walls, leaving Emile sitting on the floor. He was back within a few minutes with a bowl of water and bandages. He took off Emile's jacket and shirt carefully and looked at his arm. The bleeding had almost stopped. He had been lucky. Even though it hurt, it was only a flesh wound, as he had surmised. The boy cleaned and bandaged the wound.

"Where did you learn to do that?" asked Emile.

"My mother taught me. She was a nurse when we lived in Metz, but she hasn't worked since we came to Oradour."

"What brought you to Oradour? It's a long way from Metz."

"We had to leave Lorraine in November 1940. The Germans evicted us from our house. They gave us only one hour to pack a maximum of thirty kilos of belongings and leave. As soon as we left, a German family moved in. Many families have been evicted all over Lorraine. The Germans want to make it part of their fatherland again."

"But why come to Oradour? It's not much more than a village. Most people outside the Limousin have never heard of it."

"That's part of the reason. My father wanted us to get away from the war. He had some friends who'd moved here, and they wrote to tell him it was a very quiet town, so he decided we should join them. There are forty-four of us now from Lorraine living in Oradour. The locals call us Ya Yas because we still say the German *ja* for yes. It is a hard habit to break. We even have our own school," Julien said proudly.

"Are your parents here?"

"No. They left on the train this morning to go to Limoges. They will not be back until this evening. They left me in charge of the shop. It's good they aren't here. My father hates the Germans for what they did to us in Lorraine. If he were here, he might do something stupid and get himself killed."

"I don't blame him. Do you know what the Germans are doing here?"

"They banged on the shop door about a quarter of an hour ago. They were shouting that everyone had to go to the marketplace for an identity check."

"Identity check? In Oradour? There have been attacks on their convoys all across the Haute-Vienne and they come to sleepy Oradour-sur-Glane? Doesn't make sense."

"No, and they are an SS Panzer division. They don't usually waste their time with routine identity checks."

"I don't like it," Emile said. "They're here for something else. Why did you not go to the marketplace as ordered? You're taking a big risk."

"My father told me to hide if the Germans ever came to our house again. Many of my friends in Lorraine were forced to join the German army. He didn't want that to happen to me. I think he would rather I was dead than fighting for Germany."

Loud voices outside interrupted their conversation. Emile assumed the two Panzers were nearby. He gestured to Julien to be quiet. Emile heard the soldiers nearing the shop.

"They've found traces of your blood in the street," whispered Julien, translating the soldiers' conversation. "They will find where you hit your head on the pavement. I do not think we are safe here. We must leave now," Julien said agitatedly.

"I don't see another exit."

Julien hurriedly hid the bowl of water and bandages under a table festooned with fresh strawberries. "Come with me."

He heard one of the soldiers outside shout, this time in perfect French, "Come out into the street immediately or we will shoot!"

"They are Alsatians," Julien said. "There are many of them in the SS. Some were forced, but many others volunteered to prove they were more German than French. They can be worse than the Germans."

At the back of the shop was a long table covered in produce. The wall behind it was covered by a green cloth hanging from the ceiling. Julien fumbled under a bin filled with endives; his hand emerged holding a large black key. He reached over the vegetables and lifted the curtain to reveal an old cracked door on large metal hinges. In the middle of the door was a carving of a bunch of grapes; the paint had long since faded. Julien unlocked the door, pushed it open, and dived under the table. He emerged in the open doorway and beckoned Emile. Once Emile was beside Julien, Julien let the cloth fall back into place over the door. The thick cloth made the room dark.

"There are some stairs here," Julien said. "Go down and wait at the bottom."

Emile descended the stairs as Julien tried to close the door behind them. The deafening noise they heard next was all too familiar to Emile—machine-gun fire. The Panzers were firing into the shop. Julien strained to close and lock the door, which muffled all sound outside and left them in complete darkness.

Emile could hear Julien fiddling around as if searching for something. He heard a match strike and saw Julien's face in the orange glow of candlelight. "I'm afraid there is no electricity down here."

"What is this place?" asked Emile quietly.

"A wine cellar. This used to be a wine shop when it was built. Most people have no idea it's here. We should be able to hide here until the Germans go away."

Emile looked around in the flickering light. The cellar had a long, vaulted ceiling. The storage racks for wine bottles were empty save for a few bottles close to them.

"My parents had to leave all their wine in Alsace," said Julien, reading Emile's mind. "My father prays it has all turned to vinegar. He hates to think of the Germans drinking it."

The thick, stone walls and the heavy oak door sealed them in a world without danger, a world without time. As worries for his safety gradually receded from his mind, they were replaced with worries for his family. He had left them in the middle of a happy family gathering. *What if they went out looking for me?* "I have to go back to my family. I have to get them out of Oradour."

"You will have to wait. Listen," Julien said.

They heard dull banging outside followed by another long series of dull crackling.

"The Germans are still here. They are firing into the shop," said Julien.

Another series of loud thuds was followed by loud but unintelligible voices. Emile and Julien waited. Emile held the bandage on his arm and became more nervous.

Finally, Julien nodded encouragingly. "I think they are gone. We can go out now." He put the key in the lock. "Hold the candle."

He turned the key slowly, trying not to make any noise, but the lock was old and had not been oiled for many years. He grimaced but relaxed. He grabbed the handle and started opening the door. "Blow out the candle."

Emile did. They were once again bathed in the light coming through the curtain. They stood motionlessly. They listened for the slightest sound. A sudden bang caused them to jump and their hearts to race until they realized it was only something falling off a shelf.

Julien slowly lifted the curtain. Emile had a nightmare vision of two Germans with machine guns pointed at them. He was wrong, but the scene was nearly as frightening. The Panzers had destroyed nearly everything in the shop.

Julien walked out into the chaos, trying to step over lettuce, potatoes, beans, cherries, and other produce littering the floor. Most of the tables had been destroyed by the hail of bullets. Shards of window and door glass glistened at the front of the store.

Julien held his head and wept. "What will I tell my parents? They have destroyed everything. I was supposed to look after the shop today. We have lost everything."

Emile realized he had been treating a boy as if he were a man. Julien was mature for his years but not hardened to life, not to the horrors of the past few years.

"No. Your parents have not lost everything. They can replace all this but not you."

Julien tried to dry his tears.

"I think you should come with me. It is not safe to stay here," said Emile, feeling responsible for the trouble he had brought upon the boy. None of this would have happened if he had not called out to save him from the Germans.

Julien nodded. He followed Emile to the door. The street was clear. Emile headed cautiously back up the street the way he had come.

"Where are we going?" asked Julien.

"To Mr. Compain, the baker."

"I will show you a back way. The main streets aren't safe," said Julien, still in shock. "Germans are everywhere."

Julien turned down a narrow alley in between the houses. It led to an area where some townsfolk had small allotments for growing vegetables. Around the field was a low stone wall. "If we walk behind this wall, we will not be seen. Then we can cut back into the town close to Mr. Compain's house. We have a garden here; I often come by it after fetching bread from Mr. Compain's bakery," he said with unexpected cheeriness.

The two shuffled, crouching under the wall until they reached a well-worn footpath that turned into town. Emile listened but heard nothing. It was quiet, too quiet for Emile's liking. He put a finger to his lips and walked cautiously in the direction of the tidy stone buildings and narrow, cobbled streets. As they got closer, Emile became more concerned. Things were anything but normal. No children were playing in the street. No noise was coming from any of the houses. Emile noticed many of the doors were open. It was as if the town had suddenly been deserted. Emile hurried to Mr. Compain's bakery.

When they got to the bakery, they saw its door was open. Inside, bread was in the ovens, but no one was tending them. Everyone had gone; his wife and daughters and his future son-in-law and his family. Upstairs, filled coffee cups were on the table. "They have gone to the marketplace like everyone else," Julien said flatly.

"I must go there too. I have to be with them." Emile was close to panic.

Julien stared at him and slowly shook his head. "You must stay hidden. You have blood all over your arm and head. If the Germans see you, they will take you as a maquisard or a spy. They will shoot you on the spot."

Emile realized the boy was right. He might not only get killed, but he could also endanger his wife and daughters, but he knew he had to do something. "I must go to the marketplace to see if they are all right. If they are, I will wait for them to be released."

Julien shook his head. "Mister, I think that would be very dangerous, but I will help you if you must. I can't go back to our shop until the Germans have left."

Emile felt guilty putting him in more danger, but he did not know the town. He would be safer with Julien to guide him. Maybe both of them would be safer together. The boy had sacrificed enough for him, so he would try not to put him in any further danger.

Julien moved to the doorway, clearly anxious to leave. After what had happened at his father's shop, he was right that they were safer outside. There was something unnerving about a house that had been deserted in the middle of life's routines. The Germans might return at any moment. Emile breathed deeply and nodded. "Okay, let's go, but be careful. There's no need for you to get shot as well."

"We will go back through the fields to the marketplace to avoid the Germans. There are some trees we can hide behind and see what's going on in the fairground."

The boy and Emile left the bakery. The street was deserted. Emile followed him along narrow footpaths through the fields as they skirted the town.

"This track leads to the fairground," said Julien. "We must be very careful. It is not far now. The Germans are sure to be watching it."

He had hardly spoken when they heard machine-gun fire. Emile listened in horror, terrified it would continue. He started sweating profusely. *What's happening to my wife and daughters? Are they in danger?* He berated himself for having left them. If only he had not gone to get tobacco, he would have been there when the Germans came. If only he had not been so selfish. But the shots were not coming from the fairground. If his family was there, they would probably be safe.

They approached the fairground and heard many people talking. Occasionally, someone addressed them over a loudspeaker, telling them to stay calm and have their identity cards ready. *My family should not have any problems,* Emile thought. Monique never allowed any of them to go anywhere without their papers.

Emile and Julien crouched behind a wall as close to the fairground as they dared get. They could see what was going on and heard some of the conversations. Emile estimated there were around seven to eight hundred people gathered in the fairground—men, women, and children. A group of young mothers had gathered in one area with their babies in prams or in their arms. Some looked frustrated while others looked angry, but there was no panic or hysteria. Emile tried to pick out some of the conversations. Most people seemed simply to be complaining they had been forced to leave their midday meals or whatever they had been doing. A few worried about family members they had left behind and hoped the Germans didn't find them. Everyone seemed anxious for the Germans to inspect their identity cards so they could go home.

Emile and Julien saw an SS command post with large machine gun on a tripod pointed at the fairground. It was manned by several Panzers in camouflage with patches of chestnut and green. Emile saw a similar post at the other entrance to the fairground. Standard procedure to control a large crowd, he thought, but he did not like to think that such weapons of death were pointed at his family. Emile studied one Panzer behind a machine gun; he was holding it tightly with both hands, his finger on the trigger. It was clear he would not hesitate to spray death into the crowd if given the order.

Where is my family? He raised his head a little higher to locate them.

"Mister! Keep down or we'll be killed," Julien begged, pulling on Emile's jacket.

Emile ducked down a bit but continued to look for his family. He saw them. They were with the Compain family and others he presumed were friends. Sophie and Pascal were holding hands. Emile was frustrated they were on the far side of the fairground; that made it impossible to get their attention. *Probably just as well though.*

They heard a commotion in the street; noisy schoolchildren were laughing and talking. A few adults—Emile took them to be teachers—were leading them to the fairground. Behind them, urging them on with machine guns, were three Panzers. The children looked excited to have a reason to get out of school. Emile estimated there were at least a hundred and fifty of them.

Some of the girls started skipping rope, and a few boys started kicking a ball. Most, though, seemed fascinated by the soldiers. One group stood close to the Panzers with the machine guns in seeming admiration. One of the Panzers spoke to them with a friendly smile. Another group of children hung over the wall screaming at each other and pointing excitedly at the tanks and half-tracks.

"See those children?" Julien pointed to a group of about thirty very small children. "They are refugees from Lorraine, like me. I know most of their families."

Emile observed some less-willing participants coming up the main street to join the gathering in the marketplace. An old couple who were having trouble walking and a middle-aged lady in night clothes were being pushed and herded like cattle by a couple of Panzers. The Germans appeared to be whistling and laughing at them.

Just then, a car came down the street and turned toward the fairground entrance. Several of the Panzers turned their machine guns on the car. "Halt!" they shouted.

CHAPTER 8

A Day to Remember

The mayor came running up to the entrance. "Stop!" he cried. "That is my son. He is my partner in our medical practice. He has been attending to a childbirth out of town."

The Germans relaxed a little but kept their guns pointed at the car. One soldier went to the car and demanded the driver's identity card.

"He is Doctor Jacques Desourteaux," stated the mayor proudly.

"Okay. He can join you," agreed the Panzer begrudgingly, apparently satisfied with the doctor's Vichy papers. He waved the car in, and the Panzers cleared a way for him. Jacques got out of the car and joined his father.

As the mayor talked to his son, a large, open, camouflaged truck pulled up outside the fairground. It was full of people. The tailgate fell. Everyone was ushered out and into the fairground. The tailgate was hitched again. The truck drove off, presumably to round up more people.

When a group of cyclists, five men and a girl, attempted to ride by the fairground, a pair of Panzers leaped in front of them, their weapons ready to fire, and ordered them to stop.

"We are from Limoges," shouted one bicyclist. "We came to buy eggs and cherries."

The Germans were unimpressed. One, in perfect French, ordered them off their bicycles and into the fairground.

The mayor was getting tired and frustrated with having to keep assuring everyone there was no need for concern. He desperately wanted to get back to his surgery.

A Panzer came through the crowd toward the mayor. "The major wants to see you," he demanded.

At last, thought Dr. Desourteaux. *They are finally going to check our papers and we can all go home.* He followed his escort to Major Diekmann and Otto Kahn, who were in animated discussion. He could not understand more than a few words of German, but they stopped their discussion when they saw him. A Gestapo officer in his intimidating, jet-black uniform stood behind them.

"Mr. Mayor," the major said, "we believe this town is the center of terrorist activity against the Third Reich. We believe citizens of Oradour have killed German soldiers and participated in the kidnapping of a German officer. I intend to search all the houses in town thoroughly. To help ensure the cooperation of the townsfolk while we search, I require you to designate thirty hostages."

The mayor was horrified. He had heard of what was rumored to have happened in Tulle when the SS had taken hostages there. The people of Oradour-sur-Glane placed their trust in him; they looked to him as a father figure. He had brought many of them into the world and was indeed close to being their fathers. He could not offer them up to slaughter.

"Major," he said as diplomatically as possible, "these accusations are preposterous. As I told you before, we are a peaceful town. No one here has attacked your soldiers. As for hostages, I will answer for all the population. I do not have hostages to indicate to you. If somebody must be held responsible for an unspecified act, I indicate myself first, and after that, you can take other members of my family, including my four sons, who are all here."

The mayor's response was translated for Major Diekmann, who seemed angered by it. He and Captain Kahn began arguing. When they had finished, Major Diekmann addressed the mayor. "You will accompany me to the town hall so we may discuss this matter with my superior, Colonel Städler."

"If that is your wish." The doctor nodded condescendingly.

Major Diekmann, Captain Kahn, and the Gestapo, Sergeant Joachim Kleist, led the mayor the short distance to the town hall and posted guards in front of the building.

"You will explain to the colonel your unwillingness to provide hostages," demanded Adolf. "I am sure he will explain to you the consequences of noncooperation." He turned to Captain Kahn. "Get me headquarters." The captain picked up the phone and dialed for the operator. After a few minutes, he was agitated. "There is no reply. I cannot get through. The operator is not picking up my call."

Dr. Desourteaux smiled, but just to himself. "That is because the town operator, Odette Bouillere, is in the fairground along with everyone else you have rounded up. There is no one at the exchange."

Adolf banged the table with his fist. "Very well! We will return to the marketplace, and I will decide what we shall do."

Once back at the fairground, Adolf spoke to Eugene Patry and Léon Pitrud, who had told him Major Kämpfe was being held in Oradour. "My men have searched most of the houses and so far have found nothing. Where is Major Kämpfe? You were confident we would find him here!"

The two looked at each other nervously. Léon nodded slightly to Eugene. "Major, the news is not good," Eugene said. "We believe the maquis grew impatient and killed Major Kämpfe before we arrived. They have probably buried him somewhere in the area, but it will be difficult to find out where."

"No! That cannot be! Helmut cannot be dead. Not after all we went through together in Russia. To be killed here in this meaningless little town by stupid peasants? It cannot be. He deserved more than that. Sergeant Kleist, did you learn anything?"

"No, Major. I interrogated several suspects, but despite my methods of persuasion, I could learn nothing about Major Kämpfe. I do not believe they have seen him."

"Captain Kahn, did your men find any hidden weapons or evidence of involvement with the terrorists in the houses you have searched?"

"No, Major, not so far, but we have not had time for a thorough search. They may have hidden weapons and uniforms in the forest, a common practice with the resistance."

Léon Pitrud stepped forward. "Major, we believe the maquis left town this morning before we arrived and took Major Kämpfe and their weapons with them. If they followed their usual pattern, they gave him a mock trial and shot him as a traitor to France."

Adolf fumed. "Traitor to France? He was trying to make this country great again, part of a new European empire. Their lives are worthless next to his!"

Adolf took off his hat and nervously rubbed the back of his head. "So we have no idea of where to find Major Kämpfe or who took him? We have no idea of who is maquisard and who is not?" he screamed.

The others looked around sheepishly, slowly shaking their heads, each wanting to avoid direct eye contact with the major. Captain Kahn finally dared break the silence. "No, Major. At this time, we do not."

Adolf breathed in deeply several times. When he turned his attention to those around him, he seemed to have calmed. The anger was gone from his expression. His eyes had a clear look of resolution. "Very well. This is the situation as I see it. We believe that at least some of the residents of Oradour-sur-Glane are responsible for the abduction, murder, and possible torture of a Waffen SS officer. Not any officer, but a hero of the Third Reich, decorated many times over. We cannot identify the conspirators in this despicable act, which must be taken as an act of war. Is that correct?" he asked, staring down each of them in turn.

"That is correct, Major," replied Captain Kahn with an abrupt nod.

Adolf paced in front of them a few times before continuing. He had the look of a judge deliberating on a sentence for an accused. "We have orders from the high command to strike with the utmost power and rigor against those who aid the maquis. The orders call for us to use intimidatory measures against the inhabitants when necessary and to break the spirit of the population by making examples. I suggest we have such a situation here."

"We do, Major," agreed Sergeant Kleist enthusiastically.

"Killing Major Kämpfe cannot go unpunished. Those responsible must be seen to pay a heavy price for such an action." Adolf looked at the others. He saw no sign of dissent. "Very good. The decision is made. We will set an example for the Communists today they will not forget. We will show them that fierce retribution can be expected for all future attacks on the SS and its officers. Captain Kahn, here are my orders."

Emile and Julien were getting more on edge with each minute. Nothing much seemed to be happening in the fairground. They could see German officers arguing among themselves, but no one was checking identity papers, and no one had been released. In fact, further disparate groups of people were continuously being brought to the fairground.

A volley of shots rang out from the forest behind them. The strain was taking a toll on Julien. He was coming out of the shock he had been in since the incident in the shop and only then realizing the seriousness of their situation. "My father will kill me when he sees what they did to our shop," he lamented, close to tears. "We have lost everything. We will be refugees again. I am so tired of running."

Emile held him tightly. "Pull yourself together. You're alive, and your parents are safe. My family is in the fairgrounds with German machine guns waiting to mow them down. Consider yourself lucky." He quickly regretted scolding the boy. He should never have done it, but his patience was running thin.

Some men close to them in the fairground were smoking pipes and cigarettes. The breeze blew the smoke in their direction, and he tried to inhale some. He would have given anything for a cigarette, but then he remembered that was the cause of his current situation.

As the men smoked, he overheard them gossiping about the Germans commandeering all the food in the area. Their conversations were interrupted by a shrill whistle from the loudspeaker. The crowd fell ominously silent.

"Attention. Attention," boomed the voice in perfect French. "This is not a simple identity check. We have reason to believe certain citizens among you have been involved with terrorist activities against Free France and the Third Reich. We intend to search all your houses for weapons and evidence of resistance activity. During this process, it would be easier if the women and children would wait in the safety of the church."

A murmur swept over the crowd. Emile saw by their expressions that the announcement had unnerved people. Some began to look very anxious.

An elderly man with a white goatee pushed out of the crowd toward the German officers. A group of people who were vigorously protesting accompanied him.

"That is our mayor, Dr. Paul Desourteaux, and his sons," announced Julien proudly. "He is a good man."

"Good man or not, it doesn't look like they have any interest in what he has to say."

"Look," urged Emile, pointing at the command post.

The mayor and his entourage were being barred from approaching the German officers by Panzers, their machine guns leveled. A woman in the crowd shouted something. In response, there was another announcement over the address system. "A mother says that she left her babies at home to sleep and is worried about them. She may go and get her children. Ladies, if any of you have children at home, fetch them and bring them back here so you can take them to the church."

Some women came forward and were escorted away. A short time later, the women returned with their little ones. The women and children kissed their fathers, husbands, and brothers. All were clearly anxious about when they would see each other again. In tears, the women and children filed out of the fairground toward the church. The children were encouraged to sing. Emile saw Monique accompanying his two daughters and Mrs. Compain. The sight made him relax a little. At least for a while they would be safe.

Once the women and children were gone, more instructions screamed out from the address system. "You will line up in three rows facing the north wall of the fairground."

When the men had complied, the announcer called out again. "All those who have arms, ammunition, and other prohibited merchandise hidden in their homes are to come forward immediately. If you declare them now, you will be dealt with leniently. If you do not come forward and such items are found in your home, you will be dealt with most severely. Our soldiers have orders to conduct a thorough search, so do not expect anything will remain hidden from us."

Emile heard one elderly farmer declare he had a rifle for which he had a permit. One of the German soldiers standing near the loudspeaker quickly dismissed his declaration with a swipe of his hand. No one else spoke.

"Very well," continued the announcer. "As a precaution, you will be locked up while we conduct the search. You will be divided into six groups. Do as you are told and you will come to no harm."

A group of armed Panzers moved toward the men. The soldiers began shouting orders to separate the men into groups. One after the other, they were led out of the fairground. Emile watched the mayor leading one group up the street, while his son Jacques led another.

"I do not like this," said Emile. "Why separate the men into several groups and take them out of the fairground? It would have required fewer soldiers to guard them all together in one group. Something is not right."

"I do not trust the SS. They are not like the regular soldiers. I saw what they could do in Lorraine," Julien said.

"Can we get a better view of the church?" asked Emile. "I want to make sure at least that my family is safe."

"If we are careful," replied Julien. "We can hide behind the infants' school. I know the area well. It is close to the school for the Lorraine refugees."

Cautiously, keeping low, they crept through the fields toward the church, saying nothing. The most dangerous point came where they had to cross the main road. A German machine-gun post looked directly up the street. Fortunately, the parade of men from the fairground distracted the guards for a few minutes; they took the opportunity to run across the road.

They lay down in the field. They had a clear view of the church and the square in front of it, which was swarming with activity and heavy vehicles. They saw a couple of buildings to one side being guarded by soldiers.

"That is Madam Laudry's barn over there, and that one is milord's barn," said Julien, pointing out two buildings. "They must have locked up some of the men in those barns."

Emile wanted to get closer but dared not. The soldiers were not simply standing around, as he would have expected if they were simply on guard duty. Instead, they were running in all directions, carrying things that he could not make out.

A covered truck drove up to the Laudry barn. He could make out the officer in charge screaming orders. Four Panzers ran to the back of the truck and lowered the tailgate. They climbed into the back. After a brief delay, they emerged, struggling with a heavy machine gun on a tripod they set up opposite the barn. One Panzer held a long belt of bullets feeding into the gun while another stood behind the gun, holding it with both hands.

"What are they doing?" asked Emile. "The men in the barn are unarmed. They don't need such a large weapon to keep them from escaping."

"Mister," said Julien, tapping him on the shoulder. "Look! They are setting up a machine outside milord's barn as well."

Emile saw two Panzers manning a heavy machine gun on a tripod and aimed at the barn doors.

Julien looked terrified. "Are they going to shoot everyone?"

"No, of course not," replied Emile confidently. "They may be Germans, but they are soldiers, not butchers. Even the SS has some honor. They don't shoot unarmed civilians for no reason."

But as he watched the situation develop, he became less confident of his own words. A second machine gun was unloaded at each site and set up beside the first. Trucks then drove up loaded with bales of hay.

"Why do they need those? What possible use could they have for hay? They have no livestock."

"I don't like it," cried Julien. "Something bad is going to happen. I can feel it. It was like this when they came to our town in Lorraine."

"Pull yourself together! It's probably just a precaution. They will finish searching the houses, and the men will be released."

Their conversation was interrupted by shots from somewhere just outside the town. Julien sank to the ground with his eyes closed, covering his ears. Emile could only imagine what his family must have gone through in Lorraine.

The next ten minutes were an eternity for Emile. From their vantage point, they could see little. Occasionally, a lone motorcyclist would ride up and down the main street, but apart from that, there were few soldiers around and no action taken regarding the hostages. Emile imagined that most of the soldiers were searching houses and prayed that when they returned empty-handed, they would release all the hostages and leave. Previous encounters with the SS warned him against such a favorable scenario, but as long as his family was in danger, he would continue to hope for it.

A loud commotion in the church square broke the strange calm. Emile saw many Panzers running around frantically and shouting orders. He dared hope they had decided not to waste any more time in Oradour after a fruitless search.

What he saw next terrified him. Instead of preparing to leave, the Panzers were getting into several tanks in the square outside the church. The engines had been running since the Germans had driven them into town, but they started roaring and spewing out black smoke as they began to move. Emile tried to rationalize the situation. "Maybe they are withdrawing the tanks from the town?"

Julien shook his head. "Mister, if they were going back to St. Junien, they would all be heading south. Each is headed in a different direction."

Emile agreed with Julien's reasoning. His hope for a peaceful outcome became more tenuous. "Then what are they doing? You don't need tanks to fight unarmed civilians."

As the tanks rumbled down the cobbled streets, Emile could feel the ground shaking. One stopped between the two barns and aimed its gun in the general direction of the barns. Julien looked aghast. A loudspeaker on a truck blared out something in German.

"What did they say?" Emile asked, but Julien had covered his ears to drown out the noise of the tanks.

They heard a loud explosion from close to where the loudspeaker was, and almost immediately, as if on cue, they heard machine-gun fire from multiple locations in town, including the two barns. Emile strained to see what was going on and was horrified.

The doors of both barns had been thrown open, and machine guns were strafing the insides mercilessly. Emile could not see inside the barns, but there was no need to, nor did he want to. Merely the image in his mind of what was happening brought him close to vomiting. The SS Panzers, the pride of the German Reich, were slaughtering men and young boys without quarter. He could not hear any screams over the sound of the machine guns, but he could hear them screaming in his head. He could see them writhing in his mind as the bullets tore their bodies apart.

"No! They can't be doing this! Not even the Germans!" Emile screamed. "Why? Why are they shooting them? They have done nothing. They are all innocent."

Emile was in shock. He had seen many people killed in the bloody war, but never like this, never on this scale, and never without any warning or reason.

Julien pressed his hands more tightly over his ears in a vain attempt to keep out the sound of the tanks and the shooting, but he was not succeeding. His face grimaced in pain.

In the streets around, bullets were flying everywhere. The soldiers were shooting at anything that moved. Emile watched as they shot dogs, cats, and even rabbits unfortunate enough to have been caught up in the mêlée. He saw a group of six young people walking toward the fairground to seemingly turn themselves in shot dead where they stood. Soon, there was blood over all the buildings from the violence of the attack, which flowed over the cobblestones down the side of the street. It was all too much. Emile turned away, fell on all fours, and vomited.

When he regained a modicum of composure, Emile lifted his head, desperately hoping the nightmare was over. It was not. The shooting continued throughout the town, in the streets, inside the houses, the barns, the cattle sheds, and in the fields around them. It was a level of violence and brutality beyond anything Emile had imagined. He had surely strayed into the hell that Monique and Father François had always warned him about, but he was not dead. He wanted to scream.

The machine guns at the barns stopped abruptly, having done their work, as did some of the shooting elsewhere, but sporadic gunfire continued. Emile saw soldiers shooting randomly into houses and at people trying to get out. He also watched soldiers emerging from several of the houses carrying bulging tablecloths and sheets clearly stuffed with family belongings. As they walked away with their booty, the soldiers would frequently turn back and launch a burst of machine-gun fire into the house they had just exited as if to ensure the owners would not pursue them.

Emile looked at the two barns and saw soldiers carrying the bales of hay inside. They lit several phosphor grenades and threw them in. "They're going to torch the buildings!"

Shockingly, and in stunning contrast to the macabre events around them, one of the Germans then turned a radio on loudly and blasted out music from a German station. It felt so surreal to Emile that for a moment he almost convinced himself he was in a dream. But his escape from reality was only fleeting.

The two men watched as the flames rapidly took hold of the buildings and shot out from the open doors. Emile wanted desperately to save anyone he could, but he knew that would be futile. Even if the Germans left immediately, by the time he could get to either building, it would be too late. Everyone would have been incinerated.

"Can we go now, Mister?" cried Julien. "It is not safe for us to stay here any longer."

"Yes, yes, we should go. We can do no more here, but I have to make sure my family is all right." Emile's voice trembled. "I cannot leave while they are in danger."

"They will be safe. That is why they sent them to the church."

"I hope you are right, but after what we have just seen, I cannot rest until they are back with me. I have never seen or heard of anything as horrific as that in this entire war. It was senseless. It makes me fearful of what else they might do."

"They are Hitlerian bastards," Julien spat out. "I hope the Americans and the English kill them all."

Emile looked at the church. Everyone appeared to be safe inside, but he knew that they must have heard the shooting and were terrified. He pictured women crying, not knowing the fate of their husbands and sons, and of children crying and asking their mothers if their daddies had been shot. If only he could let his family know he was safe.

Emile watched the church, hoping against hope an SS officer would go to the large, ancient oak doors riddled with woodworm and fling them open to release the women and children. Instead, he saw two Panzers approach the church carrying a large wood box. They waited for a few moments while a group of Panzers opened the doors for them. They entered the building with the box, accompanied by an armed escort.

"What are they doing?" asked Julien nervously.

"I don't know. I hate to think what they might be planning."

The soldiers emerged. The relief that brought to Emile did not last long. He saw that the soldiers had left the large box inside and worried about what it contained. When he saw the soldiers were running away from the church, he panicked. "Why are they running?" He strained desperately to look inside the church through the still-open doors, but it was too dark inside to make anything out.

Until he saw something that filled him with absolute dread.

On to the floor, he could see the glow of a fuse wire, a sight he was familiar with. As he stared at it, transfixed in horror, he noticed a second glow some distance away, another fuse wire. As the last soldiers emerged, they slammed the heavy doors behind them.

"No, no, no!" he screamed in horror. "They're going to blow up the church! For God's sake, they are soldiers, not butchers! There are more than four hundred women and children sheltering in there!"

Emile had never had much time for religion or churches, but he held the ancient tradition of sanctuary in a church as an absolute. Churches were respected as places of nonviolence, where the weak could seek safety. It had been so through the ages.

Ignoring the danger, Emile stood. "I have to go. I must to try to save my family!" he yelled frantically, not caring who might hear him.

"But there is nothing you can do for them. We must go," Julien said.

"You can go. You have done enough for me already. I will not ask any more of you. Find your family. I must find mine."

"Mister, you'll be killed! We both will if you don't get down!" Julien was terrified.

"I cannot leave my wife and daughters to be burned alive. I brought them here. It's my fault they are in there. I left them alone. My life is unimportant. My daughters are so young. I would gladly give mine to save them. You will be fine without me. Go."

"Mister, there is nothing you can do for your family. I am sorry, but they would not want you to die too. Come with me. We can escape."

Emile ignored his pleadings. He ran to a group of trees, planning to dart between them to get to the church square. Julien followed him. As Emile was about to run to the next tree, Julien jumped on him and began hitting him wildly.

"You cannot go. You cannot get yourself killed. I won't allow it! I have seen enough people die. There is nothing you can do for your family. You will be cut down before you get to the church."

Emile hit him back, but the boy was bigger and stronger. As they tussled wildly, Emile's arm wound opened. The excruciating pain sapped his strength. Julien was on top of him. Emile tried desperately to throw him off, but the boy held on tenaciously like a rider on a wild horse. He looked into Julien's eyes, which were filled with terror. Emile realized that Julien's survival depended on Emile's and he was not going to let him go.

As the two struggled, they heard loud bursts of machine-gun fire followed by a series of explosions. Julien relaxed, as if coming out of a trance. He let Emile up. From behind the tree, they looked at the church. The doors were open. Dark, acrid smoke was billowing out. Several Panzers fired machine guns inside while others were throwing in hand grenades.

"You see? There's nothing you can do!" screamed Julien. "It's too late for everyone."

Emile howled. "No! No! No!" He tried to pull out his hair. He banged the tree with his fists and his head. Blood started streaming down his face again. "The bastards! The murdering devils! How could they murder innocent civilians? What had they done to them? Many of them are only babies!" cried Emile. "I swear I will kill them all!"

Through the blood and tears clouding his vision, Emile looked at the church, desperate that the killing would stop and that maybe a few survivors would be allowed to emerge from the sanctity of the chapel of St. Anne. He prayed that maybe his beloved wife and daughters had found a place to hide.

A woman appeared in the doorway, her face blackened with soot and her dress partly burned. "I am German like you," she cried out in perfect German. "I am German, not French. I am here from Alsace, visiting friends. Please spare me," she begged.

Her plea was unheeded. A hail of bullets caused her to crumple. She fell back into the building like an empty sack.

Along the side of the church, shards of stained glass glistened on the cobblestones. They were shards from the scenes of the saints that had inspired the faithful for centuries but had been shattered by the heat or bullets. Emile watched soldiers walking around the building and throwing hand grenades into any openings they came across. Worst of all, though, was that occasionally he could hear screams coming from inside. They tore his soul.

"Look!" said Julien, pointing toward the rear of the church. A woman was crawling out of a broken window behind the nave. She was completely blackened by the smoke. She fell hard on the cobblestones. She miraculously picked herself up and ran like a wounded animal toward the small stone wall. Another woman appeared at the window with a baby. In desperation, she threw the infant to the ground. Emile gasped as it hit hard, fearful it would not have survived the fall. The mother threw herself down and picked up the child. After looking at it briefly, she ran in the same direction as the first woman.

The Germans spotted the two would-be escapees and opened fire. With a surge of energy, the first woman flung herself over the wall to safety, but it was too late for the second woman and her baby. She fell, her child in her arms, cut down by the deadly fusillade.

By the time the screaming inside the church stopped, Emile was numb. Without hope. Soldiers were throwing gasoline and straw into the gutted building that until only a short time ago had been a place of safety and solemnity. Flames quickly began to consume what was left of the building. The ferocious heat forced the soldiers to withdraw.

Emile wept. Everything he cherished had been destroyed in front of his eyes.

"Mister, we need to go. There is nothing for us here anymore," Julien said as he looked around, fearful they would be discovered.

Emile shook his head. He could not find the words. It was only with Julien's help that he managed somehow to pull his gaze from the church and follow Julien from the place where his life seemed to have come to an end. Julien headed north, away from the town center. Emile followed him like a ghost, walking in a daze. He swore he would never return to that place of death.

Far to the south, the torrid summer heat had caused a deep meteorological depression to grow over Spain; its enormous energy drove the winds around it in a turbulent vortex. As the winds blew ever stronger over the dark-blue Mediterranean, they picked up moisture produced by the relentless sun. It moved over the southeast of France, just to the north of the Pyrenees. The winds turned inland to complete their spiral, carrying the moisture with them. The moisture gave rise to billowing, black clouds that clashed with the jagged mountain peaks. Surging up the valley of the Canal du Midi between Perpignan and Béziers, the winds blew past the impregnable mass of the Black Mountain at the southern extremity of the Massif Central.

Canvas on the sails of windmills was shredding as the wind turned them furiously. It was an ancient wind that has always been associated with foreboding by the inhabitants of the region; a wind that has been known by many names, the Black Autan, the Black sailor, the wind of the Devil, or the wind of deaths. They have long said that it blew when the gods were angry and man was to be punished for his evil deeds.

CHAPTER 9

Flight

"Captain Kahn, it looks as though you have everything under control here. I will return to Limoges to report to Colonel Städler," Adolf declared.

"Very good, Major. We will finish cleansing the town of all the insurgents before we withdraw. It will be a lesson to the Communist thugs. It will show them the price they will pay for killing an SS officer."

"Excellent. Burn all the buildings before you pull out. I want no witnesses of the events here today. It would be better for all of us."

"Understood, Major. We will be very thorough."

"As always."

Major Diekmann got in his staff car. It had been a stressful day. He had gone to Oradour hoping to rescue his closest friend, Helmut Kämpfe, but they had failed to find him. The maquisard, a despicable rabble, had probably killed him before they arrived, but they had paid a heavy price for that act of barbarism. He had taught them a lesson they would not forget. He had avenged his friend's death and hopefully saved the lives of other SS officers by discouraging attacks on them.

On arriving at headquarters, Major Diekmann went straight into Colonel Städler's office and informed him of the events in Oradour. The colonel's reaction was not what Adolf had expected.

"You did *what?*" Colonel Städler fell back into his chair in shock. "You killed everyone in the town? Women and children too? What are you, some kind of animal? That is not the way of the German army!"

"But Colonel—"

"Major, you disgust me. You have disgraced the SS. We do not machine gun women and babies in churches. I asked you to bring me hostages, and instead you killed everyone!"

"Colonel, but they killed Major Kämpfe."

"What proof do you have? How do you know that he is even dead? If indeed he is, how do you know the citizens of Oradour were responsible? You bring me no evidence of that."

"The Milice—"

"The Milice!" screamed the colonel. "Since when could we rely on anything the Milice tell us? They are liars. They tell us only what they think will further their agenda."

"Colonel, the high command ordered us to take the offensive against the terrorists."

"Offensive, yes! Butchering women and children, no! If it becomes widely known, this affair will bring disgrace on the whole Das Reich Division."

"My intention was to deter further attacks against our officers."

Colonel Städler grimaced. "Major Diekmann, your actions were unbecoming of an officer of the Third Reich. I will recommend a court martial be convened against you. It is my responsibility to uphold the good name of the division, and I will not have you destroy it. Go back to Oradour and clean up your mess."

Adolf stood mute, angry, in shock. He put his cap on and gave a sharp salute to the Colonel. "Heil Hitler," he said loudly and out of character.

"Get out of my sight," ordered Colonel Städler, ignoring the gesture. "Erwin Dagenhardt from the motor pool will drive you to Oradour."

Adolf left, full of inner conflict. He believed he had acted in the interests of the fatherland, but the colonel's angry reaction caused him to reflect on that judgment. Whatever the case, right or wrong, there was no undoing it. It was a decision like all the others he had made in the heat of battle he would have to live with.

"Take me to Oradour as fast as you can," Major Diekmann instructed Dagenhardt.

Emile and Julien were making slow progress in their escape from Oradour-sur-Glane. They had walked, crept, and run before repeatedly being forced to lie on the ground for endless minutes. Numerous German patrols were aggressively searching for escapees from the town and nervously shooting anything that moved. They encountered bodies everywhere—by the sides of the road, in ditches, lying where they had been shot. Emile and Julien had retched at the first few they had encountered, but by now, they had become numbed to even the most evil atrocities they stumbled across.

Near the cemetery, to the north of the town, they passed a man who had been shot and had fallen against a wire fence. The soldiers had tethered a horse to his outstretched hand in some sort of barbaric gesture. Emile and Julien stared in horror, angry it was too late to help him and frustrated they could not kill those responsible. They came close to screaming at those who could have committed such atrocities, but they managed to restrain themselves. Survival was all that mattered. Revenge would come later, but only if they survived.

After more than an hour, they finally made it to the north of the town, across from the cemetery. They saw a Panzer standing guard at the entrance to the graveyard.

"We need to cross over there," whispered Julien. "The woods are just behind the cemetery. We should be able to hide there until nightfall. The Germans will not be able to search them thoroughly. They do not have enough men."

"They are clearly trying to stop anyone escaping by that route," Emile said.

The guard turned away from them. "Halt!" he shouted, before firing his automatic weapon. They looked in the direction he was targeting and saw a man darting between headstones, which were being chiseled away by the bullets. The Panzer ran after him.

"This is our chance. Run!" yelled Emile.

Emile ran in a crouch across the road into the cemetery, Julien close behind. They ran to a pair of large headstones and hid. Ominously, the shooting stopped. Emile assumed the worst and grieved for the man who had given them their chance to escape but had possibly paid for it with his life. They heard the scuffing of the heavy boots of the Panzer as he returned to guard the entrance.

The two waited for a good fifteen minutes to give the guard time to relax and become less attentive. They knew they could not remain there for long in safety. Their impatience to move was growing. When everything seemed quiet, Julien pointed to the woods over the low stone wall. Emile understood and nodded.

While crouching, Julien darted to one headstone after another. He was making good progress. Emile wanted to wait until Julien had made it safely over the wall. Only then would he bolt for the forest. There was no point risking both of them being caught.

When Julien reached the low wall, he started to climb it. Emile cringed when he heard his boots make a sharp noise on the dry stone. The guard had heard it too. He shouted and fired at Julien. Emile saw Julien fall over the wall, not knowing if he had been hit. The Panzer ran toward the spot where Julien had gone over the wall. As he dashed by Emile's hiding spot, Emile kicked his feet out from under him. Taken completely by surprise, the trooper crashed to the ground like a felled tree, banging his head severely on a headstone.

He was face down on the ground, helmet off, apparently unconscious. Emile grabbed a large rock and hit the soldier. Again and again. He hit him for his wife, for his daughters, for the man Emile and Julien had seen him kill, and for all the people in the town.

Blood on the stone caused it to slip from his hands. Emile sobbed. He knew he could not bring back all the people who had died that day. He felt powerless. He felt his existence no longer mattered any more than that of the person whose lifeless body lay at his feet. His violence had only added to his guilt. He turned over the trooper to see the face of his adversary, the face of evil. It was that of a young boy, twenty if that. Emile's sense of self-esteem dropped even lower. He was a teacher who had dedicated his life to improving the minds of adolescents and had just smashed one as if he had had no value. Nothing was safe from corruption in this hideous war.

"Emile! Over here! Come on!"

Emile saw Julien on the other side of the wall, waving, seemingly unhurt. He regained his senses. He looked around for any other soldiers, then down at the gun lying beside the boy, splattered with his blood. He reached down to grab it, but was overcome by a sense of revulsion. He wanted nothing that would remind him of this place of death. A souvenir of Hades. Besides, their survival would depend on staying hidden from the Germans, not getting into a fire fight with them.

Instead, he bolted for the wall. With Julien's help, he made it over quickly. The two took off into the forest.

When they paused for breath, Julien patted Emile on the shoulder. "Well, Mister, I now owe my life to you, so I guess we are even. That Panzer would have come after me in the forest if you hadn't killed him."

"Yes," said Emile, not feeling any pride. "I suppose he would have."

After running themselves to exhaustion, they found a large, fallen tree and crawled under it to await nightfall. With the two hours extra daylight savings the Germans had decreed to save energy, it would not be several hours before they could safely attempt their final escape.

Major Diekmann arrived at Oradour-sur-Glane around 7:00 p.m. He found Captain Kahn and his senior officers in the house of Mr. Dupic, the town draper. The house was at the western entrance to the town on rue Émile-Desourteaux. Inside, the tables were covered with opened and unopened bottles of wine and champagne.

Captain Kahn saluted Adolf. "Major. I trust things went well with Colonel Städler. We have searched most of the buildings and are burning them."

"No, things did not go well," Adolf barked. "Did you find anything? Arms, supplies, uniforms? Anything that shows evidence of their involvement with the maquis or their involvement with the kidnapping of Major Kämpfe?"

"No, Major. We found nothing, but that does not prove—"

"That is most unfortunate. The colonel is most upset with our actions and intends to call for a court martial. I suggest you try to 'discover' some evidence of resistance activity with the utmost priority," he said coldly.

Otto Kahn swallowed heavily, his smile gone. "I will see to it immediately, Major."

"The colonel wants the town cleaned up. He wants as little evidence left as possible of our actions today. Dispose of as many of the bodies as you can."

"But where? They are all over the town. It would take all night."

"Then take all night. Have your men stay here until the job is done. Incinerate the bodies in the buildings, bury them, or throw them down the well. I don't care. Just get rid of as many of them as you can. Let no one reenter the town until your job is complete."

"Very good, Major. We will do our best."

"You had better, for I fear we will both have to answer for our actions today. Colonel Städler is old-school military, less willing to use the extreme measures we know are required to win this war. If there is a court martial, I am confident the Führer will understand and we will prevail. However, it will be easier if we leave the colonel as little evidence as possible to support his charges."

"Understood, Major. By morning, we will have wiped Oradour-sur-Glane off the map," boasted Otto. "There will be little evidence that anything happened here today. I give you my word."

"I am depending on it," replied Adolf.

Dusk was coming. Emile and Julien were preparing to move when they heard the crackling of broken twigs. They froze. Their first thought was that the Germans had tracked them from the cemetery. They tried to squeeze down farther under the log. They listened. Voices grew louder. When they realized they were hearing not German but French with an Oradour accent, they were relieved.

Emile and Julien watched cautiously as five young men passed. One was being helped to walk by the others. Excitedly, Julien extracted himself from under the log and stood excitedly. "Robert! It's me, Julien!"

The five were terrified at having been caught by surprise. However, when they recognized Julien, they calmed down. Julien ran and hugged each in turn. In a joint expression of relief, they all broke into tears.

Seeing the tearful sight, Emile showed himself. Since he would be a stranger to them, he did not want them to panic. He approached them slowly, cautiously. When they saw him, Julien reassured them Emile was no threat.

"These are my very good friends, Robert Hébras, Yvon Roby, Clément Broussaudier, and Matthieu Borie," he said of the men standing. "They are from Oradour."

Julien recounted what had befallen Emile and his family. Hearing it proved too much for Emile, who started sobbing. Embarrassed and completely drained by the day's events, he sank to the ground next to the fifth man, who was sitting apart from the others.

"Good day, Mister," he addressed Emile. "I am Marcel Darthout. Those bastard Germans put four bullets in me, so you'll excuse me if I don't get up."

"I understand. They shot me too, but I am more fortunate than you."

The boys talked for a short while, all the time looking around nervously. They decided to move on. Two men helped Marcel up. They set off to put as much distance as possible between themselves and the carnage behind. They exchanged horror stories of the events they had experienced. Robert Hébras, who had bullet wounds in his temple and forearm, seemed to assume the role of leader and did much of the talking. "They locked us in the Laudry barn," he said. "None of us thought we were going to be shot. We thought they were just going to keep us there until they had finished their search."

"We weren't worried because none of us knew anyone in the town who even had a gun let alone anyone who was a resistance fighter," Clément said.

"The worst thing we thought might happen was that they would take us to Limoges as hostages. We heard that major ask the mayor for a list of hostages," said Robert. "When the barn doors were opened, I thought we were going to be released."

"Then that infernal music blasted out and four Bosch came in with their machine guns on tripods," Marcel said. "They asked us to line up across the barn, and without any warning, the bastards began shooting us. In cold blood. The worst of it was they looked as though they were enjoying it."

"They will pay for what they did today," Robert Hébras hissed. "After they were finished with the machine guns, one animal came around shooting anyone in the head who was still moving. When he had finished, they threw straw on us and set fire to the barn."

"How did you escape?" asked Emile.

"We were lucky. We managed to squeeze under a large oak door at the rear of the barn that had been bolted shut from the outside."

"Pierre-Henri Poutaraud went first," said Yvon Roby, "but they shot him, so we were more careful."

"We ran down an alley into a second barn to hide because there were still bullets flying everywhere," Robert said. "A big, red-headed brute urinated on us, but we said nothing, of course. A little later, they set fire to that barn too, so we had to flee again. Matthieu, Marcel, and I hid in the rabbit hutches."

"Yvon and I made it to the cemetery," Clément said. "We hid in a vault until dark."

When they had walked for a couple of hours without encountering any soldiers, their exhaustion overcame their fear. They had heard no shooting for some time; that gave them confidence they would survive. It was scant consolation, given the horrors they had witnessed, which brought with it feelings of guilt and emptiness that they had somehow been the few lucky ones.

When they came to a road, they lay in a ditch to discuss what they would do next. Most of the men, including Julien, wanted to stay in the area to try to pick up their lives, but Emile could not face returning to his now-empty home. At Robert Hébras' suggestion, Emile decided to accompany him to Limoges the next morning and join the FTP resistance group headed by Georges Guingouin. Until then, they needed sleep.

CHAPTER 10

𝔎𝔢𝔣𝔬𝔠𝔲𝔰

Emile had a restless night. Tired as he was, sleep eluded him. He tossed and turned on his bed of leaves. The previous day's events haunted him. For much of the time, he wasn't sure if he was awake or asleep, whether what he had been through was dream or reality. From time to time, he woke up sweating, terrified by something he was running from.

Each time, Emile would reassure himself that they were only dreams and that his mind was trying to adjust to the horrors he had witnessed. When he would try to relax, anxiety overwhelmed him as he remembered that the horrors of his dreams were real. His family that had meant everything to him had been brutally slaughtered before his eyes. He despaired and sought refuge in sleep.

Throughout the night, the image that most haunted Emile was that of the children singing as they marched into the church that was to be their crematorium. He could not get their singing out of his head. It tortured him pitilessly. Recalling songs that he had played countless times on his guitar to bring the children happiness, now brought him only pain.

He saw again the unrelenting flames that consumed the young, the innocent. He remembered the nightmares he'd had many times before and wondered if they were connected. It couldn't be, he told himself, for there was no way he could have known. Besides, there had been something different about the flames in his nightmares. He had never seen any buildings or explosions in those imaginings. He had simply seen an unquenchable fire whose flames roared to the heavens. Yet in both cases, his feelings had been the same; in his nightmares and the previous day in Oradour, he had wanted to run into the flames to save something he cared desperately about, something he would have gladly sacrificed his own life to save from the flames.

Sunday, June 11, 1944

Emile was relieved that the sun woke them early. Anxious to be on their way, he and Robert Hébras said their good-byes to the others and set off to Limoges. By midmorning, they were starving, so they stopped at a farm to beg for food. Despite having had much of what they had produced requisitioned by the Germans, the farmer and his wife took pity on them and generously offered to provide them a hearty breakfast.

The food looked and smelled better than most Emile had seen since the war began, but despite his hunger, Emile had little appetite. As they ate, Emile and Robert described to the elderly couple the horrors that had taken place in Oradour. The couple listened incredulously, even after their five years' experience of brutal occupation.

When Emile and Robert were ready to leave, the farmer offered them a couple of old bicycles he had in his barn. They would not go very fast, he apologized, but they would be quicker than walking. They accepted them enthusiastically and set out for Limoges. Benefitting from their increased mobility, they arrived in Limoges by early afternoon.

It was no surprise to find the town full of Germans, though seeing it firsthand still shocked Emile. Soldiers and vehicles filled every street. It was the temporary headquarters of the Der Führer Regiment. Emile and Robert had trouble controlling their emotions as they walked among soldiers wearing the same uniforms as those who had burned young children and pregnant mothers alive less than twenty-four hours earlier.

Robert had relatives in Limoges; he took Emile to a house where they could lie low for a couple of days. Robert's family was kind to Emile, and while he was with them, he met several members of the FTP. Word spread rapidly in the town of the terrible retributions exacted by the SS against innocent people in Tulle and Oradour for actions of the resistance.

In consequence, the maquis decided to stop all attacks until the Panzer regiment had left for Normandy.

As the days passed, Emile grew increasingly impatient for action. The slaughter of his wife and daughters was tearing him apart. He either slept all day or could not sleep at all. His appetite had not returned. He was losing weight. Emile knew he had to do something or the wound inside him would never heal.

He decided to leave. He no longer had ties to the area, so he wanted to find somewhere that would give him a reason to go on living, somewhere he could take a more active role in expelling the Fascists. He no longer cared if that meant sacrificing his life. Some days, he prayed it would.

Wednesday, June 14, 1944

"Robert, I am going to join General Leclerc's Free French Forces in North Africa," Emile announced at breakfast. "I will go south and slip over the Pyrenees into Spain, since they are neutral. I should be able to get a boat from there to North Africa and join Leclerc."

"Why would you want to join Leclerc? He is with de Gaulle! They are reactionaries. I thought you were a Communist," Robert said, surprised.

"I am a Socialist. I will always be. We all have a duty to help each other and our country. Right now, our first priority must be to destroy the Germans. The resistance will never be able to do that alone; only an army can. Besides, the SS division that killed my wife and our precious daughters went up to the front in Normandy. I want to have a chance to kill them, to make them pay for what they did."

Robert looked sympathetic. "I hate them as much as you do. Maybe that is the best way to fight them, but I do not like de Gaulle. He is controlled by the Americans. They do not want to see a Socialist state in France. We will be no better with them than we were before the war."

"Then we will just have to try to make sure that doesn't happen," replied Emile. "It will be up to the people of France to decide, not the Americans. Everyone in France has suffered greatly and will not stay silent as before. They have seen what silence can lead to."

"I hope you are right. But you seem to have made up your mind, so I will not try to change it. I wish you good luck. I choose to stay here and fight. I have much to take care of. We will both be fighting on the same side though in different ways."

"I hope we will meet again soon in a free France," Emile said.

"I'll drink to that," cried Robert, going to the kitchen for wine.

Around midmorning, Emile left Limoges and headed south on his bicycle. He was nervous about encountering any German patrols on the road as he did not have any travel papers authorizing his journey. If he was stopped, he could be shot on the spot.

A little south of Limoges, Emile passed an old man in a cart pulled by two large packhorses. "Good day, Mister. What have you got in the wagon?"

"Coffins. Coffins needed in Tulle. They have run out of them."

"Any chance you could give me a lift? I do not fancy my chances on the open road with all the patrols about."

"No problem. I'm too tired to have to build another one, so I'll help you," he smiled. "Hop in the back. Hide in a coffin. The Germans won't bother looking inside if I'm stopped. After all, they ordered them," he added dryly.

Emile threw his bike down and climbed into a coffin. He pulled the lid over him, leaving a small gap. The old man whipped the horses, and they started trotting. He knew it would be a long and rough ride to Tulle, but at least he might get there safely. He and the old man exchanged horror stories about the events in Oradour and Tulle. It seemed the war had descended to an even deeper level of depravity.

It was early evening when they arrived in Tulle, not soon enough for Emile, who was hurting all over. The road had had many potholes from five years of neglect and the tanks that had used it to move north, and the casket had been hard. He felt bruised all over, and it was with some difficulty that he climbed out of the coffin. Emile vowed he would not be put in a casket again until he was ready to remain in it. The old man dropped him off on the outskirts of town. Emile thanked him and walked into town.

Emile remembered Tulle as an attractive place. He knew no one in the town but had been there a couple of times on fishing trips. The medieval town was on the steep sides of a narrow valley cut by the fast-flowing Corrèze River. To the west was the valley of the Dordogne, and to the east were the vertiginous slopes of the Massif Central, the plateau that dominated south central France. Even the name of the town had a pleasant resonance for most people, having been given to a type of fine silk that used to be manufactured there.

As he approached the town, everything looked as Emile remembered it. The twelfth-century cathedral stood unchanged. For a few moments, he even dared hope nothing had changed, but he could not fool himself; the old man had warned him what to expect.

Emile had believed that after the horrors he had seen in Oradour, he would be unaffected by anything he saw in Tulle. He was wrong. He saw the bodies of men and even young boys hanging from lampposts. Feelings of revulsion welled up inside of him, making him nauseous. Strangely, he found the feelings reassuring that there was still some humanity left in him.

Before long, he had seen as many distorted faces and bloated bodies as he could stomach. To avoid having to look at any more, he determined to keep his head down and tell himself the long shadows on the ground were cast by hanging baskets gracing the lamps. It might have worked but for the stench of death.

German soldiers were on the streets of Tulle, but thankfully, they were not SS. He learned the SS had left a few days earlier after "liberating" the town from the maquisards and had put the local garrison back in charge. He was grateful they were much less thorough than the SS, as none asked him for his papers.

In the center of town, Emile slipped into a bar, thankful to escape the rotting corpses outside. Tattered curtains with sunflowers covered the small windows, which were deeply set back into the thick stone walls. The air was acrid with the stale smell of pipe tobacco and of Gitanes cigarettes made with low-quality French tobacco. Emile sidled up to the bar; he was tired. Tired of the war, the killing, the running, the hiding. He was tired of life. At least when he had had his family, there had been something to live for, but they were gone. The only thing that kept him going was hate, revenge. He asked the barman for a beer, then another, and another. A rough-looking farm type beside him offered him a cigarette. He accepted it gladly and inhaled it furiously in between beers. He wanted to leave reality behind, at least for a while.

"Where are you from?" asked the barman. Emile told him what had happened at Oradour a few days earlier.

"They were here too, those murdering bastards, the SS," cursed the barman. "They left their calling card outside, as you have seen. We had retaken the town from the regular army before the SS arrived. Butchers, all of them, especially that Major Kowatsch."

"What did he do?" asked Emile in an inebriated haze.

"He ordered the Panzers to round up one hundred twenty men, three for each of the German soldiers who had been killed. He said they'd be hung and then thrown into the river. Changed his mind though the day after. He decided to let us cut them down and bury them. But don't think it's because he got soft-hearted. I hear they decided it would be too much of a health risk to throw them all into the river."

"In Oradour, they killed everyone. All the women and children too, even the babies."

"I am sorry to hear that. All the men they killed here were innocent too. They did not deserve to die. The maquis fled when the SS arrived, so they ended up hanging just a bunch of kids who were unlucky enough to still be on the streets when they arrived."

Emile looked at him with glazed eyes. "Did they really hang a hundred twenty?"

"Would have, but they ran out of rope. Can you believe that?" he asked despairingly. "They ran out of rope. Took the ones away for questioning who were lucky enough to avoid hanging."

"Don't know about that," slurred Emile. "They might have been better off dead than where they're going. You will probably never see them again."

"You might be right. Anyway, what brings you to Tulle?"

"I am going to go to Spain and then to North Africa to join de Gaulle."

The barman waved his hands frantically. "Keep your voice down. That is not a name you can safely say out loud around here. The Milice have their informers everywhere." He looked nervously at the other patrons. "How will you get to Spain?" he asked in a whisper. "The Germans patrol the roads. They're bringing troops up to the front from the south."

"I know. I saw them in Limoges. I haven't given it much thought," Emile said. "I will just have to be careful to avoid them," he said flippantly.

"I may know someone who can help you if you wish. I—" The barman stopped talking abruptly as two soldiers entered the bar.

"Papers," they shouted. "Get out your papers for inspection."

Emile barely heard them; he was too busy draining the last of his beer. He flopped his head on the counter and was gone, oblivious to everything.

After checking others' documents, the Germans prodded Emile, who didn't move.

Worried that Emile almost certainly lacked the necessary travel papers to be in Tulle, the barman decided to intercede.

"I can vouch for him," he said quickly. "He's my cousin. His wife just left him, so he came in here to get blind drunk."

One of the Germans laughed. "I'd be celebrating if my wife left me."

His companion, a sergeant, looked more serious. He appeared to be close to deciding whether to arrest Emile.

"How about a drink on the house?" asked the barman.

The sergeant shook his head. "No, not while we are on duty. It is not allowed."

The sergeant turned to Emile. As the barman had hoped, the distraction seemed to have weakened any interest in arresting Emile. "Well, take your cousin here home to sleep it off, and make sure he causes no trouble!"

"I will, certainly, Sergeant. You have my word."

"I will hold you responsible if he does."

Emile was still passed out a couple hours later when the barman shut up for the night. Fortunately, the barman was both strong and sympathetic. He put his arm under Emile's and dragged his limp body up the stairs. After a pause to catch his breath, he continued down the hallway to a spare bedroom, where he opened the door and threw Emile on a bed. "Goodnight, my friend. Spain will have to wait until the morning. If you have a head to go anywhere after tonight," he said quietly as he closed the door.

When Emile woke the next morning, he was disoriented by his surroundings and a pounding headache. It was dark in the room. He climbed out of the unfamiliar bed and stumbled to the window to open the shutters. Immediately, he regretted it. He was blinded by sunlight. As his eyes gradually adjusted, he saw many people on the streets. The sun was high. He concluded it must have been around midday.

Cautiously, Emile unlatched the door and saw a narrow, well-worn, stone staircase that wound downstairs. Holding onto the handrail like a vise, he descended carefully, not knowing what to expect at the bottom. The reek of beer and cigarettes made him suspect he was in a bar, a suspicion confirmed by the time he arrived at the last step. He vaguely recognized the place from the night before, though he had no recollection of the evening. The barman, who looked familiar, was cleaning the floor in the empty establishment.

"Oh, Mister, you're awake. Quite an evening you had. Sometimes it's good to just forget everything."

"Seems I managed to do that. But my head. It's making me pay the price."

The barman laughed. "Ha! I will give you a little cognac. A good cognac can take care of everything, but you must eat as well."

Emile followed him to the back of the building, where there was a small kitchen.

"Here, my wife cooked this mushroom omelet this morning," he declared, thrusting it at Emile. "The eggs will do you good, and the mushrooms are fresh. I picked them myself in the forest this morning."

"Where is your wife?" asked Emile.

"At the market. She sells some small snacks in the bar in the evening and is getting what she needs. Of course, like any woman, she will have to stop to gossip to find out what is going on. When I go, I'm back in half the time."

"You have been very kind, Mister. I'm afraid I don't remember your name. My name is Emile. I'm from—"

"Yes, I know all about you. I heard your life story last night. I'm truly sorry about your family, truly sorry. Nothing will bring your family back, but the German swine will pay soon for what they did in Oradour and here. The latest news from the north is that the Allies are advancing everyday toward Paris. Soon, France will be a free nation again."

The barman offered his hand enthusiastically to Emile. "My name's Yves."

Emile received a firm shake he was in no state to match. "I apologize for whatever I might have done last night. I'm afraid I don't remember much about it."

"Hey, forget it," said Yves. "Any man would have done the same in your shoes."

Somewhat reassured, Emile ate the omelet and some fresh bread. "This omelet is delicious. The herbs your wife used are wonderful," Emile said.

Yves moved close to Emile and put down the glass he was drying. "Last night, you said you wanted to go to Spain. Is that really your plan?" he asked in a low voice.

"Yes, I want to fight for de Gaulle. I have nothing else to live for since Oradour."

"Well you will not get there unless you are more careful about whom you talk to. There are collaborators everywhere, even in Tulle. The roads to the south are crawling with Germans. You will not get far without papers. Even if you make it to the border, you will find it heavily patrolled by the Milice." The last word caused him to spit hatefully on the floor. "You will not find your way across the border without help."

Emile stopped eating. He collected his thoughts. He looked at Yves. "I have to try. I owe it to my wife and daughters. I have nothing else to live for."

Yves paused, clearly trying to make his mind up about something. "I might be able to help you. I have a friend who is coming here this afternoon. He has contacts that could get you out of France," he whispered.

Emile could not hide his excitement. "I would be forever in your debt, Mister. I cannot repay you now, but after the war, I will find a way."

"Hey, don't thank me too quickly. You haven't met my friend yet. He may not agree to take you, and if he does, I warn you, he lives dangerously."

"I am prepared to take the risk. Better with him than with the Germans."

Starting to feel alive again after the food and the cognac, Emile left the bar to explore the old town. Most of the bodies had been cut down from the lampposts overnight, and Emile assumed the casket he had been lying in the day before was occupied. The town looked better in the sunlight; it was bustling with people. It gave the impression that life had returned to normal, but that was superficial. Everyone he talked to exuded revulsion at what had befallen them, a hatred for the Germans, and a burning need for revenge.

When Emile returned to the bar, it was busy. Yves was leaning over the counter talking to a thin man with a moustache and a faded beret. The man was leaning over too, simultaneously talking and smoking. As Emile entered, their conversation stopped. Both men looked at him. Yves nodded to Emile to join them at the bar.

"Emile, this is Jacques. He is the one I mentioned might be able to help you."

Emile held out his hand. "Emile Garnier. Pleased to meet you."

The other man looked at his beer. "You are serious about this?"

"Absolutely."

"How do I know I can trust you? You could be with the Milice. Those murdering collaborators have their spies everywhere."

Emile was taken aback. It had not occurred to him anyone could have suspected him of working with the Germans. "I do not know what I can say to convince you I hate the Milice and the Germans as much as you do. I can show you my identity papers, though I know they will prove nothing. You will just have to believe me, and if you find I have been lying to you, you will be welcome to slit my throat. Until then, I assure you I am a lowly schoolteacher from St. Junien. I was a member of the local maquis, and I led the group that blew up the bridge over the Vienne," he said proudly.

"You say too much," Jacques scolded. "If you keep your mouth shut, you will live longer. I will check out your story. If it seems plausible, I will consider your request. If not, you would be better off not being here when I get back."

Jacques downed the rest of his beer, bid them good-bye, and walked out.

"Not too friendly, is he?" asked Emile.

"He's okay once he trusts you, but that can take time. He trusts no one he doesn't know. He's had too many friends tortured and killed by the Gestapo and the Milice."

Jacques returned in the evening, a cigarette hanging from his mouth and his arm around a young girl. He left her at a table and walked to Yves and Emile at the bar. Jacques paused and looked Emile over, saying nothing. His expression was blank. "Your story checks out. Robert Hébras with the FTP in Limoges vouches for you. But if I find you are working for the Germans, I will kill you myself."

"I will provide the knife."

"We understand each other."

"That deserves a drink," said Yves, setting up three shot glasses he filled with cognac. "To victory over the Fascist pigs! Vive la France!" he proposed in a quiet but firm voice as they clicked their glasses together.

"Now, I have other important things to attend to," said Jacques, sounding more relaxed. "The little bird over there is waiting for me." He smiled, rolled his eyes suggestively, and nodded toward the young girl, who was smiling back at him. "I will be here in the morning, early. Be ready by five or I'll leave without you."

"How many days will it take to get to Spain?" Emile asked.

"We will not be going there directly. We have a little detour to make."

"Where to?"

"I have to take some cheese to a white mouse," Jacques said enigmatically. Emile looked at Yves.

"You have not heard of the White Mouse?" Yves asked in surprise. "She has quite a reputation around here. She leads the maquis to the west of here in Auvergne, and she has been giving the SS quite a headache. Madame Andrée she goes by, though I have heard she's English. The Gestapo has put her at the top of their most-wanted list. They named her the White Mouse because she is so hard to catch."

"Can she help me get to Spain?"

"You will have to ask Jacques."

Friday, June 16, 1944

Emile was ready to leave well before five; otherwise, he knew Jacques would not hesitate to leave without him. Jacques showed up a couple of minutes past five. As they walked down the steep steps of a narrow street toward the river, Emile saw the shutters on the houses were still closed. However, the smell of baking bread told him some people were already at work. The summer solstice was approaching. The sun had risen earlier than they had. Its reflections were shimmering brightly on the surface of the Corrèze.

To Emile's surprise, even at such an early hour, people were starting to arrive to set up their stalls for the market. He had gone there the previous day and had been impressed by the wide assortment of cherries, cheese, hams, live chickens and other fowl, vegetables, mushrooms, and pâté. People could obviously still eat well there in spite of the war.

Jacques struck up a conversation with someone at a stall; their words were clearly not meant for Emile's ears. When he was done, he came to Emile. "You ready? I hope you're in good shape, for it will be a long ride."

"Where are we going?"

"To Chaudes-Aigues. It is on the high plateau of the Massif Central. Quite a climb."

"Are we walking?"

"No. We are taking those bicycles over there. We have some produce to deliver," he said with a smile.

Emile saw two bicycles with trailer carts loaded with cherries, dry-smoked country ham, and as Jacques had mentioned, cheese.

Jacques thrust a bunch of papers at Emile. "Here are your travel papers. Take them. We need to get going."

CHAPTER 11

Pilgrimage to the Sky

Emile was tired. He and Jacques had been riding hard all morning with scarcely a break. His legs were aching. The road from Tulle climbed steadily. The sun had been beating down on them unforgivingly. Only where the forest grew close to the road or where a mountain's shadow fell on the road were they spared its onslaught.

Until then, Emile had always considered himself an accomplished cyclist. He had ridden everywhere in St. Junien, but that was in the Limousin, without a trailer, and only for a few hours at a time. In the Auvergne, the terrain was much harsher and the roads steeper and more tortuous. If he had not been used to riding, he was convinced he would have expired hours ago, but he managed to find strength to keep going. To Emile's frustration and embarrassment, Jacques looked as though he could go on cycling forever. Despite smoking constantly, he never seemed to be out of breath or to show any signs of exhaustion.

At last, to Emile's relief, Jacques proposed that they stop briefly for lunch after they crossed a bridge over a swiftly flowing river.

"That town over there is Aurillac. It gets its name from the Latin for gold. They say there used to be gold in this river, but I never managed to find any, and I tried many times as a kid. I used to dream of becoming rich and buying a chateau one day," Jacques reflected.

Emile saw sadness in his eyes. He was not sure whether it was nostalgia or something deeper.

"We will not go into town; we might attract attention. There are many German troops in the area. It will be safer to picnic off the road, by the river."

"Sounds great." Emile was anxious not to have to ride any farther.

Jacques climbed up on a boulder and looked about them as he ate a slice of smoked ham. "What do you think of this country? Beautiful, isn't it?"

"It's magnificent," Emile said, filling his lungs with pristine air. "What are those mountains to the northeast, behind Aurillac?"

"They are the Monts du Cantal. The tallest one, the Plomb du Cantal, is eighteen hundred and fifty-five meters. We will be going right by it. They are old volcanoes. If you go there, you can still see the peaks and the cones that used to burn with fire thousands of years ago. The lava helped build the plateau of the Massif Central. I have heard it was three hundred meters deep in places. It must have been an incredible sight. Hopefully, we shall have no such excitement today. The volcanoes have been dormant for a long time, but they are beautiful all the same. They are very green in the summer and white in the winter as they catch all the rain from the clouds coming in from the Atlantic. This land is my home. It is what I am. I was born in Murat, just up the road, where we will sleep tonight. You will need your strength for tomorrow. We have a long climb ahead of us up to the plateau."

"A long climb tomorrow? What have we been doing today? We seem to have been climbing ever since we left Tulle."

"Ah, you are not used to the mountains." Jacques laughed. "We have only climbed about four hundred meters since leaving Tulle. We have another three hundred meters to climb before we reach Murat. Tomorrow, we will climb onto the plateau above Chaudes-Aigues. Over a thousand meters."

Emile almost choked on the bleu de Tulle cheese he was eating. "Over a thousand meters! I don't know if I can make it. I am only a schoolteacher. You are right. I am not used to riding in these mountains. The Limousin was much more forgiving."

Jacques looked at him unsympathetically. "You will think of the German swine that are infesting our country and you will make it. You will think of your family and you will make it. You owe it to them. You owe it to France."

Emile nodded. He knew Jacques was his only hope for survival. "I will make it." Still, he worried he might not be able to keep that promise, but kept that to himself.

As they got back on their bikes, Emile looked at the slate roofs and towers of Aurillac. They looked so different that he yearned to explore the town. However, this was not the time. Maybe, some day he could return for a visit.

The River Jordanne, which they were standing beside, flowed through Aurillac on a vast plain that stretched southward toward the Languedoc. Its waters originated in the mountains to the north and east. It was clear Jacques was right. Their ride would get only harder from that point.

The afternoon was worse than the morning. They wound their way up the narrow valley of the River Cère. The road was steep and winding, and it was getting hotter. The only saving grace was the steady breeze coming from the mountains blowing in their faces. Without it, Emile was sure that he would not have been able to go on. As it was, his head was pounding. He was exhausted. His legs were dead weights though they still were going up and down. They were functioning independently of him.

As they approached the base of the massive Plomb du Cantal, they left the valley of the Cère and wound their way around the mountain to another valley carved by the Alagnon River. This land of volcanoes, deep gorges, valleys, fast-flowing rivers, and waterfalls was completely alien to Emile. He was homesick for the softness of the Limousin. As they climbed steadily upward the vegetation slowly changed. They were entering a mountainous environment where the winters were long and harsh. The flat, green fields of the plain below were giving way to steep hillsides and cliffs lightly forested and covered with a patchwork of clearings dotted with sheep that stared at them as if to say they this was their domain and intruders were unwelcome.

Suddenly Jacques shouted, "Murat is just around the next bend. We should be there in fifteen minutes."

Emile felt a surge of relief. He was going to make it, at least that day.

As they rounded the next bend, Emile saw a town nestled on the hillside. It was an old fortified town with some of the ramparts and guard towers still standing. All the buildings and roofs were of stone, built probably from the local basalt he had observed on their climb. The roofs were all very steep, and several were conical to throw off heavy winter snows. Emile made one last push to get inside its walls.

"Jacques, what is the news from Tulle?" someone yelled as they entered the town.

"Not good! I will tell you tonight."

They rode through narrow lanes into the heart of the old city. It was so different from anything Emile was used to in the Limousin. Surrounded by medieval buildings, he could easily believe he was no longer in twentieth-century France. He imagined shining knights in armor might come down the street to greet them. The ancient walls of the isolated town made him feel protected against the outside world. It was easy to believe there was no war, no German occupation there. It was the first time in a week Emile had felt any security. He could understand why Jacques was proud of his birthplace.

"Stop." Jacques raised his arm abruptly.

They pulled up beside two heavy, carved doors in an alley behind a small row of shops. Jacques pulled on a rope beside the doors. Emile heard a bell ring inside. In a few minutes, an old woman peered through a small grill in the door. "Ah, Mr. Jacques. It is you. Welcome home." The old woman unlocked the doors, and Jacques pushed them open.

"Be quick," he said to Emile. "Bring the bikes in."

Emile did so, and they bolted the doors behind them.

"This is my grandmother," he told Emile. The two hugged as if they had not seen each other for a long time, but Emile suspected they had been parted less than their heartfelt reunion implied. Emile sensed that bonds between the people there ran deep and that they were not afraid to display their emotions.

Jacques' grandmother led them to an interior courtyard and beckoned them to sit. She left for a few minutes and returned with wine, bread, and pâté. Emile was dog-tired. The wine only amplified his fatigue, but the smell and sight of the food convinced him to eat. The next day would require an inordinate amount of energy.

"We will sleep here tonight," said Jacques after his grandmother had left them. "She has gone to prepare us some food. You are tired. When you have eaten, you should go to bed. Do not wait for me. I must take care of some things in the town, but I shall not be long."

"I can help you if you need."

"These things do not concern you. It is better that you know nothing of them and that you rest, for we will be leaving early. We have a long day ahead of us."

Emile was more than happy to follow his advice. After dinner, Jacques' grandmother led him up three flights of stairs to a small room with large ceiling timbers just under the roof. After she left, he looked out a small window and saw in the moonlight that the room had a clear view down the valley. He pulled back the shutters and climbed into bed. He fell asleep almost as soon as his head hit the pillow.

Saturday, June 17, 1944

It was still dark when Emile was awakened by loud banging on his door. "Emile. Wake up. Come downstairs for breakfast. We need to get going."

Emile was still tired; against his body's wishes, he dragged himself out of bed and stumbled to the window. He lifted the catch and threw open the shutters. The sun was just starting to cast its first rays down the valley. He looked at his watch. It was nearly 5:30 a.m.

Emile pulled his clothes on and picked his way down the old stone staircase to the ground floor. It was hard to see, as he was still half-asleep, so he held on firmly to a rope strung along the wall. As he approached the kitchen, he heard voices and smelled coffee.

Jacques and his grandmother were in the kitchen with a girl Emile did not remember seeing the night before. The girl smiled.

"Good morning, Mister. I am Renée, a friend of Jacques."

Jacques chuckled. "This is my girl. Beautiful, isn't she?"

Emile smiled. He was by then accustomed to Jacques' rhetorical questions.

The girl was very young. She was wearing a white dress with big black dots and heavy red lipstick, a bit garish for Emile's taste. Jacques removed the cigarette from his mouth and took the coffee pot from Renée. He put it back on the stove before putting his hand on the girl's backside, causing the two to start kissing passionately. Emile marveled that they seemed completely uninhibited in the presence of Emile or his grandmother. Renée was clearly one of the "things" Jacques had run off to attend to the previous night.

The grandmother poured Emile a bowl of hot chocolate. When Renée and Jacques had finished their long embrace, Renée poured coffee for Emile and handed him a croissant.

"I went out this morning to get these from the baker myself. He opened specially for me. I think he likes me," she said, looking teasingly at Jacques, who shrugged dismissively.

Grandma handed Jacques a small bundle wrapped in a red and white checkered cloth. "I have packed you food for the journey. There is homemade pâté, some of our local goat cheese, and a couple of baguettes. You will need your strength."

"Thank you, Grandma. You look after me too well."

"Someone has to. I have also packed wine. It will help your leg cramps."

The two men splashed water on their faces and went to their bicycles. After several rounds of kissing and hugging from the two women, Jacques and Emile set off. Emile was sorry to leave Murat behind, especially when he thought of the daunting ride ahead.

"The first part of the journey will be relatively easy," Jacques said. "It is mostly downhill to St. Flour, and then down again to Chaudes-Aigues, which is about two hundred meters lower than Murat. We shall stop there for lunch."

"After that?" asked Emile with concern.

"After that it will be difficult. You will see. It is not worth worrying about now."

St. Flour was another medieval town but on a volcanic spur overlooking a river. It was a "perched" village typical of those farther to the south in the Midi built on rocky outcroppings to protect the inhabitants.

"We will have to be careful today in Chaudes-Aigues. Friends in Murat tell me there are reports of Germans in the area. If we are stopped, let me do the talking."

"Gladly."

It was fairly flat leaving St. Flour. The day was not yet hot, and the two enjoyed a cooling wind. Emile was confident he would be able to make it to Chaudes-Aigues. He had slept well, and his legs had recovered from the previous day.

"I like your grandmother," said Emile. "She looks after you well."

Jacques looked at him angrily. "Do not ever mention my grandmother! If anyone asks, I do not have a grandmother! If I did, you would not know her or where she lived. Understand? And we never went to Murat. Is that clear?"

"I understand." Emile was embarrassed. "I only wanted to thank you for—"

"There is nothing to thank me for! If you ever speak to anyone of last night, I will kill you."

"I will never speak of it. You have my word. I would have done anything to protect my own family. I understand how you feel. I will do nothing to put yours in danger."

Jacques relaxed a little. He looked regretful for his outburst. "I am sorry. I know you meant no harm, but my grandmother, she is all I have."

"What about your parents?"

"My mother died when I was born, and my grandmother brought me up. My father was mayor of the town, so he had little time for me."

"Where is your father now?"

"I do not know. The Germans took him away. We have not heard from him since. They accused him of being a Communist."

"Was he?"

"Of course. I joined the maquis to take his place when he was arrested."

"I am sure he would be proud of you."

"It doesn't matter now. He is probably dead. Now I fight for myself, not for him."

"And for your grandmother?"

"Yes. I fight for her too."

Around midday, they arrived at Chaudes-Aigues. Emile had long heard of the town and its hot-water spas, but had not known what to expect. He was pleasantly surprised. The buildings were constructed of sandstone, which gave the town an unexpected softness amplified by the harshness of the surrounding mountains. The town was nestled at the head of the gorge of the Remontalou River, which tore through it in an impetuous torrent. The river was obviously the lifeblood of the city, for it had been built along it lengthwise down the valley, never straying far from its banks. As they rode in, ahead of them was the imposing plateau of Aubrac, which rose abruptly and dominated the skyline. Emile gulped.

"We are going up there this afternoon?" he asked Jacques.

"Yes. The fortress of France, they call it. Magnificent, isn't it? We have many people up there. The Germans do not dare come after us, for it is part of Free France. Soon, the resistance will descend from there and other such places all over France to chase the Germans out."

"I can see why Germans don't want to go up there. An impossible climb."

Jacques smiled. "It won't look so bad after you have eaten." He slapped Emile on the back. "You have been doing well. You will make it, but we must be up there by nightfall, so we will have to eat quickly."

Emile did not share Jacques' confidence in his abilities. "How high is it up there?"

"Around thirteen hundred meters."

"That's about six hundred meters above here!"

"I know a tavern that serves a good beer. That will take your mind off it."

They cycled through the town. Emile looked in amazement at the steaming water that poured from public fountains.

Jacques noticed his reaction. "It is a magical place here. There are thirty hot springs in the town, one of which is the Par, which can reach eighty-two degrees Celsius. They say it is the hottest waters of any thermal spring in Europe. The volcanoes may look dead, but beneath our feet are raging fires. I think of them as I think of the resistance. The Germans do not see us, but we are there, and one day soon, we will rise up and destroy them."

"Jacques, you should have been a philosopher."

"Everyone is a philosopher here. There is not much else to do than think, especially during winter. That is why the monks built their abbey in the middle of the plateau. They make good cheese. Laguiole is made from raw cow's milk. You will have to try some."

"What about the cheese your gran—" Emile caught himself. "What about the cheese in our backpacks? Will we eat that now?"

Jacques looked at him sourly. "No. We will save that for later. We will have to stop several times on our ride up the mountain. We will need to replenish our energy."

They pulled their bicycles up outside the tavern Jacques was looking for and went in. From the greetings he received, it was clear that he was a regular. They sat and were served beer and salad with *pâté de campagne*. Emile felt uneasy as Jacques appeared to be constantly looking for someone, expecting trouble. Before he had finished eating, he joined a couple of men at another table. Emile couldn't hear what they were saying, but the conversation was animated. The three constantly surveyed the other patrons as if to see who was watching.

The innkeeper came over and made small talk with Emile. That only added to Emile's sense of insecurity as he wasn't sure of the innkeeper's intentions or sympathies. He knew one wrong word from him might put them in danger, so he said as little as possible.

"Try the spa while you are here," said the innkeeper. "It is good for muscle aches."

"I would love to," replied Emile. "Unfortunately, we don't have much time. We will need to get going soon." *How I am really going to need it tonight, though.*

"The hot water runs everything here. In the winter, we heat our houses with it, and in summer, we use it to repair our bodies. We wash our dishes and our clothes in it, and we even cook eggs with it! It has been that way since anyone can remember."

"You're lucky to have that resource, especially as coal and oil are so hard to come by nowadays."

At long last, Jacques returned, and the innkeeper flitted away. "Well, finish up your beer. It's time for some exercise," he said with all the joy of a medieval executioner.

Emile drained his glass. They began the last tortuous leg of their journey. The road headed southeast up the valley toward the mountains. As they climbed out of the town, Emile looked down the valley of the Remontalou. It was a more comforting sight than the imposing peaks of the mountains of the Cantal looming ahead. Emile had to admit that Jacques was right; the place was magical.

Before long, they entered the valley of Bès with its steep escarpments, cascading waterfalls, and deep gorges. "I can see why the Germans do not follow you up here," panted Emile, pedaling hard. "It would be difficult country for tanks and heavy vehicles."

"You are right. That is why they have not come, but lately, we have been causing them increasing problems, so they are getting bolder. People in the town have seen some Germans on this road recently, so we must not assume anything."

It was hard cycling, as the road twisted and turned ever upward. Their old bikes had only three gears, which didn't help them much with their trailers that seemed to get heavier by the minute. At times, when the road was especially steep, Emile found it was easier to get off and push. At other times, he found it easier to stand up on the pedals rather than remain seated. Despite the tortuous ordeal, however, Emile's spirits were higher than they had been since he had left Oradour-sur-Glane. Any thoughts of turning back or giving up had vanished. He would go on no matter what it entailed, no matter if it killed him. The mountains were somehow liberating. They gave him hope.

The rushing water around them was in harmony with the constant wind that descended from the highlands. As Emile looked at the dark-blue sky, he saw two eagles circling. He was envious of their freedom, but soon too, he would be free. He would be across the Pyrenees and then make his way to Algiers.

"I will be glad when we finally reach this plateau of yours. I've never cycled this hard or as long in my life," Emile panted. "At least it will be easier coming down."

"You'll probably have to walk down. That can be harder on legs than cycling up."

"You sure your friends are up there?" asked Emile. "We've seen no one."

"They're up there. You'll see them when they want you to see them. Not before."

They stopped and ate bread and cheese. Perched on the edge of a cliff overlooking the valley, Emile felt a great sense of accomplishment as he saw how high they had come. The wine helped wash down the food and numb the aches. Jacques would not allow them to stop for long. After packing what was left of the food, they set off.

"The last stretch. Two more hours." Jacques said encouragingly.

The road wound around the mountain, doubling back in places to snake its way up. For much of the way, there was a sheer drop on one side, and the other rose steeply from the road. Emile saw large goats that jumped effortlessly between rocks to graze on patches of grass. They had shiny brown bodies and white legs. Most striking of all, though, were their large, spiral horns.

"They are magnificent," said Emile. "I've never seen goats like that before."

"They are *mouflon*. Years ago, they were introduced from Corsica or Sardinia, I forget which. They make a very good cheese."

Emile watched the proud-looking, sure-footed animals that were at home in the rugged environment; he needed something to take his mind off his exhaustion. He was paying little attention to the road when Jacques slowed to come alongside him. To get Emile's attention, Jacques elbowed him sharply on the arm. Emile was about to complain when he saw Jacques gesture with his head to look up the road.

Emile looked and became terrified. Lying on the grass on the side of the road were two motorcycles painted in mottled-brown and dark-green camouflage. Two German soldiers in helmets and camouflage were across the road, admiring the view down the gorge. Emile wanted desperately to turn around and head back before they were seen, but Jacques showed no sign of doing that. He continued pedaling. Before Emile could ask him why, he realized it was too late. They had been spotted. The soldiers had straightened up and were pointing their machine guns at them.

"Stay calm. Say nothing," whispered Jacques. "I will take care of them."

Stay calm? How can I stay calm? The Germans just burned my wife and daughters to death and wiped out all of Oradour. The horrendous events of that day flooded his mind. He felt only pure hatred that made him shake.

"Control yourself," ordered Jacques. "We must not make them suspicious."

Emile tried to calm his anger, but it was not easy. As they approached the soldiers, one of them walked into the middle of the road.

"Halt!" he shouted. "Your identity papers and travel documents," he demanded in perfect French.

Another Alsatian, like those in Oradour, thought Emile with revulsion.

Emile and Jacques reached into their pockets slowly so as not to cause alarm. The soldier approached them suspiciously and took their papers. He looked over the documents carefully, scrutinizing their photographs and comparing them to their faces. He shouted something in German to his colleague and handed their papers back. The soldier walked around the back of the bikes and looked at the trailers. "What is in these?"

"Food," replied Jacques. "Food for the monks in the Monastery of Aubrac."

"I thought the monks were self-sufficient," the soldier said.

"They are, but from time to time, even monks like a change." Jacques shrugged.

The soldier's expression remained cold. He opened Emile's trailer. Emile's pulse started racing. His breathing became labored. He realized he had no idea what was in there. He had only Jacques' word for it that they were transporting only food. He'd never thought to check. *What if there were guns in the trailers? That would be the end of my short journey. I'd be shot or worse, deported to an internment camp.*

The soldier rummaged through the contents with one hand while he tried to keep his machine gun leveled on Emile with the other. He threw several of the items on the ground as he burrowed to the bottom of the container. Finally, in apparent frustration, he shouted "Nichts" to his companion.

Emile breathed a sigh of relief. His knowledge of German was poor, but even he understood the soldier, who moved on to Jacques' trailer. Again, he found nothing of interest, which seemed to anger him.

"Okay, you may put the food back," he said.

Emile and Jacques dismounted their bikes to repack the food.

"The monks will not miss a little, though." The soldier laughed as he put some cheese in his pocket.

"Help yourself," Jacques said.

"Have you seen any partisans on this road? Anyone with guns or camping in the mountains?" the soldier asked.

Jacques shook his head. "No. We have seen no one since we left Chaudes-Aigues."

"No, no one," repeated Emile.

"You are free to go, but take care. We have reports of maquisards in the area. They may want to steal your food."

"Thank you for the warning," Jacques said, raising his hand to his forehead in a gesture of salute. "We will be careful."

The soldier walked to his colleague. As soon as Emile and Jacques were finished packing, they remounted their bicycles. As they moved off, they waved at the soldiers who stared begrudgingly back at them.

"That was close," said Emile. "I thought they were going to find something."

"Ah, you do not trust me." Jacques chuckled before his expression turned serious. "That is good. Trust no one. It is the best way to stay alive."

Emile started to pedal with renewed enthusiasm. He wanted to leave the Germans behind as fast as possible. It had been close, but at least they had made it, he thought, just before two warning shots rang out from behind them.

"Halt! Come back!" cried a soldier. Both soldiers were pointing their guns at them.

"Shit!" cursed Jacques. "Now what?"

Emile and Jacques did as commanded.

"You!" shouted the soldier pointing at Emile. "Take your jacket off."

"My jacket?"

The soldiers raised their guns higher, their fingers on the triggers, making it clear it was not a point for discussion.

Emile took off his jacket.

"What is that blood on your arm?"

Emile looked at his arm. Blood had soaked through his jacket. He had not noticed until then, but the wound he had received in Oradour had opened up with the exertion of riding up the mountain.

"Take off your shirt," ordered the soldier. "And the bandage." He gestured with his machine gun.

Emile did. The soldier inspected his arm. "A bullet wound. How did you get it?"

Emile hesitated. He was not used to thinking on his feet, especially when he had a machine gun in his face. "I was in Tulle and got caught in the crossfire," he stammered. "It was when the maquis attacked the town. I was trying to flee when I was hit. I just kept on running, and that is how I ended up here." Emile knew that did not sound convincing, but it was the best he could come up with at the frightful moment. He cursed himself for not having prepared a better excuse for such a situation.

The soldiers were not satisfied. "Get off you bicycles. You are coming with us," one said. "You can tell your story to the Gestapo. They will find out if it is true."

Emile shuddered. He and Jacques got off their bicycles.

The Alsatian thrust his gun roughly into Emile's back. "Put your hands on your heads. Sit on that rock. My friend will go to arrange transportation for you."

Emile and Jacques walked to the hillside. The other soldier walked to his motorcycle. He slung his machine gun over his shoulder and bent down to pull it up. As he was lifting it, he screamed. The bike fell from his hands. Emile saw him reach to clutch his chest. The black handle of a large knife was protruding from it. The soldier's hands clutched it. His face showed shock and terror. He stumbled backward, lost his balance, and fell over the precipice. They heard him scream as he fell.

Uncertain of what had happened to his colleague, the Alsatian guarding Emile and Jacques was terrified and began pointing his gun around wildly, looking for a target. Emile worried that he might shoot them in his confusion, but the soldier no longer seemed to care about them. He was too concerned with looking up the hill above them to see whomever had killed his companion. Emile looked but could see nothing but some mouflon that appeared unconcerned. The soldier moved away from the two men and started firing randomly around them. After a long burst, he stopped and looked for signs that he might have hit the assassin. It turned out to be the last mistake he made. A young woman emerged from behind a large boulder and fired several shots in his chest that threw him backward.

"Hey, Jacques!" cried the young woman, raising a fist.

"Azeri!" Jacques screamed. He raised his fist. "Buenas días. Are we glad to see you!"

"You looked like you needed a little help," she said. "Who is your friend?"

Emile saw her studying him intently and decided it would be best not to move until he had been introduced.

"He is from Oradour-sur-Glane, up in the Limousin. The Hun wiped out the whole town and his family last Saturday. He wants to go to Spain and then Algiers to join the Free French Army."

"Are you certain of him?" she asked, eying Emile.

"I checked out his story with some of our people in Limoges. They confirmed what he had told me. The Fascist pigs butchered everyone in the town, over six hundred. They burned all the women and children and shot the men."

"The bastards will pay. They will all pay soon for everything they have done." She let her gun drop to her side and stepped down the hillside to them. She was striking. She was not dressed like anyone he had seen before. Her dark, wavy hair was tied up tightly at the back of her head; on top of it was a black beret. She wore black trousers that widened at the bottom and a black jacket with intricate embroidery around the buttonholes and cuffs. In stark contrast, a vivid red blouse showed through the opening in her jacket. Her French was good, but she spoke it with a strong Spanish accent. She held out her hand to Emile. "Welcome to our family," she said.

"Buenas días," replied Emile, shaking her hand.

She raised her eyebrows. "Habla español?"

"Si. Soy un profesor de español."

"Very good," she said, reverting to French. "That will make it much easier if you want to go to Spain."

"How did you get so close to us without disturbing the mouflons?"

"I am Basque. My people have lived in these mountains and herded the animals for generations. We were here before the goats, before the sheep. Some say we were here before the mountains. The animals know it. They accept us among them."

"I have heard and read much of the Basques, but you are the first one I have had the pleasure to meet. Maybe you will teach me more of the Basque culture."

She smiled. She paused. "We shall see. This is not a time for teaching but for killing. We must put aside our pleasures until we drive the Fascists from our homelands."

"Hey you two," Jacques said. "We have a body to get rid of."

"Throw him over the cliff to find his friend," said Azeri. "It is wild country down there. They will not be found for weeks. Take the guns."

"And the motorcycles?"

"We could use those. I will ride one to camp. Hide the other in the trees over there. I will send someone to fetch it."

Jacques dragged the body to the edge of the cliff and threw it over while Emile hid one of the motorcycles. Azeri picked up the machine guns. She gave Jacques a hug and kissed him on his cheeks before starting a motorcycle and roaring away up the hill.

"Quite a woman. You didn't tell me anything about her," said Emile. "Are there many more like her in your group?"

"There is only one Azeri."

"It's an unusual name."

"It is the name she goes by. I am told it means 'fox' in Basque."

"Seems to suit her."

"Yes, but now we must get going," replied Jacques nervously. "It is not wise to stay around here. We need to be on the plateau before nightfall."

As Jacques had predicted, it took them nearly two more hours to reach the maquis' encampment on the plateau. Emile was thankful the last part of the journey had been relatively flat; he was grateful to have some time to recover from the climb. As they rode into the camp, the sun was setting. The west was aglow in burning shades of red and orange. Emile felt as if he were on top of the world, Zeus looking down from Mount Olympus.

Jacques continued riding past many makeshift campsites and a disheveled array of people, all of whom seemed to know him. Finally, they arrived at a large tent with oil lamps glowing inside and a multitude of silhouettes visible on the canvas walls.

"This is where we get off, my friend," proclaimed Jacques. "You have done well."

A short, rotund man ran up to Jacques and hugged him. "Ah Mr. Jacques. You are here. It is good to see you. I hope you brought fresh supplies. We are running low, and we have many mouths to feed. The Germans have been making things difficult recently."

"I know. We ran into a couple of them not far down the road. They are getting bolder. Fortunately for us, Azeri took care of them."

The man smiled "Azeri. I'm sure she did. I wouldn't want to upset her. She has sworn to kill every German for what they did to her town. I think she may just do that before this war is over."

"Remember to thank her for the food," said Jacques. "If it were not for her, the Germans would be enjoying it. It's in the trailers."

"Who is your new friend?" asked the man. "I haven't seen him before."

"He is new. Maurice, this is Emile. Emile, this is Maurice. You need to be very nice to him. He is our cook."

"Glad to have you join us, Emile," Maurice said, holding out his hand. Having dispensed with the formalities, he turned to Jacques.

"Jacques. Did you bring any cigarettes? Or did you smoke them all on the way up?"

Jacques reached in his jacket and threw him a pack. He was busy trying to pull the handgrip off one of his handlebars. After struggling for a while, he succeeded. He put a finger inside the hollow tube and withdrew a rolled-up paper. He threw the grip at Maurice.

"Here. You can put this back on. I have what I need for Madame Andrée."

Jacques walked toward the command tent. "Take care of Emile," he shouted. "Get him some food. Show him where to sleep."

Maurice did as Jacques requested. After they had eaten and cursed the Germans for more than an hour, Maurice gave him a sleeping bag and an old rifle. "Time for bed. The camp rises early. I will show you where to sleep. Always sleep out in the open with your rifle. If there is a surprise attack, you will not be caught inside a tent and will be ready to fight."

"I will try to remember to not roll over and shoot myself."

"That would not be good." Maurice laughed.

Emile followed Maurice to a small copse of trees sheltered from the winds by a rocky outcropping. Several men were already there, gathered around a fire and drinking wine. Maurice introduced Emile to the group and wished him a good night.

The group was friendly and Emile was glad for the company. The warm, bright fire was reassuring in the windswept, dark, desolate place. As each told his story of what had brought him there, he listened, not anxious to say anything about himself. It was too soon and too painful. He knew that eventually it might help to talk about what had happened, that it might help to begin the healing process, but that time was in the future. He simply wanted to push out of his mind everything that had happened to him in the last week. He tried to think only of how much he hated the Germans and how he would avenge the deaths of his family. There was no love left in his life. He would have to survive on hate.

Emile listened to the conversation and drank the wine they were passing around liberally. His gaze was transfixed on the flames. He could see in them the church in Oradour burning in front of him. Out of the flames, the faces of his wife and daughters appeared, screaming out for him to save them. He missed them dearly, but he could not bear to look upon their faces or hear their screams. He wanted them to go away so he would be spared the guilt he felt for abandoning them to die so cruelly.

However, the faces of his wife and daughters would not leave him. Emile drank in hopes it would numb his mind. Numb it to the point that he might never have to face another day. The alcohol began to disorganize his mind. The voices around him faded to an incomprehensible buzz. The night air lost its chilly bite. Emile managed to find his sleeping bag and collapsed into it. Looking up at the stars took him back to the innocence of his childhood. As he lost consciousness, hypnotized by their magic, he prayed that when he awoke in the morning, he would find himself a child again and that everything had been merely a bad dream.

CHAPTER 12

𝕿𝖍𝖊 𝕱𝖔𝖗𝖙𝖗𝖊𝖘𝖘 𝖔𝖋 𝕱𝖗𝖆𝖓𝖈𝖊

Sunday, June 18, 1944

Despite the wine and the exhaustion, Emile had trouble falling into the deep sleep he craved. The ground was hard, and the chatter continued into the early hours. A further aggravation was the shooting pains in his legs caused by the two-day ride up the mountain. But his body slowly adjusted to its discomforts. The camp quieted down. He heard only the wind and the hooting of an owl. Its call was a welcome distraction from the world of man he wanted to escape. It cleared his mind. He fell asleep.

In a recurring dream, Emile saw himself running in a place he was completely unfamiliar with. The landscape was populated with tall, dry, rocky peaks, quite unlike those in the Limousin or Auvergne. Always ahead of him was a range of high, snow-capped mountains. As he tried one more time to reach the mountains, he felt a pain in his side and instinctively rolled over to avoid it. His relief was only temporary. He felt the pain again on his other side.

"Hey, Emile. Wake up. Bad night?" someone shouted.

Emile squinted at the man standing over him.

"You've got to get up now. Madame Andrée runs this group like the army. She says that for now, we are the French army, and we have to be ready to fight the Germans at any time. She does not like us oversleeping. Breakfast is by the fire. Want some hot chocolate?"

"Chocolate? Can I have coffee?"

"Coffee? Not much of that around, but I might be able to find some. Hangover?"

"Yes. I'm afraid I overdid it a bit last night. My head feels like a lead weight."

"You'll get over it. The air is so fresh up here. It's like medicine. It will clear anything away. Let me go scrounge you up some coffee. It would help if you had cigarettes to trade."

Emile reached into his pocket, remembering some Jacques had given him. He took one out, lit it, and inhaled deeply before throwing the rest of the pack at his companion. Emile looked at his face. He strained to remember his name.

"Martin," he said, reading Emile's blank expression. "We met last night, but you seemed to have a lot on your mind."

"I'm sorry, but—"

"Don't think of it. There were many people. I'll get coffee with these cigarettes."

Emile looked around. The camp was waking up. The sun was burning the mists off the fields. They were a motley bunch, these maquisards, Emile thought as he studied them. Looking at each, he tried to imagine what they had done in civilian life. They looked like a cross section of French society brought haphazardly together by circumstances. Many were simply young boys. Emile could guess why most of them were there. Many young Frenchmen had fled to the maquis rather than be drafted into the hated, forced-labor organization, the Service du Travail Obligatoire, the STO. The Vichy government had set it up to work for the Nazi regime. Some of boys reminded him of Julien, and he wondered how he was doing. Had he been united with his parents? And where would his family go?

Emile imagined that many of the older men had probably experienced personal tragedy as Emile had and had sought a place of comradeship where they had a chance to fight back. They were all reluctant partisans. A minority were clearly die-hard revolutionaries, anxious for any opportunity to establish a new worldwide social order. He sympathized with their dreams but distrusted their ambitions. He watched them greet each other with raised fists. It reminded him too much of the Nazis.

Emile was lost in his thought when Martin returned with coffee. "Drink this. It's good and strong. Only cost two cigarettes. A good deal."

Emile handed what was left of the pack to Martin, who was already smoking one, his compensation for his efforts. "Thanks. So what are we doing today?"

"Don't know yet. They never tell us until the last minute. More secure that way. I hear we got a new arms drop last night, so we'll be doing something. There's rumor about someone new in the camp with Madame Andrée. An explosives expert, they say."

"You're a lot more organized and supplied here than we were in the Limousin. We couldn't do much more than cut telephone wires and blow up a few bridges. We didn't have the arms to fight them. I wish we had."

"We are lucky. Madame Andrée has good ties to the English. She had to escape to England last year when she was betrayed. They trained her how to fight the Germans and then dropped her back here by parachute. When she got back, she learned the Germans had tortured and killed her husband. She hates them even more."

"I can understand," said Emile. "I'd do the same."

"Anyway, now the English drop arms to us all over the plateau. There have been many drops recently. Madame Andrée says we are preparing to liberate all France."

"It cannot come too soon. I hope she's right. Our people cannot endure this occupation much longer."

"We all have great confidence in her. We would follow her anywhere. She's quite a woman. Wait till you meet her."

"I look forward to that."

"Just last week, during a raid on a German gun factory, they say she killed a sentry with her bare hands to keep him from alerting the guard. She also led a raid on the Gestapo headquarters in Montlucon. I was told she executed a woman who was a German spy."

Martin was clearly in awe of Madame Andrée. Whether his confidence in her was justified or not, Emile thought she must have been a good leader to inspire such adulation. "If she's such a thorn in the side of the Germans, I'm surprised they haven't tried to eliminate her," Emile said.

"Tried? Oh they've tried. They're always trying, but these mountains are our friends. With all the allied attacks, the Germans do not have enough planes to attack us here, so the only way up for them is along those steep, narrow mountain roads. It would be very difficult for them to bring much heavy armor up. Plus, we know the terrain. We are safe here."

"I hope you're right. We ran into a couple of Germans just outside Chaudes-Aigues. That's not far away."

"No," said Martin, spitting. "But that's still a ways down the mountain. They wouldn't dare come up here."

"Emile," called a woman from behind them. "Enough of your women's chatter. There is work to be done," said the voice in Spanish.

Emile saw Azeri standing confidently with her black beret and a rifle over her shoulder. He stood. "Azeri, it is good to see you again," he said. "I owe you a debt for yesterday." He turned to Martin. "She saved our lives."

"Perhaps today you can repay me," Azeri said.

"I see you remember her name, eh?" said Martin. "Don't worry. I would too."

"How is the lovely Spanish señorita?" he asked Azeri.

"I am Basque. I am fine, thank you."

Azeri gave them hugs. Emile noticed she smelled good, in sharp contrast to the mass of unclean bodies in the camp. There was the faintest wisp of a perfume that seemed incongruous with her guerilla attire.

She looked Emile up and down. "Jacques tells me you want to cross into Spain."

"Yes. I want to join General Leclerc in Algeria."

"How patriotic of you," she said dismissively. "I have to take someone else across the border in a few days. I suppose I could take you too, but only if I can trust you."

"What must I do to earn your trust?"

"Madame Andrée has entrusted me with a mission today. We have a little demolition work to do. I heard you have some experience in this area."

"A little. I am no expert."

"That is no problem. I have an expert. I need someone to help carry explosives and plant charges."

"That is certainly within my level of expertise. When do we leave?"

"Fifteen minutes. I hope you are well rested. It will be a difficult trail."

"I'll be ready."

Azeri left.

"She's a tough one too," said Martin. "Bit of a loner, but everyone respects her. She's killed more than her share of Germans."

"I saw that firsthand yesterday."

"Get ready for your mission. It wouldn't do to keep her waiting. Good luck."

"Thanks, though I probably won't need it with her along."

In half an hour, they were on a trail, heading east.

"We must go down off the plateau to the valley of the Truyère. There is a railway line heading north to Clermont-Ferrand. The Germans are using it to move troops to the front. Our mission is to close it down," Azeri said to the five, each one laden with backpacks filled with explosives. In addition to Emile and Azeri, there were two other maquis and the demolition expert, Antoine.

Azeri fell back alongside Emile. "We must change your name. No one uses his real names in the maquis. It is too dangerous for those left behind."

"There is no one left behind. The Germans killed my family."

"There is always someone. The Gestapo will find someone, even if it is only one of the children you taught. They are very good at it, believe me. I know it firsthand."

Emile had thought everyone he had cared about was dead, but when she expanded it in that manner, he realized she was right. There were still people he cared for. It heartened him and scared him equally.

"What name do you suggest?"

"If you do not have a preference, I will call you Zori. Basque for 'luck'."

"Right now, that name does not seem appropriate."

"On the contrary. You survived Oradour when everyone else perished. Most people would say you had lots of luck."

"I don't feel lucky. I would rather have died back there than see my wife and daughters burned to death."

"It is understandable you feel that way now. Your life has lost its meaning. I went through the same thing after my family was killed. But in time, you will find a new path. It is that way in the mountains where I come from. Sometimes, high up, after searching for a sheep, you lose the trail and have to wander around until you find another one to take you down the mountain. With patience, you will find a new path."

"Right now, I feel so lost that I might be tempted to just jump off the mountain."

"You must tell yourself you were spared at Oradour for a purpose. The Lord has a plan for your life, and with patience, you will find it."

"Have you found yours? You are Basque. What are you doing in France?"

"I came here to kill Germans. I am from Guernika in northwest Spain. Have you heard of it?"

"I have heard of it, but I am afraid I know little about it. I believe it is one of the major Basque cities. I remember it was bombed during the civil war."

"Yes, it was bombed, but not like any city before it, and not by the Spanish. It was bombed by the Luftwaffe on twenty-sixth of April, nineteen thirty-seven. They were supporting Generalissimo Franco and his revolution against the Republican government. The Germans pounded it relentlessly for four hours with wave after wave of bombs. When they were finished, they had killed over a third of the inhabitants, including all my family, and they had destroyed the city. The Germans said it was an experiment, a new military tactic the Nazis had dreamed up, the 'blitzkrieg', they called it."

"I am sorry to hear that. You must hate them for it."

"Yes I do, so now my purpose is to kill every German I can find until I have avenged the deaths of my people."

"There is no end to vengeance," said Emile. "It is a dark, bottomless hole that lets in no light, and you can't crawl out of it. I have no wish to fall into it. I hate the Germans too for what they have done, but I could not justify my existence by simply killing them."

"For me, it is not a dark, bottomless hole. There is a light shining in that gets brighter every time I strike against the Fascist war machine. That light is the independence of Euskal Herria, the land of the Basques. I will crawl out of this pit of yours when my people are free again to govern themselves under the *Guernikako arbola*, the tree of the Basques."

"Then I wish you luck, or should I say zori. The Basques are a great people, survivors. If you are an example, I can see why. I am not sure if I have your strength."

"You must search for it. It does not come without effort. First, you must realize there are few people who have not lost someone they loved in this war. You are not alone. It is the duty of those of us who survive to prevent further suffering."

Emile felt ashamed. "You are right. I'm sorry. It's been difficult thinking of anyone but myself lately."

"That's normal. Your loss is recent, but unfortunately, this war does not give us much time to mourn or we risk being mourned ourselves. We have to act."

"When it is over, will you go back to Guernika?"

"Yes. It was my father's dream to restore the Basque homeland. I must go back to help unite our people again."

"I hope you make it. You have the determination to make a great leader."

"God willing," replied Azeri.

As Azeri had warned them, it was a long hike, and the boxes were heavy. The first part across the plateau was not too difficult—gently rolling pastures crisscrossed by fast-running streams. There were few trees, and those were relatively small. The winds and the harsh winters challenged the survival of anything bigger. They saw sheep and the famous Aubrac cattle that grazed any budding sprout quickly to the ground.

The group stayed off the roads to avoid detection and because it was more direct to cut across the fields. They were guided by a local maquis who knew every centimeter of the plateau as well as Emile had known his garden in St. Junien. Fortunately, they had seen no German planes. There would have been few places to hide.

Toward the edge of the plateau, the terrain became much more difficult. The volcanic plain was cracked with large fractures that rivers had carved into steep gorges, but trees offered cover. As they climbed gingerly down the mountain, Emile was bolstered by the fact that they would not have the weight on their backs on their return. At one point, he slipped and came close to spraining his ankle. Rocks cascaded off the edge of the rock face. They peered over the edge to make sure the noise had not attracted attention.

A little before noon, they made it to the plain. Ahead of them was the River Truyère, and beyond that the railway line. If all went well, they would have time to plant the charges and return to the encampment before night.

Emile heard the river just as Gérard, who was leading, crouched and waved for them to stop. He put his finger to his mouth to silence them. Azeri went forward to join him, keeping low. The two whispered for a few minutes and pointed down the path. Emile saw nothing blocking the route, but he realized they were leaving the cover of the forest.

Azeri crept back. "We have a problem. There is an armored car on the bridge with a heavy machine gun and two Bosch."

"How far is the next bridge?" asked Emile.

"The nearest one was about five kilometers," said Benoît, the maquisard. He shook his head and laughed quietly. "Unfortunately, we blew it up last week."

"Wonderful," said Azeri sarcastically. "Then we must cross here."

"How?"

"We will kill them like they killed my people without any pity, throw their bodies into the water, and walk across."

There was a coldness in her voice that scared Emile. "I assume you have a plan," he said, fearing the answer.

"I do, but I will need your help. Can you swim?"

The answer was worse than he had bargained for. He was hesitant to answer. "Well, I used to swim in the Vienne as a boy, and I believe I can swim as well as most people, but the Truyère looks too treacherous to swim across."

"You will not need to swim across it. Here is the plan."

Emile and Azeri split off from the group. Emile kept to the forest and walked parallel to the river, as Azeri had instructed. When he was a few hundred meters upstream of the bridge, he crept to the riverbank. Wading into the swift flowing water, he shivered. It was freezing. His teeth chattered. But there was no turning back. They had to get across the bridge. Staying close to the bank, he allowed himself to drift slowly downstream. As the river turned sharply, he saw the bridge ahead of him. He could see the Germans. One was in the armored car on the bridge, manning the machine gun. The other was standing at the edge of the forest on the same side of the river as Azeri and the others. Both were smoking and talking loudly to one another.

When neither of the soldiers was looking in his direction, Emile let go of the bank and pushed himself out into the river. Almost immediately, the swift current took him and sped him downstream toward the bridge. At the mercy of the river, he had to fight frantically at times to avoid being smashed against boulders. Due to the constant rushing sound of turbulent water, he had little fear the Germans would hear his struggles. As he approached the bridge, he strained furiously to put himself on a collision path with one of the supports in the middle of the river.

He succeeded only too well. The river slammed him against the stone column. Excruciating pain shot up his leg; it was all he could do to stop himself from crying out, but he managed, knowing the consequences. Emile fought to keep his grasp on the bridge. He struggled to pull himself up out of the water. More than once, the river almost succeeded in pulling him back in and sweeping him away in the torrent, but he knew Azeri's life depended on him. He did not want another life on his conscience. Emile climbed onto a small ledge and sat. He shivered. He hoped he didn't have to wait long.

The German heard a bell. He turned from his colleague and looked down the path into the forest. He saw half a dozen sheep running toward him. He raised his gun, but then he laughed at his friend, who was clasping the machine gun tightly in the armored car. Emile leaned out a little from the bridge to see what was going on.

The sheep were not far from the bridge. Emile saw the soldier on the bank getting nervous. He pointed his weapon at one sheep and then another.

Then she appeared, running out of the forest far down the path, waving frantically at the sheep. It was Azeri, though she was difficult to recognize. She had taken off her beret and allowed her long, wavy hair to fall freely down her back. She had also exchanged her distinctive embroidered black jacket for a more worn one.

"Stop! Stop!" she shouted, flailing her arms.

Both the Germans aimed at her. With their attention diverted, Emile made his move. He climbed the stone footing, which was rough enough to offer foot and handholds. As he pulled himself over the low stone wall onto the bridge, the warm rays of the sun lessened his chill. Crouching, he began to make his way to the car. To Emile's relief, their plan seemed to be working. Both soldiers were preoccupied with Azeri and had their backs to him.

"Halt or we shoot," shouted one German in French with an Alsatian accent.

Azeri froze. "The sheep! I have to get the sheep back or my father will kill me!"

"What are you doing here? You are not authorized to be here."

"My sheep are not authorized to be here either. My father will kill me if I lose them."

The German laughed. "What do you say to a leg of lamb, Heinrich?"

"Sounds delicious."

"Please do not shoot them," begged Azeri. "They are all we have to live on."

The German sneered and fired. The shot echoed through the forest. One of the sheep fell, blood gushing over its white coat from a head wound.

"Good shot!" Heinrich said. "We will eat well tonight."

"Okay, Mademoiselle. You may round up the others," yelled the soldier. "You can keep us company too. We have some wine and chocolate. If you are really good to us, we might even let you share some lamb for dinner."

Emile was just behind the car. He had never killed anyone up close before and did not know if he could do it. Then he remembered Oradour and knew he had to find the courage. He drew the long hunting knife Azeri had given him out of his wet jacket and climbed up the back of the car. Raising the knife, he prepared to strike the German in the back of the neck. Suddenly, he heard the German on the bank cry out, "Heinri—"

In a panic reaction, Emile plunged the knife downward, into its target. In the split-second of delay, Heinrich had turned to face him. He was only a young boy, younger than Pascal, who had been engaged to his daughter. He saw the horror in his eyes as the knife slashed his throat. Emile realized his was the last face the young man would ever see. He slumped to the bed of the vehicle, blood rushing from the gaping neck wound. Emile recoiled in horror. He looked at his bloody knife and threw it over the bridge. Nausea overcame him. He climbed out of the car and threw up into the angry stream, hoping it would cleanse him of what he had done.

Azeri strode up to the car and looked inside. "Good. These two will not be troubling us again. We can get on with our mission." She patted Emile on the back. "Good job. It was a close call because you hesitated, but that is normal. The first time you kill someone up close is always difficult, so much more personal than blowing a train up or sniping at soldiers from behind a tree. The next time will be easier. You will see."

Emile did not want to think about the next time. There was nothing in the war he liked to think about other than its ending.

"Okay, Zori, enough delay. We need to get rid of this car and the bodies. I need your help to push it into the forest." She was calm, in control, unnerved by the experience. Her wavy hair belied her fanatical determination. Emile admired her strength, which he had seldom seen in a man let alone a woman.

As they pushed the car off the bridge, Emile saw what had become of the other German. He was lying face down. A large knife protruded from his back. Emile understood why his cry had been interrupted. As he had turned to warn his colleague about Emile, Azeri's razor-sharp reactions had sent her knife flying through the air and into his back.

"Looks like you saved my life again," Emile said, nodding toward the body.

"Today we were a team," replied Azeri. "We saved each other."

On the bank, Emile and Azeri picked up the dead German and threw him in the armored car alongside his companion. Azeri started the car and drove it as fast as she could into the underbrush, jumping out before it crashed into a tree.

She let out a very shrill whistle. A few moments later, the others emerged on the trail from out of the forest, lugging their heavy boxes.

"We have lost time. We must move quickly," said Antoine, always short on words.

Over the bridge, the land was not as precipitous; more pastures and forest made the going easier. By early afternoon, they reached their objective. It was a beautiful area, a steep side valley that had been carved out by the glacial river flowing at its bottom. The rocky sides of the valley were covered in beech, chestnut, and oak trees. As they had hiked through the forest, Emile admired the profusion of wild mushrooms that sprouted abundantly. He had thought of picking some on the way back to cook at the camp that evening. His *cèpes aux fines herbes* had been a favorite of his wife.

At the bottom of the valley, running alongside the river, was the railway line. Antoine looked at the line through binoculars. "Over there." He pointed. "That is the entrance to the tunnel. Azeri, take someone with you and two of the boxes and place the charges all around the opening, exactly as I showed you. According to the rail resistance network, a troop transport is due here around three. Wait one minute after the train is completely in the tunnel. Then blow the charges. Understood?"

"Understood," Azeri answered as if to a commanding officer.

"You other two come with me and bring the remainder of the explosives."

Gérard and Bênoit obeyed unquestioningly. The two groups separated.

"Where is he going?" asked Emile.

"He is going to mine the other end of the tunnel," replied Azeri. "Our orders are to destroy the train and make sure the tunnel cannot be used for the duration of the war. Madame Andrée's English commanders do not want the Germans clearing the line."

"Antoine seems very secretive," said Emile. "How long have you known him?"

"I never saw him before last night. He arrived just before you did. He was loaned to Madame Andrée for this mission. When he is finished, he will go. It is best not to ask too many questions. They can only get you into trouble," Azeri said.

Emile and Azeri, lugging a box of explosives each, made it down to the tunnel entrance with about one and a half hours to spare before the train was due. Azeri unlocked the boxes. Emile drew his breath when he saw what was inside. The boxes contained TNT, plastic explosives, bickfords, detonators, primers, and *crayons de mise à feu*. Azeri carefully unpacked it all and organized it on the ground. She took a sketch from her pocket.

"This is where we must place the charges," she said, pointing to an illustration. "They must all be in place in time."

Climbing along the rocks that surrounded the entrance of the tunnel was arduous. Emile was more nervous than usual. His group in the Limousin had never had any experience with TNT, so he was unsure how to handle it safely, but Azeri took it all in stride. As she climbed among the rocks, he fancied the Basques were mountain goats themselves. She never seemed unsure of her footing.

By around 2:30 p.m., the charges had been laid. Emile and Azeri had retired a safe distance into the forest away from the tunnel. Azeri lay on the ground, her hands on the detonator plunger. Emile stood behind a tree, looking down the track. The line was empty.

Time passed slowly. Emile hated the waiting. His mind kept straying to his horrifying memories. In a lighter moment, he thought of Julien, the young Ya Ya who had befriended him in Oradour and had hidden him. He hoped his father had forgiven him for destroying his shop. He could not imagine otherwise.

Emile saw something down the track. Wisps of puffing smoke. They could hear the train rattling the rails, breaking the silence of the forest. Azeri's expression tensed.

The first carriage was an empty platform, a safeguard that would be destroyed by any mines. Behind it was a large car with tools and maintenance equipment. Following that was an armored car, no doubt containing Nazi plunder. The next carriages, though, were what they had come for—five or six carriages stuffed to the brim with Wehrmacht soldiers on their way to Normandy. This was what the Allies had wanted them to stop. Emile looked at them as they passed in their verdigris uniforms, many festooned with medals for atrocities he was sure they had committed against civilians.

Emile felt mixed emotions as he watched the train enter the tunnel. He pitied them but did not feel sorrow. He had seen too many horrible things done by their kind and in their name. It was an evil that had to be destroyed. He felt angry that through their doing, he now regarded the mass slaughter of fellow humans as acceptable. The Age of Enlightenment had been betrayed.

As the last armored car entered the tunnel, he raised his hand. Together, he and Azeri began counting. As the count approached sixty, Emile crouched and covered his ears. On sixty, Azeri pushed the plunger down with all her might. The explosion was tremendous. It seemed the whole mountain was coming down on them. They ran into the forest to escape errant rocks crashing through the trees.

The dust began to clear. Azeri and Emile picked their way through the forest toward the tracks. They saw no sign of the tunnel. Iron rails terminated in a pile of rocks. If it were not for the enormous trees uprooted like matchsticks, it would have looked as though the mountainside had always been that way.

The ground shook again, and they heard another thunderous roar. Fearing another landslide, Emile covered his head and fled into the forest. Azeri stood, hands on hips. He heard another explosion, not as loud as the first two but enough to make Emile jump.

"Relax," cried Azeri. "That is Antoine setting off the other charges."

"Why two?"

"The first one was to seal off the tunnel at the other end, and the second to destroy the air shaft. The train and all its passengers are entombed. None of them will make it to the front. It will be a long time before that track can be used again."

Emile thought of the panic that must have been sweeping through the soldiers in the blackened tunnel. He imagined it was similar to the horror the mothers and children of Oradour felt when they realized they were going to die in the church. He felt nauseous. "Why not just blow up the train? Wouldn't that have been quicker?"

"This is war. We can have no pity. We did what was necessary to cause maximum disruption to the German plans. We did what was asked of us."

Regrettably, Emile conceded maybe she was right. But it bothered him that their actions now seemed little better than the Germans'. He had always consoled himself with the thought they had been fighting a more moral war. It had been an easy delusion because until the massacre at Oradour-sur-Glane, the Limousin had been spared the ravages that had taken place elsewhere. He was coming face-to-face with the reality of war.

Without the boxes to carry, they made good time back. After about a half hour, Gérard and Benoît came trekking up the trail.

"Where is Antoine?" asked Emile.

"He is gone. He said farewell and went off," replied Gérard.

"Don't worry. He is not expected back," Azeri said.

Back at camp, Azeri reported on their mission to Madame Andrée, and Emile sought out Martin. He found him engaged in a heated debate around a man who was squirming on the ground and who had been badly beaten.

CHAPTER 13

Settling In

"Who is the man?" asked Emile.

"Milice!" Martin said with venom. "I hate them worse than I do the Bosch."

"How did he come here?"

"We caught him in the bar in the village. One of the men in camp recognized his girlfriend and forced her to write a note, inviting him to meet her. When he showed up, we grabbed him and brought him up here."

"What happened to the girl?"

"She was slapped around a little. We shaved her head and released her. Her boyfriend will not be as lucky. He turned people over to the Gestapo. Many in the camp have lost friends and family members because of him."

"We hated the Milice too in St. Junien. They are all traitors. After the war, those left should be shipped to Germany. They have no right to call themselves French."

"You are right, but this one will not survive to see that day."

"Why did they bring him to the camp? Why not just shoot him in the village?"

"They thought the proceedings of a trial would help bring a sense of justice to those he has made suffer."

"Did it?" asked Emile.

"Well, I don't know about the trial. It wasn't much of one. He didn't deny anything. He claims he is a patriot. He convicted himself with his own mouth. After the guilty verdict was read, several people set about him.

That seemed to bring them some relief. He will be executed on the hour. Everyone in the camp is invited to watch."

Emile had little stomach for such a spectacle, but he sensed it might be viewed as treasonous if he did not witness the summary application of justice.

When the time came, the man refused a blindfold. He raised his bloodied head proudly in the air, facing down his accusers. "Messieurs, Vive la France," he screamed as the Enfield rifles tore the last breath from his body.

It had been a long first day for Emile in this camp atop the world. Life there was a far cry from teaching all day and going home to a loving family in the evening, which had been his reality until only a couple of weeks previously. Nothing had prepared him for what had befallen him since. Azeri was right. If he was to go on living, he had to find a new purpose, but that still escaped him.

Emile found a spot protected from the winds by a large rock. He threw his sleeping bag down on the mossy rocks and climbed in. He saw the mica schists and large white feldspar crystals in the rock trapping the moonlight and glistening like a myriad of stars. It did not take him long to escape into his dreams. Out of sheer exhaustion, he slept soundly and did not wake up until the camp stirred early the next morning.

Monday, June 19, 1944

At daybreak, Emile was told to go with Martin and two others to pick up some weapons dropped in a field a few kilometers away by the English during the night. It took most of the morning, but Emile enjoyed the mission for it did not involve killing anyone. There was also unexplored nature to observe. The high plateau of Aubrac was a new world to Emile after the pastures of the Limousin. He marveled at the wild beauty around him.

As they walked along narrow trails through long grass, Emile watched the winds rippling through the long grasses. He focused on the noise to help wash away his thoughts in a place seemingly untouched by everything going on in the world below. They crossed numerous streams fed by snowmelt. Emile could readily understand what could attract a man to hide from the world in the Monastery of Aubrac.

The journey back to the camp with the arms was more difficult. The ground was very wet in places, and a man could sink into bogs to his knees if he was carrying a heavy load, but they were in no hurry. The sunshine warmed them despite the constant wind.

They arrived at camp in time for lunch. Rations were sparse but of high quality. The maquisards had friends all around Auvergne, many of whom were farmers. They gave what they could to support the maquis rather than allowing the Germans to confiscate it.

In the afternoon, a new commotion erupted in the camp. A young Alsatian who had claimed to be a deserter from the Waffen SS was accused of being a spy. He had been caught the night before signaling to his accomplices. After "interrogation," he admitted he had been sent to spy on them and report on their number and capabilities. The maquisard who had brought him into the group was also accused of working with him.

Emile felt little sympathy for the Alsatian, a member of the Waffen SS, the same detestable regiment that had been responsible for the abomination at Oradour. When he talked, his Alsatian accent brought back the memories of that day more vividly than he could cope with. He remembered Julien's description of how he and his family had been driven from their homes by neighbors such as this boy who had cooperated with the Germans.

Both were tried before another kangaroo court, found guilty, and shot.

The afternoon was uneventful. Emile sat with other members of the camp discussing the war and politics. They were a very mixed bunch thrown together by circumstances and united only by their hatred of the Germans. Few were without an opinion, and there was little consensus about what should be done after the Germans were defeated.

Politically, the maquisards ranged from right-wing Nationalists to Communists. Most were French, but in addition to Azeri, there were many Spaniards, either Republicans or Communists who had been defeated by Franco's forces in the Spanish civil war. Once again, they were thrust on the same side of a conflict though they distrusted each other. However, the largest number of the group was young French boys fleeing the Milice, the Gestapo, or the forced-labor Nazi draft.

Emile learned that since being parachuted back into France at the end of April, Madame Andrée had increased the number of maquisards from three or four thousand to around seven thousand in preparation for a final push against the Germans. He marveled at how she had united and organized such a disparate bunch into a very effective fighting force. Despite being outgunned by the Germans, their morale was very high; all were confident of eventual victory.

Azeri sent for Emile in the evening. She had the luxury of her own tent. Emile entered it and noticed a man he was unfamiliar with. He had several deep cuts on his face, and his left arm was in a sling. He held his hand out to Emile.

"Pleased to meet you," he said in passable French but with a thick British accent. Emile shook his hand.

"Zori," said Azeri, "I present Wing Commander Frank Rossington of the RAF."

"Pleased to meet you," Emile said.

"The commander was shot down on a bombing raid over Clermont Ferrand."

"Spot of bad luck, I'm afraid," interjected the Englishman with a shrug.

"Madame Andrée has asked me to take him over the border into Spain so he could make it to Gibraltar and back to England. She has agreed to let me take you with us if you haven't changed your mind," Azeri said, piercing him inquisitively with her dark-brown eyes.

"I have not," replied Emile after a short pause during which he tried to discern the meaning of her look. "I still want to go."

"Then it is settled. You will come with us. We leave on Wednesday. I will prepare everything we need for the journey. Commander, we will try to get you home safely. Be ready to leave at daybreak on Wednesday, and talk to no one about our plans. Even here in the camp, no one is to be trusted."

"Understood."

"If you will excuse us," Azeri said to the commander, "Zori and I have to talk."

The Englishman stood, looking slightly embarrassed. "Of course. I have some work I must take care of. I will see you Wednesday. Thank you again."

"Don't mention it," replied Azeri as she closed the tent flap behind him.

"So you still want to join Leclerc?" Azeri asked in rapid Spanish, not giving Emile the time to respond. "I do not see you as a soldier. I can read it in your face. You are a teacher, not a killer. I saw it at the bridge. You are not like most of the men out there."

"All men can be killers if they have to be. I will learn."

"Perhaps, but there is no time. The war is coming to a climax. Soon, the armies of Leclerc and de Gaulle will be fighting here in France, God willing, and the only training you will get will be on the battlefield. It might be better for you to remain in Spain and sit the war out until it is over. Europe will need all the teachers it can find to rebuild after the war."

"I am pleased you value learning," said Emile. "But I cannot hide while others die in my place. I owe it to my family to fight against those who murdered them and to prevent them from killing anyone else."

"If your wife could speak to you, is that what she would say?"

Emile paused. "No, but it is what I must do for myself."

Azeri nodded. "I understand. Now for something more pleasurable. You told me you played guitar and knew many Spanish folk songs."

Emile was taken off guard. "I used to play them to my students to get them interested in the language, but it has been a while."

Azeri reached behind a chair and produced a fine-looking Spanish guitar. "I borrowed this from a countryman in the camp. He was reluctant at first, but I told him that if I liked the feel of it, I might allow him to give me private lessons."

"Do you play?"

"No, not at all, but he doesn't know that." She smiled. "Would you play?"

Emile tuned the instrument. It had a fine tone. Just holding it made him relax. Music had always flowed through his veins. His mother had told him he had tapped out tunes on his crib. No one could tell him where he had inherited it from; neither parent had any musical ability. He felt he owed someone a debt of gratitude for his love of music.

"What would you like me to play?" he asked, plucking at the strings.

"Take me to my childhood. Play the children's songs my mother used to sing to me."

"I'm not sure I'll make a good substitute for your mother, but I'll try."

Emile started singing and playing nursery songs. Azeri sang as well. It was a side to her he hadn't seen. A sensitive young woman, a girl even, hid behind the stoic figure she presented. Azeri loosened her hair and sat on the floor next to him with a bottle of wine.

"Don't you wish sometimes you could be a child again?" she asked.

"We never stop being children. We just go into denial as we grow up. That is why I always liked being around children. They have no pretenses."

The two laughed and drank as they sang. Azeri corrected Emile's Spanish and sang verses to some of the songs he had not known. They moved on to French songs, and it was Emile's turn to add verses Azeri had not known.

The night was drawing in. Azeri lit a candle. "Have you written any songs?"

With reluctance, Emile nodded. "Yes, but only for myself."

"Please share one with me. Music and poetry are rich traditions with the Basque people. Music is the eye into a man's soul. I would like to see into yours."

"A scary thought. Now you embarrass me."

"Then have some more wine. It will allow that child in you to come to the surface. Seriously, play me one of your compositions. I promise not to be critical."

Emile thought for a moment, and then very slowly, quietly at first, he began singing one of his earliest compositions. The song was sad, telling the story of two lovers who could not be together, so the woman drowned herself in a lake. He sang others that were happier and told of love fulfilled.

"Zori, you are a poet. Your songs tell stories, like those of the troubadours. They remind me of some ballads passed down for generations. Where did you learn that style?"

"I didn't. I write only what comes into my head. I'm afraid I may have an overactive imagination. I will not sing any more if they bore you."

"On the contrary, they are captivating. I think you should have been born in another time. The world today is not a place for romantics."

"I doubt it ever was," lamented Emile.

Azeri put her head in his lap. "Play on. I would like to hear more."

Emile played a few more songs until his exhaustion and the wine overcame him. "I had better be going. It's getting late," he stammered.

"There is no need," Azeri said softly, pulling him down toward her.

Emile could not resist as she unbuttoned her blouse for him to caress her breasts. She was beautiful in the candlelight. He had seen so little beauty in the past few weeks.

She pulled him toward him. They enjoyed each other's touches. As they consummated their relationship, each gripped the other in a tight embrace as if they never wanted to let go. It was so difficult to hold on to anything of real value in the war.

The two pulled blankets over them and fell asleep. Emile expected to have a good night's sleep, but it was not to be. In the early hours, he awoke in a heavy sweat. Azeri was staring at him. "Were you having a nightmare about Oradour? You have been tossing and turning all night, screaming about a fire."

"I'm not sure. Maybe that was it. I remember a fire, but I'm not sure it was the church in Oradour. I was having these same nightmares in St. Junien, before Oradour. There was a fire, and I had to put it out or the ones I loved would perish."

"You must have had a premonition. These things happen even though we can't explain them. It must have been your wife and daughters you were trying to save."

"You are probably right, but usually in my dreams, I see Monique as clear as day. In this dream, she looked different, older. There was no church in my dream, just a field."

"I have seen battle-hardened soldiers have nightmares of things that never happened after traumatic incidents. The mind is a strange thing. You have been injured not physically but mentally. It will take a long time to heal." Azeri rubbed some water on Emile's forehead. "Try to get some sleep. We can talk about it in the morning."

They lay down, hoping for several hours of restful sleep.

CHAPTER 14

To Catch a Mouse

Tuesday, June 20, 1944

Heavy machine-gun fire began before dawn. It was followed by what sounded like mortar shells. Emile jumped up and saw Azeri was already up. He rushed around frantically to find his clothes and dress. In the midst of the confusion, a rough-looking, unshaven Spaniard poked his head into the tent. "Azeri! We have to leave immediately. The SS have surrounded the camp. They have brought tanks, armored cars, trench mortars, and artillery, and they are backed up by planes. They mean business. It is time to go!"

The man noticed Emile. From the expression on his face, it looked as though he had just seen a German. When his glance chanced upon the guitar lying of the floor, he froze for a moment as if in disbelief.

Azeri frowned, grabbed it, and handed it to him. "I will be out in a moment. Get the men together," she ordered calmly.

The shooting noises were getting louder.

"It looks as though there will have to be a change of plan," Azeri announced sarcastically to Emile. "I will see Madame Andrée to find out what her new orders are."

Azeri ran out of the tent. Emile finished dressing and followed her. A man was handing out rifles, and Emile wanted one.

Azeri returned shortly. "Information is that that there are over twenty thousand SS surrounding the plateau. They are trying to obliterate us, but they do not know these mountains. They will regret their folly. Madame Andrée has ordered us to abandon the plateau and regroup in St. Santin-de-Maurs."

"How far is that?" asked Emile.

"About three days' rough walk across the plateau and into the valley of the Lot. Let them try to follow us. Their tanks will get stuck in the bogs, and their armored cars will not be able to follow us over the cliffs. We also have a few surprises in store for them."

Azeri's confidence gave Emile hope in spite of the odds against them.

"Madame Andrée wants some help loading last night's weapons onto a truck. Can you help?" Azeri asked some of the men.

"Show me where," volunteered Emile.

Madame Andrée was a smaller woman than he had imagined from her daunting reputation, but he had no doubts of her abilities. After the truck was loaded and safely dispatched, Madame Andrée jumped into a car hidden under a camouflage blanket and sped away. Two planes appeared. People began shooting furiously at them but to no effect. The planes took up the pursuit of the car containing Madame Andrée.

"No, no. She must escape!" screamed Azeri. "They cannot kill her."

One of the planes, a Henschel 126, began strafing the vehicle. They saw bullets riddling the back of her car. Madame Andrée kept slowing down suddenly, and then speeding up, to confuse the pilot's aim, but the tactic was of limited effectiveness. The pilot was tenacious. It was clear he would not give up until he had destroyed the vehicle. Accepting the inevitable, they watched as she abruptly drove the car off the road and into a ditch. Taking advantage of the momentary confusion of the pilot, the door opened and Madame Andrée jumped out, fleeing into the forest.

"At least she's alive," cried Azeri.

The plane pulled up away from the car and turned for another run, possibly to try to locate her in the woods. As he did so, Madame Andrée reappeared and ran back to the car.

"What is she doing?" screamed Emile. "She'll be killed."

The two watched aghast while she unloaded what looked like a few supplies and a saucepan from the car.

"She's crazy," yelled Emile. "How did she ever stay alive this long?"

"By sheer determination," Azeri said proudly. "Nothing intimidates her."

The drone of the plane increased. They saw the Henschel dropping in altitude and increasing in speed. It was headed straight at the car. Madame Andrée ran back into the forest. Seconds later, a torrent of bullets raked the vehicle, which exploded in flames.

"We will see her again. I am sure of it," proclaimed Azeri.

"I hope so," said Emile.

"With luck, the White Mouse has escaped again."

Emile and Azeri turned back to camp. It was mayhem all around. People were running everywhere and firing in all directions. Mortar rounds were exploding very close to the camp as the SS pressed their assault. Despite their overwhelming numbers and equipment, the Germans were taking heavy casualties. The main road was blocked by a damaged tank. Farther down the road, a couple of armored cars were burning in the ditch.

"We have been preparing for this attack for a long time," boasted Azeri. "They will not swat us like flies. Just the opposite, it is they who will get stuck on the flypaper."

"I hope you're right," hollered Emile. He admired her defiance in the face of overwhelming odds.

"We cannot hold the plateau. Guerillas hit and run. Now is the time to run." Azeri put two fingers in her mouth and let out a penetrating whistle while waving her arm to beckon her men. They came running.

"We are to evacuate the camp and regroup with Madame Andrée in St. Santin-de-Maurs, to the southwest. It is around one hundred and fifty kilometers from here. It will take about three days to get there. Split up into small groups. There are many trails off the side of the plateau and down to the valley of the Truyère. All of them are very steep, so take only what food and ammunition you need. There should be plenty of water along the trail. Good luck."

Two others, including the guitar's owner, joined Emile and Azeri. He was introduced as José, and he shook Emile's hand, though Emile wondered if that was all he would have done if Azeri had not been with them. José carried his guitar across his back and a rifle in his hand. Several grenades dangled from his belt. He was an ex-Republican soldier, an excellent fighter, Azeri assured him. Emile had no doubt of it. He just hoped they remained on the same side.

Azeri led them down a steep trail off the plateau to the northwest. The other maquisards split up as ordered into many groups, each taking a different route off the plateau. The plan was for the groups to follow a number of routes and rendezvous once they were clear of the Germans.

According to Azeri's map, the path they were taking was one of the shortest routes to their assigned trail. However, it appeared they may have waited too long to take it, as an SS armored car was already a good way up the long, narrow road leading to the camp. As they jumped and slid down the narrow trail, they came into the sights of the gunner on the back of the vehicle. Suddenly, the rocks around them spat and splintered.

"Hurry, hurry, behind the rock," yelled Azeri.

The firing continued in bursts. During one of the pauses, Emile glanced quickly down the mountain and saw several soldiers piling out of a truck a little farther down the road. The soldiers were starting to climb the mountain toward them. "Looks like we need to get out of here in a hurry," suggested Emile with urgency.

Azeri nodded. "A good idea. We need to climb up to the plateau and find a different route. It will take longer, but we will stay alive."

The climb up was tiring. By then, smoke from mortar rounds and bombs that had been dropped on the camp permeated the air, but casualties on the resistance side appeared low. From the top of the plateau, they could see a huge force moving up the road toward them. The temptation was too much for the Spaniards. Finding covey holes in the rocks, they fired down at the troopers, picking them off like plastic ducks at a shooting gallery.

Emile fired a few rounds to less affect, but his firing attracted the attention of a plane. It turned and came at them for a strafing run. They had heard the roar of the engines and ran to cover. As they did, smoke from an exploding shell blew across their path and covered their retreat.

"The woods!" screamed José.

Everyone followed him into the trees as the pilot shot blindly into the trees. When they were safe from immediate danger, Azeri took out her map. "We will have to go to the south to get off the plateau. We will double back along the valley of the Truyère to reach the crossing point."

The trail was very rough and much rockier than the others Emile had been on. As they got closer to the edge of the plateau, the gorges became steeper and more difficult to traverse. Just as they were about to descend the side of the mountain, José called out in a low voice. "Pssst, Azeri, over there." He nodded in the direction he wanted her to look.

Emile saw nothing at first, but then he saw the cause of José's concern. Two camouflaged storm troopers were following the same trail. They were some distance behind, but they could call for backup at any moment. All four fell to the ground.

Azeri gestured to José. "You two stay here. We will take care of them."

Sometime after they had left, Emile heard an explosion, like a hand grenade, and then some small-arms fire. He worried for the safety of Azeri and José, but his fears proved unfounded. The two returned.

"They will not trouble us again," proclaimed Azeri coldly.

Near the edge of the plateau, the trees disappeared, battered by unrelenting winds. Emile saw the turbulent River Truyère in the valley below. He estimated it was a near-vertical drop of about a thousand meters. Numerous waterfalls cascaded over the precipice. "How are we supposed to get down there?" gasped Emile.

"Very carefully." Azeri laughed.

"You're serious?"

"Do not doubt it. It is not as bad as it looks, you will see. The secret is never to look down, only around you and up. The alternative is to go back into the hands of the SS."

Emile studied Azeri as she looked and mentally picked out a path down. Terrified as he might was, he had to trust her.

As Azeri had predicted, the descent was not as bad as he had feared, though it was long. It took them the better part of the day. By the time they were over the worst part, Emile's calf muscles were killing him, and he had blisters on his feet and ankles.

"This will be good training for our walk across the Pyrenees," Azeri said as she watched him massage his legs.

"I'm ready," replied Emile defiantly.

"You will not have to walk much farther today. It is getting dark. The river is not far below. We will have to wait for morning to cross it. We need to find somewhere to camp."

After a short hike, they found a cave that would shelter them for the night.

"No fires!" ordered Azeri. "SS patrols all over this area will be searching for us."

They had no blankets. Their food was just some dried bread and sausage. It was a rough night sleeping on the cold, hard floor. However, José played his guitar and sang quietly. His repertoire was mostly of the Spanish revolution, propaganda, and patriotic ballads, but it did not matter. It was music, and he had an excellent voice.

Wednesday, June 21, 1944

The shining sun woke them up early. It cast rays through the mist that rose from the cold water of the river. Emile ached all over. He brushed the dirt from his clothes. His left side was damp and cold from lying on the ground.

There was nothing to eat for breakfast, so after taking care of their toiletries, they headed off. On the way, Azeri told them the plans for the day. "Our main objective today is to cross the Truyère. The Germans will be guarding all the bridges, so we will have to find another way across."

"Can we swim across?" asked Emile naively. The others laughed.

"We will let you go first," cried José, causing still more laughter.

"The river is too cold and too fast to swim," explained Azeri.

"Then how do you plan to cross?"

"We will walk on water," declared Azeri. "We were well prepared for this day."

They stayed up in the forest as they walked parallel to the river to avoid detection. The trail was difficult. The sides of the bank were steep and treacherous, and no one wanted to risk falling into the river. Several large trees had fallen across the path, and the trail had been washed out in places by erosion. Emile twisted his ankle a couple of times.

On most of the trail, the sound of the river was merely background to the forest sounds, but occasionally, as they got closer to the river, the noise rose to a steady roar. Emile was intimidated by the river's power. Through the trees, he could see water churning and angry. Large, frothy white crests pounded boulders that had dared fall in its path. He could not imagine how Azeri intended to cross it.

Their path took them across a road that led straight to a bridge. *Please let there be no one on it,* Emile prayed. But Azeri had been right. The SS had set up a roadblock on the bridge reinforced by a tank whose turret pointed down the road toward them.

"We need to walk another two kilometers," she said. "That is where we shall cross."

It was all the information she would give them. It was another two hours of walking before Azeri gave the order to stop. Holding out a map, she indicated an *X* beside the river. "This is our crossing point. We should find it right over there," she said, pointing.

Emile looked in that direction. The river was calmer than it had been downstream, but it still looked much too deep and fast flowing.

"How will we cross?" asked Emile incredulously. "Is there a rope hidden somewhere we can all swing from?"

"Something like that." Azeri smiled. "Let us find out."

As they started down to the river, they heard voices from the far bank.

"Sssh. Get down!" whispered Azeri.

They crouched in the underbrush and saw two SS troopers patrolling the opposite bank with machine guns in hand.

"They are searching for the maquisards who escaped their trap on the plateau. I expect many came through this area yesterday," whispered Azeri. "But we did not come all this way to be caught."

The foursome waited about fifteen minutes to be sure they were clear of the patrol before starting again toward the river. Azeri went ahead and appeared to be tugging at something behind a large rock. Then she launched herself into the river. Emile was sure she would be swept away, but she was progressing in a straight line across the river. He looked down. She was holding something just below the water. It was a rope.

"Follow me," she cried.

Emile ran to join her.

Gingerly, he waded into the water where Azeri had entered and felt down for the rope. It was of heavy braid, so it did not take him long, but covered in a green slime. Grasping it tightly, Emile started across.

Azeri had now reached the far bank. "Don't let go of the rope," she shouted over the noise of the river. "Watch your footing, there are some big rocks."

Emile kept going. José and the second Spaniard, whom he knew by then as Miguel, followed behind him.

As Emile set foot on dry land, he felt confident they were going to make it for the first time since they had left camp. José was nearly across, and Miguel was not far behind. Everyone's spirits had rebounded from the previous day's grueling descent from the plateau. They anticipated meeting up with their comrades. Then all hell broke loose.

Emile heard voices screaming in German. The forest echoed with shooting. Emile looked back and saw Miguel about to exit the river, but it was too late. His body danced as it was riddled with bullets and he fell back into the water. His blood turned the frothy white crescents pink. Emile saw source of the shouting and the bullets. An SS patrol on the opposite bank had probably picked up their tracks and had followed them to the crossing.

"Halt!" they screamed as they ran toward the river.

José and his guitar had made it across. He was hiding behind a large beech with Azeri. The Germans made it to the river and discovered the submerged rope. Two of the soldiers started across. Azeri and José fired their Enfields but could not hold off the soldiers with their automatic weapons.

Emile saw Miguel's body had snagged on a low-hanging branch at the river's edge. He had to do something. He was not involved in the fire fight, so for now he had managed to go unnoticed. Crawling along the beach, he made it over to Miguel's body.

There, he removed a large knife from Miguel's belt, crawled over to a large rock at the water's edge and ducked behind it. Next to the rock was the stake that anchored the rope across the river. Ignoring the intense cold, Emile slipped into the water and began slashing at the rope. It was both thick and strong.

He was nearly done when he was spotted by one of the Germans on the opposite bank. The soldier cried out a warning to the two in the river. In response, they pulled harder to speed up their crossing, as a soldier on the bank took aim at Emile. Just then the extra tugging on the rope did what Emile had been hoping for and tore the last strands of the rope apart. Instantly, the two soldiers were swept away screaming by the angry waters. In the confusion, Emile managed to climb back onto the bank and lay on his back, exhausted.

"Bravo!" cried José, running toward him.

When Emile had recovered his breath, José helped him up. Emile stumbled to his feet, wet and shivering. Undeterred, José embraced him with a force that Emile feared might crack his ribs.

"I said you would bring us luck, Zori," she said. "You have paid me back for the times I saved your hide. Consider us even."

"I just want to get warm." Emile's teeth were chattering.

Azeri hugged him with a softness that had been lacking in José's embrace. She rubbed his arms vigorously. "Start walking. The exercise will warm you up."

José walked to the riverbank and knelt. He crossed himself. He put his hands together in prayer, then freed Miguel's body from the tree. It disappeared in the white foam.

"We have no time for a burial today," explained Azeri.

"I understand," Emile concurred.

"He and Miguel were together a long time in the civil war," said Azeri. "It is a great loss for him."

"I'm very sorry."

"He will get over it. We have all lost many friends in this war, but it takes time."

"Sometimes a lifetime?"

"Sometimes, but I have observed that most people are more resilient than they believe. Life must go on, just as we must today. I hope everyone else got across the river."

Azeri estimated it would take them another two days or more of hiking to reach St. Santin-de-Maurs. As they set out, Emile shivered in his wet clothes. However, relief came as the Midi sun rose high in the clear sky. Its rays warmed him and dried his clothes.

The climb up the side of the valley and away from the river was long and tiring. While not nearly as steep as the descent had been the day before, it was nonetheless uphill, which made it almost as exhausting. They walked the rest of the day with only a few short breaks to rest and drink mountain water. The sun was hot. By mid afternoon, Emile's clothes were dry though his boots were still soggy.

The landscape was still very sparse, and the trail was rough, rocky. Emile was convinced the trail had been made by goats rather than people, which probably explained why Azeri seemed perfectly at home. At least they had encountered no more German patrols. For much of the day, they remained relatively high up, but as they walked farther south, they began to descend.

By nightfall, all three were exhausted. They found a protected spot in a small ravine and made camp. They risked a small fire.

Azeri and Emile slept together for warmth. José did not seem to mind. He was in shock at the loss of his friend. He sat by the fire, playing guitar and singing quietly. The songs he sang were sad, not patriotic or revolutionary. They reminded Emile of his loss. The painful memories churning in his mind kept him from falling asleep.

At one point, when he had nearly drifted off, a large owl with black tufts on its head landed on the top of a nearby tree and started calling. Its deep, resounding hoots echoed eerily. Before taking off in search of prey, it spread its wings, silhouetted against the moonlight. As it beat its great wings, Emile marveled that they did not make a sound, even in the quiet of the night.

Thursday, June 22, 1944

By morning, the three were ravenous. They had exhausted their food, so José and Emile went out to gather wild berries, likely not enough to sustain them for the exertion ahead, but they had no choice. They had to press on and regroup with the others.

In time, they cleared the mountains and descended to the flatter grasslands, which were dotted with small woods and pastures. The walking became easier, but without food, they were becoming drained. To conserve energy, they talked little. They focused their efforts on getting to their destination as soon as possible.

In the early afternoon, they heard gunfire erupt some distance away. All three dived for cover. It was a stark reminder they were still in danger. They were a long way from the plateau, the lair of the White Mouse, yet even here, the SS were sure to be searching for them. For the rest of the day, they remained more on edge and on the lookout. Each time before they had to move out from the cover of the forest to cross open ground, they would first look up and listen for a while to make sure there were no German aircraft around.

Increasingly anxious to catch up with the other maquisards, they walked until late in the evening. As the light started weakening, along with their bodies, Emile spotted some cows in a field. His stomach rumbled loudly as he imagined the taste of refreshing milk. "I wonder if the farmer would spare us some food," he said.

"Worth a try," Azeri said. "I doubt they'll turn us in to the Germans just for asking."

They walked another kilometer and saw a small farmhouse. José's French was poor, so they decided he would stay behind with their things while Emile and Azeri went to beg food from the farmer. As it was a dairy farm, they hoped they could get some milk and cheese.

The farmer's wife answered the door. She appeared reluctant to talk to them at first, peering out over their shoulders. The impasse was broken when her husband appeared and beckoned them in.

"Forgive her," he said. "She has not been herself since the Fascists killed our son. They took him into town and shot him against a wall along with five other young boys in reprisal for a resistance attack on one of their trains. They told us they would kill more people if the attacks did not stop."

The farmer's wife burst out sobbing and left the room.

"I am sorry to hear that," said Azeri. "We will leave if our presence troubles you."

"Not before I feed you," thundered the farmer, rising angrily from the rough wooden table. "I hate those vermin. I would die ten times over to see them all go to hell!"

"We would be grateful for any food you can spare us," Azeri said. "We will not stay. I think that would be too much for your wife."

"She wants to give into them, but I don't. I want them off our land. Out of France!"

"God willing, that will not be long," said Azeri.

"Amen. If it's food you want, then food you shall have."

The farmer strode into the kitchen and returned with two fresh loaves of *pain de campagne*, some pâté, and several chunks of cheese. As he put them down on the table, his wife returned and scolded him. "How are they supposed to carry that?" she asked, wiping her tears. "I will wrap it in some linen for you."

"You are too kind," said Azeri softly.

"I will give you a pail of cow's milk. It's still warm," she said.

"That sounds wonderful," said Emile gratefully.

The woman left and returned with a large tin can filled with milk. She wrapped the cheese and bread in a cloth. She paused and looked above the fireplace. "That was our son," she whispered, almost choking on her words. "He was such a good boy, barely sixteen. Yet he would get up each morning with me to help milk the cows. I don't know what we will do without him. We have no one else."

Azeri walked to the picture and studied it carefully. "He was very good looking. You are right to be proud of him."

"We are," replied the farmer. "Very. He was a gift to us who has been taken away. We will have to find a way to go on without him, but sadly, we are not alone. I know of so many people who have suffered worse than us in this war." The man's voice wavered. His stoic resolve was little more than a veneer.

"Do you two have any children?" asked his wife.

Azeri looked at Emile and smiled. Emile hung his head and looked at the table to avoid her eyes. A lump formed in his throat. "We are not married," he replied quietly. "I had a wife and two wonderful daughters, but they were all killed earlier this month."

The woman put her hand on Emile's. "I'm very sorry."

After wiping more tears, she finished wrapping the food. Emile and Azeri bid the farmer and his wife good-bye and went to rejoin José.

With full bellies, they lay on soft earth and slept more soundly than they had for many nights.

CHAPTER 15

Sweet Albi

Friday, June 23, 1944

The sound of the cows mooing woke them, though they could not complain; they had eaten their cheese the night before. With the expectation they had not far to go to St. Santin-de-Maurs, everyone's spirits were high. They finished off the small amount of cheese that remained.

The walk was relatively easy, and very soon, they reached the outskirts of the town. By midmorning, they began to meet up with other small groups of maquis who had fled the plateau. The news they heard was encouraging. Most of the maquisards had escaped the German assault, and the SS had paid a heavy price for their attack.

The small town was overflowing with Madame Andrée's disparate band of fighters. Azeri sought Madame Andrée while Emile went to find food. It was a couple of hours before he met up with Azeri, by which time he was relaxed from sampling the local wines. "What is the news from Madame Andrée?" he asked.

"Nothing short of miraculous. According to our informants, the SS sent twenty-two thousand against us on the plateau with the best equipment the Nazi machine could muster. Despite the odds, most of our people escaped. By last count, out of around seven thousand, we only lost one hundred. I grieve for everyone, patriots who gave their lives for France. But their sacrifice was not in vain. We hear SS losses were over fourteen hundred. Someone will be court martialed and shot for incompetence."

"I wish they'd all be shot," declared Emile. "Maybe the war is turning in our favor."

"We can hope. Madame Andrée plans to take advantage of the Germans' disarray. She is organizing another offensive. A truckload of weapons and ammunition made it through and is being distributed now."

"Do we need to collect some? When is she planning to leave?"

"It is none of our concern," stated Azeri. "We have other orders."

"What might they be?"

Azeri's deep-brown eyes widened. She looked around cautiously. "We are going to Spain, as planned. We leave in the morning."

"At last! That's wonderful news."

"Tell no one. The English pilot will be going with us. You will have to find a place to sleep tonight. I have to tend to some of my men. A few of them were injured. If I am leaving tomorrow, I need to spend time with them tonight."

"I understand. I just hope my feet will hold up long enough. I have never walked so far as I have in the past week."

"Don't worry about them. We will be driving." Azeri grinned.

"Driving? Who's driving us?"

"You are. Ask no more. You will learn everything in the morning. Be at the church in the marketplace at sunrise. Everything will be ready."

As Azeri parted with a wave of her hand, Emile said, "Sleep well."

That night, Emile found a place on the floor in a small house along with several other men. The townsfolk were very accommodating, especially as there seemed to be increasing confidence that the days of the Third Reich were numbered.

Saturday, June 24, 1944

Despite the camaraderie of his fellow lodgers, Emile did not enjoy a good night's rest. The stone floor was hard and cold, and they had no blankets. People came and went all night, making sleep almost impossible. Emile spent most of the night in a restless, semiconscious state, constantly turning to relieve the discomfort he felt on one side and then the other. He was glad to get up at dawn. His only worry was falling asleep behind the wheel.

The marketplace was easy to find. He was there before Azeri but did not have to wait long before she came strolling toward him with Commander Rossington. "Our car is in one of the stables on the outskirts of town. Take this," she ordered, thrusting a package wrapped in brown paper into his hands. "You will need to change into it, but for your safety, not here."

Emile tore open the package and saw a dark-blue, baggy uniform like those worn by the Milice and a pair of black boots. He understood why it would not have been safe for him to don it in a town overflowing with maquis. The thought of wearing it anywhere repulsed him. The Milice stood for everything he hated; they were tools of the Vichy régime. "You can't be serious! You're not expecting me to wear this."

"Either that or walk to Spain," Azeri said. "Some of our people came across the previous owner of that uniform, he was gracious enough to donate it and his car. It will make the perfect cover for our trip south. You will wear the uniform. You should be flattered, by the way. He was a captain. You are to drive Captain Rossington and me as your prisoners. The car and your uniform will deter most questions. If we are stopped by the Germans, you can simply say you are taking us to the SS headquarters in Carcassonne."

Emile paused. It was not a plan he liked, but he had to admit it could work, and they would make much faster time in a car.

"If all goes well, we should be at the Spanish border in a couple of days. Then you can burn the uniform," Azeri said.

"And if the resistance see us and tries to take a shot at me?"

"The resistance, the Germans, anyone could try to shoot us whatever we do. There is a war on. We'll have to take our chances."

"Well, I'll give it a try," murmured Emile. "providing you promise that if I am killed, you will take this off me before I am buried."

"I promise," Azeri said.

"Now, let's find the car."

The car was not far away. Emile reluctantly put the Milice uniform on, which chafed his skin. Merely by wearing it, he felt he was betraying everything he stood for. It would not be soon enough before he could change back into his own clothes.

He bundled his clothes and threw them into the trunk, which was full of jerry cans. Azeri noticed his surprise. "It will take a lot to get us to Spain. We can't ask the Germans to fill the car up. This should be enough to get us there."

Emile admired her thorough planning. "I hope no one shoots at us. There'll be nothing left of any of us."

"Then we must take care that no one starts shooting at us, or if they do, we had better pray they are bad shots," replied Azeri sarcastically.

"I'm not putting my clothes in there or they'll smell like gasoline."

"There's plenty of room in the car, but keep them out of sight."

Emile stuffed his clothes under the driver's seat as Azeri handcuffed herself to the English pilot and sat in the back. The first part of their journey took them southeast to Rodez along narrow, twisting roads that rose and fell over the escarpments of the mountains of Cantal. Save for a few farmers with their livestock and horse-drawn carts, there were few people on the road. Emile began to relax.

The small town of Rodez was built on high ground above the River Aveyron and was visible for some distance. Its massive red sandstone Cathédrale Notre-Dame pierced the landscape like a lighthouse on the ocean beckoning travelers. As they entered the town, Emile noted that it appeared to be much poorer than those he was used to in the Limousin and that there appeared to be little industry. Nonetheless, the medieval cathedral with its tall, ornate belfry built into the town wall was impressive.

They passed only a few Germans in the town; they did not trouble to stop them. Once through the town, they turned south onto the main road to Albi and Toulouse. The road was much busier than those they had been on earlier. They saw frequent German military vehicles and convoys, most traveling north. Emile became concerned. "How far do we plan to go today?"

"To Albi. Arrangements have been made for our accommodation there this evening. If you don't break any speed limits, we should get there safely," Azeri said.

Emile saluted each German patrol they passed, and they returned his salute. He was starting to grow more comfortable again. By late afternoon, they were nearing Carmaux, a few kilometers north of Albi. Emile thought that they might reach Albi without incident and that all his worrying had been unjustified. However, as he turned a bend, his heart stopped. He saw a German roadblock. He had no time to turn around without drawing attention. There was no choice but to try to pass through it.

The guard looked inquiringly into the vehicle. "Papers!" he snapped.

Emile jumped, close to panic.

"They're in the glove compartment," said Azeri in Spanish.

The guard looked at her menacingly, but he clearly did not understand what she had said. Emile opened it and handed the papers to the guard, who looked them over carefully. "You are going to Carcassonne with these prisoners?" he asked.

"Yes," Emile nodded.

The soldier paused to look at the papers again.

Emile put his foot lightly on the accelerator, ready to floor it and try to run the blockade if necessary. He knew it would be futile as they would have little chance of getting far, but he would prefer to die fleeing than surrender and be tortured by the Gestapo.

"Okay. You are free to go," said the guard abruptly, handing the papers to Emile.

At first, the words did not register with Emile. He had been so prepared for the guard to tell them they were under arrest that he hadn't been prepared to hear anything else.

"You are free to go!" repeated the guard impatiently.

"Er, thank you. Heil Hitler!" Emile managed to stammer.

"Take care, though," said the guard. "We have had reports of increasing terrorist activity in the area."

"We'll be careful," Emile said.

The guard raised his straightened right arm. "Heil Hitler!"

"Heil Hitler!" Emile repeated with less enthusiasm as he drove away.

"If there are resistance around, I will be in more danger than you two in this uniform. I'll be glad to get out of it."

"But it suits you so well," the commander joshed.

It was late afternoon as they drove into the outskirts of Albi. "We must go around the town to the north," instructed Azeri. "Our host does not want us driving through town and drawing too much attention in this car."

Emile sighed. "I don't blame him. If I had been seen entertaining the Milice in St. Junien, I would probably have risked being shot by my best friends."

"Turn here," yelled Azeri, waving to a small side road.

The road was very bumpy. Emile was forced to slow down and concentrate. After nearly fifteen minutes, the ride was becoming unbearable. "How much farther?"

"Not far. We will be there soon," Azeri said. "Our host has a small blacksmith shop with a large barn we can hide the car in."

"Does he know you? I wouldn't want him shooting at us, mistaking me for a real Milice officer."

Azeri laughed. "You worry too much. I know him well. I have used this escape route many times. There will be no problem."

It took another ten minutes of suffering on the tortuous road before they arrived at their destination. A small, sculptured sign hanging by the side of the road showed three black anvils and the name of the shop, Les Trois Enclumes.

They turned into the drive and saw two redbrick buildings crisscrossed by large, weathered timbers. One was almost covered by a wisteria vine, whose old, knurled trunk had the girth of a good-sized tree. The buildings' tiled roofs were in need of maintenance, and all around the roofline were the cup-shaped mud nests of martins. In the warm evening, the birds were already flitting about and performing their aerial acrobatics with their mouths wide open in search of insects.

The larger of the two buildings had two large wooden doors that were wide open. Inside, a bright-orange fire glowed and gave off wisps of smoke that rose into a large exhaust vent and out a small chimney. The insides were blackened by smoke.

Emile drove over the gravel yard in front of the building. He heard the characteristic clanging of metal being pounded. A dog barked, and the hammer fell silent. A heavyset man in a leather apron appeared at the door, a long rod of iron glowing at one end in his hand. He had a short beard, and his face was blackened by soot. Enormous muscles rippled on his arms. He stared anxiously at the car, his eyes clearly unadjusted to the bright light outside. The blacksmith's face registered relief as he recognized Azeri.

"Hold on while I put this back in the fire," he yelled. "I'll be right with you. Drive the car behind the smithy. We'll have to cover it up. The Gestapo has eyes everywhere."

Azeri rolled down the car window, and the dog jumped inside and licked her face. It was scrappy looking and reeked of metal from the shop, but neither aspect seemed to bother Azeri.

"You have a way with animals," Emile remarked.

"I trust them more than I trust most people, and in return, they trust me. Animals kill only to eat, and they are open with their emotions. They have no pretense. They do not betray you as people can. Yes, there is much to admire in animals."

"I say. I detect some bitterness there," proclaimed Commander Rossington. "Was it something specific, or just this goddamned war that caused you to lose faith in humanity?"

Azeri threw her head back. "Which war are you talking about? My people have been at war for centuries. I have been fighting myself since the beginning of the Spanish civil war in thirty-six. In that time, I have seen nothing but the worst of your so-called humanity. So many atrocities. They will never leave my mind."

"We can hope all the killing will be over soon," he said.

"I am afraid I do not share your optimism," replied Azeri sternly.

Emile parked behind the shop. There was only a small clearing between the shop and a line of trees with thick underbrush, so the car was not likely to be found inadvertently. Just to be on the safe side, the blacksmith came around with a pile of old sacks. When all three and the dog had alighted from the car, he covered it with the sacks.

"Azeri, it is good to see you again," the large man bellowed. He kissed her several times on her cheeks while squeezing her like a bear. Emile thought that if it had been any other woman, he would have crushed her, but he knew Azeri could look after herself.

"We think of her as a daughter," the man explained. "It has been too long since she left us, and we are always happy to see her return."

"She is very special," Emile said. "I have never met anyone quite like her."

Azeri introduced the blacksmith to them as Henri. He shook Emile's and Commander Rossington's hands. Emile felt bones in his hand crack.

Despite his obvious strength, Emile sensed a gentleness about him that was calming. Thanks to his stature, he had probably never needed to defend himself.

"Let us go into the house for some wine. My wife has been baking all day for your arrival, Azeri, and will be overjoyed to see you."

In contrast to the shop, the house smelled wonderful. It was rich with the scents of fresh bread, garlic, and roast chicken.

Mireille greeted them enthusiastically. She was a petite woman with an apron tightly wrapped around her covered in flour. Emile was sure Henri was well taken care of.

"I'm so glad you made it safely," she said, fussing over Azeri. "These are terrible times. You never can be too careful … Henri killed one of our chickens for you. I have a nice meal prepared."

"You're too kind," Emile said.

Henri went into the cellar and returned with a large pitcher of red wine. He poured everyone a glass and raised his. "Vive la France!"

They all stood and reciprocated. As Emile drank the toast, a flash of deep sadness swept through his mind. He felt completely alone. The wine and the smell of the fresh bread brought back the memories of the afternoon at Mr. Compain's bakery. The happiness he had felt there had been taken from him so quickly, so cruelly. He was brought back to the present by Azeri, who seemed to have read his thoughts.

"Emile here just lost all his family up north. The Germans killed them all," she announced loudly. "He plans to go to North Africa to sign up with General Leclerc."

Mireille shook her head sorrowfully. "I'm so sorry. These are terrible times, terrible."

"It is good that you go to join Leclerc's forces. Our son is with him," announced Henri proudly. "Azeri took him across the border to Spain. That is how we first met."

Azeri smiled unpretentiously. "Have you heard from him?"

A worried frown appeared on the woman's face. "No, no," she muttered nervously.

"Oh the boy's all right. He can take care of himself. He's like his father," Henri declared confidently. "He had to go. I would not have him stay here to be killed, or worse, have to fight for the Germans or Marshal Pétain."

Mireille looked uncomfortable. "Let me serve dinner. You must all be starving."

Emile wanted to change the subject. He did not wish to talk about the war, and he was not ready yet to talk intimately to casual acquaintances about his family. It was too soon. "This seems a beautiful part of the world," he said. "I noticed the white cliffs that surround the town. They are very impressive. The buildings in the area too. Many look very old."

Henri nodded. "It is a beautiful part of the world. I was born here and shall gladly die here."

"Not too soon, I hope," laughed Azeri.

Henri smiled. "Albi was founded by the Romans. It got its name from the white cliffs. Many of the buildings are very old. We have a lot of history around here."

"Much of it very bloody," added Azeri.

Henri frowned and nodded. "Yes, that is true, unfortunately. The crusades against the Albigensians, who were accused of heresy by the Church of Rome, were dark times indeed for the whole region. Many still prefer not to speak of them."

"Are you referring to the Cathars?" asked Emile.

"Yes, the Cathars, the Albigensians, call them what you will. Locals still call them what they called themselves Good Christians or Friends of God."

Mireille returned with plates of salad and roast chicken. "Enough talking all of you. Let's see how hungry you are," she said as she put the food on the table.

Emile had not realized how hungry he was until he started eating. It was the best meal he had eaten in weeks. Since he did not know when the opportunity would present itself again, he indulged himself.

After the meal, Emile joined Henri and the commander in the garden for a cigarette while Azeri stayed inside with Mireille. Although it was early evening, the warm, midsummer sun was still high above the horizon.

As Henri talked more about his hometown, Emile became more fascinated by it. Beyond the few facts he had learned in school, he knew little about the area, known as the Languedoc. He knew that the name was a contraction of the words "Langue d'Oc" meaning the language of Oc, and that Oc was the word for yes in the Gallo-Roman province of Occitania. The region was said to have been large and influential, stretching from Bordeaux and Lyon in the north to parts of northern Spain and regions of northwest Italy. Emile lamented that he knew so little of its people or its history.

The Languedoc had seemed of little importance to Emile in the Limousin, but being there gave him a new perspective. Maybe Henri was just a good storyteller, or maybe Emile was just looking for something other than the war to occupy his mind. Whatever the reason, Emile found himself wanting to know as much as he could about Albi.

After all the questions, Henri finally proposed they walk into town. "The commander will have to stay here, but I can take you and Azeri if you like."

"I would love to," Emile said. "If you are sure it will be safe for us. I would not want to put you or Mireille in danger."

"It will be safe as long as we do not do anything stupid to attract attention to ourselves. Do not bring any guns. We may be stopped and searched."

Commander Rossington did not object too strenuously at having to stay behind with Mireille. His French was passable, and they shared an interest in flowers. She guided him through her garden.

Azeri borrowed some of Mireille's clothes for the outing and let down her hair in a brocade of flowing curls. Though Emile admired her appearance, he worried it might attract more attention than if she had remained in her own clothes.

The three walked down a narrow track, barely wide enough for a cart, with Henri's dog, Pastis. He was running wildly up and down alongside them, overjoyed with all the attention. The track eventually joined a small road that led into Albi.

"We will walk through the old town and then to the river," said Henri. "That is the heart of Albi, which is dear to my own. It is always sobering to walk down its streets and think my parents and grandparents and generations before them all walked the same streets and saw them just as we see them today. They have changed little over the centuries."

Many of the buildings in Old Albi were of the same brick and tiles with oak framing as Henri's blacksmith shop. Emile thought it gave the town a warm appearance.

"The brick was made from red clay from the banks of the River Tarn," explained Henri. "For centuries, the town was famous in the Languedoc for its brick."

In addition to smaller houses, Emile saw several large, ornate houses screened from the narrow streets by high brick walls with sumptuous gates. "It looks as though Albi was a very rich town at one time," Emile said. "It must have taken great wealth to build some of these mansions."

Henri nodded. "You are right. For most of its history, Albi has been a wealthy town. It began with the building of the old bridge across the Tarn in 1035. That put the town at the crossroads of trade between France, Italy, and Spain. The growth of wealth in the area led to the heresy by creating a burgeoning middle and upper class that was well educated and critical of the church; it was totally corrupt at the time."

As Emile listened to Henri's impassioned historical narrative of the town, he looked around at the old buildings with admiration. Despite all the trials and turmoil that had occurred there, they had survived. The struggles that had dominated the lives of their inhabitants were mostly forgotten, but the buildings remained as silent witnesses. *There is some permanence in life after all.* He hoped the war blighting the world would likewise fade into history and the beauty of life would once more reassert itself.

As Emile walked down the old streets with their ancient overhanging buildings and shuttered, multi-paned windows, he felt a strange familiarity with the town. There was nothing specific he could put his finger on; he just a feeling he had been there before, although he knew that was impossible. He decided the town resembled some older sections of St. Junien his parents had probably shown him as a child.

At the center of the old town was the cathedral of Sainte-Cécile, a magnificent Gothic building with a tall, brick bell tower that dominated the area. It had solid, round bastions on each corner and tall, thin windows that looked like arrow slots. It reminded Emile more of a fortress than a place of worship. However, a short distance on, Emile saw the true fortress of the town.

"The Palace of the Berbie," proclaimed Henri. "Magnificent, isn't it?"

"That depends if you were the ruler or the ruled," replied Azeri. "I always look at such places and wonder what terrible things the people inside must have done to require such thick walls to hide behind."

"Ha," scoffed Henri. "Spoken like a true revolutionary. I sympathize with your viewpoint, but sometimes, even you should just allow your eyes to open and see the beauty of what is in front of them."

Azeri looked at him warmly. "Perhaps, but it is difficult for me to see beauty where others have seen so much pain."

"Then you will have difficulty appreciating Albi, for I'm afraid that despite its quiet appearance today, it has seen much suffering."

"When was the palace built?" asked Emile. "And who built it?"

"The palace and the cathedral were built toward the end of the thirteenth century after the crusades against the Good Christians. Berbie comes from the Occitan 'Bisbia,' which means bishopric. The building of the palace and cathedral were ordered by Bishop Bernard de Castanet. He wanted to intimidate the people into submitting to the power of the pope again after the pogrom against the heretics. The fortifications were added to by subsequent bishops of Albi to protect them from the hatred of the populace."

"How romantic," Azeri said cynically.

"That was centuries ago. Today, we enjoy them for what they are, exquisite works of art and engineering. They are monument to man's creativity. There is so much destruction in the world today that it's reassuring to gaze at some of the good man can achieve."

For such a proletarian and physical exterior, Emile was impressed by his host's learning and sensitivity. "You are extremely well read," Emile said.

"It has always been that way in this region," replied Henri. "The people of the Languedoc have always valued culture and learning."

"Is that why the bishops built such a large wall around the old town? To keep learning out?" asked Azeri caustically.

"There is some truth to that. Education caused the people to question authority, so they feared it. Fortunately, they never succeeded in completely suppressing the creative spirit here. Less than a hundred years ago, in 1864, Toulouse-Lautrec was born here."

"I love his work," said Azeri enthusiastically. "It is so vibrant."

"He was a wonderful painter, but did you know he was also an aristocrat? He was the last descendent of the counts of Toulouse. They used to hold power over the whole Languedoc region, back when it was Occitania."

Emile was surprised. "Fascinating. I never imagined Toulouse-Lautrec as a count. He always seemed to me to be more of a revolutionary."

"He was, but the aristocracy here always had a tendency of siding with the common people. It was what got them into trouble."

They walked around the great palace and into the formal French gardens along the river. The sweet smell of flowers permeated the air. The river was wide and fast but smooth, not angry as the Lot and the Truyère had been.

"Historically, the river was very important to the town for trade because it flows all the way to the Garonne and out to the Atlantic," explained Henri. "There used to be thousands of boats on this river that carried everything—coal, pottery, corn, wine, hemp, wood, saffron, glass. Today, alas, they are almost all gone."

They walked along the riverbank as far as the old bridge. Built of stone and brick, it spanned the wide river above eight arches. Emile could see what a triumph over nature it must have seemed to the people of the area a millennium ago. They dared not go on the bridge; German sentry posts were at each end. They stood below it by the river and admired its beauty while Henri and occasionally Azeri threw sticks into the river for Pastis to fetch.

"There is a bar near here we can go to for a drink before we go back," Henri said.

"Sounds great," Emile said, in no great hurry to leave the old town.

The bar was not far from the cathedral, and Henri seemed to know and be known by everyone in it. He introduced Emile as Azeri's fiancé, while she in turn was acknowledged as Henri's niece from previous visits to the town. Emile found the introduction flattering.

They drank a couple of beers with the locals while Pastis sat obediently under their table. Finally, Henri burped loudly, pounded his chest, and rose from his chair.

"It is time we were going. I am sure my wife has talked herself to death by now. We have a long walk ahead of us."

Emile and Azeri nodded.

Henri threw some money on the table, and they headed to the blacksmith's shop.

Picking up where he had left off earlier, Henri continued his history lesson. "After the bridge, in the Middle Ages, the town grew rich on pastel."

"Pastel?" Emile asked.

"Yes, pastel. It was the blue gold of Albi, a blue indelible dye in much demand throughout Europe for dying cloth. It was made from the leaves of a plant with yellow flowers, I am told. Many of the fortunes that paid for those huge mansions you admired were made from the sale of pastel. Napoleon I even required that all the soldiers of the empire be dressed in uniforms tinted by the pastel."

"Is that still an important trade?" asked Emile.

"No. Pastel was supplanted by indigo from India in the sixteenth century. It was easier to work and less expensive."

Unexpectedly, Azeri squeezed Emile's arm. He was about to tease her but refrained when he saw her expression. Far from being a romantic look, it was one of concern.

"Henri, did you notice a man sitting in the corner of the bar? He was smoking and on his own. I didn't see him talk to anyone."

"Oh, you mean Gilbert. He is our postman, but he is not from these parts, and people do not trust him, so he pretty much keeps to himself."

"Why?"

"These days, people have learned not to trust anyone they do not know. Even then, it can be dangerous. They say he reads their letters, but I am not sure. Why do you ask?"

"Because he was watching us the whole time."

"I do not blame him. You are a pretty girl." Henri laughed.

"That is not what I read in his eyes. They were probing, searching for something."

Henri shook his head. "You are too paranoid, my young friend. You were probably imagining it. I'm sure he meant no harm."

"Then why is he following us?"

Emile and Henri stopped in their tracks.

"Keep walking! Do not turn around," she whispered insistently. "He will know we have seen him, and he may run."

"Are you sure he is following us? I saw no one," murmured Henri.

"Nor I," said Emile.

"He is there. He appears well trained in his pursuit. I have spent too long tracking others not to know when I am the prey."

"What do you suggest we do?" asked Emile.

"We will split up. I will double back and slit his throat." Azeri stated.

"No!" protested Henri. "If he is in the pay of the Milice, or worse still the Gestapo, that would bring only more trouble to the town. They have been rounding up young boys from town and shooting them for each German or Milice officer who is shot. I do not want anyone's death on my conscience. I have a better idea."

"He must not have a chance to alert the authorities before we are gone in the morning," warned Azeri.

"Do not worry. He won't."

Henri led them to another bar by the city walls, close to the entrance to the old town. There was a clay-covered courtyard out front, and men were drinking and playing pétanque. Henri walked to a table, ordered drinks, and went inside. He returned with a set of *boules* to play. He handed a pair to Emile, another pair to Azeri, and threw the small, white wooden ball, the *cochon*, on the ground.

"I have never played before," Emile said.

"Watch us," said Henri. "You will learn. The object is simply to leave your ball closest to the cochon. It is easy."

Emile quickly learned that while the rules of pétanque were simple, winning was not. While Henri and Azeri dueled it out, Emile was constantly pushed to the sidelines, his boules sent careering away when one of the other boules came crashing down on it.

After they had been playing for around ten minutes, Henri cocked his head over to one of the other tables some distance away. Emile looked over and saw a man fitting Azeri's description sitting by himself with a beer and a cigarette.

When one game was over, Henri picked up the cochon and threw it down. It rolled close to Gilbert's table. Henri threw his first boule and went to examine where it had landed. Emile watched him casually talking to Gilbert. He could not hear the conversation but could tell by his hand movements and mannerisms that it appeared he was saying no to something Henri was proposing. Henri appeared to be insistent. With a reluctant look, Gilbert got up with his beer and walk toward their table.

"Emile, Azeri, this is Gilbert. He is our postman. He has agreed to join us in a game of pétanque."

Gilbert's faint smile faded as he sat down.

They played several rounds of pétanque and Henri kept the beer coming. As Gilbert's glass emptied, he would fill it up again and encourage him to keep up with his own consumption. Gilbert actually appeared to appreciate the attention, and Emile started to feel sorry for him. He was clearly a lonely person.

Unfortunately for Gilbert, his frame was no match for that of Henri's. The alcohol was clearly beginning to take its toll on him. His game went downhill until even Emile was beating him. He began to slur his speech. He sank into his chair, looking very pale. "I don't feel very well. I think I'm going to be sick."

"Oh, that's too bad," said Henri. "Can we take you home?"

"That would be very good of you." His words were slurred. "I don't live far."

"Then it's no problem," Henri said.

Henri picked him up and put his arm around his neck. He guided him to where he lived above the post office. Gilbert had passed out completely, so Emile and Henri carried him up the stairs to his room and threw him on his bed.

"He will not wake up until morning," sighed Henri. "And when he does, he will not be rushing off anywhere to cause us problems."

"How are you holding up? You drank almost as many beers as he did?"

"Ah, beers, yes. But after the first few, we started fortifying Gilbert's with a little absinthe. He was too drunk to notice. He will wake up with quite a hangover."

Emile shook his head and laughed.

CHAPTER 16

The Black Mountain

Sunday, June 25, 1944

Mornings began early for Henri. Despite drinking so much beer the night before, he was out in his shop just after sunrise to stoke his furnace. Mireille also rose early to collect eggs from the henhouse.

The smell of bacon and eggs was all it took to wake up Emile and his companions and entice them to the kitchen to eat.

Henri was the last to sit down after he had washed his blackened hands. "Where will you go today?" he asked Azeri.

"South is all you need to know. It is best for your safety and ours. I have to meet some friends to make arrangements to cross into Spain. The route we take will depend on their information."

"Well, whatever you do take care and come back to us when you can."

"I will."

Mireille looked anxious. "I worry for you. You have a long way to go and I am sure it will be very dangerous. You will need plenty of food. I will pack some for you."

"You have been incredibly kind, madam," Emile said.

"It is the least I can do. Henri and I always seem so useless tucked away here while others die trying to free us from the Nazi yoke."

The old man turned to Emile. "You, young man, take care of yourself. If you should meet our son in Algiers, tell him we love him and long for him to come back."

"I will. Though I am sure he does not need to be told you love him. I am sure you are in his thoughts every day."

Henri seemed uncomfortable with the conversation and excused himself from the table. "I need to get to work. My forge is waiting. I wish you all a very safe journey."

The three stood, and he hugged each one in turn. He hugged Azeri as if he would never see her again.

"Don't worry," she said softly. "I will be fine."

"I hope so," said the gentle giant.

"You are worried about your son, aren't you?"

"Yes, but I don't want to alarm Mireille. We have heard nothing from him for over a year. Not a good sign."

"If he is like you, I would not give up hope. There could be many reasons why you have not gotten letters from him."

"You are right," he said, squeezing her hand. "You are right."

With great reluctance, Emile put the Milice uniform back on and stuffed his own clothes into a small bag Henri had given him. He went out to retrieve the car. Henri had already removed the sacks. Emile pushed the bag of clothes under the driver's seat. He retrieved a jerry can from the trunk and filled up the car. Then, he backed the car out from behind the building and drove it to the house to pick up his "prisoners," each of whom was carrying a sack of food Mireille had prepared for them. Azeri handed a third to Emile.

"Here, this is for you. Mireille packed a feast for each of us. We shall eat well today."

"We have already eaten well. I am beginning to feel guilty about it. Still, I am sure the rations in North Africa will be meager, so I will enjoy the food while I can."

Azeri held out a small envelope for Emile. "Take this," she whispered. "It is a picture of their son. She hopes you might recognize him over there."

Emile sighed. "Maybe our paths will cross. Life is full of surprises."

"We have pâté, cheeses, bread, and chicken. That should get us to Spain," the commander said after peering into his bundle.

"Let's get going," Emile said as he stuffed his sack under his seat.

Azeri handcuffed herself to the commander, and Emile started up the car and waved at Herni and Mireille. "It will be good for us to be gone from here as soon as possible. We have put them in enough danger. I'd hate to have their deaths on my conscience as well."

"I understand," said Emile. "So where are we headed today?"

"We will go south toward the Pyrenees. If all goes well, I would like to camp outside Perpignan tonight. Tomorrow, I will go into the town and make arrangements with my contacts to cross into Spain."

"Just give me directions and I will do my best to get us there."

"First, we head to Castres and then to Carcassonne," Azeri said as she looked at a map. "We should be in Spain in two days."

"Never listen to a backseat driver," teased Emile.

Azeri directed Emile along a complex maze of narrow country roads, anxious to avoid the town center and reduce their chances of being stopped. The condition of the roads was very poor. They were stopped a couple of times, but it was only by cows blocking the road, not Germans. Emile had lost his sense of direction when south of town, they emerged onto the major route Azeri had been looking for. Montauban was west. Castres was south.

"Montauban!" cursed Emile. "Thank God we're going south. I have no wish to go to that town."

"What have you got against Montauban?" asked the commander.

"The Waffen SS bastards who killed my family and incinerated a whole town of men, women, and children came from Montauban."

"Yes, but surely, you cannot blame the people of Montauban for being occupied by the Germans. I am sure they didn't like it any more than you did."

"No, but I will never be able to hear that name without thinking of the terror that was unleashed from there."

The day was warming up, so they rolled down the windows. The road was little traveled apart from a few farmers with their carts and locals on bicycles. They passed one car that appeared to belong to a doctor, but to their relief, no German convoys.

The road was relatively flat and less tortuous than those in the mountains. The countryside was green and outwardly peaceful, making it easy for Emile to look around and forget the war for a moment. Life there looked as though it had not changed in centuries.

In a little over an hour, they reached Castres, a relatively quiet industrial town split in two by the Agout River. As Emile drove through it, a policeman surprised him by saluting him on account of the Milice uniform. Hurriedly, he fumbled to return the gesture.

Along the river were many old houses whose upper floors hung out over the river.

"Those houses were built for tanners and weavers," Azeri said. "They needed the river for curing the leather and dying the wool."

"It must have smelled really terrible back then," declared Emile. "How do you know so much about this town? It doesn't look like your sort of place."

"I have visited it several times because they have a wonderful Goya Museum with the largest collection of Spanish paintings in France. Goya was a great artist. They call him the father of modern art. It is a wonderful museum. You should visit it."

Emile laughed. "Someday. Not today."

They quickly passed through the small town with its neatly lined streets of white stone buildings and red tile roofs. They took the road up the valley of the Thoré River, which climbed to Mazamat at the foot of the Black Mountain. They were only forty-five kilometers from Carcassonne, but between them and the city lay the mountain, a natural barrier rising to over five hundred meters and forming part of the High Languedoc region.

The road climbed continuously. The car's engine strained. Emile watched for the engine temperature light to come on, praying they did not break down in such an isolated place. Just keeping the car on the road required concentration as the road zigzagged up the mountain. As they gained altitude, the trees became fewer, the landscape noticeably drier.

"Your goats would be very happy here," remarked Emile.

"So would I. It is like home to me. You can breathe up here," she said, sticking her head out the window and taking deep breaths of the mountain air.

The region was completely different from the Limousin, Emile reflected. There countryside was soft and green, with rich and productive pastures. Here, the land was harsh with sharp, jagged mountains that pierced the deep-blue sky. Where there was life, it seemed forever challenged to maintain its existence in the rugged terrain. It should have felt foreign to him, yet somehow it did not. He felt a strange sense of familiarity. It did not seem alien or unwelcoming. Quite the opposite. The sensation had been growing in him since the evening they had arrived in Albi. The sound and smell of the wind carrying the sweet fragrances of the oil-rich shrubs and trees accentuated the feeling.

Azeri read his emotions. "You like this land. I can see it in your face. You are like me. This land is captivating and primordial. The Languedoc has always been that way. That is why so many have fought to possess it."

Emile was unsure of his feelings. Maybe Azeri was right, or maybe he was drawn to it because it was so different from his home and his past, which he wanted to escape.

After stopping once to let the car cool down, they reached the mountain village of Saissac. The town was very small, some distance off the road and on the spur of a mountain ridge. It looked very old and poor. Emile marveled at how anyone could have made a living in such a harsh environment. Few people were out in the hot, midday sun, giving the town an aura that it had long ago been deserted.

Just as Emile had dismissed the town as being of little interest, they passed a gap in the buildings. Emile looked and slammed on the brakes. Standing at the far end of the village, on a promontory reaching out over a confluence of deep ravines, stood the ruins of what had once clearly been a mighty fortress. It stood in stark contrast to its surroundings as a reminder that this sleepy little town once enjoyed great stature in the region.

"Many of these castles were built by the Cathars," explained Azeri. "They built hundreds across the Languedoc, or what was then Occitania. Unfortunately, most were destroyed by French invaders from the north, and they left us only these ruins."

Emile shook his head. "It's incredible. This region seems so poor, undeveloped, unimportant. Yet I look at a creation such as that and realize there must have been great wealth here at some time to produce such a fortification."

"Like Albi, the whole area was rich before the crusades, but the church laid waste to the land. It never recovered."

"It must have been impressive in its day," Emile said.

"I think it was," Azeri said.

The road continued to thread its way up between jagged ripples on the face of the Black Mountain. The land was parched, mostly barren. Only a few shrubs and thin cedars dotted the otherwise arid landscape of rocks bleached white by the sun. It was hot, too hot for Emile, and he struggled to take off his heavy Milice jacket.

They were about ten kilometers south of Saissac when Emile looked up to a ridge above them. The crest was long and thin and looked as sharp as a knife. Amazingly, perched along it were four pure-white castles against the blue sky. Emile had never seen anything like it. Though they were in ruins, they still looked magnificent. Their round, white towers commanded the area like eagles' nests, imposing a feeling of power and dominion over their surroundings that must have once been real. "How did they ever build those castles? They're incredible!"

"They are the four castles of Cabaret," Azeri said. "Lastours, I think they call them. They were Cathar strongholds against the crusaders. I don't think they were ever taken."

"I can imagine why. They're amazing. The effort and organization it must have required to build them up there, especially without the machines we have today, is hard to comprehend. Whoever built them must have been obsessed with security."

"They were," replied Azeri.

"I wish I had a camera," said the commander. "I would love to take a picture to show the family. Maybe I'll come back after the war, after we've kicked Jerry out. Bring the whole family for a holiday."

"With luck, that won't be very long," said Azeri.

Emile was sorry to leave the lonely fortresses behind, but he vowed that one day he would return to appreciate them more fully.

After Lastours, the road descended rapidly to the plain of Carcassonne. The valley of the River Aude and the Canal du Midi lay in front of them. In complete contrast to the High Languedoc behind them, the valley was lush and fertile. It was a patchwork quilt of small farms and vineyards profiting from the rich, alluvial soils. There were a few windmills here and there. Their giant sails turning slowly in the sultry air blowing up the valley.

"There is Spain!" cried Azeri excitedly. She pointed. "We can see my homeland."

Emile saw mountains rising up in the distance across the valley. They filled the width of the panorama, and the highest peaks were capped with snow.

"I wish I were an eagle and we could just fly there," Azeri said.

"If I still had my bomber, I would gladly fly you there, young lady," the commander said gallantly.

Emile felt his spirits rise. He had never been to Spain. It would be a new experience, maybe the beginning of a new life. The Pyrenees looked impressive and beautiful, but as he admired them, he felt apprehension. They were a massive obstacle in his path to freedom.

"How will we cross the Pyrenees?" asked Emile, trying to hide his concern.

"My friends in Perpignan will take us across," replied Azeri confidently. "Since the time of the Cathars, these mountains have always had their secret ways known only to a few. The goat trails and hidden paths through the mountains are impossible for outsiders to find. The Germans cannot close them today any more than the church could when the Cathars walked those trails to spread their heresy among the common people. I hope you feel like walking?" she asked rhetorically.

Emile's and the commander's smiles were strained. "I believe the Cantal prepared us for anything," Emile said.

The road descended. Emile's foot became tired from having to keep pressing hard on the brake. Azeri leaped from her seat in excitement and pointed out of the window. Emile panicked for a moment, expecting someone was about to start shooting at them.

"Look! Over there. You can see the old city of Carcassonne. Isn't it like a fairy tale?"

Emile agreed it was an impressive sight. On a slight rise on the southern bank of the river was the old walled city. It was, as Azeri described, right out of a fairy tale, untouched by time. Emile could make out the high, double curtain wall of massive stones that surrounded the town. At each bend in the wall and by every gate were tall towers, most of which were capped with slate or tile roofs rising to a point. Within the ancient walls, he could make out many ancient buildings, including a castle and a cathedral.

Emile had heard stories of Carcassonne, but he had never dreamed he would see it. The sheer scale of the town exceeded his expectations. "It's magnificent. It looks too perfect to be real, as if knights in armor will ride out of the gates at any moment. How old is it?"

"Much of it is at least eight hundred years old. Like Albi, Carcassonne was on the trade routes between Italy, France, and Spain, so there were always people here. The Celts, the Visigoths, the Romans, and Charlemagne all added to the fortifications. But much of the building dates to the times of the crusades against the Cathars."

"The Cathars again," Emile said. "They have certainly left their mark on this land. They were clearly wealthy and industrious. I can't imagine what the area would look like today if their culture had not been wiped out."

"No. It was a crime. At the time of the Cathars, around the beginning of the thirteenth century, the region was one of the wealthiest and most peaceful in Europe. Who knows? If they had been left to prosper, we might not have this war today. Unfortunately, we shall never know. The envy and greed of a few brought about its destruction."

"Very sad," Emile said. "It seems that mankind never changes. Today, the whole world is at war, fighting over everything of value and destroying it in the process. It's depressing to realize that in eight hundred years, we have not progressed at all."

"Maybe people will finally be ready to change all that after the war. Maybe they will finally realize we must change if we want to call ourselves civilized."

"Maybe. But I'm not optimistic. It will take an act of God."

"I hope you are wrong," replied Azeri.

To the north of the town, they crossed over the Canal du Midi, an important waterway linking the Mediterranean to the Atlantic. They had lost sight of the old city, which was hidden behind the contemporary buildings of the new town.

There was a substantial German presence in the town. Nazi flags flew on many buildings, and soldiers walked the streets or rode noisy motorcycles over them. They reminded him of when the Das Reich Division invaded St. Junien. He was feeling increasingly uncomfortable smiling at the soldiers who met his gaze and pretending to be sympathetic to them. To allay suspicion, he began saluting automatically at any German who showed the slightest interest in them.

"Fortunately, we do not need to cross the Aude here," Azeri said. "We can stay on this bank for now. The river turns south ahead of us as it comes down from the Pyrenees."

"South sounds good to me," Emile said.

"We will follow the river for a while. I am sure with all this activity, the Germans will have posted sentries in the town on all the bridges across the Aude, so it would be impossible to cross here even if we wanted to."

"There seem to be a lot of troop movement," Emile said after they passed a long convoy of trucks loaded with troops. "They are probably getting ready to go north. I hear there's heavy fighting in northern Italy. If the Americans and the British break through, they will have to withdraw from this region and regroup with their forces fighting in the north."

"You're probably right. They already sent the Panzer division north from Montauban to reinforce their forces in Normandy."

"With luck, within a month or so, there will be no more cursed Germans anywhere around here," Azeri said.

"I am hoping that within six months there should be no bloody Germans anywhere in France," proclaimed the commander.

Emile wanted desperately to believe it, but as they came closer to the river, he looked to the east, and the reality of the present reasserted itself. The old city was visible again. They were much closer. "I want to believe the Germans will be gone too, but for now, they are very much here. Look over there."

Azeri and the commander looked in the direction Emile was pointing. "A beautiful site ruined by that sacrilege," cussed Emile, an expression of loathing on his face. Disgusting red and black flags on the gates and flying from the towers. Swastikas and the German eagles defacing a national treasure of France. "From all the guards on the gates, it looks as though they have turned it into their headquarters."

"It is a good choice," the commander said. "Our orders are never to bomb historic sites like that even if the Bosch are using it as headquarters."

"Cowards!" yelled Azeri. "Let them come out and fight."

The road along the Aude turned south as Azeri had predicted. About twenty-five kilometers from Carcassonne, they reached the small town of Limoux. They were making good time. Emile was once again optimistic they would make it to Perpignan by evening. The Germans they passed seemed preoccupied.

The Aude became narrow; a few fishermen stood on its banks. Azeri and the commander had dozed off from the heat. Emile was having trouble staying awake himself.

A loud cracking sound seemingly from nowhere sent a sudden surge of panic through Emile. The road was empty. He had seen no threats in the countryside. He heard the sound again. Someone was shooting. At them. Adrenaline sped through his veins. He tried to realize what was going on. His companions were now wide awake.

"What was that?" asked the commander.

"Gunshots," said Emile, trying to stay calm.

"Who are they shooting at?"

"Us!" cried Emile as a bullet went through the front of the car.

"They are not Germans," shouted Azeri. "Look! They're hiding behind that house." Emile zigzagged to confuse their aim. "I see them. They must be resistance. They are firing at us because they think I am Milice."

"We have no time to explain," cried Azeri. "Turn off here. Take that road to the right," she shouted, pointing frantically at the intersection.

Emile swerved violently to the right as another bullet hit the roof just above Emile's head. He pushed down harder on the accelerator, desperate to put as much distance between them and whoever was firing at them.

When the panic was over, Emile turned to Azeri. "Where to? Does this road take us where we need to go?"

"It will be fine," she said, though she was troubled by the diversion. "This road will take us a little out of our way, but we can turn back toward Perpignan farther ahead."

The road was narrow and winding through the fields and orchards on the edge of the fertile valley farmlands. Ahead of them and to the south, the foothills of the Pyrenees rose steeply. Emile looked at them longingly.

Azeri studied her map. "When we reach Chalabre, we need to turn south to get back on the road we want. The town should not be too far ahead."

"South it will be," Emile said.

The road twisted and turned, but they made it to Chalabre. "At last," cried Emile with relief and frustration. "We can get back on track."

Emile drove slowly through the small village, not wanting attention. They found the road to Puivert. The road began to climb steeply, but Emile's optimism returned. He started singing a Spanish children's song, and Azeri joined in. Everything was going well again, until to Emile's horror, they saw two German motorcycles followed by a staff car and an armored car coming their direction. At the back of the armored car, a soldier was manning a machine gun. Emile gulped nervously. His stomach churned noisily.

"Stay calm," commanded Azeri. "Salute them as we pass."

Emile brushed his hand quickly through his hair before donning his beret. He sat up as straight as he could and assumed a severe look. The two outriders passed them first, looking at them menacingly but riding on. The staff car passed. Emile could see two SS officers. He saluted them, trying hard to stop his hand from shaking. The Germans returned the gesture. *Maybe we'll have no problems?* The armored car passed them without incident.

"That was close," Emile said. "No, wait!" he screamed, looking in the rearview mirror. "Shit! I spoke too soon."

The convoy had come to a halt. Emile watched nervously as one of the officers leaned out of the car to talk to a soldier on a motorcycle. After a short exchange, the soldier turned around and sped toward them.

When he got to the car, he waved to Emile to stop. He had no choice but to pull over. There was no way they could outrun him. They would have to take their chances.

"Papers," he demanded. Emile complied.

"These papers say you are taking two prisoners to Carcassonne."

"Yes," replied Emile curtly.

"You are going the wrong way. Carcassonne is to the north."

"Well, we encountered some terrorists in Limoux and were forced to go out of our way," Emile explained, thinking quickly. "Look, you can see the bullet holes."

"For your safety, we will escort you to Carcassonne. We are going there," said the soldier, whose uniform showed him to belong to a Panzer division.

"Thank you for the offer, but it's not necessary," insisted Emile. "I am sure I can find my own way. I wouldn't want to trouble you."

"It is no trouble. The colonel insists. Please follow me."

CHAPTER 17

Into the Land of the Cathars

Emile was sweating profusely. If he tried to drive away, they would be killed. He had no alternative but to obey. However, somehow, before they reached Carcassonne, he would have to risk escape from their escort or they be shot as spies after lengthy, horrific interrogations by the SS, or worse, the Gestapo.

Emile turned around and followed the motorcycle. When he arrived at the convoy, he was ordered to follow the staff car with the armored car behind. Emile had never felt as trapped and helpless since he had left Oradour-sur-Glane. By a miracle, he had survived that day while most of those around him had not. At the time, he would have given anything to have died in their place, but it was not to be. For some unexplained reason, he had been spared. Surely not just so he could die in the dungeons of Carcassonne. "We must make a run for it," he announced. "We cannot let them take us back to Carcassonne."

"I agree," said Azeri. She unlocked the handcuffs. "I think our best opportunity will be in Limoux, especially if the resistance attempts to ambush the convoy. We will have a better chance of fleeing in the confusion."

"Sounds as good a plan as any to me," agreed the commander.

They continued along the road to Limoux. Emile observed uncomfortably in the rearview mirror that the machine gun in the car behind was trained on him. They were a few kilometers from the town when Emile heard a humming that grew louder until it was a sharp, buzzing sound, reminiscent of a mosquito as it flies quickly past the ear. Emile couldn't determine where the sound was coming from. He saw the motorcycle soldiers looking back into the sky. They were panicking. Emile saw in the rearview mirror the machine gunner had pointed his weapon the other direction, where the soldiers were looking.

"It's a plane," cried Azeri. "An English plane! I recognize the sound of the engine. Shit. I think we're about to be attacked!"

"I say, that's bad form for them to attack us," complained the commander. "I probably even know the chaps flying the damn thing."

Emile swallowed. "This might be our opportunity to escape."

"I agree," shouted Azeri. "As soon as the shooting starts, grab whatever you can and run to the forest. Climb to that ridge and wait until we find each other."

Emile looked over where she was pointing. A daunting climb, but he was sure fear would give them the energy they would need to climb the mountain.

"Sounds good to me," he cried back.

All hell suddenly broke loose. He could not tell whether the Germans or the plane had starting shooting first. He could see bursts of fire spitting from its wings as it descended to begin its strafing run on the convoy.

"It is an RAF Spitfire," cried Azeri. "A very nice plane!"

Emile didn't share her enthusiasm. "It would be if it weren't shooting at us."

The pilot was focusing his attention on the machine-gun turret in the armored car behind them. Emile watched as the car light up in a shower of sparks from bullets tearing through it. The soldier was hit. His arms flew up in the air, and his body danced like a puppet as the bullets raked his body.

The pilot pulled up and circled. Soon, he was coming at them again with cannons blazing. Bullets ripped through the staff car and hit one of the motorcycle soldiers. What was left of him careened off the road into a ditch.

As the plane circled for another run, Azeri grabbed the door handle. "We were lucky that time, but I would not trust our luck a third time. We must get out now."

"What are we waiting for?" shouted Emile, grabbing his bags from under the seat.

The three ran from the car into the ditch. The Germans had done the same. Emile saw the Spitfire coming straight down the road toward them. He remembered the mostly empty gasoline cans in the trunk. "We need to get farther away. If our car is hit, it'll explode." Emile saw the others' look of acknowledgement. They ran across the field toward the woods.

A German screamed "Halt!" but there was no turning back. The soldiers shot at them, and the runners zigzagged instinctively. Emile ran faster than he had imagined he could toward the forest.

Another round of bullets hit the ground around them. Emile heard a cry. He cast a quick glance back and saw that the commander had been hit and lay bloodied and on the ground. He did not move. Emile thought of turning back but decided it would be futile.

Just as Emile made it into the trees, the Spitfire began strafing the cars again. Emile saw Azeri still in the field and the soldiers shooting at her. To his horror, he saw her get hit. Blood streamed from her arm. She went down.

Emile wanted to vomit. Everything he cared about was being destroyed. *Why not me? Why everyone else?* As Emile was about to run to help Azeri, he saw one of the Panzers running across the field toward him, clearly intent of taking care of the last escapee. He had no option but to run. If Azeri could manage it, he knew she would meet him on the ridge. At least if the soldier chased him, there would be one less for her to worry about.

Emile had barely started running when he felt a tremendous explosion. The forest lit up. Emile knew their car must have been hit and had blown up. His hope was that the explosion had taken most of the Germans with it.

The edge of the forest was spotty. Large, open spaces of grass had been grazed down between the trees. Emile held his breath as he to run across the open patches, not daring to look back. He started to pant as the hill became steeper, but he kept running for his life.

The hill became steeper and rockier. Emile slowed. He had to climb rather than run. But the forest was becoming more dense, giving him more cover. He stopped to catch his breath and to listen. Thankfully all he could hear was birds. Above him was the ridge where Azeri had proposed they meet. He would not rest until he got there.

Picking up his bags, Emile resumed his climb. He was sweating profusely. The late-afternoon heat and strenuous exertion were wearing him out. At least he had the consolation that he could soon throw his Milice uniform away. Incentive enough to keep moving.

Emile finally reached the ridge, exhausted. No one was there as he had expected but not as he had hoped. Walking along the ridge, he looked down at the road. The armored car and staff car were ablaze. In between were remnants of their car. Emile saw no signs of life.

Emile looked at the field where the commander and Azeri had been shot, but he could not get a clear view. He walked away from the ridge to wait. He ripped off the loathsome Milice uniform and threw it under a bush. At least if he were to die, he would be seen to die as an honorable Frenchman, not as a traitor.

Emile found a secluded spot and lay down to rest and wait. As long as he did not see any Germans, he would wait for a couple of hours to give Azeri and the commander a chance to reach him if they had survived. But he couldn't rest. He thought about what might have befallen his companions and how he could possibly get across the frontier without Azeri. She had called him Zori. Maybe she was right. Maybe he was lucky. He had survived again, but he felt anything but lucky. If he had been lucky, Azeri would be there with him.

As Emile lost himself in his thoughts, he heard gunshots near the road. One after another. Emile ran to the edge of the ledge but could see nothing. Despondent, he returned to his resting place to resume his wait, fearful of who might have been shooting.

As the sun descended, Emile faced the reality that no one was coming, and he could not stay. He clung desperately to the hope the others were alive but lost or had been forced to flee in another direction. Anything but that they were dead or had been captured. He convinced himself they would manage to find refuge. He had to do the same.

Emile picked up the bag with what was left of the food Mireille had given them. He walked southwest toward the Pyrenees. He had no idea of what he was going to do, but walking was better than doing nothing.

He reached the top of the hill. His spirits were lifted by a splendid panorama. He gazed at wide valleys separated by steep mountainsides that rose steadily toward the Pyrenees. They seemed so far away yet so close. He saw the distance he had to traverse was daunting, but the mountains pulled him toward them. He was undeterred. He owed it to his family. He would make it to Spain and fight to avenge their deaths.

After walking a couple more hours, Emile found a sheltered spot to sleep. He cleared away branches and stones, but the ground was hard so he gathered some leaves to lie on. The ground was at least dry. He finished the last of his food and slept.

Monday, June 26, 1944

It was a cold morning. Emile rubbed his arms briskly to warm up and stop shivering. Looking at the sky, he saw the cold would not last long. Only a few wispy clouds were drifting overhead. It would be another hot day.

Emile stood and stretched. He could feel bruises all over his body from sleeping on the ground. He longed for coffee and a cigarette. Looking over the rugged, unfamiliar landscape, he had no plan to get to Spain. All he knew was that on the other side of the mountains was Spain, so he would head that way.

Emile stayed off the roads in favor of the forest as much as possible. He stumbled on a primitive trail that led west. He wondered if it was one of the goat trails Azeri had mentioned, though he had seen no goats.

Emile walked for most of the morning. It was difficult on an empty stomach, but at least he had found a few streams. He soaked his hair in one of them to cool off. He had walked farther in the mountains in the past month than he had in his prior lifetime. Another new experience was walking alone, which he did not find pleasurable, especially in unfamiliar terrain.

At midday, Emile found a shady spot and lay down. He was not accustomed to such heat, and he was hungry. He couldn't risk eating the unfamiliar berries he saw, though he knew he would have to find food before long. He was prepared to work for it if necessary.

The mountains rose steeply. Emile did not have the energy to climb them that day. He knew his chances of finding shelter for the night would decrease the higher he went. The mountains were intimidating. Without a guide, he was sure he would perish if he tried to cross them alone. He would have to find a guide to replace Azeri.

Emile did not want to descend to the plain for fear of the Germans. He kept walking west along the sides of the mountain. He hoped to encounter a village where he might risk showing his face. He had a little money, so he might be able to buy food if he was lucky.

Around midafternoon, the path he was on led him to a small road. He thought it might lead him to somewhere to stay for the night. After walking for another two hours, Emile's legs were aching and his stomach was growling. He imagined having the Milice car or even the bicycle he had ridden on with Jacques from Tulle. He was losing hope just as the road began to descend into a valley. His vision led him up a river that ran the length of the valley to a small town. Reinvigorated, he stepped up his pace.

The town was like many others in the region. It was clearly very old, with half-timbered houses, narrow streets, and red-tiled roofs. Several of the houses connected on their upper floors over the street. The houses looked poor but well kept; he thought the town had seen wealthier times. His feeling was confirmed when he reached the center of town. Overlooking the town was a commanding escarpment on top of which was an imposing castle with three tall towers and a high defensive wall.

Emile walked into a baker's shop and ordered a large *croque monsieur* sandwich. He would need more to eat, but that would stave off his immediate hunger.

"What is the name of this town?" he asked the elderly woman serving him.

"You do not know? Why, this is Foix," she declared with pride.

"Foix?" Emile echoed with a blank look.

"You are obviously not from around here. In these parts, everyone knows of Foix. Its name commanded great respect throughout all the courts of Europe until the end of the Middle Ages. We used to be our own county, and a powerful one ruled by the great counts of Foix, who lived here. I would have been born nowhere else."

"I am sure you wouldn't. The town still looks a wonderful place to live."

The old woman looked at him forgivingly. "Yes it is." She handed him his sandwich. "Where are you from? What brings you to Foix?"

Emile was unsure of how open to be. Trusting any strangers at all could get him killed. "I am from the north. My home was destroyed. I came south looking for work."

"There's plenty of that around here. The Germans and the Vichy government took most of the young men away, so we are always shorthanded."

"Do you know where I might find a job and a bed for the night?"

The woman thought. "If I were you, I'd go to Jean-Pierre Navarro's farm just up the valley. He came to town the other day looking for help to pick his peaches and apples."

"Is it far?"

"No. Follow the main street to the outskirts of town. You can't miss it. He has a sign on his gate saying he is looking for help."

"I'll go there right away. Many thanks for the help."

"Tell him that Sylvie from the baker's sent you. That way, he'll probably drop me off a bunch of peaches when he next comes to town."

Emile followed her directions and found the farm easily. He opened the gate and walked up the long drive to a solid fieldstone building with heavy wooden shutters. The hill around it was covered with fruit trees. Emile knocked on the door and offered his services, which were gratefully accepted.

"You can sleep over there in the barn with the others," said the farmer. "You will find some food there and some wine, but don't drink too much," he warned. "I need you all in the fields at dawn. I have a lot of trees to pick."

"Thank you," Emile said, relieved to have found a place to stay. He walked to the barn and found a half-dozen men at a long wooden table drinking from one of several bottles of wine and talking. Emile introduced himself cautiously as Zori and looked for a spot to bed down. The others had already chosen their places, so he grabbed one of the blankets from a pile and threw it down with his bag of belongings on a patch of straw.

The others directed Emile to a large covered pot on one end of the table. Opening the lid, Emile was happy to see a couple of helpings of warm cassoulet. He emptied it onto a clean plate and wolfed it down. Despite the sandwich, he was ravenous.

It had been an exhausting couple of days. After a few glasses of wine, he was ready for bed. He excused himself and lay down. The others played cards and argued loudly among themselves, but it didn't bother him. Within a few minutes, he was lost to the world.

Tuesday, June 27, 1944

Cocks' crows woke Emile. The barn door creaked, and the farmer came in with bowls of hot cereal that were quickly consumed. The farmer divided them into pairs. Emile was paired with a young boy, Alain. Their pay would reflect how much they picked.

The peach orchard was up the hillside on a gentle slope. Emile saw many empty baskets under the trees and stepladders. Standing on top of a ladder, Emile had a clear view of River Ariège, whose waters came down from the Pyrenees.

Emile learned Alain was from Toulouse. He had come to Foix to escape being drafted into the forced labor organization, the STO, and he had been in Foix for six months. It was the first time he had been away from home, but he had made many friends in the town and did not wish to leave.

Each time the boy picked a piece of rotten fruit, he would curse it and throw it to the ground as hard as he could. He explained to Emile that he imagined each was a German soldier and he was single-handedly destroying them. It helped to relieve the monotony of filling the scores of baskets with the fruit even if it did not directly help the war effort.

Gradually, Emile became more confident that Alain was not a spy. He was anxious to learn whether he might have come across anyone who could help him get to Spain. As they ate lunch, he decided to risk asking the boy for help.

"Do people from Foix ever go over the border to Spain?" asked Emile casually.

"I don't know. Why would they? There are Fascists in charge there just like here."

"Yes, but if someone wanted to go there, do you know who they might talk to?"

The boy looked at him quizzically. "You want to go to Spain? Why?"

"Shush. Yes, I want to go to Algiers to join up," he whispered.

"Wow! That sounds exciting! Maybe I'll come with you. No. On second thought, my mother would kill me if I did that."

Emile felt like pointing out the Germans would probably kill him before his mother could, but he thought better of it.

"I know some people who might help you," he stammered, "but I'm not sure."

"Can you take me to them?"

The boy fidgeted. "I'm not sure. I'll have to check. They don't like strangers. They might even kill you and me too if they thought I'd put them in danger." Alain stopped eating. "You are not a German spy, are you?"

"No I'm not. I promise you. I hate the Germans as much as anyone. If I were a spy, why would I come down to the Languedoc? I would have been more useful to them as a spy if I'd stayed at home in the Limousin, where I knew everyone."

"That makes sense," he muttered, not looking entirely sure, however.

"Will you ask around for me?"

"I will try, but I can't promise they will agree to see you."

"That's all I ask," said Emile.

For the rest of the afternoon, the two filled basket after basket. Periodically, the farmer and another farmhand came by with a cart to pick them up. By the end of the afternoon, the farmer said, "You've done well between you. You've earned good pay."

In the evening, they returned to the barn, where there was again hot food and wine on the table. It had been a long day in the hot sun, and they had worked up good appetites.

After dinner, the men talked about when the war would be over and chatted about their girlfriends. Emile tried to reveal as little as possible about himself, saying only that his family had been killed and he wasn't ready to talk about it yet. No one pressed him after that.

At one point that evening, he realized Alain was not at the table or in bed. When he had still not shown up by bedtime, Emile was concerned. Alain could have been a German spy. Emile imagined Germans bursting into the barn to arrest him. On reflection, it was a stupid thought. He quickly dismissed it.

The lights were blown out. Everyone turned in for the night. Emile had almost fallen asleep when he felt a sharp stab in the ribs. It was Alain.

"Shush," he whispered, putting his finger to his mouth. "They will see you tomorrow night. You are to come with me. Say nothing to anyone."

"Understood."

The boy walked quietly across the floor to his own bed. Emile fell asleep.

CHAPTER 18

To Another World

Wednesday, June 28, 1944

Emile and Alain worked hard the next day. The farmer was a likeable man who treated his workers well. During the midday siesta, he brought them a bottle of peach wine he had made in his cellar of his large house. It was the best Emile had ever tasted.

As Emile picked the fruit and carefully placed it in the baskets, he looked down the valley and reflected on the tranquility of life there compared to the killing he knew was going on in Normandy and the butchery he had experienced in Oradour. He felt guilty, but at the same time, he felt a temptation to hide there until the war was over or stay there forever.

The few days he had been in the Languedoc had left him with the impression that life there had changed little for centuries. Whatever happened in the rest of France or the rest of Europe seemed to be of little consequence in that area. Life seemed untouched by time or the outside world. At the center of the small town, the mighty castle of the counts of Foix, with its three great towers, sat high on its commanding crag as it had done for countless centuries, a testament to the continuity of life there.

Emile liked what he had seen of the Languedoc since he had arrived. Albi had captivated him completely. It had touched something deep inside that made him want to stay there forever. Yet he knew that he could not remain there in good conscience while others were dying. He had a duty to do his part in the war. He had to try to join up with General Leclerc and free his country. After the war, if he survived, maybe he would return.

After the evening meal, the workers drank and smoked as they had on previous nights. Emile was on edge. To keep his wits about him, he drank less than usual.

A little after nine, Alain cocked his head toward the door, indicating it was time to go. The boy left first, and then a short time later, Emile slipped out discreetly. He saw Alain waiting outside. "Do we have far to go?"

"Only a few kilometers, but uphill, so it may take a while."

The first part of the hike was relatively easy along the bank of the Ariège, but then, as Alain had warned, their path turned to the west and up the steep, rocky hillside of the valley. The climb was difficult. The trail was lightly traveled; many loose rocks on it were difficult to see in the fading light. Emile slipped a couple of times but didn't twist his ankle.

Emile noticed they were now much higher. The ground was drier, the vegetation more sparse, and the wind was stronger than down on the farm. The trail took them along a rocky escarpment. Alain turned to Emile with a large red cloth. "Wrap this around you head to cover your eyes. I will guide you the rest of the way."

Emile was surprised and nervous. "Is this really necessary?"

"It is if you want to meet the people you said you wanted to see and you don't want either of us killed. I warned you they don't trust anyone they don't know."

Reluctantly, Emile tied the cloth around his head. Alain pulled the knot tight from behind and grabbed his hand. Emile felt helpless, blind, and lost, his fate literally in the hands of a young boy he had known for only days. He felt as if he were a child again.

To Emile's relief, they walked slowly, giving him time to feel out the uneven ground. Alain held his hand as they walked on relatively flat terrain for about ten minutes. He released his hand. "Here's the tricky part. We have to climb these last few rocks and then we're there." He felt Alain put his hands on his hips and turn him gently. "Just climb straight ahead. It's not far."

Emile fell to his hands and knees. For a second he panicked, fearing he was about to climb over the edge of a cliff, but he calmed down again, realizing Alain had already had adequate opportunity to lead or push him off the side of the mountain.

After a short climb, Emile felt the ground flatten again.

"Pull yourself up and wait for me," Alain's voice called out from below.

Emile heard other voices, muffled, in front of him.

Alain had joined him. "Let's go inside."

"Inside what?"

Alain did not reply. He grabbed Emile's hand and tugged him forward. As they advanced, the voices became louder, clearer, though they had a strange echo to them. It also seemed very dark. He could not sense any light at all through the cloth. Emile felt his arms brush against rocks on either side of their path. At one point, Alain warned him. "Lower your head here. The ceiling is very low."

Of course, thought Emile. *We're in a cave. That's why the voices sound strange.*

The path turned sharply, and the voices became loud and close. Light once again diffused in through the blindfold.

"Sit him here," someone ordered. Alain led him over to a cold but smooth rock.

"So you want to go to Spain?" asked the unidentified voice.

"Yes. I want to join Leclerc's forces in Algeria to liberate France from the Fascists."

A couple of voices cheered his reply.

"Why are you here in the Languedoc? How do we know you are not a spy?"

"I am a schoolteacher from St. Junien, a small town in the Limousin. The SS butchered my family. Burned them alive along with the rest of the people in the town. Why would I be a spy? They have taken from me everything I cared for."

The man grabbed Emile's hair and pulled his head backward. He could feel him breathing into his face. "Why are you wearing Milice socks?" he yelled, as Emile felt the cold, sharp edge of a knife at his throat. Emile heard people gasp.

"You are right. They are Milice. I kept them because my own socks were worn out. I was with the maquis in Aubrac, and they gave me a Milice uniform and a car. That is how I got here."

"Which group of maquisards were you with?"

"The group was led by Madame Andrée."

"The White Mouse," he said with recognition and respect. Others repeated her name. "Why would she give you a car?"

"We were supposed to take an English pilot across the border into Spain."

"Where is he now? This pilot of yours."

"I do not know. We were stopped by Germans who insisted we accompany them to Carcassonne. Just outside of Chalabre, an English plane fired on us. I managed to escape, but I think the English pilot was killed."

Someone shouted out excitedly from the group around him.

"Jean-Louis, his story is true. One of our people reported seeing two burned-out German vehicles in the road and the remains of another car in that area on Sunday. There were many Germans dead, together with a civilian. We found papers on him identifying him as an English pilot. We did not understand why he was not in uniform. Our people went looking for his plane, thinking he had been shot down."

"There was a girl with me," Emile said. "She was Basque. She fought with the resistance. I think she may have been wounded. Did anyone see her?"

"There were no reports of a girl, but our people did not have a lot of time to search before the Germans arrived to recover the bodies."

Emile sighed, worried about what had befallen Azeri.

The man released Emile's hair. "You are not from around here. Your presence will attract attention if you stay. After the incident in Chalabre, the Germans will be looking for you. You must leave soon."

"I have no wish to stay," Emile said, though it was half a lie. "I want to go to Spain."

Emile heard the men discussing what to do with him. He realized they might kill him rather than risk having him around. The discussion died down. He heard the man he knew to be Jean-Louis walk to him. He felt him grab his head again and feared the worst. Instead, he tore the red cloth from his head.

"Okay. The men have agreed to help you get to the border, but you must leave quickly. Once you're in Spain, you're on your own."

"I will leave as soon as you are ready so I don't put you in danger any longer."

"Good. Welcome to our group," said Jean-Louis, holding out his hand. He was thin and young, quite the opposite of the image Emile had formed from his deep voice while he was blindfolded.

Jean-Louis embraced him to seal their camaraderie and stepped back. On that signal, the other members of the small maquis group introduced themselves and welcomed Emile. Some had questions for him, but most wanted to hear about the maquis in Aubrac and the recent battle with the SS, rumors of which were spreading like wildfire in the region.

Emile had barely begun to answer their questions when Jean-Louis interrupted them with a loud handclap. "Comrades, we are not here to chat. We have to pick up the arms the Allies will drop at midnight. Let's move. We have a long walk."

Not another walk, thought Emile, but he wanted their help, so he would help them. There were about ten in all, a cross section of society united only by their hatred of the Bosch. As they walked toward the drop-off site, the talk was of the war and what was going on in Normandy. Each of them speculated about what he would do after the war.

It was growing dark. Emile stayed close to the group. He had no idea where he was. Dark shapes darted around them. They reminded Emile of the martins at Henri's blacksmith shop, but their flight was more haphazard.

"They are bats," Alain said with a smile. "Lots of them around here. All the mountains around here are honeycombed with caves."

"It's amazing how fast they can turn, especially in the dark," Emile said. "I hope our pilot can fly as well in the dark. How does he know where to drop the ammunition?"

"We will light a signal beacon when we get to a prearranged place. It is different every time. Only Jean-Louis knows where. We will pick up the boxes and leave quickly."

The going became suddenly more treacherous when clouds obscured the moon. A few men took out small lights, but their pace slowed significantly.

It was not long before Jean-Louis signaled they were at the drop-off point. The area was relatively flat and rocky with some underbrush and a few tall cypress trees swaying in the wind like artists' brushes painting the dark clouds. They scoured the area for branches and twigs and arranged them in three piles that formed a large triangle. One man stood by each pile with a dimmed lantern. Jean-Louis peered at his watch and the sky in turns.

Emile shivered in the cool breeze, He become more nervous as each moment passed. He hated waiting, which made him feel vulnerable, helpless.

Jean-Louis waved his arms. "Light the beacons. The plane will be here soon." The three piles burst into flames, sending sparks up. The fires warmed the air blowing toward Emile and stopped his shivering for a moment. Everyone cupped his ears with his hands.

Emile heard it. The droning of a plane flying low. Jean-Louis directed them away from the drop site. They ran for cover. Within a few moments, a plane was overhead almost invisible against the darkened sky. It flew over the flaming triangle so low and loud that Emile had to cover his ears. He saw a string of packages drop from its underbelly, just as dragonflies dropped eggs into the pond, which he had seen as a child.

The packages crashed to the ground. The plane disappeared as quickly as it had appeared. Jean-Louis ordered his men to douse the fires and recover the ammunition. Emile ran to help. It took time even with their flashlights to locate all the boxes. The last two were some distance up the hill. The men broke open the boxes and stuffed rifles, ammunition, and hand grenades into sacks, which were divided equally. Jean-Louis gave the order to begin the trek back to the cave. Emile felt relief it would soon all be over and he could get to bed to catch some precious sleep before morning.

Unfortunately, it was not to be. They had barely started to leave when they were doused in bright lights that caused Emile to jump.

"Halt!" a distant voice screamed in a strong German accent. Then more screaming Emile did not understand, followed by "Halt. Halt or we shoot!" in French.

"To the rocks! Take cover!" yelled Jean-Louis. "It's a German patrol. They must have seen the fires."

Each man ran. Emile heard the fire of a heavy machine gun. He ran as fast as he could. Two spotlights danced around him. Emile ran erratically as he had done before. Bullets hit the rocks around him. He saw two men fall very close to him.

In front of him, the mountainside rose steeply and was strewn with large boulders. Emile ran toward them and managed to make it behind one just as a line of bullets traced a horizontal line past his position. Jean-Louis and the others who had made it had also taken up positions on the hillside and had begun shooting. Emile, his heart still pounding, snatched an old rifle from his sack and loaded it. When the machine gun stopped to reload, he peered out from behind the rock. He aimed and fired. The gun was old but accurate. He destroyed one of the spotlights.

Machine-gun fire started up again. The maquisards returned fire and changed their positions when the machine-gun fire allowed it. The exchange went on for some time. Near where the Germans were dug in, there was a bright flash and a small explosion. Someone had thrown a hand grenade. Though it had fallen short, the Germans turned off the other spotlight to make their position more difficult to target. In consequence, they shot randomly, and the shots were coming from a wider area. The Germans were spreading out.

"We need to get out of here now," ordered Jean-Louis. "It's each man for himself. Take whatever you can and find your way to the cave."

Our own way! Emile panicked. He would have to follow someone.

As they prepared to disperse, they heard a loud buzzing. The spotlight turned on. "German plane!" someone screamed. "Take cover!"

Emile lay on the ground halfway under a large boulder. The plane flew low, machine guns blazing. As Emile lay under the boulder, he heard a whistling sound he knew well. He covered his ears. A few seconds later, two thunderous explosions started a minor landslide above the maquisards' position, sending rocks down on them.

"We must leave now before he comes back," cried someone. Emile heard people running just as the soldiers started firing again. He had no idea which direction to flee, only that it should be away from the bullets.

Most of the firing was directed close to the ground, so Emile threw his rifle down and clambered up the loose rocks. It was very tiring, but he found large boulders along the way that he could rest behind. By the time the plane came by for a second pass, he was well above where the light was directing its firing.

Anxious to get clear of the area, Emile climbed until he was exhausted. He found himself on a narrow mountain path and crawled under a bush to hide. In the dark, with no idea which way might lead to safety, he decided he would wait until morning to make his escape. It was now quiet all around him, so he lay down and quickly fell asleep.

Thursday, June 29, 1944

Emile awoke to shouts below him. He dragged himself from under the bush where he had spent a very uncomfortable night and looked between the rocks. The area below was crawling with Germans scouring the area for any weapons dropped the night before and picking up bodies. One waved his arm and shouted orders. Emile watched as his troops began spreading out farther afield. To his horror, three soldiers in menacing metal helmets and machine guns headed up the mountain toward him.

Emile looked around in panic, trying to decide whether to run or hide. The sun was just coming up. He might be able to escape into the shadows, but if he was seen or an errant rock rolled down the mountain betraying his position, he would have no chance of escape from so many pursuers in daylight.

As Emile was torn by indecision, a lizard ran along the trail and stopped in front of him. It raised its head to look around for danger. Emile moved a little, and the lizard darted behind a large rock a little below him. There were shards of rock around it, and some plants appeared to be crushed under the rock. He strained to look where the lizard had gone and could just make out a dark opening behind the rock. Emile thought he might be able to hide there. With any luck, there might be enough room. He slid down the mountainside on his rear end, trying to dislodge as few rocks as possible. He could see that the opening was a narrow slit that appeared to have just been opened up by the recent rock fall caused by the bombing. He hoped that with a little effort he would be able to squeeze in it.

As the soldiers closed in on his position, Emile slid his feet into the narrow opening. He had expected he would have to squeeze his body in behind, but instead, he found himself falling into an open chasm.

Unprepared, he bruised his arm and his face on the way down but resisted the temptation to cry out. He could hear the soldiers nearby. He lay in silence, nursing his wounds and hardly daring to breathe.

Save for the few rays of light coming through the slit, the space around Emile was black. The air was cold but fresh. As it blew on him, he felt a flow of warmth down his face. He had gashed his forehead. Rubbing his bruised elbow, he tried to stand. The hole he had fallen into was about three meters deep. He decided to allow the Germans a few hours to clear the area before he would clamber back up and out.

Emile sat on cold stone. He wondered what he would do when he regained the surface. He was unsure about finding his way back to Foix or what might be waiting for him there. He imagined Navarro was upset two of his best workers had not shown up.

Emile became more aware of the cool, steady breeze blowing over his face. *If this is just a small void in the mountain, where is this breeze coming from?* As he tried to think of explanations, he remembered the flashlight he had been given to help him find his way. He felt it in his pocket. He turned it on and was astonished. In front of him was a long passageway. He was not in a small hole in the mountain but rather at the entrance of a cave, one that had apparently been closed off for many years.

Impressive as it appeared, Emile had never liked closed spaces. He decided to remain where he was and go back to the surface when it was safe. He would rather be lost outside than in a cavern. However, with little else to do but wait, he succumbed to his inquisitiveness. He walked a bit into the passageway with his flashlight. He noticed the ground was very smooth, as if it had been walked on for many years by many feet. *Whose feet? No telling how long this cave has been closed up.*

Emile shone his small light on the walls of the passageway that led into the dark. The walls were mostly of a deep-brown color interspersed with some rock crystals that glinted in the light. Along the ceiling were a few white stalactites that sparkled as well. Emile shone his light into the darkness. Even in the faint light, something grabbed his attention. He thought he could make out a drawing on the wall ahead. He walked farther down the pathway. As his light brightened the wall, he was sure he was looking at a drawing, several drawings. Spurred on by a sense of discovery, he could not resist exploring a little further.

Emile neared the drawings and shone his light up and down the walls. He saw images of knights with symbols he recognized as belonging to the Knights Templar. A little farther on, he saw drawings of white doves. The drawings looked very old. Their colors were faded, and in parts, they were covered with deposits of lime. Emile gasped. He realized the paintings could date to the time of the Cathars, even before the building of the magnificent palace in Albi.

Emile did not want to get lost in the caves, but something inside him urged him on. He saw more drawings, beyond which everything was black. Uncharacteristically, he found himself unable to resist exploring this underground world just a little further. He moved slowly until he found the narrow tunnel he had come down from the surface opened up into a large cavern. His feeble light was insufficient to reach the roof, so he shouted "Allo" to try to ascertain its size. The sound reverberated around him for several seconds.

Emile knew he had to go back or risk getting hopelessly lost. He turned, but as he did, the fading light from his flashlight passed across a small grotto off the main cavern. It seemed to beckon him. He felt forced to enter it. He walked toward it, feeling manipulated by an irresistible force. He entered the grotto and froze. On the floor, on what looked like a makeshift bed, lay a skeleton. Its arms were folded across its chest, and it was covered in what appeared to be vestiges of dark-blue cloth. Emile shone the pale light from his flashlight over the body. It fell on a gold ring on a fleshless finger. The ring glistened like an orange star in the night sky.

CHAPTER 19

𝔗𝔥𝔢 𝔉𝔞𝔩𝔩𝔢𝔫 𝔥𝔢𝔯𔬀

Thursday, June 29, 1944 – Noyers, Normandy

Three days after leaving Limoges, the first soldiers of the Das Reich Division arrived in Normandy. They had been harassed all the way by sabotage, attacks by the maquis, and allied bombing raids that had taken their tolls on the regiment. Many men had been lost. Morale was low. They were being bombed daily. Men were arriving and being deployed to defensive positions along the front.

Adolf Diekmann had been served with official notification of his upcoming court martial for the events in Oradour-sur-Glane; no less than Field Marshal Erwin Rommel had agreed to serve on the commission. Until that morning, the prospect of a court martial had not intimidated Major Diekmann. He had been confident of vindication, but the news he had received earlier that day had changed everything. It had taken a heavier toll on him than all the allied shells dropped on him there or in the Russian campaign. The dispatch had informed him that his friend, Major Helmut Kämpfe had not been taken to Oradour and that he had still been alive on the day Adolf had burned the town to the ground along with all its inhabitants.

The Gestapo had learned from captured maquisards that Major Kämpfe had been taken as a hostage to trade for captured resistance fighters with the SS, just as Colonel Städler had surmised. He had been shot only after the massacre at Oradour and in reprisal for it. Adolf would have to live with the knowledge that his actions had led to the death of his friend. If he returned to Germany, he would have to face Helmut's widow.

As allied bombs rained on their positions, Adolf contemplated his future. The court martial would surely find him guilty of killing the men, women, and children of Oradour, but more important for him, of actions that had led to Helmut's death. He determined that honor demanded he bring no further shame upon the regiment.

With quiet deliberation, Adolf took off his helmet and put on his soft-peaked major's cap with its outspread eagle. He looked proudly at his image in the mirror one last time. He adjusted his cap and straightened his back. He walked out of the shelter and from under the camouflage netting. He could see allied planes dropping their deadly payloads. The major stood unmoved as the ground exploded around him. A few minutes later, it was over. There would be no need for a court martial. A bomb dropped close to where Major Diekmann was standing and shattered into a hundred pieces. One struck him in the head. Those who had survived the horrors in Oradour-sur-Glane and had to live with the nightmares had been denied a chance for justice and retribution.

CHAPTER 20

Rebirth

Thursday, June 29, 1944 – County of Foix

Emile turned his flashlight from the supine skeleton to explore the rest of the grotto. The space was small compared to the cavern outside, but like the passageway, the floor was smooth as if it too had been worn down by many feet. A depression in the center of the entrance confirmed his suspicion. *But whom did the feet belong to? Why had they come here? More importantly, when had they come here?* Dust on the floor indicated no one had walked there in recent times.

Emile's light illuminated a large wooden table. *How many men did it take to get it here? Had they come in along the passage? Are there other entrances to these caves?* Emile saw an empty oil lamp on the table. A quill was parked in a holder as if waiting for its owner. Beside the quill was a bottle of ink. Emile noticed a bottle on the floor about a third full of a pale yellow liquid. He took the lid off to smell it. Oil. He unscrewed the wick from the lamp on the table so he could fill it with the oil and preserve his flashlight.

He noticed a tinderbox and flints. He might try them if needed, but he still had some matches in his pocket along with a few crumpled cigarettes he had been holding back on. He lit one of the matches and put it to the wick. The flame was reluctant to catch at first, but then gradually, just before the match had burned down, the wick began to glow orange and then yellow as fresh oil from below infused its weave. The flame brightened and cast a flickering light. He lowered the glass over the wick and turned off his flashlight.

Emile saw small cutouts hewn into the wall at the end of the room. They looked as if they had been used for storage, but they were empty. On the wall behind the desk were what looked like images of doves flying toward the ceiling; the whites of their outlines were in sharp contrast to the brown rock. He looked at the table for more clues as to what had happened here or what had been the purpose of the chamber. The quill indicated someone had been writing at the desk, but he saw no parchment, no written word to explain what their purpose had been. It appeared that whatever had happened in the room hadn't been violent. He saw no signs of struggle. Everything on the table was arranged in an orderly fashion.

Emile walked to his silent companion to see if he could help explain the mystery, but he was not forthcoming. Other than the ring he wore, there was nothing that would identify him. It was clear he had been a big man; a large belt with an ornate clasp encircled what had been his waist. His feet were encased in large leather boots with fine stamped buckles. Emile concluded that despite the coarseness of his cloak, he had not been a poor man, clearly not a local shepherd who had wandered in here to die. Most certainly, he had been highborn. *But if so, why had he come here to finish his existence alone? Had someone brought him here, or had he come alone?*

Emile looked around the room. The oil lamp was spitting and flickering, painting dancing shadows on the rocky walls that sparkled in places from crystals in it. On the floor, just past the feet of his unknown friend, was a small, very solid-looking chest in a recess in the rock. He pulled the chest away from the wall. It was heavy and did not slide easily on the stone floor. In the light of the lamp, he could see the chest was reinforced with strong metal bands. On the front, it bore a coat of arms that meant nothing to him. Emile had never been interested in heraldry; it ran counter to his Communist leanings.

The lid would not yield. He saw it was locked in two places. He looked for something to force it open but saw nothing. Emile tried lifting the box to determine if he could drag it out of the cave, but it was too heavy. He had to find the key.

Emile crawled over the floor to feel in the dim light if his silent companion might have dropped the key, but found nothing. He checked and rechecked all the storage places in the wall and ran his hands over the table and again found nothing.

Where on earth could the key be? Emile was convinced it was in the cave. Surely, the chest had belonged to his reclining friend. He must have had the key. Emile looked at the cloth-draped skeleton. It remained resolutely silent. As he stared at the neatly laid-out white bones, a thought entered his mind. *What if he had not hidden the key? What if it was still with him?*

Emile looked at the pockets of the blue robe still adorning its owner. He had seen plenty of dead people during the war, but he had always had a fear of skeletons. He had had it since childhood; he had heard scary tales of Egyptian mummies rising from the dead and had never grown out of his fear. The thought of putting his hand in the pockets of a skeleton sent a shiver down his spine. However, if he was to have any chance of opening the chest, he would have to search them. Reluctantly, he knelt beside the bed. Turning away, he let his hand explore one pocket. It was as if he was putting his hand into a dark pit filled with vipers. His fingers searched the pocket, but all Emile could feel were bones under the thin, rough fabric. Emile withdrew his hand.

On the other side of the robe was another pocket, Emile's last hope. As he reached across the bed, he briefly caught sight of the face shrouded in its dark-blue hood. It seemed to be staring at him, smiling even. Emile closed his eyes. His hand found the pocket. He shuddered when he felt something cold. His hand clasped what he knew by its shape was what he had been seeking. He felt something else also. A rolled-up parchment. Emile pulled the items out and walked to the table. He slid the lamp closer and unrolled the parchment.

The penmanship was exquisite. The characters were written with flourish and precision. *"But what could be so important to merit such effort?"*

At first, Emile had trouble interpreting the text before him. But then he realized and was in awe of what he had chanced upon. The manuscript was written in the ancient language of Occitan.

Occitan was the old language of southern France. It was similar to Catalan, still the native language of the people of Catalonia just across the border in Spain from the Languedoc. Up until the fourteenth century, the Languedoc and Catalonia had been united under the Kings of Aragón. Emile had been introduced to Occitan when he studied Spanish at university and been struck by its beauty. He had taken supplemental studies in the language so that he might read the wealth of poetry and troubadour songs in the language. Still, it had been a long time, and he feared that he had forgotten most of it.

However, as he looked at the richly-scrolled letters, the words slowly came back to him and with some effort, he managed to decipher what was written on the parchment. The text sent a chill through him:

> You have come, as foretold.
> Take this key.
> It will unlock your past and your future.
> To you is entrusted the future of all.

Emile did not know if the message was intended for him or if he had stumbled into something that had nothing to do with him. There was only one way to find out. He walked to the chest and inserted the key into the first lock. It fit, as he knew it would. He turned the key. The lock responded with a resounding click. Emile removed the key and inserted it into the second lock, which also yielded as if it had just been oiled.

Emile released the catches and lifted the lid. He was half-expecting to see gold and precious stones, but what greeted him was a pile of carefully wrapped parchments. The uppermost was tied with a wide ribbon and sealed with wax. He saw that the impression in the seal had been made by the ring on the fleshless finger. Taking the scroll back to the table, he carefully broke the seal.

Emile gasped incredulously at the first line.

In the sixth month of the year of our Lord, June 1244.

Could it really be that the chamber and its occupant have lain undisturbed for exactly seven hundred years? What have I discovered here? After the date was a letter written in the same hand.

Welcome. As you read these words, know they are your own.

The Chrysalis of Oc

The journey of your soul will have been long and arduous to return to this place. But be assured, it has come for a reason, that the time is now right to fulfill our destiny. The year of your existence is immaterial, for time and all that is material is Lucifer's creation. All that matters is that the prophesy is about to be fulfilled and the long darkness is about to be lifted from the earth. It will not be long before your soul can rejoin those whom it loved and have journeyed on ahead.

During my existence, I was known as Raymond de Péreille, Lord de Montségur and descendent of the House of Mirepoix. I and my family were overlords of the people and much of the land around this sanctuary. We were subject only to the counts of Toulouse and the great kings of Aragón. It is true that this is of little importance, for as I have said, all material things are of no value.

What is important for you to know is that for the people, this was a land of plenty, of culture, tolerance, and happiness. All this was a reward for dedicating our lives to the Good God and for following the path along which he leads us.

Tragically, however, the evil one is strong, and he could not abide us worshipping the true Creator, so he amassed his hordes and sent barbarians from the north to despoil our lands, kill our young men, rape our women, and even set fire to us while we still breathed in our places of worship.

Emile recoiled in horror. He let the parchment drop to the table. *What was the writer talking about? How could he possibly have written these words? Is this a trick?* It sounded as if he were describing the present, Emile's present, not something that had happened seven hundred years earlier. *Who was this man? Who was he writing to?* Emile was apprehensive, but he knew he could not leave without reading the rest of the letter. He continued where he had left off.

> Those who had dedicated themselves to the Good God tried to reason with the invaders. They did not fight as the Good God commands of them, "Thou shall not kill." But those serving the Bad God had no such inhibitions. They struck down the enlightened ones in the most cruel fashion and all those who would give them shelter even if they also worshipped the Bad God. I and the other Occitan knights did our best to defend the innocent against the onslaught, but it was hopeless. Wave after wave of the dark Lord's forces descended upon us and eventually overwhelmed us.
>
> However, all is not lost, for in the middle of the darkness, I was exposed to the light. I found it close to heaven in the citadel of Montsegúr, which is perched high on the pog. For the last year of my temporal existence, I lived in the clouds with the angels, and they instructed me in their ways. They explained how a long, dark period would pass over the earth but would eventually pass and the Good God would triumph. They chose me to be their tool for this resurrection, and that is what brought you here this day.

A crazy old man, a long time ago. It has nothing to do with me. I'm nobody's savior. I'm not even religious, Good God, Bad God, they're all the same to me. Emile had seen enough. He thought the Germans should have passed on and he could resume his trek to Spain to fight the dark forces he was more familiar with. Emile wanted to return the parchment to the chest. He had never taken what was not his, and the letter was clearly not for him. But before he rolled it up, he read the final paragraph in its wonderfully ornate hand.

I fear my writings may seem incoherent, irrelevant to you whose eyes are first cast upon these words. That is understandable, for you were not prepared to be ensnared by events that had been set in motion probably long before your current existence began. But let me assure you that these words are meant for you and for no other. You did not stumble into this place by chance, but rather it invited you in.

What I have to tell you is as important to you as it is to me. I ask only this of you. Take the contents of the chest from this place for safekeeping. Among the papers is a true account of what befell us here so that you will understand and know your part in these events.

Do not linger. If you have been brought here, the forces of darkness may not be far behind. The contents of this chest must not fall into their hands, for many have already died to preserve them for the forces of good.

Take the ring from my finger. You may need it.

May the Good God speed and protect you, and may you have a good end.

Raymond de Péreille

  Emile rolled up the parchment and tied the ribbon around it. He went to return it to the chest but was uncertain of what to do. This ancient Lord of Montségur seemed so certain that Emile had a role to play in a history he had no knowledge of. *How could that possibly be?* There was certainly a darkness over the world, and Emile was hopeful it would soon be lifted, so the words were not out of place. He certainly enjoyed history, so reading the accounts in the chest might be interesting, he thought. *No. Maybe another time, another place.* He was in the middle of a war, fleeing for his life. He was in no shape to save humanity.

He thought of returning in the future, after the Fascist menace had been vanquished. He was about to close the lid when he heard noises, voices. He listened intently. He became terrified. The shouting echoing down the passageway was in German. He realized the soldiers must have discovered the opening to the cave and were searching it. *The forces of darkness may not be far behind.* He shuddered. The writer, he thought, had foreseen these events. *How could this ancient lord have known?*

Emile decided he could not refuse the burden that had been assigned him. If the lord had given his life seven hundred years ago to protect the contents of the chest, he could not in good conscience see them fall into the hands of modern evil. Emile hastily took the pile of parchments from the chest. Beneath them were several small packages, all carefully wrapped. He saw a neatly folded, dark-blue robe similar to the one the late lord was wearing. At the bottom of the chest was a heavy leather bag. Emile realized the ancient Lord had planned everything for him—a bag to carry his precious artifacts and a robe to keep him warm. It reminded him of how his wife had taken care of him. He felt deep sadness and anger.

It was rather cold in the cave, so Emile put the robe on. Curiously, it was a perfect fit and surprisingly comfortable, though it made him feel somewhat like a monk, however, far preferable to being a member of the Milice. *If Raymond here had only packed some food for the journey, I'd be all set.* His stomach growled at the thought.

Outside in the passageway, the noise was getting louder. *Time to leave.* Then, he remembered the ring still on a bony finger. The thought of taking it off made him shudder. *Will I be cursed like those who had disturbed mummies?* He convinced himself it wasn't the same. This spirit from the afterlife had commanded him to take it.

The noise outside grew closer. Surprising himself, he rushed to the body, slipped the ring off the white sliver of bone, and put it on his own finger. He raced out of the grotto and ran down the corridor he had been in before, but in the other direction.

He had no idea where he was going. He had no map and only the flickering light of the oil lamp to save him from eternal blackness. The sack over his shoulder was heavy, so he had to stop running to catch his breath.

"Who is there?" he heard someone shout in German and repeat it in French. "Stay where you are or we will entomb you forever!" cried another voice.

Emile could not see anyone. He reasoned they had not seen him either, but the glow from his oil lamp had probably given him away. He turned down the wick and headed deeper into the cave. The going was difficult without much light.

Unfortunately, Emile could not throw off his pursuers. They seemed to be gaining on him. He could hear them running. He snatched a glance back and saw their flashlights not far behind. Ahead of Emile, the path narrowed and fell off to one side. Water dripping down the wall here and there made the path slippery. Emile was forced to slow down.

His pursuers, however, were less encumbered and almost certainly had boots more suited for walking in caves. It was not long before he saw them. Two soldiers from the division that had ambushed them the night before. They saw him. "Halt or we shoot!"

Emile did not stop. He would as soon die there with the former Lord of Montségur than in a Gestapo cell. The Germans shot at Emile, who ran as best he could. The cave walls were rough and not straight, and there were areas of fallen rocks and limestone formations that gave him some protection from ricocheting bullets. Stalactites that had been growing for countless millions of years rained down upon him like icicles.

Emile decided he would have no hope to outrun them unless he left the satchel. He thought of simply tossing it into the abyss at the side of the path and abandoning it to whatever was down there rather than leaving it for the Germans, but he could not bring himself to do that. He had no idea what he would be destroying.

Forced to act if he were to survive, Emile took a risk. The path turned slightly, and as soon as it had done so, he covered the oil lamp with his cloak and pressed himself against the wall. As the soldiers neared, Emile held his breath and waited for the right moment. When he could hear their arms scuffing against the cave wall near where he stood, he lurched out and threw the oil lamp at the wall above them. Bullets from their guns went wildly in all directions as the glass of the nearly full reservoir of the lamp shattered and showered both soldiers with oil. In just seconds the cave lit up as the oil ignited. The soldier closest to Emile was enveloped in flames.

With a blood-curdling scream, he dropped his gun and fell off the edge of the path. Emile could see from the light that they were in a vast cavern. The soldier seemed to fall for an eternity until the light was extinguished. Emile heard a loud splash.

The other soldier was also on fire, and his machine gun too had fallen away. Despite his pain, he was fighting to subdue the flames. Emile dared not move as he succeeded in extinguishing the flames. The cave returned to its perpetual darkness. Emile could hear the soldier groaning. A few minutes later, a flashlight came on.

"You will die slowly here!" the soldier screamed. "You will be entombed forever in this dark, accursed world. You will never see the light of day again. May you rot in hell!"

Emile remained motionless, scared that the soldier might still have a gun. The light from the flashlight began moving away from him, down the path along which they had come. It was only when the light had faded and there was only darkness that Emile felt safe to come out of hiding, but he did not know where he was or where the cave system led. Maybe he would die there as the soldier had promised. He was certain he would not be able to leave the way he had entered. The soldier would see to that.

If only Raymond de Péreille had left me a map. Maybe he had? He seemed to have been prepared for everything else. He frantically searched the robe's pockets. Sure enough, in one was a small piece of parchment. Emile prayed it would be a map. He extracted his flashlight. Its light was feeble compared to the oil lamp, but it was enough to illuminate a map of the caves, but they were far more complex than he had anticipated. Emile studied a labyrinth of passageways.

Anticipating his plight, Raymond de Péreille had marked the grotto he had been lying in. It was up to Emile to find a way out. He traced out where he had already been and chose one of several exits on the map. Picking up the satchel, Emile prepared to set off. As he did so, he heard a loud but distant noise. He felt a rush of air from down the passageway that almost knocked him over. He knew the Germans had blown up the entrance he had used.

Emile walked for an hour or more trying to get to the exit marked on the map. It was slow going. The sack was heavy, and he needed food and sleep. He periodically rechecked his map; he seemed to be on the right track. However, the battery in his flashlight was close to giving out, so when the path seemed safe, he would turn it off and walk in the dark. It was an unnerving experience. The darkness was a weight pressing on him.

As he walked in darkness, Emile felt a puff of wind pass his face. Then another. And another. He heard nothing. The air seemed to be coming from random directions. He turned on his flashlight and saw he was surrounded by bats hanging from the walls and flying past him as if he were merely another rock. Despite their aerobatic skills, Emile covered his face until they were gone.

At long last, Emile approached the exit marked on the map. He wanted his ordeal to end. He wanted to feel the sun on his face again and fill his lungs with the fresh air of the Languedoc. It would be none too soon. Body and flashlight were nearing exhaustion. He saw that the path ended. The cave wall rose before him. *There must be an opening in the rock. My flashlight is just too weak to reveal it.*

Emile became increasingly concerned. He could see no sign of the exit. All that stood before him was a pile of rocks. He started pulling at them frantically, clawing away at them and tossing them aside in anger. The more he moved from the path, the more fell from above. With his flashlight battery expended, he was totally in the dark. Devoid of hope, totally exhausted, Emile lay on the ground and wept. All the feelings he had been suppressing since that heinous day in Oradour-sur-Glane rushed to the surface.

CHAPTER 21

Metamorphosis

Friday, June 30, 1944 – County of Foix

Emile could not decide if he was dead or merely dreaming. His head was turning. His thoughts were confused. He could hear ethereal voices. He struggled to understand the meaning of their words but could not. Finally, it dawned on him he was hearing not French but Occitan, the ancient language of the Languedoc, the "tongue of Oc." With great concentration, their words began to take on meaning.

"Oh good Lord of Montségur, wake up! We, your servants, have long awaited your return," they were calling to him.

Must be a dream. Lord of Montségur. Then he remembered the title on the letter he found in the cave. I'm still in the cave but have become delirious.

He lay back to accept his fate, but felt a soft touch. He thought it was a hallucination, but it made him shiver. The sensation had been real. Emile strained to open his eyes. He could make out the roof of a cave high above him and sensed he was lying on something very soft, definitely not the floor of a cave.

Emile tried to prop himself up, but his arms were too weak. From somewhere behind him, hands appeared and gently raised him. He could see more clearly now. He was in a large cave, much larger than the one he had been in before he had lost consciousness. It was well lit by several lamps.

"Where am I? How did I get here? I do not know how I came to be here. All I remember is passing out in the darkness before an endless wall of rocks."

"We heard your cries, oh Lord," a voice replied in Occitan. "We heard it through the wall of the cave when we were dedicating ourselves to the Good God. He chose to answer us with your cries. None of us knew until then there was a passageway behind those rocks. It took us many hours to clear away enough to pull you through."

"I owe my life to you. I never expected to see light again," Emile said.

Emile was looking at about a dozen people, men and women, simply dressed. The men wore earth-colored long blouses and brown, baggy trousers. Their shoes were well worn and caked in mud. The women wore pastel-covered dresses covered by short aprons. Their hair was wrapped in scarves. They were more rustic than anyone he had met before in the region. People he had never imagined could exist in the middle of this brutal, all-consuming war. Their faces reflected only kindness. He felt in no danger.

As Emile struggled to stand, as he did so the people fell to their knees, palms on the ground. Each bowed deeply three times and began imploring Emile to do something for them. It was difficult to understand so many voices at once, especially in a language not his own, but he finally understood they were asking him to pray for them. Emile, a Communist at heart and with no faith in any Creator, tried to think of a polite response.

"Bless us, Good Christian. Pray to God for this sinner that I might have a good death," one demanded.

Emile thought they had confused him with someone else. *Who do they think I am? And who are they?* He decided to play along. He beckoned them to rise with upturned palms. They obeyed him without question, more submissively than any of his students had ever done.

"You call me lord, but I am no lord. My name is Emile Garnier," he said in French. "I am a mere schoolteacher from the Limousin who was trying to get to Spain. I became lost in the caves. I do not know who you think I am, but I am neither lord nor knight nor preacher."

The people looked at each other. One stepped forward hesitantly. He had a small grey beard and receding grey hair and carried a short crook. Emile guessed he was a shepherd and clearly in a leadership position.

"My Lord—" he began in Occitan before catching himself. To Emile's great relief, he resumed in French.

"Sir, if you are truly who you say you are, why do you wear the seal ring of the Lord of Montségur? Why do you carry a satchel embossed with the crest of the Mirepoix?"

Emile saw heads nodding. Some people muttered quietly to each other.

After acknowledging the response of his fellows, the old man continued. "We would also ask you why you wear the habit of one of God's chosen ones. These are not the clothes of a mere teacher of children but of a teacher and leader of men. You came to us from the sacred caves of our ancestors that have been sealed for hundreds of years and ask us to accept that all this is not miraculous."

A loud murmur of affirmation came from those behind him.

"We have been expecting your return for generations. The song of the troubadour from the thirteenth century tells us, 'At the end of seven hundred years, the laurel will be green once more.' This year, it is seven hundred years since the terrible evil triumphed over good in God's citadel. The time has come for the good balance to be restored."

The old man bowed, humbly awaiting Emile's response, as did the others. Emile realized he had a lot to explain. To get their help, he could tell them he was the spiritual leader they had placed their hopes in, but he could not lie. He did not know how to convince them who he was, so he decided at least to explain away the artifacts.

"I tell you truthfully, I found the body of Raymond de Péreille, whom I now know to be an ancient Lord of Montségur in a grotto in the caves. Close to the body, I found a letter he had apparently written just before his death in 1244. In that letter, he implored me to take the contents to a place of safekeeping. He asked me to take the ring from his finger."

"What else did this letter ask?" demanded the old man.

"It was confusing. He evidently believed that whoever found the letter was predestined to play some part in restoring this balance you speak of."

The old man's eyes glistened. A smile crept over his face as if he had some secret knowledge Emile had just corroborated.

"Raymond de Péreille was a great lord," the man said. "He is a hero to all the people of the Languedoc. He protected the good ones at his own peril until the forces of Lucifer overwhelmed him. He paid a heavy price for his sacrifice. You have touched the hand of that great man. I am envious of you. If Raymond de Péreille writes even from beyond the grave that you have a mission to fulfill, it must be so. You may have been a teacher in your former life, but when you entered that grotto, a new life began for you. Henceforth, you will have to find your new path. We will help you."

The others nodded animatedly in agreement.

Emile did not know whether to thank them or protest their offers of help. He certainly did not feel capable of being anyone's savior. In the past month, he had failed abysmally at helping even those he loved most, and these people were strangers. Even so, they appeared to be good people, increasingly hard to find those days, so he had no wish to offend them. He did indeed need help. He thought it would be best to go along for a while with their wishes and not destroy whatever hopes they had for him. If it brought them happiness, what harm could there be? They would soon see he was no savior, and he could part company with them amicably.

"What is this religion you follow?" asked Emile.

"We are Christians who remain true to the teachings and ideals of the earliest Christians. We follow the Good God, unlike the many who call themselves Christians yet have strayed from the true path and unknowingly worship the idolatrous Bad God. The Church of Rome pursues this wrong path. We refer to ourselves simply as Friends of God or Good Christians, though our enemies call us Cathars. It is a name with many connotations, the most favorable one being 'the pure ones,' but is not a name we care to use ourselves."

"I have heard of the Cathars," confessed Emile. "But I thought they had all been wiped out centuries ago."

"It is sadly true that many of our believers were brutally tortured and murdered by those who could not allow people to hear the truth of our message, but that message is still alive and is preserved by many in the region. We believers dedicate our lives to spreading that message to others in the belief that one day soon, people will turn away from the Bad God, the material God of the Church of Rome, and other blasphemies and again know the Good God. Our message is one of peace and nonviolence, something the world has great need of today."

So they're not totally out of touch with what's going on around them. Maybe they can help me get to Spain. With no other options, he decided to comply with their wishes. "I will go with you. In removing the contents from the chest of Raymond de Péreille, I made an implicit commitment to take them to a place of safety. I will do my best to fulfill that commitment. However, I can make no promises beyond that."

The old man smiled. "We will ask no more of you. My name is Guillème, and this is my wife, Maurina. We will take you to our dwelling. You will be safe there. You can stay with us as long as you need."

"I am very grateful. My life has been torn apart in recent weeks. I would be glad for somewhere to recuperate, but I have no wish to burden you and will be glad to do whatever work I can to help you."

"Whatever Raymond de Péreille commanded of you, that is what we wish you to do. That and no more. That is how you can best help all of us."

"I will try," Emile said, unsure of what he was committing too.

"Now, let me take the satchel," Guillème said. "It is heavy. We have a long walk ahead."

Emile was in no shape to protest. He followed them along a confusing network of interconnected passageways and caves. In places, he saw more drawings and what looked like crypts cut into the limestone. At one point, they walked alongside a fast-flowing underground river. When they emerged into the bright light of the Mediterranean sun. Emile had to shield his eyes from its glare. There would be no way he would have ever been able to find his way back into the cave they had been in on his own. The location of their meeting place was safe with him.

The worshippers parted company not long after leaving the caves, each taking a different trail home. Emile stayed with Guillème and Maurina. They were not terribly talkative. The hike was arduous and long, as Guillème had warned him. Emile felt they were climbing ever upward. "Doesn't it get cold up here in the winter?" he asked.

"Yes," the old man said. "That is why we spend the winter in the valley. After the snows pass, we bring our herds up to the mountain pastures to graze, and we stay with them all summer. We are going to the summer house right now."

"Which do you prefer? Mountains or valley?"

"That is easy to answer. The mountains of course. You are closer to the Good God in the mountains. In the valley, mankind has lost its way. People are obsessed with material possessions. They think nothing of killing each other to obtain them. That is why we have prayed for your return so you can teach them once again that such things are of no value. Remind them that all that is truly important is that they lead peaceful, virtuous lives if they are ever to find redemption."

Maurina looked at him with a puzzled expression. "My Lord, if you are truly from the Limousin, how is it that when we found you in the cave you were rambling in Occitan? It is not a language still spoken outside this region."

Emile was surprised.

"I learned some Occitan at university. I learned it while studying Spanish, but I hadn't remembered much of it until now. I think it was after reading that letter from Raymond de Péreille. I must have been dreaming about it."

"That may be so," Guillème said, "but I think there is more to it than that. I think there is a plan behind all this that has not been revealed to you. It will be. We are patient."

Emile did not reply. He was worried he wouldn't be able to live up to whatever expectations these people had of him.

Few words passed between them for the remainder of the journey until sometime around midafternoon, as Emile was about to die of exhaustion, a sheepdog came bounding over the rocks toward them, eyes bright. It ran to Guillème, lay down in front of him, and cocked his head from side to side as if to ask what was required of him.

Guillème was clearly overjoyed to see him. With the aid of his stick, he knelt slowly on the ground and rubbed the dog's head. Master and devoted servant embraced. "Good boy, Pedro, good boy. I named him after Pedro II, one of the greatest kings of Aragón."

Emile smiled politely, having no knowledge of what he was talking about.

"If King Pedro had lived just a little longer—" He shook his head sadly, "—things might have turned out very different for the Languedoc and the rest of the world. You might not be speaking French now but Occitan."

A glint of hope seemed to flash in Guillème's eyes for a moment before being washed away by tears. "Alas, that was not to be, so we must find another way."

"Come," said Maurina. "Our house is just over the rise."

The old couple's house was built on a rocky, south-facing hillside in a small valley. Emile was struck by its construction. It was built entirely of stone. No wood, not even on the roof. Large, heavy limestone rocks constituted the walls and thin, layered ones the roof. The roof had a steep slope, Emile assumed it was to cope with heavy snow.

"Did you build the house?" inquired Emile.

The old man chuckled. "Me, build that house? No. It has been in my family for generations. Each of us in our turn has worked to repair it after each long winter, but I have no idea who built it. My family has been herding sheep in these mountains even before the time of the crusades against the Albigensians."

"You must know these mountains well then, old man."

He nodded. His eyes glazed over as he looked around. "Yes, they are my friends. I grew up in these mountains, and I will die in them. I would have it no other way. They are a part of me. I am a part of them. It is the same for most people from this area. I may not have many years left of this existence, and my soul may have to return to earth. All I pray is that it will again be in Occitania. I care not if it will be as a human, a goat, or a bird so long as it is here."

It seemed strange to Emile to hear a Christian talk about reincarnation. He had certainly never heard his brother-in-law Father François mention it. "If you know these mountains that well, could you take me to Spain?" Emile asked nervously.

Guillème stopped. He turned to Emile. His deeply wrinkled brow registered disapproval. "I could, but first I ask you to do what Raymond de Péreille has requested of you. After that, if you still wish to go, I will take you."

It did not seem an unreasonable request to Emile. All he had been requested to do was read the account the Lord of Montségur had written for him. That should not take him long, and then he could leave. It seemed only a small inconvenience to keep them happy. At the most, it would delay his journey only by a few weeks. "Guillème, you have a deal."

Emile put Raymond's satchel on the floor beside his bed. The bed was no more than a few blankets thrown over a layer of straw, crude and uncomfortable compared to the soft bed he and Monique had shared, but that life was behind him. In his new reality, the bed would suffice. Maurina had freshened up the room with sprigs of lavender to sweeten the air. After straightening up around the house, Maurina went to the kitchen to begin cooking.

"Let me show you around while she is busy," Guillème said.

Emile agreed, though he was not anxious to go far after their long hike. He need not have worried; Guillème was clearly tired as well. After a short tour of the house, they went outside. Almost immediately, Pedro was at their side.

"He never comes in the house," said Guillème. "He likes to keep his freedom and to go wherever he pleases. I could not manage the flocks without him, and he is also our protector. I have seen him chase off a hungry wolf more than once."

The dog ran and leaped in the air beside them with excitement as they walked down the hill. Guillème pointed to a small stone hut just ahead.

"That is our toilet. It is very basic but serves its purpose. Be careful in the dark, though. The path can be a little difficult."

The path? What about the wolves? I will have to make friends with Pedro.

In one area, where the hillside was less steep, there was a small garden enclosed by a low stone wall. The land was terraced to hold back the thin but clearly fertile soil.

"The soil here is very red," remarked Emile.

"It is. When the rains come in the spring and autumn, they wash down into the Aude and turn its waters into an angry torrent of bubbling red. People in these parts say that it is the blood of the Cathars," he said with such conviction that Emile thought he believed it.

"Your vegetables look very healthy."

"They are, but I can't claim credit for that. Maurina looks after them. She grows much of the food we eat. You will taste some tonight."

"I look forward to it. What is that tower?" asked Emile, pointing up the hill.

"That is our telephone," replied Guillème with an air of sarcasm. "Come and see."

Emile heard cooing before he got there. It was a pigeon loft.

"These pigeons carry our messages to other believers in the area. It is how we stay in touch and organize meetings. You owe them your thanks that we were in the cave today."

"You will have to show me what seeds they eat around here so that I can gather some to feed them." Emile laughed.

The last building they visited was a small stone barn where a particularly friendly goat with a bell around her neck approached Emile.

"That is Florence. She is the lead goat around here, and she is just checking you out. She's a smart girl, smarter than many of the people I have met."

"I don't doubt it," said Emile as he stroked her head. He was surprised how solid it felt. Pedro seemed jealous at the attention and began fussing and barking.

Guillème shook his head knowingly. "Don't mind him. Those two always compete with each other for attention."

The dog nipped at the goat's leg. The goat leaped into the air and brought her forehead straight down on Pedro's. The poor dog started whining and limped away.

Maurina called to them.

"Dinner's ready," declared Guillème.

"Better not keep her waiting," said Emile, remembering the trouble he would get into with Monique when he delayed too long.

The two walked to the back of the house, where there was an entrance to the kitchen. Emile could smell Maurina's creations. Until then, he hadn't realized how hungry he was. He felt famished and stepped up his pace.

Just outside the kitchen, Guillème showed him the deep well they depended on for drinking water. "Water is more precious than gold in these parts during the summer. It is very hot, and you can go for three months without a drop of rain up here. Without water, everything dies. The animals, the crops, the people."

"Does the well ever run dry?" asked Emile.

"It can in the driest summers, but we also have that tank there to help with the animals and the garden. It fills with rainwater from the roof in the spring, and if we are sparing, it lasts most of the summer."

"You are very enterprising."

"And very independent. You have to be to survive in these parts."

The meal began with Guillème reciting the Lord's Prayer. The words were a little different from those Emile remembered from childhood, but only subtly. The meal was a white-bean stew without any meat. It smelled and tasted delicious.

"This stew is wonderful," said Emile. "Do you also put lamb in it from your flock occasionally? Lamb is very popular in the Limousin."

"We avoid meat," replied Maurina. "It is allowed to us as we are only believers, but we aspire to be Good people one day, and it is forbidden for them to eat meat as another's soul could be trapped there."

"I have much to learn." Emile felt stupid for having asked.

"You can start in the morning," Guillème said. "I am sure the papers you found in the lord's chest will explain everything to you. When you have read them, I hope it will be you who can teach us to become better people."

Saturday, July 1, 1944 – County of Foix

A shaft of light pierced the slit between the shutters on Emile's window, waking him up. The bed was too hard for him to get back to sleep, so he decided to make an early day of it. He entered the kitchen and found Maurina at work.

"Guillème is with the flock. He and Pedro left about an hour ago. He says not to expect him back before dark."

After a quick breakfast of berries and goat cheese, Emile returned to his room to begin his assignment. He opened the satchel and retrieved the bundles of parchment. They were numbered, so he broke the seal on the first. There were several sheets, all written in the same hand he had seen in the letter he had read in the cave.

> I do not know in what time these words will find you, for Bernard Marty, a leader among those who have dedicated their souls to the Good God, has predicted that the period of darkness ahead for mankind may endure for many

> generations. However, I go to my rest untroubled in the certain knowledge that the day will come when good will again triumph over evil and the darkness will be lifted from us as the cloud is lifted from the mountaintop.
>
> Have faith that as you read these words that time is now before you. The charge that I accepted is to prepare you as best I can for the part that is your destiny in the rebirth. Right now, you are as a child who does not know his past or future. If you read what I have put before you, I will show you both. Have patience and take my hand.

Emile reflected. He had been a schoolteacher for many years and was not sure he was ready to play the child again. *What did this knight from seven hundred years ago believe he could teach me about myself that I don't know?* The concept seemed preposterous, but Emile was intrigued. He wanted to learn what had motivated such a highborn man to sacrifice himself to send a message into the future.

> If you are to know your future, you must know your past. I am troubled to know exactly when to begin this narrative, for the evil that befell us did not appear spontaneously on a single day I could name.
>
> Rather, it grew insidiously, gathering unseen, until like a tumor, it showed itself when it was too late to remedy. I have decided therefore to begin my account when my memories begin, in my childhood, for it was not long after that the clouds of evil began to blow across our lands.

CHAPTER 22

The Tale Begins

I, Raymond de Péreille, was born in 1190, the second son of Guillaume-Roger de Mirepoix and my dearest mother, Fournière de Péreille. As you may observe, I took my family name from that of my mother, which was a common Occitan practice, for in our lands, we respected our womenfolk and treated them as equals to men. This practice was one of the many grievances that finally brought down upon us the wrath of the barbarian French from the north and their ally, the Church of Rome.

I shall recount to you as best I can the tragedy that unfolded in this blessed land of Occitania so you may learn from it and be better prepared for your task. For the events in which I participated, I swear to relate to you their true occurrences to the best of my ability, as the Good God is my witness. For others, my account of the events was relayed to me by those who had full or direct knowledge of them. These accounts came from numerous sources sympathetic to our cause and yet in whom I have absolute trust. Among these sources were many from inside the Church of Rome itself, who after witnessing the horrors perpetrated against our people, turned against their offices and rejected the brutality demanded of them. I hold it in faith that this knowledge will prepare you to restore the balance of good over evil that the Creator intended.

I begin my account with an event that was to bring me much personal happiness yet was also blackened by a harbinger of future danger. It was in the autumn of 1203. My memories of that day are still as clear as if it were yesterday. My father, Guillaume-Roger, and his brother, Pierre-Roger, co-lords of Mirepoix, had organized a large reception in my honor. All the Occitan nobility was invited. They came to celebrate the announcement of my betrothal to Corba de Lanta. It should have been an entirely joyous occasion, but as I shall recount, our happiness was dampened by an unanticipated event that cast a gloom over the gathering and gave us a warning of the dark days that lay ahead for all of us.

1203, Autumn – Castle of Mirepoix

It had been one of those perfect autumn days beloved by all in Occitania. A thunderstorm that passed quickly through the night before left the air crisp and fresh. The sky was a deep blue, like the Mediterranean. At first light, I had gone hunting with my father and my uncle, and we had killed two of the largest wild boars I had ever seen.

It took most of the day to roast them, smothered in herbs, over an open pit for the evening banquet. By the time our guests arrived, the castle was permeated by the mouth-watering aroma of roasting meat. The castle was adorned with flags of all the royal houses of Occitania, and we had many jugglers and troubadours for entertainment. My spirits could not have been higher as the evening began.

While we ate, the troubadours sang to us songs of courtly love and others that mocked the northern French lords and their uncivilized ways. Our guests were in rapture over the entertainment. For me, the evening was magical.

At the end of the meal, my father stood. The great hall fell silent. There was loud applause as he announced that Corba de Lanta and I were to be married. I could not have been happier.

Politically, it was a perfect match for our two houses. Corba was the daughter of Raymond de Lanta of the family Barbavaire, relatives of Raymond VI de Toulouse, the overlord of Occitania, and the Maquèse de Fourquevaux. It was the Occitan custom for the lines of inheritance to be passed down through either male or female descendants, and thus our marriage would unite our two great houses.

Politics aside, I am glad to say Corba and I were truly in love. I had fallen in love with her the first time I saw her, long before there was any suggestion of a marriage contract between our families, at least that I was aware of. The first time I saw her, she was playing the harp. I perceived her as an angel. Nothing since that day has caused me to change that opinion. At the time, I timidly expressed my appreciation for her playing. It was not until a few weeks later that I realized my feelings for her were reciprocated. She was walking by in the castle grounds when I was practicing my swordsmanship. I had not realized she was there until I heard her soft voice. She commented that I handled the sword better than she did the harp, which was not true. I told her so without hesitation.

From that day on, we searched for excuses to be together. We did nothing more than talk and walk, for we knew from the songs of the troubadours that only tragedy could result from an unchivalrous relationship between a virtuous man and his lady. Though we were barely in our teens, we were conscious of the duties and obligations we owed our families.

I believe our parents took notice of our friendship, for one day, they surprised us by announcing our families had agreed we should be betrothed. We received the news as a gift from heaven and were overjoyed the night my father announced the happy news. It was a night we had dreamed about for weeks and one we wanted to be entirely joyous, whose memories we could cherish forever. Unfortunately, it was not to be. My father had barely finished his speech when the herald's trumpet announced two uninvited guests who wished to be received. My father had no choice but to honor their request in the long tradition of Occitan hospitality.

The herald came forward with two monks adorned in exquisite robes. Putting his trumpet under his arm, the herald announced them. "My Lords of Mirepoix and of Foix, I present legates to the lands of Occitania from his Excellency Pope Innocent III."

The herald turned to the monks. One stepped forward and slightly tipped his head in a manner of acknowledgment but not of submission.

"Pierre de Castelnau," announced the herald.

"Welcome to Mirepoix." My father greeted him sincerely.

"Raoul de Fontfroide," announced the herald. The second monk stepped forward.

"This is quite an honor," my uncle said sarcastically. "Two legates in one night. The pope must truly be worried about our souls."

Pierre de Castelnau scowled, clearly not seeing any humor in the comment. "The holy father worries about all men's souls. He is the shepherd of all men."

"And of women too I hope," cried out Esclarmonde de Foix.

Pierre turned to her. "I am pleased to see you again, my Lady," he said coldly, his expression indicating the opposite. "My condolences on the death of your husband. He was a good and devout follower of Christ. You may be consoled by the fact that he has surely taken his rightful place in the house of the Lord. If you follow his example, one day, you too may follow him to the eternal paradise."

"What are you implying, legate?"

"I am implying nothing, my Lady. Just giving you humble advice."

Esclarmonde de Foix glowered at him.

The legate smiled condescendingly. "Regarding your question about the holy father, there is a natural order to the universe ordained by God, the Creator of all things. In this order, those at each level are responsible to those above them for the ones below. Thus, the pope is responsible only to God for all mankind. Since woman is subservient to man, it is up to man to take care of woman. Thus, when the pope prays for the souls of men, he also indirectly prays for those of women."

"That is so reassuring, friar," Esclarmonde said sarcastically. "I shall sleep so much more soundly this night knowing that my fair sex is always in the thoughts of our men folk." A suppressed but audible laughter swept the banquet table.

Esclarmonde had a tongue rarely equaled in Occitania or beyond. It was not without cause that she was known as "the Great." My father was well aware that Pierre de Castelnau was no match for her oratory, so he tried to spare him further embarrassment by turning the discussion.

"Archdeacon, I understand you were recently received into the Cistercian order. I congratulate you, as do we all. To what do we owe the honor of your visit?"

Pierre de Castelnau tipped his head in acknowledgment. "Thank you, Guillaume-Roger. We come directly from Rome. His holiness, God's representative on earth, just reaffirmed us as his legates and charged us with eradicating the heresy infecting this region. We wanted all here to know of this and to give us their support in carrying out this obligation we have sworn to take on. It is an onerous task but one we welcome and intend to pursue with fervor and dedication until all heretics are eradicated from these lands."

Another powerful voice interrupted him. The frame of the man matched the deepness of his voice. The self-confidence he exuded gave caution to any man that he was not to be trifled with. He was Raymond-Roger de Foix, Esclarmonde's brother. He approached the legate from where the troubadours had been playing, for despite his mastery of the art of warfare, he was also a renowned troubadour and poet. Raymond-Roger was a close relative and ally of Raymond VI de Toulouse, and there was no one more devoted to the cause of Occitania than he was. Raymond-Roger held the rebec he had been playing.

"Legate, it would seem to me that your time would be better spent in saving the souls of the French in the lands to the north. You will find no truer Christians than the citizens of Occitania. We trouble no one and are better fed and more cultured than any in Europe, save perhaps for Venice and Rome. Our language and our literature have become synonymous with civilization. Why, even the great Lionheart, the king of England, and his mother, Eleanor of Aquitaine, preferred to converse in Occitan."

The legate started to protest, but Raymond-Roger was not ready to yield the floor. "The people of Occitania love God and read the scriptures more regularly than you will find in any other land. I'll wager you they can debate the scriptures with any man. Or woman," he added with a nod to his sister.

The passion in his words built as he spoke. "You will find no people more tolerant than those of Occitania. Why would the Church of Rome want to send emissaries to save their souls? Are their souls not already more pure than those of the French, the English, and the Germans, who butcher each other while claiming to follow Christ? They have no culture other than that of the sword. Go save their souls, legate, and hold up Occitania as a shining example to be followed by others."

Pierre de Castelnau looked at him respectfully and paused to allow the power of his words to dissipate. "Raymond-Roger, most eloquently spoken, as usual. I value your words, for I know you to be a true Christian and a great soldier of the cross. Your distinguished service in the crusade under King Philippe-Auguste of France to the Holy Land in 1190 is an example to us all. Your triumph over the infidels at Acre is also a legend that will never be forgotten. You fought valiantly against those who reject our Savior and the cross on which he died for our sins. I would ask you to join us again in the same cause."

Raymond-Roger set his rebec on the table and looked around at the guests. He held his arms outstretched. "Good legate, I see no Saracens in Occitania threatening to tear down our places of worship. I see most people diligently studying the Bible, not the Koran. It is true we tolerate a few heathens in our lands and allow them to worship as they please, but that should not threaten the faith of a true Christian."

"Raymond-Roger, it is not the heathens in your lands the pope most grieves over, though he is greatly troubled their presence will corrupt the souls of innocents whose faith may be weaker than yours. For that reason, he commands all the heathens convert or be expelled from your lands without delay. What concerns the pope the most, however, is the distortion of Christianity that has infected many of the faithful in your region from the humblest shepherd to even the royal houses of this land." Pierre de Castelnau paused to look accusingly around the room. "Even some of our own clergy have been infected with this pestilence," he proclaimed with dread in his tone.

"Those who have been infected have renounced the cross and no longer accept that Jesus died on it to save all our souls. In subscribing to such blasphemy, they have become as heathen and lost to God as any Saracen. The tradition of Occitan tolerance has blinded you to this disease as it has spread among you. The disease I speak of is Catharism!" he thundered, causing his companion Raoul de Fontfroide to make the sign of the cross.

When reaction to his words had died down, my uncle, Pierre-Roger, rose to restore calm. "My dear friar, I know of no one in these lands who calls himself a Cathar. It is true some among us call themselves Good Christians, but in large part, they are well loved, honest, and less corrupt than most who profess to be Catholic. They bring honor and respect to the practice of Christianity when others bring disrepute."

"Pierre-Roger, you play with words. I have heard where your sympathies lie. Do not jest with me. Those who call themselves Good Christians or Friends of God are heretics in the service of the Devil, and they must be excised from your society as a bad apple is removed from the barrel. They have no right to call themselves Christians for they do not follow the path of Christ."

Esclarmonde looked angered and stood. "Legate, you surely have heard the same about your priests. They say it is the Church of Rome that has become corrupt and no longer follows the path of Christ. They say it is they who have remained faithful to the teachings of the gospels while the Catholic Church has been lost to the Devil."

"That is the vilest of heresies," screamed Raoul de Fontfroide, his voice shaking. "You shall be excommunicated."

Pierre de Castelnau waved his hand restore calm. "My brother is right. Such accusations are the purest heresy and warrant immediate excommunication. However, on this occasion, I shall assume you do not subscribe to such falsehoods and cite them only to test my faith and to strengthen yours with my response. I would answer these accusations simply by reminding you we are guided by God's representative on earth, Pope Innocent. Since he is guided by the Creator himself, his word is infallible. Hence, the Church of Rome cannot stray from the path of righteousness. The words of the Cathars are clever, for they are from the mouth of the Devil, who tries eternally to turn us from serving God."

Esclarmonde shook her head in rebuke. "Legate, it is hard for many here to keep faith in the church when most its servants lead their lives in the gutter."

"Your priests are the worst debauchers in the town," bellowed Raymond-Roger to shouts of load approval. "None of them works for a living, and most are completely worthless. They gamble, are drunk most of the time, and fornicate with man and beast."

"Yet the church demands that the poor who labor in the fields from dawn to dusk must tithe to support them," Esclarmonde added.

A mounting swell of approval for their words could be heard among the guests. As it died down, Pierre de Castelnau prepared to speak, but Raymond-Roger was not ready to yield the floor. He had more words of vitriol to impart to the representatives of the Church of Rome. "The Good Christians who preach to us, whom you call Cathars, could not be more different from the lecherous parasites that constitute the Catholic clergy. They live and work among us and do not expect to be kept by another's labor. Their morals are above reproach. They do not lie, steal, or rape our sons and daughters. The church named them Cathars to denote they were 'pure' heretics, yet their lives are such an example of piety that most now take it to refer to their purity."

"It is the souls of your clergy you should have come here to save," cried Esclarmonde, "not those whose lives are unblemished by sin."

The legate spoke. "Some of what you say is true. I concede that the state of moral decay of some of our clergy may have encouraged the spread of the heresy. The church will take care of any problems in its own family, but such problems do not excuse the illness we have been sent here to cure."

"How do you propose to cure this illness?" my father asked.

"The pope has just reconfirmed me as first inquisitor. In this role, I shall seek out those who have been corrupted by the heresy. Since God is merciful, I shall save their souls by reminding them the only path to salvation is through our Lord Jesus Christ and his apostolic descendants, the Church of Rome."

"And if they are not repentant?" demanded Esclarmonde. "Will you tie them to a stake, even women and children, and burn them as they did in Vézelay? Is that how you will seek to show the people the mercy of your God?"

Pierre de Castelnau's expression soured. "If their souls are lost to the Devil and cannot be reclaimed, then regrettably, they will have to be destroyed. If not, they will remain a threat to all the faithful. The Cathars were declared heretics by the Third Lateran Council in 1184. This ruling was recently confirmed by the Catholic Council of Montpellier. As heretics, they are an anathema and are to be excommunicated from the church and from all interaction with the faithful. Any man giving them shelter or who does not reveal their heresy to the ecclesiastical authorities is likewise subject to excommunication. If any noble does not aggressively extirpate known heretics from among his vassals, he is to be dispossessed of his estates, and no man will owe him homage."

"Praise be to the Father, the Son, and the Holy Ghost," added Raoul de Fontfroide for good measure, crossing himself again.

"My fealty is to Raymond VI, as is everyone's here," boomed Raymond-Roger. "I do not take my orders from a young upstart in Rome."

While many heads nodded in agreement, Pierre de Castelnau smiled derisively. "Ultimately, we all take our orders from Rome. We are on our way to visit Raymond VI with a message from the pope. The pontiff is very unhappy with the progress Raymond has been making to suppress the heresy and urges that much stronger measures be taken immediately. I think you can anticipate that very soon these too will be your orders." He was gloating.

My uncle looked very unhappy. "Honorable legates, much as we appreciate your visit, this is a family occasion, not one of state, so if you have finished your business, I ask you leave for Toulouse without delay. You still have a long journey, and the sun is sinking."

Pierre and Raoul bowed politely if insincerely and walked from the hall.

For the rest of the evening, people talked of nothing but the threat of an upcoming conflict with the Church of Rome. The event that they had come to celebrate, my betrothal to Corba, was close to forgotten.

The next day, my uncle, Pierre-Roger, moved by the prior evening's events, ordered that all young men must rededicate themselves to perfecting their skills in warfare.

1203, Late Autumn – Castle of Toulouse

Count Raymond was forty-six, and had succeeded to the title of count of Toulouse only ten years earlier. He had numerous other titles, including duke of Narbonne; count of Quercy, Rouergue, Saint-Gilles and Agen; marquis of Provence; and count of Melgueil, but his overlordship of Toulouse, Béziers, Carcassonne, and the county of Foix consumed most of his time. With so many familial obligations, he had not found it easy to govern. His mother, Constance, was a daughter of the king of France, which made him a cousin of the current King Philippe II. He had been married five times, once to Jeanne, the sister of King John of England, which made him a son-in-law of Henry II and Eleanor of Aquitaine and brother-in-law to the late Richard the Lionheart and the current King John. Currently, he was married to Eleonor, sister of King Pedro II d'Aragón, to whom he also owed allegiance. Since most of his relatives were constantly fighting each other, it was impossible to keep them all happy at once and very difficult to not be seen taking sides in their disputes.

Raymond had never much cared for warfare. It was not an option that would serve him well since his potential adversaries had much larger armies than he could muster. He had survived by diplomacy, by convincing those to whom he had obligations that it was in their best interest to leave him and Occitania to prosper. He had mastered the art of communication rather than swordsmanship. The policy had worked well. At least until now.

Increasingly, however, the very success of Occitania was threatening to be its own undoing. Spared from the ravages of war that had bled the other areas of Europe, Occitania had become one of the wealthiest lands in Christendom. Its inhabitants were literate and cultivated. They had developed the arts of literature, poetry, and music to levels never achieved before. Their tolerance of other people and their religions existed nowhere else on the continent and had brought them great benefit. Catholic, Cathar, Jew, and Moslem worked together without fear of persecution, and the country's access to Mediterranean ports had brought them great prosperity. Occitania had become a significant power in international trade; Raymond hoped one day it might supplant even Venice.

Other differences also distinguished Occitania from its neighbors. Occitania had long had a strict policy of delegating public office only to those who were most qualified, which even extended to allowing Jews to run town councils. As a result, Occitan society was well and efficiently run, and the policy enjoyed widespread support among the people, who benefitted greatly from it. In contrast, in the rest of Europe and the Church of Rome, corruption was widespread, institutionalized. Appointments were bought and sold; people were appointed to positions of authority based solely on their connections to powerful relatives and friends.

The great success of Occitan society had been a blessing to Raymond and a source of great pride for all Occitanians. It had only been recently that Raymond had begun to realize there might be a terrible price to pay for it. Others looked increasingly envious at the wealth of Occitania, and he was finding it increasingly difficult to rely solely on the arts of diplomacy.

To compound these dangers, a new young pope in Rome had dangerous pretensions. He had announced he wanted to expand his spiritual dominion to the temporal one, claiming kings and clergy alike should owe homage to him. It was a dangerous new concept, one that put fear into Count Raymond.

Raymond was signing papers when his squire walked in. "My Lord, two legates from the pope arrived last night. They are demanding an audience with you."

Raymond shrugged. "I suppose I must see them. Tell them I will see them after my midday prayers. That should make me sound suitably pious."

"But my Lord, they demand to see you immediately."

"They will have to wait. I am not one of their sheep to be ordered around."

"No, my Lord. I will tell them you are preoccupied with matters of state."

"Leave out my comment about the sheep. I cannot afford to vex them too much."

Raymond knew he was playing a dangerous game. The pope would be a powerful enemy, one he did not need with all his other difficult relationships, but the church could take it as a sign of weakness if he submitted too readily.

On the first stroke of the midday hour, the legates appeared promptly at his audience chamber. His squire announced them. "Pierre de Castelnau and Raoul de Fontfroide of the Abbey of Fontfroide, legates of his holiness."

"Greetings, my brothers," Count Raymond said. "I am told you are just back from Rome. How is our new pope? Well, I trust?"

"His eminence is extremely well, thank you. He said to tell you he remembers you in his prayers and sends you his blessings. He hopes your reign will be long and peaceful and dedicated to the service of God," recited Pierre de Castelnau as if reading a script.

"I am glad to hear that. I shall certainly sleep more soundly knowing the pope is praying for me. Please tell the holy father the lands of Occitania under my protection have no serious disputes with our neighbors, so I see no reason why peace cannot endure in the region as he wishes."

The friars looked at each other and at the ground.

"Archdeacon, I sense some hesitation. Is this just a visit of protocol, or do you have other business with me? If so, speak promptly, for I have much to do."

Pierre de Castelnau raised his shaved head. His expression was cold. "Count, the pope is greatly troubled by the Cathar heresy that has taken hold among your subjects. He is concerned for their souls and commands you to suppress it without delay."

"I have tried to suppress it since I took office," protested Raymond. "It is a difficult task, and I am not alone. There is heresy in all kingdoms. We are no different."

"The heresy is strongest in Occitania, and it is growing faster here than elsewhere. If you do not take urgent measures to suppress it, in addition to the souls lost here, it risks spreading outside your domains to corrupt many thousands of others across Christendom. It is a contagion wrought by the Devil that must be extinguished aggressively, just as a fire in the forest must be extinguished or it risks burning down the entire forest."

"What more would he have me do?" asked Raymond. "I have tried to set an example to my people. I take Mass every day, I confess, and I frequently attend services in the cathedral to encourage others to take their religious devotions equally seriously."

"Your piousness is commendable, Count, but unfortunately, it is insufficient for the task you face. The pope commands that you commit yourself totally and wholeheartedly to eliminating the heresy. You are to actively seek out heretics and make them abjure their false ways. They must be forced to recommit themselves to the cross."

Raymond looked at him in disbelief. "And what if they will not? I am certain many will not. What then? The Cathar elect, Good Christians, they call themselves, have promised never to abjure their faith even in the face of death."

"Then death must be theirs," declared Pierre de Castelnau. "For if their souls are already lost to Satan, they are already dead. Destroying what remains of their mortal shells is necessary to prevent others from being infected."

Raymond felt outrage. "You would have me burn these people?" he screamed. "How can you ask me to do that? As a Christian, I cannot. The heretics you speak of are all good people. They study the Bible and can quote it verse by verse, better than most of your priests. They faithfully try to follow the teachings of Jesus, and yet you say they are not Christian. They do not lie, steal, kill, or cheat. They live in obedience to the commandments brought down to us by Moses. I wish all my people upheld such high moral standards."

"The Devil is cunning. He is an expert in the art of temptation, which he has been perfecting since God created man. He deceives you into believing these Cathars are Christians when they are clearly imposters. A Christian must submit to the sign of the cross and acknowledge Jesus died on it to redeem our sins. They must accept that the pope is God's sole representative on earth and that his word is the word of God, thus infallible. They must accept the Eucharist, infant baptism, and all the sacraments. Yet the Cathars reject all these things. Therefore, their claim to be Christian is false."

"Doctrinal differences do not make them unchristian. Surely, those who follow Christ cannot be called heathens. Would it not be better to resolve your differences with them by debate rather than by bloodshed?"

"Those who do not accept Christ as their Savior and the Son of God cannot call themselves Christian," insisted Pierre de Castelnau with a venomous tongue. "We have tried to correct the error of their reasoning, but Satan has poisoned their minds to God's message. The Bible tells us, 'If any man love not the Lord Jesus Christ, let him be Anathema Maranatha.' Even the gospel of John, which these Cathars have taken as their own, declares, 'He that believeth not is condemned already, because he hath not believed in the name of the only begotten Son of God.' Thus they are condemned by God himself."

"But they do hold true to the teachings of Jesus more faithfully than most of their Catholic brethren. I beg of you, do not give up hope of reconciliation. If you pursue this course, it can result only in terrible tragedy and much bloodshed. Cathar beliefs are widespread in Occitania. They are not held by a sect I can easily suppress or expel. They are dispersed among even the most devout Roman Catholic families. If you demand people turn against those with Cathar sympathies, you will be calling them to civil war."

"Heretics are to be rejected since they are subverted, and sinneth, and condemned by God," recited Raoul de Fontfroide from the scriptures.

"These words attest even more to the seriousness of the situation," asserted Pierre de Castelnau. "With these words, you admit the heresy has already spread its roots deep into Occitan society, where it is poisoning the soil of humanity. It must be uprooted now before all the good that remains has been choked out of existence by its pestilence. If some of God's faithful are also destroyed, it is a small price to pay, and the Father will reward them in heaven for their sacrifice. God did not hesitate to destroy Sodom and Gomorrah when he learned their people were beyond redemption. You too must be equally committed to routing out this evil."

Raymond was despondent. He felt himself tremble, whether from anger or fear he was not certain. This young upstart of a pope with his lust for power and his pompous self-righteous zealots was threatening to destroy everything he had worked for. He could not persecute his friends, neighbors, and relatives or watch them burned alive to satisfy the megalomaniacal ambitions of that Roman tyrant, but what was he to do? The Occitan forces were weak. They had devoted few resources to the art of warfare for many years. It was imperative he avoid an open conflict with the church. All he could do was play for time.

"Honorable legates, please tell the pope his message is clear. I will take more-aggressive measures to eliminate heresy from my lands as he demands. He has my word."

"Count, his holiness will be pleased to hear that. The pope has also asked me to organize a crusade against the Cathar error and requests you join it. Shall I tell him you agree to this?" asked Pierre de Castelnau.

Raymond hesitated. "No, I cannot join a crusade at this time. Bloodshed is not the way we settle disputes in Occitania. There are other measures I prefer to try first."

Pierre de Castelnau scowled. "Count, I warn you that if these measures do not quickly begin to suppress the heresy and that if you refuse to join the crusade, you risk being excommunicated. All your vassals, all your subjects will be freed from their vows of allegiance and you will be dispossessed of your lands."

"How dare you threaten me! I will take care of this problem in my own way. I have promised you that. Now leave before I have you thrown into the dungeons to rot."

Pierre de Castelnau remained defiant. "We are leaving. We go to Béziers to prepare the crusade. I pray for your sake it will not be necessary."

Pierre de Castelnau and Raoul de Fontfroide pulled their habits over their heads. They left the hall, leaving Raymond to ponder what he would do next. He would need an ally if he was to be plunged into a dispute with the church. It did not take him long to decide whom that would be. He would call for help from his brother-in-law and his most important overlord, King Pedro II d'Aragón, a renowned, powerful knight held in great respect throughout Christendom.

CHAPTER 23

The Problem of the Heresy

1203, December – Rome, Palace of the Vatican

Lotario di Segni was still very young by papal standards. Elected Pope Innocent III in January 1198 at age thirty-eight, he was filled with ambition. Coming from a long line of popes, he viewed the papacy as his birthright. He had no doubt of the mission God intended for him. He would extend the power of the papacy in all matters, spiritual and temporal, over common man and nobility alike. It had long been accepted that the pope spoke for God in all matters that were spiritual, but he had had a revelation. If the pope was God's representative on earth, since God was the king of kings, the pope must also be recognized as the king of kings in all temporal matters. Therefore, he would seek to force all to recognize that the papacy was the ultimate power in the feudal system. He would force the monarchs to acknowledge they held authority only by virtue of God's grace.

To Lotario, the concept of *imperium mundi*, "emperor of the world," seemed such an indisputable truth that he was growing frustrated by the reluctance of several monarchs to submit to his authority. Philippe-Auguste, the king of France; John, the king of England; and the Germanic emperor were all recalcitrant. He was determined not to back down, for to do so would be to deny God's authority over man. He would hold the threat of excommunication over their heads to force their submission. It was a heavy sanction. Once excommunicated, no serf or vassal would be required to honor his oath of allegiance to the monarch. Thus, the king would lose all authority over his subjects. It was, therefore, a powerful negotiating tool, as intimidating as the armies at the disposal of his opponents.

One of the servants was clearing the pope's breakfast away when Cardinal Marcellini entered to review the pope's appointments for the day and brief him on any news.

"Ah, Cardinal Marcellini, what news of the crusade?"

"Nothing good, I'm afraid, your Eminence. The crusaders continue to give siege to Constantinople, but they have not yet taken it. The reports are that they continue to bombard it relentlessly and that much of it is in flames."

"What can Cardinal Capuano be doing?" the pope shouted. "I ordered him to warn the crusaders not to attack Zara and Constantinople under threat of excommunication. They are Christian cities. I organized this fourth crusade to free the Holy Land from the infidels, not to spill the blood of fellow Christians. The liberation of Jerusalem was to be the glorious beginning of my pontificate. It has turned into a murderous venture of opportunism."

"I fear that it is the fault of the Venetians, your Eminence. The crusaders could not pay them the eighty-five thousand silver marks, the price agreed to for preparing the ships, so they forced them to do their bidding. The Venetians care nothing for saving the Holy Land. They see only the riches of Constantinople, which they seek to plunder."

"But the crusaders wear the sign of the cross. To kill another Christian is sacrilege. Venetians and crusaders alike, they are all excommunicated. Issue the bull immediately. I will not have them doing this abomination in my name."

"Very well, your Eminence."

"Now to other matters. What do I have this morning?"

"Abbot Arnaud Amaury, from the abbey of Fondfroide at Citeaux near Narbonne in Occitania, is here to see you. He wishes to discuss the growing heresy in the region."

"Ah yes, I summoned him. I sent two legates to demand that the count of Toulouse extirpate these Cathar Devil worshippers with the utmost vigor, yet I hear that the heresy is spreading. I want to hear a firsthand account of the problem. I cannot allow this challenge to the Church of

Rome and my authority as pope, to fester and grow. Send him in. Oh, and bring us some wine, for I am sure he must be thirsty after so long a journey."

Amaury was middle aged, bald, and overweight. In the white robe of his monk's habit under a dark-blue outer robe, he did not look impressive, thought Innocent. Yet he knew otherwise. He had heard reports that this abbot was of stern resolve, a man of action, not words. He was also said to be very ambitious, which could be useful, though it also carried its own risks. Men of ambition were rarely troubled by their consciences and could therefore be depended upon to perform whatever tasks serve their self-interest, the pope thought. Innocent was in need of such men with so many challenges to his authority, but he had to be careful not to create another.

"My dear Abbot, welcome. Pray be seated," Innocent said, gesturing to one of the sumptuous chairs covered in white silk with gold embroidery. "Tell me what has become of my two legates to your region. I have had no news recently. Does the heresy persist?"

The abbot frowned; the wrinkles in his countenance grew deeper. "Holy Father, it saddens me to tell you the heresy persists. In fact, it grows worse. Many of our clergy are penniless and forced to beg as the people refuse to pay their tithes."

Innocent was displeased. He unconsciously began turning one of the large gold rings on his fingers in frustration. "And what of my legates Pierre de Castelnau and Raoul de Fontfroide from your abbey?" he asked impatiently. "I sent them there to organize a crusade against the heresy. What are they doing?"

"They are trying to carry out your wishes, Holy Father, but the situation is very difficult. I fear the church has waited too long to act. The Cathar poison is now deeply implanted throughout the region, even among the nobility and some of the clergy. Pierre de Castelnau visited all the bishops to instruct them to preach vehemently against the heresy. He warned them they would be suspended if they did not threaten anyone suspected of subscribing to the heresy with excommunication, but it was to no avail. They do not heed his counsel."

Innocent's blood boiled. "Will no one do what I command? First the kings, then the crusaders, and now my clergy! Damn them all! How dare they defy the word of God? For my words are his. I am simply his meager servant charged to do his bidding."

"Yes, your Excellency. No one should doubt that," declared Arnaud in as fawning a manner as possible. The abbot bowed his head and clasped his hands as if he were begging the pontiff for redemption. "They sin when they do not do your bidding."

The pontiff was somewhat assuaged by his act of submission. He stood and paced the floor to collect his thoughts. "And the clergy shall burn in hell alongside the heretics they protect. For God demands they cast them out. The Bible says of those who worship the false God, 'Thou shalt not hearken unto him; neither shall thine eye pity him, neither shalt thou spare, neither shalt thou conceal him: But thou shalt surely kill him.' Why would they risk their eternal souls to protect these sinners?" he cried out.

Bishop Amaury maintained his pose of contriteness. "Holy Father, I am afraid we cannot depend on the faith of any in the region, even those who profess to belong to the Church of Rome. For those people have no respect for the moral code of a civilized society. They still strive to live by the laws of Charlemagne and a social code that is an abomination, a contradiction of what we know from the Bible is the natural law. In their language, it is called *paratge*, which roughly translated means 'parity.' It calls for all men and women, rich and poor, Christian and non-Christian, to be treated as equals."

"But that is against God's law! It is an abomination to treat a heathen as one who has entered the body of Christ!" Innocent screamed.

"It is, your Eminence. All true Christians know that is blasphemy. Their transgressions know no bounds. They are inspired by the Devil. If it were just the peasants who had erred, the problem might be more easily treatable, but most of the nobility live by these false doctrines also. They do not enforce serfdom. They treat Jews and infidels as equals to Christians, and they even delegate their authority to elected assemblies. Worse still, they allow women to hold office and to preach the gospels."

Innocent walked over to the lead-glass window to look into the courtyard below. It was raining hard. "God is crying to hear such words." He turned to the abbot. "The woman shall not wear that which pertaineth unto a man, neither shall a man put on a woman's garment: for all that do so are abomination unto the Lord thy God," quoted Innocent. "What you tell me is an abomination against God. We have allowed Satan too much freedom to do his work. These evil ideas must be expunged without mercy or they risk to threaten the very order God has decreed for man."

Amaury nodded. "I agree, your Grace, but they mock those we have sent to restore God's rightful order. The Occitan troubadours roam the kingdom entertaining people with their poems and songs that revile the clergy and those who do God's work. They travel beyond their borders to all the courts of Europe to spread their contempt for the church and even yourself. Many are nobles, and some are even women. Our ability in the region to suppress this heresy becomes more impossible by the day. If we do not take aggressive measures immediately, the entire region will be lost to the church and their souls with them. Much of the population no longer tithes and laughs at the threat of excommunication. Even our abbey grows short of wine and meat. The villagers no longer come to us for confession."

Pope Innocent adjusted his robes. "Brother Abbot, I thank you for coming to tell me this. I had not appreciated just how grave the situation had become in Occitania. It angers me to think that we have allowed Satan to get such a strong foothold in the region."

"I am grateful to you for permitting me the audience, your Eminence."

"How would you advise we suppress this heresy and bring the population back to the church?" asked Innocent. "Should I send missionaries to reclaim these lost souls, or should we slay every heretic until the rivers of Occitania run blood-red like wine?"

"I fear the error runs too deep to be uprooted by preaching. We tried tirelessly. Our monks gave numerous sermons throughout the region to point out the fallacies of Catharism and to warn the people that to save their souls they must return to the only true church. Sadly, they were met only with hatred and derision. In many places, the populace complained that our sermons were in Latin or French and refused to listen if we did not address them in Occitan, a language most of our clergy are unfamiliar with."

"Have they no respect for the word of God? To speak the word of God in Occitan would be sacrilegious. Latin is the only language fit for the holy scriptures."

"Yet the Cathar priests have translated the Bible into Occitan, and they distribute these 'bibles' among the people for them to read on their own."

"They compound one heresy with another," Innocent said. "Are there no limits to this blasphemy? It is a crime against the Creator to translate his word into so base a language as Occitan, and it is double the heresy for a serf to own a Bible. Without a priest for guidance, the Devil can twist the word of the good book and bend it to his own ends."

"I can attest to the truth of that, your Eminence, for I have witnessed with my own eyes shepherds arguing with priests over the interpretation of the scriptures."

"This evil has gone deeper than I feared," the pope said. "It must be crushed, utterly and completely, without delay!" He banged his fist on the table. "Those who challenge the authority of the church can expect no mercy, for they seek to destroy the basis of society. The whole feudal system is threatened by this heresy."

"I could not agree with you more, Holy Father," declared the abbot with obvious delight. "I believe the Bible is clear on what we must do. The scriptures command we put on the armor of God and take a stand against the Devil's schemes."

"Abbot Amaury, I am convinced you are truly committed to cleansing this evil from your land, and I take it you are prepared to do your part."

"Holy Father, you have but to ask."

"You are a true servant of Christ. Your services will be amply rewarded."

"Doing God's work will be reward enough, your Eminence, though should the church wish to show its gratitude, I would not refuse its generosity."

"Very good. It is settled. I intend to take stern measures against these Cathar heretics. I will be satisfied with nothing less than their complete extirpation. If you are willing, I shall appoint you as my chief legate in this matter."

"Your Eminence, it would be a great honor." Amaury knelt and groveled at the pope's feet while the pope kissed the abbot's hand.

"You are to return to the region and join your brothers, Pierre de Castelnau and Raoul de Fontfroide in this mission to restore God's order to the people of Occitania. I shall expect you to report back regularly on your progress."

"I will keep you informed of each triumph against the heresy."

"Good. Now arise. What is the latest news from your brother friars?"

"It is not good, I am afraid," Amaury said, shaking his head. "They were recently preaching and attempting to organize a league against the Cathars in Béziers, an important town to the east of the region. Indulgences were offered to anyone who would take up arms against the heretics, but there were no takers. Instead, the friars were ridiculed and attacked by the inhabitants, even by those who professed to be Roman Catholic. The attacks became so violent that they feared for their lives and had to flee."

Innocent shook his head. "All men who persecute a soldier of Christ, a member of the Church of Rome, declare themselves pagans whose lives are without worth. They will feel the wrath of God if they persist in rejecting him."

Amaury smiled. "I would propose that the town of Béziers be made an example of, your Eminence. Its walls should be made to crumble like those of Jericho. It is the only way to restore respect and fear of the church in its inhabitants."

"And how far would you go to restore respect?" inquired Innocent, seeking to explore the limits to this man's commitment to the church. "Would you demolish the walls and burn everything, including its inhabitants, as did the Israelites?"

"God has often demanded that sacrifices be made to reassert the power of his word over mankind. The Church of Rome represents his will on earth, and I am prepared to do his bidding," replied the abbot without hesitation or emotion.

Excellent! thought Innocent. *Here is a man of unquestioning obedience, without reservations, and totally devoid of a conscience for his actions.* "Your devotion to the church reveals the great love you have for God and gives me confidence you will reclaim these lands lost to the Devil."

"Holy Father, I give you my word that as your legate, I shall move heaven and earth to eliminate the scourge of Catharism from the lands of Occitania."

"I do not doubt you. Go then. Begin God's work." Pope Innocent held out his hand laden with gold rings for the abbot to kiss.

Amaury rose and knelt to kiss it. "Very good, Holy Father."

The pope raised his arm. "I have one more question. I was told these Cathars are pacifists, but you say your friars had to flee Béziers to save their lives. How could that be?"

The abbot's cowl nodded gently. "It is true that the Cathar preachers, the 'Perfects,' as they are known, are pacifists and forbidden to kill man or beast. However, they have many supporters who have no such qualms. The common people, including Roman Catholics and even the nobility, often rally to their side. Several of the most revered Cathar perfects, in fact, are from noble families."

"And what of their overlord, the count of Toulouse? Where do his sympathies lie?"

The abbot paused. "I do not believe he actually practices Catharism. Certainly not openly. He professes to being a faithful Roman Catholic and accepts all the sacraments of the church. However, it is clear he does not truly love God in his heart, for he refuses to persecute the heretics. He is well aware that many of the nobles under him, his vassals, protect family members who are known Cathars or Cathar sympathizers. The viscount of Carcassonne and Béziers, the count of Foix, and the count of Mirepoix are known by all to have Cathar sympathies, yet he does not move against them. Pierre de Castelnau has implored him to do this, yet he has refused."

"Did he refuse to join a crusade of the faithful to eliminate the heresy?"

"He did, your Eminence, so Pierre de Castelnau excommunicated him. He promised to work harder to suppress the error, but so far, he has not taken any effective measures. I am convinced he will need to be replaced if we are to succeed."

"The nobles, even those outside Occitania, are much opposed to direct interference by the church in their lines of succession, so you will have to tread carefully."

"I am a patient man, your Eminence. I can wait. The time will come, and when it does, I will be ready." The lines on his face hid a smile that revealed a cold, inner satisfaction with that prospect.

"God will reward you for your patience," Innocent said. "God speed you back to Occitania." The pope made the sign of the cross over the abbot and pronounced a blessing in Latin. "Be sure to send me frequent reports of you progress against the heresy."

"I will not forget, Holy Father."

After the abbot departed, Innocent pulled the sash to summon the cardinal. He arrived, carrying the pope's appointment book with him.

"Your Excellency, your next meeting is on the hour."

"Good. That gives me time to take care of a couple of things. Abbot Amaury has told me of the deepening crisis for the church in Occitania. These Cathar heretics are becoming a serious challenge to the church. Many there have apparently stopped tithing or even attending church, and they no longer fear excommunication. Without income, the church will perish, so I have decided to act to prevent this pernicious doctrine from spreading. I intend to crush it without pity. The survival of the church depends on it."

"It is your duty to protect the church, Pontiff. Your word is God's. No one has a right to question it. The faithful will follow where you lead."

"Good. Then I will start by reinforcing the bulls against heresy. Write this down."

Cardinal Marcellini dutifully moved over to the desk in search of a quill and parchment and settled into a large, white chair trimmed with gold leaf and awaited the pontiff's words.

"First, I declare anyone found guilty of heresy will forfeit all his property to the church and will be excommunicated. Second, anyone who attempts to construe a personal view of God that conflicts with church dogma must be burned. Third, the church will issue indulgences absolving all sins to any man who takes up arms against the heretics."

Cardinal Marcellini seemed well satisfied with the bulls. "These will help to motivate the faithful, your Excellency. They shall see clearly that you speak the word of God. I shall post them immediately for all to read," he said as he blotted the ink.

"I have also appointed Abbot Amaury as my legate to the region. He will coordinate the crusade against the Cathars locally, with the other legates."

"Can he be depended upon?" asked the cardinal guardedly.

"I am convinced he will diligently pursue the heresy. However, he is a very ambitious man, so some caution must be exercised. I suspect he might even dream of becoming pontiff. My greatest concern is that he might not be patient enough to wait for me to die first," the pontiff said jokingly.

"I shall ask my sources to stay close to him then, your Excellency, and to keep me fully informed of his ambitions."

"Thank you, Cardinal."

The cardinal carefully filed the parchment in the bundle he had brought. Opening a ledger, he ran his finger down the page. "Pontiff, have you made a ruling yet on the matter presented to you last Tuesday?"

"Which one was that?"

"The monk accused of murder for persuading the girl he lay with to abort the fetus."

"Oh, yes, that case. I remember. The law is quite clear, so there was nothing for me to decide. He is not guilty."

"Not guilty?"

"Yes. She had been with child for only about two months, and the aborted fetus was said to have been a girl. Canon law clearly declares that a male fetus is not animated until forty days after conception and a female fetus not until eighty days after conception. Therefore, the fetus was not animated, so the monk cannot be found guilty of taking a life. There was no life to take."

The cardinal nodded. "I will inform his abbot of your verdict, your Eminence."

"Also be sure to tell him that the girl be must be castigated for her whoredom. She clearly tempted the monk away from his devotions to the church and thus is a tool of Satan. 'Bring her forth, and let her be burned,' was Judah's admonition for she who played the harlot. I shall let the bishop decide on what her punishment should be."

"Very good, your Excellency."

"Tell them to fetch me more wine. I have grown quite thirsty with all this talking."

After Cardinal Marcellini left, Innocent sat, took some parchment from a drawer, and dipped his quill into the inkpot. He knew it would take more than a few monks to rid Occitania of its heresy and return it to the Church of Rome and his stewardship. It would take swords and men prepared to use them, but where was he to get them?

The lands of Occitania were under the tutelage of King Pedro II d'Aragón, which lay to the south. To the north, King Philippe II of France was aggressively trying to expand his territories around Paris by doing battle mainly with the English monarch, King John. If Philippe-Auguste could be persuaded that Occitania was a richer prize and one easier to pluck, he might be turned to doing God's work for him. It would not be easy, for he and Philippe were locked in a stubborn battle of wills, but where there was mutual gain to be made, he was sure that some accommodation could be found. Innocent put his quill to the parchment and began to compose his missive.

CHAPTER 24

The Growing Threat of Conflict

I shall always remember February of 1204 as one of the happiest times of my life. Corba and I were still very young, betrothed, and deeply in love with each other and the land in which we lived. We felt very blessed as we talked of our future and recited poems of the troubadours to each other. I remember Corba playing the flute one evening as I looked out at the mountains around Mirepoix. It seemed that the sun would never set on our happiness and that time stood still. How I wish it had been so.

Corba and I were naïve. We thought only of the future and dreamed that one day the beloved culture of Occitania would spread throughout all Europe. We believed that all would share our freedoms and that our children and grandchildren would live in a world that valued learning and the arts more than bloodshed and warfare. Since then, time has made me cynical, but I do not regret our youthful naivety. They were precious moments I treasure.

Late in that month, events started to draw me into the reality of the world that was closing in around us.

1204, February – Castle of Carcassonne

It was late February, and in response to the returning warmth of the Midi sun, the wildflowers were blooming in the fields around the great castle of Carcassonne. Their rich fragrances sweetened the air that washed gently over its warm stone walls. Festooned with many colorful banners, the castle appeared to be a spectacle fit for a king, and in 1204, a king came to Carcassonne. He was the young King Pedro II d'Aragón. Barely thirty, he had already been king for eight years, though he had not yet been crowned and would not be until later that year by Pope Innocent III.

Pedro II was the overlord of Raymond VI de Toulouse, who was in turn the overlord of most of Occitania. He came at Raymond's request to heal the rift between the Catholics and the Good Christians that was threatening the peace, but it was a hopeless task.

I was with Corba when King Pedro rode in through the city gates, resplendent on his white horse. The crowds were crying out loudly for him.

"Corba, come look at the young king. See the majesty with which he rides. I have heard that he is a great warrior against the Moors," I said.

"And I have heard he is a great troubadour," she replied with admiration. "Tell me, would you rather see him sing or shed blood?"

"You cannot ask a young man such a question. Certainly, I would love to hear him sing, but I cannot forget I am also a knight of Mirepoix. I have sworn an oath to defend the kingdom. My ultimate allegiance is to King Pedro, and I do not know of any young man who does not marvel at the tales told of his battles."

"Would that they marveled at his poetry instead," she said. "My mother believes one day, people will no longer kill each other but help each other lead better lives. I would like to think our children will be born into such a world."

"Corba, your mother is a dreamer. She is a Good Christian and a kind woman who does not see the cruelty and selfishness also in man."

"My love, if there were not dreamers like her, this world would never change."

"That is true, but we shall see if the Church of Rome is ready to leave the Good Christians of Occitania to follow the Savior in their own manner. I am not optimistic."

Corba laid her head on my shoulder. She squeezed my hand. "Raymond, I hope you are wrong. Pedro is said to be a very skillful politician. Surely, they will listen to him and leave us in peace. After all, Christ was a man of peace. My mother says anyone who claims to follow him must live by his example."

"Your mother is an idealist who lives by the principles she espouses. The Catholic bishops, on the other hand, live duplicitous lives. They claim to follow the path of Christ when the only path they follow is one of self-interest. The Good Christians and the believers who follow them refuse to tithe to the church and refuse to recognize the pope as their spiritual superior. They are chasms apart. Even the greatest diplomat in Christendom would be challenged to persuade the Catholic clergy to give up their income and power. If they cannot reach an accommodation, I fear there could be dangerous times ahead for all of us."

A profound sadness overcame Corba. "I do not like to think about it," she murmured. "I will pray to the Good God to protect us."

As I feared, the conference broke up in disagreement after two days of vitriol. The Catholic bishops demanded nothing short of a total submission by the Good Christians to the will of the Church of Rome and a complete cessation of their heretical teachings. They demanded that all those who refused to renounce their erroneous beliefs be burned at the stake. Reluctantly, King Pedro admitted defeat and returned to Aragón. Corba and I returned to Mirepoix. The next day, I had an unexpected meeting that profoundly changed the course of my life.

1204, February – Castle of Mirepoix

"Raymond," Corba called out excitedly, "I have brought you some visitors."

I saw our mothers and two men dressed in long, dark-blue robes. Their attire left me in no doubt they were Friends of God, Good Men, or as the Catholics called them, perfects of the heretical Cathar Church. "Mother and Marquèse, this is an unexpected pleasure. To what do I owe this honor?"

My mother smiled politely, but her expression could not hide the seriousness of her mood. "Raymond, I would like you to meet Raymond Blasco. He is a Good Christian and a deacon of the church. This is Raymond de Mirepoix, who is also a Good Christian. We have come to ask you a favor."

"A favor? What can I possibly have that could be so important? Why did you not just send Corba? She knows the way to my heart."

Corba blushed. My mother straightened up. "It concerns your inheritance and future responsibilities. I could not burden Corba with making the request I am about to make."

"Mother, if you need anything, you have only to ask. You know that."

"I do, my son, but I had hoped we would not have to involve you in this. Now, I regret I see no alternative."

Deacon Blasco said, "My Lord, there is a castle high on the pog above the village of Montségur. I believe you are familiar with it."

"Yes. I have ridden by it many times, though I have never ventured to climb up the steep sides of the pog. The castle is abandoned. I have watched eagles on its walls looking into the valley for prey."

"That is true. The castle has been abandoned for some time," said my mother. "But it has been in my family, the Péreille family, for generations. As the firstborn, your brother Arnaud-Roger will inherit the lands and title of your father, Lord of Mirepoix, but as the second born, you have taken my name and will inherit my possessions. Thus, the castle and the title of Lord of Montségur will belong to you."

"You have told me about my inheritance since I was a little boy, mother. I promise I shall do my best to be a good steward for all the land and people you give to my charge. The Péreille family name has always been respected, and I shall not let you down."

My mother clutched my hand. "I have never doubted it, my son."

"But why do you come to me now to raise these matters? And why do you talk of Montségur? Surely a dilapidated castle is of little importance."

Deacon Blasco looked at me from under his hood. His expression was calm and kind, yet his eyes seemed to look deep into my soul. "Today, the castle is of little importance, my Lord. But in the future, it might be all we have to preserve the freedoms we have been blessed with in these lands for so many years."

I did not fully comprehend the meaning of his words. I looked to my mother.

"Raymond, the castle is in a near-impregnable location. It is not called Montségur, 'the safe mountain,' without reason. If you were to restore its fortifications, it could become a place of safety for many who are persecuted. We might need to live there ourselves."

"In Montségur? Why would we need to go there for safety? Surely we can continue to live in Mirepoix, or Foix, or even Toulouse."

"I hope that is the case, but the rumors are growing of a conflict that could put us all in danger. If we are to be prepared for it, we must begin now."

"Is this a result of the failed talks in Carcassonne?" I asked.

"Yes," replied Deacon Blasco. "I am afraid the debates with the Roman Catholics did not go well. We tried to reason with them. We had hoped to persuade them to leave Occitania in peace, but their minds have been poisoned by Satan's great disciple, Pope Innocent. They would not listen. We fear they are even more resolved to destroy us. My Lord, we are asking you to provide sanctuary for the faithful in the fortress at Montségur."

It was not a request I had been prepared for, so I was not sure how to respond. I looked to my mother and saw her tremendous sadness. Her eyes were pleading with me for help, which grieved me greatly. Corba's mother too, the Marquèse de Lanta, was subdued but anxious in her demeanor. I knew as I contemplated my response that I did not have the strength to look into their faces and say no. My mother had given me everything, and the castle was her inheritance. In conscience, there was no way I could refuse her request. "Mother, if it is that important to you, then of course I will do as you ask. But hopefully, things will not turn out as badly as you fear, for we all worship the same God and the same Savior. We should be able to find a way to live together in peace."

"I pray you are right," she said, her eyes glazing over with tears. "But we must be prepared for the dangers in case you are not and that our fears come to pass."

Deacon Blasco nodded. "My Lord, as Friends of God, we are sworn to peace. If there is conflict, it will not be our doing. However, the more we talk with the Catholics, the clearer it becomes we do not worship the same God. We worship the Good God, the Creator of all the souls in the universe and all things immaterial. The Roman Catholics worship the Bad God, Jehovah, the Creator of all material things, which he created to separate us from our heavenly spirits. The Catholics are overwhelmed by avarice. They seek only wealth and power and care nothing for their souls. They are so obsessed by greed that they will resort to any depravity to obtain that which they lust for. The Devil has them in his iron hand."

"Surely Deacon, you cannot condemn all Catholics in such a manner," I protested. "I have many friends and family who remain Catholics and are truly good people. I would trust them with my life."

The dark-blue cowl covering the head of Raymond de Mirepoix moved slowly up and down in agreement. "What you say is true. In Occitania, we have a tradition of living in peace with our Catholic brethren. The vast majority is tolerant and understanding. They are good people, who like all true Christians aspire only to lead good lives with the hope of eternal resurrection. Unfortunately, that is not true of the Catholics beyond our region. There, the population is not so enlightened, and the Church of Rome preaches hatred and fear and spreads its lies about us. The pope and all the clergy are tools of the Devil bent on preserving their own power and privilege above all else."

"I hear your words and know the wisdom in them. Yet I hope to avoid a bloody conflict and find a way to preserve the peace."

"Blessed are the peacemakers, for they will be called sons of God," Deacon Blasco said. "You know that as true Christians, we have sworn to harm neither man nor beast even if to save the mortal shells that currently house our souls. However, the Roman Catholics ignore Christ's words and thus show themselves not to be Christians. The Church of Rome has a murderous history against those it views as a threat to its power."

My mother tried to feign a smile of reassurance, but she could not hold it. She looked as if her life depended upon my decision. I began to fear she might have been right.

"Mother, do not worry so. I promise you I shall give orders to begin work immediately on restoring the fortifications and the accommodations of the castle. Once it is livable again, anyone who requests sanctuary there will be granted that."

My mother breathed a sigh of relief. The two Good Men bowed. "My Lord," said Deacon Blasco, "may the Good God bless you. In his name we are truly thankful."

My mother smiled for the first time in a long while.

1204, March – Palais de Louvre, Paris

King Philippe II of France, or Philippe-Auguste as he preferred to be called, was only thirty-eight, yet he had been on the throne for close to twenty-four years. He had accomplished much, and he was rightfully proud of that. When his father died, his kingdom had comprised only the lands around Paris and Orléans in the center of the country, but by marriage and conquest, he had succeeded in nearly doubling the size of his domain.

Unfortunately, holding on to his lands had proven almost as difficult as winning them. King John of England, the emperor of Germany, the counts of the other regions of France, and even his own barons were continuously scheming to steal them away from him. But Philippe-Auguste did not back down from a fight. He had accompanied Richard the Lionheart on the Third Crusade to the Holy Land. It had failed and had damaged his relations with the English crown, but it had established his reputation as a respected knight of Christendom.

Philippe threw down the letter he had just received from Pope Innocent. "Damn the ambitious meddler! He is as much a thorn in my side as are my barons. Now he seeks my help in trying to disinherit my cousin Raymond VI of his lands. For all I know, he has sent the same request to Raymond, asking for his help in disinheriting me. I swear he will not stop until he has disinherited us all. Why should he expect me to help him when he continues to deny me my freedom from that awful hag I'm married to?"

"If he wants your help, make him pay, your Majesty," proposed Sir Thomas de Marly, a close friend of the king's.

The two were sitting across from each other with large mugs of ale in hand in front of a large stone fireplace. In the grate, logs blazed furiously to stave off the winter cold.

"The pope is the richest man in Europe. He can afford it," Sir Thomas said.

"Ah, but he is a stubborn bastard," countered Philippe. "I've been trying to get him to grant me a divorce from Ingeburga since I married her eleven years ago, but he steadfastly refuses. 'You are to reconcile with her,' he commands. Reconcile be damned! I've locked her up in Etampes, and she can stay there until she rots."

"Why does he not release you from your vows? Does he have a theological objection?"

"Theological be damned! No, it's all politics. This young pope is pretentious beyond his years. It's not enough for him to be God's representative on earth. He also wants to play God. He has proclaimed himself the 'king of kings' and demands we acknowledge we govern only through his good grace. Ingeburga is the sister of King Canute of Denmark. He does not want to lose his favor by siding with me against her. He refused to acknowledge my divorce even when I announced my intention to marry Agnès, a woman I deeply loved, God rest her soul," he said, crossing himself. "During our marriage, he demanded I repudiate Agnès and take back Ingeburga. The obdurate fool. The thought of it repulsed me."

"But I thought he and you had made your peace recently."

"Of sorts. He finally agreed to pronounce that Agnès' children were not bastards. Only after her death, mind you, and only to persuade me to bring back Ingeburga as my queen. When I refused, he issued an edict against me, but I warned the bishops that if any of them posted the edict, his property would be confiscated. I had to make a few examples of the bishops of Paris and Senlis, but after that, the rest quietly forgot about it. It was gratifying to demonstrate to that pompous ass in Rome that his servants were every bit as self-centered and selfish as he is. There are limits even to his power whether he speaks with the word of God or not."

"I admire your stamina. You remind the world that France is ruled by a French king from Paris, not by an Italian noble in Rome," Thomas de Marly said. "For now, it would seem the two of you are at a standoff. Unfortunately, the pope is young, so he will be around for a while. I would counsel you, therefore, to find a way to make peace with him. It would be costly to be at war for too long with the Holy See. Your enemies would exploit it."

"You are right. He is indeed young. Though believe me, that has not prevented me from praying to the Lord on more than one occasion to take him to his bosom and relieve me of him," Philippe-Auguste said with a laugh. "God has not yet answered my prayers."

"Maybe you've been praying to the wrong God," joked Thomas. "Perhaps you would have better luck with Satan."

The two laughed heartily.

"That is a wonderful idea. Maybe I'll give it a try tonight."

The two banged their glasses, but Thomas de Marly's expression turned more serious. "You know, Philippe, Occitania would be a rich prize to add to your possessions."

Philippe-Auguste reflected for a moment. "You are right. Believe me, it has not been out of my thoughts, but there are impediments."

"What could stop the great King Philippe-Auguste of France when there are lands waiting to be taken and added to his kingdom?"

"Well, first, there is John Lackland, Richard's despicable brother who now sits on his throne in England. He has his eyes on my lands. If I were to send my army to Occitania to fight for the pope, it would be the perfect opportunity for him to invade France. I must remain strong here to discourage any such ambitions."

"And what else?" asked Thomas.

"The overlord of the region, Raymond, Count of Toulouse, is my cousin. I will not scheme against him for the pope. If the pope is encouraged to believe he has the authority to dethrone a lawful king, then none of us is secure on his throne." Philippe threw some scraps of food at the dogs, which began fighting over them.

Thomas de Marly nodded. "It is true the pope considers himself the head of the feudal system. If he had his way, we might all become priests." He laughed.

"You might enjoy it, Thomas, since you like women," Philippe said, teasing Thomas. "You would make a good priest. They are the most notorious lechers in all Paris, and they drink their fill of ale, I hear."

"I cannot deny enjoying such pastimes," replied Thomas. "I just don't think I could be sanctimonious enough to become a priest."

When their amusement had died down, Thomas asked, "How do you intend to respond to the pope's demands?"

"I will have to put him off. I will tell him that I do not have any forces for his crusade but that I might consider participating in the future."

"I have an idea," Thomas said. "Why not ask some of your barons to go? It would be difficult for them to refuse you, and while they were away, it would neutralize the threat they pose to you. The fighting would weaken their armies, and any land they won would ultimately belong to you. You would win all around."

"A brilliant idea!" bellowed Philippe. "I love it. I shall do just that."

As they continued scheming, a beautiful young girl entered their chamber. She was wearing a long, dark-green, silk gown with a pearl headpiece atop long, deep-brown hair that flowed softly down her back. Philippe smiled to acknowledge her and inwardly admired how gracefully she moved. He looked at Thomas. He was clearly struck by the young woman.

The girl curtsied elegantly. "Gentlemen, I hope I am not disturbing you," she said with a charming Spanish lilt to her French.

"Not at all, my dear. It is a pleasure to see you. Allow me to introduce my very good friend Sir Thomas de Marly. Thomas, this is my daughter-in-law, Blanche de Castile."

"I am delighted to meet you," she said, nodding deferentially.

"The pleasure is mine, Princess. His majesty did not tell me how beautiful you were."

Blanche smiled but otherwise ignored the compliment and turned to the king. "Tell me, your Majesty. What important matters of state are you discussing today?"

"Oh, nothing very important." said Philippe. "We were speaking of the pope and his problems in Occitania."

"Occitania?" Blanche raised her eyebrows. "It is good for us he has problems there, is it not? While he is busy in Occitania, he will not have time to trouble us in France."

Thomas repressed a smile. "You are very astute, my Lady, but politics is not that simple. The pope always looks for others to do his work for him. He asks for our help."

"If he would use us, I would use him. All the lands from Normandy to the Mediterranean rightfully belong to the king of France. Make that your price for helping him. Swear to acknowledge him as the leader of all Christians if he swears to acknowledge you as the leader of all France," Blanche said with a seemingly innocent smile.

Philippe-Auguste marveled at his daughter-in-law's precociousness. "Blanche, your enthusiasm is admirable, but we must tread carefully. You know your uncle, John Lackland, has ambitions for our French territories. We cannot afford to show him any weakness."

"John!" she uttered contemptuously. "My uncle John is a weakling and a coward. His mother, my grandmother, Eleanor d'Aquitaine, told me so herself. His own barons despise him. We have nothing to fear from him."

"Powerful words, my Lady. I hope you are right," Thomas de Marly said, clearly impressed with the girl.

"You will see I am," she said. "Now, gentlemen, I must go. My husband needs me." Blanche picked up the sides of her long dress and strode from the room, leaving the two men lost for words. It was as if a strong gust of wind had just blown between them.

"Well, you've met my daughter-in-law. Impressive, isn't she?" boasted Philippe.

"She was quite a prize for Louis to win."

"I'll say. She is old beyond her years. She could be quite a handful for him too though, I'll warrant," de Marly said.

"She inherits that from her grandmother. She was too much for her husband Henry II to manage. Blanche's mother was also named Eleanor. She is the sister of Richard and John. I can see a lot of Richard in her too. She certainly has a lion's heart. Fortunately, there is little of her uncle John in her."

"How did you ever win her for Louis?" Thomas asked.

"It was her grandmother's doing. Eleanor is one of the most formidable women I have ever known. She was devastated by Richard's death and has little love for John, who was his father's favorite. Eleanor fears John will destroy everything she worked so hard to build. Rather than see the Plantagenet line disappear, she decided to try to unite the English and French thrones with this marriage."

"That may be, but why did John agree? That did not seem to be in his best interest."

"He still does what his mother tells him. Besides, he is weak. Even his barons plot against him, so he was anxious for a truce. I agreed to recognize him as the lawful king of England if he agreed to the marriage."

"When were they married?"

"Four years ago, on May twenty-third, 1200. The agreement John and I signed called for them to be married before the first of July. Do you know that even though Eleanor was seventy-eight, she traveled all the way to Castile, crossing the Pyrenees in a terrible winter to bring her granddaughter to France for the marriage?"

"I can see that determination in her granddaughter's eyes."

"Yes, it is there."

"She will make a fine wife for Louis. He will need a strong woman. The only pity is that I couldn't give them a better marriage ceremony."

"And why was that? Was your treasury running low?" Thomas jibed him.

"No. It was that cursed pope again. Because of his damned edict against my kingdom, all marriages, divorces, and religious ceremonies in France were and still are invalid in the eyes of the church. To prevent him from nullifying it, they had to be married at a quick ceremony on John's land in Normandy."

"How unfortunate."

"It was worse than that. When they returned to Paris, on the pope's orders, the bishop of Paris refused to allow a single bell to be rung for them. I shall never forgive him for that. I think it is because of that Blanche sank into a deep depression immediately after the marriage. Louis had to work hard to get her out of it."

"He seems to have succeeded. She looked happy enough to me."

"Yes, she is much better now, I am glad to say. Mind you, she still chastises us from time to time for being uncultured heathens in comparison to the court she was used to in Castile. She grew up with the poetry and music of the troubadours. That is probably why she would like France to acquire Occitania. If we did, she might be tempted to set up court down there," said Philippe in jest. He checked himself to wonder if there was some truth to it.

"Any sign of offspring?" asked Thomas.

"No, not yet. Give them a little more time. Blanche was only twelve on their wedding day, and Louis but thirteen. They have plenty of time. She comes from good breeding stock, though. Look at her grandmother. She sired ten."

A page entered the room and handed the king a scroll. The king broke the seal. He read it and threw it down on the table, a grim expression on his face. "Is there no good news today? Blanche will not take this well."

"What is the news, your Majesty?"

"It concerns Eleanor d'Aquitaine. I am just informed she died at Fontevraux Abbey a few days ago."

1204, April – The Palace of the Vatican, Rome

Cardinal Marcellini came running into the room. *Shuffling* might have been a more appropriate word to describe the motion of the cardinal who was no longer young. "Your Eminence! We have news of the crusade. The crusaders have taken Constantinople. They have sacked the city!"

"Sacked the city? Damn them!" Innocent said. "I warned them they would all be excommunicated if they attacked Constantinople.

The cardinal was shaking. "It appears the crusaders were unaware of your threat of excommunication. Apparently, it was not communicated to them."

Innocent looked at him in disbelief. "What do you mean, not communicated?"

"Er—"

"Speak, man! Oh, I understand. Cardinal Capuano is responsible for this. I will excommunicate him and anyone else involved. Prepare me a list."

"From the reports, I believe you are right, your Eminence. However, the Venetians gave him little choice. He had to repay the debts owed to them for furnishing the armada."

"And what of Constantinople? Is the city destroyed?"

"I am afraid so, your Eminence. According to most accounts, much of the city was set ablaze. Worse yet, holy relics, churches, and imperial tombs were plundered for their riches. Even crosses are said to have been melted down for their silver and gold."

Innocent crossed himself. "Such desecration by men bearing the sign of the cross on their chests is blasphemy. I fear we will pay a heavy price for this 'victory.'"

"I fear so also, your Eminence, for there are reports of widespread and indiscriminate killing of men, women, and children, Christian and non-Christian. By all accounts, the crusaders also raped many of the women in the city, even those in holy orders in their places of worship."

Innocent threw his hands up in horror. "This is a nightmare! The crusade was supposed to glorify my name, but now it will be a terrible stain on it. I will have to work for years to repair the damage. Is there any good at all to come of this disaster?"

"Possibly," replied Cardinal Marcellini. "The crusaders deposed the Orthodox Christian Emperor and installed Baldwin of Flanders. He owes his allegiance to the Church of Rome." The cardinal offered the pope a sealed letter. "This letter is from him to you, your Grace." Cardinal Marcellini tried to restrain himself while Innocent read it. "What does he say, Holy Father?"

"He describes the sack of the city as 'a miracle God has wrought.' We shall see what this miracle brings us, for it is not the miracle I sought. However, he does at least swear allegiance to Rome, so we may yet salvage some benefit from this sordid affair."

"Holy Father, you must also know that to show their contempt for the Byzantines, the crusaders threw out the Greek patriarch in Sancta Sophia, the Church of the Holy Wisdom, the most sacred church in all Christendom. They hacked the crosses to pieces and tore down the icons. They set a prostitute on his throne to sing lewd songs while they drank wine and pillaged. I have received many complaints about this outrage and would propose we set a Roman Catholic patriarch in place as soon as possible."

Innocent was in shock. "How can these crusaders be so debased after they swore an oath to God to use their swords to do only his work? I intend to compose a letter to the crusaders to inform them of my disgust for their actions. Instead of turning their swords on the Saracens, they have steeped them in Christian blood to gain earthly rather than heavenly riches. This time, I will charge you personally to see they receive it. Understood?"

"Yes your Eminence. What of your threat of excommunication and the crusaders' pledge to continue their pilgrimage to the Holy Land? Will you relieve them of it?"

"They have at least achieved a victory for the Latin Church over the Byzantine Empire, so I will remove the threat of excommunication for now. It is clear this must be God's will for this crusade, so we should give thanks to him for our victory. This crusade is already a spent force. We will have to organize another to free the Holy City."

"Very good, your Eminence. I will order the papal legate, Peter of Saint-Marcel, to issue a decree absolving the crusaders from having to proceed farther to fight the Moslems."

"Good. Now to other matters. Any news from our new legate to Occitania?"

"Yes, Holy Father. Arnaud Amaury is working from the Fondfroide Abbey and coordinating his efforts to fight the heresy with Pierre de Castelnau. Unfortunately, they are getting no help from the nobility there. Throughout the region, they continue to be ridiculed and driven out of town or their lives threatened if the preach against the heresy. Arnaud has begun offering indulgences to anyone who will take up arms against the Cathars, and he is requesting you to appoint a military leader to organize and lead such men in a crusade against the Albigensians."

"I have little knowledge of military matters. Tell the abbot to find a suitable candidate himself. A crusade might be the only way to eradicate these menacing heretics from Occitania, but we have just seen what can happen to a crusade that lacks a strong leader. Arnaud needs to find a true man of God, one who will put his devotion to the church above his devotion to himself."

CHAPTER 25

A Woman Loved and a Man Despised

In the summer of 1204, Corba and I were married in Mirepoix to much fanfare. It was a beautiful wedding attended by all the Occitan nobility. The Mirepoix, Péreille, and Foix families in particular turned out in full force. I remember the day being hot, but the wind was blowing, as it often does in these mountains, for I can still see Corba's hair blowing in ripples over her dress like waves on the sea. That day, we forgot all the problems that beset our region. We looked into each other's eyes and saw only our future happiness together.

For the first year or more of our marriage, we continued to live under the illusion that what my mother feared would not come to pass, that the pope was far away and had forgotten us. It was a naivety, like the shepherd who looks only at the sun and does not see the storm clouds building behind him. However, my mother's concerns continued to grow.

The rebuilding of the castle at Montségur began as I had promised. Its fortifications were supplemented, and it was stocked for a siege. It was a requirement that at the time I thought quite unnecessary, but my mother insisted. My mother also delegated supervision of the work on the castle to Esclarmonde de Foix. She was a remarkable woman, so full of energy and passion. I will never know where she found such strength. Esclarmonde had been widowed in 1200 and had long been a fervent believer in the church of the Friends of God. Since being widowed, she had devoted herself to receiving instruction to become a Good Woman whose soul would be committed entirely to the service of the Good God. In 1206, Corba and I were invited to attend her ordination.

1206, Summer – Fanjeaux

The town of Fanjeaux had been built like many towns of the Midi, for defensive reasons. It sat on a rock whose approaches could all be defended. In 1206, most of the town's inhabitants had rejected the degenerate Roman Catholic clergy and had started following the Good Christians who lived and worked among them. It was there that Esclarmonde de Foix went to receive the *Consolamentum*. After years of preparation, she had achieved the ultimate level of purity required to receive the rites of passage to the highest spiritual level of a *"perfect."*

"Greetings, my friends. I am glad you could join us," roared Esclarmonde's brother, Raymond-Roger de Foix, with a friendly slap on my back when we arrived.

"We are honored to be here," replied Corba politely. "Nice to see you again, Philippa," she added with a smile to Raymond-Roger's wife.

Philippa smiled. "Nice to see you, Corba. And a good day to you, my Lord. Your mothers are already here. It is quite a family gathering."

Corba's expression lit up. "Indeed so. Our mothers admire Esclarmonde. It would not surprise me if someday they follow in her footsteps. I have tremendous admiration for her. She is an inspiration to us all."

I shot a worried glance at Corba. "Don't you go running off and dedicating yourself to God any time soon. I still need you by my side."

Corba smiled reassuringly. "Don't worry, my love. I am not planning to do it any time soon. One day, though, who knows? I might consider it. Until then, I shall simply lead a good life and follow the path of the Good God."

"My love," I said, pulling her close, "I have never seen you be anything but good."

Corba blushed.

"Let us walk to the house of Guilhabert de Castres," Raymond-Roger said. "It is at the top of the hill with a wonderful view over the rich plain of the River Aude. To the north, you can see the Black Mountain, and to the east, you can see all the way to Carcassonne."

"I prefer to look at the snow-capped peaks of the Pyrenees from the house," Corba said. "The mere sight of them makes me feel cooler in the summer."

Raymond-Roger nodded. "She speaks truly. She knows the house well."

"Yes, my mother comes here often, and increasingly, yours too, Raymond, to receive instruction from Guilhabert and his sisters on how to better dedicate their lives to God."

"I have heard of this Guilhabert de Castres," I said. "People tell me that he is the most famous of all the Good Christians and that one day he will be the bishop of Toulouse."

"I don't doubt it," Raymond-Roger said. "He is a truly remarkable man. It is impossible not to like him. Unlike the Catholic preachers, who are indolent and lascivious leeches, he tirelessly travels around ministering equally to the poor and the highborn. If you need someone to confide in, you will find no truer friend than Guilhabert."

"It is hard to see how anyone could live up to the picture you paint of him, Raymond-Roger, though I have heard my mother describe him similarly. Let us go, for it is time I meet this living legend," I said.

"You will not be disappointed by him," Corba said.

The house of Guilhabert de Castres and his sisters impressed me by its plainness. It was built of limestone with almost no ornamentation. Inside, the only objects were the basic necessities. This was in stark contrast to the houses of the Catholic clergy I was familiar with; theirs were filled with rich tapestries, crosses of gold and silver, and chalices studded with precious stones designed to impress the mere mortals they claimed to serve. Guilhabert clearly had no interest in worldly possessions.

Besides Guilhabert and his sisters, there were other people living in the house, believers similar to Esclarmonde de Foix, who were likewise receiving instruction on how to become Good Christians. One of Guilhabert's sisters dressed in a long, black habit greeted us as we entered. Corba bowed to her three times.

"Bless us, good Lady," Corba said. Following the third bow, she said, "Pray to God for this sinner that he delivers me from an evil death and leads me to a good end."

The woman put her hands on Corba's lowered head. "May God bless you. Let him make a Good Christian out of you, and let him lead you to a good end."

"Thank you," Corba said.

The woman smiled at Raymond-Roger and me before addressing the gathering. "Today is a wonderful day we have all come to celebrate with Esclarmonde. For this day, she will dedicate herself to God and he will adopt her as one of his own. I know it brings her great happiness that you have all come to share this day with her and witness her baptism."

"I am very happy for her," declared Raymond-Roger. "It is the path she has chosen." He turned to me and with a chuckle, whispered, "I just hope God can handle her. She has the will of the Devil."

Based on appearances, Guilhabert was not an impressive man. He was stocky, especially in his dark-blue robes, and he had long, unkempt hair and a wiry beard. His well-worn sandals were open. However, it did not take long to understand why he had earned such a dedicated following. He spoke humbly and yet with great certainty. His passion and enthusiasm were infectious. It was a refreshing experience compared to the typical exchange with Catholic preachers who spoke in Latin and raised themselves on pedestals above their congregation. Guilhabert spoke in Occitan and quoted the scriptures in the same tongue so common people could understand them. The contrast could not have been more stark.

Guilhabert seemed to know more about what was going on in Occitania and with its people than even the count of Toulouse. In just our short conversation, he told me of several personal problems troubling some of the people in my charge. He brought up their problems as a caring parent would when speaking of children. It embarrassed me to realize I had been unaware of what was going on in the lives of people with whom I had grown up and interacted with daily. Yet here was someone who seemed to know every detail of their personal lives and obviously cared enough to ask. I vowed that when I returned to Mirepoix, I would be more caring of those around me.

In place of the Catholic threats of fire and eternal damnation, Guilhabert promised only eternal salvation for all and the certainty of a loving, forgiving God. It became clear to me why Esclarmonde, Corba, my mother, and many others in Occitania had chosen to follow Guilhabert's message over that of the Church of Rome.

The Consolamentum was administered to Esclarmonde by Guilhabert assisted by his sisters. Each laid hands on Esclarmonde's covered head while Guilhabert recited the sacrament. In accepting the vows of the Consolamentum, Esclarmonde acknowledged that her soul was hence free of the mortal body in which it had been imprisoned by Satan and that its cycle of birth and rebirth had ended. When her flesh died, her soul would reunite with her spirit at the side of the Creator, as would all souls in the course of time. For the remainder of her time on earth, Esclarmonde would be a walking soul already united with the Holy Spirit. She would be as an angel walking upon the earth, and as such, worldly possessions would no longer have any power over her.

After the service, I saw that Corba and our mothers were in tears. "Corba," I asked, "why are you crying? This is a happy occasion. It was what Esclarmonde desired."

"We are happy for Esclarmonde, but we are sad for ourselves," she said. "For Esclarmonde is no longer of this earth, and so we have lost a friend. I know it is selfish, but I am not yet like her and still have many faults."

I held her close. "No, my love, it is not selfish to lament over the loss of a friend, but I am sure Esclarmonde's love for you will be no less now that she is a Good Woman."

"That may be true, but as one of God's adopted children, she will now have to share her love with everyone, for that is what God demands."

"Maybe you are being just a little selfish," I teased her. "But I am sure Esclarmonde will forgive you."

Corba smiled and slapped me gently on the arm.

On the way back to the center of Fanjeaux, we heard a great commotion in the square. As we got closer, we saw a crowd huddled around a lone figure standing by the fountain. His hand was in the air as he screamed at his listeners. Some were shouting back, but most were just laughing at him.

"Who is this man?" I asked someone at the back of the crowd.

"He is Domingo de Guzmán, commonly known as Friar Dominic. He came from Spain to save us from ourselves," he said, scoffing at the idea.

We moved in closer.

"Unless you repent, you shall all perish!" screamed the friar.

The crowd responded with loud jeers.

Undeterred, the friar opened a Bible and began reading aloud. "Whoever believes in the Son has eternal life, but whoever rejects the Son will not see life, for God's wrath remains on him—"

He was interrupted by shouting. "Friar, we've read the Bible. We don't need you to read it to us," shrieked one man. "It is you who need repent, not us, for we are true believers. You are a disciple of Satan. You worship the evil one."

"That is blasphemy," the friar shouted. "The Roman Catholic Church is God's one true church. The Cathars you follow and their perfects are heretics. It is they who are Satan's disciples!"

We heard loud booing and cursing. The crowd was getting angry. One woman raised her fist at the Spaniard. "Do not speak so of the Good Christians in this town. For they walk with God. They teach us how to know the Lord, and they come to us when we are in need. They are not like your sodomizing clergy who come to us only when they are in need. Go back to Spain before we follow the example of the Bible and take you to the town gates to be stoned to death."

Her words caused loud cries of approval.

The friar was clearly starting to appreciate the delicate nature of his predicament. He adopted a less-confrontational stance. Instead of menacing his audience, he opened his arms and pleaded with them. "The holy father has sent me to show you the error of your ways as it pains him to—"

"Do not speak of the pope here," an elderly woman yelled. "For he is the Devil's whore!" She flailing her arms menacingly at the friar. "The pope is not pained by what we think. He is only pained he can no longer steal from us. He the richest man in Europe. He sits on his backside and drinks his wine from golden chalices while we labor in the fields. Where is his humility? His soul will have to suffer many more rebirths before it is cleansed enough to escape this world and rejoin the Creator."

There were loud cheers of support. Amid the din, the friar tried to resume his proselytizing, but he had lost them. They were more interested in lecturing him than being lectured to. He pulled his cowl over his head, put his Bible under his arm, and marched off.

"I am afraid of that man," said Corba, trembling. "He has been in our region for more than a year, preaching against the Friends of God and condemning them as heretics. It is said that he is not corrupt like the clergy but that he is obsessed with converting us back to the Church of Rome whatever the cost. I fear such men. If he fails in his mission, I fear what violence that could provoke in him."

"Well, maybe if we pray hard, he will be recalled to Rome or sent to another country that needs saving," I said in jest. However, it was clear from her expression she could see no frivolity in the situation. She glared at me as if to say she saw evil in the man that I could not.

"What if he remains here? The pope has already called for a holy war against us and decreed that heretics must be burned. What if there is a conflict? Which side will you be on, my love?" she asked.

I shook my head. "I do not wish to think of such things. I hope the Friends of God and the Catholics will find a way to live together. We here have such a deep tradition of tolerance that words of hatred and intolerance from preachers like that fall on deaf ears."

"But that is not the way outside our region. Good Christians have been burned alive in France, Lombardy, the Germanic States, and Flanders."

"I do not believe the count of Toulouse would permit such things to happen here, for he even has Good Men and Women in his family."

"But I hear the papal legate has threatened him with excommunication if he does not rid Occitania of all who will not swear allegiance to the Church of Rome and accept the infallibility of the pope. Pope Innocent is said to have ordered the count to dismiss all the Jews, Muslims, and other heretics in his service," Corba said.

"That will never happen," I replied with confidence. "The count could not do that or his kingdom would be ungovernable. He relies on such people to run his affairs. It is their good governance that has made Occitania wealthy."

"And that is why others envy and hate us," she insisted. Corba's expression was clearly one of anguish. "Raymond my love, if the count, as your overlord, ordered you to burn Esclarmonde for being a heretic, would you do it?"

I pulled away in horror. "You should not ask me such a question, for I cannot answer it. I have sworn an oath of fealty to my lord on my honor as a knight. Yet Esclarmonde is close to family, and I know her to be fair and gentle. I cannot give an answer to your question that does not force me to betray some of the deepest values that make me what I am. You put me in conflict with myself."

Corba continued to press, as was her nature. "I understand. That is why I ask you the question. I fear that sometime in the future, it may be one you will be forced to answer."

"I hope to God you are wrong," I replied.

We passed a shepherd bringing sheep to the market and then a weaver's shop. Corba seemed to know them all and they her.

"You are happy here, are you not, my love?"

"There is nowhere else I would rather be."

I breathed the warm air in deeply. It was fragrant from the herbs and flowers on the mountainsides. "This is a beautiful land," I said looking at the lush valley below. "Let us enjoy it while we can and put aside your worries that may never come to pass. If they do, at least we will have happy memories to treasure."

Corba smiled at me with cheeks that were rosier than usual. "You are right. We should enjoy the present. I shall not allow the pope to rob us of that, at least not yet."

"Good, and tonight, we will enjoy ourselves at Puivert. I hear a new band of troubadours has just arrived at the castle. The gossip is that they are very entertaining. They bring an amusing tale about the pope's latest disastrous crusade to the Holy Land. It seems they mistook Constantinople for Jerusalem. If the pope is that incompetent, maybe we don't have anything to fear."

"I hope you are right," said Corba, trying to sound more upbeat. "I would love to go. I have not heard any troubadours in a long time. Besides, my mother has just made me a beautiful, new, blue-silk dress. I think you will like it," she said suggestively.

"I am sure I will, but I always find you irresistible. I have no doubt you will drive all the young knights to distraction and test their code of chivalry. I am sure I will have trouble keeping my own hands off you until the party is over."

Corba elbowed me playfully. "You will just have to control yourself for a while and treat me gently, for I have some news."

"News? Something wrong?" I asked.

"No, it's nothing to worry about. I just found out … I'm pregnant!"

"Oh that is wonderful news!" I exploded with joy. "I promise I won't touch you until after the baby is born."

"That sounds a little extreme," she said teasingly. "Why don't we make tonight an exception?"

I hugged her warmly.

Puivert Castle was decked out with the flags of all the Occitanian nobility for the night's festivities. Wine and food were plentiful—wild boar from the forests, fresh fish from the sea, and exotic fruits from North Africa. Best of all, though, was the entertainment. As we ate, troubadours sang poems set to music. Many told tales of unrequited love between a lady and her knight, all sung, of course in the fair Occitan tongue. The troubadours encouraged audience participation, and there was plenty of shouting and laughter.

Some of the songs, particularly those sung by Raymond-Roger de Foix, were rather explicit and caused the women to blush. More interesting to me were the satirical accounts some gave of recent events and personalities coming from outside our blessed land. They poked fun at the French barbarians to the north and how their king, Philippe-Auguste, seemed to be at war with everyone—the German emperor, the English king, the pope, and even his own barons.

"At least with all those enemies to fight, he won't have time to trouble us," someone shouted cheerfully, raising his mug.

"I wouldn't count on that," cried another. "War is the only thing he knows. The French have no culture other than killing people. They are heathens with no appreciation for the fine arts of music, poetry, or contemplation."

As always, a recurring target of their scathing wit was Innocent III. Most dwelt on his obsession with his power and his dilemma of trying to decide whether he was God's servant or whether it was the other way around. They also mocked his recent crusade to the Holy Land and how he had been outmaneuvered by the Venetians.

"Maybe we should ally with the Venetians against the pope," a young knight said. "At least they appreciate culture."

"Yes, but I doubt you would find the taxes they would levy upon us worth the price," shouted an older man. "It would be cheaper to hire mercenaries."

Corba broke her happy news to our families and friends, and soon, everyone in the castle knew it. As we walked around after the meal and danced late into the evening, we were constantly stopped and congratulated. It was good to see Corba so happy for a change. The evening would have been perfect save for one unpleasant encounter.

"My Lord de Péreille," called out a voice from behind us. I turned and found myself face-to-face with the new bishop of Toulouse, Foulquet de Marseille. "I hear congratulations are in order for you and your lovely lady," he croaked insincerely with a forced smile.

Foulquet was not a man I much cared for, and I knew that Corba and her mother despised him. Behind the bishop stood two monks of the Cistercian order, to which he also belonged. Their faces were obscured by their cowls and tipped toward the ground as if to deny our presence. Foulquet's face was rough and unshaven, and some of his teeth were darkened from decay from overindulgence in rich food. I could smell the heavy stink of alcohol on his breath. "Thank you," I responded politely.

"We offer you our congratulations on your appointment to the bishopric." Corba nodded perfunctorily.

Foulquet looked at her dismissively for a moment, his expression clearly sending the message that a woman's opinion was of no importance to him. He turned to me. "It was certainly a great honor to be trusted with such an important position by the holy father, especially in these troubling times. I will be his humble servant and represent his needs to the best of my abilities."

I could sense Corba tensing. She could not restrain herself from speaking. "I hope you will not forget to also represent the people of Toulouse to the pope when you are next in Rome. I trust you have not forgotten you were a citizen of Occitania before you became a servant of the Church of Rome."

Foulquet scowled and turned to Corba, his eyes filled with derision and hatred. "My Lady, we are all born servants of the Church of Rome, for we were all born to serve God, and the church is his representation on earth. Unfortunately, it appears that some in this region have forgotten that truth. I hope you are not among them."

Corba hesitated before responding, "I am a true servant of God," she replied guardedly.

I was becoming very concerned of where the exchange might go, so I decided to change the subject. "Bishop Foulquet, are you enjoying the music of the troubadours? It is not so long ago that you were one yourself. Maybe you would care to sing to us?"

The bishop reluctantly turned his attention from Corba; he was a hunter forced to release its prey. "I do not have time for such triviality any more. Some of the lyrics I heard earlier I consider blasphemous or even heretical. I shall counsel those involved against repeating such offenses."

"But surely you would not begrudge us entertainment that harms no one," I said.

"Heresy is not entertainment but poison. It steals men's souls and corrupts the innocent. The pope has ordered that anyone preaching heresy shall burn at the stake. I intend to carry out those orders."

Corba turned away, no longer able to bear looking at the bishop. I felt her shiver.

"And who will decide what is heresy and what is not?" I asked.

"The Church of Rome. Whatever contradicts the teachings of the church is heresy, for the word of the church is the word of the pope, and that comes directly from God."

I decided to take the risk of probing to see whether there was any small grain of humanity left in the shell of this former troubadour.

"Bishop Foulquet, you know this has long been a tolerant region. That tolerance has helped us prosper. The vast majority are Christian, even if there are differences in how they express that. Surely, as a Christian, you would not advocate burning a fellow Christian."

"These other 'Christians' you are referring to these—Cathars—" He appeared to choke on the word, "—who plague our region are not

Christians. Only those who profess faith in the Church of Rome can be considered Christian. All others are pagans or disciples of the Devil, and they will be dealt with as all Christians are instructed by the Holy Book."

Bishop Foulquet's companions nodded. I felt Corba pull away from me to face him. I tried unsuccessfully to pull her back, fearing what she might say.

"I wonder how with so much hatred in your heart, assuming you still have one, that you dare call yourself a Christian," Corba blurted out.

The bishop turned to Corba and looked at her in the manner of a snake trying to decide where to strike. "Jesus is my Savior, and I do only his bidding," he pronounced as if delivering a sermon. "For did he not say, 'Think not that I have come to send peace on earth: I come not to send peace, but a sword.' Thus, Jesus demands we stand ready with a sword to do battle against God's enemies. I am simply his humble servant."

"You twist the savior's words to support your selfish interests and those of a church that has lost its way, for Jesus was a messenger of peace," argued Corba.

"Be careful, my Lady, for even though you are a noble, criticizing the church or its sacraments is heresy and punishable by death. You would be wise not to repeat such accusations. I would also advise you both to talk to your mothers, for they have been accused of having sympathy for the Cathars."

Corba grew even angrier at the mention of her mother. "I know no one who would go by that name," she shouted at the bishop. "It is a slanderous invention of the Church of Rome. My mother—"

"The Marquèses de Lanta and my mother are true Christians," I interrupted Corba to save her from herself. "Do not draw our mothers into your intrigues. They have only kindness in their hearts and malice toward none."

"It is for the church to judge if they are true Christians," retorted Foulquet, content at having gotten under Corba's skin. "When did each last go to confession?"

"That is a matter between them and their priests. It does not concern you. Besides, going to confession is not the ultimate test of faith. I am not an expert in the scriptures, yet even I remember Jesus advised his followers to pray in secret, where God would hear them, rather than in public as hypocrites who wish only to be seen and heard."

"The disciples knew how to talk to God, but the common man does not," the bishop said. "The church exists to help them. Through apostolic succession, Jesus granted the Church of Rome sole authority to intercede between the faithful and the heavenly Father. The pope has decreed that only confession given in the presence of a priest will be heard by God."

"Enough!" I announced. "I grow tired of this conversion. Take your hatred elsewhere, for we do not need it in our lands. You take advantage of our tolerance."

Foulquet looked at me with flames in his eyes. "It is you and witches like your mothers who take advantage of the tolerance of the church," he shouted hatefully. "You have all been offered the chance to repent. Those who do not shall be swept away. The Bible commands that all heretics are to be rejected. They are sinners, and all who consort with them will likewise be condemned by God. We shall be doing God's work. My Cistercian brothers Arnaud Amaury and Pierre de Castelnau have already begun to rid us of these sinners."

"Burning women and children at the stake is doing God's work?" Corba screamed.

"It is doing God's work if they are in the service of Satan," screamed Foulquet. "We must purge them before they pervert more innocents. The church will issue indulgences to any man who takes up arms against the heretics. My Lord de Péreille, it is still not too late for you to join us in this crusade against Satan. If you side with God, you will be allowed to keep your lands. Otherwise, the pope has declared that all the southern fiefs will be forfeit."

My anger was at the boiling point. "First, you question the faith of my family, and now you threaten me. I hold my lands under obligation to Count Raymond VI de Toulouse and in turn to King Pedro II d'Aragón, not to the pope. I will answer to them and to them alone, not to some new young upstart who has bought the papacy."

Foulquet cursed. "Raymond de Péreille, you will come to regret those words. As God is my witness, you will regret those words."

CHAPTER 26

Disaccord

The Church of Rome made no effort to rein in the abuses of its clergy. It continued to abuse and threaten the people of Occitania, leaving little doubt in most men's minds that they cared not for their eternal souls but only for wealth and power. As a result, the popularity of the preachers of the Friends of God, the Good Christians, and their message of love and tolerance continued to spread. As the Catholic pews emptied, the clergy, rather than reforming their ways, increasingly appealed to the pope for help to defend their privileged positions in society and to act more aggressively to eliminate the heresy.

In response, the pope's legates became ever more active in seeking out those who criticized the church. They traveled the region, arbitrarily arresting those upon whom suspicion had fallen and extracting "confessions" in secret by the most heinous methods. Those who refused to abjure their supposed heresy were burned at the stake.

Rather than suppress the heresy, these actions had the opposite effect. The number of Good Christians and believers continued to grow. The threat of excommunication no longer intimidated the people, so the Catholic clergy lost their source of power and income alike. For the first time in their lives, many clergy had to give up the cloth and seek an honest day's work. Some of the more moral priests even became Good Christians and joined in the fervor to spread the word of the Good God.

The pope and his legates became increasingly frustrated and angered by their failure to quell the growing uprising against their authority. They became fearful that if unchecked, it would spread to other regions beyond Occitania. In desperation, the pope called for a crusade against the Cathar heresy, a holy crusade against the Albigensians. In May 1207, the pope ratified the excommunication of Raymond VI, setting the church formally against the Occitan nobility.

Later that year, there was one last attempt to head off an all-out conflict between the church and its Occitan detractors.

1207, Summer – Pamiers

Esclarmonde de Foix, in the company of Benoît de Termes and other Good Christian leaders of the Friends of God, had come to Pamiers, a short distance from Mirepoix, to debate their differences with representatives of the Church of Rome. The Colloquy of Montréal, as it was being called, was to be one last attempt to reach a peaceful conciliation between the two churches. Esclarmonde did not hold out much hope, as it was not they who were threatening bloodshed but their adversaries. Only recently, the church had committed several acts of unrestrained, murderous savagery against them in an effort to reassert its position of wealth and power. The persecution of those accused of heresy was growing more intense by the day.

Aware of the rapidly deteriorating situation, Esclarmonde anticipated that the debate would not revolve around religious philosophy at all, which she would have preferred, but merely around self-interest. The pope had been adamant in his latest pronouncements that nothing short of a complete capitulation to his demands by the Church of the Friends of God would be acceptable. He was to be acknowledged as the king of kings in all matters spiritual and temporal. Nothing less would satisfy his megalomania.

The problem for Esclarmonde and her entourage was that they and any other Good Christians could never agree to swear allegiance to a pope or any earthly potentate. By accepting the Consolamentum, they had renounced all obligations to the material world and had sworn allegiance to the Father. Their allegiance was no longer theirs to give. There could be only one sovereign for a Good Christian, the Creator. Since they had a direct relationship with God, they had no need for any mortal to intercede on their behalf. Likewise, they could not feign such an oath as they had also committed themselves to a life of absolute truth.

The meeting thus seemed doomed from its inception, and Esclarmonde had at first planned not to attend. However, she learned the Catholic delegation would be led by Domingo de Guzmán. In stark contrast to the majority of the local Catholic clergy, in the two years he had been preaching in Occitania, he had earned a reputation for austerity and honesty comparable to that of Good Christians. He had also shown himself ready to debate to win converts back to the Catholic Church rather than merely using threats and bloodshed, the pope's approach. If there was any chance of a real debate with the Church of Rome, this was it, so she decided to take it.

The two sides sat across from one other at a long oak table. The high, vaulted ceiling was richly adorned with the flags and crests of all the noble families of Occitania. The Good Christians were dressed in their usual simple hooded robes of dark-blue and black cloth. Esclarmonde de Foix and Benoît de Termes sat at their center. Domingo de Guzmán sat opposite them and was dressed in a similarly austere fashion, mimicking their own. His head was closely shaven, and yet he had a beard. Benoît de Termes opened with a lighthearted compliment. "You dress like a Good Christian, Friar Gúzman. Maybe you are on the wrong side of the table."

"I freely admit to being a good Christian, but one who accepts that the Church of Rome is the only true church of Christ. I think I will remain where I am, thank you."

The other members of the Catholic delegation had bedecked themselves in rich garments of fine red, with gold chains and ornate sashes. Heavy gold rings adorned their fingers.

Standing around the table were supporters on both sides in the debate. Monks and clergymen had come to support their Catholic brethren, while on the other side, a much greater number of Occitanians from all levels of society had come to support the Friends of God. The gaudy dress and gold pendants of the Catholic clergy had clearly been intended to assert their superiority. However, Esclarmonde knew well that it was sure to have the opposite effect on the Occitanians and only confirm their prejudices against the church.

Benoît de Termes stood. "Welcome to Pamiers, fellow Christians. We are glad to have this opportunity to resolve our differences with the Church of Rome by debate rather than by sword."

"I too prefer the tongue to the sword," replied Dominic. "We will surely do God's work if by debate we can correct those who have erred and return them to the true path of Christ."

"That is something we can both agree on then," cried Esclarmonde to mild laughter from her supporters.

One of the bishops grimaced. "It is your fault we are all here today. Your perfects bear a heavy responsibility for leading the people of Occitania astray with your Cathar heresy. You have put their souls at risk of damnation."

"Bishop, we are neither perfects nor Cathars," Benoît de Termes shot back. "You show only your ignorance by using such terms here. They mean nothing to us. They were created by your church, your new ministry of 'propaganda,' I believe you call it, to denigrate us. Only the Father—that is, the one in heaven, not in Rome—" he said, pointing up, to howls of cheers and laughter, "—can attain perfection. Unlike some, we do not claim to be God or even infallible."

More cries of support echoed from the Occitan supporters.

The bishop's face turned the color of his robe. "To question the infallibility of the pope is the greatest of heresies, for he speaks only the word of God!" he said, to loud cries of support from the Catholic side.

Esclarmonde rose. "Where in the Bible does it say any mortal can be infallible or speak for God?" she asked, holding a Bible high. "I cannot find it in mine," she declared with humor. The Occitanians laughed. "Even Christ did not claim infallibility. In one instance, he even admitted his own witness was false."

Etienne de Metz, a follower of Domingo de Guzmán, clumsily tried to silence her. "Go to your spinning, Madame. It is not proper for you to speak in a debate of this sort."

The Occitanians erupted. "We respect our women in Occitania, unlike the Catholic Church, which treats them as whores whose only purpose is to lead man to sin," yelled one.

Dominic, showing clear signs of embarrassment, tried to restore calm. "My friend's words were well meaning but ill chosen. I am afraid he is not used to debating with women."

"Women cannot wear men's clothing and vice versa—it's an 'abomination unto the Lord,' say the scriptures," countered an unrepentant monk.

"You quote from Deuteronomy in the Old Testament," fired back one of the Good Christians. "The Old Testament is the book of Jehovah, the Bad God, the false one, the Devil. That is why you spout words of venom. The contrast between the Good God of the New Testament and that of Jehovah, the God of the Jews, is as night to day. True Christians must follow Christ and worship only the Good God of the New Testament."

Diego de Acebo, the bishop of Osma, objected strenuously. "A true Christian cannot pick and choose which passages to accept from the Bible. It is all the word of God. He must accept the God of the Old Testament as he accepts the God of the New Testament. For there is only one God, and it is he we worship in the Church of Rome."

However, the Good Christian was not backing down. "From your actions, I submit that the Church of Rome does worship only one God, but that God is not the one I worship. By its greed and murderous intent, the church has shown to all that it worships only one God, Jehovah of the Old Testament, for he is cruel, unforgiving, and hateful. The Good God whom true Christians follow and of whom Jesus spoke is loving and forgiving. Look to yourselves. The Devil has twisted you into his ways. The Church of Rome no longer cares for souls but only for the riches and power it can acquire. You have strayed from the path of Christ. Reform your church, and we will join you."

"The Church of Rome is the church of the Devil," repeated an Occitanian from the crowd to loud cries of support.

Dominic stood to speak but waited until both sides stopped screaming at each other. "The Bible is the word of God! If you call yourselves Christians, you must accept that."

"We do not!" responded Benoît de Termes with a steely coldness in his voice. "The Bible is the creation of the pagan emperor Constantine. It does not reflect the teachings of Christ and as such has nothing to do with Christianity. Therefore, we reject it, as did the majority of practicing Christians when it was forced upon them under pain of death."

The room erupted. The two sides came close to physical combat. When he could finally make himself heard, Diego de Acebo shouted over the uproar. "These accusations are absurd. The Council of Nicaea in the fourth century declared that the Bible was the true word of God. It was voted on by all the bishops present."

"Your words are true but full of deceit," countered Esclarmonde. "It was voted on by all the bishops present for the vote, but by then, their number had dwindled to less than three hundred. At the opening of the conference, there were more than two thousand bishops at the council. The vast majority supported Arius's contention that Jesus was not divine and that the world was ruled by two opposing forces, good and evil, as we continue to believe. However, the emperor threatened them and forced over seventeen hundred bishops to leave the council before the vote. Later, he butchered anyone who refused to accept the version of the Bible that he had forced through the council. The Bible you follow is thus not the word of God but the word of a pagan emperor."

The Occitanians cheered. "The pope is the new Constantine!" shouted several.

The Catholics began yelling, "Heretics, you shall all burn in hell!"

When order had been restored, Benoît de Termes stood. "The Friends of God are not the heretics. You have heard Esclarmonde's words and know them to be true. Thus it is we who remain faithful to the beliefs of the earliest Christians. It is we who reject the material world in favor of the spiritual world, as did Jesus. It is we who practice humility and dedicate our lives to helping our fellow men. It is we who obey the commandment 'Thou shalt not kill' and reject all violence, as did Christ. Tell us then, what would you have us do to be more Christian?"

There was a pause as the Catholic representatives looked at each other to see who would respond. When no clear decision could be made, several voices spoke together.

"You must recognize the pope as your spiritual leader and accept his word as infallible," cried one.

"You must accept that Christ was mortal and died for our sins and that he was not a mere spirit sent by God to speak in riddles as you teach your followers," cried another.

"We will never accept the authority of the pope over the Church of Christ. We cannot, for it would be blasphemy!" yelled a Good Christian. "The pope is a mere mortal, and like all mortals, he is impure and fallible!" he cried. "We have seen many times that the popes do not even speak the truth when they know it. They try to deceive us for their own ends as they did with the Donation of Constantine forgery. They make up passages to support their arguments and insert them into the Bible as they did with the Holy Trinity. They promulgate dogma such as infant baptism, for which there is no foundation in the Bible and which was explicitly rejected by Christ. If the popes truly spoke the word of the Good God, they would not speak such falsehoods, such blasphemies. Only a fool would believe the pope speaks only the truth, and only a greater fool would believe him infallible."

Most of the Catholic delegation started banging violently on the table. Some began chanting, "Burn them! Burn them! Burn them!"

Domingo de Guzmán tried to calm their passions, but it was becoming increasingly difficult even for him to do so. "Benoît de Termes, I fear this debate is tearing us further apart rather than bringing us together," despaired the friar. "I grieve for the future if we do not reach reconciliation here today. I have prayed ceaselessly to the Lord that we can succeed in showing you the error of your ways. I am offering you the opportunity to rejoin the Church of Rome, the church of all true Christians, and to end this heresy. If you agree to that, the pope is prepared to forgive your error, and you will be permitted to continue your dispute on doctrinal issues from within the body of the church. I beg you to see reason."

Esclarmonde stood, a picture of serenity compared to the pandemonium surrounding her. "Friar Gúzman, I respect your intent, for I truly believe you mean good. However, we cannot accept what you are offering. We do not seek forgiveness, for we do not believe we have erred. If we had, forgiveness could be obtained only from God. We have committed our lives to God and shall continue to follow him, not the pope or any mortal, who are equal in our eyes. If a condition of rejoining the Church of Rome is to accept that the word of the pope is infallible, all debate within the church is meaningless."

Benoît de Termes rounded out the words of Esclarmonde. "The pope's position seems very clear to us: 'Renounce the Father in heaven and worship me or I will destroy you.' Jesus faced the same ultimatum, and we must give the same answer he did."

Dominic shook his head despondently. "Speaking on behalf of Christ, I tell you that only slavery and death can come from this decision. Kings and peasants alike will rise up and arm to strike down this aberration of the faith you have created. Take care, for God can be merciless with those who transgress him."

One of the Good Christians stood. "Jehovah can be merciless and vindictive. There are many examples of it in the Old Testament. The Bad God created all material things and trapped men's souls in their bodies, but we no longer fear him. We have committed our souls to the Good God, the Creator of all immaterial things. Jehovah does not threaten us."

"You will burn in hell for eternity, heretic!" shouted a Catholic bishop.

"Your curses are meaningless to us, for we do not fear your hell," countered the Good Christian. "We know hell is merely the earthly existence we experience. The Devil trapped the souls of angels in physical bodies and created the material world in which to imprison them. Man's goal is to reach a sufficient level of purity so his soul can be freed from the material world and return to his spirit by the side of the Creator. After sufficient cycles of birth and rebirth, all men's souls will eventually be freed, so no one need fear eternal suffering. There is no hell other than the here and now."

Someone shouted, "Don't worry, Bishop. I'm sure that with your level of impurity, you have a lot of lives left to get it right!" Laughter erupted.

"It is the Cathars who are impure!" screamed a priest. "You do not believe in copulation between a man and a woman, as God intended. You fornicate with animals."

A Good Christian sprang to his feet. "That is a lie created by your ministry of propaganda. As Good Christians, we have forsaken all sexual relations, for we have committed the remainder of our material existence to the Creator."

"But is it not true that you condemn sex for procreation, thus sex between a man and a beast is more acceptable for you than sex between a man and a woman? Is that not what you believe?" asked Friar Dominic.

"We believe that the act of procreation traps another soul in the material world, which serves only the Devil," replied Benoît de Termes. "However, procreation must be tolerated until all men's souls have reached the level of purity that will no longer require them to be reborn. The majority of our faithful, the believers, practice procreative sex."

"It is not us who fornicate with sheep and young boys," yelled an Occitanian. "It's your priests!"

The howls of protest from the Catholic side were countered by jeers from the Occitanians.

Esclarmonde looked at Dominic from under her hood, her expression as sharp as ever. "Tell me friar, why do the Catholics practice cannibalism?"

Domingo de Guzmán looked confused, as did the rest of his delegation, who objected loudly to the accusation.

"My Lady, why do you ask such a thing? It is an abomination, a blasphemy you know is a lie. I thought as a perfect, you had taken a vow to always tell the truth, yet your own words betray you, for you know this to be false. All men here know that the Church of Rome does not practice cannibalism, nor has it ever. I had expected better from someone with your reputation."

The monks started to chant a canticle as if they were trying to ward off evil spirits Esclarmonde had brought down upon them.

"Women are Satan's whores," screamed one of them. "They exist only to tempt a man's faith and lead him into sin as Eve did Adam."

Esclarmonde remained resolute, unmoved by Dominic's words or the insults being thrown at her. "Friar Gúzman, I do speak only the truth, for at each Mass, your priests allegedly turn bread and wine into the body and blood of Christ and give it to the congregation to consume. Surely this is cannibalism. We find this concept revolting."

People cried out loudly in support of her words. A young woman yelled, "The Spanish canon should go back to his ignorant flocks in Spain!" Another cried, "He insults us by coming here to lecture us on what the Bible says when most Occitanians can recite each word of it! We have no need of a priest to interpret it for us and weave his lies into its truth."

Domingo de Guzmán tried to protest over the din, but it was no use; he could not be heard. Scuffles broke out. Benoît de Termes gestured aggressively for order.

Diego de Acebo stood with his papers under his arm, anger and hatred burning in his eyes. "I see no point in continuing this meeting!," he thundered.

"You are all beyond redemption. You are lost to the Devil. I shall tell the pope this and advise him that all our efforts now should be directed to containing the infection so it does not spread to other lands."

Benoît de Termes stood to face the bishop. In stark contrast to Diego, he appeared calm, in control of his emotions. "Pray tell the pope we are simple Christians leading ascetic lives and are dedicated to God. We do not lie, cheat, nor steal. Neither do we kill man or beast for any reason. He has no reason to fear us, for we shun wealth and power, which he seems to crave. Tell him we wish only to lead lives of peace that will prepare our souls to return to the heavenly Father when we are freed from this material world."

Domingo de Guzmán shook his head vigorously. "In the name of Christ, I warn you to reconcile with the church, or face your own destruction. I shudder for what you have set in motion this day. I beg you to change your ways. I have prayed for you, yet you have rejected all my entreaties. You ask for peace, but you will not find it on the path you have chosen. May the Lord be merciful upon you, though I fear he will not."

The delegations rose and filed out. After they had left, arguments between the followers of both camps continued long into the afternoon.

CHAPTER 27

The Die Is Cast

The Colloquy of Montréal sealed the schism between the Church of the Friends of God and the Church of Rome. From that day on, Pope Innocent III gave up any pretense of trying to convert those who denied the Church of Rome and began to call for their destruction. His legates, independent of the clergy and answerable only to him, became more aggressive in their witch hunts for those suspected of heresy.

The accused had no right to a defense and no right to know their accusers or what they were accused of. The legates acted as judge and jury. Men, women, even young children and Catholics were condemned to be burned alive merely on their authority. However, the campaign of terror continued to have the opposite effect the pope intended. The Occitan people had long valued their independence and rebelled against this attempt to subjugate them to the will of Rome. The pope and his legates became increasingly hated figures, and rather than scare Occitanians away from the heresy, the terror pushed more people toward it.

As the pope realized his efforts to rein in the challenge to his authority were not working, he became increasingly angered and frustrated. His legates Arnaud Amaury and Pierre de Castelnau tried ever more energetically to persuade the Catholics of the region to join a crusade against the heretics, but their efforts proved futile. None was willing to take up arms against fellow Occitanians at the behest of a foreign potentate.

Finally, the pope realized that nothing short of a full crusade such as he had launched against the infidels to free the Holy Land would rid him of the Cathars. If he could invoke a crusade, the promise of redemption and the spoils of war would bring men to fight for his cause from all Europe. From the highest born to the dregs of society, all would come to fight in the name of God even if motivated principally by self-interest.

The major impediment to his plan was that he needed to find adequate justification for such a crusade. It would be more difficult than customary, for this crusade would be directed not at infidels but at those who also called themselves Christians. To initiate such bloodshed, Innocent would need to have good reason, a *casus bellum*. Early in 1208, that reason presented itself.

1208, 14 January – St. Gilles-du-Gard, Provence

It was early morning, and Raymond VI cursed as he and his entourage of knights and foot soldiers entered the small Provençal town of St. Gilles-du-Gard. It had been a long ride from Toulouse. He was tired, soaked, and frozen and had no wish to be there. They had traveled the Via Tolosana, the southernmost route for pilgrims that ran from Arles, less than a day's journey to the east, to the tomb of St. James in northwestern Spain.

At that time of year, the route was little traveled, but by spring, it would be flooded once again with pilgrims. Arles was a much larger town on the Mediterranean at the mouth of the Rhône, which drained much of the heartland of France. Raymond would have much preferred to continue to Arles, but that day, his business was in St. Gilles.

He had been summoned there to meet with the papal legate Pierre de Castelnau. Raymond had taken an instant dislike to the legate at their first meeting, and subsequent interactions and reports had done nothing to improve his opinion of the man. Tale after tale had reached Raymond of the papal legates' bloody deeds as they traveled his lands, spreading fear among his people and perpetrating the worst cruelties in the name of the church. Hardly a day passed that someone did not petition him for protection from the pope's henchmen and beg that he banish them from Occitania. He would have dearly loved to do so, but unfortunately, there were limits to his power.

The pope was the richest man in Europe; he had alliances with all the royal households. Raymond could not afford to push him too far, for he would be a powerful enemy and Occitania was ill prepared for a war. The region's great prosperity was based on education and trade, not warfare. Though Raymond resented the pope's incessant meddling in his affairs and loathed his legates, he had little choice but to meet with them when summoned.

Raymond needed to heal his rift with the pope if he was ever to get his excommunication lifted. It was fortunate that the southern nobles paid little attention to the pope, for while he was excommunicated in the eyes of the church, all their and all his serfs' allegiances were officially absolved. Furthermore, all Catholics were obliged to shun him, and his authority to pass laws or sign treaties was revoked. The situation was beginning to make life difficult for Raymond; he was anxious to restore his rights and position.

The abbey church of St.-Gilles-du-Gard loomed tall ahead of them, its three arched doorways reminding Raymond of the crucifixion and planting the thought in his head that he may have been summoned for his own crucifixion. His stomach churned as he thought of the treacherous negotiations that lay ahead. He would rather face a battle on an open field than negotiate with the pope or his envoys.

On the battlefield, Raymond could see the enemy, assess its strengths and weaknesses, and decide on a plan of battle. It was always clear who was fighting with him and who was fighting against him. However, with the pope, nothing was ever clear. There was always some intrigue festering unseen until it was too late to act. The pope was an elusive enemy, one of the most treacherous he had ever faced. In the eyes of the faithful, which comprised most of the population in Europe outside Occitania, he held the power of eternal damnation or salvation over their souls. When this was coupled with his position at the pinnacle of the feudal system and the unmatched wealth the church had amassed, the pope had the power to wage war against even the mightiest king. He had no need to wield a sword himself, for there was no shortage of volunteers to do that. That left the pope free to talk of peace while waging war. The day's meeting would test all of Raymond's diplomatic skills. He looked forward to heading back to Toulouse. There were unseen dangers in this place, and he would not sleep soundly until he had left it behind.

Raymond rode up to the front of the church. An old friar came out to receive him. "I trust you journeyed well from Toulouse, my Lord," he asked.

"We did not," replied Raymond tersely. "The weather was foul crossing the Black Mountain. It snowed or rained on us for much of the way, and my party is exhausted. Show me where to clean up."

"Certainly, my Lord. The legate has been anxiously awaiting your arrival. He is looking forward to the meeting."

Raymond opened his mouth to reply but thought better of it.

Pierre de Castelnau and several other friars joined Raymond in a small chapel. The legate was wearing a long, white robe that bore a large cross on the back embroidered in the finest gold threads. Pierre clearly intended to remind his guests he was there to negotiate with the full authority of the pope, thought Raymond, who was accompanied by three of his most trusted knights.

The legate held out his hand for Raymond to kiss. On one finger was a large, gold signet ring bearing the seal of the Vatican. Raymond dutifully obliged, bowing politely in an act of submission. Pierre de Castelnau smiled pretentiously. "Count Raymond, we welcome you to the St. Gilles Abbey. His eminence will be highly gratified to learn you have accepted his request for a meeting. The Father sends his love as always and wants you to know he continues to pray for your soul."

His smooth and silky tone came close to making Raymond recoil and withdraw. He already deeply distrusted the man, and his feigned compliments deepened his suspicions. "I trust the pope is well also," Raymond replied insincerely.

"Good. Now that the pleasantries have been dispensed with, we can get to business, for I am sure that as I am, you are equally anxious to conclude these negotiations. My time is short, for I must be gone from this place before nightfall."

Pierre ordered a chair to be brought up behind him. He sat slowly and deliberately, almost ceremoniously. The event clearly intended to convey to Raymond that the meeting was to be conducted as the legate saw fit and that Raymond was merely to be regarded as a subservient participant.

Two fellow friars sat on either side of Pierre, while other monks hovered behind them. After a well-punctuated wait, the legate gestured toward small chairs and beckoned Raymond to sit. "I would be glad to go right to the heart of the matter," he said in a calm but supercilious tone. "The pope has summoned me to Rome to give him a full account of the situation in Occitania regarding the heresy. He is particularly anxious to hear what progress you have made since you last met with him."

"That is good news indeed," replied Raymond excitedly. "I am anxious for you to tell the holy father that I continue to be a good and devout Catholic and that I was excommunicated unjustifiably. As legate to our region, I ask you to petition the holy father to accept me back into the communion of the church."

One of the friars whispered something into the legate's ear. Pierre de Castelnau tipped his head slightly toward Raymond and smiled coldly. "Count, if you were truly repentant, I would gladly plead your case before the pope. The holy father is full of love for all his flock and always ready to joyously welcome back those who have strayed but have found their way back to the church. He would share the same joy that Jesus tells us the father in the scriptures did when he welcomed home his prodigal son."

"But I am truly repentant," protested Raymond.

"Then what you have done to save the souls of your subjects and to wipe out the heresy as the pope has demanded? You have sworn many times you would eradicate the heresy from your lands, yet we watch it flourish."

"I have fulfilled my promises," cried Raymond. "I have labored tirelessly to eliminate the heresy, but it is deeply rooted, and my efforts will take time before they yield the results you seek. The church must show me more patience."

"Raymond, Count of Toulouse, you were given your title by the grace of God, and by accepting it, you also accepted the responsibilities of the office. You are the steward over these lands and their people. Their material and spiritual well-being are in your trust. We are gravely concerned that while you may have fulfilled your material obligations to the people, as the lands of Occitania have grown rich, you have not provided them with the spiritual guidance that is equally your duty."

"What more would you have me do?" Raymond asked.

"Burn the heretics!" screamed one of the friars.

Bernard de Casenac, one of Raymond's knights stood and shook his fist angrily at the friar. "I was always taught that it is the Devil who burns souls, not the Good God," he yelled. "The God I worship is a God of love, not hatred. Whom do you serve, friar? God or Satan?"

The friar crossed himself hastily at the mention of Satan lest his soul be stained by the accusation. "It is you who speak with the tongue of Satan," cried the friar. "I am a soldier of the cross, and I know blasphemy when I hear it."

Pierre de Castelnau ignored the knight and addressed Raymond. "The words of your servant are the very language of the heresy itself. Your servant speaks of the 'Good God,' the language of the heretics. His very words betray you and give clear witness to all that you continue to encourage and support the heresy."

"Surely a man cannot be condemned as a heretic for saying God is good?" argued Raymond. "That is no proof I encourage the heresy."

"It is proof enough for the pope. For there is but one God, who is without fault. To call him the Good God implies there is another god who is not good, and that is heresy, but there is much more than this that demonstrates you continue to support the heresy. Even today, you bring a perfect heretic who defiles this hallowed ground with his presence."

"I do not support the heresy," objected Raymond. "I have done my best to encourage those who have erred to return to the church. However, the Occitan people do not switch their allegiances lightly. Their beliefs and tolerance are deeply held and cannot be changed overnight."

"It is your duty as a sovereign and a servant of Christ to do so. It is an insult to the church and an affront to the pope and the hand of friendship he has extended to you not to act more aggressively. You must crush the heresy mercilessly. When we see that you do not, we conclude your true sympathies lie not with the church but with the heretics."

"That is false!" shouted Raymond.

"I know it to be true!" yelled Pierre de Castelnau. "I have reports that wherever you go, you travel with two or more perfect heretics in lay attire. You keep them close so that if you die, you will die in their arms and with their blessing rather than in the arms of a Catholic priest. Is this true?"

"Who told you such lies?" cried Raymond.

"Bishop Foulquet testified you declared to him that the Devil made this world and that the Cistercians cannot hope for salvation as they have amassed too many earthly riches to enter heaven. The bishop also testified that one night, you invited him to your castle to hear the heretics speak, that being something you do often at night."

"Bishop Foulquet is a deceitful liar!" screamed Raymond. "He seeks to destroy me for refusing to acknowledge that he has higher authority over my lands than I do."

"You only add to your crimes by disdaining a bishop of the church," replied the legate. "The bishop is not alone in his accusations. Others have claimed that you wanted your son brought up by the perfects so he would have their perversion, or so-called 'faith.' Also, that you offered to pay one of your knights to follow in the Cathar heresy."

"These are all lies!" bellowed Raymond.

"Can you deny that you accept gifts from the heretics and bow to them subserviently, asking for their blessing, as many have born witness to?"

"I treat all men with respect. It is the Occitan way!" Raymond answered.

"Men of true faith are not required to treat infidels with respect!" retorted the legate. "It is your duty as a Christian to eradicate them, not show them respect. When you shirk this responsibility, they continue to contaminate others. Our priests and other legates have sworn to me that on many occasions, they have identified heretics to you, yet you have not apprehended them or raised a finger to stop them spreading their blasphemy!"

Raymond's patience was wearing thin. "For my part, I partake of the Eucharist, and I remain true to the Church of Rome and to all its sacraments. It is true many of my subjects have abandoned the church, but that was not of my doing, and I would bring them back if I could," thundered Raymond. "But many are my friends and counselors of long standing, some even my relatives. I cannot persuade them overnight to return to the church that has lost them through its own faults. Until they do, I have a duty to treat all my subjects with equality and respect whether they be Catholic or heretic, man or woman, Moslem or Jew. To do otherwise would be to destroy the society Occitanians treasure so much. Our Occitan culture is based on tolerance, culture, and learning.

It has long welcomed different cultures and traditions, and that attitude has benefitted us greatly. I am acting only as my forebears have done, as my people expect of me, and as I believe Christ demanded of all of us: 'Do not judge, and you will not be judged,' if I remember rightly from the scriptures."

Pierre de Castelnau murmured something inaudible in Latin. "Do not dare to quote the scriptures to me, Count! The pope's interpretation of the scriptures is incontrovertible, and he grows impatient with your intransigence. The time for tolerance of these heretics has passed. If you will not extirpate the heresy from your lands, you will remain excommunicated and shunned by all civilized men. The pope will dispossess you of your lands and titles and convey them to someone ready to do God's work."

Hugues d'Alfaro, one of Raymond's most trusted knights, reacted furiously at the threat to his master and reached for his sword. Sensing the danger, Raymond seized his arm and ordered him to stand down. "How dare you threaten my lord, you wretched traitor!" cursed Hugues d'Alfaro angrily. "You were born in Montpellier, which makes you Occitanian. You know only too well our principle of paratge, generosity, tolerance, courteousness, and self-sacrifice we all swear to live by. That is what distinguishes us from the French barbarians to the north and even those who hide in Rome. Have you no shame that you would seek to destroy the very culture that nurtured you? Have you too been corrupted like the parish priests who sell their forgiveness to the highest bidder?"

"In insulting the legate, you insult the Church of Rome and the pope," cried a friar.

"I mean to," d'Alfaro shouted.

"Then you too will be dispossessed and excommunicated," swore de Castelnau.

The legate glared at Raymond's knights in turn. "Which among you will reaffirm his allegiance to the Church of Rome?" he demanded. "Which among you has the courage to swear an oath in this holy place before God to put every heretic to the sword?"

Silence ensued. The knights looked at one another as the legate waited for a reply. When it came, it was not what he was looking for. All three spoke up and loudly reaffirmed their allegiance to Count Raymond.

Raymond looked at the legate with disappointment more than malice. "Has the church sunk so low that it is no longer content with just turning Occitanians against the heretics but that it now seeks to turn us against one another? Would you have a civil war in Occitania?" Raymond asked.

The legate was unabashed. "If God decides that is the only way to return the people of Occitania to the true path of Christ, so be it. We shall do his bidding. We enjoy the blessings of Christianity today only because of the sacrifices others have made before us to preserve the faith. Jesus Christ sacrificed himself to save others. As soldiers of Christ, we must be prepared to follow his example."

"You hypocrite!" spat Hugues d'Alfaro. "How dare you compare yourself to Christ? You are not proposing to sacrifice yourself as Christ did. You are proposing to sacrifice others so you and your kind can bleed the people dry with tithing and taxes."

"I am prepared to sacrifice myself for the church if that is what is asked of me," the legate replied.

"Do that and leave us in peace," yelled d'Alfaro, advancing toward the legate.

Raymond pulled him back again. "Legate, your presence in our lands is vitriolic. Your methods are an anathema to the Occitan people. Violence, threats of excommunication, and bloodshed may work elsewhere to force people back to the church, but they do not work in Occitania. The populace here is well educated and expects to be persuaded by debate, not intimidation. You and your fellow friars have become figures of hatred wherever you go, and you have driven more people from the church than to it. You have made my task of trying to suppress the heresy nearly impossible."

Raymond felt a near-uncontrollable surge of anger. *How could the pope have sent such loathsome hypocrites to represent him? How can I negotiate with those who demonstrate only bigotry and ignorance of the region? How can I hold any meaningful negotiations with those who appear to have no interest in anything I say?* Raymond decided the discussion was futile. "My counsel to you, legate, is to go back to Rome and stay there. Tell the pope your presence here only exacerbates the heresy. Tell him to lift my excommunication and restore to me the authority of the church and I will fight the heresy."

"Hah," Pierre de Castelnau said caustically. "You expect the pope to entrust these lands to you? To rely upon you to eliminate the heresy? Do you think him too stupid or too young to know better? I assure you he is neither. He sent us here because you failed the trust he gave you. At best, you sympathize with the heretics. At worst, you are one of them."

Raymond squeezed his fists. "If you accuse me of heresy again, Friar, I swear I will kill you myself! You and your brothers are the heretics, not I. For your presence here in my lands serves only to inflame the heresy, and I see no example of Christian love in your ruthless persecution. You say you have come to save the people of Occitania from the Devil, but in your actions, people see only the face of the Devil. You did not come to save the people of Occitania, you came to claim them. The only thing the pope is interested in is stealing the wealth from our lands and our labors. If the pope were truly concerned for the Occitan people, he would have sent you here to listen to their complaints about the church, but instead, you come only with demands."

Pierre de Castelnau drew himself up. "I do not need to accuse you of heresy, for you condemn yourself with your own words. To question the word of the pope, let alone accuse him of seeking worldly gain over spiritual gain, is the vilest of heresies."

The other friars loudly voiced their support and vigorously nodded agreement. One monk cried out, "Count Raymond, you employ mercenaries whose employ has been forbidden by the pope, and you use them to attack the church and confiscate its property. They have even destroyed monasteries in their excesses!"

"No one could call you a Christian!" cried another. "You kill priests, expel bishops, and do not respect the Sabbath day or Lent."

"I take back only what the church has stolen in the first place!" Raymond said. "And I practice the faith better than any of your clergy."

Pierre de Castelnau was unmoved. "How can you claim to be a true Christian?" he cried, "when you cherish heretics and Jews and bring them into your bosom? You protect and encourage them in your lands when it is the duty of every Christian to persecute them."

"I employ those in my service who are honest and efficient. I care only how they serve Occitania, not how they serve God. Better a heretic than one who claims to be a Christian but is corrupt. You are well aware that the Church of Rome in Occitania is putrid with corruption. It is no wonder the people reject it."

"The church is not anywhere perfect," the legate argued. "I am aware some changes may need to be made, but those issues do not relieve the people of their obligation to remain in the church and to support its clergy and accept its sacraments."

"Not perfect!" fumed Bernard de Casenac. "Around here, the morals of your priests are lower than the purveyors of flesh in brothels, and at least, the latter work for their living. The priests live as parasites, extorting monies from the poor for the forgiveness of sins that they themselves excel at. They come to visit the sick and rape the women in their own beds, telling them it is God's will that they submit. If the pope wishes to know why the Occitan people have turned away from his church, tell him that the Church of Rome in Occitania stinks and that the heresy will continue to flourish until the church is purged of its rot and the people associate it once again with spiritual virtue."

"I say throw them all out!" yelled Savaric de Mauléon, the third of Raymond's knights. "Occitania would be better without any of them. The pope is misguided in seeking to launch a crusade against the Occitan people. He would be better off organizing a crusade against his own servants if he wanted to restore his church."

"Yes, and I would suggest he start with you!" cried Hugues d'Alfaro. "Leave our lands and let us look to our own souls."

The Cistercians started hurling insults and threats. Pierre de Castelnau's face was red with rage. "Count Raymond of Toulouse, you dare criticize the morals of our priests when your own morals are the extreme of depravity! All have witnessed how you treat the sacred sacrament of marriage with utter contempt in like manner to the heretics. When you tire of a wife, you cast her off to seek another. To this day, you have already had four wives, three of whom are alive. Your first wife, Beatrice, was the sister of the Viscount of Béziers. After her, you married the daughter of the duke of Cyprus, and after her, the sister of Richard, the king of England. When she died, rather than mourn her loss, you married the king of Aragón's sister. To confound your infidelity, you now seek to rid yourself of Beatrice by forcing her into a convent."

"Legate, be careful of your words or I will run you through even within these sacred walls. Do not dare impugn my personal morals or those of my wives, whom I have loved. I do not need lecturing on matters of holy matrimony by a man who has never lain with a woman. But I might ask you how many brothers you have shared your bed with."

The legate reacted with disgust. "You are truly an apostate who reeks of the excrement of sin, for you have not only sorely mistreated those women you have taken in wedlock but others over whom you have had dominion. I have been told that you abused your own sister and that from boyhood, you have sought to sleep with all your father's whores. The depravity of your vileness sickens me and all men of faith."

"These are lies from the mouth of a viper!" yelled Raymond.

"They are truths!" screamed Pierre de Castelnau. "As you know them to be! You are an executioner of Catholics, a firstborn of Satan, and the instigator of countless treason against the Church of Rome and the cross of Christ it represents. I shall recommend firmly that your excommunication remain."

"Leave these lands and do not return. Your words make me question whether you are not truly the servant of Satan as many say. It is impossible to imagine you are truly the servant of a good God as you claim."

"You will all pay dearly for your heresy, Count Raymond. One word from the pope and all of Christendom will descend upon you. You will experience firsthand the wrath of God. You dare to challenge the might of the Church of Rome? Others have tried it, and all have failed, as shall you. If there is nothing left of Occitania when this is over, I will not weep, for you will have brought it upon yourselves."

Raymond approached him menacingly. "In condemning the Occitan people, you expose your own perfidiousness. Be gone from my lands before I do something even I might regret. Tell your master in Rome your mission here has been an abject failure. Tell him nothing will unite the Occitan people more against him than his threats to send barbarians against us. Until he understands that, we have no need to talk further."

"We shall be glad to be gone from this place, for it reeks of sulfur. You have sealed your own fate and that of your people. You dare to question the understanding of the pope when he speaks with the unchallengeable authority of the Almighty. It is you, Count of Toulouse, who must gain understanding. You have no hope of your excommunication being lifted until you dedicate yourself completely to the annihilation of the heresy by all means possible. If that means burning your friends alive in front of you, you shall do it, for that is the will of God. If you refuse your duty, others will be found to do your work for you."

It was only with great effort that Raymond restrained himself. "It would give me great pleasure to run you through where you stand, but I fear your blood would corrode my sword, for clearly nothing but venom flows through your veins. Tell the pope to send another legate if he wishes to restore his hegemony over these lands, for you will not be welcomed back. You belong in hell, not in any church of Christ."

"Do not doubt that I shall give the pope a full account of our meeting today and of your complicity in the heresy. By morning, I shall have crossed the Rhône and be gone from Occitania. I will give thanks when we are once more among Christians."

Raymond stormed out of the chapel, followed by his companions. Outside, he took a deep breath. "That man brings out the worst in me. When he speaks, all I can feel is anger and hatred. I truly came here to negotiate an accord with the church. I want to spare these lands and their people from the ravages of a conflict with the papal empire, but it would seem I have failed. I have worse than failed, for I fear that our exchange this day will only exacerbate the situation. Pierre de Castelnau will go back to his master and spread his vile lies about me and the Occitan people. Maybe I should have run him through?" he asked rhetorically.

"They are scum," declared d'Alfaro. "Their self-righteousness makes me vomit."

"I shall pray they all drown crossing the Rhône," said de Mauléon.

Raymond nodded. "That would be nice. But I fear God may not be so kind to us."

"Then I will pray for a miracle," de Casenac said.

Raymond slapped them heartily on their backs. "Enough! Let us round up the men and be gone from this place. I do not trust the treachery within the walls of this abbey. We shall make camp on the road tonight and continue to Toulouse in the morning."

1208, 15 January – St. Gilles-du-Gard, Provence

It was early morning. The papal flags were hanging lifelessly over the small, round tents in the encampment on the banks of the Rhône. The embers of the campfires were still glowing. Dawn was approaching and the camp was gradually awakening. Some servants were preparing breakfast for the legate and his retinue while others were packing the wagons to make ready for the ferry crossing of both men and beasts across the great river.

In the cover of the forest close by, three knights placed their hands one upon the other to seal the pact.

"We are agreed?" asked Bernard de Casenac.

"Aye," said Savaric de Mauléon.

"Aye," added Hugues d'Alfaro.

"We do this for Raymond but not at his bidding," de Casenac said. "His hands must remain clean. But I do not hesitate to soil my hand in the name of Occitania."

"Let us draw straws to decide whose hand will strike the blow that rids us of this foul inquisitor," said de Mauléon, holding straws. "It does not matter whose hand is chosen to spill the guts of this ogre. That hand strikes for all of us. We will be equal in the deed."

"Agreed," swore Bernard and Hugues as they drew straws. The choice having been made, one knight threw a white blouse over his breastplate to cover the family crest he usually displayed with pride. He pulled his visor down and rode quietly toward the road.

On the road, his horse found better footing and quickened its pace until it was running on the well-traveled path toward the river. It did not take long before horse and rider reached the encampment. The knight paused in the clearing and peered through the slit in his visor. The camp was already busy with servants packing up the last of the tents and others preparing for the short trip to the ferry. He slowly studied each of their faces until he found the one he had come for. The loathsome creature was at the head of a group of monks who had just left the camp and were beginning their journey.

The rider crossed himself, patted his horse, and committed himself irreversibly to the purpose that had brought him there. He dug his heels deeply into the side of his horse. The animal responded immediately with powerful thrusts from its legs, surging the pair forward in a gallop down the road and through the camp. People shouted angrily as they were forced to run out of its path. Others cried as they fell, startled by the rush of wind behind them or the thunderous pounding of the horse's hooves. The rider heard none of them as he forged on single-mindedly toward his goal.

As he came up rapidly behind the line of monks, he drew his long sword and held it out straight and defiantly. It glistened as the first rays of the morning sun found it in the darkness. Looking back and seeing the sheer power of the beast hurtling toward them, the monks were overcome by terror. All ceased chanting. Some knelt and began frantically crossing themselves while looking to heaven for salvation. Others tried running to the side.

As if in a trance, the rider pressed on toward the object of his hatred. He raised his sword and swung downward. It found its mark. He felt blood spurt on his hand. He pulled on the reins. His horse reared as it tried to arrest their charge. Coming to a halt some distance down the road, man and beast turned to inspect their handiwork. The crumpled figure in the road was torn open, his guts a tangled mass of red. There was no need to go back. His mission had been accomplished. The hated legate, Pierre de Castelnau, would terrify the people of Occitania no more.

CHAPTER 28

Penance and Treachery

1209, January – The Palace of the Vatican, Rome

It had been one year since the Blessed Pierre de Castelnau had been so brutally cut down by the servants of the Antichrist in Occitania. Pope Innocent had taken that savage act to be a declaration of war against the church by Raymond of Toulouse. In the year that had passed, he had been aggressively preparing to fight that war. It was one he did not intend to lose. He could not afford to lose.

The pope was returning to his chambers after vespers with Cardinal Marcellini. It had been a good day, and he would sleep soundly that night. In the afternoon, he had received two monks recently arrived from Occitania. The monks had brought excellent news from legate Milo, newly appointed to the region in place of the martyred Pierre de Castelnau. Since the assassination, which all placed at the feet of Count Raymond, he had been under relentless and ever-mounting pressure to repent of his crime and make his peace with the church.

For Innocent, there was no longer any question of making peace. He would not be satisfied until the count was dispossessed of his titles and lands. He had challenged his authority, murdered his representative, and allowed the heresy to flourish. Each of these crimes was worthy of excommunication in its own right, but together, they forfeited any claims he might have to hold Christian office. He was an abject sinner who deserved no pity.

Innocent was resolved to use him as an example to the European nobility that they must all acknowledge him as their overlord and accept they held their power only through his good grace. His predecessors had been lax and not forceful enough when it came to asserting their rightful authority, an error he was determined to correct. If he was to be remembered for anything, it would be for restoring the rightful dominion of the papacy over all spiritual and temporal matters. It was his duty to sit God back on his earthly throne. To do otherwise would be to neglect the sacred commitment he had made in accepting the papacy.

"Cardinal Marcellini, it would seem that we make excellent progress against the Count of Toulouse."

"Indeed, your Grace. Count Raymond's excommunication finally seems to have broken his spirit. I am optimistic the time will soon be opportune to dispossess him of his lands in the name of the church."

"That is good news, but I counsel patience. Do not move too swiftly, my dear cardinal."

"Agreed. It would be better if the church were not seen as the aggressor in this affair but as the wronged party. We do not want it to be perceived that we are out to destroy the count of Toulouse since by all accounts he is well-loved by his people.

"It would be better if the count were seen to destroy himself."

The cardinal looked confused. "But why would the count do that, your Grace? There are no reports of him wanting to take his own life."

"No, and I do not expect he will." Innocent smiled. "I meant that literally, that he will be his own undoing. Like any monarch, he craves power, and we shall use that against him. We will give him no option but to take the side of the church, and that will eventually turn his people against him. When they have rejected him, we shall be free to do what we want against him. All will agree that the church had no choice but to move against an unpopular ruler who was consorting with Satanic worshippers who threaten all Christianity. The faithful will flock to defend our cause."

"A wonderful plan, your Grace. That would truly be a righteous outcome."

"Most righteous indeed, Cardinal. It will also serve as a lesson to the other recalcitrant monarchs of Europe of what they risk if they do not acknowledge the omnipotence of the papacy."

"It is hard to imagine how they could ever imagine themselves to be above God, your Grace."

"Indeed. Now back to legate Milo. I believe he is awaiting my response to the request he relayed to us from Count Raymond."

"Yes, your Grace. Count Raymond petitions you again to grant him a pardon for his transgressions and to lift his excommunication. I assume you will deny his requests?"

Pope Innocent smiled and drank a little more of the heavy red wine to ward off the evening chill. "On the contrary. I shall offer to lift his excommunication and welcome him back into the bosom of the church."

Cardinal Marcellini caught his breath. "But—"

"On certain conditions, of course."

"Ah," replied Cardinal Marcellini, a renewed sparkling in his eyes. "And what would those conditions be, your Eminence?"

"First, he must express contrition for tolerating the heresy and allowing it to flourish in his domain. He must declare publicly he will dedicate himself to its extermination."

Cardinal Marcellini rubbed his hands gleefully. "Very good, your Grace. If he agrees, that should certainly incite a civil war. If not, his refusal will invite further condemnation of him by the faithful."

"Second, he must agree to turn over to the church seven of his key defensive castles as proof of his contrition for his sins and proof of his allegiance to the church."

"That is only just, your Eminence. What more?"

"Third and most important, he must humble himself before legate Milo and submit himself to be publicly flogged by the legate in the square in St. Gilles, near the tomb of the Blessed Pierre de Castelnau. It will be seen by all as an admission of his guilt in that perfidious act of savagery against a peace-loving servant of God."

"You are truly inspired by God, your Grace. That should humiliate him in front of his supporters and further condemn him in the eyes of the faithful."

"At least the death of Castelnau will not then have been in vain. I will write down the terms in full, and you shall deliver them to the monks to take to Occitania."

"Certainly, Holy Father. Are you confident he will accede to these terms?"

"He has no choice," replied Innocent confidently. "He will have to."

"But to be humiliated in front of his people? How can he expect to keep their allegiance?"

"It will be a challenge, but one he might hope to overcome. Henry II of England was punished in like manner for the murder of Thomas Beckett. He managed to hold on to his crown, so Count Raymond will not be without hope. We must always offer him hope if we are to get him to acquiesce to our demands. The trick each time is to push a little farther until we have isolated him from his power base and it is too late for him to recover it. Then he shall become an irrelevancy, and we can dispense with him as we please."

"That is why you are the pope and I a mere cardinal. God gives you vision that is denied to mere mortals."

Innocent tried halfheartedly to feign embarrassment, but it was difficult, for the cardinal spoke only the truth.

"I shall write my response to legate Milo and you shall have it by morning."

1209, January 18 – St. Gilles-du-Gard, Provence

Raymond was tired. His legs were numb. Yet somehow, they continued to carry him forward. He was not wearing his normal garments made of fine flax or wool that set him above common men. He was meagerly attired in a long robe of coarse cloth that chafed his skin. He was not wearing fine leather boots but rather open-toed sandals whose thongs had given him blisters. He was a mere pilgrim.

It had been a long, tortuous walk along the Via Tolosana. On the path, he had encountered many other pilgrims who suffered in like manner, but unlike Raymond, they welcomed it. For them, it was a penance for the suffering Christ had endured as he walked to his crucifixion. For Raymond, it was a price that had to be paid to appease the pope. The other pilgrims were walking to the west, to the tomb of St. James in Spain. However, Raymond's pilgrimage was to the east. He had walked the long distance from Toulouse through Castre, Lodève, Saint-Guilhem-le-Désert, and Montpellier to arrive at his destination, Saint Gilles-du-Gard. It was a place he had hoped never to see again.

The abbey church that dominated the town loomed just ahead. He could think only of the duplicitous Cistercian monks who had been the cause of much of his grief. He had disliked the town on his previous visit, and this time, he despised it. Last time, he had come to talk to the loathsome papal legate Pierre de Castelnau. This time, the same loathsome creature had called him back from beyond the grave to visit his tomb.

Raymond was numb, a broken man. He longed only for the day to be over. He had already agreed to use all his efforts to eradicate the heresy, but that had not been enough for the king of Rome. Most painful was that he had to turn over several of his most prized fortifications to the church, which would cripple his defenses. He had to suffer the humiliation of a pilgrimage to honor the memory of a man who had been universally despised by most of his subjects. His death had been a cause of widespread rejoicing in Occitania, for which Raymond could feel no remorse.

As Raymond and his few companions entered the town, monks and clergy cursing and taunting him lined the streets. Many spat on him. Fortunately, in his near trance, it was easy to ignore them. He continued to the abbey church. The new papal legate was waiting for him.

"Pilgrim, in the name of Jesus, do you confess your sins and repent them?" Milo shouted for all to hear.

"I do," muttered Raymond.

"Louder, so that all may hear your confession."

"I am a miserable sinner, and I confess before Jesus," screamed Raymond.

Shouts rang out from the crowd, but Raymond avoided making them intelligible.

"Do you accept responsibility for the murder of our brother in Christ, the Blessed Pierre de Castelnau, who campaigned tirelessly to redeem the people of Occitania before his untimely martyrdom?"

"I do," screamed Raymond. "I am responsible for his death."

The crowd cursed Raymond, who was on the ground, kneeling. Some pelted him with stones. A sharp one hit him on the side of the face and drew blood.

The legate raised his hands, beckoning the crowd to stop. The hail of stones stopped, but the cursing and expressions of hate continued. Legate Milo took the long, narrow strip of cloth from around his neck and shoulders and tied it around Raymond's neck. He tugged sharply on the cloth, jerking Raymond forward and up. Dragging the count behind him like an animal, the legate walked through the town. A column of hooded monks walked behind them chanting in Latin, while all along the way, the crowds continued their screams of abuse.

They arrived in a square before a small chapel that had been built to house the body of the murdered legate. A crowd pushed in on them but was held back by the monks.

"Raymond, Count of Toulouse, you have sinned against God. By your own words, you have admitted complicity in the death of one of God's servants who sought only to spread compassion and love. He came to these lands to save your people from the abomination of a heresy, which seeks to deny your people the chance of everlasting life, and you rewarded him with death."

The crowd's screams reached a crescendo. Milo allowed them to vent their anger.

"Take off your robe, pilgrim," ordered Milo. "You come here seeking absolution. Absolution for such a heinous crime as you committed can come only after your body has been purified by suffering and the demons inside have been driven out."

Raymond took off his robe and shirt, baring his delicate, pale skin to the bright rays of the Midi sun. One of the monks gave Raymond a leather thong to chew on and tied his hands to a pole. The legate picked up a many-tongued leather strap and brought it down with as much force as he could on Raymond's back. Raymond winced in pain, but the legate was in no mood for pity. He hit him again, and again, and again. The pain was unbearable. Raymond came close to losing consciousness. He had no idea of how many thrashings he had received, but when they finally stopped, he felt blood flowing from the gashes and soaking his soiled trousers.

The monk who had tied up Raymond released him. He handed Raymond his shirt and robe. The pain was excruciating as Raymond pulled the coarse cloth over the open furrows on his shoulders, but he bore it. He had no choice. He had to show the assembled crowd that he still had the strength to be the leader of Occitania. He would submit to the authority of the church, but it would not break him.

"Count Raymond, you have sworn to the holy father you will seek out the heresy and destroy it wherever you find it and will join a holy crusade to free this land of those who led the people away from the true path of Christ. Do you reaffirm those vows in front of all those here today?" Legate Milo almost thrust a large cross into Raymond's face.

"I do," stammered Raymond, kissing the crucifix.

"Then go back to your castle and be reborn as a soldier of Christ. Let your people see that the heresy will no longer be tolerated in your lands and that no mercy will be shown to those who profess it and profane Christ's name."

"Amen," roared the monks.

"You are to dismiss all the Jews and infidels you have allowed to infect your offices of government or have been given any authority over Christians."

The legate was interrupted by loud jeers and cursing from the crowd

"For such is an anathema against the natural will of God," continued the legate. "You are to dismiss all mercenaries in your service, for too often they defend the heresy. You are to restore to the church all property the heretics have taken from it, and you are to keep the roads safe, abolish all arbitrary tolls, and observe strictly the truce of God. Do you swear by these things?"

"I do," repeated Raymond, kissing the outstretched crucifix once more.

"Then go repent and atone for your sins by destroying those who criticize the church or its doctrines in these lands. Seek out the servants of Satan and show them no mercy."

The crowd roared its approval.

Slowly, Raymond strained to stand against the pain in his back that burned as though it were on fire. He began walking the way he had come. His only thought, his obsession, was to get out of that place. He felt he was going to die, but if he was, he was determined it not happen in St. Gilles-du-Gard.

1209, January – Mirepoix

"Raymond, we have a visitor." My wife, Corba, surprised me. She sounded cautious. "He would speak with you of recent events I think you should hear."

"Let him come. I will hear what he has to say. These are dangerous times, and it is wise to stay as informed as possible."

Corba hurried to fetch her visitor. When she returned, I was shocked to see Guilhabert de Castres by her side. There was no mistaking him in his dark-blue robe. This, and the fact that despite being hunted by the church as perhaps its number one enemy, he had been able to avoid capture for so long was testimony to the love the Occitan people held for him.

I bowed to show him the respect I truly held for him. "Guilhabert de Castres, you honor us with your presence. What brings you to Mirepoix?"

Guilhabert smiled. "My Lord de Péreille, I always enjoy having the opportunity to debate with such avid learners as your mother and your mother-in-law. Even your good wife Corba is becoming adept at debating the scriptures."

Corba blushed with embarrassment.

"Preacher, my wife is a skilled debater on many topics," I said with a smile. "But I understand you did not come just to hone your debating skills. Corba tells me you have come with news I should hear."

"Yes, my Lord, I am afraid I do," replied Guilhabert, his smile gone. "I bring grave news that concerns the count of Toulouse and does not bode well for our homeland."

"How grave can this be? Your countenance bears a look of despair that is not in keeping with your reputation."

"It is extremely grave. I fear that Raymond has betrayed us all to the Church of Rome. He has sold his soul and his people to the pope to safeguard his lands and title. It is a bargain I am sure he will regret, for the church does not seek equals but servants. By the time he realizes that, it will surely be too late for him to atone."

"I have heard rumors he was considering taking the side of the church against our people, but I could not believe them."

"I am afraid they are true. Only a few days past, in the square of St. Gilles-du-Gard, several of our followers heard him swear allegiance before all to the Church of Rome and to promise to hunt down all those who oppose it."

"This cannot be! He knows that could cause civil war!"

"Yes, he knows that well, but there is even worse. Raymond agreed to join a holy crusade against Occitania to exterminate all those they declare to be heretics. As we speak, French forces are gathering. Raymond will fight on the side of the barbarians against his people. While he wages war upon us, his possessions will be under the protection of the church."

"This is monstrous! I would never have believed him to be capable of such treachery after the loyalty we have all given his family."

"The Catholics are masters of deception and treachery. They have honed their skills over the centuries to subjugate the people. I am sure the count was under great pressure."

"Nonetheless, he is still the count, and as such, he must put the needs of his people above the needs of the church."

"It seems he put his needs above both," Corba said quietly.

"It would appear so, but until I have talked with him, I will continue to hope that there was some misunderstanding, that he had been forced to make this declaration."

"I will pray for that also," said Guilhabert.

"But if your prayers are not answered, what will you do? I must organize the southern lords to prepare for this onslaught. What of Trencavel and the rest? Have you talked with them?"

"No. You are the first I have visited, but I will go to them with this news."

This turn of events was a great shock. I imagined the horrors a crusading Christian army could bring to our homeland. All had heard the tales of the recent unspeakable atrocities of the crusaders against fellow Christians in Constantinople. What might they do against those they do not consider Christian in our lands?

I looked at Guilhabert, a man who epitomized the Occitan spirit of tolerance and nonviolence. "What will the Good Christians do if this invasion comes?" I asked, knowing the answer before he gave it.

"We will not fight, for we have foresworn all acts of violence against any man or beast. We will continue to spread the true word of the Good

God, help the poor, and tend to the sick. We shall counter their brutality with compassion so the people can see it is we who are the true Christians."

"And when they seek to burn you at the stake?"

"We will go willingly," he responded without the slightest hesitation. "The flesh is merely a cage for the soul and is of little importance. It would be a poor bargain indeed to betray one's eternal soul for a body that is by nature transitory."

I was impressed by his calmness and honesty. Studying the expression on my wife's face, I saw she revered him. As I listened to his words, I began to understand why.

"Is there anything I can do to help?" I asked.

"Yes, my Lord. I said we would willingly accept death, but we will not seek it out, for we have a duty to show the people what the Church of Rome really is, an imposter that seeks worldly riches and power and is possessed by Satan. It is time the people were led again down the path of Christ. If the crusade comes to our lands, it will become very dangerous for us to continue to minister publicly to the people. In the past, you were kind enough to allow some of our brethren to take shelter in your castle at Montségur when needed. I ask simply that you will continue to allow this."

"Brother Guilhabert, I gave my word to Deacon Blasco, and I will not go back on it. Any Good Christian or other man of peace is welcome to shelter in the castle."

"Thank you, my Lord de Péreille. You are a true Christian. Maybe someday you will also be a good one," he jested.

I laughed. "I am not a terribly spiritual man, preacher. I do not have time to think about such things. I am a Christian. That is enough."

"It may not be enough in the times ahead, I fear. Events may force upon you a deeper reflection before you answer."

A loud wailing from the kitchen interrupted us. We rushed there and found one of the cooks in anguish. She could not even express herself to us because of her sorrow, so a serving man beckoned me aside to explain the cause of her grief. She had just learned her young daughter was dead. She had been stoned by monks while shopping in the town after they accused her of being a heretic.

It was the beginning. The horror had come to Mirepoix.

1209, January – The Palace of the Vatican, Rome

Pope Innocent applied his seal to the letter he had written to Count Raymond that granted him absolution of all his sins and welcomed him back into the Church of Rome. He thought on it with great contentment as he ate another olive. If all the Occitan lords were as naïve and easily manipulated as Raymond, his task would be easier than he had imagined. It would certainly be much less costly than trying to retake Jerusalem from the Arabs.

The northern lords were so much more sophisticated than these southern bumpkins in the arts of politics and warfare. Music and poetry had made the southern lords soft and their lands ripe for the taking. If only Raymond's uncle, King Philippe-Auguste, was so easy to deal with. However, the southern lands would be a useful bargaining tool with Philippe-Auguste, for Innocent knew he desperately sought a port on the Mediterranean from which to launch his crusades against the Holy Land.

CHAPTER 29

The Crusading Horde Assembles

1209, Early June – Lyon

Arnaud Amaury was a proud man. He had every right to be. He was the abbot of Cîteaux and commander general of the crusade against the Cathars, also known as Albigensians, for the seat of their heretical church was in the provincial town of Albi. Amaury had risen far from his humble origins in Catalonia through hard work. Years of relentless planning and diligent maneuvering had helped him eliminate all obstacles in his way.

Amaury viewed his meteoric rise as proof that God had indeed chosen him for greatness. As one of God's chosen, he expected, in fact demanded, the obedience and subservience of all those around him. To oppose him was to oppose God and thus was heresy, pure and simple.

Amaury saw the crusade as a gift from God that presented him with the opportunity to demonstrate to those who had not yet realized that he was the rightful heir to St. Peter's chair. It also provided him with a means to crush those who opposed him or refused to acknowledge his authority. High on this list was the count of Toulouse.

As overlord of the lands over which the abbot had spiritual stewardship, the count should have been the first to recognize the abbot's authority, but instead he had treated him with only derision and contempt. The man was an obvious lecher and Antichrist. He claimed to be a Catholic but surrounded himself with heretics. It was said he never traveled without a Cathar perfect in his entourage in case he fell ill and needed the Consolamentum administered to him on his deathbed.

Amaury blamed the heresy in the southern lands in large part on Raymond. Occitania would have no chance of freeing itself of the heresy until it was freed of Raymond. The abbot's mission was to accomplish that goal, and he would not rest until he had accomplished it.

As Amaury waved from the balcony, even he was overwhelmed by the enormity of the gathering below him. It was a magnificent sight that made him feel he commanded all mankind. The crusader flags with their red crosses on white cloth billowed in the wind. Sunlight glinted off bright armor. Black smoke rose from the blacksmiths' fires as they beat red-hot steel into swords that would soon run with another red. Before him, stretching farther than the eye could see, were nobility and scum from all over Europe gathered for a glorious cause, a holy crusade against the Albigensians.

King Philippe-Auguste II of France had not come, but that did not matter. He had encouraged the French nobility to participate. Besides, without King Philippe-Auguste, there would be more opportunity for Amaury to claim the accolades.

Among the French nobles were the duke of Burgundy, the counts of Nevers and Saint-Pol, the marshal of Anjou, numerous other lesser nobility, and a vast number of knights and bishops. They had come seeking indulgences for their sins or to seize the lands of the southern lords. While on a crusade, the pilgrims' possessions would be under the protection of the church, their debts would be suspended, and they would earn a place in heaven.

As always when the drums of war sound, the mercenaries were there too as thick as ants. Together with the knights, they swelled the number of the crusaders to over one hundred thousand. Their motives for participating in this Christian army were much baser than those of the nobles. Like flies around animal droppings, they smelled pillage and plunder, the spoils of war, women and possessions to be taken from those too weak to resist and to be disposed of any way they chose. At other times, they would have been hung for such actions, but under the banner of the crusade, they could be sure that whatever atrocities they perpetrated would be forgiven or even praised in the name of God. For participating for forty days, a *quarantaine*, all participants would receive forgiveness for all their sins. With the indulgence, they could return to their homes rich and purified.

It was the greatest army Christendom had ever assembled. Amaury had prayed so long for this moment. It hardly seemed real. God had answered his prayers, as he always did. God had given him the tools he needed, and with them, he would do God's bidding.

The abbot cut a diminutive figure above the crowd, but as he waved to them, they roared. They were charged up, ready to go. He rejoiced. *I will not let their enthusiasm go to waste.* He addressed the crowd. "We are assembled in God's name to purge the lands of Occitania of those who have turned away from Christ, those who reject the Eucharist, infant baptism, and the other sacraments of the true Church of Rome. Those who reject the infallibility of the holy father!" He made the sign of the cross over them and wiped his brow. He waited for his words to percolate through the huge crowd by word of mouth of monks relaying what he had said. The mob thundered its agreement and raised their fists.

After indulging their anger a little while, Amaury outstretched his hands and gestured for quiet. "The Bible tells us what we must do. I read to you the word of God, from Deuteronomy thirteen, verses twelve through sixteen. 'If thou shalt hear say in one of thy cities, which the Lord thy God hath given thee to dwell there, saying, Certain men, the children of Belial, are gone out from among you, and have withdrawn the inhabitants of their city, saying, Let us go and serve other Gods, which ye have not known; Then shalt thou enquire, and make search, and ask diligently; and, behold, if it be truth, and the thing certain, that such abomination is wrought among you; Thou shalt surely smite the inhabitants of that city with the edge of the sword, destroying it utterly, and all that is therein, and the cattle thereof, with the edge of the sword. And thou shalt gather all the spoil of it into the midst of the street thereof, and shalt burn with fire the city, and all the spoil thereof every whit, for the Lord thy God: and it shall be a heap forever; it shall not be built again.'"

Once more, it took a while, but his words spread throughout the crusaders. Their reaction was even stronger. They raised their pikes, swords, and lances. "Burn them! Burn them! Burn them!" they chanted.

Amaury was pleased. "In a few days, we march south down the valley of the Rhône to confront those who confess to worshipping the false God.

Let them tremble at our coming, for we shall show them no mercy. Just as the Lord rained upon Sodom and Gomorrah brimstone and fire, so shall we rain fire down upon the people of Occitania."

Amaury raised his hands. The crowd cheered. The ground below him was a sea of white and red. Amaury was a happy man. Red was his favorite color.

The following days were absorbed with preparing the massive army for its march. It was a daunting task. Huge quantities of food and provisions for man and beast had to be requisitioned and packed. Weapons had to be prepared. Many of the large armaments had to be disassembled for the journey. Blacksmiths hastily loaded cartloads of supplies they would need to build siege engines. Most of the southern towns were well fortified and in naturally defensive positions, so it was anticipated they would have to be taken by siege. Amaury did his part. He prayed constantly, in public, for God's help and blessing with their crusade. He toured the camp with other Cistercians preaching the righteousness of the church's cause to all who would listen and vilifying the heretics they would be fighting.

One of the abbot's prayers was answered when a much anticipated but lowborn French noble, Simon de Montfort, rode into the camp. His arrival was heralded by trumpets Amaury had ordered to impress the teeming masses under his control. As captain of the crusade, he considered it important to establish his authority from the outset.

Simon was accompanied by most of his household—his wife, children, and personal priest and confessor. He waved to the adulating crowd along the route, who fought with each other to catch a glimpse of the famous crusader who had waged war against the Saracens. He had come to lead them. A fever of confidence swept through the camp that victory would surely be theirs.

Amaury was anxious to capitalize on the new enthusiasm in the camp and begin the march south. He ordered the French nobles to assist Simon in planning a strategy for the campaign. However, most were less than enthusiastic to take orders from a near-landless Anglo-Norman noble who appeared to be more motivated by financial gain than by spiritual redemption. In the end, Simon decided to take charge on his own.

In a week, the crusader army was ready to march. As the first rays of the sun began evaporating the clouds hanging over the forests on the mountains, Amaury held an invocation to bless everyone wearing the sign of the cross and to promise them success in their sacred mission. "There could be no holier a cause than the one you are embarking on," he said. "Everyone who participates will be richly rewarded by God."

With Amaury and de Montfort at its head, the mighty army set out down the Rhône Valley. The river was an impressive sight to most of the crusaders, who were from northern France and had never seen it. Morale was high as they followed the river's lush and productive valley that cut between the high mountains of the Massif Central to the west and Alpine terraces to the east. Many of the numerous vineyards they saw dated from the sixth century before Christ, when the Greeks sailed up the river to Avignon.

It took several days for the mighty army to snake its way down the valley and arrive at the ancient city of Avignon, the gateway to Provence. The journey had been hot and arduous under the relentless summer sun, but Amaury was not discouraged. On the contrary. The closer they came to the southern lands, the more impatient he became that they reach their objective and begin the purification task.

Avignon was a great city with a new bridge across the wide, swift-flowing Rhône. It was the only crossing point between Lyon and the Mediterranean, which endowed the city with a source of wealth and power as an essential transit point on the trade routes between Spain and Italy. The abbot viewed the town as hostile territory; it owed its allegiance to Count Raymond. However, the count had inherited these lands from his mother and held them as count of Provence under the patronage of the German emperor. For the time, the town would be spared from the crusaders' onslaught.

On the outskirts of Avignon was a large encampment. As they approached it, cheering broke out when they saw red crusader crosses flying high on white banners. It was the camp of Count Raymond.

As they rode into the camp, Amaury smiled. "See this fool," said the abbot to de Montfort with a nod to the count's camp. "He pretends to be a crusader to save his skin and his possessions. He pretends to be a Catholic but is a heretic, as are all in his family."

"And yet he betrays them?" asked de Montfort. "I had heard these Cathars were resolute in their beliefs."

"Yes," stammered Amaury. "That is true of the elite, the 'perfects,' as we call them. However, most of the believers are less obsessive in their virtue."

"I had also heard they forsake all violence and would not take up arms even in their defense, that they would not swear allegiance to any man."

"You are well informed," Amaury said. "Again, what you say is true of the perfects, but many of the believers are not bound by such vows and will take up swords readily."

"I have always made a habit of understanding my enemies," replied Simon. "I have found the practice to be conducive to a long life."

"Quite," grunted the abbot. "But mark you, the count is no Salahuddin. He is not worthy of such respect. He is a coward and a profligate who has devoted himself to womanizing and poetry rather than to the task he was born to, to serve as a soldier of Christ and protect his church. All the Occitan nobles are the same. They have known peace for so long that they have forgotten the art of warfare. You need have no fear of them."

"Only a fool does not fear his enemy," de Montfort said. "Anyway, the issue appears academic for now, as the count fights on our side. Surely, he cannot be a good Cathar if he swears allegiance to the crusade and wields a sword against the heretics. Maybe you have misjudged him and he is a true Catholic after all."

The abbot cursed then crossed himself. "I tell you before God that the count is not a Catholic. I have heard his confessions, and they were insincere. You may be right that he is also not a true Cathar. If so, he is thus nothing but an opportunist who will profess to any faith to protect his position. In either case, he is unworthy to lead the people of Occitania."

Simon de Montfort looked at the abbot. He was unconvinced. "Since he now fights under the crusader flag, I will have opportunity to judge him for myself."

"His conversion is but a temporary deception, as you will see," warned Amaury. "He will not last long in the crusader camp."

Count Raymond's tent was at the center of the encampment. He walked out to meet his guests in a white tunic with the red crusader cross.

"Abbot Amaury, welcome to Provence. I am here to keep my vow to the pope and to offer my services to you."

"Bless you, my son. God is always joyous to receive back into his flock one who has erred. Console yourself with the certainty your past sins will be washed away with the blood of the heretics you will spill in God's name."

"Thank you, Abbot," replied the count, kneeling and kissing his hand.

Amaury gestured to his companion. "Allow me to introduce the captain of our crusader army, Simon de Montfort. He is a truly devout Catholic and has much experience with soldiering under the cross."

"Your reputation precedes you," said Raymond, sounding sincere. "It will be an honor to serve under you."

Simon paused before replying. He ran his fingers through his bushy brown beard. He was sizing up an adversary. He replied in his own time. "Your reputation precedes you also, Count, though yours is more colorful than mine. I hear you are accomplished in many arts of which I know little. I am afraid we northern lords have little time for much else than our obligations to our king and the church, but I trust you will find me a swift learner."

"We will make a troubadour of you before you leave us," joked Raymond.

Amaury cast a piercing glance at de Montfort.

Simon shrugged off the count's comment. "Alas, there are some limits to my learning," he said with a smile.

1209, Late June – Castle of Carcassonne

Raymond-Roger III of Trencavel was youthful and energetic. At only twenty-four, he was the latest to assume the family's hereditary titles, including the viscounties of Albi, Béziers, and Carcassonne. The Trencavels were one of the oldest noble families of Occitania, and Raymond-Roger, like his father before him, was well loved by most of his people. Like a majority of his fellow Occitan lords, he was openly tolerant of the Jews, non-Christians, and heretics in his domains. He wanted only to encourage learning, commerce, and literature among his people so the region would continue to develop its riches and the standard of living of its people.

Count Raymond was uncle and overlord to Raymond-Roger; the two families had been allies for generations. However, that relationship had been severely ruptured. When the count decided to join the crusade, he had tried to persuade Raymond-Roger to join him. He had also commanded him to allow the inquisitorial tribunals of the church into his towns to rout out and burn heretics and expel Jews and other non-Christians.

Raymond-Roger had refused both requests and had accused his uncle of treachery in allying himself with the pope and the French barons. The count had warned him that he was putting his own survival at stake, but his youthful idealism had led him to place the security of his people over that of his own. Raymond-Roger knew that non-Catholics were deeply integrated in his administration, the government of his towns, and the economy of the region. To purge them would have had disastrous consequences. Many of his family and friends were sympathetic to the Friends of God if they were not Good Christians themselves. In no way could he turn them over to be burned.

Guillaume de Laurac, captain of the guard of the castle in the fortified city of Carcassonne, came running breathless into Raymond-Rogers' audience room. "My Lord, I fear we are in grave danger," he sputtered. "The latest reports place the crusader army just to the east of Montpellier. By all accounts, it is the greatest army ever raised in Christendom. I do not see how we will be able to withstand them. We do not have nearly enough men."

"What do you advise?" asked Raymond-Roger.

Guillaume de Laurac took off his helmet, knelt, and looked at the ground. "My Lord, I advise you to seek terms for surrender," he said in a subdued tone.

"No! Guillaume, I value your advice, for you served my father well, but I cannot accept that the situation is as dire as you suggest. Albi and Béziers are strongly fortified, and we have two thick walls around Carcassonne. Surely there is a chance we could withstand their sieges long enough for these crusading zealots to give up and return home."

Guillaume shook his head. "Our cities could hold out for some time, that is true, but I fear that the cost would be high and that in the end, the result would be the same. The towns will fall, for the forces against us are overwhelming. To make matters worse, they say the crusade is led by two fanatics obsessed with our destruction. One of them is the Abbot Amaury, who blames us for the murder of the papal legate. The other is a northern noble dispossessed by John Lackland of England who seeks our lands in redress. He is a knight who earned himself a formidable reputation in the Holy Land. There is even a rumor that the pope has ordered them not to yield until they have sacked Occitania as a warning to others who dare defy the church."

"And you think that if we surrender, they will spare us?" asked Raymond-Roger disbelievingly.

"We have no other option than to place ourselves at their mercy. It will surely be better for us than if we resist. Besides, your uncle is with them. He will speak for us."

"The count of Toulouse is a traitor!" snapped Raymond-Roger. "We cannot depend on him to protect us. He looks only to his own survival."

"Then we must prepare our cities for siege and pray the Good God will protect us," said Guillaume despondently.

Raymond-Roger paced. His anguished expression added years to his appearance. He looked vacantly out of the tall, vaulted window as if hypnotized by the turbid waters of the Aude. His expression was blank, emotionless. "There may be another way."

Guillaume's puzzled expression encouraged the young lord to continue. "If I cannot prevent this abomination of the Church of Rome from descending upon my people, I must at least save as many as I can from its savagery. Order all the Jews and infidels out of my cities. Arrange safe passage for them over the Pyrenees into Aragón. They will find safety there. I will ride to the crusader camp and offer to join the crusade."

"But my Lord!"

"I have made up my mind. It is the only way. If I join this cursed crusade, my lands and my cities cannot be attacked by the crusaders. They will be placed under the protection of the church until my quarantaine is complete."

"But my Lord, the church will send inquisitors to seek out the Good Christians among us. They will all be slaughtered."

"I know that!" cried Raymond-Roger in torment. "But if we resist, you tell me more will die. I know my people well. They will not surrender the Good Christians to the inquisitors. They will not find their job easy. I pray the Good God will protect them."

"And what of you, my Lord? How will you stomach riding among such demons?"

"I will not think upon it. I will remember only that I am there to save my people. I would ride with the Devil if it would spare the people of Occitania."

"From what I have heard of de Montfort, you will be close to doing that."

"Go quickly. Clear my cities of all those the crusaders would put to the sword. Prepare a detail for me. I ride out this afternoon."

As the captain walked out, his footsteps were masked by the cries of a young boy. "Daddy!" cried the child, running toward Raymond-Roger. Before he could reach his father, his nanny who had been chasing him snatched him up.

"I am sorry, my Lord. He heard your voice and took off. It will not happen again."

"Do not apologize. Give him to me. I would hold him for a while."

CHAPTER 30

At the Gates of Béziers

1209, Early July – Crusader Camp outside Montpellier

Amaury thanked God for his beneficence. The crusaders' camp had now swelled to two hundred thousand or more, with additional recruits arriving every day. He was aware most had not come to perform a service to God but for the promise of spoils. That did not trouble the abbot. They would still be doing God's work.

The army was divided into three groups all under the command of de Montfort. The first and largest contingent comprised the nobility and inhabitants of the Loire region and was led by Amaury himself. They were known as the French. The second contingent comprised groups from the western province of Aquitaine and was led by the archbishop of Bordeaux. The third contingent, from the Cantal, was led by the bishop of Puy-en-Velay.

The abbot was reclining in a large, padded, red-backed chair with gold trim and savoring delicacies of the region. A young boy fanned him to ward off the summer heat. He held his glass of red wine up to the light to study its clarity. "You will enjoy the life here, my Lord de Montfort. The wines take their body from the limestone slopes of the Rhône Valley and are so much richer on the palette than any you find up north." He raised the glass to his nose, swirled the wine, and inhaled deeply.

"You will also find a wonderful abundance of fruit, vegetables, cheeses, fish, lamb— anything you wish for. Plus, it is available all year. It is the land of milk and honey God promised the Israelites. That is why the southern lords have grown soft. Life is not the challenge that it is up north. But we will change that, will we not?"

"If God wills it," answered Simon de Montfort more cautiously.

"Oh God wills it most assuredly. The pope wills it, and he speaks the word of God. These heathens, these pagans, these Devil worshippers have no right to live at all and even less so in a land the Lord has blessed with such abundance. They were given ample chance to repent, but they refused. For years, I committed myself to walking among them and preaching God's word. I warned them that if they did not change their ways and accept Jesus as their savior and the Church of Rome as his one true church, they would bring God's wrath down upon them, but they spurned my teachings. They mocked me and the church. They even mocked the pope. For that, they shall feel God's pitiless wrath."

"I am here as a simple tool of the Lord," declared de Montfort. "With his divine guidance, I will seek out his enemies and deliver them to the church for judgment. You have my word, Abbot, that I shall tirelessly strive to cleanse these lands of all those who deny God's word. It shall be as we did in the Holy Land."

"Excellent," replied Amaury. "How I have been waiting for this moment." The abbot walked to a large map on a table in the tent. He pressed his finger down. "We should start here in Montpellier. The town looks rich enough."

Simon de Montfort shook his head. "No, alas, we cannot. It is a possession of King Pedro. The pope would not permit it, for he is an ally of the church against the Moors in Spain. We are only a few days' march from Occitania, so you will not have long to wait before there will be plenty of towns to choose from for cleansing."

Trumpets heralded the arrival of someone of importance. A squire came into the tent. "My Lord, Abbot, Lord Raymond-Roger III of Trencavel begs an audience."

Simon de Montfort and Amaury exchanged glances. "Well, well. This is unexpected surprise." Amaury gloated. "If he has come to beg for mercy, he will find none here. The Trencavels are one of the oldest and most influential families in the region. We must make an example of them, for they have given much support and protection to the heresy. They have done nothing while our churches were emptied of their congregations and our priests starved as the people were allowed to forgo their tithes. When we excommunicated them for not upholding their duties to the church, they laughed. We shall see who laughs now."

"I suggest first we see what he wants," de Montfort said. "Maybe he has come to surrender. It would truly be a blessing from God if we win our first battle without a fight."

"Ha! These southern lords will never surrender until they have suffered God's vengeance! I know them well. He has come to bargain but is not ready to yield anything. The Trencavel lands are some of the richest in Occitania. They will make a fine prize for the victor and for the church," the abbot declared cynically.

Raymond-Roger entered the tent with two knights.

"Ah, my Lord Trencavel," the abbot said. "We were not expecting to see you so soon," he declared arrogantly. "Allow me to introduce Simon de Montfort, who commands the soldiers of the cross who are with us in the name of his holiness."

The two nobles inclined their heads slightly to each other.

"What is your business with us?" demanded Amaury coldly.

"I have come to join your crusade."

The abbot came close to choking on his wine. "And what has brought about this change of heart? Has a miracle occurred? Did the Virgin Mary come to you in the night perhaps?" He looked at the young noble with disdain. "I am a great believer in miracles, but this stretches even my credulity. The Trencavels have long protected the heretics and the Jews and Saracens from the church. I am told half your family members are heretics. Do not take us for fools to believe you have suddenly reformed!"

The young lord stood his ground. "I am a Catholic. I attend Mass daily. I have never been a heretic, yet it is true I tolerate them among us. I do not deny it. But Abbot Amaury is of this region, and he knows well the Occitan tradition of tolerance. It runs in the veins of every Occitanian. It is what we are."

"But God demands the faithful to cast out from among them all those who preach against his word. As a leader of the people, it is your duty to impose God's will on them if they have strayed from it," exclaimed the abbot.

"But surely it is not un-Christian to show mercy?" responded Raymond-Roger. "Did not Jesus say, 'Blessed are the merciful, for they shall receive mercy'?"

Amaury reacted with rage. He put down his wine goblet and stood. Raising his hand, he walked to Raymond-Roger. "Lord Trencavel, do not quote the scriptures to me! The Bible also says, 'Believers must not commune with unbelievers. What fellowship hath righteousness with unrighteousness, light with darkness, believers with infidels?'"

Simon de Montfort joined the debate. "If you would protect these heretics, why do you offer your sword for the crusade?"

"I offer it to protect my people. I offer it that you will heed my counsel and show forgiveness to those you may find to have erred."

Amaury fumed. "God demands we strike you down!" He picked up a heavy Bible on a table. He flicked quickly through the pages. "Here it is. Deuteronomy fourteen, verses six to ten. 'If thy brother, the son of thy mother, or thy son, or thy daughter, or the wife of thy bosom, or thy friend, which is of thine own soul, entice thee secretly, saying, Let us go and serve other Gods, which thou hast not known, thou, nor thy fathers; Thou shalt not consent unto him, nor hearken unto him; neither shall thine eye pity him, neither shalt thou spare, neither shalt thou conceal him: But thou shalt surely kill him; thine hand shall be first upon him to put him to death, and afterward the hand of all the people. Thou shalt stone him with stones, that he die; because he hath sought to thrust thee away from the Lord thy God.'"

The abbot paused, content to let the words sink in. He stared at the young lord with pure hatred. "You see, the Bible is unequivocal. As a protector of your people, it was your duty to God and to the church to destroy the heretics in your possessions. By not doing so, your sin is greater than theirs."

"Abbot, if you believe I have sinned, hear my confession and punish me alone. Spare my people. Accept me into the crusade. I pledge to join you in casting the heretics out of my lands and reasserting the Church of Rome as the only true church among my people."

"And the Inquisition? Will you allow the inquisitors to rout out the heretics from among your people?" de Montfort asked belligerently.

Raymond-Roger froze. His expression revealed his revulsion at the mention of the hated inquisitors. "If it will spare my people from a worse fate, I will allow the inquisitors into my towns," he stammered. "However, I would beg of you that they spend more effort on conversion than persecution. Their brutal practices in our region have served only to engender more hatred of the church and increase the heresy."

"I think you come here as a serpent of the Devil to speak with a serpent's tongue! But you will not beguile us as the serpent beguiled Eve. You come here to shield the heretics from God's wrath, not to betray them!" Amaury bellowed.

"No! It is not true," cried Raymond-Roger. "I came to do your bidding in hopes that it would bring peace to the region. I do not want to see any more bloodshed on the fair soil of Occitania. Those who follow Christ should not shed one another's blood."

"Those who reject the sacraments of the church are not Christian!" Amaury screamed. "They are infidels, heathens. It is the duty of Christians to strike them down."

Simon de Montfort remained above the fray. "If you have come to aid the crusade, tell me the battle plans of my adversaries. Bring me details of their fortifications."

"And give me a list of those in your family and those in your court who practice the heresy. I will burn them first," cried Amaury, his eyes filled with hatred.

Raymond-Roger addressed de Montfort. "I am not privy to the battle plans of others or to information about their fortifications. I cannot betray the trust others have in me."

"Then you are of no use to us!" screamed the abbot. "Be gone. Go back to your Devil worshippers. Tell them their hour of judgment is at hand."

Simon de Montfort said nothing, but his gaze did not leave the young Trencavel. He was studying his every reaction as a lion sizes up its prey before striking. As tempers flared, de Montfort's hand moved closer to his sword.

"Where is my uncle?" demanded Raymond-Roger. "Let him speak for me. He knows the Trencavels are not enemies of the church and that it is a grave injustice to send an army of the cross against my people."

The abbot laughed. "He knows no such thing. Your uncle will not speak for you. He told us all about you. How you refused his pleadings to join the crusade because of your sympathies for the heretics." Amaury looked pleasurably upon Raymond-Roger's tortured expression. "He will be happy to see you burn with your heretic friends."

"You lie!" screamed Raymond-Roger. "He would never say that. I don't know what you have done to blackmail my uncle into joining this heinous crusade of yours, for he is a good man. Your mind may be twisted, but his is not."

The abbot smiled triumphantly. "Now we see your true sentiment of the crusade, a 'heinous venture of a twisted mind.' Well that is not the crusade of which you speak. That is the error of the heresy you and the other southern nobles have encouraged in your lands. That is what more than two hundred thousand faithful Christians have come to eradicate."

Simon de Montfort stood to attention, his hand on the hilt of his sword. "My Lord, I will see my men give you safe passage to the edge of our camp. When we meet again, it will be on the field of battle. May God protect his own."

Raymond-Roger was burning with anger but could think of nothing more he could say. He had failed to avert a conflict. He would have to prepare his people for war. It seemed that the Good Christians had been right. The Church of Rome had strayed from the path of Christ and was following the path of Satan.

Raymond-Roger felt dread and hatred as he looked at the threatening stance of de Montfort. Barbarians such as he had no comprehension of paratge, the principle of equality held dearly by all southern nobles. It was a way of life he would gladly give his life to protect.

"Abbot, you and your henchman here have no right to call yourselves Christians! You are here not for a solemn purpose but for greed. You intend to pillage our lands, steal our riches, and kill those who follow the true path of Christ. You make a mockery of the commandment 'Thou shalt not covet.' For to you, nothing is sacred."

Simon de Montfort started to withdraw his sword from its scabbard. Raymond-Roger and his companions reached for theirs.

Amaury gestured for them to stop. "Here and now is not the time for swordplay. That day will come soon enough."

Simon was disappointed. "Go, Lord Trencavel, before I withdraw my offer of safe passage. We will meet again."

Raymond-Roger stormed out of the tent and collided with a knight who was intent on entering. The two looked at each other in surprise and then in astonishment. The man Raymond-Roger had run into was his uncle, the count of Toulouse. They paused for a moment but said nothing. Raymond and his companions left the camp at full gallop. They had much to prepare and little time in which to do it.

"Back to Carcassonne, my Lord?" asked the captain of the few knights Raymond-Roger had brought with him.

"No. Béziers. We must make haste. It is the first town over which I am overlord that is in the path of the crusader army and is much too great a prize for them to pass by. They will reach it in a few days. We must prepare the townspeople for a long siege."

"Béziers? But the town is well fortified. Surely they could not hope to take it."

"You did not see the hatred and the greed I just saw in the eyes of the abbot and this northern lord. They are obsessed with killing our people and stealing our lands. They have recruited the scum of Europe to do their bidding. We must pray the walls of Béziers will be strong enough to stem their tide."

1209, 19 July – Béziers

Béziers was a pearl on the banks of the River Orb. It was an ancient, well-defended town high on a promontory at a bend in the river. It was forever bathed in the warm Occitan sun that bestowed upon its inhabitants an exceptional spirit of kindness and hospitality. The town's wealth was based on the vineyards that surrounded it and dated back countless centuries.

Benefiting from its long history and location on the eastern extremity of Occitania, Béziers had a well-earned reputation for having a rich and tolerant culture. People of all beliefs sat on the town council, intermarried, and worked together freely. Contrary to the teachings of the church, Catholics saw no reason to shun their Cathar brethren or those of other faiths. As elsewhere in Occitania, even Jews were eligible for public office.

The gates of Béziers were flung open in welcome as the heralds announced the unexpected arrival of their young and popular lord. Raymond-Roger tore through the gates at full gallop, followed by a few knights. The men and their horses, near exhaustion, rode the narrow streets into the heart of the city. Dismounting, Raymond-Roger commanded that a meeting of the town elders be convened immediately.

"The crusader army of Arnaud Amaury will be upon you in days," Raymond-Roger warned the council. "You must make preparations for a long siege."

The response to his plea was muted. The elders muttered among themselves at the news with no show of excitement. Most maintained stoic composures. Many shook their heads. The head of the council stood.

"My Lord, you are most welcome here, and we are very grateful you have come to warn us of the approaching army, but there was really no need. We have known for some time the crusaders were coming and have already made preparations. Extra provisions have been stored, our livestock has been brought within the city walls, and our wells are full. We are confident we could hold out for weeks if necessary. So do not worry on our account, for we are in no danger from the crusaders."

"By God you are in danger!" thundered Raymond-Roger. "You underestimate the enemy. I have seen the hordes of barbarians who now wear the cross of Christ and masquerade as Christians. Do not fool yourselves that they have come to convert you or that they will go away after a few weeks' siege. They have come to pillage your lands, rape your women, and eat your livestock. They will not be content until they have done so."

"Our walls are strong. They cannot hurt us," boasted one councilman.

Raymond-Roger glared at him. "You have never seen an army like this. It is the greatest army ever assembled in Christendom. They are sure to bring many siege engines. They are led by a French knight, Simon de Montfort, who has had much experience on crusades in the Holy Land."

Another councilmember spoke. "After their quarantaine, these northern barbarians will melt away to their homes. Four years ago, they demanded we turn over to the church all those they accused of being heretics, and we refused. After a short siege, they gave up. They shall do so again."

"I pray you are right, but I fear you are not," Raymond-Roger said. "This time, they are led by a man who is utterly obsessed with hatred of our independence and his lust for power. The pope's legate, Abbot Arnaud Amaury, has dedicated himself to our destruction. His master, the young pope in Rome, sees himself as the king of kings and cannot tolerate the indifference the people of Occitania show him. Together, they are determined to bring us back under the iron fist of the Church of Rome."

The elders looked at each other, their expressions more serious. They debated among themselves, and several heated arguments sprang up between members. Finally, when they appeared to have reached a consensus, the council leader addressed their overlord. "My Lord, your concern for our well-being is greatly appreciated. The people of Béziers have great respect for you, but you are young. Many here have more experience in these matters and do not share your concern for our safety. Our town is well fortified and provisioned. We will take additional measures for our defense but are confident we will be able to hold out long enough to send these barbarians looking for easier spoils elsewhere."

Raymond-Roger shook his head. He wondered how he could persuade them to take the threat more seriously.

Seeing his frustration, Renaud de Montpeyroux, the Catholic bishop of Béziers, spoke. "My Lord, you paint a dark picture of Arnaud Amaury, but he is an abbot of the Church of Rome. I have to believe he has some Christianity in him and is not quite the ogre you make him out to be. In the unlikely event the town was to fall, the townspeople would almost certainly be well treated as most are practicing Catholics."

"And what of the others?" demanded Raymond-Roger. "What of the Good Christians who live among you? What of the Jews and the Saracens?" He pointed at one of the elders at the table. "Isaac? What of you and your people? You will be slaughtered if the town falls to this abbot and his northern crusader knight. Simon de Montfort's hands are already washed in the blood of countless non-Christians in the Holy Land."

Isaac held his hands out. "My Lord, what do you propose we do?"

"Take your people and warn all the other infidels to flee the city and go south to Aragón. You will be safe there. If all goes well and in a few months the crusaders leave, you will be free to return."

Isaac rubbed his beard and nodded.

Raymond-Roger turned to the others. "For those of you who remain, I implore you to make preparations for a long siege and pray for deliverance."

His plea instigated more discussion at the council table. When it was concluded, the council leader spoke. "So be it, my Lord. We will follow your advice, but we pray your fears prove to be mere nightmares without reality."

"So do I," sighed Raymond-Roger. "So do I."

Raymond-Roger beckoned his knights to leave. "I ride to prepare defenses in Carsassonne. I leave Béziers in your trust. May the Good God protect you."

The council members continued deliberating as Lord Raymond-Roger and his companions rode from the city. They turned west and headed up the valley of the River Aude toward the great, fortified city of Carcassonne.

1209, July 20 – Servian

Like a swarm of insects, the vast crusader army overwhelmed the small hilltop village of Servian, east of Béziers. It was the first battle of the Albigensian Crusade and the first blood for de Montfort. The town was a useful staging post to prepare for the siege of Béziers, but otherwise, it had little to satisfy the voracious appetite for spoils his army demanded. For that, he would have to give them Béziers.

1209, July 21 – Béziers

Some crusaders had arrived the night before. By midday, the crusader army stretched nearly a league around the city. As the Midi sun beat down, vast plumes of dust rose high in the sultry air from the encampments being built on the plain below the town.

In addition to the knights and peasants who had sworn their service to the cross, the crusader camp had swollen further with the arrival of the king of the Vagabonds. He brought with him fifteen thousand or more cutthroats and thieves who made no pretense of being about God's work. They came for whatever they could make off with, and they were prepared to take it any way they could. Unkempt, unclean, and clothed in rags, they would readily stab each other in the back if it were to their benefit. They were akin to hyenas ready to move in and grab scraps after the lions had killed the prey and finished their feast.

It appeared a strange sight to the people of Béziers as they gazed over their walls. What had been a rich, green plain to the south had become a chaotic quilt of tents, flags, cooking fires, horses, and men. It stretched as far as they could see.

"That army won't last more than a couple of weeks," speculated the blacksmith to his companion. "They will never be able to feed such a rabble."

As the crusaders began encircling the city walls to lay siege to them, the inhabitants thronged to the battlements to shout insults and throw garbage and the contents of urinals on them. They jeered at the proud French knights sweltering in their coats of mail under the unfamiliar, blazing Occitan sun.

Despite the confidence of the townspeople in the face of the crusader threat, the town elders called another meeting. They decided to try to defuse the situation by attempting to negotiate. Since it was a Catholic army, Bishop Renaud de Montpeyroux was nominated to ride to the crusader camp to speak with the abbot.

In the camp, Amaury was in no mood to receive him let alone negotiate. Against his better judgment, he relented and granted him an audience.

The bishop bowed reverently to his superior and clasped his hands in deference. "Reverend Abbot, I am here to ask you to withdraw your crusader army from Béziers. There is no need to besiege the city, for it is a Christian community. I am a bishop of the Church of Rome, and my large flock is faithful to the church. I beg you to take your army to the Holy Land, where you will find the true enemies of Christ. They are not in Béziers."

"You think me a fool?" shouted the abbot. "A Christian community that defies God by concealing many heretics in its midst? They insult the very name of the savior by daring to call themselves Christians. Such impiety is a greater danger to the church than is Satan. Many of our priests go begging in the streets because they have lost their congregations to the Cathar perfects. As the bishop of Béziers, you have betrayed the church by permitting this. You have tolerated the heresy and allowed it to spread until it has become like a wildfire, out of control. We have come to extinguish it."

"But your Grace, it was beyond my power to stop it. The people ignored my pleas because they have long been accustomed to having people of differing faiths among them. Many families have at least one member or a friend who is sympathetic to the heresy."

"Your very words betray the depth of your damnation and disobedience of God's commandments. A true Christian is not permitted to extend any tolerance to those who reject the divinity of Christ! A true Christian must slay all such infidels. It is his duty to God to silence the mouths of Satan!"

"But my Lord Abbot, that is not the Occitan way."

"It is the Christian way! As a bishop of the church, it is your duty to lead your flock and to show them what is demanded of them to keep the faith. I have no doubt you are familiar with some of these heretics yourself. Set an example that the faithful might follow. Burn all the heretics known to you in the center of the town. It will be an inspiration for those among you who are truly Christian to denounce all the heretics in your midst."

"But your Grace," stuttered the bishop, "the people would never permit it! Forty years ago, when one of the knights of Raymond-Roger I murdered a Cathar, the townspeople murdered him. The Good Christians are loved even by those who are faithful to the church, for they minister to the poor and take care of the sick."

"Good Christians! Never use that term before me!" bellowed the abbot. "Call them what they are. perfects! perfect heretics! They are the foot soldiers of Satan and must be hunted down. They poison the minds of the faithful against us."

"Your Grace, may I suggest that it is our own clergy who have poisoned the minds of the people against us. They have set a poor example to the people, buying their priesthood and then selling their indulgences to the highest bidders. The Cathar perfects work within the community while our priests live off their tithings and lead debauched lives. We should look to ourselves if we wish to win back the souls we have lost."

"You are a bishop of the church and yet you mouth the very words of heresy!" thundered Amaury. "How dare you question the ways of the church? It is for the pope alone to question the ways of the church. Anyone else who questions the church is guilty of heresy."

"Your Grace, I did not mean to criticize—"

"Enough! I will hear no more of this. All I wish to know from you is whether you will bring to me all those in Béziers who practice the heresy. If you will not do your job, we will have to do it for you. They will all burn, and you may come to celebrate the spectacle."

"Your Grace, I am uncertain of who are heretics, for they do not preach to me, and the people would never give them up."

"Then allow me to help you." Amaury grinned. He held out his hand. A monk put a scroll in it. "Here," said the abbot, thrusting the scroll into the face of the bishop, giving him no choice but to accept it. "Here is a list of all the people in Béziers known by the church to be heretics. We shall start with them."

The bishop nervously unrolled the parchment and gasped in horror.

"There are over two hundred names on that list, and you are encouraged to add more." The abbot gloated. "I shall expect you to bring them to me in chains. When they have been burned alive for the greater glory of God, we shall talk of lifting the siege. Those are my terms."

The bishop began to read the names and started shaking. His face registered horror and revulsion. "But these are good people!" he protested, close to tears. "I know all of them. They are no threat to the church. They are good citizens who seek to harm no one. In fact, most are well loved for they are honest and caring souls. I can personally testify that one woman on this list gave medicine to my wife when she was near death and saved her life."

"Witchcraft! All the more reason she must be burned!"

The bishop shook his head and muttered incoherently. He clasped his hands and started praying, looking away from the abbot, up to heaven.

The abbot returned to his comfortable seat, picked up his wine glass, and held it out. A servant quickly filled it. After savoring a mouthful, he looked at the bishop as if he were despoiling his view. "Go back to the town and take my demands to your council. I need a reply urgently or God's mercy will rapidly become God's wrath."

With a nod from the abbot, two monks came forward to assist the bishop out of camp. With his spirits completely beaten down, the bishop made no further attempt at protest.

When the bishop was gone, Simon de Montfort came out from behind a curtain where he had been concealing himself.

The abbot smiled contentedly. "Have no fear. They will never accept my terms. Domingo de Guzmán and Pierre de Castelnau preached in Béziers only three years ago. They warned the townspeople that they would have to yield up the heretics among them if they were to save their souls, yet they refused. So do not concern yourself they will not do so now. The salvation of Béziers will be entrusted to you."

"I am eager to do God's work," declared de Montfort with satisfaction.

Bishop Renaud de Montpeyroux rode despondently back into Béziers and made his report to the council. The list was passed around for everyone to read. The reaction was unanimous. They would never give up the citizens demanded by the abbot. To condemn them to death was unthinkable. Many had at least one friend or relative on the list. To give them up would have been to betray their communal oath of paratge.

"Take a message to the abbot," dictated the council leader. "Tell him his demands carry little more weight than that of a peeled apple. We will never betray citizens of Béziers to barbarians. We have fought too long and hard for the religious and economic freedoms we enjoy and would rather drown in a sea of tears than alter our beliefs."

Everyone let out cries of support. When they had died down, he said, "Tell him we will resist his siege to the end even if we are forced to eat our own children. Only then will he understand how dearly we hold the culture of Occitania."

Amaury had anticipated the town would refuse his demand, but he had not expected such a defiant tone. It only added to his hatred for the Occitanians that these southern lords still dared to treat him with contempt. "Who do they think they are?" he thundered. "I am the personal legate of the pope. To defy me is to defy the pope. It is the vilest of heresy!"

The abbot tore the note to shreds and trampled on the pieces. "Bring me the emissary who delivered this!"

The man cowered as he was led to the abbot.

"Bring me a Bible," Amaury commanded. A monk dutifully obeyed. "I have a message for you to take to your elders. Tell them to seek out their bishop to pray for their souls. Have him read to them Deuteronomy, chapter twenty, verses ten to sixteen. Allow me to read it to you now. 'When you march up to attack a city, make its people an offer of peace. If they accept and open their gates, all the people in it shall be subject to forced labor and shall work for you. If they refuse to make peace and they engage you in battle, lay siege to that city. When the Lord your God delivers it into your hand, put to the sword all the men in it. As for the women, the children, the livestock and everything else in the city, you may take these as plunder for yourselves. And you may use the plunder the Lord your God gives you from your enemies. This is how you are to treat all the cities that are at a distance from you and do not belong to the nations nearby. However, in the cities of the nations the Lord your God is giving you as an inheritance, do not leave alive anything that breathes.'"

The abbot glowered at the man groveling at his feet. "Tell your city elders they have provoked God's anger, and in retribution, he will destroy them utterly with fire and brimstone. Béziers will be an example to the rest of Occitania of what befalls those who dare challenge the authority of the church!"

The poor man said nothing.

"Go before I decide to crucify you to appease God's anger."

The man ran from the tent. He did not stop until the city gates closed behind him.

The fury of the abbot's response panicked the bishop, who decided to leave the city with a few of his priests. However, the majority of the Catholic priests decided to stay with their parishioners rather than abandon them to the wrath of their own church. If the army of Amaury were to enter the city, they would at least be able to plead for clemency for those they knew to be truly faithful.

During the night, there was frenetic activity both inside and outside the city. In the crusader camp, siege engines and attack towers were being constructed and catapults and arbalets assembled. The few trees around were quickly hacked down for construction and firewood, and rocks were quarried to provide ammunition. Hot fires glowed brightly as blacksmiths repaired old weapons and forged new ones from steel that were to be put to the service of God. Over other fires, huge caldrons bubbled and hissed as cooks struggled to prepare enough food to satisfy the insatiable appetite of the vast army. Some soldiers drank heavily to ward off their fears while the more devout prayed for protection in the battle ahead.

Anticipating what the morning would bring, few slept soundly in the crusader camp. Those who tried found it next to impossible because of the noise. In addition to the human activity, there were the noises of the animals and the livestock. Thousands of horses whinnied loudly as their owners tried on their harnesses for battle; they were spooked by the noises in the camp.

Goats, sheep, pigs, chickens, and cattle were as essential to the army as were their weapons. All had been brought along with them. In addition, many had brought their dogs for hunting, protection, or companionship. These roamed the camp, barking incessantly and frequently attacking those with whom they were unfamiliar. Then there were the smells; smoke from fires permeated the warm night air and mixed with the smells of human waste. Thick, black smoke from the coal of the blacksmiths' fires clung stubbornly to the encampment without the winds that during the daylight hours might have borne it away.

Amid the crusaders were many monks and priests who had come to witness God's work. Makeshift churches were scattered about to provide absolution for those who might face death in a few hours. For those who did not wish to go to the churches or could not because they were too busy with their labors, bands of hooded monks roamed the camp, each led by a monk carrying a large crucifix and followed by his brothers holding candles and burning incense. The smoke and flickering orange light gave the processions an almost ghostlike appearance amplified by their chants in Latin, a language incomprehensible to the vast majority in the camp. In fact, the majority in the camp could neither read nor write even their own dialects let alone that of the ancient Romans.

Inside the city, the council elders debated all night on the best strategy to defend the city. In the end, they decided to organize a small sortie in the morning to try to destroy some of the crusader siege towers and earthworks being built close to their walls. They knew they could not win an all-out battle with the soldiers of the cross, but they hoped to demoralize them enough to cause them eventually to leave.

CHAPTER 31

In the Name of God

**1209, July 22, the Feast of Mary Magdalene –
The Crusader Camp**

At first light, the abbot summoned his commanders and their engineers and tacticians to plan the siege. It would not be an easy task. The city was well placed and well defended. The city was close to the river, so the wells in the city would provide its defenders an adequate supply of water. The military planners did not know how much food was in the city, but the town was wealthy, and the inhabitants could well have stockpiled adequate provisions to resist a siege of six months or more.

"We cannot wait six months," complained the abbot. "Our army will melt away after forty days if they do not see rewards."

"We will have to probe the city for weaknesses. The defenders are overconfident. That may prove their downfall," Simon de Montfort said.

Amaury drove his staff down forcefully. "Go find their weakness. I want this town destroyed! They have cast down a gauntlet before the pope and with it condemned themselves to suffer God's anger. I want no one in this town to be spared, neither man, woman, nor child. I want not one stone to be left standing upon another, for that is the way of the Lord against those who transgress him."

Amaury stormed out of the tent. It was up to his commanders to implement his orders. The abbot had placed his confidence in de Montfort, who would have to demonstrate his confidence had been justified.

Simon de Montfort systematically evaluated all the possibilities for breaching the defenses of the town. Some proposed tunneling under the walls until they collapsed. Others proposed setting large fires at the walls to weaken them. Still others proposed a direct assault with large siege towers that would allow their troops to surmount the walls. There was no shortage of ideas. In his campaigns in the Holy Land, de Montfort had seen all of them used and knew that none assured success because every siege was different. He decided they would try each in turn until one brought them success.

Béziers

Normally on the day of the Feast of Mary Magdalene, Béziers would be festive with free-flowing wine and food from the bountiful lands and seas of Occitania. People customarily celebrated and danced in the streets to give thanks to the Good God for their blessings.

That day, however, the mood was far from festive. Surrounded by a large, hostile force, few people were in the mood for celebrating. The populace remained confident they could resist the assault of the barbarians, but most realized the conflict would be more arduous than they had anticipated.

As the sun rose over the endless sea of tents and battle flags around the town, few inhabitants of Béziers ventured out. The guard on the city walls had been doubled. The sentries nervously waited for signs of activity from the crusader camp.

The night had been hot and oppressive. For those in the crusader army from the north who were unaccustomed to the southern heat, it had been especially burdensome. To make matters worse, the summer heat had parched the land, and throughout the camp, the constant activity churned up dust.

Many of the lowly chores in the crusader camp were performed by boys who had been brought along to serve their masters. Among these were such tasks as cleaning up after the animals, peeling turnips, or polishing suits of armor or boots. As the camp began to stir, a small group of boys gathered to complain about their conditions. Many had not slept, and all had dry throats from the dust. As they faced the daunting prospect of another hard day's work, the first rays of the sun glinted off the fast-flowing River Orb.

One boy had an idea. "Let's go down to the river to bathe. We can be back before anyone realizes we are gone."

Everyone agreed, so they sneaked quietly out of the camp and down to the river by the closed southern gates of the city. As they cooled themselves in the river, the city guards looked at them from the walls. "Go back to your mothers!" shouted one of the guards.

"Satan worshippers!" shouted back one of the boys.

The insults mounted, and some of the youths began throwing stones at the guards. One particularly brash young youth ran naked onto the bridge. "Your mothers are whores!" he screamed.

Some of the town's youths heard the commotion and joined the guards. "Your mother must have slept with a pig!" screamed one from the battlements.

The catcalls escalated until before long, a full-scale shouting match was taking place between the crusader youth and the youth of the town. Tempers flared. Some of the town's youth were unable to endure the taunts any longer. They descended from the ramparts, cracked open the city's gates, and charged the boy on the bridge. Cursing and screaming, they hurled him into the water.

Rather than appease their anger, the act served only to incite the boys' anger. Instead of returning to the city, the boys ran across the bridge to pursue the other crusader youth by the river. Raising their lances with small white pennants atop them, they screamed loudly and menacingly as they charged. A crusader passing by the area ventured onto the bridge only to be killed by an arrow shot by one of the town's youth.

The commotion began to attract the attention of others. Peasant crusaders near the river saw what was happening and rushed toward the bridge to protect the youth. Before long, the king of the Vagabonds became aware of what was going on and saw an opportunity. He blew on his horn as loudly as he could to alert the camp. His disheveled band of followers sprang up to follow him as he charged to the river. Most were dressed in rags, some barely dressed at all, but each carried a fearsome weapon—a mace, a pike, an axe, or a lance, and each knew how to wield his weapon.

The city youth were no match for vagabonds and were quickly cut down. With nothing between them and the open city gates, the vagabonds rushed toward them. The city guards panicked and tried frantically to lower the ramparts, but they were too late. The vagabonds began pouring into the city in an unstoppable swarm.

Simon de Montfort and his knights were debating their plans when the shrill sound of the hunting horn reached them. A young squire burst into their tent. "No time for talk, your Lordships! The gates of Béziers are open! The city is ours for the taking!"

The nobles ran out and were greeted by chaos. People were running everywhere, grabbing any weapons they could find. Simon de Montfort saw the gates opened wide and people streaming from the camp toward the bridge and into the town.

"To horse," he commanded. "Order all the knights into the city. We must regain control of this attack from the mob."

The knights, feeling slighted they had not led the attack, charged through the gates. It mattered not to them whether they trampled townsfolk or crusader. All that mattered to the knights was that they reclaim their honor by retaking control of the campaign.

As the attackers poured through the gates, the bells of the town's churches began clanging to sound the alarm. In response, people rushed out of their houses to find out what was going on. From the battlements, the sentries fired arrows at the attackers in a futile attempt to stem the onslaught. Enraged and despondent that Christ had abandoned them in their hour of need, some of the sentries began tearing pages out of their Bibles and attaching them to their arrows. Others shrieked in horror at the bloodbath occurring below.

When Amaury was informed of what was happening, he was overjoyed. "No one will now doubt God is on our side! Get me my horse. I must join the crusaders in their victory and claim the city in God's name."

When the abbot reached the gates, he saw mayhem and disorder. A knight in command of a group of crusaders galloped over to seek his advice. "Your Grace, my men cannot distinguish between the Christians and the heretics. What are they to do?"

"Slay them all! God will know his own!" the abbot shouted.

As the vagabonds, mercenaries, and crusaders poured into the city, the fighting became more intense. The city's defenders fought valiantly, but the sheer weight of numbers was against them. First the ramparts and then the streets fell to the invaders. The knights fought with some constraints of civility, but the vagabonds and mercenaries had none. They slit the throats of any man, woman, or child they came across so they might steal from them or merely for the pleasure of doing so. Young girls were raped and then disemboweled.

The citizens of the town sought refuge in the churches with the hope that soldiers of Christ would not dare desecrate consecrated ground. They were wrong. The doors of the church of St. Mary Magdalene were broken by the crusader army, and around seven thousand terrified inhabitants who had taken refuge in the basilica had their throats slit. Human blood and entrails flowed abundantly across the floor of Christ's temple wrought by those who claimed to be doing Christ's work. The crusaders stripped all belongings of value from the bodies and the church before setting it ablaze and slamming the great doors shut.

In the cathedral church of St. Nazaire, around twelve thousand townspeople, whole families with babes in arms had sought sanctuary from the abomination outside. More than half the number was Catholics who had remained faithful to the teachings of the Church of Rome. To calm the frightened gathering, two priests commenced a Mass to pray for God's forgiveness and protection. The crusaders burst into the magnificent edifice just as they had in the church of St. Mary Magdalene.

In their white tunics bearing the cross of their savior, they set about slaying everyone they could. It was hard work, and their tunics became blood red; the crosses on their garments were no longer discernable. The priests who had been ministering to the congregation were slaughtered on the altar. When the crusaders had plundered everything of value, they streamed out to seek more plunder. Before leaving the holy sanctuary, they set it afire to complete God's work.

The Chrysalis of Oc

As they slammed the massive doors shut behind them, those inside who had survived the attack and those still alive though mutilated, howled and screamed for salvation. The flames rose. Smoke filled the air. It became difficult to breath. The lucky few who could still walk rushed to the doors but found them barred. Hungry flames leaped into the air and began to lick the carved, vaulted ceiling. In no time, the dry, wooden beams caught fire. As their strength diminished, they cracked and yielded to the weight of the roof. In a mighty roar and rush of air, the ceiling fell. Those who were not killed instantly were burned alive. Within hours, what had been the magnificent cathedral of St. Nazaire had been reduced to no more than a charred pile of stones reeking of burned flesh.

As the day wore on, the vagabonds and the crusader foot soldiers grew weary of the tiresome business of killing and plundering. The town was theirs, so the threat of dying at the hands of their adversaries no longer loomed over them. They had also amassed more spoils than they could carry, so they sought amusement as a reward for their hard day's labor. Captives were tied up and mutilated. Girls and boys were raped and abused while others were thrown alive from the city walls. Some were used for target practice. Others were dragged by horses through the cobblestone streets. The depravity practiced by the crusaders against the townspeople was limited only by the victors' imaginations.

By nightfall, with no more Occitanians left to kill, the crusaders fought among themselves over the spoils. The disputes were aggravated by the fact that many of the disparate groups in the army hated each other and had nothing in common save for the crusade itself. The northern barons, fearful of a full-scale riot, sent their knights into the town to try to quell the mayhem and regain control. It was a fearful task. Drunken gangs of crusaders roamed the streets, fiercely armed and ready to kill at the slightest provocation. The knights used their swords and lances or struck them with their staffs.

The king of the Vagabonds was furious with the knights. When they demanded his followers restore most of the property they had taken to the church, he was enraged. "Burn the town. Destroy it all!" he screamed to his gangs of villains. "If we shall not have what we have rightfully earned, then neither shall the church."

In no time, the whole town was on fire. Every home, every church, every shop, every schoolhouse was set ablaze. The flames consumed everything that had been Béziers—all its wealth and all its people.

From the crusader camp, Amaury watched with joy as the funeral pyre that was Béziers lit up the night sky. "My Lord de Montfort, this has truly been a blessed day. Like Sodom and Gomorrah, God's mighty hand has vanquished his enemies."

"Indeed, your Grace," said de Montfort, standing close with his personal priest. "I will admit even I did not expect to take the town with so little effort."

"You underestimate God. When he is on your side, his gifts can be unexpected, and you must be prepared to exploit them. The citizens of Béziers brought their destruction upon themselves with their vile infidelity to God."

"Indeed, my Lord Abbot," a monk said. "On today of all days, the feast day of our Lady Mary Magdalene, many of them were screaming at us from the battlements saying that Mary Magdalene was the concubine of Jesus Christ."

The priests all crossed themselves and muttered blessings.

"For such blasphemy, God demands no less than their total destruction," declared the abbot.

"If you will excuse me, I wish to confess to my priest and give thanks to the Almighty for our victory," said de Montfort.

"Of course. I will remember you in my prayers this evening, but first I must write to the pope to inform him of God's glorious victory here today." The abbot made the sign of the cross over Simon.

"Scribe, take a letter to the pope."

Obediently, his scribe sat at his feet with a clean sheet of parchment and a quill. The abbot began. "Today, your Holiness, at least twenty thousand citizens were put to the sword regardless of rank, age, or sex. From my reports, around seven thousand enemies of the church were destroyed in the church of the Madeleine and around eight thousand in the cathedral of Saint-Nazaire. It was a miracle sent from God. The workings of divine vengeance are wondrous to behold."

In Rome, the pope was well satisfied with the report on his crusade against the Albigensians.

CHAPTER 32

An Ignoble Death

1209, Late July

The crusaders marched west from Béziers. Their next major objective was the town of Carcassonne, the family seat of Raymond-Roger, an even richer prize than Béziers.

News of the crusaders' victory at Béziers and the fate of its inhabitants had wreaked fear and dread across the Occitan countryside. The hundred or more small, fortified villages in the path of the invading army had surrendered without a fight. On the coast, in Narbonne, the town readily gave up all its heretics to be burned. They also turned over to the church all the property of the Jews who had lived there or in Béziers. The abbot made daily reports of their progress to the pope, who responded with his blessings for the continued success of the crusade.

Carcassonne

Raymond-Roger had hurried from Béziers to Carcassonne to prepare its defenses. News of the fall of Béziers and the slaughter of its inhabitants had hit the young lord hard. He had been friends with many of the dead; they had been influential in his upbringing, and he had depended on them for advice. Their lives had been so cruelly taken.

The captain of the guard, Guillaume de Laurac, entered the chamber in panic. "My Lord, we have news the crusader army is advancing rapidly from Narbonne. They will be outside our walls by the end of the month. I am not sure we can withstand a siege mounted by such a multitude. They have many large and powerful war machines, and our soldiers have little experience of a siege."

"What do you suggest we do, Captain? Raymond-Roger asked calmly. "Surrender? If we submit to the army of the pope, they will demand we turn over to the church all the Good Christians within our walls. You know what their fate will be. Do you have friends and family who do not acknowledge the legitimacy of the Church of Rome?"

The captain was nervous. "Er, yes I do, my Lord."

"Could you stand by and watch them burned alive?"

The captain shook his head shamefully. "No, my Lord. I could not."

"No. That is not the Occitan way. It is the way of the Church of Rome and its allies the French, but their ways are not ours, and that is what we are fighting for."

The captain paused. He was ashamed but still reluctant to commit to a course of action in which he had no confidence. But he knew there was but one reply for him to give. "Yes, my Lord. I will do my best to prepare the city for a siege."

"Thank you, Guillaume. Although our situation may appear dire, there is hope we may yet prevail. Our walls are thick and tall, and we have nearly thirty watchtowers. The city will not fall easily."

"No my Lord, but the population of the town is greatly swollen by many Good Christians and others who have fled before the crusaders. I am worried about our supplies. If it is a long siege, our provisions could run out."

"Then we must begin rationing them immediately."

"Yes, my Lord. I will order it."

"I will play one last political card I have to see if we might yet avert this conflict. The abbot would not listen to me, but he may listen to King Pedro."

"But my Lord, he came to Carcassonne five years ago to try to heal the rift between the Church of Rome and the Friends of God, but the meeting ended in failure. In fact, it made matters worse. Do you really think he could help us now?"

"I do not know, but the stakes are much higher for all of us now than they were then. I must try everything to prevent my people from suffering the same fate as those in Béziers. I took an oath to protect them, and am prepared to do whatever I can to uphold it."

1209, August – Carcassonne

At dawn on the first day of August, the unending crusader army began arriving before the walls of Carcassonne. As they had done in Béziers, they cut down trees to satisfy their many needs and built defensive earthworks. Throughout the day, the crusaders poured in by the tens of thousands, covering what had been green fields with their tents and animals. By nightfall, the city was surrounded by a city five times the size of that within the walls. The siege had begun.

The next day, before any serious fighting had begun, King Pedro arrived in answer to Raymond-Roger's plea for help. He immediately called for a truce between the two sides so they might find a negotiated way to avoid the conflict.

Abbot Amaury was in no mood to negotiate and stated his position forthrightly at the outset. "My demands… that is, the demands of the pope, are simple. The basic ones are first, that the man before us, Raymond-Roger III de Trencavel, must give up all claims to his lands and titles. In not moving to extirpate the heresy in his lands, he has shown himself unfit to hold office. He has thus been excommunicated by the pope. Henceforth, no man owes him allegiance or should have any dealings with him.

"Second, all known or suspected heretics in Carcassonne must be declared to the church and brought in chains before tribunals of the church so their fate may be adjudicated before God.

"Third, the property of all Jews, other infidels, heretics, and all church properties that have been seized by others must be turned over to the church."

The abbot stopped. "There are others, but we will discuss those later."

"But I could not eradicate the heresy. It was impossible!" Raymond-Roger protested.

King Pedro's firm, loud voice cut him short. "My dear Abbot, are you not being a little too demanding? The heresy is deeply rooted in this region. No one should know that better than yourself, for you are from this region."

"Yes, but unlike Lord Trencavel, I have dedicated my life to eradicating it and restoring God's order. He has done the reverse. He has knowingly allowed heretics on his town councils and to hold other positions of authority. He has even allowed Jews to hold power over Christians. These are abominations before God, as you well know, King Pedro."

"Abbot, you know there is no more loyal Catholic or friend of the church than I. I have fought tirelessly to expand the dominion of the church in Spain and rout the infidels. Yet even in Aragón, the heresy flourishes. Raymond-Roger here is young and inexperienced. I know him to be a good man and a faithful Catholic. If the church were to give him more time and help, he might suppress the heresy and we could avert much bloodshed."

The abbot was unmoved. "These southern lords have been given adequate time and have been warned repeatedly they must act to protect the interests of the church, yet they have done nothing. Indeed, worse, they have encouraged the heresy and allowed it to spread to the point that it now endangers all of Christendom. The patience of the pope is exhausted. He was left no choice but to organize this crusade to liberate the region from the clutches of the Devil."

"And you seek to spread God's word by butchering innocent people, even those who have remained faithful to the church? All have heard tales of what your holy warriors did in Béziers," roared King Pedro.

"God can be vengeful when he is angered," thundered Amaury. "It is best all remember that. He owes no apology to any mortals be they serfs or kings."

"Are you threatening me, Abbot?"

Before the abbot could respond, de Montfort spoke. "King Pedro, I am sure the abbot meant no threat. He only wished to remind everyone that God is all powerful and that if we transgress him, it is at our peril."

"You must be Simon de Montfort," the king said. "I have been told of you. Tell me, why is a northern landless lord so concerned about the souls of Occitanians?"

"He was chosen by the pope," cried Amaury.

"To do God's work or steal our southern lands for the pope or maybe even King Philippe-Auguste?" King Pedro demanded.

King Pedro and Simon de Montfort reached for their swords. The abbot sat. "My Lords, I think these negotiations are concluded. I do not see us reaching agreement on the major issues, so we will have to put ourselves in God's hands. The crusade against the heresy will continue until God wills it to stop."

Raymond-Roger returned with the king to Carcassonne and summoned his wife. "The siege will not be lifted," he said. "I have failed you and my people. What happens now is beyond my control. I can no longer guarantee your safety or that of anyone in Carcassonne. You must take our child and go with King Pedro. He will accompany you to Foix, where you can take refuge with the count and Esclarmonde."

"No," she said. "I will not leave your side."

"But you must. I will not be able to concentrate on defending the city and its people if I have to worry about your safety. You must go. When this is over, you can both return."

His wife clutched him. "I am afraid we will never see you again. They will kill you! That abbot is a demon sent by Satan to destroy us. Come with us. Do not remain here."

"I cannot abandon my people. Go. I have much to do."

"I have seen few cities as well fortified as this one," de Montfort said to Amaury after a brief reconnaissance. "It could be a long siege."

"We will stay here until the city falls," vowed the abbot. "God will not abandon us."

"It will please me to be his instrument, your Grace. With his help, we will succeed."

The battle raged for several days. *Ballistas, mangonels, trebuchets,* and all manner of powerful catapults and rotating-beam artillery were employed by each side. The defenders attempted to set fire to the crusader camp, while the crusaders tried to weaken the walls by pounding them with large stones. However, the walls held firm, and the crusaders quickly extinguished the fires with water from the river.

On the seventh of the month, de Montfort came unexpectedly smiling into Amaury's tent. "I have found it. Their weakness. The city will be ours. God has shown me the way."

The abbot hid his annoyance at being interrupted in his meditations. He strained a smile. "This is truly good news. Pray tell me what the Lord has revealed to you."

"You see here," he said, pointing to a map. "There are two poor quarters of the city that lie just outside the walls. They extend from the walls to the banks of the Aude."

"What is the importance of these peasant dwellings?" the abbot asked as if just to acknowledge their existence might soil him. "They will surely be infested with rats and filthy urchins. Our men will risk the plague there."

"Your Grace, we have been observing these quarters carefully and noticed that each day, a nearly endless line of peasants comes down to the river to draw water. Yesterday, we captured some with buckets in hand. They revealed that unlike Béziers, there are no wells within the walls. If we take these quarters, we will cut the city off from water."

"Excellent!" exclaimed the abbot. He rubbed his hands with joy. "Do we know how much water they have stored inside the city?"

"No, Abbot. Unfortunately, the prisoners did not have that information. However, none was aware of any large holding tanks. Since the river has always been there to supply their needs, they probably never thought to build any."

"Excellent news indeed, my Lord. God has guided you well. Take all the men you need. Overrun those quarters. Destroy them if you have to. Burn them. We shall cut this umbilical cord. The city will shrivel up like a prune in the scorching Midi sun."

"I have already given the orders, your Grace. They will be ours before dusk."

"I shall thank God for his blessings and reflect on what to do with the city when it surrenders. God will see you are well rewarded, my Lord."

"Thank you, your Grace."

The fighting in the two quarters was fierce, hand-to-hand. It lasted most of the day. Raymond-Roger's soldiers had the advantage of fighting on home ground and with the support of the dwellers of the suburbs, but the crusaders had the advantage of numbers. No matter how many crusaders the defenders killed, there were always more to take their place. By late in the day, the defenders had no option but to abandon the two quarters and withdraw behind the city walls.

Conditions in the city quickly deteriorated. People prayed for rain though they knew they were asking for a miracle; the summer rains in the Midi rarely arrived before the end of August, and they knew they would not be able to hold out that long. After a week without water, the population was weakening. Many became delusional from thirst. Disease was spreading, and Raymond-Roger knew that if he did not act soon, there would be no one left to save. Their numbers were too few, and they were too weak to consider attacking the enemy. He was left with only one option. Surrender.

The night of the fourteenth of August was a long one for Raymond-Roger. His thoughts were occupied with the onerous task that lay before him in the morning. Just after dawn, he summoned the captain of the guard for his daily update. As he had feared, the situation had deteriorated further overnight. He had to follow his conscience. "Saddle my horse. I ride out to the crusader camp to seek terms of surrender."

"My Lord, you cannot! They—" cried Guillaume, checking himself.

"Guillaume, you know I must. We can hold out no longer. I have failed my people."

"No, my Lord, you did not fail them! The count of Toulouse failed them. The pope, the Church of Rome, the king of France all failed them, not you! Do not blame yourself. The people know you did not desert them. No one could have done more than you."

"Nonetheless, I can no longer protect them as they deserve. I fear they will pay a heavy price. It grieves me terribly to have to invite these savages into our fair city. The Good God has deserted us. I can only pray he spares our citizens from the fate that befell their brethren in Béziers. I have no choice but to throw us all on the mercy of the abbot. We will see if he truly has a soul."

"I will accompany you, my Lord."

Raymond-Roger, surrounded by a few knights, rode into the crusader camp under a flag of truce. They were received under a promise of safe conduct and escorted to the tent of the abbot and de Montfort. "Abbot Amaury, I come to negotiate terms for the surrender of Carcassonne," said the young lord, kneeling before the abbot.

"I do not negotiate with a heretic," replied the abbot. "You have no authority to negotiate anything. You have been excommunicated. No man, let alone a legate of the Holy See, should give you quarter."

"But your Grace, I swore to you at our last meeting I am not a heretic. I have always kept the faith, and I have remained true to my vows to the church."

"If you had remained true to your vows, you would not have tolerated the heresy. I am told you have sent your wife and child for protection to a family of avowed heretics. What greater proof could there be of your heresy?"

"But, your Grace—"

"Silence! I wish to hear no more from you. I will deal with Carcassonne as the Lord directs me. I need no advice from an apostate. You forsook your people when you allowed the error to spread. It is too late for you now to claim you care for their well-being!"

"But, your Grace, I love my people—"

"Guards, take him away!" screamed the abbot. "I do not wish him in my sight."

A few of de Montfort's men grabbed Raymond-Roger, took his sword, and dragged him out of the tent. The knights with him were likewise removed as they protested the outrage of the crusaders' oath of safe conduct.

When they were gone, the abbot clapped his hands and smiled. "Well, my Lord de Montfort, it would appear Carcassonne is yours for the taking."

"Indeed, your Grace. A rich prize indeed. Do you think yourself not a little too hard on Trencavel? He is, after all, the nephew of the count of Toulouse, our ally."

"That is why he shall be sacrificed. He is but a pawn in the game, but one I shall take to get to his uncle. He is our real enemy. The count of

Toulouse is the key to reclaiming this region for the church. Until he is dispossessed, the threat of heresy remains."

"But we cannot attack the count or any of his possessions while he participates in the crusade. They are under the protection of the church," Simon reminded him.

"That is why we must force him out of the crusade. We shall then be free to move against him. But all that is for later. Let us return to the matter in hand, Carcassonne. It should make a fine base in the region for our campaign."

"Yes, your Grace."

"Prepare your men to enter the city. I do not want a repeat of the anarchy in Béziers. If we are to reclaim these lands for the church, we must preserve something of value. They say Béziers burned for three days after we left it and is now no more than a charred, black mound. That is of no value to the church."

"Understood, your Grace. I will instruct the knights to remain in control. What are your orders regarding the population? Are we to put them all to the sword as in Béziers?"

The abbot hesitated. "No. I will demonstrate God's mercy this time. After all, King Pedro may have made a valid point. In Carcassonne, we shall surrender to God's judgment only those who are known heretics. The rest of the inhabitants will be forced out of the city and permitted to take with them nothing but their sins. When the inhabitants are gone, you can allow the army to enter in an orderly fashion. They may pillage whatever they want provided it does not belong to the church. That way, they shall receive their reward and we will not have a riot on our hands."

"A wise strategy, your Grace. It shall be done exactly as you command."

That evening, the abbot dictated his daily report to his master in Rome. "Holy Father, I am pleased to report to you that today the Lord smote our enemies in the city of Carcassonne and laid open the gates to the soldiers of your crusader army. As an example to the people of the region that God could be merciful as well as vengeful, I decided to allow those not known to be heretics to flee the town with their lives but without their possessions. I believe that will lead to the greater glory of the church among the population rather than being seen as a sign of weakness."

1209, Autumn – Region of Carcassonne

After Béziers and Carcassonne were conquered, most of the small towns in the region surrendered without resistance. Albi, Castelnaudary, Castres, Fanjeaux, Limoux, Lombers, and Montréal all fell in quick succession. However, as autumn arrived, there was renewed hope that the nightmare for our people might be short lived.

Having completed their quarantaine obligation to the church and with all their sins forgiven, many of the crusaders began to melt away. It was important to them to return north to their homes and families before the winter. New recruits would not arrive to replace them before the spring. Thus, defending and administering the newly conquered lands during the winter months posed a significant challenge to the crusaders. Most Occitanians prayed the challenge would be too great and the few crusaders remaining would melt away to leave us in peace once more. Unfortunately, that was not to be.

Abbot Amaury declared Raymond-Roger, rotting in a dungeon far below them in the castle of Carcassonne, to be dispossessed of all his lands. He convened a meeting of the nobles to elect his successor.

In the Holy Land, it had been customary to award the captured lands to one of the high-ranking crusader nobles. Following that custom, that would be either the duke of Lorraine, the counts of Nevers and Saint-Pol, the duke of Bourgogne, or another major representative of the French nobility. This time, however, that was not the will of the abbot or the pope.

The lands had been conquered in the name of the church, and the pope had no wish to turn them over to a French noble whose first loyalty would be to the king of France. Furthermore, the crusade must continue until the church gained control over all Occitania. To ensure the success of the crusade, it had to be led by a capable military leader with no land in the north that might distract him. One man fit these requirements.

"The pope appoints Simon de Montfort, Count of Leicester, as viscount of Béziers and Carcassonne," declared the abbot. "With these titles, he will also be responsible to the church to administer the town of Albi and the Razès area. He will also remain commander of the crusader forces that will eradicate the heresy from all southern lands."

Simon de Montfort bowed to the other nobles, feigning humility. "It is a great honor the pope bestows upon me. I will try to do justice to the confidence the church places in me."

There was little surprise at the meeting. The abbot had previously informed the nobles of the pope's decision. Most of the nobles were only too anxious to leave the crusade and return to their French estates. They knew it would be an ongoing struggle to hold the southern lands they had taken. They had no stomach for more fighting.

With the main issues of the initial campaign resolved and the crusaders having firmly established a foothold in the southern lands, the majority of the French nobles returned to their northern domains. Only the duke of Bourgogne, with a small contingent of around three hundred, remained with de Montfort. They continued to rout out the Cathar menace and restore the authority of the church over the population.

However, as the crusaders' numbers diminished further, to protect his new possessions, de Montfort had to offer double wages to retain a minimum garrison of about five hundred men.

1209, November 10 – Carcassonne

Raymond-Roger had languished in isolation in the depths of his own prison for nearly three months. During that time, he had been allowed no visitors, and no news had been given of him by the crusaders. Many had forgotten about him; none knew whether he was alive or dead. With the region firmly under the authority of the church and de Montfort installed as the new viscount of Carcassonne and Béziers, the continued existence of the young Trencavel was becoming a liability to the abbot and de Montfort.

The cell door opened into the blackness. The youthful prisoner was gaunt, emaciated, and blinded by the light of the torch a soldier held. One went to where the prisoner was chained to the wall and held him up. Another poured a foul-tasting liquid into his mouth and forced him to swallow it. He had no strength to resist. They left.

Later that day, Abbot Amaury announced the regrettable death of Raymond-Roger from dysentery. He had been only twenty-four. When the news reached his wife in Foix, she screamed in grief. It was left to the Good Christian, Esclarmonde de Foix, to console her.

1209, November – Council of Avignon

With the death of the young Occitan noble, de Montfort's control was firmly established over the Trencavel lands he had been ceded. Simon was pleased but not content, for both he and his masters, the abbot and the pope, had much greater ambitions. They would not rest until the church exercised absolute authority over all the possessions of the count of Toulouse. Thus, at the church's urging, de Montfort began attacking the lands of the count of Foix, including Mirepoix, Foix, and Saverdun. However, with an army only a shadow of what it had been in the summer, his attacks were easily repulsed. Moreover, many of the inhabitants under his control, realizing his weakened military capacity, rose up against him. This forced him to spend much of his time retaking towns.

It continued to vex the abbot that he was still not free to attack the lands of the count of Toulouse. As long as he remained an ally, he kept his good standing with the church and his lands remained under its protection. Somehow, he had to find a way to drive Count Raymond from the crusade and have his excommunication reinstated by the church. To advance his plan, he convened a meeting in Avignon of the principal Catholic hierarchy in the south.

The Council of Avignon was well attended. Two papal legates, including the abbot, four archbishops, and twenty bishops, constituted an ecclesiastic council of unchallengeable legitimacy in the eyes of the faithful. The council was to reassert the church's control over the newly conquered territories and to clarify the dogma the inhabitants would be required to adhere to. However, that was not the abbot's first objective.

Amaury moved before the council that Count Raymond be newly excommunicated and thus dispossessed of all his lands, properties, and vassals. He presented no evidence to the council to justify the excommunication. The abbot charged simply that the count had not lived up to his commitment to the church to aggressively eliminate the heresy in his possessions. The fact that he had been participating in the crusades was not taken into account, nor was the count given the opportunity to defend himself against the charges.

The council voted overwhelmingly to support the excommunication. Seizing on the mood of the council, the bishop of Toulouse, Foulquet de Marseilles, petitioned the council to go even further and act against the heretics in his city. He described how his brutal attempts to restore the power of the church over the inhabitants of Toulouse had met with failure, so much so that he dared not walk alone in the city for fear he might be killed.

On hearing that, the council voted to excommunicate all the inhabitants of Toulouse for their continued support of the count and their tolerance of the heresy. Henceforth, all Christians would be free to kill any citizen—man, woman, or child—of Toulouse as an infidel and appropriate their possessions for themselves.

The council also ruled against many of the social practices the Occitanians valued so greatly and that set them apart from the rest of Europe. All were despised by the church, which viewed them as heretical or a direct threat to its authority.

The council took aim at the troubadours, a long and much-loved Occitan tradition. Much to the anger of the church, they had become wildly popular throughout all the courts of Europe. Many troubadours were self-confessed heretics who sang of the virtues of the fair sex, of the equality of men and women, and brotherly love. Such values were in conflict with the teachings of the church, and the troubadours rarely missed an opportunity to point that out. They ridiculed the church, even the pope, and exposed the corruption of its priests.

To suppress the troubadour art, the council forbade in churches "all play acting, hopping dances, indecent gestures, ring dances, and sung love-songs or ditties." It also declared, "Nobody shall on such occasions sing devilish songs or play games or dance."

Second, the council took aim at the Occitan principle of tolerance to those of other religions or ethnicities. The council mandated laws against the hiring of Christian servants by Jews and warned the faithful not to exchange services with Jews but to avoid them as "pollution." The council nullified all marriages between Christians and Jews and forbad "Jews and harlots" from touching bread or fruit exposed for sale.

The council enjoined all bishops to call upon the civil power to exterminate heretics. The council reconfirmed the papal bull that threatened princes who refused to extirpate heretics from their realms with excommunication and forfeiture of titles and possessions.

Amaury was most gratified. "My fellow soldiers in Christ, you have done well. The actions of this council are the first important steps in reclaiming these heathen lands from the servants of Lucifer. More work is ahead of us, but with God's help and the guidance of his eminence, we shall triumph over those who have erred and led the people of Occitania from God's church. In the struggle ahead of us, we shall save as many souls as possible, but we shall be unrepentant in seeking out those who reject God's order and will destroy them."

The abbot looked around the council for acknowledgment. It came only in the form of a polite handclap, but that was enough to satisfy him. "I have an announcement to make," Amaury proclaimed with a smile. "I have received a communication from the pope." He held up the scroll with the papal seal clearly visible. "His eminence has asked me to assume the post of the archbishop of Narbonne. Of course I humbly accepted."

Several archbishops raised their glasses in a toast.

"It should not be lost on our enemies, of course, that the count of Toulouse is the duke of Narbonne," Amaury added contemptuously.

1209, December – Lastours

The situation was growing steadily more desperate for what remained of the crusader army. It was now a mere shadow of its former self. Only those with no homes to go to or those hoping to further enrich themselves by offering their swords in the service of the cross remained.

Despite his weakened situation, de Montfort had not been content to cower behind Carcassonne's walls and wait for new crusaders to arrive in the spring. It was in his blood to be the aggressor, not the defender. He had waged limited campaigns with his few forces.

Ever mistrustful of the intentions of the count of Toulouse, de Montfort was anxious to control as much of the countryside around his new possessions as possible. Since early autumn, he had pursued all those who opposed him openly, and until the beginning of December, the campaign had gone well. He had added many small towns to his possessions. However, the campaign faltered when the crusaders arrived in the Valley of Orbiel, a strategic passageway controlling access to the Black Mountain.

The three castles of Lastours perched precariously on a long, thin, rocky crest that ran down the middle of the valley. The castles dominated the valley. The largest was Cabaret, encircled by a thick wall and fiercely held by Pierre-Roger de Cabaret, an Occitan knight owing his allegiance to the Trencavel family.

Since his arrival in the valley, Simon had discovered much to his cost that Pierre-Roger was a more formidable adversary than any of the Occitan lords he had encountered. He had shown himself to be a skilled commander on the battlefield. Simon's position was made even more difficult by the strength of his enemy's defensive position. Flanking the castle of Cabaret on opposite sides sat the two round towers of Fleur-Espine and Quertinheux. They formed a defensive chain Simon had been unable to break, but that had not been for lack of trying. Simon had applied all the tactics of warfare he knew. He had painstakingly analyzed the castles' defenses for weaknesses by probing them with small attacks. He had then launched full-scale attacks, but his efforts had all been unsuccessful. The weather was now turning sharply colder and the steep slopes were white with snow.

Simon had already lost more men than he could afford, and his men were not equipped to sustain a siege through the winter. If the day's attack failed, he would have to retreat to Carcassonne and wait for the spring. It would be a bitter pill to follow for Simon, who was not used to failure. He studied the maps as the cries of battle grew louder outside.

The duke of Bourgogne strode into the tent, his armor clanging. "Simon, we must withdraw. Our attack on Cabaret was turned back. They cut us down with stones and arrows. We are trying to assail a mountain! Lastours cannot be taken except by siege, and for that, we will have to return next year."

"What of my cousin, Bouchard de Marly, Lord of Saissac and his men? They were to attack the Quertinheux tower and take out its defenders.

If they can destroy that tower, it would greatly weaken the defense of Cabaret."

"I fear they have failed. I saw a large group of knights led by Pierre-Roger coming to augment the defense of the tower. They can see our every move from their eagles' nests on top of that damned ridge."

"That may be, but do not lose hope. We have a higher vantage point. God sits above all in heaven, and he will show us a way. There are many Cathar heretics under the protection of Pierre-Roger. The Lord has led us here to destroy them."

"I hope he acts soon, or it is we who shall be destroyed."

Simon de Montfort's son, Amaury, burst into the tent. "Father! They have captured Bouchard de Marly!"

"How?" screamed Simon. "When? I must rescue him."

"It is too late!" Amaury de Montfort cried. "They have taken him inside Cabaret. They came at us from all sides. We had no chance. I barely escaped myself."

"Yet you are here and he is not!" shouted Simon. "You do not flee the battlefield when one of ours is under attack!"

"Father, Bouchard himself ordered us to retreat."

"You are too hard on the boy," interjected the duke. "He fought bravely. I saw so myself. He is only seventeen, and this is his first crusade. He still has much to learn."

"He is a de Montfort. That is all the experience he should need," snapped Simon.

"Father, Pierre-Roger came at us like a mountain lion. We did not see him, and suddenly they were all around us. We were greatly outnumbered. Many of our men were killed or captured as they pursued us down the mountain."

"We can stay here no longer," thundered the duke. "It is as I said. We will all freeze to death if we are not cut down first by Pierre-Roger. He can see our numbers. It will not be long before he turns the tables and attacks our camp. I am returning to Carcassonne with my men. You would be wise to follow." The duke stormed from the tent.

"Damn this cursed Pierre-Roger!" screamed Simon. "If any harm comes to Bouchard de Marly, I will slay him myself." He plunged a dagger into the table. He looked wearily at his son. "Tell the men to break camp.

We leave for Carcassonne before nightfall." The words caused him pain. "But we shall be back. Lastours will be ours." He strained to retrieve his dagger. "The Lord has told me it will be so."

1210, January – The Palace of the Vatican, Rome

The pope reached for another slice of venison to be washed down by yet another goblet of rich, red wine. He was in particularly good spirits after reading the latest communication from Amaury. The situation in Occitania was apparently progressing well. With the port city of Narbonne firmly in the hands of the crusaders and with Amaury as its archbishop, it would be much easier to bring in fresh troops and supplies in the spring to continue the campaign. Narbonne was a jewel Philippe-Auguste would love to have. It would be a powerful bargaining chip to bring to the negotiating table with the wayward king of France.

Once the heretics were crushed and Occitania once again paying tribute to the church, the recalcitrant monarchs of Europe would all fall in line and acknowledge his authority over them. His mission of establishing the papacy as the unchallenged authority over the spiritual and temporal worlds would be accomplished.

"Your Eminence, Count Raymond arrives tomorrow to make his case that we revoke the excommunication against him. How will you respond?" asked a bishop.

"I intend to be polite and to offer him hope that his excommunication will be lifted. Otherwise, I fear he might try to organize the Occitan lords against us."

"But surely you do not intend to lift his excommunication?"

"Certainly not. The count is a spent force we no longer need. Archbishop Amaury is particularly adamant that he remains banished from the church, and I am in agreement. I still hold the count responsible for the murder of my legate, and he continues to tolerate Cathar sympathizers in his court. Amaury's plan is to replace him with de Montfort. There is a man whose loyalty to the church is beyond question. When we are ready, we will sweep the count away with the rest of his Cathar heretics."

CHAPTER 33

The Blind Will Follow

1210, February – Carcassonne

Alix de Montmorency was the sister of the commander in chief of the Kingdom of France and wife of Simon IV de Montfort. A strong and pious woman, she had dedicated her life to the service of France, the church, her husband, and to her ambition. Angered to obsession by the dispossession of their English estates by King John Lackland, she was determined to restore the family's fortunes.

Alix was busy on a tapestry when her husband marched energetically into the room, as always, with his priest just behind him. "It is truly a glorious day," he remarked. "See how the sun is streaming in the windows. It will melt the snow on the mountains where the infidels seek the protection of Satan. Soon, our crusader army will again move against them."

"Is the army strong enough?" asked his wife.

"No, but it soon will be. See how the pilgrims stream through the front gate, anxious to redeem themselves before God by slaying heretics. The winter has not yet released the French lands from its icy grip, and yet already they come to join us."

"You have the church to thank for that, my Lord. I have heard that never a sermon goes by in the north without the priest administering to his flock on the obligation of the faithful to defend the church against the heretics."

"You are right. The church makes a powerful ally. Unfortunately, most do not come in answer to the true message. They come simply for selfish reasons. It was always that way with the crusades to the Holy Land. They come to gain absolution for their sins, for that is the reward the church has offered them. It is surely cheaper than paying the indulgences the church would otherwise demand of them. Many are also tempted by the worldly spoils they can gain by pillage and plunder."

"My Lord, you impugn the honor of those who are true Christians like ourselves. Whatever the reasons for joining us in the holy crusade, all will be doing God's work."

"You are right. I only wish all pilgrims put their duty to serve God above all. Then, they might not be so ready to abandon our cause when they have fulfilled their quarantaine."

"It certainly would benefit the crusade, and it is regrettable that many do not put the Lord first in their hearts," Alix said.

"Yes, it is sad many do not see their service to the crusade as the path to eternal salvation but as a path to earthly convenience."

"You are not a member of the clergy. That is not your concern. It is between them and God. The church will forgive their sins for their service in the crusade, which will give them another chance to lead sin-free lives and enter heaven. If they forsake that chance by sinning again, they will have no one to blame but themselves."

"Yes, and it will give the church another chance to sell them indulgences." Simon laughed. "I fear most of them will never attain salvation." He shook his head and paused for a moment. Then he clapped his hands. "Enough of that. I must focus on the task God has given me for my own salvation. I care not if these pilgrims are illiterate or untrained in the arts of warfare. I care only that they are here, for I grow restless trapped within these walls. I will find a way to use them all in my campaign. I shall shape them into the tools I need to eradicate heretics."

The priest bowed his hooded head and made the sign of the cross over Simon.

Alix put her tapestry down. "We shall defeat them. That is certain. Our cause is just. We have the blessings of the holy father while the heretics have merely the faith of old men who pray in caves or on the tops of mountains."

"That is true, but the Devil has long had the region to himself to work his evil," replied Simon. "He has dug his horns deeply into the people. It will take years to draw him out completely. How many will depend on the number of crusaders who rally to our cause."

"You will get all you need. I have that assurance from my brother," Alix said. "King Philippe-Auguste takes a keen interest in your crusade. He is too occupied at the moment with the English and the Germans to become involved directly, but he offers us his support. However, he is concerned that these lands do not become territories of Rome after the conflict. They rightfully belong to France."

"Ah, the pope and the king. The eternal struggle for power. We shall have to walk a delicate line to please them, I fear. They make powerful allies or deadly enemies."

"I do not see a conflict in serving both masters," stated Alix. "The pope will not be able to hold these lands when the crusade is over without a powerful noble to administer them for him in the name of the church. He will need a new count of Toulouse."

"Indeed, Archbishop Amaury has already assured me of that title."

"Exactly. The pope wishes it, and so does the king providing that as a noble of France, you reaffirm your oath of allegiance to him. His cousin Raymond, as count of Toulouse, owes his first allegiance to King Pedro, which does not sit well with Philippe. You will serve his needs as you will not be subject to the influence of Aragón over these lands."

"An admirable compromise that will satisfy all concerned," Simon said. "There is no time to waste in clearing these lands of heretics. As the new count of Toulouse, I shall no longer have to beg that cursed John Lackland to restore our estates in Leicestershire."

"No. You shall be a lord of Occitania, wealthier than many a northern lord. These lands are fertile, with access to the Mediterranean and control of the trade routes to Spain and Italy. The family name of de Montfort will once again be respected, and our children shall have an inheritance to be proud of," Alix said.

"Indeed. Amaury will inherit the title of count of Toulouse when I am called to heaven. His younger brother, Simon, can try to regain the earldom of Leicester."

"How has Amaury served you of late?" asked Alix. "I was disappointed he did not show the courage and initiative on the battlefield expected of a de Montfort last year."

"He is still young, inexperienced. He does not show the natural aptitude for battle I did at his age. Still, I will strive harder to mold him into the leader of men he will need to be."

"If he is to be count of Toulouse, he must earn the title," said Alix coldly. "If he is not up to the task, there is always Simon, who is more adept at wielding a sword."

"I will prepare Amaury to assume his responsibilities when they come due to him."

"Good. When do you begin your campaign?"

"I shall be ready in a few days if our numbers are sufficient."

"Do not let the number detain you. I shall take charge in your absence and ensure all new pilgrims are equipped and trained. When they are ready, I will ride out with them to the battlefield."

"No man could have a better wife than you," Simon said. "God has truly blessed me. Now where is Amaury? We must plan the campaign together."

The young Amaury arrived obediently in response to his father's summons. "Good day, mother," he said quickly, barely acknowledging her presence. "Father, rumor is we shall be resuming the crusade in a few days. Is that true?" he asked excitedly.

Simon was pleased with his son's enthusiasm. "Yes. Happily, it will not be long. See how the Almighty sends us fresh souls to replenish his armies. They come in greater numbers by the day. I believe God is as impatient as we are to see his work done."

"Do you plan to defeat the count of Toulouse this year?"

"Not so fast!" Simon laughed. "You will learn patience is as important on the battlefield as is courage. The count has the strongest army in Occitania, and Toulouse is large and well fortified."

"But you said our army swells in number every day. So soon they should be numerous enough to take the city?"

"Numerous enough yes, but they are inexperienced. Few have tasted the heat of battle. Until they have tested their mettle in a few skirmishes, they will be little better than an organized mob. If I were to attempt to lay siege to Toulouse today, I would be bogged down for months. I would risk them returning to their homes before the city fell. We will wear down our enemy. We shall challenge each of the hilltop fortresses that dominate these lands and tear down any that oppose us, one rock at a time. We shall tear out the roots of the southern nobility from this earth until they lose their grip on it. When that is done, we shall be ready to end the reign of the count."

Amaury smiled. "So we shall wage a war of attrition against the southern nobles who swear allegiance to Raymond?"

"Yes, it is in our favor that they are divided and have little experience in warfare. Individually, they will be no match for our army. When the count of Toulouse is isolated, he will not stand against us for long."

Amaury was excited. "How long do you think it will take, Father, to defeat the count? Will it be this year or next?"

"Hah. The impatience of youth! Rome and the church of our Savior were not built in a day. There is much to do. We must fight each battle one at a time and keep our faith in God. With God's help, we shall prevail, but do not ask God how long his work will take. It will be finished when God determines. Not before."

"No, Father." Amaury's smile was gone. "Where do we begin?"

"At Bram! It is a small town west of here. It is of little consequence, but by all reports, it is infested with the heresy. I intend to rout it out and set an example to the rest of these southern peasants of the wrath of God that will befall those who reject his word."

"But what of Lastours? Pierre-Roger de Cabaret still holds our cousin, Bouchard de Marly, in his mountain stronghold."

Simon de Montfort clenched his fists. "You need not remind me. We shall attack his nest in the sky again when we are strong enough, and I shall see our cousin freed. I shall bring down the vengeance of God on the lord of Cabaret and all those at his side if Bouchard de Marly is harmed. I have pledged this before God."

Alix de Montmorency moved to her son. "Take care, Amaury. Do as your father commands, and make us proud of you. My prayers will be with you both."

"I will do my best, Mother. Your prayers are welcome, and I am sure the Lord will protect us. Brother Arnaud promised me this morning he would pray for us three times daily while we are waging this holy war."

Alix strained a smile.

"Fetch me the maps," Simon shouted to a soldier.

Alix curtsied. "I will leave you to plan your campaign, for I have much to do. I know you will bring only honor to the name de Montfort."

1210, March – Bram

Bram was a small, insignificant village, little more than a small cluster of stone houses built in concentric circles around a square and an ancient church. The village was not fortified, nor did it sit in a strategic location such as by a river, on a craggy hilltop, or by a major route. It was not home to any of the southern nobles or of any of the rich and powerful families of the region. It was merely the home of simple people who struggled daily to raise a living from the parched earth of the plain below the Black Mountain. They were farmers, merchants, and weavers hoping only the turbulent world around them would pass them by. Unfortunately, that was not to be.

The inhabitants of Bram were overwhelmingly sympathetic to the Friends of God though no more so than most of the towns around them. Like many Occitanians, many had stopped tithing to the Church of Rome, which they saw as cruel, avaricious, and corrupt. However, none in the town had attacked the church or the crusaders or posed any threat to them. The town could not have been more typical of all the towns in the region.

It was precisely because Bram was so average that de Montfort decided to make an example of it. He would vent his anger upon them to set an example to others of the price they would pay for resisting him.

To the buzzards that rose high on the thermals from the craggy limestone cliffs of the region, Bram would appear no more than a small dot on the landscape. To de Montfort, its appearance was much the same. He knew the town would be easy prey for his inexperienced army and would give them their first taste of warfare. It would be good for their morale. They would experience the excitement of overwhelming and slaughtering an enemy and reap the rewards. It would prepare them for the more difficult battles ahead.

The town had prepared as best it could for the onslaught. The outer streets had been barricaded by carts and piles of rocks, but there was little that could be done to make the town truly defensible. Furthermore, there were no stockpiles of food or water that might allow the town to hold out against a siege even if the fortifications had been adequate.

As a prelude to their assault on Bram, the crusaders began with a massive bombardment by numerous trebuchets and other large catapults. It did not take long before many of the buildings had been reduced to rubble under the merciless pounding. Many others were set afire by the hail of burning bales of oil-soaked hay that rained down on the town.

By the second day, the situation for the defenders was becoming hopeless. It was clear it would be only a short time before their meager defenses would be overrun. On the third day of the siege, the town elders saw no alternative but to sue for peace. Almost immediately, the town became lost in a writhing sea of white flags and red crosses that enveloped their prey like a swarm of ants.

"My Lord," cried Bishop Hurepel, running into de Montfort's tent. "The town has fallen. The town elders have agreed to accept your terms of surrender."

"Most gracious of them," mocked Simon. "And after only three days. I almost wish they had put up a more spirited resistance. It would have been better training for our army. Still, they will have other opportunities."

"What are your orders, my Lord?"

"My orders? The same as yours. Cleanse the town of the heresy. Reconsecrate the churches. Destroy any symbols of blasphemy. Have each man, women, and child in the town kneel down to kiss a crucifix and swear fidelity to the Church of Rome."

"Certainly, my Lord. And what are we to do with those who refuse? The Cathars will not swear an oath to any man."

"Burn or stone any who refuse, for they are an abomination unto God, but wait. Do not slay them all. Send one hundred or more to my guards. I have use of them. They will take a message from me to Pierre-Roger de Cabaret in his lair of heretics at Lastours."

"Gladly, my Lord," agreed the bishop, excited at the prospect. "You are truly a soldier of our Savior. Your rewards shall be great in heaven."

"I would have my rewards first in this world, bishop," proclaimed Simon. "Giraud de Pepieux betrayed me at Puisserguier and joined the heresy. He abused two of my men and sent them to me through the winter snows, dying and naked, to bring me his message. I shall send my message today to the heretics, one they will remember."

"You are truly God's servant."

"Thank you," said Simon humbly.

The bishop left with great enthusiasm to begin his task of cleansing the town of the heretics, accompanied by equally enthusiastic priests.

Simon de Montfort and Robert de Mauvoisin, a French lord and comrade at arms, rode triumphantly into what was left of Bram. Only three days before it had been a quiet, nonbelligerent collection of dwellings, now it was little more than a pile of rubble. The nobles were greeted by a thunderous welcome from the hordes of crusaders in their white and red tunics whose spirits had been lifted by the rewards they had come by in looting the town. There were few inhabitants to be seen. Those who had not been killed, raped, or mutilated in the name of the cross were in hiding. Most of the dead had not yet been cleared from the streets. Simon took great pleasure in the sight. *Who in the region would now dare oppose me?*

In the central square, by the village church, Bishop Hurepel and his lieutenant Alain de Roucy greeted them. The bishop stepped forward as a footman grabbed the reins of Simon's horse. "My Lord de Montfort, you have truly done God's work here. The pope will hear of it and will surely ask the Almighty to bless you for your deeds."

"I would be humbled by that, but I am only fulfilling my duty to God."

The bishop nodded and smiled. "Indeed. The Bible tells us 'the Lord rained upon Sodom and upon Gomorrah brimstone and fire from the Lord out of heaven. And he overthrew those cities, and all the plain, and all the inhabitants of the cities, and that which grew upon the ground.' Those who sin can expect no more than God's justice."

Alain de Roucy beckoned for Simon's attention. "My Lord, everything has been prepared as you asked," he announced, his voice a little unsteady.

Simon smiled. "Excellent. Bring them forth, for we have a long way to go. We must attain the walls of Cabaret before nightfall so all may tremble at their sight."

"Yes my Lord." The lieutenant gestured to one of his men, who disappeared behind the church. He emerged followed by a long procession flanked by monks and clergy. Many of the latter were chanting or praying with Bibles, relics, or crucifixes in hand. The procession came slowly into clear view. The crowd gasped. Many vomited. The grim procession comprised a hundred prisoners, each chained to the prisoner in front and behind. They were all ages, all professions, male and female. The only thing they had in common was that they had all refused to swear fidelity to the Church of Rome.

The appearance of the prisoners was horrific, as Simon had intended. The clothes of each of them hung in tatters on their listless frames and were soaked in their own blood, making them resemble the tunics of the crusaders. Each prisoner had a hand on the one in front, for all but the lead prisoner were blind. Their eyes had been torn out by the holy warriors of de Montfort and Innocent III. The lead prisoner had been luckier. Only one of his eyes had been gouged out so he might lead his companions.

There were no pleas for help from the procession, no singing as the unrepentant heretics were renowned to do as they march to their funeral pyres. Simon had taken measures to prevent it. Nor were there any cries of pain. There were only groans. They could not talk. In God's name, the pilgrims of Christ had cropped off their noses, cut off their lips, and cut out their tongues. They were the walking dead.

"It is a glorious day for a ride, is it not, my Lord de Mauvoisin?" asked Simon as they rode behind the ghoulish procession.

"It is indeed, my Lord. I hold that spring is the best season in these southern lands. The air is warm and clear. By summer, it is too hot and oppressive for me. I shall return to my lands in France before then."

"You do not wish to become a noble of Occitania?"

"No. I wish only to see these lands rid of the heretics lest the infection spreads from here onto French soil."

"You are a good Christian, Robert. God will reward you."

"In heaven, I trust. Though it would seem that you will be rewarded in this life. I hear Archbishop Amaury intends to appoint you as the new count of Toulouse."

Simon shrugged. "The archbishop is a devout soldier of Christ, and I am honored by the trust he has put in me. He has dedicated himself to removing Count Raymond, for he is a Cathar sympathizer and many of his family are heretics. While he is overlord, the heresy will persist in this region. It is premature to discuss who will replace him."

"I cannot think of a better person than you."

"If I am asked, it will be a great honor," said Simon self-effacingly. "Before that day, though, there is much to do if we are to overthrow the count of Toulouse. It will not be an easy task, for his family has ruled over this region since the days of Charlemagne. He has allowed the people too much freedom. It has made him a very popular ruler, but is also the origin of his problems. The heretics took advantage of his weakness to take root and prosper in his lands like weeds. It is a lesson to all of the danger in being a weak ruler. God decreed that the people should have monarchs chosen by him to rule over them and keep them on the path of righteousness."

"It is the natural way," de Mauvoisin said. "Left to himself, the common man would be too open to temptation."

Simon nodded. "If we are to bring down the count, we must first eliminate his basis of support, and one of his strongest supporters is Pierre-Roger, lord of Lastours, where we are headed. It is a string of castles built along a long, narrow, high ridge. Many say the Devil himself must have built them for it is hard to imagine how they were put there by man. I tried taking Lastours by siege last year, but my engines were ineffective. The mountain is tall and steep."

"They must be very formidable to resist Simon de Montfort," teased de Mauvoisin.

"They are indeed. You shall see for yourself. But this has become more than a simple matter of weakening the count. During the siege, Pierre-Roger took my cousin Bouchard de Marly as a prisoner. I have sworn I shall not rest until he is free."

"You think that if you cannot take his castles by force, you can scare him out?"

"More or less. This gift we shall deliver him today will show him what I am capable of when angered and make him think twice about harming Bouchard de Marly."

Robert de Mauvoisin smiled. "You are devious, but that is why the archbishop put you in charge of the crusade, a man who fights with his head as well as his sword."

"I follow only God's word. This morning, my priest reminded me of a passage in the book of Nahum. 'The Lord is a jealous God, filled with vengeance and wrath. He takes revenge on all who oppose him and furiously destroys his enemies.' If I am to do God's work, I must not show pity to heretics or those who support them such as Pierre-Roger."

It was a long walk for the hundred tortured souls from Bram to Lastours. As they approached the castles of Lastours, most were near death. The sentries on the parapets of Cabaret high above had seen the procession heading toward them and alerted their lord.

Pierre-Roger looked out from a high tower, trying to ascertain the nature of the threat. Only when the procession had snaked its way up the mountain was he able to make out the macabre vision before him. At first, he refused to believe his eyes, assuming they were playing tricks on him. As the ghoulish procession came closer, there was no denying what he saw. "What sort of a butcher could have done this?"

Other soldiers flocked to the walls. As they screamed, wept, and vomited, Pierre-Roger saw the answer to his question. Simon de Montfort and his soldiers had followed the poor souls but remained in the valley floor to gloat.

The procession arrived at his gates. Pierre-Roger ordered the gates opened and wept as he watched the gruesome entourage enter. "This was done in the name of a god? Surely their god can have nothing to do with the Good God we worship. From their foul deeds this day, no man can doubt that the Church of Rome is the church of Satan!"

His sergeant at arms hung his head weeping. Straining to speak, he asked, "My Lord, what shall we do with them? For they suffer greatly."

"We must care for them as best we can. Send the Good Christians to minister to them, and see they are offered the Consolamentum so they might at least have a good end to their suffering. I have to believe that after their sacrifice, God will accept their souls into his kingdom. They will not have to suffer in this world again."

The sound of trumpets from outside the walls pierced the thin mountain air in a seeming affront to those in torment in the courtyard below.

"Who dares interrupt the solemnity of this hour?" demanded Pierre-Roger.

"My Lord, there is a courier from Simon de Montfort. He is at our gate and demands our surrender. How shall we respond?"

"Tell them to go back to hell where they came from!" he screamed.

CHAPTER 34

The Safe Mountain

In the autumn of 1209, Corba and I were forced to abandon our castle in Mirepoix. It had been the family home for generations. We had always known peace there until the armies of the cross invaded our lands. They came like the swarms of locusts I had seen in the Holy Land, insatiable and unstoppable, devouring all in their path, a dark cloud upon the land.

The castle was in the rich and gentle plain of the River l'Hers, a tributary of the mighty Garonne, which flows through Toulouse. After the fall of Béziers, Albi, Fanjeaux, and other towns, it became clear our castle would not be defensible against a siege by the crusaders. When I learned of the savagery they had inflicted on the inhabitants of these poor towns, surrender became unacceptable. I moved my family and courtiers to the greater protection offered by my castle at Montségur.

Thanks to the foresight of the three most important women in my life—my wife and our mothers—the castle had been greatly fortified in recent years. The walls had been raised and strengthened, and our accommodations, though meager, were habitable. Only those close to the family and the garrison were to sleep within the walls of the castle, for its quarters were cramped.

A small town of Good Christians and believers had by then grown up outside the walls, seeking our protection. Though conditions on the top of the pog were harsh due to winter winds bearing down from the Pyrenees, the people were warmed from the inside by the fellowship of their small community. Unlike the priests of the Catholic Church, every man and woman, whether Good Christian or a stable boy, gave freely of their labor to support the settlement. As the crusaders' onslaught played out on the plains below, all felt protected in Montségur.

1210, March – Castle of Montségur

Corba came smiling into the room. Our eldest child, Philippa, chase behind her, though it did not take long for the nanny to catch up with her and whisk her away.

"Raymond, mother and I just had a wonderful lesson from Blanche de Laurac. She is visiting the castle with her daughter Mabilia. They are Good Christians and work tirelessly to take care of the sick and the orphans who have lost their parents to the crusaders. She is an inspiration. You should meet her."

"I have heard good things of her. I have heard her called the Mother of the Cathars. I believe she became a Good Christian some years ago after she was widowed. Her son still holds extensive possessions between Albi and Carcassonne."

"She seems to have such a deep understanding of everything and to be truly at peace with herself. I have never seen anyone so accepting of our existence in spite of all the terrible things going on around us. How I envy her."

"Envy? I thought envy was a sin." I teased her.

Corba gave me a scolding with just her eyes. "It is not a sin to want to be pure like her. To be a Good Christian. To help give people meaning to their lives instead of killing them. My mother and your mother both agree."

"So they do, but they are older and widowed. They have time to contemplate the meaning of life. We on the other hand are young and have responsibilities to those who depend on us, our people and our children. We must accept the realities of life."

Corba looked at me with a hint of sadness. She said nothing for a moment. She looked lost in another world. It was a look I had seen increasingly of late.

"Raymond, do you believe there is a Good God and a Bad God, or do you still cling to the dogma of the Church of Rome?"

It was a difficult question to answer, one I had been increasingly trying to cast from my mind since we had come to Montségur. I wanted to pass it off lightly, but it was clear Corba would not be content with anything less than a serious answer. "I have not had much time to dwell on such matters. You know my father believed in the Good God, as does my mother. Indeed, she is shortly to receive the Consolamentum and become a Good Christian, a member of the spiritually elect, alongside your mother. However, I have a large household and estates to run. We live in a world dominated by the Church of Rome. Many lives depend on my decisions. If I were to deny the authority of the church, I would put their lives at risk. I could not do that in good conscience even if it were to save my soul. So I try only to lead a good and pure life and leave matters of spirituality to others."

"I understand. It is right that your first responsibility is for your people. It is what makes you a good leader. If only everyone were like you ... But alas, they are not. However, despite your best efforts to protect them, they are being tortured and burned in front of you. You cannot keep your head in the sand forever."

"As always, you are right." I said, trying to console her. "Recent events have been enough to shake any man's faith, especially when perpetrated in the name of the religion he follows. I am trying to sort through my thoughts but do not see any good outcome."

"You must follow your conscience. When the time is right, the Good God will show you the way."

"I trust you are right," I replied in all sincerity.

I postponed telling Corba the bad news I had received until late in the day, when she had calmed down from our earlier exchange. "Corba, I must go to Foix. I fear I shall be there a while. Simon de Montfort and his crusader armies are laying siege to the town. Raymond-Roger has asked for my help with its defense. I cannot stand by and watch Foix fall into their hands, especially after the terrible news from Bram."

"You must go. You have no choice. May the Good God protect you, but what news is there from Bram?" asked Corba, her voice trembling. "I heard the crusaders were besieging it. It is but a small hamlet of weavers; why would the crusaders bother with it? It is no threat to them"

"Sadly, de Montfort decided otherwise. His crusaders took it and brutally massacred most of the inhabitants. The barbarity of their crimes is so horrific that I will not speak of them. I will never again be able to look upon the red crosses of the crusaders without seeing them dripping with blood. Satan could have done no worse a deed."

Corba stood up, sobbing, and grabbed hold of me tightly.

"No!" she screamed. "This nightmare goes from bad to worse. How can civilized men be capable of such evil? And in the name of Christ? What have we done to deserve this? The church and these French treat us like animals good only for slaughter. Blanche de Laurac is right. They are the servants of Satan!"

Corba ran to seek refuge in a corner of the castle to be alone with her grief.

For several months, I remained in Foix, fighting off the attacks of Simon de Montfort's devils. The castle was attacked no less than four times, and the bombardments from his war machines were unrelenting. Fortunately, thanks to the thick walls of the castle and its commanding position on top of the rock that overlooks the town, the crusader attacks were repulsed. Though there was much suffering among the defenders and the townspeople, never once did I hear cries for surrender. The memory of Bram was etched on everyone's mind.

Though Foix was spared from 'salvation' by the Christian hordes, Minerve was not so fortunate. In the foothills of the Black Mountain, to the west of Béziers and to the northeast of Carcassonne, the River Cesse and the River Brian cascaded into one another. Over the millennia, their turbulent waters carved out a rocky plateau from the white limestone on which sat the fortified village of Minerve. The present town of Minerve was built mostly by the Romans, and to this day, it looks more Roman than Occitan. The village was well protected with double surrounding walls and overhanging ledges. Perched high on the rock with near-vertical cliff walls and ringed by fast-flowing rivers, the fortress town was considered impregnable. With ready access to the fertile plain of the River Aude below and surrounded by warm, sunny slopes ideal for vineyards, the area had been fought over since prehistory. Mystical dolmens, monuments of giant rocks constructed by ancient man for purposes long forgotten, dot the hills and attest to the presence of man for millennia.

After the fall of Béziers the previous year, many Good Christians and believers had fled there for protection. The castle was defended by Viscount Guilhem de Minerve, a good man I knew personally, and a garrison of around two hundred men. Guilhem was not a believer but as a loyal subject of the Trencavels and an Occitan noble bound by the honor code of paratge. It was his obligation to protect all those seeking refuge from the foreign invaders.

1210, June 20 – Minerve

"Ah, my good Archbishop. It is an honor that you join us here in our struggle to reassert the dominion of God over those who have strayed. How is the holy father?" de Montfort asked, bowing courteously bow.

Archbishop Amaury smiled agreeably. "I am pleased to say well, especially with the reports he has been receiving of your progress against the barbarians. He grows daily more confident these lands will soon be sanitized of the heresy and returned to Christendom. He wants you to know he remembers you daily in his prayers and asks for God's help in your campaign against the forces of Satan."

"I am grateful to the pontiff and have indeed felt the presence of God alongside us in our struggle to liberate these people from the clasp of Satan. God gave us a glorious victory over his enemies in Bram, and I am confident he will also give us victory in Minerve."

"What is the importance of this village to our crusade? I have been told Guilhem de Minerve is only a minor Occitan lord and the village is of little strategic importance."

"Both are true, your Grace, but the town has become a sanctuary for many Cathars and their perfects. From here, they continue to spread the error and their infectious teachings throughout the region. If we are to eradicate the heresy, we must show we will permit no sanctuary for those who resist the will of God."

"Your thoroughness is commendable. It is good to send a clear message all will understand. There must be no doubt among peasant and noble alike that none can escape paying a heinous price for disobeying God's will."

"There will be no misunderstanding of my message, your Grace, I promise."

"Excellent. When the town has fallen, I will assist you in cleansing it of the heretics."

"Your help will be most graciously welcomed, Archbishop. My skills are in warfare, not in cleansing souls. You would take a great burden off my shoulders."

"Gladly. But first the town must fall. That looks to me to be a considerable challenge, but then my skills are not in warfare. What gives you such confidence? Amaury asked.

"Your Grace, it is well placed. The rock walls are too steep to climb, and if we tried we would be attacked from above with rocks or boiling oil. Fortunately, that will not be necessary. I brought four siege engines with which I will attack the town from neighboring hills. The defenders of Minerve will soon see the damage these magnificent trebuchets and mangonels can inflict. They will tremble at the very sound of their ropes hissing and straining. They will rain God's wrath down upon the defenders. It is a glorious sound indeed, one I am sure you will enjoy. A most heavenly chorus. The town will not resist our bombardment for long."

"It heartens me that you do not anticipate a long siege. I am anxious to move against the more powerful nobles of the count of Toulouse. Time spent here distracts the crusade from its ultimate mission. Do not forget our true enemy is the count. He must remain the focus of our campaign. This crusade will not be complete until Raymond is overthrown and you are put in his place."

"How could I forget that, your Grace? It is always uppermost in my mind."

"Good. In turn, I bring you good news. Just a week ago, King Pedro and the Occitan lords met in Montréal. They were seeking Pedro's support in fighting the crusade in return for their offer to swear allegiance to him. Fortunately, Pedro's forces are currently too occupied fighting the Moors in Spain for him to offer them any assistance."

"I thought King Pedro was a champion of our cause in Spain."

"He is, and he is very much in favor with the holy father."

"Why would he want to aid the Cathars?"

"He is truly a Christian knight. But his sister is married to Count Raymond and he dreams of a greater Aragón, one that extends across the Pyrenees and incorporates the Occitan lands. There is the danger his faith may come second to his lust for territory."

"But these lands belong to France. I have sworn that to King Philippe-Auguste."

"And rightly so. The pope has already ruled as such. But King Pedro may not see it that way. We will have to watch him. Once he succeeds in driving the Moors from Spain, he will be free to turn his attentions to Occitania. He could become a powerful adversary."

"I shall heed your warning. But first, to a more pressing matter, I have a town to take."

"Indeed. Do not tarry on my account. I shall pray for your victory with the confidence we shall meet soon in Minerve."

The din from the crusader army filled the normally quiet mountain air as Viscount de Minerve addressed the defending garrison. "The forces of evil knock at our doors. We hear them desecrating our beloved lands and can smell their cooking fires like the infernos of hell. A foreign noble, the bishop of Rome together with his army of French barbarians demand we surrender and give over to them all those who refuse to bow before them, but we are Occitanians. Our forefathers gave us the spirit of paratge, generosity, tolerance, courteousness, and self-sacrifice. We must fight to defend that spirit so we will remain a beacon of light. If we submit to the crusaders and agree to extinguish that light, it will be a dark day for mankind. What say you all?"

The garrison erupted in a loud roar of approval.

"We all know we do not have the strength to oppose our enemy in open battle. But our walls are thick, and the Good God has blessed us with his sculpturing of the rock and the torrents that flow from the mountain for our protection. With his blessing, we shall hold out until these foreign invaders tire and leave. Our food and water are in good supply."

The soldiers cheered again.

"Pray to the Good God for deliverance from this pestilence. Now go to your posts"

By the end of the first week of the siege, the bombardment had become intense. "What is our situation, Etienne?" asked Guilhem of his captain of the garrison.

"The crusaders have placed their war machines well, my Lord. They have set up four trebuchets on the surrounding hills to pound our defenses with heavy shot. Three of them are aimed at the city gates, but the gates are strong. I have confidence they will hold. But the fourth—" He stopped in midsentence, lowering his head.

"The fourth? What of the fourth?"

"The fourth, the largest trebuchet, is targeted at the stairs and walls down to St. Rustique's well at the base of the village. If they cut us off from the well, we will have no source of water. I fear we will not be able to survive more than a few more weeks."

"So his strategy is to deprive us of water. He is truly as wicked and as devious as I have heard. Is there anything we can do?"

"My Lord, a party has volunteered to venture out tonight to destroy this *malvoisine* or 'bad neighbor' as they have named the monstrosity. They will try to burn it."

"At best that will grant us only a temporary reprieve. But let them go. The people of Minerve will be grateful for each day they can win for us against the crusaders."

"Very good, my Lord."

That night, Guilhem felt a rare moment of joy as he watched the night sky light up on the mountaintop where the malvoisine was positioned. He wondered how long if ever it would be before he felt such joy again.

Within a couple of days, as Guilhem had feared, the mighty trebuchet was pounding their well again, more heavily than before. Rock by rock, the ancient walls crumbled under the relentless assault until the ancient stairs crashed down angrily into the well and were lost in its waters far below in the bowels of the mountain. The sound of the destruction of the well sent a feeling of dread throughout the townsfolk. With no access to the well, all knew their cause was lost. The crusaders had only to wait for them to surrender or die of thirst. On Guilhem's orders, they had stored water in whatever they could muster, but after taking stock, the estimate was that it would last them barely another three weeks.

The defenders tired from the heat and began to weaken. Simon de Montfort continued hurling boulders upon the town. Many buildings were destroyed. People lived in constant fear of being mutilated or killed.

The ferocity of the attacks only strengthened the hatred the people had of the crusaders and their determination to resist them. However, determination cannot quench thirst. As the water ran out, the weakest died or became delirious. Guilhem realized they had no option but to surrender. Under a white flag, the viscount sent an emissary to the crusader army to negotiate terms of surrender. However, he returned much quicker than Guilhem had expected.

"My Lord," said the emissary, "Archbishop Amaury and Simon de Montfort refuse to negotiate any terms for our surrender. They demand that the gates be opened immediately and unconditionally and that all heretics be surrendered. Until we agree, they will bombard the town to rubble."

Guilhem's head fell heavily into his hands. "This is a grievous day for all the people of Minerve and all of Occitania. The Good God has thrown us to these devils. Now we must beg for their mercy, though I fear they have none to give."

"My Lord, the archbishop gave his word you and your men would be spared if you abandon your defense and lay down your arms."

"What of the people? What of those they brand as heretics?"

The emissary said nothing. He shook his head.

Guilhem tried to straighten himself to increase his stature, though he had never felt so small. "It would seem I have no choice. Go back to these Philistines. Tell them Minerve is theirs. We will lay down our arms. The gates will be opened, but plead with them to show the same compassion to those they consider to have transgressed them as Christ showed to those who transgressed him."

1210, July 22 – Minerve

Amaury and de Montfort rode triumphantly through the gates of Minerve followed by a procession of monks, clergy, knights, and leaders of their army. As they streamed endlessly into the small hilltop citadel, panic broke out among the citizenry. Weakened as they were in body and spirit, they had to watch helplessly as the marauding army fought among themselves to steal anything of value.

"Brother Vaux de Cernay," called out Amaury. "Take a few of your fellow brethren and go through the town. Seek out each man, woman, and child and demand they swear allegiance on the Bible to the Church of Rome. All those who refuse are to be chained and brought to the square. Take care that none are overlooked."

"Certainly, your Grace. I will deliver the heretics to God's justice."

"I quite enjoy this mountain air," de Montfort said, not hiding the pleasure he took from his conquest. "God's creation will be only more beautiful without the stain of heresy upon it."

"Certainly, my Lord," said the archbishop. "If you will give the order to erect a large pyre in the town square, I will set about cleansing it."

"Gladly. It will be good for the army. The faith of each crusader will be renewed as they witness they have played a part in the administration of God's justice."

In all, one hundred and forty men and women refused to swear the oath. They professed openly and proudly to being Good Christians, or perfects, as the Catholic clergy insisted on calling them. They received the opportunity to recant their heresy and affirm their faith in the Church of Rome, but each refused. "Neither death nor life can separate us from the faith to which we are joined," cried out one.

Amaury read from his Bible. "'There were false prophets among the people even as there shall be false teachers among you: which privily shall bring in damnable sects, even denying the Lord that hath bought them, and bring on their own heads swift damnation.'"

The prisoners appeared unmoved.

"You bring destruction upon yourselves! Your souls will be lost to eternity!" Frustrated by his failure to provoke a response, the archbishop addressed the monks. "Take them to the pyre that their souls may be returned to hell from where they came."

The monks led the chained procession toward the large pile of kindling and branches. Spontaneously, the prisoners began singing a canticle as they climbed upon the branches and allowed themselves to be tied to posts in the middle of the pile. There was joy in their voices instead of fear. Crusader, priest, and townsfolk alike looked on in awe.

A monk, realizing the power that Cathar singing was having over the onlookers, even many of the crusaders, began a chant of his own. The other monks quickly joined in trying to drown out the haunting song of the Cathars.

"Captain, set fire to the kindling to end this scourge," bellowed Simon.

Soon, the crackling of angry flames drowned out even the chanting of the monks. The air stank with the smell of burning flesh.

"It is a glorious deed we have done this day," exclaimed Amaury. "The pope will rejoice that more of his flock has been returned to the fold and the pestilence of heresy lifted from their backs."

"It is gratifying to see such progress," Simon said. "But there is much of God's work left to do."

Viscount Guilhem, who had been forced to watch the spectacle, vowed to take up his sword again to free Occitania from the horror that had befallen them this day.

CHAPTER 35

The Present Intrudes

Monday, July 3, 1944 – County of Foix

Emile had slept deeply after putting down the testament of Raymond de Péreille. In his dreams, he had found himself increasingly pulled into the ancient world of the Occitan lord, unable to distinguish it from his own life in the twentieth century.

As the first rays of the Midi sun grazed the horizon, a cock's crow woke him. He thought he heard another noise—someone calling to him. He sat up.

"Emile! Emile! Get up, we need your help," pleaded Guillème outside his door.

"I'm coming," Emile shouted. He rose and dressed quickly. When he entered the kitchen, he saw Maurina preparing food as usual. However, when she turned to greet him, the anguished look on her face told him things were far from usual. An old woman he had not seen before was sitting at the long, wooden table. She was wearing a pale, olive-green wrap around her head and a white smock over a long, olive-green skirt. The clothes were simple and reminded Emile of those he had seen Guillème and his fellow Cathars wearing when they had found him in the cave. She looked at him with a gaunt expression. She had been crying heavily. In spite of her pitiful state, the woman got off her chair and fell to her knees in front of Emile. With her palms to the ground, she bowed deeply three times. As she did so, she cried out to him.

"Bless me, Good Christian. Lord, pray to God for this sinner that he deliver me from an evil death and lead me to a good end," she demanded of him on the last bow.

Emile was taken by surprise. "I'm sorry, but you must be confusing me with—"

Guillème cut him off. "Emile, not now. Bruna has been through a lot this night. She and many others believe you are indeed the lord de Péreille come back as a Good Christian to restore the faith. As Friends of God, we believe life is a cycle of birth and rebirth until our souls are pure enough to rejoin the Father in heaven. Let her keep her belief for now."

Emile felt uncomfortable but did not have the heart to deny Guillème's request, at least until he better understood what was going on.

"Why did Bruna come to us? And what can I do to help?" asked Emile.

"She wishes to tell you herself," said Guillème.

Bruna appeared nervous and at a loss for words, but she began her tale. "My Lord, last night, we went to the grotto to hold our services as is our custom. We thanked the Good God with all our hearts for bringing you back to us. Everything was normal until we emerged from the caves. As we did, bullets rang out. Rixende, a true believer, gasped and fell on the ground beside me. She was clutching her chest. Her white apron was stained with blood. There was nothing I could do for her. She died in my arms."

The distraught woman wept and covered her face with a cloth. When she regained her composure, she continued her tale, straining hard to put the words together. "Suddenly, Germans soldiers were all around us, looking for the one who had fled from them in the cave. When they could not find him, they became angry. They said they would kill us all if we did not tell them where to find him. No one spoke, so they shot Gregory. Oh, it was terrible," she cried.

Maurina put her arms around her. After a short time, she was ready to continue.

"They threatened again to kill us, but still no one spoke, for it is not our way to put another soul in danger to save our own. One of the Germans seemed to know our ways, for he suggested to the captain that instead of killing anyone else, they set one of us free to deliver their message."

"What is their message?" asked Guillème.

Bruna was reluctant to answer.

"Tell us what they said, Bruna," Guillème asked more forcefully.

"They said that if the man from the cave does not come to them, they will shoot everyone they are holding."

The woman fell to the floor again at Emile's feet, her hands clasped in prayer. "Oh Good Christian, please tell us what we should do. My husband and I do not fear death, but our daughter is very young. She is not yet ready to relinquish her body, for she has not been adequately prepared for a good end."

"Did they say what they want of this man?" asked Guillème.

She looked at Guillème, her face bereft of hope. "They said he stole something from a chest in the cave which they believe can lead them to the fabled treasure of the Cathars. They want him to bring it to them."

"All people think of when they hear of the Cathars is treasure!" cursed Guillème. "The Friends of God place no value in earthly treasures. They serve only to trap our souls in this material existence. Why do they not seek the true treasure of the Cathars? Their Gnostic understanding of our existence and of the scriptures."

"I must save these people," declared Emile.

"No! You cannot surrender to them," objected Guillème.

"Their lives are at stake because of me. I will not see others die on my account."

"They will surely kill you, and we cannot allow the legacy of Raymond de Péreille to pass into the hands of the Nazis. It has remained hidden for seven hundred years. We cannot now allow it to fall into the same dark hands he gave his life to save it from."

"But these are Nazis we speak of, not crusaders," Emile said.

"The armies of Satan have had many names, but their purpose has always been the same, to enslave men's souls. Did not the Nazis burn your family just as the soldiers of the cross burned the Cathars? They are one and the same."

Emile said nothing. He found the analogy troubling. Guillème's words only exacerbated the confusion he was having in keeping apart the two worlds in which he had been living.

"Do not get me wrong, for I have no wish to see my friends die," Guillème said. "We must try to think of a way to save our brethren that does not cost your life or give the Germans knowledge they turn to evil purpose."

Maurina looked at Emile warmly. "Master, you did not come to us on your own. The Good God guided you on your path for reasons I am sure he will reveal. The evil one has taken our friends to thwart God's plans. We cannot allow him to triumph. I know every one of our brethren would gladly give up his body of flesh to protect you and the contents of the chest of Raymond de Péreille."

Emile knew she spoke from the heart. A thought suddenly came to Emile. "Do you have any guns in the mountains?" he asked.

Bruna looked surprised. Guillème shrugged. "That is not our way. The Friends of God pledge never to take life of man or beast, for each houses a soul. As mere believers, killing is not forbidden to us, but if committed, it would require a lengthy atonement before our souls would again be pure enough to escape the material world."

Emile shook his head in disbelief. There was a world war going on only kilometers from where they were. People were being killed daily and without conscience by the thousands. Yet these people, who had clearly lived their lives apart from the realities of the modern world, were not prepared to kill even to defend themselves.

Guillème saw the frustration on Emile's face. "Give me a chance for the Good God to guide me. You must keep faith," he said as he left to walk outside.

When he returned to the kitchen, he smiled. "I have a plan," he announced.

"We have much to do, and little time. Come with me."

Their plan agreed to, Bruna led the two men to where she had left her fellow believers. It was an arduous hike across rough terrain. The white rocky outcroppings were covered by small, scrubby plants and stunted evergreen, oaks, and junipers that somehow clung to life in the mountain environment. It was a world totally alien to that in which Emile had grown up but one that he felt strangely at home in. By the time they reached their destination, Emile was exhausted.

Staying out of sight of the Germans, Guillème nodded reverently to Emile. "May the Good God protect you," he said before setting off down another trail.

Bruna went ahead to talk to the Germans. When she waved, Emile followed her down, hands high in the air. Two soldiers pointed machine guns at Emile as he descended the rocky trail.

What Emile had not expected was the reaction of Bruna's companions. Despite being prisoners who could be shot at any moment, they fell to the ground and bowed to him just as Bruna had. Emile watched their lips. They were mouthing the same incantation.

At Guillème's insistence, he was wearing the dark-blue hooded robe he had taken from the cave of Raymond de Péreille. Guillème's reason had been to help convince the Germans he was indeed the man they were looking. But Emile realized it also transformed him in the eyes of the Cathar followers into the legendary figure of an ascetic, one to be venerated and followed. It would thus make it easier for him to execute the plan.

Emile was surrounded by soldiers as soon as he reached Bruna and her friends. Each one was pointing a gun directly at him and seemed anxious to use it. Emile's heart pounded, but he told himself they would not shoot him until they had what they were looking for.

Their captain approached. His gait was slow, measured. He held himself stiffly. His hands were crossed behind his back. "Where are the things you stole from the cave of the ancient lord?" he demanded leisurely.

"What things do you mean?"

The captain paused and smiled. "Whoever you are, you obviously like to play games. I see that from your attire, but my men and I are tired. We have already spent too long on this cursed mountain. Do not try my patience. If you do not answer my questions or I believe you are lying to me, I will have your friends here shot one by one. Is that clear?"

Emile nodded reluctantly and muttered "Yes" under his breath.

"Good. I will ask you again, more explicitly if you wish to avoid misunderstanding. Where are the things you were seen fleeing with in a satchel from the cave in the mountain? What exactly was in that chest you found? Treasure perhaps?"

"No. There was no treasure. Just parchments. They would be of no interest to you."

"To me perhaps not, but they are of great interest to the Reichsführer, Heinrich Himmler. He has ordered me to recover them. I will not disappoint him."

"They are just a bunch of old parchments. What interest could the German high command have in them?" asked Emile dismissively.

"Do not take us for fools. No one goes to all that trouble to hide parchments that are without value. We know of the Cathar treasure. If it was not in the chest, the papers probably tell where it is hidden."

"You are right. The parchments are of great value, but not the kind you seek. They contain a wealth of knowledge and of the spirit, but they are not of material value."

"What then of the Holy Grail?" asked the captain excitedly, allowing his emotion to surface. "The German archaeologist Otto Rahn was convinced the Cathars had hid the cup of the Holy Grail somewhere in these mountains. He searched for it for many years. The SS in Carcassonne is convinced you have found it."

"They are wrong."

"You will have the opportunity to tell them yourself. I have orders to take you to Carcassonne with the contents of the chest. They will have many questions. You will find they can be very persuasive. Where are these parchments?" he demanded, drawing his pistol.

"They are in a cave. The writings of the ancients are sacred to us. We placed them in one of our places of worship."

"Take us there immediately. The contents are the property of the Third Reich."

"I will take you, but it is a long hike up into the mountains."

"It had better not take too long. That would not be good for you or your friends."

"Understood."

"Good. Then we had better get going. Your friends here will come with us. If I find you have been lying to me and the papers are not in the cave, I will shoot them all."

The soldiers forced Bruna and her friends to stand. They all set off following Emile.

In his head, Emile tried to focus on the map Guillème had drawn for him. If he strayed from the path he had been shown, he would risk killing them all.

The group had been walking for close to two hours when Emile was relieved to see the limestone plateau in front of them. It looked exactly as Guillème had described. The summer sun was beating down on them. The soldiers were sweating in their heavy uniforms.

"How much farther?" complained the captain. "My men are exhausted!"

"We are nearly there. It will be cool in the caves. They can rest there."

"What is the name of these caves?"

"The one we are going to is called the Cave of Life. It is one of our places of worship." The believers cast a strange look at Emile but said nothing.

"Everything you took from the chest is there?"

"Yes. Will you allow the others to go free when you have the parchments?"

"They will be allowed to go, but you must come with us."

Emile prayed even harder that Guillème's plan would work. If not, he could imagine dying in the same dungeons as the young lord, Raymond-Roger de Trencavel had more than seven hundred years earlier.

The narrow trail zigzagged up a steep slope to the top of a plateau.

The captain was very unhappy at the prospect of the climb. "Do you expect my men to climb all the way up there?"

"No. That will not be necessary," Emile said. "The entrance is halfway up," he said, pointing. "It is where the trail disappears behind that rocky ledge."

"Very well. But you go first. If this is a trap, my soldiers will shoot you first."

"Killing is not the way of the Cathars, captain. If you had studied anything about them, you would know that. You have no need to be fearful."

"I have stayed alive by being fearful. Let us go. I want to be out of these mountains before dark."

The trail was steep and narrow, requiring the party to walk in single file. Emile was captivated by the view of the towering Pyrenees. They promised the freedom he had been searching for. His head was pounding. He had had no water since early morning. The Germans, never intended for the parching sun, had nearly emptied their canteens.

At long last, they neared the place where Guillème had told him the entrance to the cave would be. The trail narrowed more and dropped away steeply to one side. Unaccustomed to hiking, he worried he might slip on the chalky gravel and pull everyone to their deaths. At one point, he came very close, but he managed to grab a small bush just in time. He saw the cave opening ahead. He breathed a sigh of relief. Just then, one of the Germans let out a terrifying scream.

Emile saw a soldier clinging desperately to a small juniper bush that hung off the edge of the path. The soldier had clearly missed his footing just as Emile had come close to doing. The bush was straining under the weight. Its roots were tearing from the ground.

Emile watched with surprise as Thomas, one of the believers, went back down the path to where the soldier was clinging for dear life. Lying down with one arm around a rock, he reached over the edge. The soldier grabbed his hand. Thomas pulled him to safety. When the soldier had overcome his fright, he thanked him profusely in German while the captain looked on disapprovingly.

Who are these people, thought Emile, *that they would help those who had every intention of harming them?* In the five years he had been fighting the war, he had never encountered anyone quite like them. The world of Raymond de Péreille became more real.

As they all regrouped at the cave entrance, the captain asked impatiently, "How long will it take you to get the papers?"

"The cave where they are stored is less than half a kilometer from the entrance."

"Get them. We will wait for you here. You have one hour. After that, I will begin shooting your friends."

"I will need a torch."

"I will prepare one for you," volunteered one of the believers, an old man with a mop of white hair. "That is always my job."

A boy ran off with him to tear branches from small shrubs. The old man wrapped the bundle tightly with a scarf he borrowed from a woman.

"These bushes are rich in oil," he said, handing the torch to Emile. "They will burn for some time in the caves. We use them to light the way for our services."

Emile fidgeted nervously. He did not want to go alone into the caves. It was not part of the plan. "Captain, I do not know these caves well. I had a guide to show me the way. It would be much quicker if you permitted the Cathar brethren to accompany me. They know these caves like the backs of their hands. They use them for their services."

The captain looked annoyed and ready to say no, but a black cloud passed overhead, blocking the sun. They heard a loud crack of thunder. It began to rain heavily.

The captain moved into the entrance for cover. "It would seem we have no choice. Very well. We will all go with you, but you shall all be tied together. I would not want anyone getting lost."

Emile marveled that maybe there was a Good God after all.

"Fritz, tie one arm of each of the prisoners to another," shouted the captain. "The prisoners will go first into the caves. We will follow. If they attempt to run, shoot them."

One of the soldiers lit the torch. Emile led the procession. Close to the entrance, the air was cool and dry. As they ventured farther, the air becoming damp. From time to time, he pretended to confer with Thomas for directions, but they were not necessary. He knew where he was going. Guillème's map was etched in his mind. As Emile looked at his fellow prisoners, he could see confusion on their faces. He had lied, for this was not one of their places of worship and none had probably ever been here before. In spite of that, they did not seem concerned. The look of complete trust they gave Emile told him they would follow him anywhere. It was much to his relief. Shortly, their lives would depend on it. Guillème must have counted on this when he insisted Emile wear the dark-blue robe.

The walls of the cave began to part from each other as the ceiling receded into the darkness above. They were soon in a large cave. They could hear the rush of running water. As the noise grew louder, the flickering orange light of the torch revealed an underground river that had carved a path through the limestone. Emile guessed the river had created the cave. In the winter months, the cave would probably be inundated, but in June, with only the occasional summer shower, the water level was low.

After walking along the river for about fifteen minutes, Emile saw what he had been looking for. It was time. His heart rate soared as he prepared to execute Guillème's plan.

After taking a deep breath, Emile flung the flaming torch into the air as high as he could. The Germans and his companions were taken aback. The torch rose for what seemed like minutes until it plunged into the river. The cave became darker than the darkest night.

Adding to the sense of disorientation in this alien world was the eerie noise that had continued to grow since the torch began to descend. The sound was loud enough to drown out the sound of the rushing water. As the last rays of light from the torch had lit up the surroundings, many were terrified to see the air around filled with fast-moving shadows.

"Get down! Get down!" Emile cried in French. "They are bats. They will do you no harm. Follow me quickly. We must get out of here."

Emile tugged on the rope around his wrist to drag the next man along behind him. After a few intermittent jerks, he found himself free to move. One of the girls started to cry. Her mother silenced her.

"Where can we go?" someone demanded.

"Trust me," replied Emile. "I know the way."

The Germans were shouting in confusion. A shot echoed through the cave. The captain ordered them to stop lest they killed one of their own. The noise of the shot caused even more bats to fly from their roosts and encouraged everyone to follow Emile's tugs.

Emile groped his way along the cave wall. Before unleashing the torch, he had focused intensely on where the opening he was seeking was. He was nonetheless terrified he wouldn't find it and all would be lost forever.

However, Guillème's description had been precise. The opening was exactly where he had said it would be, at the bottom of a narrow shaft that led steeply upward and away from the cave. The floor of the shaft was worn smooth, but loose rocks here and there made the climb treacherous. It also did not help they still had their arms tied to one other.

When they had climbed some way up the shaft, Emile looked below them and saw a faint glimmer. He surmised one of the soldiers must have found his flashlight and they were following them. "Hurry," Emile whispered. "We must get out of this cave!"

"How much farther?" someone asked. "I do not see any light."

"We should soon be there. After a bend ahead, we should begin to see daylight."

They continued climbing the steep incline. Instead of a piercing light as Emile had anticipated, the change was much more subtle. Gradually, the walls around them began to appear out of the darkness. The light was weak, barely perceptible at first, but as they climbed, it grew stronger. Unfortunately, the sounds of pursuit in the tunnel below them also grew. The Germans were gaining on them.

"Push as many of the loose rocks down on them as you can. It will slow them down," cried Emile. "We must go faster. The surface cannot be far."

As they sped up, exhaustion set in. One of the older members fell. Fortunately, he was held by the others, and he regained his footing, but Emile was worried the soldiers would catch up. He had nearly lost hope when he felt something on the ground. A rope. Guillème was waiting for them as planned.

Emile grabbed the rope and started to pull himself up the incline. The others did likewise. Very soon, their rate of ascent increased. *We're going to make it!*

A few minutes later, and they saw the opening to the world. Their pace quickened in the light. Emile could see the silhouette of someone looking down at them. *Guillème!*

After Guillème had helped them all out of the shaft, he quickly pulled the rope back up. He helped untie the ropes that bound them. "Emile, come here! I need your help."

Emile saw Guillème standing by the edge of a large pond. Near him was what appeared to be a sluice gate.

"Help me. We need to open this gate. The water will flow into the shaft and will slow down the Germans. The rock is slippery when wet. I know that well from experience."

The two struggled to raise the wooden gate that had obviously not been moved for a long time. When they finally got it to move, the water began pouring into the channel that led to the opening they had just exited. Emile imagined the unpleasant surprise in store for the soldiers climbing in the dark up the narrow tunnel.

"The water will not kill them, but it should push them back down a ways," Guillème said with satisfaction. "It should give us plenty of time to be long gone. They will also be cold and wet when they get out, so they will probably return to their barracks than look for us."

"How did you know of this place?" asked Emile in awe.

"I came upon it several years ago. There was a small stream flowing down into the cave opening you came up. That stream cut the shaft. I had the idea to dam up the stream to create a holding pond for my goats. It is dry up here in summer. It worked out very well."

"I see," nodded Emile. "And the bats?"

"Oh yes, the bats." He chuckled. "A couple of years ago, a goat had gone down the shaft, so I went in to find him. I was surprised the shaft was so wide, so after I got him out, I went back to explore the caves. I hoped there might be a good cave for us to worship in. Like the original Christians who worshipped in the catacombs, we do not believe in building fancy churches with ornate trappings to talk to the Good God. They separate us from him. We hold true to the teachings of Christ and praise the Good God in his creation, not in those of man. The Catholics build gilded temples to pray in. That was not the way of Christ. The Devil has lured them into an idolatry of material possessions."

Emile wondered what his brother-in-law Father François would have said to Guillème's philosophy. Emile found himself more sympathetic to it than to anything he had heard on the occasions he accompanied Monique to Mass. He had always found the Catholic dogma to be too ritualistic, too rigid, and too cold for him. It had never made him feel closer to his soul, the way he felt as he listened to Guillème. He and his fellow believers seemed to have a deeper appreciation of life and death than anyone he had met before, and they were closer to the forces of nature that ruled their daily existence.

"I take it you didn't find these caves suitable to worship in?"

"No. They were already occupied by those bats. Gave me quite a shock when I disturbed them and they started flying all around me. I hoped it would have the same effect on the Germans."

"You were right. Thanks to you, everyone is safe."

"Let's keep it that way. We need to get going just in case those Germans decide to chase us after they have dried off."

"Lead the way. I've no idea where we are."

Before they could leave, Bruna and the other believers thanked Emile and Guillème. They bowed to Emile. "My Lord—" began Bruna.

Emile cut her off. "I have told you before, I am not a lord or a Friend of God. I am not even sure I am a Christian. I am merely a schoolteacher. My name is Emile Garnier."

"But you wear the ring of Lord de Péreille," one cried out.

"Yes, and the robe of one of the pure ones," cried another.

"The ring, the clothes—they are not mine. I will gladly give them to you. You have more right to them than I do."

Thomas stepped forward respectfully. "Kind sir, you underestimate your involvement in this affair. We believe you did not chance upon the cave but were led there by the Good God in his wisdom. His possessions therefore rightfully belong to you for what little value worldly possessions have anyway. Keep them, for in time we are sure the Good God will reveal to you the purpose he brought you here to fulfill."

Emile was embarrassed that anyone would believe he had been "chosen" for anything. For him, it was mere happenstance he had discovered the cave. However, he did not doubt Thomas's sincerity and had no wish to undermine his or the others' beliefs. "Thank you. I promise to take great care of everything I found. From what I have already read, this ancient lord was an honorable man, and I will treat his writings with the utmost respect."

The group nodded and muttered in agreement.

"We must go quickly," Guillème said impatiently.

CHAPTER 36

Aragón and Rome Divide

Tuesday, July 4, 1944 – County of Foix

Emile had slept very soundly. The previous day's adventure had exhausted him. The sun was above the horizon when he awoke. Maurina had prepared a breakfast of fresh berries, which she had just gathered.

"I am glad you can still walk after your clambering about in those caves yesterday," Guillème said, smiling.

Emile observed the deep creases in his face. He was uncertain how much they were due to his age and how much to the harsh Midi sun. Whatever the case, his face glowed with a mixture of kindness and wisdom Emile had never experienced before. Maurina too made him feel that he was one of the family and that she would be happy to have him stay with them for as long as he liked. Even Pedro, the dog, had taken a liking to Emile. So soon after losing his own family, it was consoling to find there was still somewhere in the world where he might belong.

Emile reflected on how much the war had hardened him, dehumanized him. Before it started, he had been a dreamer, enthusiastic about his family and the young lives he helped mold as a teacher. The war had changed all that. He had become cynical and cold, able to kill without worrying about it. It had been a subconscious transition imposed upon him by the world, which had not offered him an alternative. The only choice was to kill or be killed.

Emile had not realized how much he had changed until he met Guillème and his friends. Despite everything going on around them, they had somehow managed to reject the madness and hold true to their philosophy that killing was wrong, that fighting over earthly possessions was futile and counterproductive to a person trying to attain true happiness. It was counter to everything he had been taught, yet the people he had been among for the past few days seemed happier in their simple lives than any he had known in the Limousin.

Guillème sat beside him at the table. "Emile, yesterday, you told everyone all you seek is to be taken across the mountains to Spain. Well, Maurina and I have discussed the matter. We realize we have no right to force you to stay. You kept your bargain and read some of the writings of the Lord de Péreille. If it does not interest you to read further, I am willing to take you across the Pyrenees. Maurina and I will keep the parchments safe in case you wish to return for them in the future."

The proposal caught Emile off guard. After the tragic events in Oradour-sur-Glane, the only thing that had kept him going was the obsession to fight for his country against those who had destroyed everything he loved. Nothing else had mattered, but that was before he had met these unusual people with their unique attitude to life.

Then there were the writings of Raymond de Péreille, who spoke to him from the pages of parchment of a world long gone. If Emile left, he might never know what had driven that ancient noble to write his account of events he clearly and desperately wanted to preserve. It had been so important a task to him that when completed, he had chosen to die alone in a damp, cold cave.

Emile did not believe he had been chosen by any spiritual power to find the resting place of Raymond de Péreille, but he had apparently been the first to stumble upon it. If the ancient lord truly had a message to impart, did he not have a duty to finish reading his account? It would probably take him about a week to finish reading it. *Would it really change the course of the war if I delayed a few days?*

"I see you are hesitating in your reply," said Guillème. "That is good. You have responsibilities to weigh. Take time to think about it. The decision will alter the course of your life whichever way you decide. But you will know you have made the right decision when it comes from your heart, not from your head."

Emile knew that if he decided to set out for Spain at that moment, Guillème would take him without hesitation. As Emile pondered what to do, Guillème studied him like an all-knowing father, confident his son would make the right decision. As usual, he was right.

"I will stay and read the rest of the parchments of Raymond de Péreille," Emile announced. "I believe I owe him that much."

Guillème and Maurina smiled and hugged Emile. Guillème said, "If you will be with us for a while longer, we must make arrangements. After yesterday, the Germans will be looking for you even harder. We will probably be having visitors. They do not know us, so we will be safe, but you must stay out of sight."

"I will show you where you can go," said Maurina. She led Emile to the pantry. Maurina lifted one of several sacks of flour on the floor. Beneath it was a trapdoor. "You will be able to read uninterrupted in the cellar. No one will find you there. Take the satchel and everything you took from the chest of Raymond de Péreille with you. We would not want anything to be found if the Germans search the house."

"I will. Thank you," Emile said. "I have no wish to put you in danger."

"Our duty is to help you find the truth," Maurina said. "We would gladly sacrifice our earthly existence for that."

It was afternoon before he had moved all evidence of his presence into the cellar. Guillème had given him an oil lamp. Emile unrolled the next parchment. He felt very much as he imagined Raymond de Péreille must have as he wrote his account in that bygone age.

After the fall of Minerve in the year 1210, the armies of the pope wasted no time in spilling more innocent Occitan blood. This time they went south, to the village of Termes. southeast of Carcassonne, in the southern mountains that are extensions of the Pyrenees. Like Minerve, we considered Termes impregnable.

The fortress of Termes sat high on the pinnacle of a long, narrow, rocky crest. On the east and west sides, deep gorges fell precipitously away from the mountain, making approach impossible. To the north, a steep ascent was guarded by the tower of Termenet. The fortress was encircled by a mighty wall, and inside that, the habitation for the defenders was protected by a second wall.

The village of Termes lay below the castle on the southern slope. A defensive wall that abutted those of the castle surrounded it. The entrance to the castle in the southeast corner was by way of ramps overlooked by two high guard towers. I had been to the castle many times and always been in awe of its defenses. I never imagined such a formidable defensive position could succumb to an attacker. In early August 1210, however, Simon de Montfort and his murderous band of crusader pillagers laid siege to the fortress.

1210, August – Termes

Simon de Montfort crossed himself and bowed to the cross on the makeshift altar in a tent that had been set up as his chapel.

"God will be with you in your struggle, my son," said the priest. "He will smite down his enemies before you."

"Thank you, Father," replied Simon.

"Raymond, the lord of Termes is a heretic. He is surely a Cathar, if not a perfect, for he has not held Mass in the castle chapel for thirty years."

"So I have heard, Father. He is surely lost to God."

"I fear he is. The Devil beguiles those who are weak and uses them to spread his blasphemy. His whole family is infected with the heresy. They work to bring more innocents into Satan's fold. His brother, Benoît de Termes, was one of the perfects who argued against Domingo de Guzmán at the Colloquium of Montréal three years ago."

"The error runs deep among most of the Occitan nobility," Simon said. "They are all infected. It is an infection we must purge so the people can be restored to the true path of the church. I have dedicated my life to that task, Father."

"God is a witness that you speak the truth. It is written, 'Righteous people will be rewarded for their own righteous behavior, and wicked people will be punished for their own wickedness.' Your deeds have shown you to be righteous, my Lord. You shall surely be rewarded in this life and in the next." The priest held out his hand for Simon to kiss.

Obediently, Simon knelt and kissed the ring.

"I am told the pope prays for you daily," said the priest.

"So I have been told, Father. It is a source of much strength and comfort to me."

"As it would be to all. Do God's work. Slay this Antichrist and bring me his head!"

"If God permits."

It was early morning, but already the sun was creeping into a cloudless blue sky. Simon knew it would be another day of relentless heat. "Is the siege laid firmly?" Simon asked his commander.

"Presently, my Lord. The last of the siege engines are nearly in place."

"As soon as you are ready, begin bombarding the town. Pound them into submission. I have had enough of these Occitan lords and their blasphemy."

"My Lord, I will show them no mercy, but their position is strong. We are firing up, and their trebuchets prevent us from getting close. Their catapults' range exceeds ours."

"Then you shall have to make your stones count more than theirs. We shall not leave this place until the town is ours, for God demands it. Is that clear?" he yelled.

"Yes my Lord."

After two months of siege, Simon was growing restless. His war machines had been pounding Termes relentlessly, but the town still held out. He watched as massive boulders continued to fly angrily through the air between the crusaders and the defenders. The trebuchets groaned and creaked as the heavy rocks were loaded into the baskets, and then heavy counterweights were raised to power them. Each time the baskets were released, the machines seemed to sing as they relieved themselves of the strain and hurled their deadly load at the enemy. As heavy as the rocks were, the miracles of engineering seemed to toss them into the air as if they were mere pebbles.

Simon grimaced as some of the crusaders were struck by an incoming rock. Two were crushed beyond recognition. The others groaned, with their limbs shattered. His one consolation was that the same fate was surely befalling the defenders. It was getting late in the year, and soon, many of the crusaders would have fulfilled their quarantaine. He would have to try another tactic if he was to succeed before that.

"Frédéric," he yelled to his chief engineer. "We have wasted enough time attacking the fortress. I will lay siege to the tower of Termenet on the north side instead. It is less well defended. If it falls, we can attack the town from the north, where their defenses are weaker."

"It will take some time to reposition the trebuchets to attack the tower, my Lord. They will have to be torn down and the timbers carried up to be rebuilt there."

"Then begin immediately. I grow impatient. Take as many men as you need. You must be bombarding the tower within the week."

"But my Lord—"

"See that it is done or I shall have you thrown from one of your own machines against the tower."

For several weeks, they had been throwing every rock the crusaders could find against the tower. However, to Simon's frustration, the Occitan engineers had been very skilled in their art. The tower still stood.

As Simon was discussing their situation with his commanders, a knight rode in frantically from the north of the valley, his red cross indistinguishable from the blood spattered on the white cloth. "My Lord, Pierre-Roger de Cabaret and his men attacked our supply train. They slaughtered everyone. Hacked them to death, crying, 'Remember Bram.' They were surely sent by the Devil," he screamed, scared almost to madness.

"Pierre-Roger again!" screamed Simon in a rage. "That man is a plague. He hides in his mountain nest and descends to attack those doing God's work. But Lastours will submit to the will of God. I shall destroy it and all the other bastions of these heretics. God will show me the way."

The crusader fell off his horse in exhaustion and wept. "My Lord, when Pierre-Roger was done with his butchery, he destroyed the trebuchets that were bombarding the keep. As I rode away, I saw his men hacking at them with axes."

"Captain," screamed Simon. "Take fifty knights and ride north. Pierre-Roger's men are destroying our siege engines. Drive them off. Kill him or capture him if you can, but your first priority is to protect the trebuchets."

1210, November 22 – Termes

A chill had set in. Cold air rolled down the mountains. Simon threw the remains of his meal on a crackling fire. "Curse this place. It would seem they have Lucifer himself protecting them. What more proof is needed that they are true enemies of God? It is nearly four months now, but the town still holds out against us. I was planning on their cisterns running dry by now, for I am told there are no wells in the town. They would have been forced to surrender. Yet by some miracle, it rained heavily two nights ago, enough I fear to allow them to hold out for several more weeks. That is assuming it doesn't rain again. This late in the year, I worry my army will desert me."

"I believe most will stay, my Lord. They feel victory is near. They do not wish to return empty-handed."

"Spoken honestly. If not their faith, their avarice will keep them on God's mission."

Simon turned to go to bed. Barely had he entered his tent than Amaury ran in. "Father! They have broken out! The inhabitants are fleeing the castle!"

"What?" asked Simon. "Why?"

"It is said many in the city are sick. Their cisterns filled with rainwater, but the water was polluted by dead rats. It has given everyone dysentery. Everyone is fleeing to escape the sickness."

Simon knelt down and crossed himself. "Thank you, Lord. Forgive me for doubting you. You have delivered a plague upon your enemies. I shall strike them down in your name. Sound the alarm! Wake up the camp! We shall ride into the city before dawn."

The next morning, the carnage from the night before was visible outside and inside the city. Most of those trying to escape had been cut down by the hordes of crusaders who had been obsessed with battling their way into the city before everything of value was looted by their companions. Some of those who had not managed to flee were being used for target practice, while others, especially women and young children, were being abused carnally to satisfy the crusaders' lust.

Simon looked from the ramparts over the ravaged town. After four months of effort, it was finally his. He rejoiced in his victory. A short time earlier, he had attended what was surely the first Catholic Mass to be said within the walls of the castle for many years. *God has returned to this place,* he thought.

"My Lord," announced one of Simon's captains. "We have Raymond de Termes in irons in the dungeons."

"What of his son?"

"We cannot find him. His father says he escaped last night and will avenge him."

"That is most unfortunate. At least we have one of the heretics. Take him to Carcassonne and throw him in the deepest dungeon. Tell the jailer I do not wish to be troubled by him ever again."

1211, February – Castle of Toulouse

"You have been looking after my sister well. She has put on a little weight," joked King Pedro. "It must be all this good food," he said in jest, patting his stomach.

Eleonor blushed in embarrassment. "You have put on more weight than I have," she rebuked her brother. "I do not have time to enjoy as many banquets as you, for there is much to do running the castle here and we do not have enough servants."

Raymond spoke in his wife's defense. "Eleonor looks healthy, and I am glad of it. She has filled out only in all the places a woman should. It makes her even more irresistible."

His wife blushed, but this time with a smile before bowing in modesty. After her brother chuckled, Eleonor changed the subject. "Enough of me. You men have more-serious matters to discuss. At least it will be on a full stomach. I trust you enjoyed the meal?"

"Indeed I did, good sister. The pork, olives, and sweet onions were the equal of anything I have eaten in Aragón. I shall not worry about you eating well again."

"You need not, but there are other troubles that ail us. My husband seeks your help. The pope and the king of France are conspiring against us." Eleonor's voice was no longer light or jovial. "When they conspire against Occitania, they conspire against Aragón as well, for these lands are more a part of Aragón than they are of France."

King Pedro looked at her sympathetically. "I am here to discuss these matters with Count Raymond. Like you, my sister, the blood of Aragón flows deep in my veins. I will protect it with my life. We shall see what can be done."

As in on cue, a herald announced the arrival of an unexpected guest. "My Lords, Arnaud Amaury, archbishop of Narbonne and legate of the holy father, begs an audience."

Eleonor's face went ashen. She rose. "You must excuse me. I cannot face this man. I have heard of his wickedness. Speak with him if you must, but beware of his evil. He is devious. His hands are bloodied." She stormed out of the room, followed by her attendants.

Raymond and Pedro exchanged grimaces. "We have little choice but to hear him," Raymond said. "Show him in."

As the archbishop entered, both men rose reluctantly and bowed politely but without sincerity. Raymond was the first to speak. "Archbishop, I am told you convened an ecclesiastical council in Montpellier recently. Do you bring us news of it?"

"I do, my Lord," he replied with a barely a nod in Raymond's direction. He turned to King Pedro and bowed his head respectfully toward him.

"Has my excommunication been lifted and my lands and titles restored?" asked Raymond. "I fought with the crusader army. I have kept my word to the pope."

Amaury repressed a sneer of satisfaction. "No, my Lord, your excommunication was confirmed by the council," he stated. "It ruled you had not done enough to fight the heresy and has issued this charter of demands against you."

"That is preposterous," protested Raymond.

The archbishop ignored him. He pulled out a scroll from his habit. It was bound by a large, gold ribbon and sealed with red wax bearing the impression of the legate's ring. Commandingly, he held up the scroll and beckoned a servant to take it to Raymond.

Raymond tore open the seal and read the document. It was not long before his face had turned red with anger. "This is an abomination! You seek to bind me and my heirs to these outrageous demands?"

The archbishop smiled with the charm of a snake. "My Lord, the council was acting only in your, and your people's best interests. If you abide by the terms in the charter, you will restore yourself in the eyes of God and save your soul from eternal damnation."

"I am to accept damnation in this world for salvation in the next? Is that the bargain you offer me?"

"Even Christ had to atone for his sins, my Lord. Surely you do not put yourself above Christ."

"But Christ did not have the responsibilities I have to protect my people. How can I do that if I can no longer collect tolls? If I am to send home all the soldiers I pay to protect my lands? If I am to dismantle my castles and their ramparts? How, if I and all my knights are to be banished from the cities? Who will look after the people I have sworn to protect?"

"The council has relieved you of that oath and of your responsibilities." The archbishop smiled. "The Church of Rome will assume those responsibilities."

"Ha! The Church of Rome?" bellowed King Pedro. With his disdain for the archbishop clearly visible, the king walked to Amaury. His large frame completely dwarfed the diminutive figure of the clergyman. "Whom do you mean by 'the Church of Rome'? You? The pope? Or maybe this de Montfort I have heard so much of? They also say he owes dual allegiance to the pope and the king of France. Is this true?"

The archbishop was uncharacteristically silent as if cowering beside an angry bull.

"Let none forget that the lands of Occitania pay homage to Aragón!" King Pedro hollered in the archbishop's face. "I will not have them usurped by a puppet of the king of France or an Italian pope in Rome."

The archbishop shuddered. He recovered his composure. "King Pedro, all Christendom is inspired by the bravery you have shown against the infidels in Spain. The lands of Occitania will retain their obligations to Aragón. The council has no issue with you, only with your vassal, Count Raymond, for his support of the heretics. No one questions your faith or your commitment to the church."

Count Raymond was furious. "Archbishop, you and your council are not worthy to call yourselves Christians for you do not even keep the commandments. You bear false witness with the pretense that you brought your crusade to our lands to save the souls of our people. In truth, you came here to steal our lands. You care nothing for our people or you would not slaughter them in the most cruel fashion! This charter is no more than an act of thievery. You seek to impose demands upon me you know I cannot meet for crimes of which I am not guilty. You accuse me of supporting the heretics, yet I have fought alongside the crusaders. I have remained faithful to the church and have done everything in my power to suppress the growth of the heresy in my lands."

"Not in the eyes of the church," Amaury said.

"You expected the impossible of me. The actions of your priests and bishops made it even more so. The widespread corruption, idleness, and debauchery demonstrated by the clergy only drives more into the arms of the heretics, whom they see as pure and incorruptible. It is not I who need to reform but the church itself!"

The archbishop seemed invigorated by Raymond's outburst. "The very words you speak are heresy. If you were not the count of Toulouse, I would have you burned at the stake for such utterances. Only the pope has the God-given authority to criticize the church."

"I speak only as a true Catholic wanting to strengthen the church," Raymond said. "The church could reclaim many more Occitan souls by demonstrating Christ's love to them rather than by sending French barbarians into their lands who hide behind their crusader crosses, kill our kinsfolk, and burn our dwellings."

"It is what God demands. Does not the Bible say, 'Let the praises of God be in their mouths, and a sharp sword in their hands—to execute vengeance on the nations and punishment on the peoples, to bind their kings with shackles and their leaders with iron chains, to execute the judgment written against them. This is the glory of his faithful ones.' You were warned repeatedly to rid your lands of heretics and infidels, yet you did nothing. Your people must pay the price for your transgressions."

"Those you speak of with such hatred have lived and worked peacefully in our midst for generations. They are accepted by the people of Occitania. We are not like the French, who seek to kill those they do not understand."

Amaury sneered. "The French do not kill those they do not understand, only those who have been declared enemies of Christ. They are true Catholics who have shown themselves prepared to fight for the Lord against those who deny him. Because you refused to join this fight, the crusaders had to come among you to purge the heathens."

Raymond finished reading the charter and threw it to the feet of the archbishop. "You would have me abstain from eating meat six days a week and wear garments cut in rough, brown cloth? You accuse me of supporting the Cathars, yet as a punishment, you demand I behave like one?"

"The proverb tells us, 'Before honor is humility'," the archbishop said.

"If that were not enough, you would have me go to the Holy Land under the guard of the Knights Hospitallers and not return to these lands until the pope permits?"

"Those are the terms stipulated by the council."

"What would be left of my lands to return to?" screamed Raymond. "By then, you would have exterminated half the population, and those spared in your divine mercy would be no more than subjugated serfs in a province of the king of France."

"I cannot speak of the secular arrangements that will be made for these lands. That is not my domain. My only concern is that these lands once again return to God's dominion and that those who follow Satan are extirpated."

"If you did not come with the authority of the pope, I would gladly extirpate you from this room," the king said menacingly. "You are a worm. You know Raymond can never consent to these terms. What is your intention? That Simon de Montfort usurp these lands and claim them in the name of the pope and the king of France?"

"The church will free them in the name of God, in the name of France, and in the name of Aragón," Amaury responded. "All Christians should rejoice at God's triumph over his enemies."

"It is not God's triumph that concerns me," Pedro said. "It is man's! I see the church's self-interest in this more than I see God's."

"Take your charter back to Montpellier," cried Raymond. "Tell your fellow bishops I reject their demands. Tell them they leave me no choice but to withdraw from the crusade. Tell them to withdraw their unholy army from our lands before any more blood is spilled and leave Occitania in peace, for that is all we seek."

"Your response was anticipated and serves to confirm only the correctness of the council's decision to excommunicate you for a third time," Amaury said smugly. "All your lands and possessions are forfeit to the church. No man will owe you allegiance, and all oaths sworn to you are hereby annulled. No man of faith is to offer you shelter or sustenance under threat of damnation until you undertake the penance for your transgressions against God. Similar decrees will be issued against many of your nobles who are likewise diseased with the heresy. I can assure you the crusade will continue until these lands are completely free of Satan's influence."

"Be gone!" barked King Pedro. "Be gone before I slay you as the infidel you are. I shall take this matter up myself before the pope."

"You are most welcome to, your Majesty." The archbishop was confident. "You will find him as resolute as I am in this matter."

King Pedro paced agitatedly after the archbishop left. "I see the hand of Philippe-Auguste in this plot. He has long lusted after these lands that rightly belong to Aragón. He craves a port on the Mediterranean to launch his crusades against the Holy Land. He shall not steal them while I am their guardian. You must organize the other southern lords to resist these crusaders," the king said. "I will help you as I can."

"The crusaders greatly outnumber us. They more-skilled in the arts of warfare than most in Occitania. I fear we are no match for them. Amaury and the bishops are confident of that and determined to take from us our riches and our lands."

"That is true, but Toulouse appears to be well fortified. You should be able to hold off a siege. Hopefully, that will allow you the time you will need to unite the counts of Foix, Mirepoix, Comminges, and the others against the crusaders. Together, you might stand a chance."

"I shall try, my Lord, but it will not be easy. I see dark times ahead for all in Occitania."

1211, March – Castle of Montségur

On the top of the pog at Montségur, the winter's snows had melted. The days were becoming warmer. Life in the confines of the small, drafty castle was becoming more bearable. People's spirits were lifted by the coming of spring.

Corba was pregnant again. She was anxious to tell me of her latest instruction from one of the Friends of God our mothers had introduced her to. She had some fresh spring flowers woven through her hair.

"Raymond, you should come with me to hear what the Good Christian Maurina Maury has to teach about reaching eternal salvation. She says we are all equal, men and women, and none of us is a sinner as the Church of Rome teaches. She says that no person, priest or otherwise, can open the doors to heaven for us, that it is up to each to find his or her own way. She is so full of hope. She says all souls will eventually return to heaven when they are pure enough. Isn't that wonderful?"

"I am glad you find her words uplifting, my dear. In these times, there is precious little to comfort people."

"Why do you not come to speak with her?"

"Too many matters require my attention at the moment. Maybe later."

"Can you not make time? When my spirit returns to heaven, I want to know we will not be apart for long."

"I want nothing more than to be by your side in the afterlife, but I have much to take care of in this life first."

Corba tugged at my arm. "Come. You will see how Maurina can lift your spirits." Her irresistible smile could melt snow. "My dear, you must attend to your soul as well as your flesh. And your soul is more important, for it must last you for eternity."

I was about to give in when the knight Jordan du Vilar burst into my chambers.

"My Lord, forgive the intrusion, but I bring bad news. Pierre-Roger de Cabaret has surrendered the castles of Lastours to the forces of Simon de Montfort."

I rose in horror. "No! It cannot be. Why in God's name would Pierre-Roger turn his fortresses over to Montfort? Pierre-Roger is a true Occitan knight, stubborn, and ready to give his life for our cause. Montfort already tried to take his fortresses and failed. He found, as have others, that Cabaret is impregnable. What treachery did Montfort employ to accomplish this ruination?"

"None, my Lord. It is said that when de Montfort arrived at the gates of Cabaret with his army swollen with new spring recruits, he wrought dread among the inhabitants. They were terrified he would butcher them as he had the people of Bram. They begged Pierre-Roger to sue for peace. In the end, he agreed."

"What price did de Montfort exact from him to spare Lastours from the savagery and the pillaging of his crusader horde?"

"He demanded the release of his cousin Bouchard de Marly and that all the inhabitants of Lastours renounce the heresy and swear allegiance to the Church of Rome."

"Did they?"

"Yes, my Lord," said Jordan with sadness in his voice.

"This is indeed dark news for all Occitania. These crusaders will not stop until we are all enslaved to that upstart of a pope. He is innocent in name only. One day, he will answer to God for the evil he and his assassins, de Montfort, Amaury, and others, have committed."

"If there is any justice, I pray God's retribution may be felt even before then, my Lord," cried Jordan du Vilar, a steely coldness in his voice.

"We shall have to see if God is listening," I said.

"The Good God is always listening," Corba said. "But so is Satan. They do not even see they have turned from the path of Christ, for they are blinded by the worldly power and riches he bestows upon them. Those who know the loving nature of the Good God must show them they have been deceived and convince them to turn from their wicked and selfish ways the Bad God uses to keep them trapped in the physical world."

"It will be no easy task to reform the church. Its clergy lusts after earthly pleasures," I said. "Dark days are ahead for our lands and people.

We tried to live in peace with our neighbors, but the church seeks to destroy us."

Corba tried to hide the worry I saw on her face. "The walls of Montségur are strong, and the Good God is with us," she said bravely. "We must trust in him as Maurina tells us."

"I wish I had your confidence, Corba, but as the Lord of Montségur, I cannot afford to do nothing and simply trust the Good God will protect us. I must act to protect those who depend on me. I place my trust in the likes of Jordan du Vilar here and the other knights in my garrison."

Jordan du Vilar smiled and bowed in humility.

"I have no intention of surrendering this castle to that villain de Montfort," I said. "We shall wait him out here until he is gone from our lands."

CHAPTER 37

Chivalry Forgotten

Given the continued threat of the dark forces of the pope in our lands, I strengthened our defenses at Montségur. Outside the walls of the cramped castle, my mother, Forneira, had a house built to welcome other Friends of God and novices who one day hoped to also take the Consolamentum. Corba spent increasing time among the faithful, which was of concern to me. With our mothers so committed to the faith, I suppose it was inevitable, but these were dangerous times for anyone to follow his or her conscience.

Corba helped in the house of the sick. At night, she would tell me of the debates she had had with Friends and believers. She was especially taken with those Friends of God who were known as *Méditatifs*. They devoted their earthly existence to trying to understand its purpose rather than preaching as did their fellow Friends. Corba longed to understand everything, so she had much in common with them.

As life continued in its orderly and calm flow in Montségur, isolated from the world below, the armies of the cross continued their butchery across our lands.

1211, May 3 – Castle of Lavaur

Foulquet de Marseille had been appointed bishop of Toulouse in 1206 by Innocent III. A close ally of Domingo de Guzmán, he was consumed by a fierce hatred of the Cathars and had, therefore, enthusiastically embraced the crusade of de Montfort. Frustrated with the inability or unwillingness of the count of Toulouse to rout heresy from Toulouse, Foulquet had created an urban Catholic militia, the White Brotherhood. Before long, the name struck terror in the hearts of the inhabitants of Toulouse. The brotherhood went about its task with religious zeal, murdering or bludgeoning to death anyone suspected of belonging to the heresy. Foulquet had become one of the most hated figures in the city; his actions served to further deepen the resentment of the inhabitants against the church, which he represented. Unfortunately, Count Raymond was powerless to stop the extremes of the bishop for fear of further antagonizing the pope.

When Foulquet learned de Montfort and his army were planning to lay siege to Lavaur, a city close to Toulouse, he had ridden joyfully to join him with a number of his brotherhood. Foulquet and his followers were excited by the opportunity to exterminate the heretics in Lavaur and set an example for the citizens of Toulouse.

Bishop Foulquet, surrounded by a coterie of his White Brotherhood, approached Simon on the battlefield. "My Lord, glorious news. We have breached the walls," he announced jubilantly. "Members of the brotherhood and other crusaders are pouring into the city. Soon it shall be ours!"

"Excellent news," replied de Montfort. "Tonight, we shall give thanks to God for our victory over his enemies. I shall send news to the pope of our success."

Brother Vaux de Cernay looked indignant. "There is no need for you to inform the holy father. I shall do so immediately. The pope has charged me with updating him."

"Forgive me, brother," Simon said. "I do not seek to usurp your role, but I am sure the pope will not be upset to hear more than one account of our glorious victory here."

"No, my Lord, I am sure he would not," Brother Vaux de Cernay reluctantly replied.

"I will also write to his Excellency," the bishop said. "The glory of this day cannot be overemphasized." He turned to de Montfort. "My Lord, what would you have done with the Lord of Lavaur, Aimery de Montréal? I ask that you permit the church to judge and punish those who have turned against it."

Brother Vaux de Cernay spoke. "Yes, my Lord, the church should be permitted to assume that responsibility because the crusaders fight under the protection of the church."

"Very well," de Montfort responded cautiously. "But an example must be made of Aimery de Montréal, who led the revolt. I cannot permit southern lords to turn against me after they have sworn allegiance to my cause."

"Of course, my Lord," the bishop said. "You need have no concern he will escape punishment. An example will be made of him that none shall forget, together with all the knights who fought alongside him." Bishop Foulquet looked like an excited child who had been given permission to go out to play.

Simon shook his head. "No. If the knights do not themselves profess to the heresy, then it is customary under the laws of chivalry they not be harmed."

"But these are exceptional times, my Lord," the bishop said. "We are in the ultimate struggle of good against evil. We battle to save the souls of humanity from Satan. Those who fight for his cause can expect no less than to burn in hell alongside the heretics."

"The Bible commands no less," Brother Vaux said. "In Deuteronomy, we are told, 'When the Lord your God brings you into the land you are entering to possess and drives out before you many nations—and when the Lord your God has delivered them over to you and you have defeated them, then you must destroy them totally. Make no treaty with them, and show them no mercy.'"

Simon was discomforted by the proposal. "I will permit it only if you are certain the Bible commands we show them no mercy. I would not want to interfere with God's will."

"We are, my Lord," the bishop asserted forcefully.

Brother Vaux nodded.

"Very well. Do as God commands. We have shown these people great tolerance and have gone out of our way to offer them redemption, yet they have spurned our attempts to save them. Even God's mercy has its limits. Those who oppose God's will, will receive his judgment."

"The brotherhood will assist your soldiers in routing out the perpetrators of the revolt, my Lord," the bishop said. "Justice will be swift, and it will strike fear into the hearts of those who stand against the church."

Simon was confident the priests would undertake their tasks with zeal and destroy those who stood in the way of his destiny. Prince John Lackland had stolen his family's land in England. In Occitania, he had a chance of redeeming the family honor. As the count of Toulouse, he would restore his family's privileged position in feudal society. It was clear to him that God had chosen him to lead the crusade against the Albigensians. The pope had told him so. Simon had pledged to restore those who had strayed to the rule of the cross. His reward would be the restoration of his family honor.

Simon had found the ideal ally in the Church of Rome. The pope was consumed with restoring the power of the papacy and the church to the pinnacle of the feudal system just as Simon was consumed with restoring the power of his family. Their goals were compatible; they shared philosophies for achieving what they sought. Success could be best achieved by showing no mercy to those who dared oppose them.

Simon watched contentedly as the bishop, assisted by Brother Vaux, the White Brotherhood, and many other clergy set avidly about their mission. In less than a week, those who had led the resistance were imprisoned, tried, and sentenced to death.

Aimery de Montréal and eighty of his knights were paraded in chains in the town square and lined up in front of the gallows to be hanged. The townsfolk were forced out of their houses to watch and listen to the many sermons condemning the wickedness of the heresy and demanding repentance of those who had sympathized with it. When the sermons ended, two hooded brothers led Aimery de Montréal up the steps to the gallows. The monks sang spiritedly. A dread hush fell across the crowd as Simon watched discreetly from the shadows.

A priest heard the bound Aimery de Montréal's confession as another pulled the noose tight around his neck. Before the priests had finished their tasks, everyone heard a loud, creaking sound followed by the sounds of splintering wood. The gallows collapsed under the weight of the robust lord. Shrieks of surprise broke out. "Behold! A miracle! The Good God has saved him," someone cried, which set the crowd in an uproar. Many began spontaneously praying and rejoicing at the divine intervention.

Simon clenched his fists. Bishop Foulquet seethed. "They mock us!" Simon said. "You swore to me your priests would see the heretics punished and humiliated before their own people. Now it is we who are humiliated!"

The bishop scowled. "I shall show them God does not reprieve infidels." He pushed his way to the front as if pursued by a beast. When he made it to where the knights were being held, he screamed orders. A monk drew a long knife and slit the throat of Aimery de Montréal. Blood gushed out of the wound; de Montréal's body writhed. The monks chanted loudly to drown out the disapproval of the crowd. Other monks began slitting the other knights' throats until all eighty lay dead in pools of blood.

"So dies a most foul traitor who had deserted God and his appointed representative in these lands, Count Simon de Montfort!" screamed the bishop above the mayhem.

Brother Vaux crossed himself with joy. "God is great! Their blood runs as red as the fires in hell. We vanquish all God's enemies!"

The townsfolk looked on in horror. Many wept. Others hid their faces for fear a similar fate might befall them. The clergy and the crusaders were alone in their jubilation.

With the blood of Aimery de Montréal still flowing, his sister, Giralda de Lavaur, was led before the crowd, her hands tied in front of her. Her clothes were shredded. Her breasts hung limply from her garments. Her face was bruised and bloodied. As she was pushed along by her captors, they goaded her, insulted her, spat on her, and boasted about the many pleasures they had taken with her in the few days they had held her captive. Clergy and crusader alike seemed to take immeasurable pleasure in her suffering.

"You stand convicted of heresy! Of working for the Antichrist!" roared the bishop in her face. "Do you repent the wickedness of your ways? Do you renounce your vows of Catharism and accept that the Church of Rome is the only true church and that Pope Innocent is God's sole representative on earth? This is your last chance for redemption before you stand before the final judgment!" he shrieked.

Her body but not her spirit was broken. Proudly, and painfully, she raised her head. Through swollen eyelids, she looked at him. "I shall never renounce the true God. The Church of Rome is corrupt and heathen, and the pope is a messenger of Satan."

Bishop Foulquet struck her face with the large cross he held, causing her to bleed profusely. "Take her!" he screamed. "Take her to where her words will never again offend the ears of the faithful. She is a heretic of the worst sort. Bury her in the bowels of the earth where only her master Satan can hear her."

The monks restraining the woman tugged harshly on the ropes to drag her from the bishop's presence as they would an animal being led to slaughter. They took her to a deep well just inside the castle walls. Crusaders and priests raised her in the air, crying benedictions for their own souls and vile curses for those of the witch they bore. Wary that they might be contaminated merely by contact with her, they hurled Giralda down the well as if they were discarding a piece of odious rubbish.

Giralda's cries echoed eerily out of the well. To the crusaders' horror and annoyance, they continued even after she hit the bottom. There was some water in the well, so she remained alive. From her screams, it was apparent she had suffered great injury from the ordeal. She began to cry for mercy from her captors. In response, they hurled rocks down the well. The more she screamed, the more angry they became and the more foul their taunts became. Her cries became weaker, until finally they stopped. The valiant Giralda was no longer of this earth.

For several more days, the trials of the Cathar perfects continued in Lavaur. Bishop Foulquet took the greatest of pleasure in his mission. "Do you confess your heresy?" he would demand of the accused.

The reply was always close to the same. "No, I do not, for I am not a heretic. I am a true Christian. It is the Church of Rome that is heretical."

"If you do not confess your heresy and denounce your fellows who have also sinned against the church, you shall be burned at the stake until your soul is banished forever to the fires of hell!" the bishop screamed.

"My body is of little value to me," was the repeated reply. "I have sworn my soul to the Almighty, and he will take care of it. You are powerless to separate me from him."

At first, Foulquet had been angered by their unrepentance, but he grew to welcome it. There was no doubt that these people were truly evil and that God had delivered them to him to be destroyed. Man, woman, or child, they were all the apostles of Satan, and God demanded and would rejoice in their destruction.

Outside the walls, large pyres of straw, branches, and small trees were set around massive stakes. The four hundred or more who had willingly confessed to being Good Christians or perfects of the Cathar Church were tied to one another and led to the pyres. Ladders were thrown on the piles so the prisoners could mount them and be tied to the stakes, though it was hardly necessary as none resisted. None pleaded for mercy or screamed to renounce his or her faith. Instead they began to sing quietly, accepting of their fate.

Bishop Foulquet excitedly threw the first torch on the pyre. Other monks did likewise. The dry tinder roared into flame. The singing from the four hundred or more souls did not continue for long. Those who had dared defy the might of the Church of Rome were quickly incinerated. In no time, the warm Midi air was heavy with the acrid smoke of burning wood, hair, flesh. The monks sang with great joy at their victory over evil.

"It is done," the bishop told de Montfort. "Lavaur is once more in God's hands."

"This is a day for rejoicing," Simon said. "But I fear the heresy is still strong in these lands. I have learned the counts of Foix and Comminges attacked a band of pilgrims coming here from Germany to join our crusade. We still have much work before we can declare Occitania free from the terror of the heresy."

"Indeed, my Lord. The heresy is a many-headed snake. We must chop off all its heads one by one. With God's help, I have faith we will do so."

Simon continued his campaign with renewed vigor. In June, he captured Cassès, where sixty Cathars were burned at the stake. Despite the threat of a tortuous death, the Cathar perfects held to their vow of nonviolence. They were an enemy the likes of which he had never encountered. When captured, they did not resist, lie, or plead for mercy. Simon could not decide whether to admire or pity them.

The perfects, however, did not volunteer to be slaughtered. They made their apprehension more difficult. They gave up their dark-blue habits and open sermons among the people. They dressed as those around them and took to giving their sermons among those they worked with. To cope with the new menace, the church began offering rewards for those who would denounce the Cathars among them. No evidence of the accusations was required; instead, it was up to the accused to prove their innocence.

1211, June – City of Toulouse

By June, Simon's ranks had swollen greatly with the arrival of many German pilgrims. They had come as had others to have their sins absolved and to reap the spoils of war. Simon decided he was strong enough finally to move against Count Raymond and become the overlord of all Occitania, answerable only to the king of France and the pope.

"How goes the siege, commander?" asked Simon.

"Not well, I am afraid, my Lord. The city is large, and its walls are strong and well manned. They have access to the river, so I fear they will be able to hold out for many months. In addition, Raymond's forces have been augmented by those of the count of Commings and Raymond-Roger de Foix, and his son Roger Bernard."

"An unwelcome development. The southern lords have finally decided to fight together. I suppose it was inevitable. I must teach them they will pay for their resistance."

Screams, galloping horses, and other loud noises interrupted them. Simon rushed out of the tent. "What is going on?" he screamed at a soldier.

"Soldiers under the count of Foix are attacking our positions."

"Get my horse," screamed Simon. "They shall taste my mettle."

After the first attack, Simon's army suffered near daily sorties from the Occitan forces. Before long, he realized he had greatly underestimated the number of crusaders required to maintain an effective siege of such a large and well-fortified city. His supply lines were threatened by constant ambushes. His situation became precarious. After consulting with his commanders, he decided to lift the siege.

"These southern lords may think they have won, but I shall show them differently. I will exact a heavy price on the county of Foix. I shall destroy every village in Foix I can," he promised, "Such is the wrath of God!"

In Narbonne, Archbishop Amaury excommunicated all the inhabitants of Toulouse for refusing to open their gates to de Montfort, their rightful lord. All inhabitants would be denied the protection and sacraments of the church. The archbishop preached hatefully against Jews and money lenders who gave financial support to the Cathars.

Inside Toulouse, the news of the butchery by the White Brotherhood in Lavaur spread rapidly. As the brotherhood launched murderous attacks against money lenders, Cathar sympathizers banded to fight them. Angry mobs drove them, along with Bishop Foulquet, out of the city. He dared not return for fear of his life.

CHAPTER 38

A Tragic Loss

I shall not dwell upon the military events of 1212, for none was of great significance. Throughout the year, skirmishes continued across our once-peaceful lands. For a while, there was some cause for optimism on our part. Raymond VI de Toulouse and Raymond-Roger de Foix succeeded in liberating Castelnaudary from the crusaders. As constant, low-level warfare dragged on and the battles became less glorious and rewarding for the soldiers of the cross, Simon's army began to melt away. Raising soldiers from across Occitania, Raymond took advantage of Simon's weakness and managed to recapture sixty fortresses and towns that had fallen to de Montfort. However, at the end of that year, one of the greatest treacheries in our history was perpetrated against the Occitan people by the Church of Rome and its French barbarian allies.

A so-called parliament held in December in Pamiers was attended by Archbishop Amaury, other papal legates, southern bishops, and French occupiers. None of the Occitan nobility was invited. That they chose to hold the meeting in Pamiers was an insult, for the town was in the county of Foix, which had suffered greatly from the crusaders' unspeakable brutality. Most of the town's inhabitants were Friends of God. It was in Pamiers only five years earlier that Esclarmonde de Foix and other Good Christians had so overwhelmingly won the debate against Domingo de Guzmán at the Colloquy of Montréal.

With none present to defend our interests, the parliament imposed French laws on our lands. That such a decree could have been made by supposedly enlightened men is beyond belief. When I heard the news, I was in shock and finally forced to agree with those who had long said the Church of Rome cared nothing for the people but only with preserving its wealth and power. Imposing the rule of the French over Occitania for our people was the near equivalent to the sacking of Rome by the Visigoths.

Since the rule of Charlemagne, Occitania had been ruled by Gallo-Roman law, and under it, it had developed the most vibrant, cultured, and tolerant civilization in Europe. By comparison, the French were war-loving, uncultured, uneducated barbarians who spoke in a harsh foreign tongue. Under Roman law, all children were equal, and all inheritances were divided equally among them regardless of gender. The noble titles and lands in Occitania were passed down equally to male and female descendants. But the French tradition of primogeniture was to be forced upon us; the eldest male would inherit all. Females henceforth would have no rights of inheritance.

Worse still for our noble Occitan women, whom we esteemed so highly, was that they were to be barred from marrying southern nobles. They would have to seek permission from de Montfort to marry, and then only to a French knight. The consequence would be the inevitable confiscation of our lands by the northern lords and the transformation of our women into northern whores in spite of our belief that men and women were equals.

Further decrees from the parliament were equally odious. Jews, who had been well integrated into our society, were to be banned from public office. Southern nobles were to be prohibited from carrying arms, and a new tax was to be levied on all our citizens to benefit our oppressors.

Regarding the heresy, the parliament declared that all convicted heretics must be burned at the stake and that only the Church of Rome could judge those accused of heresy. To add thievery to injustice, they declared that heretics' property was to be forfeit to the church. From that point on, Occitanians were to be answerable to the church, and no one could challenge its rulings. The church, of course, would remain answerable to no one.

With the victories during the year of Count Raymond over the forces of Simon de Montfort, many in Montségur had begun to hope the darkness might finally be lifted from our lands. However, the decrees of the parliament in Pamiers destroyed all such hope.

More bad news came from the north, including reports that fervent sermons were being preached from the pulpits throughout northern France against our people. This was the result of collusion between the pope and King Philippe-Auguste, both of whom lusted after our rich lands. As a result, by the spring of 1213, Simon's army was strengthened by many pilgrims from the north, all anxious to spill our southern blood. The year thus began menacingly for the people of Occitania and the events that transpired during the year led to a great loss of hope for our people.

1213, January – Castle of Toulouse

"Send for my son," commanded Count Raymond. He continued dictating to a scribe. With his chancellor beside him, he finished the remaining sentences.

"It is done, my Lord," said the chancellor. "All you have to do is sign and seal it."

"I want my son to witness this," insisted Raymond.

"Understood, my Lord. Given the circumstances, that would be good."

When the young boy was ushered in, the count addressed him. "Raymond, I have something important to tell you. This is a sad day for me but a happy one for you." He paused. "I am abdicating in your favor," he blurted out so the words would not stick in his mouth. "You will assume the title of Count Raymond VII de Toulouse."

His son was shocked. "But Father, I am not ready! I am only fifteen and still have much to learn about running your estates. You are still in good health and popular with the people. Why abdicate now?"

"I have become a burden for our people. I bring them only death and suffering. The pope and his legate, Archbishop Amaury, our bishop of Toulouse, Foulquet de Marseille, and other Catholic clergy have determined to destroy me. They will not stop until they have driven me from power even if they have to kill everyone in Occitania. I cannot let our people pay that price."

"Father, you cannot let those loathsome outsiders dictate how we live in Occitania."

"I have struggled to prevent it, but failed. Culture is subservient to the sword. We are no match for their arms. The pope has excommunicated me, which leaves Occitania without a ruler in their eyes. That allows any French barbarian to claim it as his own. With you as count, Occitania will have a legitimate ruler again, and they will no longer have any excuse for the crusade. I pray they will leave us in peace."

"Father, do you really expect that devil incarnate de Montfort will relinquish his conquests and return to his northern estates?"

Count Raymond shook his head. "I am not naïve enough to expect such a miracle. He has grown rich on our lands, and I do not have the power to drive him out. I do not doubt the pope will also want him to stay. We will have to tolerate him."

"I despise what he has done to our people and land, father. I would like to kill him."

"If you are to be count of Toulouse, you will have to learn the art of diplomacy."

"But father, if we train enough men and the crusaders go home, surely then we can drive out this odious man."

"Only at the price of spilling more Occitan blood. Our people are more accustomed to the fine arts of the troubadours than they are to slitting each other's throats. We are no match for them in battle."

"But you recaptured many of our towns from Simon's forces last year. The people are behind you, and I believe our people can learn to fight if they have to."

"We retook some towns, yes, but we failed to retake Lastours, and de Montfort took Albi. In recent months, he has renewed his attacks across the county of Toulouse. With the church behind him, he can count upon an endless supply of soldiers. There are only so many Occitanians, and it is the duty of the count of Toulouse to protect them. The best way for me to do that is to abdicate and install you as my successor."

The boy shook his head despondently. "Father, if you allow de Montfort to keep his possessions in Occitania, you will be conceding much of our lands to the king of France."

"That nightmare scares me too, but it need not be so. All the southern lands also owe homage to your uncle, King Pedro. In your inauguration as count of Toulouse, you will reaffirm your oath of loyalty to him. It will be a reminder to de Montfort and King Philippe-Auguste that these lands are not part of France despite what the papal legates declare."

"I shall willingly and loudly swear homage to King Pedro, who is much more cultured and just than Philippe-Auguste."

"It is settled then." Count Raymond took a deep breath. With a quick flurry, he signed the document. The chancellor blotted the ink, rolled up the parchment, and bound it with a ribbon. Holding a stick of red sealing wax over a candle, Count Raymond dripped the hot wax onto the ribbon to seal the knot. He pushed his ring into the wax as his last act as count. He handed the ring to his son, Count Raymond VII, the latest in a long and proud line of the counts of Toulouse that traced their ancestry to the days of Charlemagne.

1213, January – Castle of Carcassonne

Simon de Montfort soon learned of the abdication of Count Raymond VI. "How will this affect us?" asked his wife, Alix de Montmorency, with concern.

"I do not yet know. If the pope accepts his abdication, he will have to end the crusade, for his son is not excommunicated."

Simon's son, Amaury, paced nervously. "I thought Archbishop Amaury had declared you to be the count of Toulouse, father. How can Raymond abdicate what is not his?"

"Many questions have yet to be answered," replied Simon. "I am a soldier. Such questions are not for me to resolve. They are for the pope and the archbishop to decide. But I have confidence they will not abandon us or what we have accomplished here."

"They had better not. Our family honor depends on it," cried Alix. "We were promised these lands by the church, and you did everything asked of you. You have earned them. No one has a right to take them from you."

"That is true, God willing. We shall know more shortly. The archbishop is coming to update us on the latest news. His emissary is recently returned from Rome."

Amaury arrived late that day. An impatient Simon asked, "What news from Rome?"

The archbishop shook his head. "The news is not good, I am afraid, but I do not believe all is lost," puffed the stout archbishop, out of breath. "The pope has accepted Raymond's abdication and ordered an end to the crusade against the Albigensians."

"No!" screamed Simon, slamming his fist down upon the table. "Archbishop, you know I am a faithful Catholic. I do not question the word of the pope, but he is being tricked by the Devil! This abdication is no more than a charade. Raymond's son is every bit a Cathar as is he. If the crusade is abandoned now, everything we have accomplished will be wasted and the heresy will flourish. What does the holy father expect me to do? Return home like any other pilgrim, cap-in-hand, to Philippe-Auguste?"

The archbishop sat. He smiled. "Calm down, my Lord. We are of one mind. I have spoken with the other legates. We all agree Raymond is an enemy of the church who has treated the clergy with contempt. When I was abbot of Cîteaux, I warned him what would become of his failure to rein in the heresy, but he dismissed me as a fool and refused to remove from his service the Cathar perfects he keeps around him. He was surely responsible for the murder of Pierre de Castelnau, and he still treats all the legates with derision. We cannot allow such crimes to go unpunished. God demands retribution."

"How can that come about?"

"It is quite simple," replied the archbishop, his smile revealing rotting teeth. "We shall overrule the pope."

"Surely your vows require you to accept the word of the pope as the word of God."

"The pope speaks the word of God as he hears it. That I believe, but sometimes, the Devil corrupts God's message to him. These are exceptional times. The Devil is fighting hard to keep the lands he won. He seeks to confuse the word of God to the holy father. It is up to his loyal servants to help him hear more clearly. As legates to Occitania, we know what is best for these lands and for the church, not a pope cloistered in Rome. We will correct any 'confusion' in his decisions. I am confident he will accept our judgment."

"You are a loyal servant," Simon said with a hint of sarcasm. "You have no doubt?"

"None. The pope is far too busy planning a crusade to the Holy Land and fighting the kings of England and France to be concerned with the details of Occitania. King Philippe-Auguste has assured us of his total support for our plans." The archbishop grinned. "We intend to hold councils within the month in Orange and Lavaur. We shall reject Raymond VI's abdication as a ploy and demand the resumption of the crusade. We shall reconfirm the excommunication of Count Raymond VI."

"That is good news indeed, Archbishop! My faith is reinvigorated by the knowledge that there are those such as you who are selflessly dedicated to protecting the church."

The archbishop nodded smugly. Simon and Arnaud toasted the news with wine, then Simon's expression resumed a serious nature. "I am told Raymond VII swore an oath to King Pedro, not King Philippe-Auguste. Is this true?"

"Yes," the archbishop said. "The new count wants to set Aragón against France."

"King Pedro is a hero to all Christendom after his defeat of the Moors at Las Navas de Tolosa last year. He drove the Turkish Muslims into the sea. Being the brother-in-law of Raymond, and not wanting to relinquish any of his lands to the king of France, he will surely oppose our cause."

"I am only too aware of that," replied the archbishop. "He could be our biggest impediment to asserting our will over Occitania. I will try to dissuade him from meddling in affairs north of the Pyrenees, but I am not sure I will succeed. If I fail, we might have to fight the king and the new count."

"That would be ironic. A crusader army against the hero of Christendom," Simon said. "But as you say, these are unusual times."

"And unusual times call for unusual men. You are such a man, my Lord."

"You must include yourself on that list, Archbishop. Few have done more to save men's souls."

"Quite so. History will remember us for it. Now, with our business concluded, I propose we eat. I am quite famished by the journey here."

1213, September 12 – Muret

With the legates refusal to end the crusade, and Simon de Montfort refusal to relinquish his conquests in Occitania, King Pedro was forced to defend his interests. Sharing a mutual desire to expel the French invaders from the southern lands, he led his forces across the Pyrenees to unite with those of his brother-in-law Count Raymond VI. Together they dreamed of a greater Aragón with a common culture and language.

The journey to Toulouse took King Pedro and his Aragónese forces past the castle of Muret. A small and strategically unimportant fortress. The castle stood on the west bank of the Garonne River some distance south of Toulouse. Despite its insignificant role in the conflict, it was nonetheless occupied by crusader forces, so King Pedro lay siege to it. His expectation was for a short and victorious battle after which he would continue north to sweep the French invaders entirely from Occitania, which rightfully owed their fealty to Aragón.

Having heard about the siege, the counts of Foix and of Comminges joined Count Raymond VI and rode with their forces to assist King Pedro.

Aragónese Camp

"We have assembled quite an army here to rout these invaders," boasted King Pedro.

Count Raymond smiled. "Yes, my Liege. We have assembled close to four thousand cavalry and more than thirty thousand infantry."

"Excellent. Do we know our enemy's strength?" the king asked with no great expression of concern.

"We estimate they have fewer than one thousand cavalry and three thousand infantry."

"Then we shall make short work of them. No need to wait, for there are much greater prizes than Muret ahead. I propose we attack today."

Count Raymond was more cautious. "My King, I recommend a defensive strategy. The castle of Muret is not well fortified or well supplied. The crusader forces will not be able to endure a long siege. If we dig into a strong defensive position, after a few weeks, they will be forced to come out and do battle. We are well positioned here with the river on one side and a marsh on the other. If we fortify the camp, we will be able to cut down their cavalry with crossbow fire and javelins. Muret will be ours for the taking."

The Aragónese commander grimaced. "Sire, such a plan would bring dishonor upon the army of Aragón. We attack our enemies honorably on the field of battle. We attacked the Muslims at Las Navas de Tolosa; we did not hide from them."

Raymond-Roger de Foix spoke. "Sire, I know nothing of the Muslim heathens you faced in Spain, but I have fought many battles against de Montfort and I can tell you it is like fighting the Devil. He is everywhere and nowhere on the battlefield. He is totally unforgiving and ready to exploit the smallest weakness. Do not underestimate him or his men. I am told he has nearly one thousand mailed cavalry and knights, hardened crusaders who have fought alongside him in many battles and who would gladly die for him."

The Aragónese commander sensed the king was wavering. "Sire, if de Montfort and his knights are so ready to die, we should grant them their wish without delay. I say we attack them now and exterminate them as we did the Muslim infidels."

When the Aragónese soldiers behind their commander cheered his defiant words, King Pedro raised his hand. "I hear both sides. My Occitan brothers, you fear this Simon de Montfort and his crusaders because they have defeated ill-prepared defenders many times in battle. However, in fearing him, you enhance his reputation, which serves only to make him stronger. You say the walls of Muret are not strong, yet you would not attack. I say to you that while it is true we might prevail in battle by waiting for de Montfort to attack, we would risk losing the hearts of the people by appearing to be afraid of this northern lord."

The Aragónese soldiers cheered belligerently.

"I did not come here to Occitania merely to win battles. I came here also to win the confidence of the people. My decision is that we attack today," declared the king.

Castle of Muret

"What of King Pedro?" asked Simon. "Will he attack us or try to starve us?"

"We are not sure, my Lord," said Alain de Roucy, a trusted knight.

Simon studied a map. "If he is to attack, I would prefer he wait a while until these marshes dry out a little or even that he waits until spring. By spring, we should have pilgrims from the north to augment our forces. Archbishop Amaury has promised me as much."

The count of Corbeil shook his head. "He would be ill advised to wait that long. The numbers are greatly in their favor. He will want to take advantage of that."

Alain de Roucy nodded. "I have heard King Pedro is not a man of patience. He is renowned for his bravado. I do not see him waiting long for the satisfaction of victory."

Simon nodded. "Very well. I must prepare for an attack. Captain, how long can you hold the town?" he asked the commander of the town garrison.

"Not long I fear, my Lord, against the onslaught of so great an army. The castle's defenses are weak in several places. They could overrun us in any one of them. I do not have enough men to protect them all."

"Very good. Make sure they break through in only one of those places," said Simon enigmatically. "That way, you will be able to concentrate all your forces against them."

"But how—"

"I will tell you how when the time comes. But Captain, you must hold them as long as possible if my plan is to work. Can you promise me that?"

"Yes my Lord. Before God I promise you we will hold them to the last man."

"Alain, Florent, you stay with me. We need to discuss what to do if we are to turn the tides in our favor. The rest of you may leave."

As the retinue was filing out of the great hall, a bedraggled soldier came running in. "My Lord, it has started! The southern army is riding against us by the thousands. You can see them on the plain to the northwest. They will be upon us presently," the soldier cried.

"There is no need for fear," Simon proclaimed above the ruckus. "Remember that God is on our side. With his guidance, we shall win this day. If every man does as he is commanded, we will triumph! Commander, open the Toulouse gate."

"But—"

"Now! Defend it to your last man!"

The southern and Aragónese knights launched wave after wave of attacks against the castle. By midmorning, they were well inside the castle despite the valiant defense by the town's garrison supported by crusader forces. By midday, when both armies paused for lunch and to recover their dead, the attackers had overrun most of the castle.

While some crusaders were becoming despondent, de Montfort watched the events unfold with increasing satisfaction. The scenario was being played out exactly as he had planned. The enemy forces were spread across the plain. It was the moment he had been waiting for, the moment to deploy his treasured cavalry. Taking advantage of the lull in the fighting, with as little fuss as possible, he gathered his cavalry and foot soldiers and rode with them out of the castle toward the enemy camp.

The southern cavalry were camped out in two lines when Simon came upon them. The Aragónese forces were commanded by King Pedro, while the Occitan forces were under the command of their respective lords.

"We are in luck," Simon called out to Alain de Roucy. "See how they are overconfident. The cavalry has left the infantry in camp. They will be too far away to help them when we strike. Remember the plan. Strike at the head of the serpent!"

"I will, my Lord. We are with you."

"God willing, we shall triumph." Simon turned to the commander of his soldiers. "Commander, divide your men into two squadrons and attack both lines. Cause as much panic and confusion as possible. I will need distraction. Some cavalry will accompany you. As you go into battle against God's enemies, remember the scriptures, 'Cursed be he who does the Lords work remissly, cursed who he holds back his sword from blood,'" screamed Simon, raising his sword.

The soldiers cheered and raised their swords. Confident his forces were ready for battle, Simon rode to his knights. "Alain, Florent and all the crusader knights will come with me. We will cross the swamp and attack the Aragónese army on its left flank, where they believe themselves secure."

It was hard going through the swamp. The horses, weighed down by the knights in heavy army, became stuck in the mud. Mosquitoes swarmed incessantly around their faces, but they persisted. They were on a mission for God. They could not turn back. They heard shrieks and cries from the enemy lines as Simon's infantry fell upon them and created pandemonium. The cries of battle, the neighing of horses, and the clash of steel masked the noise made by Simon's cavalry as they fought their way through the marsh.

When they emerged from the swamp, the battle was raging across the plain. Simon regrouped in haste and ordered his cavalry to charge the Aragónese forces that were by then in complete disarray. Simon led the charge with lance in hand. His two best knights, Alain de Roucy and Florent de Ville, charged the Aragónese line.

At the head of the Aragónese line, a knight of large frame was fighting fiercely. He rode a white horse and was wearing a tunic bearing the red and gold stripes of Aragón. The crusader knights took him to be none other than King Pedro. Intent on executing Simon's plan of striking the head of the serpent, the two knights fought their way through the mêlée toward him. Coming at him from both sides, they charged, lances in hand. The lances sank deep into the horse's flanks, killing the mighty beast and throwing its rider to the ground. The two knights rode toward the disoriented figure. As he tried to regain his footing, they struck him repeatedly with their swords until his tunic was soaked in blood.

Alain de Roucy dismounted and ripped the helmet displaying the crest of Aragón from the lifeless body and held it high over the battlefield with its signature crest of Aragón. Removing his gloves, he tore at the straps holding the helmet and ripped it from the head. As Alain de Roucy looked upon the face, he recoiled in disbelief and bewilderment.

"This is not King Pedro! What deceit is this?" he shrieked. "What king would send others to battle to masquerade as himself? Only a coward! I ride for a man who is not afraid of battle, who does not hide his identity.

I expected better of the one they call Pedro the Great. The tales they tell of him must all be lies."

"Simon de Montfort is the only great leader on this battlefield," cried de Ville.

The two remounted and rode around the body, cursing and spitting on it.

A nondescript knight rode up. "You wish to fight with Pedro the Great? You shall have your wish."

"And where might we find the coward?" demanded de Roucy.

"Right here," declared the knight, taking off his helmet.

"It is Pedro," de Roucy said.

"Prepare to face your God," bellowed de Ville.

The knights allowed the king time to put his helmet on before attacking him. The king fought ferociously, but he was no match for the two knights. He began to tire. Alain de Roucy moved in for the kill. He ran the king through with his sword. King Pedro fell from his horse. Aragónese knights rushed to rescue him, but they were too late. The jubilant knights of de Montfort struck them down too as they cradled their dying monarch in their arms.

The news of King Pedro's death spread like a plague across the battlefield, causing chaos among the Aragónese, but it did not stop there. King Pedro had been the de facto leader of the combined forces fighting the crusaders, and no clear command structure had been established. With King Pedro dead, the Aragónese and Occitan forces were leaderless. Confused and lacking any coordination, the disparate armies descended into disarray.

Seizing the moment, Simon regrouped and attacked his enemies, cutting them down as they fled. He soon turned the battle into a full-scale rout. His greatly outnumbered but well-disciplined, battle-hardened crusaders pursued their enemy off the battlefield.

Upon hearing of the death of their king, the Aragónese knights in the castle poured out of the gate and fled. The thirty thousand or so infantry in the southern camp grabbed what little they could and fled in panic as the crusader forces bore down upon them.

Simon was triumphant. "God has given us a great victory! We have changed the face of Europe and demonstrated to all that the one true church of Christ is the Church of Rome. God will not tolerate heresy and will strike down those who profess it. God commands us in the book of Psalms to 'crush his foes before him, strike down those who hate him.' We have done so. Let all men rejoice in the work of the Lord."

The cries of victory drowned out the groans of those dying on the field around them.

After Simon had given his men time to realize the greatness of what they had done, he called for calm. "My fellow pilgrims, Christ has walked with us this day on the very grass under our feet. I ask you to walk back with him to the castle. To walk as Christ walked and as he suffered to forgive our sins, I ask you to remove your boots. We will walk to the castle barefoot in penance for his ultimate sacrifice in our name. Tonight, we will celebrate Mass."

A priest blessed the crowd, and together they cried out passionately, "Amen!"

CHAPTER 39

Intolerance Enshrined

King Pedro had been the greatest friend and hope for Occitania against the crusaders who wore red crosses they hoped to stain with the red blood of the Occitan people. The crusaders had come to enslave us, while King Pedro, a true Christian, had come to free us.

King Pedro's death marked the beginning of the end of our precious Occitan culture. The tradition of tolerance, chivalry, the troubadours, our respect for our woman, and learning had been a threat to those in power in Rome and France. With King Pedro's death little now stood in their way of to eliminate it.

Count Raymond VI fled to England to seek the protection of his former brother-in-law, John Lackland. With Raymond in exile, Innocent granted the lands and possessions of Count Raymond to King Philippe-Auguste. The pope was anxious that Philippe-Auguste administer our lands in the name of the church so the pope could end his crusade against us and launch a new one against the Holy Land.

The timing could not have been better for the French king. After a failed invasion of southwestern France by John Lackland and his defeat at the Battle of Bouvines in another invasion attempt in northern France, the French king was relieved of any further worries from his traditional enemy. That left him free to concentrate on the annexation of our lands.

It was under these circumstances in 1215 that Simon de Montfort entered Toulouse accompanied by Louis, the son of King Philippe-Auguste. Both were despised by the Occitan people, but with Count Raymond in exile in England and his young son having fled to Aragón, the people had no choice but to submit to the invaders. The much-hated Bishop Foulquet and his White Brotherhood also returned to the city, further increasing the animosity of the inhabitants to their new rulers.

It was at this time I started seriously to question my faith in the Church of Rome.

1215, August – Castle of Montségur

"What is the news from Toulouse?" asked my mother, Forneira.

"Not good. Bishop Foulquet and his thugs are again accusing anyone who speaks against them of heresy. Many are being tortured and forced to confess or to accuse others to try to save themselves. When he is finished with them, they are usually declared guilty of heresy anyway and burned at the stake."

"And the church confiscates the property of all found guilty of heresy?"

"Yes. It makes living in the city particularly dangerous for the wealthy, as the church envies their possessions. Many merchants and most of the Jews have fled for that reason."

"How can this be Christianity?" asked Corba, close to tears. "How can these people claim to worship the same God as we do? Surely they profess to follow the Christ who taught compassion. My husband, how can you share faith with those who bring only murder and suffering to our people?" she asked.

It was a question I had sought to avoid increasingly of late. I tried to think as I spoke to clarify my own misgivings. "Recent events have certainly tested my faith. But as Lord de Péreille, I have a responsibility to my people. Since the decline of the Roman Empire and the death of Charlemagne, the legitimacy of all forms of government in Europe has come from the Church of Rome. I cannot reject it without risking destroying the social fabric that binds us all. Without order, we would slip back to the days of barbarism that existed before Rome's legions brought us civilization."

"But what have we left of that civilization now in Occitania?" asked Corba. "Did the crusaders not bring us barbarianism? We had order before they came, and they have destroyed it." She wept.

I hung my head, not knowing quite how to console her. "You speak the truth, I am afraid. That has been troubling me. The Church of Rome claims to follow the teachings of Christ, as do we all. Therefore, I had believed our differences could never be great."

"Yet we do not believe in burning women at the stake!" cried my mother.

"Nor did Christ," I replied. "It would seem the church has lost its way."

Corba dried her eyes. "Guilhabert de Castres says the evil God has seduced the Church of Rome with material possessions. That they are now the church of Satan."

"I am not a philosopher such as he is in these matters," I admitted.

"I have heard the pope is not long for this world. I pray the new one will return the Church of Rome to the path of Christ," said Corba with the first glimmer of hope I had heard in her voice.

My mother shook her head. "I too pray for that, but I fear the church is too far lost for such a simple redemption. Despite the lesson of Occitania, it has done nothing to reform itself. Under Pope Innocent III, it has slaughtered fellow Christians here and in Constantinople, and the clergy have become ever more debauched."

"I cannot deny that," I agreed. "Since the crusaders entered Toulouse, I have heard that many of the clergy have returned to their old ways. They frequent brothels and gambling houses, they even wager indulgences. Some are said to fornicate with young boys, and most are drunk more than they are sober."

"Indeed," my mother said. "And yet the people must pay extra taxes to support the clergy who have been forced upon them, for they do no labor, unlike the Good Christians who live and work amongst us."

Corba's eyes were bloodshot. "Guilhabert de Castres says that the souls of all living beings, even those as evil as Simon de Montfort and Bishop Foulquet, will eventually find their paths to God. I wish that it were not so. I cannot forgive those who throw babies into the flames. However, he assures me they will have to suffer through many cycles of birth and rebirth before their souls are pure enough to reach heaven."

Forneira touched her arm. "Some things are difficult to understand. But the elders will teach you they are not responsible for the vileness of their deeds. The Bad God is to blame. He has taken control of their souls, and before they can return to the side of the Good God in heaven, they will have to cast him out. It is up to each of us to help them find their paths to salvation."

"I do not think I am strong enough to do that," confessed Corba.

"You must spend more time with Esclarmonde. She will help you find that understanding, and when you have found it, you will find great peace, as I have."

"Esclarmonde de Foix is a wise and wonderful teacher," Corba said. "I admire her so much. If I have a daughter, I will name her Esclarmonde in hopes she will grow up to be like her."

"She is truly an inspiration to us all," declared my mother. "Esclarmonde will teach you that the evil of the crusaders is proof to all that the Church of Rome has lost its way. The Catholic Church has confused the Good God with the Bad God since Constantine forced them to declare there was only one god. They were deceived to follow the word of the Bad God, the jealous, vengeful, and murderous God of the Old Testament, the antithesis of the Good God Christ commanded us to follow."

"Guilhabert de Castres has told me that, Forneira. He is very knowledgeable, but I still have so much to learn."

"Have patience, child, and follow what he and Esclarmonde teach you. They will teach you that that the Bad God is very strong. Only today Esclarmonde read this passage to me from the Old Testament—" My mother opened her Bible, "—'The people of Samaria must bear the consequences of their guilt because they rebelled against their God. They will be killed by an invading army, their little ones dashed to death against the ground, their pregnant women ripped open by swords.' It is clearly a work of pure evil inspired by the Bad God. The Catholics are only practicing what they have been told falsely is the word of the Good God."

"Why do all not see this?" Corba asked.

"The church of Rome seeks to hide the nature of the god they follow from their flock. They keep the Bible in Latin, which few but the clergy and nobility can understand, and those who dare read the Bible outside the presence of a priest risk being burned at the stake."

1215, November – Lateran Palace, Rome

"Your Eminence, the ecumenical council awaits you," declared Cardinal Marcellini.

"Is the church well represented?"

"Very well, Holy Father. We have representatives from every corner of the Christian world. There are seventy-one archbishops, four hundred and ten bishops, and eight hundred abbots. It is a most powerful convocation, one whose word none will dare challenge."

"I am glad to hear it. I have matters of great importance to impart to them. First, I want the clergy to actively reassert the authority of the church over all temporal powers. The principle of imperium mundi must be accepted by all. None is to question the supreme authority of the pope in all matters spiritual and temporal, for the pope is answerable only to God. Monarch, noble, and bishop must accept they are subjects of the Holy See. God created the papacy to rule his kingdom on earth. It is heresy to say otherwise."

The cardinal smiled. "I am glad you will forcefully reassert the supremacy of the papacy. Some of your recent decisions have been openly challenged by John Lackland and King Philippe-Auguste, and even some of the clergy have criticized your edicts, daring to call some evil. Such heresy is an affront to God and treason against his church."

"My predecessors were too weak," complained the pope. "They were lax in reminding everyone the word of the pope is the word of God and thus no one has the right to challenge it. God's word can never be evil. Those who challenge it commit blasphemy. I intend to excommunicate any who criticize the dogma of the church."

"You will be an inspiration to the faithful, your Eminence."

The pope smiled. "I intend to speak out strongly at the council against this treasonable list of demands John Lackland was forced to sign. I believe they are calling it the Magna Carta."

"They are, your Eminence. It is an anathema to God's order."

"Indeed. The authority of the monarch over his barons is absolute. His authority flows from God through the papacy, and none has the right to intercede in God's order. This document is a sacrilege King John signed at the point of a sword. I shall annul it and release John from upholding its terms. I shall excommunicate any who seek to uphold it."

"Holy Father, another important matter before the council is how you intend to resolve the situation in Occitania. Count Raymond VI, his son, and several other important Occitan nobles have come to petition you. Simon de Montfort's brother, Guy, and a number of crusaders will be in attendance to oppose their demands. It is certain Occitania will be much discussed."

"I had expected as much. Events there are going much in our favor, I hear, though the heresy has not yet been fully uprooted. I am inclined to restore the count to his possessions if he will foreswear the heresy in front of the council and take a solemn vow to purge all those who practice it. This crusade against the Albigensians is a costly burden I wish to be rid of so I can pursue a greater glory God has set for me, the liberation of Jerusalem. While our pilgrims and our money fight these southern pagans, I am unable to launch a new crusade against the Holy Land. I wish to be remembered as the pope who freed the land of Christ, not the land of some troublesome minstrels."

"That would be a glorious achievement. However, Archbishop Amaury and many of the southern bishops and legates are sure to insist the crusade not be abandoned until the House of St. Gilles is brought down. They have a fierce hatred for Count Raymond VI and will oppose any move to lift his excommunication. I am told they intend to petition the council to transfer his titles and possessions to Simon de Montfort."

Pope Innocent frowned. Giving in to their demands would surely delay his plans for a new crusade. "I cannot dispossess the count of all his possessions and confer them to a northern noble of such low rank. It would not sit well with the other nobles. They would see it as a direct threat to their own titles. Also, if I restore Count Raymond, it may quell the resentment of the people against the church."

"Your reasoning is sound, your Eminence. Unfortunately, the southern bishops are sure to raise strong objection to such a decision."

"It would not be the first time. I have no wish to aggravate them. I need their support for my new crusade. Perhaps it would be best if I made my intentions clear but allowed some flexibility in my ruling. We will learn where the sentiment of the council lies."

"A most wise decision, your Grace."

"Between ourselves, Cardinal, I do not entirely trust these southern bishops. They assume an importance beyond their rank and have become a threat to my authority. I believe Archbishop Amaury sees himself as my successor. Hopefully, he will allow me to die first."

"Yes, your Grace."

"On another matter, I have decided to create a new order, the Dominicans, under Friar Dominic. He has aggressively pursued the heresy in Occitania and seeks additional church sanction and support for his work. The new order will conduct inquisitions into the faith of the people and eliminate the heresy by conversion. They will be more effective in the long term than waging costly crusades. And much less bothersome."

"I have heard only good things of Friar Dominic, Holy Father."

Before the great council, Pope Innocent III pronounced his dictum that the papacy was at the pinnacle of the feudal system, which made him king of kings and answerable to none but God. As God's sole representative on earth, his canons were God's laws and were thus binding without question on all men and women of faith, from archbishop to peasant.

The council received his pronouncement in silence. None rose to challenge it. With his primary message clearly expounded and understood, the pope moved to his next topic. "We have made much progress in suppressing the error of the heresy of late, particularly in Occitania. The archbishop of Narbonne has tirelessly led our crusade against the Albigensians, and for this we owe him our gratitude."

To thunderous applause, the archbishop stood and took a self-ingratiating bow. The pope allowed him his moment of adulation before continuing. "But the struggle to spread God's word is never ending. We must not rest until all Satan's disciples are defeated and his lies are erased from the minds of the common people to save them from damnation."

Loud cheers and shouts of applause erupted.

"To aid in this struggle, I am announcing today the creation of a new order that will be under Friar Dominic. The order is to be known as the Dominicans, and their principal task will be to seek out the error wherever it hides and eradicate it. It will be an onerous task but one Friar Dominic has already shown himself capable of."

Friar Dominic stood to make himself known to the council and received many cries of support and encouragement. Amaury and the southern bishops greeted the news with particular enthusiasm. When he sat, the pope continued his address.

"I need remind no one that the penalty for heresy is death, for such is commanded by God. Unfortunately, the nobility and in some cases even the clergy have not been diligent in applying God's law. This has allowed the heresy to take root and flourish in regions such as Occitania. Such a situation is intolerable to God and cannot be permitted to continue. I command each of you to return to your parishes and preach this message to all. From this day on, all those suspected of heresy are to be reported to the Dominican order. It will be their sole responsibility to decide the guilt or innocence of the accused."

Amaury stood, beaming with pleasure. "Holy Father, the people will be forever indebted to you for taking such a strong stance against the heresy. Your boldness will surely spare many souls from hell. Only through such vigilance can we avoid another Occitania."

All on the council nodded. When Amaury sat, a bishop from northern France stood. "Holy Father, our region has fortunately seen little of the heresy, which has plagued other regions such as Occitania, thus we have little knowledge of it. Can you remind us how to recognize the principal acts of heresy?"

"It is good you ask. There are many acts of heresy commonly practiced by those who deny God. I can list a few that are most easily recognized. A refusal to swear an oath to the church or to a noble is proof of heresy, as is a refusal to eat meat. By refusing to eat meat, the heretic denies God's bounty, as do the Cathars, for example. It is also heresy to deny Christ as the Son of God or to reject any of the sacraments or theology of the church.

"Translating the Bible from Latin or reading it outside the presence of a priest are also common acts of heresy. Those who insist on a literal interpretation of Christ's teaching when it conflicts with the church's interpretation are guilty of heresy. The number of heresies is too great to list, which is why the Dominicans are charged with identifying them."

The pope paused for a standing ovation. When the applause died down, he continued his address. "I wish now to turn to the problem of the Jews. It was their race that persecuted and crucified our Savior. To this day, they continue to deny Christ's deity, so they cannot be accepted into civilized society. They pose a grave threat to those who have chosen to follow Christ. All contact between Jews and the faithful should be minimized. To ensure this, I propose new restrictions on the Jews who choose to live within Christendom. First, all Jews of either sex, in every Christian province, and at all times, are to be distinguished in public from other people by a difference of dress."

When the cries of approbation died down, the pope continued. "Jews will also be required to live apart and will not be entitled to any redress for grievances in a Christian court. Marriage between a Christian and a Jew will remain strictly forbidden, and since it is unacceptable that blasphemers of Christ should exercise power over Christians, I am renewing the decree forbidding Jews to hold public office."

Count Raymond looked at those around him and shook his head gently in disapproval, anxious not to draw attention to himself. However, Raymond-Roger de Foix, having no such qualms, shouted his disapproval, but few cared for the opinion of an Occitan noble. All the clergy on the council overwhelming expressed their approval of the proposals.

Innocent was most gratified by the council's reception. He had but one important matter left to cover—Occitania. It was an issue for which he did not expect to receive such universal approval, so he introduced it diplomatically.

"Finally, to the problem of Occitania. First, let us remember in our prayers the pilgrims, the soldiers of God, the crusaders, who have been fighting to save the souls of humanity against an obdurate heresy. Their sacrifice is in the service of the Lord, and those who kill a Cathar, just as those who slay a Muslim, are assured of the highest place in heaven."

Archbishop Amaury and Bishop Foulquet stood and applauded. They were quickly joined by all the southern clergy and shortly after by most of the clergy on the council. Only Count Raymond and his companions remained seated.

"It is the right if not the duty of every man who hears the calling from God to abandon his family without explanation or farewell to join the crusade," cried the pope over the applause. "For in like manner, the disciples abandoned their families to join Jesus."

The pope made clear to the council his strong preference to call an end to the Albigensian crusade so preparations could begin for a new crusade in the Holy Land. He argued that the best way to do this would be to lift the excommunication of Count Raymond VI so he could continue the pursuit of the heresy in Occitania. As he had feared, Archbishop Amaury and his supporters voiced strong opposition. "The excommunication of Count Raymond VI must stand!" cried Amaury. "He and his family are heretics!"

The count and Raymond-Roger stood to strenuously protest the allegations, but the archbishop was undeterred. "Holy Father, we demand from this council nothing less than the complete disinheritance of the House of St. Gilles!"

Cries of support and opposition clashed. The pope sensed, as he had feared, that it would not be to his advantage to dictate a course of action on the matter. There was clearly too much passion on both sides for any decision by him to be received without rancor by one or both parties. Since he had already received near-unanimous support for the issues he cared about most dearly, he would defer judgment for the time on the issue of Occitania.

"I have given you my preference for resolving the situation in Occitania. However, I am not as well informed on the issue as are the archbishop of Narbonne, the other legates, and the clergy in the region. The council must debate this matter. I will accept its decision."

Amaury bowed to the pope with a wide smile before enthusiastically plunging into the debate. "Raymond VI was responsible directly or indirectly for the murder of the papal legate Pierre de Castelnau."

Count Raymond rose to protest but was quickly shouted down.

"He travels with known Cathar perfects as advisers in his retinue, and he allows known Cathars, their sympathizers, and even Jews to hold public office!"

Many of the delegates stood, shaking their fists angrily and booing.

"Under the count, the heresy has flourished in Occitania, the churches and collection plates have been emptied, and the population scoffs at the threat of excommunication."

"Treachery!" cried one of the bishops.

"It is only through God's good grace that a northern knight, Simon de Montfort, has recently been sent to us to restore the rule of God to

Occitania. He has led our crusading forces to victory over the forces of Satan. He has suppressed the heresy wherever he has found it, and he has crushed those who spread its vile lies. God has ridden at his side throughout the crusade, for Simon has not lost a single battle. Only this summer, he was outnumbered by more than ten to one, but God led him to victory over the invading Aragónese forces that sought to prolong the heresy."

A loud crescendo of supporting cheers rang out across around the room. Amaury continued as soon as he could be heard again. "I know Simon de Montfort to be a pious man, a man of the cross we can trust to enforce the will of God in the southern lands. God has sent him to us, and God commands we disinherit the House of St. Gilles from all its possessions in Occitania and confer them to Simon de Montfort and his heirs to hold in perpetuity in the name of the church!" screamed the archbishop.

When the maelstrom had subsided, Raymond-Roger stood defiantly to address the council in defense of his overlord, Count Raymond VI. With his large frame surrounded by a sea of hostile faces, he appeared as a bear among wolves.

"You cannot so lightly disinherit a noble from his possessions," he said in a commanding tone. "We have order in our lands because the people accept their lord's authority comes directly from God via their birthright. If you so lightly cast this principle aside, you risk tearing up the roots of all the nobility and killing the tree that is the feudal system. All men may begin to question their lords' authority over them. Simon de Montfort will never be accepted by the people of Occitania as their rightful overlord."

The words gave some pause for thought. A few ayes came from around the table. Sensing the acquiescence, Amaury and the southern legates quickly moved to counter it by crying out in condemnation to overwhelm them.

The voice of Raymond-Roger boomed. "Count Raymond does not stand accused of any treasonous or vile act against his people or against God. He is not accused of any action. He is accused of inaction. Yet few here understand the situation in our lands. He has done all in his power to restore the authority of the church, but the church has undermined his efforts. The Occitan people are among the best read and most educated in Europe and thus not easily misled. The debauchery of Catholic priests and the corruption of the church have driven the Occitan people to the heresy. It is not the count who is to blame for their rejection of the church but yourselves. The Church of Rome must be reformed!"

Archbishop Amaury jumped up. "Raymond-Roger, you are a man of great reputation who fought valiantly at the side of King Philippe-Auguste in the crusade during the siege and capture of Acre. For that, you are welcome at this council." He paused to look at the other members of the council. "However, since then, by many accounts, you have turned away from God, your mind poisoned by the heresy. Why then should the council heed your words? Your sister Esclarmonde is an admitted heretic witch, and you are accused of murdering our priests!"

Raymond-Roger was unabashed. "It is true I have murdered priests," he admitted proudly.

The reaction to his admission was instant and passionate. Threats and curses of condemnation were hurled at him from around the table. Raymond-Roger waited a short time for the protests to die down before holding his mighty arms in the air. They had the effect he desired of bringing some semblance of order to the chamber. Daring to look even directly at the pope, he continued.

"I have murdered priests, and I have had no regrets. Indeed, I regret I did not kill more. But each one I killed deserved his fate. They were not doing God's work but the Devil's work. They were guilty of thieving, raping, sodomizing, or other vile deeds. Priest or peasant, I will not tolerate such acts in my lands."

Amaury glared at Raymond-Roger. "You come to us to plea for your overlord with your hands steeped in the blood of Christ and expect us to hear you?"

"I do! For my hands are entirely without sin next to those of the archbishop of Narbonne," he exclaimed. "There is more of the blood of Christ on his hands than flows in all the members of this council. What of the good Catholics in Béziers and Bram he burned to death in God's own houses?"

The archbishop's supporters rose tumultuously to his defense. A heated shouting match ensued. Each side threw curses and accusations at the other. However, the southern nobles and their supporters were greatly outnumbered; the exchange was overwhelmingly one-sided. The southern legates and bishops were intent on destroying their archenemy and were in no mood to compromise. Their priests had been ridiculed and virtually expelled from Occitania under the rule of Count Raymond VI. The common people had stopped tithing, forcing them to beg or worse still, to seek work. It had been a degrading experience to a social class, the priesthood, who truly believed that the world owed them a living. It was time for their revenge.

The shouts and screams continued until the pope banged his staff on the floor. Gradually, the rancor and insults subsided. When order was restored, the council was ready to cast its verdict on the Occitan problem.

Raymond was dejected and resigned to the fact he had failed to persuade the council of the righteousness of his cause. However, he had never received a chance with Amaury and the southern legates dominating the council. It was clearly they who would dictate the verdict. He knew his cause was lost.

Archbishop Amaury rose and gloated with satisfaction to read the decisions of the council.

"The council declares that Raymond de St-Gilles, by his actions and by his inaction, encouraged the Cathar heresy to flourish among the congregation of the faithful he was entrusted by God to protect. In betraying that trust, he has shown himself totally unfit to hold such office, whose authority rests with God, through his representative on earth, His Holiness Pope Innocent III."

The archbishop bowed punctiliously in the pope's direction, acknowledging him with a cursory smile. "It is therefore decreed by this council that Raymond de St-Gilles and his descendants be disinherited of the titles that God had bestowed upon them. Among these titles are the count of Toulouse, of Quercy, of Rouergue, of St-Gilles, of Aquitaine, and of Melgueil. He is also to forfeit the titles of duke of Narbonne, overlord of Foix, and viscount of Béziers and Carcassonne. These titles and associated possessions will be conferred upon the house of Simon de Montfort and his descendants."

The southern legates stood and vigorously applauded. Amaury was more than happy to allow them a moment of triumph before continuing. "Simon de Montfort has shown himself to be a great soldier of Christ and a truly devout and pious Christian. After his inspiring deeds against the infidels in the Holy Land, he has of late dedicated himself entirely to liberating the Occitan people from the scourge of the heresy. With God's help, he has made much progress, but the battle is not yet won, for Satan is strong. Bestowing these titles upon him will reward him and aid him in his struggle to champion righteousness over evil."

There were more loud calls of support, at first from the southern clergy, and before long from every church member on the council. In sharp contrast, Count Raymond VI, his son, Raymond-Roger, and the other Occitan nobles sat, stony-faced, angry, and desperate at the travesty of justice they had just witnessed.

The archbishop fixed a triumphant glare upon Raymond. He had despised the count for so long for having treated him with derision and contempt and now h was relishing his revenge. None in the future would dare mock the archbishop of Narbonne. Amaury attempted to straighten his curved posture for one last pronouncement. "In its generosity, and as a demonstration of Christ's mercy, the council has decided to provide Raymond de St-Gilles with a pension of four hundred marks per year," he proclaimed with aloofness.

"But what of my son?" cried Raymond. "He stands accused of no wrongdoing. Why are his titles and lands to be forfeit?"

The archbishop looked annoyed. "The lands he would have inherited from you are forfeit, for they are no longer yours to bequeath to him. However, those of his mother are unaffected by the declaration of the council. Thus, when he comes of age, your son will still be able to assume the title of marquis of Provence and the stewardship of his mother's possessions in Provence in the name of the church. I trust he will not betray that trust as you have done."

The young Raymond started to rise but was restrained by his father.

1215, November – The Palace of the Vatican, Rome

"Your Holiness, Raymond de St-Gilles and his son are here," announced Cardinal Marcellini.

"I was expecting them. Show them in and leave us, please."

Raymond entered the pope's chambers with his eighteen-year-old son. He was nervous, not knowing what sort of reception to expect or why he had been summoned. The pope was seated. Raymond knelt at his feet as demanded by etiquette and bowed. "Holy Father, I thank you for summoning us. Pray tell me what I might do to atone for what I am accused of, for I have always been a humble servant of the church."

"Arise," said the pope. He hesitated. "I am troubled that the decrees of the council regarding the Occitan nobility may have been somewhat excessive and premature."

"Holy Father, I have never spoken out against the church," pleaded Raymond.

"That may be, but I am afraid you have greatly offended many of the clergy by shunning them and ignoring their demands to act against the heresy. You gave them no choice but to call for a crusade against your lands to recover their property, their livelihood, and their authority. I am afraid the legates will never accept returning power to you."

"But what of my son? He has done nothing to offend anyone. And what of the ten-year-old son of Raymond-Roger de Trencavel? What did he do to justify being dispossessed of his inheritance? Simon de Montfort came into our lands and cast his father to rot in the dungeons of Carcassonne, and today he is rewarded for that treachery with his title."

The pope nodded. "It was not my wish, but it was the decision of the council, and I am loath to overrule them. However, I remain troubled by any action that seeks to overturn God's order. It is fraught with peril."

"Indeed, your Grace."

"I fear some of the legates might be too close to your cousin King Philippe-Auguste. I know him to be anxious to take your lands for himself rather than for the church. In their enthusiasm, some legates may have put their duty to their monarch ahead of that to the church."

"Then what will you do, Pontiff?"

"For now, there is no need for me to do anything, for your son here is not yet of age. However, if before that time he were to recover his lands," the pope said with clear encouragement, "and swear to administer them in the name of the church, I would be open to restoring your family's lands and titles to him."

The offer took Raymond by surprise. It took him a moment to reply. "Holy Father, I am grateful for your message of hope. I am confident that if my son were to be in the position you mention, he would gladly swear allegiance to the church."

"I would," agreed the younger Raymond. "And I will gladly take up arms to drive the northern invader from our lands."

"If you succeed, you must promise me you will make your ports on the Mediterranean available for my crusade against the Holy Land and will provide troops for the venture to free Jerusalem, for that is to be my legacy."

"You have my word," young Raymond said.

"Then we have an accommodation." The pope smiled.

1215, December – Castle of Montségur

High on the plateau of the pog of Montségur, the wind was driving snow against the dark stones of the fortress. Fires were burning for people to keep warm in the ramshackle dwellings that spread out from the castle walls. As the crusaders had wrought their terror on the lands below, the population of Montségur had swollen.

Corba entered the room with her hair and clothes disheveled. Snow on her clothes and hair melted in the heat of the fire. The moisture on her face, however, came from tears. "The lady Esclarmonde de Foix is dying," she announced.

"I am truly sorry to hear that," I replied. "For she is an inspiration to us all. But I am surprised somewhat by your sorrow. Surely, as a Good Christian, she welcomes death, as her soul will finally complete its journey to heaven."

"That is true. That is why I do not cry for her but for myself and all of us she leaves behind. She has guided me with her kindness and her wisdom for many years. Despite all the terrible things that have happened in Occitania, she has always been able to see through it and to show me hope. I fear my hope might die with her."

"I understand, for I too have sought out her counsel many times. But if it is God's will she leave us, we cannot change that and should not wish to prolong her suffering."

"I know. It is selfish of me to think that way, but many others are grieving. As I walked through the castle and talked to people, I could feel a gloom over everyone. It is as if Montségur was under a cloud even darker than those above our heads."

"It will pass. We should be grateful she came among us and hope that others will come to take her place. If we are to survive these dark times, we must believe in ultimate good as she did and follow her example."

"I strive to do that," said Corba, "but I am not sure I have her strength."

"You will find it. Get some rest. You have labored for many hours by her bedside."

"I will." Tears returned to her eyes. "I am so sad our child will never get to talk to Esclarmonde as we did."

CHAPTER 40

An Unwelcome Visit

Wednesday, July 5, 1944 – County of Foix

Emile had been turning in his sleep most of the night. The long hours spent reading the chronicle of the ancient Lord Raymond were taking a toll. He had become obsessed with it. The more he read, the more horrified, yet the more engrossed he became with the account; he found it near impossible to put down. Something in it touched his soul and drove him to read on.

As he lay restless on the uncomfortable, makeshift bed in the cellar, his mind spun in confusion. It was having increasing difficulty in keeping his reality separate from that of the ancient Occitan lord. At one moment as he saw a church burning in his mind, he was back in Oradour-sur-Glane watching helplessly as those he loved perished. The next moment, he was in Béziers watching innocent Cathar women and children crying out to be saved.

Emile remembered the faces of some of his Jewish students who had to wear yellow crosses and how they had been taunted before they disappeared into the internment camps. They too blended into the world of Raymond de Péreille as he recalled the canon that he had just read of Pope Innocent III requiring the Jews to wear distinguishing clothes.

Emile had recurring nightmares of the Gestapo torturing their captives, which morphed into the hideous images of the carnage de Montfort had inflicted on his captives in Bram. He thought of Amaury and Bishop

Foulquet and his White Brotherhood and began to confuse them with Captain Otto Kahn and his fearful Waffen SS troops.

In Emile's dreams, the only comfort came when his mind took him back to the castle at Montségur. He would stop sweating and lie calmly as he imagined walking among the weavers, carpenters, preachers, poets, troubadours, and others who had come seeking peace. High on the pog, it had been a sanctuary from the madness that had enveloped the world of Raymond de Péreille and Corba. Emile felt a strange kinship with these people. On occasion, he could visualize Corba tending the sick and smiling at him to reassure him everything would be fine. In his dreams he believed her. He would invariably fall back into a deep and restful sleep.

During waking hours, Emile tried to analyze his dreams. He decided the ancient world of Montségur had not been too unlike what he had experienced on the high plateau of the Massif Central with the White Mouse and her resistance fighters. There too, people had come from all walks of life to escape the madness in the world below. They had come to help each other and to cope with the loss of loved ones. Many had fled there to escape a world they no longer understood just as the Cathars had fled to Montségur.

It will soon be morning, Emile thought as he lay sweating. He remembered seeing flames in his mind before something had woken him. That time it had not been Corba, for he did not feel calm or reassured. Quite the opposite. He felt tense, nervous. At first, he did not know what had woken him, but then he heard it.

Someone was walking heavily on the floor above. It was much too heavy to be Maurina and too quick-paced to be Guillème. Emile strained to hear what was going on. It was something that struck immediate fear into him. He heard people shouting. The words were unclear and muffled, but there was no mistaking it was German. Emile froze. His mind raced, trying to remember if he might have left anything in the house that would betray his presence.

Maurina was shouting, pleading for something. He heard Pedro barking loudly. A shot rang out. *No,* thought Emile *They have shot Guillème. I am to blame.*

Emile thought of surrendering, but he realized that would mean Maurina's immediate execution. Emile grabbed his revolver. He would rather die than be taken captive.

Emile imagined himself in the cave where he had discovered the remains of Lord Raymond. He wondered what thoughts had been going through his mind as he lay down for the last time. Had others been chasing him too? Emile would never know unless he could finish reading the chronicle. *Surely if the Occitan lord had sacrificed so much to prepare his account for him to read, it would not be denied him to finish it. I must not die now.*

It was an hour before Emile thought about emerging. He had heard loud arguments and heavy items being thrown around for much of that time, but for ten minutes, he had heard nothing. His hiding place had not been discovered, but he was heavy with guilt that Guillème and Maurina might not have been so fortunate.

With great caution and his revolver in one hand, he tried to raise the trap door, but it would not budge. The flour sacks were keeping it down. Emile put down the gun and tried again and was finally able to move it. The sacks of flour slid off the door. It became lighter. He looked around the pantry and saw no one. He picking up his revolver and ventured out.

The kitchen looked as though a herd of goats had run through it. There were cooking utensils and plates all over the floor. Most of the cupboards had been emptied. He peered into the front room. It was in similar disarray.

Gripping his revolver, he advanced cautiously into the room. He heard a noise outside the open front door. Emile paused. He heard sobs. A woman's voice. She was reciting a prayer. The voice was Maurina's. There was no sign of Guillème.

No! Emile was afraid the Germans had killed Guillème. *How can I look her in the eye again? She will surely hate me.* If he had left when Guillème had offered to take him to Spain, the old man would still be alive. He had destroyed their lives because of his obsession with reading an old manuscript. Emile hid the gun in his jacket and walked outside.

In a small grassy area some distance from the house, Maurina was trying to dig the hard ground with a spade. Emile walked somberly toward her. It was not until he had almost reached her that he could see the object of her grief. It was not Guillème but Pedro. The Germans had shot the dog that had been every bit a member of their close-knit family. Sad as it was, Emile felt relieved it was not Guillème.

The old lady was bereaved and exhausted. Emile tried to take the spade from her. At first she refused, but before long, she could dig no longer. Emile took it gently from her.

"He was our child. He was no harm to them, but they killed him just to shut him up." She sobbed. "How can such men be so evil? Surely each of them had a mother who showed him love when each was a child. How can they have lost all compassion?"

I shook my head. "I am afraid much of Europe has been perverted by this war. It has gone on for so long that many people have forgotten the values and morals they once held. They have lost all hope and will participate in the most heinous deeds without conscience if they think it will end it."

Maurina shook her head sorrowfully. "It is the Bad God, it is his doing. He tempts people with promises of wealth and power. But that is why you have come back to us, is it not? To end the dark times and restore us to the ways of the Good God so wars like this one can never happen again?"

She looked at Emile with such hope and conviction that Emile could not bring himself to contradict her, not in the fragile state she was in. "I believe this war will end soon," he replied in as positive a manner as possible. "But where is Guillème?"

"He was taken," she murmured unemotionally. "The Germans took him."

Emile flinched. "Took him where?"

Maurina ignored his question. She hugged and kissed her dog and gently placed him in the shallow grave, his white fur stained red. "Our spirits will meet again in heaven," she said. "It is only a short while that we will be apart."

Emile filled in the grave. "Did the Germans say where they were taking Guillème?"

Maurina was reluctant to answer. Emile stared at her expectantly. "Where?"

"They have taken him to Carcassonne. The officer in charge said they were taking all those suspected of being Cathars to Carcassonne."

"For what reason?"

"It does not matter." Maurina wept. "He is lost to us. They will kill him. There is nothing we can do."

Emile was frustrated. He was desperate to know why they had taken Guillème. He grabbed Maurina's arm. "What did they say? What is going on? There is something you are not telling me. Why did they take him?"

Maurina sobbed. She was conflicted. "I cannot tell. Guillème made me promise."

Emile thought they were trying to protect him from something. He had to know. He could not allow them to put themselves in danger for his sake. In desperation, Emile turned Maurina's faith against her. "Maurina, you claimed to be a believer in the ways of the Friends of God. Is that still true?"

"As long as I am of this earth."

"Is it not also true that if you strive to become a Good Woman, you must not lie. You must answer all questions truthfully."

Maurina nodded reluctantly.

"Then I ask you again. Why did they take Guillème?"

The old woman looked torn. Emile could sense she wanted to answer him, but the words would not come out. He stared until the pressure was too much.

"They said they are rounding up all the Cathars," she blurted. "They say that if the man in the dark-blue robe who fled from the cave with the treasure of the Cathars does not bring it to them, they will all be killed."

"Then I must go to them."

"No!" Maurina cried, falling to her knees. "Please! We have waited so long for your return. You cannot leave us again!"

"Maurina, I must go. I cannot ask people to die to protect me. I am not your lord. I am merely a schoolteacher."

"No. You are more than you know. You will see. It was your destiny to come to us."

"But I cannot let them die."

"My Lord, each of them will gladly yield their earthly body so you may live. It was agreed by all."

"I did not agree! Would this ancient lord of yours have let his friends die in place of him? From what I have read, I do not believe he would have. I must go to Carcassonne."

Maurina covered her face and shook her head. "No!" Totally distraught, she grabbed Emile's hand. "Lord, promise me that before you go, you will finish reading the manuscript. The Germans will allow you a few days. Please do that for all of us! Finish the manuscript!"

Emile could not resist her pleas after all the kindness the couple had shown him. Moreover, though he was loath to admit it, the manuscript had gained a hold over him. "All right. If you are sure they will be safe for a few days, I will finish the manuscript. After that, though, I will give myself up to the Germans."

Maurina clasped her hands. "Thank you, my Lord. When you are finished, you will have more wisdom to decide what must be done. Wait until then."

After helping Maurina restore the small house to a semblance of normality, Emile returned to the cellar to immerse himself again in the world of the thirteenth century.

CHAPTER 41

Uprising

The death of Esclarmonde left a heavy sadness over all of us in Montségur. Corba distracted herself by working even longer hours in the house of the sick and discussing philosophy with the Méditatifs. She was also heavy with child; she had a new life to focus on.

In April 1216, de Montfort, desirous of two rather than one sponsor for his murderous war in Occitania, went to Paris to pay homage to the French king. He ceded all the southern lands he had conquered and those he would conquer to the king. That was an odious deed. Those lands had not been his to give. The act further intensified the hatred Occitanians had for the invader and resulted in more uprisings and acts of discontent.

Sensing the opportunity later in the same month, the young count of Toulouse, Raymond VII, who was only nineteen, returned from his self-imposed exile in Aragón. His father, who had returned from England, was at his side, as was their most loyal supporter, Raymond-Roger, Count of Foix.

1216, April – Marseille, Provence

As the royal ship sailed into the harbor of Marseille flying the flag of the counts of Toulouse, the citizens of the town thronged to greet them. There was a festival throughout the town with loud cheering, flag waving, and people dancing with joy at the prospect of their rightful sovereign returning to save them.

When Count Raymond VII stepped ashore, he was greeted enthusiastically by the town consuls. "Your Majesty, the keys of the city are yours. The people are yours to lead. We pledge allegiance to you, none other."

The crowd roared its consent. Raymond was overwhelmed with the welcome. "Honorary consuls, I accept the keys to your city with humility. I will serve the people and all the citizens of Provence to the best of my ability. Provence has long been in my heart as it was in my mother's."

"Long live the king!" bellowed Raymond-Roger.

"Long live the king!" screamed the crowd.

"Where are your bishops?" asked Raymond. "I do not see them here."

Boos and jeers came from the crowd.

"Our bishops are in hiding," answered the mayor. "Since the coming of the crusaders to Occitania, they tried to impose the rule of Simon de Montfort upon us, terrorizing the people and killing or brutalizing those they accused of the heresy. They have become much hated for it and now dare to venture out only with soldiers to protect them."

"But Simon de Montfort has no claim over these lands! They are in Provence, not Occitania. Even the archbishop of Narbonne has conceded that."

"Indeed my Lord, but the bishops and clergy would like to claim these lands, as those in Occitania, for the church. They accuse us also of being too lax in fighting the heresy. My Lord, these have truly been dark times for us. The people have been praying for your return, and today, you have answered their prayers."

The young count put his hand over his heart. "I pledge you this day that I will do everything in my power to keep you free from the scourge of Simon de Montfort. With your support, we can prevail. However, the struggle ahead may be difficult and require much sacrifice. The forces opposing us are strong. Simon de Montfort has the support of the church and more recently of the king of France."

"My Lord, the people of Provence are prepared to make any sacrifice you ask if it will free our lands of the invaders."

1216, May – Provence

Lord Raymond-Roger stormed into the chamber of Count Raymond VII with a triumphant look on his face. "My Lord, all the towns of Provence have now sworn fealty to you and renounced all obligations to de Montfort. This is a great victory!"

"It is indeed, and it gives me confidence our cause is just," the count said. "But we will have to show we can defeat de Montfort on the battlefield if we are to give people real hope."

"Sire, I believe such an opportunity is at hand. Your birthplace, Beaucaire, lies on the Rhône and at the border between Occitania and Provence. It is rightfully within Provence and outside the lands ceded to de Montfort, yet his soldiers have long occupied it."

"And you believe we have the strength to retake it from him?"

"Yes my Lord. On your return, the townspeople rose against their French oppressors and are asking for your help to drive them out. It would be a wonderful victory to demonstrate to the people that de Montfort is not invincible."

"It would be a wonderful day indeed if we could succeed. However, I fear our army is no match for the French. We should wait until we are stronger."

"If we wait, Simon will strengthen his defenses and the rebellion will fail. We must strike now!" bellowed Raymond-Roger. "My Lord, all of Provence is with you. If you march on Beaucaire, they will join you. By the time you reach the town, you will have an army that will put the fear of God into the French, I am confident."

"Then we shall go. Order the commanders to prepare our army. Send messengers to Beaucaire. Let them know their son will help them expel the French. If we are successful there, we will drive de Montfort, his priests, crusaders, and troops from our lands."

"Yes, my Lord. It will be a pleasure," Raymond-Roger beamed.

1216, May – Beaucaire, Provence

Raymond-Roger had been better than his word. By the time Count Raymond VII arrived at Beaucaire, his army had swollen to overflowing by an endless number of recruits. All were driven to fight by their hatred for the French and de Montfort.

On the approach of Raymond's army, the French troops had fled the town and withdrawn for safety to the castle. Count Raymond laid siege to it.

"We must seal the castle from every drop of water and from every morsel of food. Nothing must get through. Is that understood?" Raymond ordered his commander.

"Yes, my Lord."

"It is critical that the garrison surrenders before de Montfort returns from his French master with an army."

"Nothing shall get in or out, my Lord."

Raymond-Roger gave his assessment of the situation. "I have heard from the locals that the town is not well stocked and they are cut off from the river."

"That is good news indeed. How long do you think they will be able to hold out?"

"Probably a couple of months, which I fear will give de Montfort time to come."

"Then we are lost!" cried Raymond.

"I do not believe so. He will not be able to raise enough crusaders in that time to fight his way through to the garrison, and his challenge compounds as our numbers swell."

"We must win here if we are to drive the crusaders from Occitania."

"We will win," proclaimed Raymond-Roger without a tremor in his deep voice. "The irony is that we will owe our victory to de Montfort himself, the pope, Archbishop Amaury, Bishop Foulquet, and their ilk."

"I do not understand," exclaimed Raymond.

"We will win because they are so hated by the people of Occitania and Provence that they are driving everyone who can fight to our cause. I have heard the fields are deserted in all the neighboring towns as people have put down their ploughs to fight by your side. Half the town of Avignon must be here." He laughed.

"I am thankful that they are and that they have brought plenty of food with them."

"We will not starve while we are here." Raymond-Roger rubbed his full stomach.

1216, August – Camp of Simon de Montfort, Beaucaire, Provence

Lord Lambert de Croissy walked into Simon's tent in answer to his summons.

"I want you to go to the camp of Raymond VII in Beaucaire and sue for peace," declared Simon.

"But surely all is not yet lost? We can try again to relieve our garrison!"

"I have tried many times and have lost too many men. I will shed no more blood on a lost cause. We do not have the numbers to break through their defenses. Unlike past encounters with the Occitanians, this time, they are well commanded by Raymond-Roger and his son, Roger-Bernard. The new count chooses well, better than his father. We cannot defeat them."

"But surely God is on our side."

"God in his wisdom does not always grant victory. It is clear to me he has other plans for Beaucaire. I have received word from Lambert de Thury, who commands the garrison there, that they can hold out no longer. They have been without food for more than a week and are without water."

Lambert de Croissy shook his head. "What terms do you seek?"

"Our bargaining position is weak. My terms will be modest. I shall ask only that the French garrison be allowed to leave unharmed."

"I will convey your terms, my Lord."

"I am grateful to you, Lambert. When this is over, we shall return to Toulouse. I fear this defeat for the crusade may cause some instability in our possessions. We may have work ahead to suppress it."

"I share your concern, my Lord. But you should be able to quickly suppress any insurrection now that the church and the king of France support your campaign."

"The death of Innocent III has put a question mark over the church's support. I do not yet know the level of enthusiasm Pope Honorius III will have for our crusade. I pray he will support it with the same zeal as his predecessor, but I do not know."

"From what I hear, I do not think you need be concerned. I am told he hates heretics, Jews, and infidels even more than Innocent did. In his first edict, he ordered that a new synagogue the Jews were building in Rome to be torn down. If that is the measure of the man, you should have no worry of him abandoning our crusade. If anything, he is more likely to take a more active role in it."

"That is good to hear, for we have still much work to do if we are to fulfill God's mission and defeat the heresy in these lands."

CHAPTER 42

David and Goliath

There were few tears shed in Occitania on the death of Pope Innocent. He had brought our people only death and suffering. Many hoped that with his parting, the crusade would end. But alas, it was not to be. Simon de Montfort and his crusader army continued to spill innocent Occitan blood.

As resentment against invaders continued to build, Simon was increasingly forced to suppress uprisings against him across the lands he occupied. In 1216, the people of Toulouse rose against him and barred the city gates against his return. However, through the treachery of Bishop Foulquet, he gained entrance and took vengeance out on those who had rebelled.

His subjugation of the citizens of Toulouse was not to last long. In the summer of the following year, while de Montfort was away in the Rhône valley attempting to expand his conquests, Toulouse rose against him anew. It was the opportunity Count Raymond VI had been waiting for.

1217, September – County of Toulouse

The journey across the Pyrenees had been long and arduous. The army had traveled through high mountain passes and along difficult, less-traveled paths so as few as possible knew of their coming. Many of the paths were known only to the few Good Christians among them. They were paths the brethren used to travel between Occitania and Aragón and to spread their message of hope among the common people.

With the snow-capped peaks behind them, before them lay the rich plain of the Garonne River. It was a welcome and familiar sight to the elder Count Raymond VI. Soon, he would be back in Toulouse, his home, the town that had been taken from him by the French invaders and the Catholic priests. He had returned to reclaim his birthright and to free his people from the tyranny of the Catholic crusaders.

Raymond had not come alone. He rode proudly at the head of a long column of soldiers. He had brought an Aragónese army that shared his fervor to sweep the French invaders from the lands of a greater Aragón and avenge the killing of King Pedro.

Raymond knew the troops would not be needed for him to gain entrance to the city. While in Aragón, he had received several emissaries from the city. While de Montfort was out of the city with his army, the citizens had revolted against his rule again and were beseeching him to return to lead them.

The rebels had learned painful lessons from their last failed uprising and were determined not to repeat their mistakes. This time, they had expelled the hated Bishop Foulquet and all the Catholic priests from the town along with the small garrison Simon had left. Alix de Montmorency, de Montfort's wife, had likewise been expelled and confined in the castle of Narbonne. There was none left in the city to oppose Raymond's return.

The situation was precarious, however, for all knew de Montfort would return at great haste to retake the city once he knew of its rebellion. For that reason, Count Raymond had hastened with his army over the Pyrenees with as little fanfare as possible so Simon might not learn of his return until he and his army were safely in the city.

Count Raymond VI's return to the city after his exile in England was a deeply emotional experience for him. He vowed never to leave it again. The inhabitants broke out in wild celebration of his return, though Raymond could not fully share their joy. He was troubled by his certainty that the crusaders would return and bring more suffering upon his people. When the Aragónese army was fully billeted within the city walls, Raymond ordered all the great gates to be closed and barricaded.

The latest reports had Simon de Montfort campaigning in the county of Foix. However, by now he would certainly have learned of the rebellion in Toulouse, and be hastening to return to the city with his crusader army. It would give Raymond only a few weeks to organize the city's defenses for his arrival. Simon's reputation for vengeance was legendary and so his onslaught was sure to be merciless. Recent history had also demonstrated that if the town fell, few would be spared the wrath of this pious northern noble.

During the next month, Count Raymond and Aragónese engineers worked frantically to prepare the city for a siege. Food and livestock were brought in, and hundreds of trees were chopped down to make catapults, trebuchets, mangonels, *bombars,* and all manner of weapons. Rocks and stones were brought in on carts for ammunition. Weak spots in the walls were strengthened by skilled masons. A few areas of the city were abandoned as indefensible after the inhabitants of those quarters were found other accommodation.

Raymond met with his commanders daily. Toulouse was a large town strategically situated on the Garonne River. It had high, thick walls that the pope had once commanded Raymond to tear down, but he had never got around to carrying out the edict.

Simon de Montfort would need a substantial force to effectively besiege the city. However, it was already late in the year, so Raymond was betting many crusaders would have melted away to their homes in the north. Simon would likely have only his personal army to enforce the siege. God willing, it would not be equal to the task.

Count Raymond and his Aragónese commanders planned their offensive strategy. During the long winter months, Simon could not be expected to receive any new recruits so his lines would be overstretched. Hopefully, this would lead to low morale among his men. The Occitan and Aragónese would attempt to exploit the situation by making sorties against the attackers to try to drive Simon from Toulouse before new crusaders could come.

Simon de Montfort and his army arrived at the barred gates of Toulouse in October and demanded the immediate surrender of the city.

"Tell him to go back to his estates in France," Raymond responded.

His reaction was exactly as the defenders had anticipated. Enraged by their defiance, Simon ordered his troops to lay siege to the city.

"But Simon," protested his brother Guy, "We do not have the numbers to effectively enforce a siege. We will need more men."

"I will write to the pope and the king of France for more! They cannot let the heretics make fools of us."

"But they will not be able to send us any reinforcements before spring."

"Spring! God cannot wait until spring to be avenged! These rebels seek to undo everything I have fought for and they have transgressed even further by expelling all our priests. I hear that Count Raymond has brought more heretic Cathar perfects with him to lead the inhabitants deeper into sin. They have even imprisoned my wife."

"God will punish them for their vile deeds. You can be certain of that," Guy said. "But we must have patience for him to show us the way."

"I share your revulsion of these Devil worshippers, my Lord," declared Bishop Foulquet. "I barely escaped with my own life from their murderous clutches. Yet I agree with Guy, we must be cautious in our actions. I know firsthand the town is well supplied. It will not fall easily. Without sufficient troops, our siege would have little chance of succeeding. However, if we wait until spring, when the pope can send us more pilgrims, we will be able to slaughter them all. I remind you of the proverb, 'Be patient and you will finally win.'"

"I am in no mood to be patient!" Simon thundered. "If I cannot besiege them effectively, I shall attack them directly. I will probe for their weaknesses and exploit them. It has worked for me many times in my campaigns when all predicted failure."

"You are a genius on the battlefield, my brother, there is no denying that," acknowledged Guy. "Given our situation, I grant you that it is worth a try. However, the town is well defended by a seasoned Aragónese army. They will not be overrun easily."

"Aragónese soldiers, ha! They ran from me like frightened chickens at Muret."

"I do not believe we can count on that happening again," Guy said. "At Muret, they fled because of a confusion of leadership, but here, they have only one commander, Count Raymond, and he will not venture onto the field for us to kill him as did King Pedro."

"Nonetheless, we shall attack. Inform the men."

In the following weeks, Simon launched numerous attacks all around the city to try to gain entry, but each attack was repulsed with ease. Unable to sustain his losses and with the harshness of winter making his task daily more difficult, Simon was forced to concede the task was hopeless. He had no alternative but to wait for spring and for fresh crusaders.

1218, April – County of Toulouse

Behind the walls of the city, the inhabitants of Toulouse remained safe and well fed during the winter. But rather than welcoming the coming of spring, they feared it. By mid-April, the level of nervousness in the city was palpable. All knew the snows in the north would be melting and pilgrims would soon arrive to swell the numbers in the crusader camp.

Count Raymond and the Aragónese forces were relieved to have successfully repulsed all attempts by Simon's army to breach the city's defenses. However, there was no rejoicing among them for they had failed to drive away the hated northerner. They knew that with de Montfort confident he would not have long to wait before his crusader army was replenished with new pilgrims, he was sure to continue the siege and resume his attacks with renewed vigor.

However, the city's dread of the crusaders lessened when Count Raymond VII entered the city with an army he had brought from his triumphs in Provence,. It was a cause for great celebration. Father and son embraced to wild cries of joy from the multitude. Here was the man who had beaten the invincible de Montfort in Beaucaire. What he had done once, they prayed, he could do again.

"I have to sit here helplessly while Raymond de Provence rides through our lines bringing more troops to help his father?" Simon complained bitterly. "How much longer do I have to wait until I can see their heads on pikes?"

"It should not be long," said Alix de Montmorency, who had been released by the Occitanians. "I have word from Bishop Foulquet that the drive for the crusade is going well in the north. The king is giving it his full support. The bishop expects to leave within the month with a large number of pilgrims who are ready to wear the cross for our struggle against the Albigensians."

"They cannot arrive too soon," grumbled Simon. "Raymond de Toulouse has taken something that no longer belongs to him. I will not rest until I recover it. It is a question of family honor. The pope bestowed the title of count of Toulouse upon me, and I shall not relinquish it. Count Raymond and his son shall pay a heavy price for their treachery."

"They shall indeed, and they can expect no mercy from God."

"They shall get none from me. I shall treat them as I did the young Roger Trencavel. They shall both rot in the dungeons of Toulouse, God willing, until they are forgotten."

"They deserve no better. I have had enough of these southern nobles treating us as though we were inferior to them with their cultured ways. They need to learn who is inferior," complained Alix, burning with resentment.

"I shall show them, my dear. Have no doubt of it."

Simon turned to one of his commanders, Guy de Levis. "Guy, if we are to have reinforcements soon, we must make preparations. We must make good use of these pilgrims. I will not have them leave after their quarantaine with my army still outside these accursed walls. We must take the city while they are with us!" barked Simon.

"No, my Lord. What preparations do you require?"

"Order the carpenters to build siege engines to batter the walls and send rocks and fireballs deep into the city. I have surveyed the walls. They are very thick. It is unlikely we will be able to undermine them or cause their collapse. The only way we will be able to enter the city will be over its walls. We will need grappling equipment, ladders, scaffolding, and towers to allow us to move up the ramparts and launch out troops over the battlements."

"Understood, my Lord. I will see that work begins immediately. Everything will be ready by the time the crusaders arrive."

"You will crush these heretics, my dear. Do not doubt it," Alix said while clutching his hand. "If we put our faith in God, he will show us the way to destroy them."

1218, June 25 – County of Toulouse

One morning, Count Raymond VI and his son were meeting with the commanders of the Aragónese and Provençal forces. "What is our situation?" asked Count Raymond.

One of the commanders stepped forward. "The crusader numbers have been greatly augmented by the arrival of new pilgrims. We are now greatly outnumbered, sire. Because of that advantage, we were unable to prevent de Montfort and a significant contingent of troops from crossing the Garonne River a few days ago. Despite heavy resistance from our forces, we were unable to prevent the crusaders from taking control of the Saint Cyprien quarter of the city, which was unfortified."

"Have we any recent news from there?" asked the count.

The commander looked to his companions, who returned pained glances. "My Lord, I am afraid the news is not good. By all accounts, the crusaders are perpetrating all manner of savagery against the people. They are committing rape, murder, and other unspeakable atrocities. They take whatever they want and burn everything else. The Catholic priests are encouraging them by preaching that all the inhabitants of Toulouse are heretics and that God demands they be killed. Many of the priests are even participating in the crimes."

Raymond looked away in horror. "See that this news does not spread throughout the city. It will provoke panic."

"Yes my Lord."

"And what of our position in the city?"

"Before abandoning Saint Cyprien, our forces managed to destroy the bridge across the Garonne linking it to the city. We believe, therefore, that for the moment at least, we are safe from attack from that direction."

"It is a relief to hear that," murmured Raymond.

The other commanders nodded cautiously.

"In what direction are we not safe?" the young Raymond asked.

It was Savaric de Mauléon, a knight of King John Lackland and count d'Aquitaine who stepped forward to answer. "My Lords, during the night, Simon's forces brought a large siege tower onto the field and have been steadily advancing it toward our ramparts. It is of massive construction, with huge wheels, and exceeds the height of our walls. If their sappers succeed in getting it close enough, they will drop ladders down and pour men over our battlements."

"We cannot let one crusader into the city!" yelled Count Raymond. "If they overwhelm our defenses, they will fight their way to our gates!"

"Can we destroy this tower?" asked Guy de Levis.

"We are trying, my Lord. We have turned all our heavy artillery on it. Our trebuchets are launching the heaviest projectiles we have. I believe it is close enough for us to be able to damage or disable it. However, the frame is built of mighty oak timbers, and it has heavy wooden cladding. I fear we will not be able to completely destroy it."

"We will not be safe until it is destroyed," insisted the Aragónese commander.

"Can we burn it?" asked the young count.

"Not from within the city. We hurl fireballs, but the crusaders put the fires out."

"Then what do you suggest?" asked Count Raymond.

"We will have to organize a sortie to burn it down," proposed Savaric de Mauléon. "It is the only way. I am ready to lead it."

"I will join you," came cries from around the room.

Count Raymond sighed and rose to conclude the meeting. "It is agreed then. Savaric de Mauléon will lead a raiding party. May the Good God go with you."

Simon de Montfort, with his close family at his side, was still at morning Mass when his lieutenant Alain de Roucy burst in. "My Lord, forgive me." He removed his helmet, knelt, and crossed his chest. "The Occitanians have sent a raiding party against the 'Cat'!"

Simon was on his knees before the priest. He said with no trace of urgency, "De Roucy, you should know better than to disturb us in the house of God. When I have given God his time, I shall give you mine and be better prepared for it. Return to the battlefield. Protect the tower at all costs. I shall be along presently."

"Yes, my Lord. I'm sorry to have disturbed you," he stuttered as he withdrew.

With his soul cleansed, de Montfort donned his armor and prepared to ride at great haste to the plain in front of the gates of Toulouse. He would command his troops who were already engaged in fierce combat with the enemy attempting to destroy his siege tower.

"We cannot let them destroy the Cat," Simon screamed to his brother, Guy de Montfort. "It is our best chance to pierce their defenses and get our troops into the town. If the sappers can get it up to the walls, we will end the siege this day and not spend another night in a dusty tent with the foul smell of animals and their dung. Raymond and his son will pay a heavy price for this rebellion. So will every man and his family who helped them. I shall turn the city of pink into a city of red. Red with the blood of blasphemers of Christ. Let us be about God's work!"

It was still early morning, but the rays of the midsummer sun were adding to the exhaustion of those fighting outside the gates when de Montfort and his companions arrived. The large tower cast a long, ominous shadow over the wall and into the city. Simon prayed that before the end of this day, the tower would project more than its shadow over the wall. With God's help, he would sleep that night once more in the city he had been given by the pope and thus by God. No man had a right to take away what God had given him.

The fighting was already intense. Alain de Roucy informed Simon on the situation. "My Lord, the Occitanians have sent out a strong force to destroy the tower, knights and foot soldiers. They are still bombarding the tower with rocks and fireballs from catapults on the city walls. They have immobilized it, but we have brought up large wooden shields to protect the sappers while they repair it, however, the crusaders are having difficulty holding back the attack."

"If they reach the tower, our cause is lost! Send all the men you have to protect it."

"I have already done so, my Lord, but the new crusaders have not seen battle before, and the enemy has sent seasoned warriors. We are also close to the walls, so we are under a constant fusillade from the defenders."

"We have been in worse situations than this and have come out on top," proclaimed Simon. "We will bear any losses necessary to get the Cat to the ramparts."

"Agreed, my Lord. I will ensure no man is spared from protecting it."

"Excellent. Let us join in the fray ourselves. They will need every man. I will have victory this day!"

By midmorning, dead and dying littered the field of battle. Despite the gruesome carnage, de Montfort was content. His siege tower still stood. His crusaders had paid a heavy price, but they had kept the enemy from destroying it. With God's help, he thought, it would soon be rolling again toward the ramparts.

As Simon was planning his next move, a rider brought his horse to an abrupt stop close to him. "My Lord! Your brother Guy has been hit! He is by the Cat!"

Simon jumped immediately on his horse and raced to the Cat. As he got close, the fighting was heavy, but he managed to force his way through. There, he found his brother on the ground, bleeding badly. He had been hit by a crossbow bolt. "Get him a wagon!" roared Simon. When he was satisfied his orders were being followed, Simon walked towards his horse.

High above the battlefield, on the wall of the city, a woman loaded a large stone into her mangonel. As she had done many times before, she pulled on the wooden chock to release the arm of the catapult. It swung upward, launching its deadly load toward the crusader army. She watched the stone travel in a high arch before the pull of gravity forced it to descend at ever-increasing speed toward the enemy.

The stone struck de Montfort on the head, smashing his skull wide open. His limp form crumbled to the ground. His blood enriching the dry Occitan soil he had so lusted to possess.

Knowledge of his death spread quickly throughout the city. Wild rejoicing broke out. The peasant woman who had killed the seemingly invincible and most hated man in the history of Occitania was carried high throughout the city. With their faith renewed, soldiers and peasants rushed from the gates to join the fight against the crusaders, grabbing whatever was on hand as weapons.

News of Simon's death spread equally rapidly among the crusaders on the battlefield. His son, Amaury, tried to take command, but he was not up to the task. With the leader who had given most of them confidence in the righteousness of their cause lying at their feet, most lost faith and fled. The crusader army was in chaos, and the Occitan and Aragónese forces pursued the crusaders. The battle quickly turned into a rout.

The southern forces jubilantly set fire to the tower and people danced wildly around its mighty flaming timbers. Mothers in the city took their children onto the walls so they might see the wondrous sight. All were united in joy by the certainty that the city would not fall that day.

At night in the crusader camp, Simon's death was mourned. Alix sat stoically in black all night beside her husband's body as nobles and knights filed by to pay their last respects. The tent glowed in candlelight, and the air was heavy with the sweet smell of incense from the thuribles swung by an endless line of priests and clergy.

"He was a saint," declared Foulquet de Marseille to Alix. "He did only God's work on this earth, and God shall surely reward him with eternal life in heaven."

"Thank you, Bishop. He thought only of the church. I am sure he is now with God."

"I have no doubt of it. With his passing, I trust Amaury will assume the burden of restoring the light of God to the people of Occitania?"

Alix responded with a nod. "Amaury is as faithful to the church as was his father, Bishop Foulquet. He has already sworn to continue the crusade against the Albigensians until they are all freed from the curse of the heresy. I fear, though, his military prowess does not yet match his father's. He will need time. My husband's shoes were too great for any man to readily step into."

The bishop smiled and nodded, revealing the blackened teeth in his mouth. "That is true, my Lady. I shall pray for God to help him with this task. I shall declare five days' mourning for the death of your husband. It will give your son time to adjust to his new responsibilities. I shall hold a Mass for Simon in the morning."

"You are most kind."

"It has been five days since the murder of my father!" cried Amaury. "No man was more devoted to our cause that he was. We must avenge his death by taking Toulouse!"

"But my Lord," pleaded a French knight, "the Cat is destroyed and with it any hope of our taking the city for at least two months. The city remains well provisioned and can likely hold out until winter. We lost many men. Those who remain have been badly shaken by the death of your father. We are not strong enough to overcome their defenses."

"But we must! We owe it to God and to my father. He gave his life to liberate the people of Toulouse from the heresy."

"But sire, it will not help your father's memory to send more men to die in vain, nor would he have wanted it. My advice is to withdraw to Carcassonne," Alain de Roucy said. "We are no longer able to maintain an effective siege. If we remain here, we will be vulnerable to attack. We can regroup in Carcassonne."

"Aye, aye," came cries of agreement from most in the tent.

"Then let us end the siege!" Amaury screamed. "If we throw all our forces at the main gates, with God's help we can break them down!"

"It would be suicide," protested de Roucy. "They would cut us down with artillery and crossbow fire."

"Do you think my father would have abandoned the city to the heretics? You know he would not. He would have tried to snatch victory from defeat."

Alain de Roucy shook his head.

"What about our pay?" a soldier shouted. "Your father promised us gold. When will you pay us what we are owed?"

He was joined by a chorus of angry demands from other soldiers.

Amaury raised his hands for silence. "You shall have your gold when we enter the city. There are riches within for all. Fight, and you shall have more than you were promised."

Jeers of dissatisfaction broke out. "We will not fight again until we are paid!"

"But my father's wealth was taken by the rebels. It is inside the city. They forced my mother to leave, taking nothing with her," Amaury said.

"Maybe we should fight for the rebels," a soldier said derisively.

"You shall get your gold," Amaury screamed over the laughter. "But first, let us take the city and do God's bidding."

"When God pays me, I will do his bidding. Until then, my sword stays in my scabbard," a soldier said. Others debated the matter heatedly among themselves.

Amaury tried again to turn them to his cause. "Today is the Sabbath, God's day. Let us use it to do God's work and free his people from the heresy. Each man here swore an oath to the church, and I will hold you to it."

Disgruntled and unhappy but more out of obligation to Amaury's father than the expectation of success, the knights and clergy agreed to one last attempt to take the city.

By midmorning, the crusader forces had assembled for the attack. Amaury was optimistic his forces would prevail and he would earn the respect of his mother and his men. As they marched and dragged their siege engines closer to the city, the wind began to blow and then howl. It was the anger of the White Autan, which many crusaders took as a sign from God that he had sent the drying wind to blow them away from the city.

"It is Satan!" Amaury cried to his men. "He is fighting against us for he fears we will defeat his servants." But his words were lost in the wind.

As the crusaders approached the walls of the city, they were pounded by projectiles and by Mother Nature. Their ballistas, catapults, ladders, and equipment were soon blown over or destroyed. Before long, the crusader forces were in total disarray.

"My Lord," cried Alain de Roucy. "We must withdraw to Carcassonne. Our cause here is lost."

Amaury looked despondently around the battlefield. Though it pained him to admit it, their situation was hopeless. "Very well. But let no man say we were defeated here today. We did not win, but we were not defeated. God willing and with more crusaders, we shall return and drive the cursed heretics from their fortress."

CHAPTER 43

𝔅lanche de Castile

With the death of Pope Innocent III and Simon de Montfort, some among us dared hope the darkness over our lands would soon pass and we would once again live in peace. However, when the Bad God loses a disciple, he quickly finds another.

The new pope, Honorius III, proved to be no better friend to the Occitan people than his predecessor had been. While his words were less tinged with venom, one of his first acts as bishop of Rome was to sanction the creation of the Dominican order that Pope Innocent had proposed. In the years that followed, the Dominicans were responsible for untold torture and savagery against our people. Like his predecessor, the new pope also announced his commitment to launching a crusade to recover Jerusalem. For that, he was anxious to assure free passage through our lands and access to our Mediterranean ports.

While the Church of Rome continued to threaten our lands and our culture, a new insidious enemy of Occitania was busy accumulating power in the north. At first, we were oblivious to our new enemy, but it was not long before we were to pay for that ignorance with the blood of countless innocent Occitanians. The new nemesis of Occitania proved to be every bit as ruthless as Simon de Montfort but with more guile. The Devil had found a new servant in the body of a woman. For the peace-loving Occitan people, she became a witch who cast her black magic over our lives in the names of the church and of France.

The name of our new adversary was Blanche de Castile, the wife of Prince Louis of France. She was aptly named, for her heart was as cold as the winter snow. In appearance, I was told, she was beautiful; she had long, brown hair and a beguiling smile.

Blanche was as devout a servant of the Church of Rome as had been Simon de Montfort, and after his death, she increasingly began to assume his leadership of the crusade against the Albigensians. She was dedicated to restoring the dominion of the church in the south and determined to seeing our lands incorporated into the Kingdom of France.

Simon had been a lowborn northern noble of limited resources, but Blanche could wield the full power and authority of the king. In that, she was an infinitely more dangerous foe than Simon de Montfort had been.

1219, March – Palais de Louvre, Paris

King Philippe-Auguste summoned his young son, Prince Louis, and said, "Louis, Amaury de Montfort comes today to seek our help with his Albigensian crusade. I should like you to be in attendance."

"As you wish, Father. How do you intend to answer him?"

"I have not decided. Naturally, he comes to seek our purse, but I do not dispense it readily. The pope has more gold than I do, so why should I not let the church continue to fund its crusade? Also, I would not want to do anything that might hasten the end of this crusade. It has been a most fortuitous distraction for the pope. The time he must spend managing his crusade is time he does not have to interfere in my affairs."

Louis found his father's attitude amusing. "I hear that the young Amaury does not possess his father's skills in warfare. Last year, the crusaders were forced to lift their siege of Toulouse. I have also just learned the crusaders were recently defeated by the Occitanian and Aragónese forces at a place called Baziège. It would appear the pope may need a new leader for his crusade."

Blanche de Castile strode confidently into the chamber. "Yes, my husband, you are right. And who better than you?"

"Me?" stammered Prince Louis. "You would have me make war in the south? I hear the ale is poor, and I cannot speak a word of their awful tongue. The last time you sent me off to war, it was to claim the crown of England for you. That was a misadventure I do not care to repeat."

"Occitania is not England. The archbishop of Narbonne has convinced me it is our duty to God to destroy the heretics. If we do not, we risk the infection coming here."

"I will never permit that!" the king vowed. "Your uncle, Count Raymond VI, should have acted more firmly to crush the heresy before it spread."

Blanche was not ready to back down, even to the king. "He was weak. The world does not reward weakness, but it may yet be to the benefit of France. The lands of the south are rich, with many fine ports on the Mediterranean. They would be a rich prize indeed. All France would benefit from the increased trade. And as devout Christians, we would all like to free the Holy Land from the Saracens. Marseille would be an ideal port from which to launch a crusade led by a French monarch from French soil," she said.

"You have your grandmother's spirit, my child," the king said. "Eleanor d'Aquitaine was more than Henry bargained for when he married her. I see you will also keep my son on his toes. What you say is true. I shall reflect on it."

"Now is the ideal opportunity," pleaded Blanche. "With the death of my uncle John Lackland of England, we need no longer fear invasion. Amaury de Montfort has shown himself incapable of leading the crusade. He has already lost many of the possessions his father had captured. Now is the time for France to assume leadership of the crusade. We shall be rewarded by God and by the pope. Imagine a France stretching from the Atlantic to the Mediterranean. My king, you would rule over the greatest nation since Charlemagne."

Prince Louis looked at his wife in admiration and awe. "My father is right. You have much of Eleanor in you. Like her, you are ambitious. They will be the death of me or the making of me. Father, I would hear this Amaury de Montfort. There could be more profit in this than I had appreciated."

Blanche smiled with satisfaction, bowed, and curtsied. "If you will excuse me, I have other duties to attend to," she said quietly and left.

The king looked approvingly at his son. "She will make you a strong queen someday. You will do well to listen to her counsel."

"She would have it no other way, Father," the prince replied with a laugh.

1219, June – Crusader Camp, Marmande, Aquitaine

Marmande was a small, sleepy town on the Garonne River, northwest of Toulouse. It was a bastide of no strategic or military importance, typical of many in the area. The town was lightly fortified. Its narrow, cobbled streets, stone arches, and arcades had been built around a square. Richard Cœur de Lion of England had authorized the construction of the new town in 1195 to protect an older settlement from frequent attacks.

Like Bram, the citizens of Marmande were mainly weavers, farmers, herdsmen, shopkeepers, and tradesmen. They counted none among them who fought or preached against the crusaders. In stark contrast to the fortified castles of the Occitan lords perched high on rocky peaks, Marmande was unthreatening and indefensible. It had no attributes that should have attracted the attention of the crusader army, save one. After the death of Richard Cœur de Lion, the town had passed into the possession of Raymond VI.

"My Lord!" shouted a herald. "The king is coming! He will be here within the hour."

"He is expected," replied Amaury. "Make sure everything is prepared for his arrival."

Amaury's mother, Alix, groaned disapprovingly. "Finally, the king comes to our aid. If he had recognized his duty earlier, your father would be alive and we would still be in Toulouse."

"The king has sent Louis, which implies a significant commitment to our cause. We can but hope he has recognized our mutual interests in these lands. It will not help for us to complain about what is past."

"I will not. However, do not believe the prince comes to fight for our interests. He comes only because his father has sent him for his own interests. The king has long battled the pope for power. Do not get caught up in their fight or we risk losing everything. Take care, my son. Politics can be more deadly than warfare."

"I will, mother, but we need his help. The pope is obsessed with raising an army to send to the Holy Land. He has no interest in sending any more crusaders to help our cause in Occitania, so we need Prince Louis' army to retake Toulouse."

The French army arrived later in the day to great fanfare. Amaury scurried to greet the prince. "Prince Louis, we are greatly indebted to you for joining our crusade. Welcome."

"I am glad to be here. It has been a long journey."

Amaury bowed and introduced his family. "This is my mother, Alix de Montmorency, and my younger brother, Guy de Montfort."

The prince smiled to acknowledge them. "I have come to redeem my soul and do God's work. I will fulfill my vow to the church and to serve my quarantaine," he declared, looking at Archbishop Amaury and the other nineteen bishops who had traveled with him.

"Your highness, God will surely reward you for your service to him," pronounced the archbishop.

"Good. Now, to the task in hand. I trust you are planning to bring these southern nobles to heel and in so doing strike a fatal blow against the heresy?"

"I am, your Majesty. The strength you bring should assure us of success."

"What is the situation here?" asked the prince.

"We have been besieging the bastide of Marmande since December. The town is running out of supplies. With our combined armies, we should be able to overrun them."

"Excellent! That will be a good start to my campaign." Prince Louis rubbed his hands gleefully. "We shall teach these troubadour-loving peasants that the king of France does not tolerate rebellion among his subjects."

"Nor does the king tolerate heresy," added Archbishop Amaury.

Louis was taken off guard. "No of course not," he stuttered. "King Philippe-Auguste is most distressed at the heresy against the church, and it pains him to think of the many souls at risk if this error is not expunged."

Arnaud Amaury smiled.

"Now, my Lord Montfort, when do we begin? I have brought with me thirty or more nobles, six hundred knights, and more than ten thousand infantry. Let us dispense quickly with this village and move on to more-challenging conquests."

"Your highness, we have made preparations to begin the attack in the morning. It will give your men time to rest."

"So be it," Prince Louis said. "Have wine and food brought to my tent. I am quite famished, and this heat makes me thirsty."

1219, June 3 – Marmande, Aquitaine

Prince Louis and Amaury, together with his mother and brother, attended Mass at first light. The archbishop of Narbonne led the service and reminded all that their work that day had been ordained by God. "At the Fourth Lateran Council, his holiness reminded us it was the duty of every Christian to slay those who preach blasphemy. It matters not whether they be Muslim, Cathar, or Jew! They are all an anathema to God, and he will reward you with eternal life for destroying them."

"Death to the heretics!" cried Prince Louis, who was quickly joined by all the worshippers. "We are ready to do God's work!"

"Then go forth and do as the Lord commands," the archbishop said. "The Bible commands, 'Kill without showing pity or compassion. Slaughter old men, young men and maidens, women and children.' Just as the people of Samaria, the people of Marmande must bear their guilt. For they too have rebelled against their God, and like the Samarians, they shall fall by the sword."

With their souls rededicated to God, the French knights and crusaders prepared to attack the weakened and lightly defended town.

The initial attack was overwhelming and decisive. The citizens of Marmande had no skills in warfare, no defensive artillery, and no mind-set to kill others. They wanted only to be left in peace so they could make their living from the land as their forebears had done. That day, their world was destroyed in the name of the same God they also prayed to.

With ladders and grappling hooks, the French knights and crusaders sent wave after wave of soldiers over the walls. Soon, all the gates were opened. The invaders killed and pillaged with abandon. The Catholic priests accompanied the soldiers, cursing the townsfolk and killing many at their own hands in the name of their savior.

When some semblance of order was restored, Prince Louis, Amaury de Montfort, and Archbishop Amaury, who was carrying a crucifix, rode triumphantly into town.

"Hugues," cried Louis to one of his knights. "Round up every man, woman, and child who refuses to swear an oath to the Church of Rome and to King Philippe-Auguste. The pope has commanded that we zealously seek out the heretics and destroy them, for they are an affront to God."

"They are indeed," affirmed Arnaud Amaury. "I shall have the brethren build a large pyre in the square. It is important that all witness the fate of those who follow Satan."

"Then I shall order the rest of the inhabitants to be slain, for I intend to send a message to the rest of Occitania as you did at Béziers, my Archbishop. Those who rebel against the rule of God and the king can expect no mercy."

The archbishop smiled smugly. "The Bible demands no less."

Throughout the remainder of the day and into the night, the crusaders terrorized the town. Soldiers accompanied by priests went door to door, seeking all they suspected of being heretics. Those they accused were stripped of their clothes, bound, and dragged to the square. Those who were true believers or Good Christians went almost willingly. They refused to swear an oath to the church or to renounce their beliefs. Their passivity angered the priests; many tried to incite them to violence by beating them, but it was to no avail. As they dragged the heretics away, they cursed them loudly as disciples of Satan.

By early next day, the main square was piled high with brush and other combustible materials the invaders had looted from the houses. A line of stakes stood out from the pile. Around midmorning, priests began leading the scantily clad prisoners to ladders leaning against the brush. When they had climbed onto the pile, the priests tied them together in groups to the stakes. Few offered resistance or cried out in protest.

When the preparations were ready, Prince Louis sent the soldiers through the town to order everyone to the town square. Those who refused to go or were too sick to go were slain where they were found.

The archbishop led a prayer service to give thanks to God for their glorious victory. His incantations were echoed by the other bishops and priests. A group of priests led by Bishop Foulquet climbed onto the pyre. He leaned a large crucifix toward each of the hapless and bound prisoners. "Kiss the cross that you might show repentance to your maker before you stand in judgment before him," commanded Foulquet.

From the oldest to the youngest, from grandparent to grandchild, each refused. From the midst of one group, an elderly man the others deferred to, spoke bravely. "You claim to worship Christ but ask us to kiss the very symbol of his torture. Does this not show you how far from his path you have strayed?"

Foulquet was angered. "The cross is the symbol of the sacrifice God's only Son made to forgive our sins. Now kiss it that yours too might be forgiven!"

"Christ did not die. He was never alive," the man proclaimed. "The Good God would never have trapped a soul in body, for that is the treachery of the evil one. Christ was a holy spirit sent by God to teach us through Gnosticism the path back to his kingdom."

Foulquet was furious. He crossed himself frantically to ward off the heresy. The priests around him did likewise. "Your words are venom! Blasphemy!" he shrieked.

You are about to die and yet you persist in your profanities. You deny Christ. You will burn in hell for all eternity."

"We do not deny Christ. We deny his death, but not that he walked among us. We worship his coming, and we are faithful to his teachings, unlike you. He was a man of peace, and we follow his example. We study his parables that we might gain knowledge. We worship his life, not his death. Our teachings have been handed down to us by the earliest disciples who walked with Christ. The Friends of God is the one true church of Christ. Only its adherents can call themselves truly Christian."

"The Church of Rome is Christ's only church on earth!" Foulquet cried. "And the pope is Christ's sole representative! All else is heresy! Blasphemy!"

The old man was unmoved. He showing no fear. "No. The Church of Rome is no longer the Church of Christ. It is the church of the Devil, for he has surely grown to possess it. Instead of seeking spiritual fulfillment, the church seeks worldly riches and power. It has been corrupted by lust, and it glories in death, not in life. You need only look around to see your crusaders whose business is death. Even in your sacraments, you worship death. You idolize the crucifix on which you believe Christ was murdered, and you eat his flesh and drink his blood. All such things are an abomination to true Christians."

Bishop Foulquet could bear no more. With all the force he could muster, he raised his heavy cross and brought it down violently on the man's head. With blood streaming from his mouth, the old man slumped forward. "'Let the lying lips be put to silence; which speak grievous things proudly and contemptuously against the righteous!'" quoted the bishop as he held the crucifix over the heads of the other prisoners trussed beside the dying man. It was impossible to tell whether he was threatening them or offering them some bizarre form of benediction. "Enough of this perfidy! Send them to hell. We must silence Satan's tongues before more souls are corrupted."

He led the coterie of priests from the pyre and joined Amaury and Prince Louis.

"See how even as they face meeting their maker, they refuse to repent," cried Amaury to the crowd. "It is proof of how deeply the Devil has perverted their thoughts."

The priests and crusaders cheered at his words, but the townsfolk remained in a hushed silence.

"We have much work ahead of us," Louis said. "Burn them quickly."

Lit torches were distributed to the priests, who enthusiastically threw them on the pyre. The flames caught hold. The faces of those tied to the stakes contorted from the heat and the agony of the fire. The clergy chanted. The crusaders cheered with excitement while most of the townsfolk turned their faces.

The spectacle concluded, Prince Louis gave the order to cleanse the town of its inhabitants. With zealous enthusiasm, the soldiers, crusaders, and priests moved through the crowd with swords, daggers, pikes, and hatchets, hacking and stabbing everyone. All were slaughtered without pity. The streets and fields ran red with blood. Mutilated bodies littered the narrow streets so deeply in some places that passage was impossible. By the end of the day, not a single human or animal from the town of Marmande was left alive. The purge, in God's name, was similar to many such glorious events told of in the Bible.

"Five thousand or more of God's enemies have been dispatched to their fate of eternal damnation," Arnaud Amaury wrote in his report that night to the pope. "The day's work will serve as a true inspiration for all men of faith who have this day shared in and witnessed God's terrible vengeance against those who turn against him."

In a final act of retribution, the crusader army burned the town to the ground.

1219, August – Palais de Louvre, Paris

Prince Louis had completed his quarantaine with the army in July, but it had taken him a few weeks to make the long, arduous journey back to Paris. On his arrival, his father called him to account for his campaign.

"I am informed you failed in your siege of Toulouse," the king said.

"Yes, Father. Unfortunately, that is true. We joined forces with the crusaders under de Montfort, but the city was strongly fortified and well defended. It will take more men and many months of siege to gain its surrender. My quarantaine was fulfilled, so I returned."

"You made the right decision. I need you here. The church can fight its own battles."

Blanche looked disapprovingly at her husband and king. "Surely, your Majesty, this is not just a battle for the church but a battle for the salvation of souls?" she asked beguilingly in her Spanish accent. "These heretics reject the divinity of Jesus and teach that Satan is equal to God."

The king was surprised by the forcefulness of her words. "Yes, my child. You are quite right. It is a struggle for men's souls, and in that, it is a battle for all who are faithful. Yet, as king, I have many worldly battles to fight. For those, I need Louis close."

As Blanche bowed courteously to the king, he turned to his son. "What of this Amaury de Montfort? Is he competent enough to command the crusader forces? I have heard he does not match the mettle of his father."

"What you have heard is true, Father. He is a poor commander on the field, and he has little respect from his men. I do not expect the crusade will go well under him."

The king nodded with satisfaction. "Good, then I suggest we bide our time. We shall let the church continue with its crusade and not intervene directly. When Amaury de Montfort fails in his conquest of the southern lands, the pope will have to seek our help, and we will set our terms. I would not want the church to grow too strong, or worse, have a papal state on our southern border."

"Those lands belong to a greater France," proclaimed Blanche.

The king smiled. "Indeed they do. One day, they shall become part of France. But as the Bible says, 'To everything there is a time,' and unfortunately, that time is not now. We shall have to wait for Amaury to fail before the pope will agree to such a concession."

"A wise strategy, my king," conceded Blanche. "A greater France will truly be glorious. The people will honor your for it. In the meantime, however, I trust you will continue supporting the suppression of the heresy, it is a threat to our redemption."

"Do not trouble yourself, my daughter. I fear the heresy as much as any man … or woman," he added with a smile. "I will do all within my power to prevent the heresy from spreading to France. These Cathars do not recognize the authority of any man. They refuse to swear oaths to their nobles, kings, or the church. Such beliefs menace our whole civilization. I will continue to encourage the French to offer themselves to the crusade."

"God will reward you for it," Blanche said. "Now, there are some troubadours newly arrived from Castile. I must welcome them. If you will excuse me?"

"Enjoy your music," said the king. "If you are as dedicated to helping my son rule France as you have been in your attempts to raise our culture, I need have no fear for France when I am gone."

"You may depend upon my devotion to both, your Majesty," Blanche said.

The king looked admiringly after her. "Intelligence and beauty. A rare combination. You have done well, my son."

"Sometimes, I think she would make a stronger king than I will." Louis laughed. "She has all the fire and tenacity of her grandmother Eleanor. Few men can match her resolve, and few women her beauty. I am fortunate indeed. She had some trouble adjusting to our ways at the beginning. She had become too accustomed to the opulence of King Alphonso's court in Castile. But I have seen her love for France and for you grow strong over the years. There is no one who loves France more dearly than Blanche does. You will remember she harangued us to conquer England after the death of her uncle John."

King Philippe-Auguste shook his head. "You do not need to remind me of her stubbornness over that matter. She threatened to pawn your children if I did not give you the money for your campaign. Even I had to yield to her scheming," he said with a mix of admiration and incredulity.

"You have to admire her. She will stand up to anyone. She has a lot in common with her uncle King Richard. Just be thankful she is on our side, father, for she makes a fearful adversary."

"Indeed she does. And on top of all her virtues, she has not neglected her responsibilities to you as a wife. She has borne you many children."

"Yes. I no longer worry about a successor. She will soon have borne me more children than Eleanor did Henry II of England. I lost count at six." The prince laughed.

The king shared his amusement. "She is a good mother and takes time to see they have a good Christian upbringing."

"She cares a great deal for all of them, especially Louis," the prince said. "He is clearly her favorite since our elder three died. She takes him with her to prayer each day and has the legate give him personal instruction in the faith."

The king frowned. "It is good that the church contributes to the education of your son, but take care they do not steal him from you. Be sure to remind him he is to be the king of France, beholden to no one, including the pope."

Prince Louis frowned, clearly surprised by the remark. "I will, Father, if it concerns you. But it would be wise for me to do it when Blanche is not around." He smiled.

CHAPTER 44

False Hope

I shall pass over the next few years briefly that I might hold your attention for the more important events. Through the long years 1219 until 1224, our struggle continued against the crusaders at a reduced but constant level. In 1220, when Raymond VII retook Castelnaudary, Guy de Montfort was killed.

The following year, Raymond-Roger de Foix succeeded in driving the crusaders from Fanjeaux, their headquarters. The city was very dear to his heart; it was where Guilhabert de Castres had instructed his sister Esclarmonde in the faith and where she along with many others had received the Consolamentum.

Raymond-Roger also drove the Catholic priests from Fanjeaux. Domingo de Guzmán had sent them to wage a campaign against its citizens. By murderous acts and intimidation, the priests had sought to force the people to relinquish the heresy and return their allegiance to the church. However, their efforts had met with little success, for the people were repulsed by anyone connected with the name of the Spanish priest, who had become inextricably associated with the dreaded Inquisition. To ensure that the priests would not return, and with the universal approbation of the inhabitants, Raymond-Roger burned their belongings and their buildings.

Sadly, Count Raymond VI died in 1222. In an act that served only to further inflame the tensions between the Occitanians and the church, the pope refused him a Christian burial. Consequently, with renewed vigor and with the enthusiastic support of his people, Raymond VII stepped up his campaign to drive the soldiers of the cross from his lands.

In contrast to his father, the younger Raymond was an able commander. At the same time, the situation for the crusader forces was reversed. Amaury de Montfort lacked the military prowess of his father. In battle after battle, the crusaders were defeated by Raymond VII. Sensing the weakness of the crusader army and driven by the intense hatred of the populace for the invaders, the garrisons of the few towns still held by Amaury de Montfort began to surrender to Count Raymond.

With the defeat of the invaders, Occitanians smiled and looked with optimism to the future. Our lands had been devastated, but if we were left alone, we were confident we could restore the material things we had lost and return to our traditional culture.

In Montségur, many believers and Good Friends, no longer fearing persecution, returned to their homes, and troubadours traveled unfettered again throughout our lands.

Sadly, it soon became evident, the danger had not left us, it had simply become more insidious. The crusaders were replaced by what turned out to be a more dangerous threat to our people and their way of life. The church sent an army of priests bearing crosses and driven by greed, self-righteousness, and obsession. They proved themselves even more murderous and destructive than any army.

The Catholic priests and inquisitors roamed through our towns accusing thousands of innocent Occitanians of heresy and sentencing them to be burned at the stake. None was permitted to speak in favor of the accused or to defend them against the charges for fear of being similarly accused of heresy. The 'trials' were held in secret, and the priests passed sentence without presenting any evidence of guilt. The inquisitors quickly became reviled and hated by all Occitanians, turning them only further from the Church of Rome.

As people came no longer to fear retribution from the crusaders, they began to rise up against the priests and drive them from their towns. In the fortified village of Cordes, people became so incensed by the brutality of the inquisitors that they threw three of them down a well.

For a while, I contemplated returning to our home in Mirepoix, but Corba pressed me to stay in Montségur. She argued that she was too busy to move, taking care of our two young daughters, Philippa and Esclarmonde, and that her services were still needed in the infirmary. However, in truth, she had fallen in love with the feeling of isolation from the troubles in the world below our pog. It engendered a feeling of security in all the inhabitants of our small hilltop community. That feeling was enhanced by the nature of the Good Christians and believers among us who offered friendship and kindness to everyone and eschewed all forms of violence. Sometimes, it felt even to me as if the pog pushed up just high enough above the earth to pierce a small part of heaven.

I decided to remain in Montségur after a visit from Guilhabert de Castres, who had become the most respected Good Christian in all Occitania. It was easy to understand why. He had an unusual magnetism and a powerful intellect. He was unlike any other I had met.

1223, July – Castle of Montségur

Corba bowed three times to welcome Guilhabert de Castres, an impressive figure in his dark-blue robes, and beseeched him in the softest of tones. "Good Christian, please pray to God for me that he might deliver me from an evil death and lead me to a good end."

He smiled at her. "I will remember you in my prayers, my Lady, though I have confidence your prayers are already being heard. Your mother tells me you are a true believer and think only of others. God is clearly guiding you back to his side."

Corba blushed. "Good Christian, I do not yet have the wisdom to know the path, but I am trying."

"That is all the Good God asks of us, my child. In Montségur, you are fortunate, for there are many who can show you that path. Seek them out. They will instruct you."

"I have already been doing so, but there is much I have to learn. I also have children and a castle that require my attention."

"There is no need for haste. You are young. Your soul is likely to remain in this world for some years. If your heart is open, God will instruct you in his ways so you will be ready when he calls you back to him."

"I hope so," replied Corba joyfully.

"Guilhabert, what news do you bring from Toulouse?" I asked.

"I am glad to report it is mostly good. Raymond VII has recovered most of his lands from Amaury de Montfort, and the crusader army is in retreat."

"I am glad to hear it, for I have been thinking of returning to Mirepoix with Corba and the children. There is little space for us here. I am too far removed from my people."

Guilhabert frowned. "I strongly counsel you against it, my Lord. I advise you to remain in Montségur. It may be far from your people but it is closer to God. Do not be deceived by the recent triumphs of which I spoke. Such gains may be fleeting. I foresee many more coming to Montségur to seek its safety."

"Surely Guilhabert, you do not believe the crusaders will return?" Corba asked.

"No, I do not fear another army. Pope Honorius is consumed with launching his new crusade to recover Jerusalem after the failure of the Fifth Crusade."

"Then what do you fear?" I asked.

"I fear an alliance between the church and the new king of France, Louis VIII. The king has already shown the depravity he is capable of."

"No Occitanian can forget his butchery of our people in Marmande," I said. "But that was four years ago. He has not troubled with us since. I dare hope that with all France to occupy him, he will be too busy to launch a campaign against us."

Guilhabert shook his head. "I pray you are right, but my expectations are otherwise. King Philippe-Auguste was no friend to Occitania, but many here may come to look on his death as a dark moment. It is not King Louis I fear, but his wife."

"But Queen Blanche was raised in Castile. They say she is more cultured than any in the French court, intelligent, and with a great love of music," Corba said. "Castile and Aragón have much in common. Surely we can hope she will bring enlightenment to Louis."

"By all accounts, the things you say are true. She is cultured and intelligent, and many say even beautiful. Yet she is much more. She is a pious Catholic, fiercely loyal to the church and the pope. Those attributes are menacing enough, but she is also very ambitious, a trait that runs deep in her bloodline. Together, these characteristics pose a far greater threat to our people than did even Simon de Montfort."

Corba winced. "Please do not mention his name again in my house or before my children. He was Satan incarnate sent to increase our suffering and prevent us from finding our way back to salvation. I do not believe any woman could be as wicked as he was."

"Yet you know of the wickedness that was visited on Marmande?" Guilhabert asked.

"Louis killed all those innocent people, not Blanche!" cried Corba in denial.

"No, my dear. Prince Louis may have wielded the sword, but Blanche had put it in his hand. Louis is weak. She is strong. She is clearly the power behind the throne, but what is more frightening is that the church is the power behind her."

"I cannot bear to listen to this." Corba sobbed. "The Occitan nightmare must end if only for our children's sake! Why can we not be left in peace?"

Guilhabert put his hand on her shoulders. His touch seemed to sooth her. "My child, we do not threaten them with our swords but with our ideas and our words. We challenge their authority and reject the falsehoods on which they rely for their legitimacy. They are terrified of us. They believe if we are not silenced, others will hear the truth and reject them also."

"Then there is no future for our children or any of our people. Good Christian, you have God's wisdom. What are we to do?" Corba asked.

"We must live as the Good God desires of us. We must not stray from our virtuous path. We must draw strength from our faith and remember our earthly existence is but the blink of an eye in the eternal duration of our souls."

Corba wiped her eyes and tried to smile. Our eldest daughter Philippa ran and hugged her mother.

"Your words are reassuring as always, kind friend. I will try to be guided by them. I just wish I could see as clearly as you do, as clearly as Esclarmonde did. Sometimes, I feel blind."

"You feel blind because you are trying to see further than others dare to. Your vision will come. Those such as the pope and the archbishop of Narbonne do not try to see and will remain blind to their affliction."

"Is there any evidence yet of this alliance?" I asked.

"Yes. A Catholic council was recently concluded at Sens. With the recent deaths of Pope Innocent and King Philippe-Auguste, many have pleaded for an end to the Albigensian Crusade. However, the papal legates led by the archbishop of Narbonne and the southern clergy refused to sanction it. They voted for the crusade to continue until all the voices against the church were silenced. Those I spoke to who attended told me it was clear the defeat of the crusader army had made them only more bitter and determined to crush our independence and reassert the authority of the church over all of Occitania."

"With the resurgence in the fortunes of Count Raymond VII, even I had begun to believe Occitania might be spared further adversity," I said.

"It is not the news any of us had hoped for, but we cannot hide from the truth that the evil we face is not likely to abandon us. The pope, the clergy, and the king are all obsessed with destroying the Occitan culture, as it challenges the violent underpinnings of their authority. With the help of the Good God, we will prevail, but it will be a long struggle."

"I trust your words, Guilhabert, though I do not welcome them." I looked at Corba and Philippa. I knew I had to do whatever I could to protect them. "All right. It is decided. We shall stay in Montségur and continue to offer sanctuary to those who seek it."

"My Lord, those who seek only peace will be eternally grateful to you. It is the act of a true Christian. The Good God will look kindly upon you for it."

"As you know, it is no more than the spirit of paratge would demand of me. I shall never abandon my vows to assuage these northern barbarians and war-mongering priests."

1223, September – Palais de Louvre, Paris

Louis VIII was adjusting well to being king. At age thirty-six, he looked forward to a long reign. He had added to the French possessions in the southwest with his victories over Henry III of England and was anxious to find other opportunities to expand his realm.

Louis put a note down. "I have an urgent request here from Amaury de Montfort. He is begging for help with his campaign in Occitania," he told his wife. "How would you propose I respond?"

"I would suggest you ignore his pleas for assistance for now. Assure him he has your full support but tell him your forces are fully committed to defending France's possessions."

"I like that. Defending the possessions of France. That will do nicely."

Blanche was content the situation in the south was going very much as she had hoped. "Recent reports from Occitania tell us Amaury is failing to hold onto the lands his father had conquered. The crusaders are deserting him in droves, and the southern lords are reclaiming their titles and possessions. It is only a matter of time before he is forced to flee."

"When he does, you are sure he will plead with us for his salvation?" the king asked.

"I am sure. He has nowhere else to go. The pope does not have the will right now to raise another crusader army for him. Even if he did, the pope recently appointed you as commander of the crusade, so he would still be forced to appeal to you."

"True. Amaury needs an army, and there is only France he can turn to. I will exact a heavy price for any help he wants."

"Naturally," Blanche said, "he will have to cede his southern lands to France. To maintain the family honor, you can promise to appoint him to administer the possessions as a vassal of France. That should suffice."

"But what of the pope?" Louis asked. "His representatives have made it clear he does not wish France to annex these lands. He would rather see a southern noble loyal to him as count of Toulouse than one beholden to a greater France. He thinks himself more of a king than a pope."

"He is the king of kings," exclaimed Blanche. "But that does not conflict with the God-given responsibilities of a monarch. The role of a monarch is to administer worldly affairs for the pope so he may devote himself to the spiritual guidance he receives from God. I am confident he will not oppose the French annexation of Occitania if he is confident we will administer them in a stern and Christian manner."

"And why are you so confident of this?"

"I have talked with the legate Arnaud Amaury and other clergy. They encourage us to liberate the southern lands from the control of the heretics and their sympathetic nobility. The clergy are confident they can persuade the pope to permit these lands to become part of France."

"What price does the clergy demand for their help with the pope?"

"None, my husband. Only that they be allowed a free hand to eradicate the heresy and convert the people back to the true faith once they are ours."

Louis smiled. "A fair bargain. The clergy can have the people's souls as long as France has their wealth and their land. We will both benefit."

"Indeed we will. We must simply wait for events to move in our favor. I do not expect it will be long."

1224, February – Castle of Carcassonne

The towers on the great curtain wall of Carcassonne were adorned with flags that fluttered in the cold wind sweeping down from the snow-capped Pyrenees. Their bright colors contrasted sharply with the grey stone of the castle. Each flag bore the crest of a noble family, most prominent among them those of the pope, the king of France, and the house de Montfort. The gay trappings gave the castle an appearance of celebration and festivity. Inside, however, the mood was somber.

With a jolt, the heavy gate and portcullis began to rise. Each creaked and sang loudly as the heavy chains strained to pull them upward. The ratchets clicked one at a time into the notches on the great wheel to prevent them from falling. When they had disappeared into the wall, the drawbridge was lowered. It hit the ground on the far side of the moat with a loud thud.

In the large courtyard behind the gate and flowing into the narrow streets, a multitude stood ready to abandon the castle to the heretics they had sworn to exterminate. It was a sad day for the church and an especially sad day for the de Montforts.

Brother Pierre de Vaux de Cernay conducted Mass from a balcony and prayed for everyone's safe journey back to the Christian lands of France. "The holy father and the Church of Rome will never abandon these lands and their people to Satan," he preached. "The soldiers of Christ will continue in their holy struggle until all the forces of evil have been vanquished. Those who deny Christ and his church will not be suffered to live, for they are an abomination to God!"

The crowd roared approval. "Death to the heretics!" "Send them all to burn in hell!" Those with swords raised them toward the Cistercian monk to reaffirm their pledge to commit them to the service of the church.

"The family de Montfort has truly followed the path of Christ and has sacrificed much in God's service. Simon de Montfort was a pious man committed to bringing Christ into the lives of those who had been denied him or had been seduced by the false testimony of those in the service of the Devil. He gave his life for their redemption."

Amaury de Montfort and his mother, Alix de Montmorency, stood quietly behind the monk as the crowd cheered them.

"Amaury de Montfort has followed in the righteous path of his father and continued to struggle to liberate the Occitanians from the heresy. It has been an arduous task as the forces of Satan have been allowed to grow strong by the counts of Toulouse and their infidel underlings. The roots of Satan have gone deep into Occitan soil, but the family de Montfort has fought mightily to rip them out. Their sacrifices in this holy war have been great, and it is time for them to pass the cross to others. As they leave us to finish the struggle they began, I ask you to remember them in your prayers."

"I feel ashamed. I have failed my family and the church. I have betrayed the trust God put in me to lead his crusade," Amaury de Montfort lamented.

"You have nothing to be ashamed of, my son. You have devoted yourself fully to the service of Christ. That is all that can be asked of you."

"No. God had a right to expect more of me. You had a right to expect more. I have failed you both. My father and brother died to free these lands from the sickness that assails them. My father had every right to expect me to continue the crusade in his name until all the lands were liberated. But I have forfeited all those he conquered and gave his life for. Now we must return to France as beggars and throw ourselves on the mercy of the king."

"It is not you who have strayed from doing God's work but the pope. He no longer feels threatened by the southern lands and looks to Jerusalem for a new crusade. Without his call to pilgrims to rally to our cause, you could not hope to hold onto your father's gains, but our cause is not yet lost. If we win the support of King Louis, we will no longer need a crusader army to take back these lands, for the French army is strong. It recently defeated the English under King Henry III. The Occitan nobles and their Aragónese allies would be no match for it."

"But mother, I tried to offer him homage only last year, but he refused me. Why should he now be more favorable to our cause?"

Alix raised her black shroud. "I have spoken with the pope's legates. They are close to Blanche and assure me she is committed to helping the Occitanians lead Christian lives."

"I do not question her faith. I have heard it is profound. However, I suspect she also sees the opportunity to seize these lands for France while the pope is distracted."

"That is not for us to know, nor is it our concern. The manner in which God motivates his servants is for him alone to decide. We must leave the salvation of the Occitan people in his hands."

"I am tired of the Occitan people. They are all heretics," Amaury said. "I hate them all. They deserve to perish. We have battled the heresy here for twelve years in their name, and still they refuse the sacraments, reject our priests, and kill our crusaders."

"I too feel your anger. They have taken my husband and my son. Most do not deserve salvation. Your father strove hard to do God's work in these lands, yet they rejected him, so I also have little sympathy for them."

"Yet the legate believes the Occitanians are worth saving? That we should not just kill them all?"

Alix put her hand on her son's arm. "The church believes the Occitanians have been deceived by their leaders. The archbishop blames the counts of Toulouse. He believes if the Occitan nobility is removed, the people will return to the true faith."

"For my part," Amaury said, "I have seen little evidence the Occitanians are ready to embrace the church. There is no fear of God in their eyes. I wager that many more will have to experience the wrath of God before they are ready to accept his love."

"Perhaps you are right, my son, but it is no longer our task."

"No. We must return to Paris. I will offer the Occitan lands granted by the pope to the king. If he accepts, he will be committed to defending them as part of his realm."

"Indeed. I was promised the king would continue to allow you to administer many of the possessions in his name."

Bouchard de Marly, a northern knight and devoted comrade of her late husband, interrupted their conversation. "My Lady, it is time to leave," he announced gravely.

Alix touched her husband's casket. "My husband, we shall take you back to lie in peace in Christian ground, for there was no truer servant of Christ than you."

After a few moments of reflection, she walked to the carriage and looked around one last time. When she had mounted the carriage, Bouchard de Marly shut the door. "It is time for us to leave these heathen lands, my Lord," she said with sadness. "Let our journey begin. We leave them to God and pray he will shed his light upon them yet."

Before long, the trumpets sounded. The procession began to snake its way out of the city and begin the long journey to the Île-de-France.

For the first time since the murder of Raymond-Roger in the dungeons of the castle, Carcassonne was free of crusaders.

1225, March – The Archbishop's Palace, Narbonne

The walls and rich tapestries seemed to move in the flickering candlelight. The air was heady with the smell of burning wax and incense. At the center of the room stood a heavy, ornately carved, four-poster bed around which several monks hovered.

The bedroom of the archbishop's palace in the Occitan port town of Narbonne was lavishly furnished in keeping with the rest of the magnificent building. The palace served as a monument to impress upon the people the power and wealth of the church. However, the principal occupant of the room was in no state to enjoy his opulent surroundings.

On the bed lay one of God's most humble servants, Archbishop Amaury, the duke of Narbonne, Cistercian monk, legate to the pope, and former commander of the crusader forces against the Albigensian heresy. He was close to death. A servant propped him up on a mound of pillows that he might hear his confession.

He was a shadow of his former self. His obsession and hatred of the heresy had taken a great toll on his body. In addition to physical pain, he was suffering a mental anguish as he realized he would die with Count Raymond VII still in power in Occitania. The Albigensian Crusade had failed, he had failed, and the heresy was strong. He would have much to confess to his maker.

The archbishop struggled for breath as the recently appointed papal legate, Frangipani, sat by his bedside. Frangipani was on his way to Paris, where he was to become the personal representative of Pope Honorius III in the court of King Louis VIII and Queen Blanche. "What is the latest news from Occitania?" the archbishop asked feebly.

"Not good, I am afraid," replied Frangipani. "The young Raymond-Roger de Trencavel has returned from exile in Aragón and has reclaimed his father's estates. As we speak, he sits in Carcassonne, which was abandoned by Amaury de Montfort and his forces. Cathar perfects preach again in the open, and our priests have been forced to flee."

"You must speak with the pope. I beg of you," cried Arnaud Amaury. "He must raise a new crusade against the Albigensians. I have devoted my life to it but have failed. Promise me you will continue to fight the heresy until the last heretic burns in the fires of hell."

"I give you my assurance on the scriptures that the fight against the heresy will continue. However, the pope believes that the new crusade should be led by King Louis rather than the church. The pontiff is anxious the church devote itself to freeing the Holy Land so pilgrims might travel freely in the land our savior walked."

"Just so," Amaury said. "But do not lose sight of the evil in Occitania or it will spread like an infection."

"Do not trouble yourself with such fears. The pope has decreed all dioceses will tithe to Queen Blanche to support a new crusade against the Albigensians. With her stewardship and the support of her husband, I am sure we shall finally be able to eradicate the heresy."

"I will go more peacefully with that thought." Arnaud Amaury sighed.

"Good. Now I will hear your confession."

CHAPTER 45

On the Bridge of Avignon

1225, November – The Palace of the Vatican, Rome

The old pontiff stroked his long, grey beard in nervous anticipation. He had been pope for nine years but had not realized his dream of liberating the Holy Land. His health was declining. He was having increasing doubts he would have time to fulfill his dream.

The Albigensian crusade had dragged on for sixteen years. It had been a major distraction that had sapped resources and pilgrims from the church's fight against the forces of Islam. Pope Honorius III would like nothing better than to end the crusade against the heretics. Unfortunately, he knew any challenge to the authority of the church had to be suppressed lest it undermine the legitimacy of the church. Just as God had demanded, "Thou shalt have no other Gods before me," so the church demanded, "Thou shalt have no other church before the Church of Rome."

The visitor he had been expecting had arrived. It was the legate Frangipani, assigned to the court of the king of France. The legate clasped his hands as if in prayer and bowed to the pope. The pope made the sign of the cross over him and bade him sit. "What news do you bring me of the French court?"

"The young king and queen are well, your Eminence. They ask you to remember them in your conversations with God."

The pope nodded. "That is good. Tell me truly. What is your assessment? Where do the loyalties of these monarchs lie? With the church or with France?"

"Your Eminence, their loyalties lie with both. I do not see them to be in conflict."

"Yes, but do they respect the supremacy of the church? Will they support us in spreading the faith and fighting those who oppose the truth of our word?"

"Queen Blanche is as devout a Catholic as any I have met. She takes prayers several times daily and has entrusted us with the education of their son Louis. She is extremely intelligent and ambitious. She clearly wants to enlarge the power and possessions of France."

"Ambition can be dangerous. It was with her encouragement that Louis invaded England after the death of John Lackland to seize the English throne. The church's interests are best served by moderating the power of the monarchs."

"That is true, your Grace, but in Blanche de Castile, I see little the church has to fear. I have heard her confessions and probed her inner soul. She believes the interests of France and the church are one."

The pontiff smiled. "I have heard it said she is beautiful. Is this so?"

The legate was uncomfortable. "She is very fair, your Grace. Some say beautiful."

"You are sure you are not letting that affect your judgment? And what about Louis?"

Frangipani took affront. "Holy Father, my loyalty is only to the church. I admire this young queen but only because she has a deep faith and gives herself to God. Regarding the king, he also is a loyal servant of the church. Under his wife's influence, he will remain so."

"That is encouraging. Then I have only the English and the Germans to worry about. Now how shall we address the problem of Occitania? There is to be an ecumenical council in Bourges to debate the matter."

"I am aware of it, Holy Father. Count Raymond VII intends to come to petition the council to restore to him the lands and titles his father had been dispossessed of."

"Many say I should grant his demands. He has remained in the church, and his inheritance is his birthright by the grace of God. It would be good to have rid of this problem. What is your counsel, legate?"

"I have spoken with all the southern bishops. They are united in their opposition to restoring the count. He has made no greater effort to suppress the heresy than had his father. He still permits Cathar perfects to preach in the open, even women preachers. In their sermons, they refer to the Church of Rome as the church of Satan."

"Such blasphemy must not go unpunished! Did the crusading armies of Simon de Montfort accomplish nothing? The church paid dearly for them in men and money, resources dearly needed in the Holy Land."

The legate shook his head despondently. "For a while, many Occitanians found redemption, but after the death of Simon de Montfort, the heretics poisoned their minds against us anew, and many returned to the heresy. Once more, our churches are empty and our priests are penniless."

"What would you have me do?" demanded the pontiff in frustration.

"Your Grace, the bishops ask that you excommunicate Count Raymond VII in like manner to his father. They ask that you reaffirm that all the lands and titles bestowed upon Simon de Montfort pass by succession to his son, Amaury."

"I am informed that Amaury is weak, ineffective. Surely, he is not up to the task."

Legate Frangipani nodded. "He is not, but it is no matter, for he has offered all his Occitan possessions to King Louis."

"Has the king accepted them?"

"He has, your Grace. Thus, Amaury's Occitan possessions will become the responsibility of the king of France."

"It will greatly benefit the French crown, but where is the benefit for the church?"

"Your Grace, if you excommunicate Count Raymond, a new crusade will have to be declared to drive him from his possessions. King Louis has a large army, and he sends you his assurance that if the crusade is on French soil, he will be duty bound to unite his army with the crusader forces. He promises he will crush the heresy and restore all the church's property and authority in his new possessions."

The lines in the wrinkled forehead of the old pope deepened as he raised his eyebrows in satisfaction. "It would be a matter of much relief to the church to pass this lingering problem to the king. The Albigensian crusade has been distracting us for too long."

"I agree, your Grace. Then you will support the demand of the bishops to excommunicate Count Raymond?"

"I will support it if it will end the church's responsibility to resolve the Albigensian problem, but how sure are you the king will keep his bargain?"

"I am confident of it, your Grace. I shall take personal responsibility for the king."

"It is decided then. I will inform Cardinal Romanus he is to reject the entreaties of Count Raymond and declare him an enemy of the church and of Jesus Christ. His lands and titles will remain forfeit to Amaury de Montfort."

The legate beamed. There was just one thing remaining. "Holy Father, you will need to declare a new crusade."

"Yes, the crusade. I will declare a second crusade against the Albigensians, but this time, the burden will fall on the king of France. And I shall expect it to succeed."

"With God's blessing it will, Holy Father."

With the departure of the legate, Pope Honorius turned his thoughts to fighting the supreme heresy, that of the Saracens. Frederick II of Germany would lead the crusade in his name and cut down the infidels who blasphemed the Holy Land by their presence. The Christian world would remain forever grateful to the memory of Pope Honorius III.

1226, June – Avignon, Provence

The rich city of Avignon, in Provence, sat on the left bank of the wide, fast-flowing Rhône. It was on a strategic site first chosen by the ancient Celts for a hill fort and later settled by the Romans. It was on the eastern edge of Occitania and its inhabitants were loyal to Count Raymond VII, who held the town as vassal to the German emperor. The bridge at Avignon was the only crossing point over the Rhône between Lyon and the Mediterranean.

Given its strategic position, the town was well fortified and protected by a powerful ruling council of knights who administered it as a near-independent state.

On June 10, 1226, King Louis VIII accompanied by Amaury de Montfort, several papal legates, and a multitude of Catholic bishops and clergy arrived at the head of an immense crusader army outside the walls of Avignon. It had been a long march on the eastern bank down the Rhône Valley. The king was tired and short-tempered in the scorching Midi sun. He made camp on low ground by the bank of the river, just outside the city gates. The area was buggy and damp, but it was the only open area large enough to pitch the tents for his entourage, and he had no intention of staying there long.

"Legate Frangipani," commanded the king, "go into the city and tell these Avignon knights we are on a mission from God and must pass through their city. We need to cross the bridge to wage a war for Christ in Occitania."

"I shall go immediately, your Majesty."

"I shall accompany you," Amaury de Montfort said. "I have dealt with these knights before and know something of their ways. They delude themselves with their own importance and can be frustrating to negotiate with."

"Very well," the king said. "Be sure they understand I am not here to negotiate. I intend to cross the river, and I demand passage without any delay."

Conditions in the camp deteriorated as the king waited for a response. "Sacré bleu! I have been camped here for two days, and these Avignon knights have not yet agreed to let me into the city. I do not ask for access to the city, I demand it!"

"Your Majesty, the knights debate among themselves. They cannot reach agreement," the papal legate said.

"I will gladly smash their heads together to speed up their decision making. I despise this place, the heat, the mosquitoes, and the humidity. Who are these Avignon knights that they dare to defy the king of France? The largest army in Christendom waits at their gates, ready to tear down their walls."

"Your Majesty, many of the knights are sympathetic to the Cathar cause," Amaury de Montfort said. "They are loyal to Count Raymond and do not wish to help you attack his possessions. They also believe they will be protected by the German emperor. None manifests any love for the French."

"Is that so? I do not care much for them either. If there are heretics or sympathizers in Avignon, we may as well begin our crusade here. Return to the city tomorrow and give them my ultimatum. If they do not open the gates to me by tomorrow night, I will put the city under siege. When it falls, I will exact a heavy price for their disloyalty."

Legate Frangipani nodded. "I will give them your ultimatum, but the knights are arrogant and have gone unchallenged for so long they believe themselves to be in a position of power quite beyond the reality of their situation."

Amaury de Montfort stepped forward. "Sire, the Occitanians in the city are also lobbying strongly against us. I too expect them to refuse your demand."

"Them they shall have a taste of French steel! A few hundred southern knights will not be permitted to thwart the plans of the king of France and the pope. There is no other way to cross this cursed river with so great an army than the bridge here at Avignon. If these stubborn knights stand in our way, I will crush them and walk over their dead bodies."

"It will be an unfortunate but necessary decision, your Majesty. I am confident that you will have the full support of the pope and that he will intercede for you with the German emperor," legate Frangipani said. "We are on a mission from God. All who stand in our way side with the infidels. No Christian would fault you for killing them."

"No, and I shall kill as many of them as I can until they capitulate. They shall receive no mercy from me," swore the king.

1226, September 13 – Avignon, Provence

The crusader siege of Avignon was sorely testing the patience of King Louis. He had been stuck in his foul encampment by the river for over two months, enduring the heat, humidity, and bugs. To make matters worse, the hot, dry, mistral wind had recently begun blowing, bringing in a wave of low pressure that caused discomfort to all. As the king tried to sleep off a headache, he was awakened by the blaring of trumpets followed closely by the sound of horses and great commotion outside his tent. Angrily, he went outside. "What is the reason for this noise, Brother Guillaume?"

"Your Majesty, there is great news. God has sent us a great victory. The city has fallen! The Avignon knights sent emissaries early this morning seeking terms for their surrender. Legate Frangipani and Amaury de Montfort have already gone to the city to make preparations."

"At last! After three months wasted in this hellish place, I shall be able to begin the crusade I came for. These Avignon knights shall pay dearly for my delay." The king returned to his tent. "Get me some cold water. My head is pounding, and this wind is drying my throat and nose. Be sure the legate and de Montfort are sent to me immediately upon their return. I will dictate my terms of the surrender. There will be no negotiations."

Legate Frangipani and Amaury de Montfort returned to the camp within the hour and reported to the king. "Your Majesty, the city is ours," announced Frangipani triumphantly. "The knights are offering us their unconditional surrender. The city gates are open to us, and the crusader army is free to cross the bridge without further delay. We will hold a special Mass to give thanks to God and to bless those who are to fight in his name."

"It is right to thank God for delivering the city to us. I will attend the Mass, but first, we must deal with these impudent knights."

"Agreed, your Majesty. The terms are yours to set. They have little to bargain with."

"They will have nothing when I am finished with them," hissed the king. "I will see to it that Avignon never again dares defy a king of France."

Amaury de Montfort was eager for vengeance as well. "You must set a firm example to those in Occitania who continue to refuse to pay you homage, your Majesty. You must show them you will be merciless with those who usurp power not rightfully theirs."

"I intend no less. What is the situation in the town?"

"It is exceedingly poor, your Majesty. Food is scarce, and there is much disease. With the power of the knights broken, no one is in control. There is widespread looting and mayhem," replied Frangipani.

"Let it continue for a while," King Louis declared gleefully. "How many of these knights of Avignon are there in all?"

"Around three hundred I believe," answered the legate.

King Louis turned to the soldiers in the tent. "Lieutenant, go to the city and bring me back in irons the knights who were most instrumental in opposing me. I shall demand a heavy ransom for their safe return to compensate me."

"And what of the rest of them?" Amaury de Montfort asked, sounding disappointed at the king's seeming leniency.

King Louis smiled demurely. "I will leave that to the citizens of Avignon to decide. I am told that their rule was oppressive and that they are very unpopular with the people."

"That is so, your Majesty," the legate said. "I have seen it myself. They ruled with an exceedingly stern hand."

"I will let the people have their vengeance. Proclaim throughout the city that on my authority, all property owned by the knights is forfeit and any man is free to seize it. That should be retribution enough. At the same time, it should endear me to the inhabitants."

Amaury de Montfort's eyes lit up. "Your Majesty, if we send in our own knights to join in the plunder, it will also be good for morale."

"An excellent idea. Yes, let them take what they like. They have earned it."

Frangipani likewise took pleasure at the prospect of punishing the knights. "It will be divine justice, your Majesty. It will be the end of their order. From this point on, the power of Avignon will be greatly diminished."

"Destroyed, I trust," the king said. "And to ensure that, I will demand that the ramparts around the city be torn down and the moat filled in. If I pass this way again, I do not want to have to besiege the town to gain entry."

"I am sure you will not, your Majesty," the legate said. "As for the heretics in the town, I have already sent inquisitors to seek them out. I propose that those who will not abjure their blasphemy be put to death in public to strengthen the faith of those who have not strayed. It will also demonstrate to all that the church is vigilant in protecting the faithful against God's enemies."

"I will send soldiers to accompany you," declared the king. "The people need to see that it is not only the church but also the king who is committed to protecting the faithful. In preaching against the church, these heretics also preach against the monarchy. They refuse to take feudal vows of loyalty. Society cannot function if such people are tolerated."

"It cannot, your Majesty. They are truly an abomination to all civilized men. In doing God's work here, we will send a message to those in Occitania that the heresy will no longer be tolerated. They will know Christ's pilgrims are coming to sweep them away."

"I have sworn that before God," the king said. "With his blessing, I can continue to Occitania to fulfill my promise."

It took several days for the crusader army to break camp and march across the bridge. The last few stragglers of the vast army had barely crossed the bridge when the river began to rise quickly from heavy rains in the mountains. In a few hours, the low ground where the army had been encamped was flooded by the angry river. Everything in its path was washed away. A few days earlier and many of the crusaders would have drowned. Legate Frangipani declared that it had been a miracle they had been spared and confirmation their cause was just and that God was protecting them.

The arrival of the crusader army in Occitania caused immediate and widespread panic. Few had forgotten the savagery inflicted on Marmande during his Louis' previous crusade. Most could also recount with horror tales of earlier atrocities and butchery that soldiers bearing the red cross of Christ had perpetrated against peaceful citizens in Béziers and Bram.

Fearing for their lives, most towns surrendered to the king without resistance. Those that did not were quickly overrun by the overwhelming numbers and mighty war machines of the crusader army. Amaury quickly settled scores with those who had turned against him in his absence. Their treachery was rewarded with painful death.

The vast entourage of Catholic priests and crusaders immediately set about the task of identifying and arresting suspected heretics. Many Catholics were very willing to denounce neighbors with whom they had had scores to settle or for personal gain.

Many Good Christians fled the towns to hide with their followers in the countryside. Others went for safety up to the high mountain passes to be alone with their flocks. Still others sought sanctuary in the castle perched high on the pog of Montségur.

Within weeks, the king marched triumphantly into Carcassonne at the head of his army. To spare the town from a long and brutal siege, the young Raymond de Trencavel had decided to abandon it to the invaders. However, he had not given up the fight. He fought a campaign of harassment instead against the invaders. The young Roger-Bernard de Foix II, son to Roger-Bernard de Foix I and nephew to Esclarmonde de Foix, took similar paths.

1226, October – Castle of Carcassonne

"I grow weary of this campaign," complained King Louis. "My men grow restless, and many of the crusaders are anxious to return home."

The bishop of Toulouse, Foulquet de Marseille, moved agitatedly toward him. "But your Majesty, Count Raymond still sits behind the walls of Toulouse. The heresy will never be defeated while he remains in power. I pray you lay siege to my city and rid us of this Devil worshipper so Catholics no longer have to practice their faith in hiding and suffer the blasphemy of sinners. Restore de Montfort to his rightful place as count of Toulouse."

"I will not besiege Toulouse during this campaign! It is too late in the year. The crusaders will soon be leaving me, and from my last venture here, I know the town will not be taken quickly or easily. I will not bog myself down here through the winter. France has need of me. Have no doubt I shall return when I am ready."

Foulquet frowned but decided against further argument. It was clear nothing he could say would change the king's mind. He could only hope it would not be long before the king returned. "Your Majesty, we are grateful you plan to come again to our aid. We will pray for your safe return."

"I am most grateful," acknowledged the king.

Amaury de Montfort shrugged acceptingly. "Your Majesty, what are your plans for the remainder of this campaign?"

"I shall leave Carcassonne within a few days to begin my long march back to Paris. I plan to travel north through Occitania. I may not be able to take Toulouse, but I shall do my best en route to deprive the city of as much of its lifeblood as possible. I shall give orders to burn all the crops and slaughter every animal. We shall make this winter a living hell for the people of Toulouse. God demands nothing less of me."

Bishop Foulquet smiled through his broken teeth. "God will rejoice in their suffering, your Majesty. The faithful will also be much encouraged and strengthened in seeing you are a true Christian monarch committed to enforcing God's will."

1226, November – Palais de Louvre, Paris

The carriage hurtled wildly through the gold-encrusted gates of the Palais de Louvre flanked by cavalry bearing the coat of arms of King Louis VIII. Horses and riders were near exhaustion as they rushed over the gravel drive leading to the palace.

As the carriage came to an abrupt halt in front of the palace guards, the horses' breath condensed into misty clouds in the cold air. The guards approached to open the carriage door and let down the stairs. The papal legate leaped from the carriage and hastened into the palace. He was accompanied by a small coterie of the king's personal guard who had been riding alongside the carriage and had dismounted hastily.

Queen Blanche was still in bed when her maid-in-waiting informed her the papal legate had arrived unannounced and needed to see her urgently. Knowing that only recently Frangipani had been with her husband on the crusade, she was anxious to learn what news he had brought that was urgent enough to require her attention in the middle of the night.

"Legate, what is your business here at this hour? Do you bring news of the crusade that could not await my husband's return?"

"I do, my Lady. I am afraid the news is not good."

"Has my husband been wounded?" she asked anxiously.

"Your Majesty, the news I bring is most grave. Your husband is dead." The legate rushed the words from his mouth as if they had been choking him.

The queen's face whitened. Her maids-in-waiting, assisted by two of the king's guards, helped her sit. "It cannot be! I had a communication from him last week. He wrote that the southern climate and the weather did not agree with him but that he was well. How could he have died? Did some heretic southern devil strike him down? If so, I shall go there myself and destroy them all."

"No, your Majesty. The king died of dysentery. The physicians did all they could to heal him, but the illness took him too quickly."

"Where did this happen?" the queen asked, tears welling in her eyes.

"In Montpensier in Auvergne, my Lady. He was on his way to Paris."

The young queen's head fell into her hands. She sobbed quietly.

The legate cleared his throat. "Your Majesty, I know this is a difficult time, but you must act quickly before news of the king's death becomes widespread. You must think of your son. You must ensure that he retains his right to the throne, that he becomes King Louis IX."

"But he is only eleven!"

"Nonetheless, he must be crowned king without delay before others steal the crown from him," urged the legate passionately. "You can act as his regent until he is of age. It is imperative to France and to the church that the monarchy remains with a person of devout faith such as your son and yourself."

"But who would plot against him? He is the rightful prince."

"Your Majesty, lords and barons on the crusade learned of the king's death. I have had reports they are planning to rebel against you and kidnap the boy."

The queen was in panic. "That is treason! They shall not have him! He is the rightful king of France!"

The legate tried to calm her. "He is the rightful king, and he will be if we act quickly. You must arrange for the coronation in a week or two. No more, or the rebels will have had time to organize. Some of the king's most loyal guards will protect you. We must get the people on our side to support the young prince. The church will support you in this."

Blanche wiped her tears. She felt her strength returning. She needed to protect her son. "Legate, France will be eternally grateful to the church for its help in assuring the rightful succession. It will surely serve to deepen our faith in the church and our obligations to the holy father. At times such as these, I am especially grateful to God for working through the pope to lead us along his path. I shall do as you advise"

1226, November – Toulouse

"My Lord, the papal legate Romanus has arrived and begs an audience."

"Very well, show him in. He is expected," said Count Raymond VII.

The elderly legate Romanus was accompanied by a small delegation of monks and clergy carrying scrolls and documents. "Count Raymond, at last you have agreed to see me. I trust this meeting will be a fruitful one."

"Fruitful for you, perhaps, but not for my people or me."

"If it is good for the church, it is good for all, since the Church of Rome is the house of God, and who would deny God his due?"

"I have never sought to deny God his due, only what is demanded by those who exploit him," Raymond retorted.

"Count, it is blasphemy to criticize the church, as you are well aware, but I shall let that comment pass since we are here to negotiate, not fight."

"I am much relieved to hear it," Count Raymond said sarcastically.

Legate Romanus allowed himself a small smirk at the comment. "I understand that your fortunes have changed and that you wish to, shall I say, seek an accommodation with the church," said the legate smugly.

"You have left me no choice," protested Count Raymond. "My principal overlord, King James I d'Aragón, who succeeded my brother-in-law, King Pedro II, now sides with the church against me. I have no doubt he was rewarded generously for his compliance," said Raymond accusingly, looking to the legate for a reaction.

Romanus smiled and tipped his head as tacit confirmation of his suspicions.

"As you know, my other benefactor, King Henry III of England, is too occupied with keeping his own crown to come to my aid. My first duty is to protect my people, so I am forced to try to reach a reconciliation with the church."

Legate Romanus cast a supercilious look; he was a hunter who had cornered his prey. "I will not question your motivation for returning to God. That will be between you and the Creator on your day of judgment or before then if you wish to confess your sins. For now though, it is enough that you have decided to repent."

"What are your demands?"

"Ah," replied the legate with clear enjoyment. "I have them here." The legate snapped his fingers. Two monks came forward with parchments. "We recently concluded a council of bishops here in Toulouse. They set down the terms for your reconciliation, which you will find in these documents. After you read them, I will require you to sign each of them to acknowledge you agree to be bound by them."

Count Raymond began reading, fully dreading what he would find. The terms were worse than he had even feared. "Four thousand silver marks annually for a Catholic university so you can train more priests to fight the heresy? That is an enormous sum. You have burned our lands, killed our people, and sacked our cities. How am I to raise such a sum? The people of Toulouse will starve to pay this tax!"

Legate Romanus was unmoved by his protest. "Sacrifices are often necessary for the greater good. Man needs both spiritual and physical sustenance."

Count Raymond read more of the terms aloud in utter disbelief. "All heretics are to be denounced to the church authorities. A priest and three citizens are to search every house for heretics who might be hiding. Anyone found concealing a heretic will be arrested and lose their possessions. All youths and adults must renounce the heresy under oath and swear loyalty to the Church of Rome. The heads of households must attend Mass on Sundays and holidays or pay a fine unless they have a legitimate excuse."

Count Raymond threw the papers down. "These are onerous terms on a people who have a long tradition of free thought and tolerance for others. You are asking people to betray their friends, neighbors, and relatives and to give them up to possibly be burned."

The legate scowled. "God does not tolerate heretics to live wherever they are found. There is no exception for Occitania!" The legate held a Bible. "The Psalms tell us God killed the finest and strongest of the Israelites for their sins. However, in spite of this, the people kept on sinning! They refused to believe in his miracles. So he ended their lives in failure and gave them years of terror. When God killed some of them, the rest repented and turned to God. So will it be in Occitania!"

"The people of Occitania have already suffered years of terror. It is time to put an end to it."

"The terror will end when they repent and turn back to God," the legate said.

"Amen," echoed several of the clergy.

Count Raymond felt nothing but revulsion for his visitors. "You claim to have murdered, pillaged, and raped in our lands to show our people the way to God? That is not the way back to any god that Occitanians would want to worship. Christ preached tolerance and love. That is what my people seek and have yet to see in the actions of the crusaders. You are hypocrites who seek only power and riches."

"We came to these lands not for riches but to save the Occitanians from themselves and from the likes of you, who have led them from God. We are here to reveal to them the true word of God," the legate proclaimed.

"Occitanians have no need of you to reveal the word of God to them, for they are very familiar with it. Most have Bibles in a tongue they can read and understand."

"It is blasphemy to translate the word of God into the foul language of Occitan. Only Latin is fit for his word!" cried one of the priests in horror, followed quickly by cries of protest from others.

"If you truly wish Occitanians to know the word of God, why do you proclaim here that henceforth it will be a crime punishable by death to be found with a copy of the Old or New Testaments even in Latin? How can reading the word of God be a mortal sin?"

The elderly legate sighed deeply and clasped his hands. "The Bible is the undisputed word of God, but God is so much above man in the breadth of his knowledge and understanding that his word is complex and beyond the ability of common man to comprehend. That is why people must read the Bible only in the presence of a priest who has been trained to interpret the meaning of God's word to the uninitiated. Even the Savior spoke often in parables that confuse the common mind."

"Your words are devious and false, legate. You keep the Bible from the people to use it to your favor and so they might not quote it against you to criticize the errors in your teachings or the sins of your clergy. Why else would you kill anyone simply for reading it outside the presence of a priest? What misunderstanding could be worth the life of a man?"

Legate Romanus looked uncomfortable having to argue theology with the count. He had not been prepared for it but was duty bound to defend the church. "When the Bible is read without a priest, it creates an opportunity for the Devil to poison God's word against him. The proof of it is here in Occitania. The Cathar heretics freely distribute Bibles to weavers, shepherds, journeymen, and the like to read in their homes. When their adherents seek an explanation of the biblical passages, they take advantage of them. Their perfects twist the meaning of God's word and turn them against his true church."

"In an even worse sacrilege, they allow the Bible to be read and interpreted by women!" cried a priest. "That is clearly against the scriptures."

"Your arguments are specious. I have seen candle makers in Occitania manifest more knowledge of the Bible than one of your drunken priests on many occasions."

Legate Romanus was losing patience. "Knowledge and understanding of the Bible are two different things, but enough of this. I did not come here to debate theology with you. It has served only to confirm my fears that your mind has been sorely poisoned by the heretics. It is even more imperative that we act quickly to suppress the error. It is also why you are in the regrettable circumstances you are today."

"If I sign this, will the church repeal my excommunication?" he asked heatedly.

Legate Romanus frowned. "From what I have heard today, it is clear you are not ready to be accepted back into the communion of the faithful. I suggest you seek instruction from Bishop Foulquet. For now, your excommunication stands. If you sign these documents, it will demonstrate your contrition and willingness to reenter the body of Christ. However, your excommunication will not be lifted until the church is convinced you are again living as a true Christian and energetically purging your lands of the heresy."

Thursday, July 6, 1944 – County of Foix

Emile carefully put down the journal of Raymond de Péreille. He had been reading nonstop for hours and needed sleep. The ancient world of

Raymond de Péreille absorbed all his waking hours. He was becoming obsessed by it.

He could no longer separate his world from that of the Lord de Péreille. In both, oppressive authoritarian regimes sought to impose their power by military might, fear, and unrestrained cruelty toward those who challenged them. In both, those who dared to hold true to their beliefs were hunted down, as were those brave enough to hide or protect them. Human life was treated as worthless, and people were slaughtered and burned without conscience. Sadly, these realities were only too familiar to Emile.

CHAPTER 46

Death of a Nation

1227, December – Castle of Montségur

A chill wind was blowing as I was busy working with the stonemasons on repairs to the barbican of Montségur. The fortifications, which included a small tower, were critical to the defense of the castle. On a small plateau high on the eastern edge of the pog, they controlled access to our mountain refuge by dominating the only access route, a narrow trail. The castle was on the western edge of the pog somewhat higher. Between the two, the hilltop was mostly forested.

The fortifications and tower were in need of much repair. As we labored to lift heavy stones into place, a group of around twenty approached us, begging entry to the castle. These women, children, and elderly were exhausted, gaunt, and close to despair.

"My Lord de Péreille, we come to throw ourselves on your mercy," exclaimed their leader. "Grant us your protection and sustenance. We do not ask for charity. We will gladly work in return for anything we are offered. Many have told us you are a true Christian who offers shelter to those in need."

"Where are you from?" I asked. "What drove you here?"

"We are from Toulouse. The situation in the city is desperate, my Lord. The people are starving. The French army under Humbert de Beaujeu, and our own bishop, Foulquet de Marseille, have visited this terror upon us."

"I have heard of their foul tactics," I answered.

"My Lord, they have poisoned our wells, burned our vineyards, our olive groves, our orchards, and our crops. They have demolished our homes and our villages and killed or eaten our livestock. There is nothing left for us to live on."

"How long can the city hold out? Are the defenses still intact?"

"The city can hold out only for a few more months if it cannot be provisioned. The defenses are strong. The invaders have been unable to breach them, yet it will not matter. Count Raymond will be forced to surrender if he cannot feed the people."

I shook my head. "This is grave news, friend. I shudder to imagine how many will die if the invaders overwhelm the city."

"There is panic in the city, my Lord. Many describe the horrors the soldiers of the cross inflicted on Béziers, Bram, Marmande, and other towns. They say the crusaders stripped everyone naked and hacked them to death, even the children. They say there were limbs and guts hanging from the trees and strewn on the ground. The people are terrified."

"I fear many of these tales are true. Many here witnessed the horrors you describe."

The visitors recoiled in horror. "My Lord, there were rumors in the city that the crusaders had recently massacred all the inhabitants in Labécède and set it ablaze. It is close to Toulouse, and many of us have friends and family there. Can this be true?"

I could offer them no consolation. "I am afraid it is true. Some here who fled the town tell just such a story."

Several members of the group cried. Others engaged in nervous discussion.

"Many are fleeing the city, fearing it will fall. All tremble at the thought of the return of Bishop Foulquet, a most vengeful and cruel man. He and his White Brotherhood terrorized us for many years before they were driven out. If he returns, he will surely kill all those who turned against him and any he chooses to accuse of heresy. He is known as the 'bishop of the Devil' by most people in Toulouse."

The very mention of Foulquet made me want to vomit, for I had heard much of his abominations in the name of the church. I could well understand the terror the inhabitants of Toulouse must have been feeling.

"From accounts I have heard, Bishop Foulquet truly serves the Devil, for he cannot claim to serve any loving God with the many murderous acts he is guilty of."

"My Lord de Péreille, several among us, including me, are Good Men and Women, and the remainder are mostly believers. I tell you this so you will know the danger if you offer us sanctuary. If you do not see fit to shelter us, we will leave and think no less of you. Our choices were few. If we had remained in the city, we would all have been killed."

I smiled and opened my arms. "You are most welcome to shelter with us. I am afraid my resources are meager, but we have bread and grain enough for all. You will not starve here, and none will condemn you for your words."

I have rarely seen people so grateful for such a small kindness.

When I returned to the castle, Corba was with our two young daughters Philippa and Esclarmonde. The children's faces were ruddy from running around in the cold mountain air. They were sitting in front of the fire as their mother played the flute to calm them down. Corba looked happy as she always did in front of the children, but I detected sadness in her music. She stopped playing as soon as she became aware of my presence.

"Children, time for bed. See your grandmother Fournière. She will read you a story."

When the children had gone, she sat beside me. "I talked with some of the recent arrivals from Toulouse," she said. "They told me that the people are starving and that it will soon fall to the French and the crusaders. Can this be true?"

"I fear so. By all accounts, they will not be able to hold out much longer. The French have mercilessly destroyed everything they need to live on."

"This new queen is possessed by the evil one. She seeks to finish the job Simon de Montfort began. I fear for our children. What will become of Occitania?"

I shook my head. She cried and buried her head in my shoulder. "I am afraid that Occitania, as we have known it, will probably cease to exist. The queen is said to be determined to annex us to France and bring us under the rule of the pope and the French monarch. By reputation, she is a cold and ambitious woman driven by religious fervor. It is likely that obsession shields her from any conscience."

Corba sighed. "I cannot understand how, if she is a devout Christian and a pious woman, as they say, she could be responsible for such evil. When I hear of the unspeakable horrors committed by her army and the crusaders in Labécède, I cannot reconcile her faith with any form of Christianity I know."

Corba looked at me pleadingly for some sort of explanation. I had none to give. "There were only women and children in Labécède when it fell!" she cried. "The men had all fled after the fighting. Imagine if our children had been among those they slew in the name of the Savior. It is too horrible to even imagine. How can anyone doubt the Good Christian Guilhabert when he says the Church of Rome is the church of Satan?"

I put my arms around Corba. "I thank God it was not our children, and I grieve for those who lost theirs. I too find it impossible to reconcile the actions of the church in our lands with the teachings of Christ. My own faith is torn between the allegiances I was born into and the examples of piety, caring, and charity I see every day in the Friends of God. These conflicts trouble me daily. I am finding it increasing difficult to resolve them."

"I understand," said Corba. "I understand," she reassured me as she squeezed my hand softly.

1229, March – Castle of Toulouse

The seneschal, who had been appointed by Blanche to administer Toulouse after its fall the previous summer inspected the carriage and the guard ready for the journey. "Is all prepared? Have you everything you will need? It will be cold and wet up north."

"My Lord, we are prepared and will leave at your command," a lieutenant said.

"I will send word to the count." He handed a sealed letter to the lieutenant. "Give this to the queen, none other."

"Yes my Lord. You have my bond on it."

"This is a great day for France," declared the seneschal. "Today, Occitania ceases to exist. The Kingdom of France stretches to the Mediterranean. Never has there been such a power in Europe since Charlemagne. France has reclaimed what was taken from it."

The legate, who had just emerged from the castle, heard his words and frowned. "Seneschal, the glory of God trumps the glory of any earthly potentate. Today is above all else a triumph for the Lord."

The seneschal was taken off guard. "You are right, Father. Please forgive me. The glory of God triumphs all others."

The legate smiled. "Summon my carriage. I am to return to Rome with these papers freshly signed by the count. When Pope Gregory receives them, he will most certainly give thanks to God that the Occitania problem is at last resolved. The count has agreed to all the terms of the pope. He will aggressively persecute all heretics, infidels, and Jews in his lands. They are an anathema to the Lord, his church, and all those of the true faith. No longer will the faithful suffer the servants of Satan."

"The people will be most joyous at their liberation," commented the seneschal, forcing a smile.

"It will bring comfort to many," the legate said, eyeing him suspiciously for the insincere tone of his words.

The seneschal tried to redeem himself with a comment more likely to please the monk. "Father, we can all also rejoice in knowing that when the young king comes of age, he will lead crusaders from French ports against the Holy Land. Let no one doubt our victory here was for God's purpose."

"It was for no other," insisted the legate, angered by the suggestion of a more base motive. He strode to where his carriage would arrive. He faced a long, tiring journey to Rome.

Margaret le Brun, the wife of Count Raymond VII, walked into the chamber to talk to her husband just after the legate had departed. "What did you promise him?" she asked. "Everything he asked. I have nothing left to bargain with. My soldiers are no match for the crusaders and the French army combined. Our people are starving and dying of disease. Our once-beautiful lands have been ravished by over twenty-five years of war."

"You are the count of Toulouse, the descendant of a long line of proud, great ancestors, the rightful lord of these lands and people. God gave you this authority."

"According to the legate, whatever is given by God can be taken by the pope, for he is God's custodian of all earthly things."

"Curse Pope Gregory IX!" cried Margaret in a mix of anger and sorrow. "He will bring only more suffering and misery to our people. They say he is obsessed with organizing a new crusade to the Holy Land. Why does he not just go and leave us alone? But then, what should we expect from the nephew of Innocent III? It was he who first laid waste to our lands, with his crusaders burning, murdering, and pillaging in the name of their loving God."

"I am sorry my dear. I have failed you. I have failed myself, and I have failed our people. Yet if I do not submit, I will bring only more suffering on all concerned."

Margaret wiped her tears. "And if you submit to their demands, will the pope reinstate you in the church? While we remain excommunicated, we are outcasts. Many walk on the other side of the street when I am out. We can claim nothing as our own."

The count shook his head. He could give her no assurance her suffering would end soon. "I was promised nothing. But according to the legate, if I agree to their terms, do penance for my sins, and show myself committed to routing out the heresy, the pope will consider lifting my excommunication."

"And in the meantime, will they allow you to remain as count of Toulouse?"

"Perhaps, but I am not certain. The church has no objection, but that will be a decision for the regent, Blanche de Castile. I must go to Paris to make my peace with her."

Margaret trembled. "I fear for you. Her reputation is one of a beguiling but dangerous beauty. One who, while of Spanish blood, is more driven to expanding the boundaries of France than any king before her. Take care. Watch out for treachery."

"I hear as you do, but I also hear she is cultured and shares our Occitanian passion for troubadours. Our common culture may win us some sympathy."

"I would not count on it after all the savagery her army has shown our people."

The count shrugged uncomfortably. "Whatever the outcome, I have no choice. I must plead our case and hope for mercy."

Tears streamed down Margaret's face. "Go then, my dear. Make your peace. I wish you a safe journey. I will remember you in my prayers."

1229, April – Castle of Montségur

I should have known that further sadness was about to befall our land. For two days, the Pyrenees, a long way distant to the south, had been so clear that it seemed you could touch them. It was a sure sign the Black Autan was coming. The locals call it "the wind of the Devil" and for good reason.

The Autan brought billowing, black clouds that turned day into night and winds that seemed determined to blow us off our mountain. Fearsome as it was, I knew the Autan would pass. The same was not true for the dark news that arrived along with it that plunged a knife into my soul. I knew that it would change our world forever.

Two Occitanians who shared the southern ideal of paratge and who were to become intimately tied to our family carried this news to us. If they had not come bearing such evil tidings, we would have been overjoyed to welcome them to Montségur. But there was no joy brought to us by their visit, only dread that quickly spread across the pog.

"The Lord de Mirepoix, Pierre-Roger, and his brother, Isarn de Fanjeaux, seek shelter for the night," cried the page.

"Show them in! They are most welcome."

Pierre-Roger strode to me forcefully, as was his manner, and gave me a firm hug. "It is good to see you, cousin," he bellowed. "These are dark times. I count each of my friends as a blessing sent from the Good God."

"It is good to see you too, and your brother. You are most welcome to stay for as long as you wish. I am sure Corba will be delighted to have someone to talk to and to bring her up to date with the world beyond our isolated existence up here."

Pierre-Roger and Isarn exchanged veiled glances.

"Tell me. How is life in Mirepoix and in Queille?" I asked.

Pierre-Roger looked ill at ease. "It is not good. It will bring no joy to your wife. But all Occitanians must be told of the recent treachery against them so they will unite in the fight against the satanic forces of the Church of Rome and the Kingdom of France."

"Cousin, you were always one for fighting. After all this warfare, is it not time to try to make peace? There are many in our community here, including my mother and Corba's mother, who teach that killing is not the way of the Good God; it brings only suffering."

"Cousin, you speak the words of the Good Christians. Their worldly existence is of little value to them, but you are a knight. You have sworn an oath, as I have, to protect our people. Have you renounced yours, or are you still bound by it? If so, your obligations as a Lord of Occitania must rise above your sympathies to the Friends of God."

"You speak truly, I confess, and yet lately I have been conflicted as to how best protect our people. Many have suffered greatly since the church brought this war upon us, and none more so than the Good Christians. Yet they still refuse to fight and advocate we find a peaceful solution. Corba has been spending much time among the Good Christians with us, trying to learn how she might lead a purer life. She prays for her soul to return directly to the Good God after this life."

Pierre-Roger made light of my remark. "There are few purer than Corba. If she cannot enter paradise, we are all condemned to be reborn a thousand times." He laughed. "But what is this to you?"

"She is anxious that our souls are not separated for long, so she has also been trying to guide me down her path. It is a good path but not an easy one to follow in these times."

"Nor is it one that the Lord de Péreille can follow today!" Pierre-Roger said. "The forces of the Bad God have come to destroy those who follow the Good God and everything we value of Occitania. We must fight back or lose everything we cherish."

Isarn moved to his side. "My brother is right. Like Montségur, there are many Good Christians who have come to Queille seeking our protection. They are well liked in the village, for they help the poor and the sick without extorting tithes or indulging in the lascivious behavior of the Catholic priests. Yet the emissaries of the church energetically seek them out and burn them alive."

"I grieve for them truly, but what would you have me do? I cannot fight the armies of the pope and the king of France. I have barely a few hundred soldiers and a castle scarcely big enough to house them. Even the count of Toulouse with his army and that of Aragón was unable to prevent the crusader hordes from ravaging our lands."

"This is not a struggle over mere land. It is a struggle over ideas," cried Pierre-Roger. "They seek to destroy our values of equality, chivalry, learning, and tolerance, which above all else the Church of Rome and the northern barons are desperate to snuff out. They are terrified that if our flame is not extinguished, it might eventually consume them in a mighty conflagration like the fires of hell."

Pierre-Roger had always had a fiery disposition. He was not one to suppress his feelings even when doing so might cost him dearly.

"I see you have not lost any fire in your words, cousin. I have some admiration for that, though in these times, it might not serve you well. I have tried to avoid conflict that we might survive unnoticed until the madness has passed."

"An admirable goal, but one I fear whose time is drawing to a close," Isarn said. "The forces of darkness grow stronger. Soon, even those such as you must take sides. The Church of Rome continues to soak their white tunics in the blood of our people. Blanche de Castile does the pope's bidding and sends the armies of France against us."

Pierre-Roger paced. He was full of anger. "It is true I speak freely against injustice when I see it and damn the consequences! It is in my nature. I do not apologize for it. I am proud to have fought energetically against the forces of Satan sent by the pope and the French. I wish I could kill them all! Unfortunately we Occitanians are not as practiced in the arts of butchery; but we are learning fast."

It seemed then that even the sky grew angry at his words, for the Black Autan gusted stronger than ever, making it difficult for us to continue our conversation.

"Let us go inside for shelter," I proposed. "You can rest. We will talk at dinner."

The sky was unusually dark for the time of year due to the storm. The small table we sat around was lit by candles.

"Pray tell us all about what is happening in Occitania and beyond," Corba said. "Do we have any cause for hope? I pray to the good Lord every day."

Pierre-Roger hung his head to avoid her gaze. "My Lady, I have only dark tidings."

Corba, always optimistic, tried to hide her disappointment. "Tell us these tidings so we might judge for ourselves. Maybe we can see light where you see only darkness."

"The news is from Paris and concerns Count Raymond. It grieves me to say he went there to swear an oath of fealty to Blanche de Castile."

Corba gasped.

"He had little choice," I said. "For his people are starving and his fields are burned."

"Even worse," added Isarn, "the people of Toulouse were forced to allow the priests back into the city, and they have taken what little the people had left. I saw it myself."

"What other news from Paris?" I asked. "Has Count Raymond been reinstated?"

"In name only. Blanche agreed to recognize him as count of Toulouse, a subject of France, providing he marries his daughter to the king's brother, Alphonse de Poitiers."

"But they are both barely nine!" my mother declared. "Margaret le Brun will weep to have her daughter stolen by the French court."

"Yes, but the regent had worse punishment in store for Count Raymond," Isarn said.

"I am not sure if it was Blanched de Castile or the papal legate behind it," Pierre-Roger said. "The church excels in acts of unbridled vengeance against those who oppose it. On Good Friday, the count was forced to sign an onerous treaty at Meaux, outside Paris. Then, he was taken to the Cathedral of Notre Dame, where he was made to declare his repentance while kneeling before the altar and all those who witnessed his humiliation. He was dragged into a small courtyard. In front of a jeering crowd, Blanche, and an army of Catholic clergy, he was stripped to the waist and whipped as his father had been."

"Now he is imprisoned in the Louvre," Isarn said. "They say he will remain until the key terms of the treaty are enacted."

"That is monstrous," proclaimed Corba, totally distraught.

"What is in this Treaty of Meaux?" I asked more calmly.

"It is a death warrant for Occitania," lamented Isarn.

"Not just for Occitania, but for many Occitanians also, I fear," added Pierre-Roger. "The treaty requires the count to aggressively eradicate all heretics in his lands. Before the altar of the Notre Dame, they made him pledge to persecute Cathars, Jews, and the like, all who do not hold to the dogma of the Church of Rome and swear subservience to the pope."

"This will set the clock back in Occitania a hundred years or more," I said, aghast. "But what more? Pray go on."

"In addition, the count must return all church property to the church."

"But that was stolen from the people in the first place!" protested Corba's mother.

"The church declares the land was given to it by God," replied Pierre-Roger derisively. "Not content with a return of their property, the treaty also demands the count pay a huge war indemnity and compensation to the church."

"Ah, there we have it. As always, the church seeks worldly enrichment," complained Guilhabert de Castres who had joined us at the table. "Instead of consoling the people, as would those who truly walk in the path of Christ, the priests terrify them with the threat of eternal damnation. Then they can a exact payment from them to save them from such a terrible fate. It is truly a cult of the Devil."

On that point, there was general agreement by all of us.

"But how can we be expected to pay such sums of money?" fretted my mother. "Twenty years of warfare have left us with nothing. We cannot even feed our people."

Pierre-Roger threw his head back angrily. "The church cares nothing for the plight of our people, only what it can steal from them. In addition, they would institutionalize their theft, for the treaty also calls for the establishment of a Catholic University in Toulouse whose purpose will be to force the theology of the church upon our people. Yet it is the people who will have to pay for it."

"That is truly an abomination," Guilhabert said. "The Church of Rome, dripping with wealth it has misappropriated from the starving masses, now demands the people pay to train more thieves to threaten and rob them."

"It is an abomination indeed," cried Isarn, "that the poor must be taxed to fund the opulent and debauched lives of their oppressors."

"They now make a profession of their deception," exclaimed Pierre-Roger. "They have created such a group within the church to spread their lies. They are calling it 'Propaganda.' Most threatening of all, the church plans to establish a commission of inquiry in this new university to eradicate the heresy from our lands. It will be called the Commission of the Inquisition."

"Enough of the church," I protested. "I grow weary always hearing of the church and its scheming. What of our other enemy, the French? What more concessions did Blanche demand of the count? She has long plotted to add Occitania to France."

Pierre-Roger sighed. "She has castrated him of all real power and turned him into a mere puppet. He must turn over all his castles to her and dismantle the walls and fill the ditches of thirty strongholds in his domain, including Toulouse. Even more egregious is that he must renounce his title to the lands in Provence and to Carcassonne. He inherited those from his mother, who held them under the patronage of the German emperor. France has never had any just claims to those lands. The ambition of Blanche surpasses that of any of the kings of France."

"I cannot believe this news," Maquèse de Lanta said. "It is beyond a nightmare."

"I tremble at the sound of this Commission of Inquisition," Guilhabert said. "Whenever the church sets up a commission to inquire into the correctness of people's faith, many innocent people die. Killing and terror are the church's means of purification."

Corba stood and clapped her hands. "I fear we will become too sorrowful listening to such dire news that we will forget who we are," she said bravely and to my surprise. "If we do that, they will have taken everything. We must remember we are Occitanians. Let us raise our spirits if only for one night and rejoice in our culture. Minstrel, bring in the troubadours!"

Two troubadours entered and began playing. Corba told me later they had come to the castle only that day, offering entertainment in return for sustenance.

Our daughters joined us. Like their mother, they loved dancing and singing the Occitan ballads of in our own fair tongue.

"That was true nourishment for a weary spirit," rejoiced Pierre-Roger at the end of the evening. "Montségur is surely a heavenly haven protected in the embrace of the Good God from the ravages of Satan."

"Good friendships are a gift from God. We are always glad of such company," replied Corba.

"Your daughters are most charming and quite different. Esclarmonde appears very serious, while Philippa seems very spirited, full of passion. She makes me feel a zest for life."

"We love them very much," said Corba. "And you and your brother are most welcome any time in our house when you feel in need of rejuvenation."

"Tell me, cousin, where will you go from Montségur? Mirepoix?" I asked.

"No. I am no longer welcome there. Under the Treaty of Meaux, I, like many other good Occitan lords, was dispossessed of my lands. Blanche intends to replace all Occitan nobles with French knights who will do her bidding. My lands have been given to a knight who fought alongside Simon de Montfort. His name is Guy de Levis."

I stood, enraged. "French lords have no place ruling over Occitanians! They are uncouth and do not speak Occitanian! This Spanish witch and her Italian papal master will not be appeased until they have destroyed one of the greatest works of man and the Good God, the Occitan culture. It is the envy of all European courts, yet they will not rest until they have eradicated it out of fear it will shake their thrones."

Pierre-Roger shared my anger. "It is indeed a sad time for Occitania and for all Europe. I fear there will be dark times ahead for all men of conscience," Pierre-Roger said. But fear not. I and many others will fight the forces of darkness as long as we can. I plan to go to Quéribus, where those still willing to fight are rallying their forces."

I patted him on the shoulder. "Take care, my cousin. Oft times, I have seen your passion rule your head. Temper your emotions or you will risk losing your head."

"Fear not. I have faith the Good God will protect us, but if he does not, I will not regret my fate. I live for Occitania. I will gladly die for it."

1229, May – Castle of Toulouse

The doors of the count's apartments in Toulouse shuddered under the impact they were receiving from the heavy blows of a pikeman's staff. "Open these doors in the name of Blanche de Castile, regent of France!"

After a brief wait, the doors began opening slowly, creaking under their great weight. "The count of Toulouse remains in Paris. The countess demands to know who seeks an audience with her," demanded a servant blocking their way.

"No one seeks an audience with the countess," the ill-tempered man spat back. "Out of our way or I will have you impaled."

The servant backed away in haste. Clergy and armed soldiers pressed ahead. Responding to the commotion, the countess appeared, disheveled. "With what authority do you dare break into the count's apartments?" she demanded bravely.

"With the authority of Pope Gregory and of Blanche de Castile. I am Foulquet de Marseilles, reaffirmed bishop of Toulouse by Blanche de Castile and recently given the full authority by Pope Gregory to pursue the heresy throughout this region."

"I know who you are. But what is your business here?"

"Where is your daughter?"

"She is asleep," she replied, gesturing to the child's bedroom.

"Guards, seize her!" screamed Foulquet.

Two soldiers rushed across the room to fetch the child.

Margaret le Brun ran to block their way. "What do you want with my child?"

"Your daughter is now a ward of the regent of France. She is to be married to the king's brother, Prince Alphonse de Poitiers, when both come of age. It is a great honor for her to marry into the royal house of France."

"I spit on your honor!" screamed Margaret. "The child is only nine! You would take her from her mother to a heathen court?"

"Your opinions are no longer of importance," scoffed Foulquet, his voice filled with hatred. "You are to be evicted from these apartments and banned from the city."

"No! You can't do this! Give me my daughter!"

"I can do whatever I want on the direct orders of the queen regent," he hissed. "Soldiers, take her out of my sight. See that her belongings are out of the city before nightfall. Those that are not will be burned!"

CHAPTER 47

Montségur Becomes a Sanctuary

1231, Castle of Montségur

It was early spring when we received an unexpected visit at Montségur from Guilhabert de Castres, bishop of Toulouse, accompanied by his companion *filius major* Bernard de Lamothe. They had brought with them a delegation of fellow Good Christians and believers representing the Church of the Friends of God. Their dress in dark-blue and brown robes was in stark contrast to the ostentatious garments worn by the Catholic clergy.

Many, including Corba and our daughter Esclarmonde, fell to their knees when the group entered and placed their palms to the ground. They bowed deeply three times and begged the Elect to pray for them to the Good God. "Bless us, Good Christian," they begged, and then on the third bow, they said, "Lord, pray God for this sinner that he deliver him from an evil death and lead him to a good end."

Guilhabert blessed them all.

"To what do I owe this honor?" I asked. "It is rare to receive such a delegation."

"My Lord de Péreille, you are a true friend of God, whether Catholic or Good Christian, for you have given shelter to those outcast by others but yet pure in soul."

"It is the Occitan way to accept others without judgment. Only God is entitled to judge our fellow man."

"It was the Occitan way. Sadly it is increasingly so no longer," he said with remorse. "The Church of Rome has excelled in cruelty against our people. They have demonstrated there are no limits to the depravity they will show to those who oppose them. None can now question, as we have long said, that the church does not worship the Good God. They have shown themselves to care only for riches and power. The church even dares to place itself above God by condemning others in his name."

I could see the pain in the old preacher's face and hear it in his words. He was a man of passion who truly cared for others and felt their pain. He was feeling much pain, and there was a sense of desperation in his manner I had not seen before.

"Good friend, I will not seek to defend the actions of the church, for I cannot. None can defend the brutality of its actions, yet I am afraid there is little I can do to prevent it. What would you ask of me?"

"I would ask for your continued protection against such evil."

"But there are already many Good Christians who live here among us, my mother and my mother-in-law among them. What more would you have me do?"

"The head of the church of Satan, Pope Gregory, plans to establish tribunals in Toulouse and other cities to persecute those who question or defy the teachings of the church. It will become much more dangerous for us to live and preach among the people. As Friends of God, we cannot countenance violence to protect ourselves; killing any living thing is to deny its soul the chance to return to its spirit. Thus to avoid conflict, we ask permission to move the seat of our church to Montségur and under your protection."

"This is not a request to be considered lightly," I said. "I would risk bringing down the wrath of the church and the French upon all who shelter here. We may be far from the tribunals, but the church would pursue you all the same. They fear not your swords but your words, which they will seek above all else to silence."

"You are right. We will not force you in the matter," Bernard said. "It is a matter for your conscience to be decided by you with God's guidance.

He has guided you well until now, for you have already given sanctuary to many who worship him as we do."

I reflected for some time before suggesting an option. "What of Count Raymond? He is newly installed in Toulouse and has shown sympathy to your cause in the past. Will he not offer you protection or at least protect you from the church?"

"He is without power and acts only as instructed by the regent's seneschal. Just last month, two Good Christians were arrested in Albi in his name. I watched as one of them was burned at the stake."

Corba closed her eyes in revulsion.

Bernard raised his head and pulled the dark-blue cowl from over his eyes. "All the citizens of Toulouse, Catholic and Good Christian alike, are being persecuted by the church. The count has shown himself powerless to stop it."

"I fear this is true," Guilhabert said. "The evil Bishop Foulquet has been tithing the people beyond their means. Many have died toiling to meet his demands. Others are starving because he robs them of their crops and livestock, which he gives to his fat priests, who drink and eat to excess and place no value on a day's labor.

In the past, the count would have supported the people to rise up against the bishop. But he sits idly, powerless to intervene for fear of antagonizing Blanche."

"Nonetheless, the bishop has so terrorized the people," spoke another of Guilhabert's party, "accusing anyone he dislikes of being a heretic, that in desperation, they are rising up against him. When we left Toulouse, an angry mob was on its way to evict him from the city."

"These are truly dark times for our people that sadden me greatly," I said. "Would that we could drive these foreigners from our lands. Alas, I cannot make it so."

"Nor can any of us," Guilhabert said. "The test of our faith is simply that though evil surrounds us, we refuse to be complicit in it and continue to strive to lead good, pure lives that are examples to others. That is the only way to reenter the kingdom of heaven."

"Then your soul is surely assured of regaining its place by the heavenly Father ahead of us all, for I have heard you have inspired many to lead good lives," I said. "Allow me time to think on your request," I asked.

"The church will accept your decision, whatever it is," said Guilhabert. "May God grant you a good death."

I summoned leaders of our small community at Montségur to take their counsel on Guilhabert's request. The advice I received was nearly unanimous—we should accede to what he was asking. It was clear that a deep hatred of the Church of Rome and the French burned fiercely inside them as it did in most Occitanians. The Good Christians did not put this hatred into words—that was not their way—but I could detect it in their voices. Those who were ordinary believers and even Catholics among us expressed their animosity for those who had invaded and desecrated our lands. All believed strongly we give sanctuary to anyone coming to us in peace to seek our protection. Even the knights and soldiers advised me to permit the Friends of God to move the seat of their church here.

"Sire, permitting the Good Christians to install their church at Montségur will put us in great peril of an attack by the French. Despite this, we are all Occitanians willing to give our lives to remain so. Honor requires we protect fellow Occitanians who desire no more than to live in peace."

"And what of our ability to protect them?" I asked.

"Considerable work will have to be done to improve the defenses of the castle to secure our position. We must extend the walls along our southern and northern slopes and raise and strengthen them. We must repair the barbican. But with the Good God's guidance, we believe we can protect our community from all but the most sustained attack."

Thus, I allowed Guilhabert de Castres and the bishops of Agen and Razes to take up residence at Montségur. However, Guilhabert was rarely among us. Though proclaimed a heretic and actively sought by the Catholic clergy, he traveled widely on foot throughout Occitania despite his advancing years. From the banks of the Aude to the foothills of the Pyrenees, he went by goat trails and paths known only to a select few to slip unseen from one town to the next to administer the *Melioramentum*, a blessing for a good end, or the Consolamentum to those near death.

The people responded with affection to his charismatic personality and the caring and kindness he exuded. Guilhabert toiled for his daily bread and kept true to his vow of poverty.

1232–1241 – Occitania

I will pass over the remainder of the terrible years 1232–1241 with but a brief account of them, for there were no great battles or crusades to give account of. Yet do not be deceived; during this period, the Occitan people endured such terrible suffering at the hands of the church and its murderous priests that my words cannot adequately portray it to you. It was as a river in which all could clearly see a waterfall where the course of the water changes abruptly yet its energy is soon dissipated. Much harder to perceive is the swelling of a river as it moves relentlessly onward. Untold streams flow into it and turn it into a powerful torrent. So it was with the campaign against our people.

In 1232, Pope Gregory decreed the establishment of the first holy Inquisition to apply the terms of the Treaty of Meaux in Occitania. He entrusted the newly created Dominican order with administering this savagery against our people. The tribunals were set up completely independent of the local clergy and were subject to the authority only of the pope. The Dominicans were given limitless powers to torture and burn anyone they decided was guilty of heresy. Heresy was defined as any act or spoken word the inquisitors ruled was contrary to the teachings of the church. Many were accused on the basis of seemingly innocent acts, and all lived in fear as a result.

It is ironic that the order founded by Domingo de Guzmán should have been responsible for such wicked cruelty, for when the Spanish monk came to our lands, he promised to defeat the heresy by word of mouth rather than by thrust of sword.

The pope appointed Stephen de Burnin, legate for southern France and northern Spain, to head the order, and tribunals were established in Barcelona, Albi, Cahors, Toulouse, and Moissac. In those tribunals alone, two hundred and ten people were burned at the stake. The tribunal in Carcassonne was held in a tower that became infamously known as the

Tower of the Inquisition, a name that wrought terror in the hearts of the people.

In Toulouse, Peter Seila and William Arnald were appointed as the first official inquisitors. For most of the time, Seila remained in the city while Arnald toured the region and intimidated the populace with accusations of heresy.

One particularly despised inquisitor, Bernard Gui, was said to have confiscated the homes and property of nine hundred and thirty, incarcerated another three hundred and seven, and to have burned alive forty-two. Gui, empowered directly by Pope Gregory, claimed to be following the path of Jesus and once proclaimed, "No one should argue with the unbeliever but thrust his sword into his belly as far as it will go."

Before the Inquisition, it was the duty of the accused to prove themselves innocent rather than the reverse, our practice under common law. The inquisitors acted as prosecutors and judges. Proving innocence was next to impossible as the accused had no right to counsel, no right to call witnesses, and no right to know his accusers. To make matters worse, anyone stepping forward to defend the accused or speak as a witness on his or her behalf risked being charged with heresy. The accused could be imprisoned indefinitely at the pleasure of the inquisitors. Trials were held in secret. No appeals were allowed.

In their campaign of terror, the Inquisition used the tools of torture and mass murder against those who even professed to be Christian on an unprecedented scale, all in the name of Jesus Christ. They did so with a zeal only Satan could have mustered.

Thousands of our people were burned alive screaming at the stake, without regard to age or sex by priests who gleefully lit the fagots around them and chanted praise to their God for his beneficence. The smell of human flesh burning made me vomit on more than one occasion. The Catholics enthusiasm for human sacrifice extended even to those who were dead or could not be captured. In their place, effigies were burned and prayers chanted to God that they would roast in the fires of hell for eternity.

Many more received punishment and suffered flagellation and torture. Those who were spared typically submitted voluntarily to the Inquisition or denounced others to be seized in their place. Whether or not charges were proven, all who were spared had to sign a confession that they recanted all their heretical beliefs and would henceforth accept the Church of Rome as the one true church of Christ. The church offered indulgences as a special reward for those who identified Good Christians, absolving the beneficiary from all sin in the eyes of the church and God.

The lucky few who were spared the flames and accepted back into the faith were required to wear two yellow crosses on their clothes to warn others of their sin of turning away from God. The faithful were to walk on the other side of the street to avoid risking their eternal souls by coming too close to them. In time, if the church viewed them as fully redeemed, they could remove the crosses and re-join the faithful. Jews, on the other hand, were required to wear the yellow crosses in perpetuity to identify themselves as infidels.

In 1233, the Inquisition began a campaign of exhuming the bodies of those they believed had died as heretics. Their tombs were desecrated and their bodies removed and publicly burned. The homes and possessions of the accused, though they were deceased, were then seized from their descendants. Anyone caught with a Bible was liable to be burned.

The people of Occitan hated the Inquisition, and numerous spontaneous uprisings occurred throughout the region. In 1235, the Inquisition was chased from Albi and Narbonne, and even William Arnald was forced to flee Toulouse. Bishop Raymond de Fauga, who had replaced the much-hated Foulquet, was expelled from the city.

In 1233, during an uprising in Cordes, two inquisitors were thrown down a hundred-foot well to their deaths, while in Albi, an inquisitor was thrown into the River Tarn. Sometime later, widespread riots broke out in Narbonne after the inquisitors began exhuming the bodies of dead family members for burning.

In 1235, faced with the increasing unrest in his lands, Count Raymond VII was forced to petition Pope Gregory to curb the excesses of the Inquisition in Occitania. He pleaded that the practices of the inquisitors drove the people from the church and fueled the heresy. He argued that secret trials were contrary to the long-established laws of Occitania and that the destruction of the houses of the accused, without evidence, was also unacceptable to the overwhelming majority of Occitanians.

Pope Gregory showed some sympathy and requested his legates to curtail some of their most egregious practices. However, the inquisitors gained much personal wealth from confiscating the estates of the accused, so they had little interest in complying. Much to the sorrow of the citizens of Toulouse, the Inquisition returned to their city in 1235.

One happy event from that period concerns my high-spirited cousin Pierre-Roger. In 1234, he married our dear daughter Philippa and joined us in Montségur. In addition to bringing great joy to Philippa, his joining our family also greatly raised spirits in the castle and our growing community. A renowned knight, Pierre-Roger brought with him other knights, men-at-arms, many court officials, and relatives who, like him, had been dispossessed by the French. Their numbers greatly strengthened our garrison and helped improve our fortifications. With Pierre-Roger a member of the family, I handed over full responsibility for defense of the castle to him so I could focus on the governance and provisioning of those who depended on me.

Looking back, I may have been mistaken to have entrusted so much responsibility to Pierre-Roger, for he had one great weakness I was aware of, one that ultimately brought us great tragedy. He was a man of great passion and would frequently act upon it without reflecting upon the consequences. I did my best to temper this weakness but failed, so in part, I blame myself. In his defense, the atrocities committed against our people during those years were enough to make the blood of anyone boil. The sheer wickedness of these acts drove many to commit desperate acts. But as a leader of my people, it was my duty to rise above that and protect them from retribution for ill-considered actions.

Pierre-Roger was apt to ride out frequently with his closest knights and engage in skirmishes with the forces of occupation. His increasing notoriety resulted in his being declared an outlaw in 1237 and being condemned by the Inquisition. Undeterred, however, he continued in his ways and was nearly captured by the French in 1240 while fighting unsuccessfully with Raymond de Trencavel to retake Carcassonne.

During the period, Pierre-Roger's brother, Isarn de Fanjeaux, was a great help in supplying food and provisions to us on the pog. He procured these for us in Queille and developed secret paths up the side of the pog to deliver them to the castle.

Corba became close friends with Rausanne, Isarn's wife, and traveled frequently to the castle of Queille to visit with her. It was a nice change for Corba after living in our harsh mountain retreat, to relax watching the large water wheel of the mill turn slowly as the gentle waters of the river Touyre washed over it. What excited Corba most about going to Queille, however, was the opportunity to speak with and listen to many travelers who passed through the village. There was a rarely a time when some wandering troubadours or Good Christians were not in the village and ready to entertain or preach in return for lodging and food. Our daughter Esclarmonde accompanied Corba as she became more interested in discussing with the preachers the purpose of our worldly existence as she struggled to make sense of the violence around her.

Count Raymond VII tried to win back favor with the church and the French. Unlike the late count of Foix, Raymond-Roger, who personified the Occitan spirit of culture, compassion, and chivalry, Count Raymond was weak. At heart, he remained a true Occitanian, but after the Treaty of Meaux, his spirit was broken. His actions became focused on getting his excommunication lifted and regaining independence to rule his people. To show he was suppressing the heresy, he sent knights and bailiffs on two occasions to Montségur, demanding that known Good Christians be turned over to them. Their demands were of course refused, and they left without incident.

Unfortunately, on a third occasion in 1235, they seized a deacon and three Good Christians from the terraced village growing rapidly outside the walls of the castle, where we could do little to protect them. The three were burned in Toulouse as a warning of what would befall others who defied the church. Corba was devastated at the news.

Despite the count's desperate efforts to regain control, he remained little more than a pawn in the hands of Blanche and the royal seneschal. In 1237, Count Raymond's only child, Jeanne de Toulouse, was married to Alphonse de Poitiers, guaranteeing the eventual absorption of our lands into the Kingdom of France.

In that same year, a more personal tragedy befell us. Corba's uncle Guillaume Bernard Hunaud de Lanta was captured and condemned to death by the Inquisition in Toulouse for being a Cathar. I had known him well; he had been a frequent visitor to Montségur. He strove only to lead a pure life, which for him, like many others, meant rejecting the church and its avaricious and murderous priests.

Corba desperately wanted to go before the Inquisition to plead for his life, but I forced her to accept that no good would come of it. We were already condemned by the Inquisition for supporting the heresy. If she went before the tribunal, she would be arrested and likely burned alongside her uncle. His brutal murder greatly deepened her hatred of Catholicism and led her to spend still more time among the Good Christian preachers.

In 1238, after further pleas from Count Raymond to the pope to end the murderous extremes of the Inquisition in our lands, Pope Gregory agreed to suspend the Inquisition until 1241. During these years, however, the scourge of the Inquisition continued to spread like a plague in neighboring countries. Inquisitions were established in Aragón, Castile, Leon, and Navarre, and priests and bishops were gleeful as thousands were burned.

By the summer of 1241, all the main seats of resistance against the occupation forces had been taken by the French. Carcassonne, which had been besieged by the Aragónese forces of Raymond-Roger IV was relieved by the French royalist forces and Raymond-Roger driven back into exile. Many inhabitants of the towns who had joined in the insurrection on the return of Raymond-Roger were slaughtered in retribution. The Occitan strongholds of Fenouillèdes and Peyrepertuse submitted to the invaders, leaving the only beacons of Occitan freedom still burning at Montségur and the strong fortress of Queribus.

As the persecutions worsened across the region, the community at Montségur swelled with Good Christians and believers who sought sanctuary. Our small castle, already burgeoning with our close family and the knights and men-at-arms, had no room to shelter them, and so a small village grew up on the terraces outside our walls. I am afraid conditions there were very poor; there was little to protect them from the biting winds that battered the pog frequently during the long winter months. However, despite their suffering, few complained, and all took great care of one another.

Corba and I grew closer as the world around us darkened. I was increasingly exposed to the teachings of the Good Christians in our midst, and each day, I became less secure in my faith in the Church of Rome.

CHAPTER 48

To Rile the Beast

1241, Summer – Castle of Montségur

"My Lord," announced Pierre-Roger de Mirepoix, "French troops alongside those of Count Raymond are encamped at the base of the pog. They mean to lay siege to us."

I shook my head in reluctant acceptance of the inevitable. "I was told it would happen. I had news from the court in Toulouse that Raymond had promised the new king, Louis IX, to 'destroy the Cathar nest in Montségur.' He deceives himself into believing that it will advance his cause with the regent."

"His cause is lost. These are sad days for Occitania. I could give fight to these invaders and show them there are still Occitanians who have kept their honor," he said.

"Sheath your swords until I know our position. Those we protect counsel peace over bloodshed. We should heed them. Are these invaders an imminent threat?"

"Not in their present number. Their siege is like a sieve, for many of the Occitan troops sympathize with our cause. Some are even believers. They will allow our men to pass through their lines unhindered and unseen by the French. The French do not know the ways up the pog, so for now, they are no threat to us."

"Then leave them be. We will give them no excuse to escalate their siege. God willing, they will melt away before the winter snows."

And so it was. Raymond's troops returned to Toulouse along with the French after only minor skirmishes with us. Our community had once again been spared. We hoped our existence would continue to slip by the outside world. Alas, that was not to be.

1242, May 27 – Castle of Montségur

Two knights of Pierre Roger de Mirepoix slipped unnoticed from the citadel of Montségur and descended one of the secret paths down the side of the pog. Horses were waiting for them in the valley. They rode hastily down the road to Bram.

In Bram, the two knights, Guilhem and Pierre-Raymond de Planha, sought out Jordanet of the Mas St. Puelles. He arranged for them to meet secretly with Raymond d' Alfaro, provost of the count of Toulouse and bailiff of the castle of Avignonet. Raymond had sent word to Pierre-Roger that he had urgent information for him. Raymond was an illegitimate nephew of the count of Toulouse and clandestine believer. Avignonet was a small town at an important crossroads between Toulouse and Carcassonne.

Raymond d'Alfaro reached into a leather pouch. "Take this letter to Pierre-Roger, none other. Protect it with your life. Make haste to Montségur." Raymond d' Alfaro looked slowly around the other people in the poorly lit tavern. "The inquisitors are coming back. They will be staying in Avignonet tomorrow night," he said nervously.

"But how can we act on this?" asked Pierre-Raymond in a hushed voice. "They will be well protected."

"It is all in the letter. I have made arrangements. We can strike a blow against these murderous priests." His eyes squinted with venom. He or someone close to him had clearly suffered at the hands of the Inquisition. He would exact his price from them. "May the Good God speed you back to Montségur. It would be safest if we did not leave together, the Church has its spies everywhere."

Intently aware of the importance of their task, the two knights rode to the castle at great haste, taking side roads wherever possible to avoid detection.

On their return, Guilhem and Pierre-Raymond were immediately escorted to Raymond-Roger. The knights knelt and handed him the letter. Pierre-Roger read it. His face lit with excitement. "Come. We have much to do! And much to profit from in this! But we must move quickly. The chief inquisitors of Toulouse, Etienne de Saint-Thibery and Guillaume-Arnaud, and their assistants and notaries will arrive in Avignonet tomorrow night, where they will fete the eve of the Ascension. We shall cut off the head of this serpent before it has a chance to sink its fangs into the flesh of Montségur."

"Sire, should not Lord Raymond de Péreille be apprised of this?" Guilhem asked.

"It would be best if his hands were not upon this act. I am already an outlaw, so they can do no worse against me. The Lord de Péreille appointed me commander of the garrison, and I will do what I judge necessary to carry out my duties."

1242, May 28 – Castle of Montségur

At dawn, Pierre-Roger quietly slipped from Montségur with about sixty men-at-arms, counting among them fifteen knights. They rode at great haste through Montferrier, Villeneuve d' Olmes, Lavelanet, and Mirepoix before resting at Gaja-la-Selves. There, they were joined by a second group under the command of Pierre de Mazerolles and Jordans Vilar. Most men carried hatchets and cudgels. Two had crossbows. All were well versed in the art of warfare.

Around mid-afternoon near Payra, which lies close to the castle of Antioche, the conspirators split into four groups to maximize their safety and the success of their plan. One group took up a position on the road between Castelnaudary and St. Martin Lalande. Their role would be to ambush the inquisitors if by some means they managed to flee the castle. Another group was concealed in the wastelands above the Mas St. Puelles, while a third took a position to the west of Avignonet. The last group, which included Pierre-Roger and Guilhem de Planha, hid in the Antioch Wood, close to the Mas St. Puelles on the outskirts of Avignonet. By evening, all were awaiting a signal.

Inside the castle, Guillaume-Raymond Golairan, a knight and confidante of Raymond d'Alfaro, was entertaining his guests.

"We are told these parts are rife with heretics. Is that so?" the grand inquisitor Guillaume-Arnaud of Raymond asked as he downed a glass of wine.

His companion inquisitor, Etienne de Saint-Thibery, likewise appeared to be looking forward to his work. "God demands we purge these lands of the servants of Satan. There can be no surer place to find them than near his lair at Montségur."

Guillaume-Raymond held his head down to avoid eye contact. "It is true that in the past there were many Cathar sympathizers in these parts. But since Count Raymond swore fealty to King Louis IX, most have fled to Aragón or Lombardy."

"If that is so, our trip here will have been wasted," Guillaume-Arnaud said. "But I do not think it is so, for we have been told otherwise. The heretics in Montségur could not continue to defy us if they were not supplied and fed by sympathizers. Tell me, Guillaume-Raymond, are you a good Catholic? Dou you pray three times a day and tithe?"

Guillaume-Raymond made the sign of the cross, His voice trembled. "Holy Father, I have been a good Catholic all my life. You can ask our priest."

"We intend to," declared Etienne de Saint-Thibery. "He will guide us where we might most fruitfully begin our search."

"I am full from the boar and the wine," Guillaume-Arnaud said. "It was a difficult journey here. Conduct us to our chambers. We will begin God's work early in the morning."

Guillaume-Raymond smiled politely. "Your chambers are well prepared. I trust tonight you will experience true Occitan hospitality."

"We are not here to experience the ways of Occitania," barked Etienne. "We are here to suppress them. We are here to ensure the people of Occitania learn how to lead Christian lives to be spared the tortures of damnation."

"You are doing God's work, Father," Guillaume-Raymond said as he led the entourage to their rooms. "I will pray to the heavenly Father tonight to thank him for sending you to us."

The group of twelve heavily armed men had gathered quietly in a concealed ravine near Baraigne, very close to the castle of Avignonet.

Leading them were three dispossessed knights, Guillaume de Lahille, Bernard de Saint-Martin, and Guillaume de Balaguire, the prime actors in the night's work. Pierre-Roger remained in the Antioch Wood to coordinate the affair. He was too well known to be seen participating in the attack; that could bring down certain destruction down upon Montségur.

The men were cold and growing anxious when they received the signal they had been expecting. As they emerged from their hiding place, they were greeted by Guilhem-Raymond Golairan, who had hurriedly exited the castle. He was accompanied by a companion from Avignonet, Bertrand de Quiriés. "I have lodged the friars and their scribes in the central chamber of the castle keep," Guillaume-Raymond said. "Bertrand here will guide you to the place."

"What about the guards?" asked Guillaume de Lahille.

"Do not fear. Raymond d'Alfaro will see they are occupied elsewhere when you enter. Besides, many are believers who hate the inquisitors as much as any Occitanian. They will not challenge you even if they suspect your purpose."

"When will it be time?" asked Bernard de Saint-Martin. "My sword cries out for retribution."

"Wait until darkness falls over the plain. Then Bertrand will guide you safely inside."

"And what of you?" asked Guillaume.

"I will ride back to the castle to ensure the inquisitors are settled down. God willing, this will be a glorious night for Occitania. One that will give hope to all our people."

Guillaume-Raymond knocked and entered the inquisitors' chambers. "I have brought clean bedpans and fresh linens that you might sleep more deeply tonight. Is there anything else I may bring you?"

"We are communing with God," an inquisitor castigated him. "Be gone and do not disturb us again. We have need of nothing more."

Nor will you again after this night, thought Guillaume-Raymond.

As night finally fell, Bertrand de Quiriés led his men across the plain in front of the castle. "Come in here, to the slaughterhouse," he beckoned. "I will make sure of the path ahead."

The men quietly went inside but did not have long to wait.

Guilhem-Raymond Golayran came to join them with another twenty armed men from Avignonet. He led the party from the slaughterhouse to his home, where torches were waiting for them. "All has been prepared for us. Let us avenge the innocents of Occitan who have been tortured and murdered by these most foul of men."

"They do not deserve to die quickly," cried Guillaume. "Their eyes have feasted on the agonies of those they have condemned."

"Light the torches," Guillaume de Lahille ordered. "These abominations of humanity have lived long enough. Their souls will have to be reborn many times before they are pure enough to escape this world."

Guilhem-Raymond's servants lit the torches. The men marched toward the great gates of the castle. As they came closer, the gates began to creak open. Once they were open wide enough, the knight within came out to beckon them inside and joined their number with a heavy broadsword in his hand. As the conspirators entered the castle, Raymond d'Alfaro greeted them. He was ready for action in a white quilted military tunic.

"You risk soiling that with the blood of demons tonight," someone said, laughing.

"I trust that it is so," he replied.

From out of the shadows, a knight on horseback appeared. "Follow me. I will lead you to the inquisitors' chambers."

When they reached the keep, the door was open as expected. They climbed the spiraling stone staircase. After pausing to prepare themselves, they confirmed that the heavy oak door had been bolted from the inside.

A knight, Bernard de Saint-Martin, who had been condemned to death in absentia by the inquisitors a few years earlier, raised a heavy battle axe. "I will pulverize this barrier that seeks to protect demons from their fate. It will fall heavy upon their skulls for all the loved ones they have taken from me."

The wood began to splinter as Bernard swung at it ferociously. He was not going to rest until his task was accomplished. Others helped him with their axes. The ancient gradually hardwood yielded to their assaults, the door split in two, and fell to the floor with a resounding crash.

"The gates of hell are open!" yelled one man. All lunged into the room and saw a heavy tapestried curtain shrouding the sleeping area. The two inquisitors and five monks were kneeling and praying with their heads bowed. A notary and three bailiffs cowered in their beds.

Bernard de Saint-Martin swung his axe first with a terrifying force driven by his sheer abomination for those on whom it fell. His companions hacked the monks with swords, axes, knives, and spears. The savagery the Church of Rome had visited upon Occitania over a twenty-year period, first at the hands of Simon de Montfort and the crusaders and then with the Inquisition boiled to the surface. They struck the enemy that had come to their lands with merciless brutality to avenge all the innocents who had been slaughtered. They did so with fury. The two inquisitors, the most hated, bore the brunt of the blows. They were chopped limb from limb, until there was little left that was recognizable as a human being.

When the killing orgy was over, the plotters rifled through the belongings of the monks. They found and burned the Inquisition registers that listed the names of those suspected of heresy. They took clothes, money, and other valuables. "The church has no right to any of this!" shrieked one man. "It was all stolen from those they murdered. They never did a day's honest work." He spat on their remains.

The conspirators cleaned their weapons and left for Antioch Wood, where Pierre de Mirepoix greeted them, "From the blood on your tunics, I trust you bring me good news."

"We do, my Lord. The inquisitors will torture no more," Jean Acermat said.

"These are glad tidings indeed for all Occitanians," Pierre-Roger said. "Why did you not bring me the head of Guillaume-Arnaud that I might drink from it in celebration?"

"It would do you no good, my Lord, for it is quite broken," he said with a laugh.

"No matter, I would have bound it together with a circlet of gold and drunk from it all my days!" Pierre-Roger said.

After much celebration, the men dispersed to their lodgings. Pierre-Roger and his accomplices rode back to Montségur, pleased with their night's work.

The news of the massacre of the inquisitors spread rapidly throughout Occitania and resulted in widespread rejoicing. People dared to think the scourge of the Inquisition had been lifted; the perpetrators were feted as heroes.

However, the reaction of the church and the French monarch was one of outrage and fear that the attack would lead to greater revolt against them throughout Occitania. They moved without mercy against those who showed sympathy for the revolt. Soldiers and inquisitors swept through the towns and villages, torturing and burning anyone who spoke against them or voiced support for the heresy. In the village of Baraigne, next to Avignonet, where the assassins had hidden, monks of the Inquisition came escorted by soldiers and dug up most of the bodies in the churchyard. They threw the corpses in various states of decay, many among them children, into a pile behind the church. Declaring them all to be heretics and Cathar sympathizers, they piled wood around them and set fire to it, singing as the flames consumed the remains of the loved ones of many villagers who were forced to watch.

Most of those who took part in the murders fled the region. Raymond d'Alfaro sought sanctuary in the north of Italy while Bertrand de Quiriès fled to Lombardy. Our small community at Montségur came close to being overwhelmed by the number of new arrivals each day seeking sanctuary. As I listened to their horrifying tales of suffering, I suspected my loyal but impetuous cousin Pierre-Roger as having been involved in the matter. I felt guilty; I had entrusted him with the safety of all those who looked to me for protection. It appeared his actions had lit a fire that risked burning us all.

I faced him with my suspicions. "Cousin, from many accounts, you are responsible for the massacre of the inquisitors at Avignonet. Do you deny it?"

"I do not deny it. I am proud of it. I did it for the safety of Montségur."

Anger and sickness overtook me. "The safety of Montségur? That bloody night's work may well result in the downfall of us all! You poked the dragon between its eyes. It will breathe fire on our mountain. After this, the church and Louis IX, who is a besotted Catholic like his mother, will not rest until they have destroyed us."

"They were already intent on destroying us, good cousin! Guillaume Arnaud and his companions were to establish an inquisitional tribunal in Avignonet. The safe houses, the secret rooms, the paths the Good

Christians follow to and from the pog and that we depend on for supplies would have been endangered by an inquiry so close. My actions have bought us some time to prepare."

"Prepare? Do you imagine our few numbers could hold off a full-scale attack?"

"My Lord, Montségur is well situated. We have already fought off one attack."

"That was by Occitan troops under Count Raymond. Many of them had friends or relatives in our castle. They had no heart in the fight. If we are attacked again, it will be by French troops. They will not make the mistake of trusting Count Raymond again."

"We cannot be sure of that. Count Raymond is a useful puppet the regent uses to do her bidding while she wins favor with the people."

"Thanks to you, no longer! I have word the legates renewed their excommunication against him, for they suspect him of involvement in the murders."

"Even the French will find it difficult to besiege the pog. There are no hills from which they can bombard us. The French are unfamiliar with the area. The people will give them little help. If we hold out until the winter, the French will melt away with the snow."

"I pray you are right. But as the lord and co-lord of Montségur, we must protect its people. We cannot trust in prayers alone, and there are many Good Christians here who can pray better than we can. We must devote all our energies to preparing for a siege."

"I have already given orders to do so," declared Pierre-Roger, much to my surprise. "I have sent to Queille for Arnaud de Villar to come to take charge of improving our defenses. He installed the arbalettes that helped us fend off the last siege. I will ask him to raise and strengthen the walls. My brother Isarn will see we are well stocked with food, water, and arms. They will not starve us out as Simon de Montfort did so successfully to many of the fortresses."

"I am glad to see you take the threat to our safety seriously. Pity you did not give it more thought before riding out to Avignonet. But that is behind us. Let us get to work. The first priority is the barbican and the tower on the Roc de la Tour, both of which need much work. They sit at the lowest point of the plateau and therefore are our most vulnerable points. They must be garrisoned at all times."

"I will give the order immediately. From the tower, the guards can readily hurl projectiles down upon any attackers that attempt to assail us up the narrow path on the eastern slope of the pog. I have confidence that we will be able to hold it."

Much to my relief, for the remainder of 1243, no army moved against the pog. That was not due to a lack of resolve on the part of our enemies but because the church and the French king had greater threats to contend with. Rebellious uprisings against the much-hated Church of Rome and its priests continued to flare up across the region. The church suppressed them with its usual brand of Christian brutality.

In July of that year, King Henry III of England, urged by Count Raymond VII, brought his army to Aquitaine to press his claims on the southern lands over those of Louis IX. However, the count as usual proved to be an untrustworthy ally and transferred his loyalty to Louis. With the loss of his promised support from Count Raymond and the count of Foix, the English forces suffered defeat at the battle of Taillebourg.

In January 1243, Count Raymond VII signed a definitive peace agreement, referred to as the Peace of Lorris, with the French king near Montargis. The treaty finally ended his opposition to French rule over Occitania. In return, Louis granted him a full pardon for past transgressions. However, the church, still fuming over the murder of the inquisitors, refused to lift his excommunication.

With his principal antagonists defeated, Louis was free to act against the last vestiges of opposition to his rule in the southern lands, those of us taking sanctuary at Montsegúr.

CHAPTER 49

The Vice Tightens

1243, April – Catholic Council at Béziers

"I appeal before you to lift my excommunication from the church," pleaded Count Raymond VII. "I have sworn fealty to King Louis and agreed to abide by all the terms of the Treaty of Meaux."

The monks across the table scowled. "You ask us for absolution from your sins while those who murdered our brothers Guillaume-Arnaud and Etienne de Saint-Thibery, humble servants of Christ, go unpunished," said inquisitor Brother Ferrier in anger. "Some even question whether your hands are clean of their blood."

"Before God, I swear to you I had no knowledge of or took any part in that act. It was vile and unchristian. I condemn it."

"Even so, the perpetrators of this crime have not been brought to justice," said Pierre Amiel, the archbishop of Narbonne.

"And you continue to permit the Cathar heresy to spread its wickedness from the mountain lair of Montsegúr," one of the papal legates spat out.

The count was uneasy. He had come asking forgiveness, not to be accused once more of being a heretic. He was desperate to convince them he had done all he could to fight the heresy. "My forces laid siege to the castle, but they did not have the strength to take it. The castle sits on top of the pog of Montsegúr and is near impregnable to attack. It rises nearly four hundred feet above the surrounding and dense forest of Corbières. All three sides of the mountain are near vertical in places, with treacherous rocky crags and crevasses that make them impossible to assail or pull war machines up. Access to the pog is but by a very narrow path well guarded and controlled by a barbican."

"If you cannot exterminate the heretics, we will find someone who can," barked Brother Ferrier.

"I swear to you that if you lift my excommunication and provide me with more troops, I will lay siege to Montsegúr and remain until it has fallen."

Brother Ferrier was dismissive. "I will oppose lifting your excommunication until the murderers of my fellow inquisitors are brought before the tribunal," he said, seething with hatred. "God's justice for them will be swift and unforgiving!"

Archbishop Pierre Amiel was calmer but no more positive in his response. "Your request to be included in the body of Christ will be a matter for the new pope to consider. You will have to petition him. We shall not lift it."

"Then I shall go to Rome to make my case before the holy father."

"That is your choice," replied the archbishop. "But you will not be entrusted again with the fall of this synagogue of Satan. King Louis has put that important task in the hands of one of his military commanders. You are to cooperate with him fully. Is that clear?"

The count nodded. "I will do whatever he asks."

Inquisitor Ferrier stood and raised his arm in the air. "We shall finally cut off the head of the dragon!"

"We shall strike this hydra heresy and cut off its spreading tentacles," a monk said.

The archbishop of Narbonne held his hand out for order. "It is agreed then. The excommunication of Count Raymond stands. He will give his full assistance to the king's seneschal of Carcassonne, Hugues des Arcis, to lead an assault against Montsegúr. All who fight with him will receive the blessings of the church and know they are fighting in the name of Jesus Christ. This conclave is concluded."

1243, May – Castle of Montsegúr

It had been on the eve of Ascension Day one year earlier the inquisitors had been murdered. We were to pay a terrible price for that act. French soldiers from Gascony and Aquitaine arrived to set up camp in the valley below the pog on Ascension Day. Over the coming weeks they were joined by troops from Toulouse and Carcassonne. During the day, we heard the noise of their horses and the beating of hot iron by their smithies. At night, we could smell smoke and charring meat. The quiet, contemplative world of the pog had been overwhelmed by their presence.

At the beginning of the siege, our community in Montségur numbered around five hundred souls. Among those were most members of my family, which included my dear wife Corba and our mothers, our four beloved daughters, and our son Jourdain, plus my sister Alazais de Massabrac.

My cousin Pierre-Roger had brought with him even more family members and companions. His household numbered around seventy. They were, however, much to our benefit, for many among them were men-at-arms. Eighteen were battle-hardened knights, six were skilled riders, still more were foot soldiers of various skills, and two or three wielded crossbows.

In addition to the fighting men pledged to Pierre-Roger, there were at least another ten independent knights, approximately sixty archers, additional soldiers, and hired mercenaries, bringing the total number of defenders to around a hundred and fifty. Attached to these were wives, mistresses, children, and servants.

Our number included artisans, blacksmiths, weavers, healers, and the like to support our existence, plus two hundred Good Christians and their families who had fled to us.

Contrary to the propaganda spread by the church, many in our community did not practice the heresy. They had come with friends or relatives who were believers. They saw no sin in living and praying alongside their heretical brethren. While remaining practicing Catholics, they rejected the hatred the church would have them feel toward those it had excommunicated. Their tolerance was a vile anathema to the church, but tolerance had always been our way before Pope Innocent III had sent his barbarian hordes to our lands.

Our families and most of the soldiers were housed within the walls of the castle, as were the horses and all critical provisions. Conditions were very overcrowded. The small village on the terraces outside our walls continued to expand. The Good Christians, and those who came to live alongside them, constructed their own accommodation. These were very basic and gave little protection from the driving rain or snows that battered us during the winter, but they did not complain. They continued their trades to exchange for food with the villagers.

After the assassinations of the inquisitors, financial contributions to the Friends of God increased significantly. The Good Christians, who had taken vows of poverty, could not profit directly from it. However, their church accepted it graciously and paid for much of the work to improve our defenses. Their support also paid for some of the highly trained mercenaries who came to help us stave off the siege.

1243, September – Castle of Montsegúr

"Corba, your hair is windblown," I said. "You must have been outside the castle."

She smiled gently, as if somewhat lost to the world. "Yes, I have. It is a beautiful day. I walked along the hilltop and into the forest. There is such beauty in the natural world. The Devil may have trapped our souls in mortal shells and created the physical world, but it was the Good God who gave it such beauty to relieve our suffering."

"I am envious. I wish I could see the beauty as you do. When I walk around the pog, I do not see trees, flowers, or birds. I see only the French, I hear only the French, and I smell only the French. They are intent on destroying everything I hold dear. There can be no beauty in our situation for me until they are gone."

Corba's face lit up. "Oh my dear! Do you think they will leave us?"

I scolded myself for having given her cause for premature optimism. "My love, I hope they will leave in time, but I have seen no sign of it yet. Maybe winter will force them to abandon the siege. It will depend on the resolve of their commander."

The Chrysalis of Oc

Corba took my hand. "Well, you should not be blinded to God's beauty until winter. You must spend time among the Good Christians. They can instruct you how to see the beauty before your eyes despite the evil the Devil has sent to cloud it. They will help you understand our true place in this world and explain that most of what appears of value is no more than illusion. Worldly possessions, transitory and worthless, are not worth fighting or killing for. The evil one makes man lust for worldly riches, but all that really matters is preparing our souls for heavenly riches."

"You have spent too much time with the preachers. I fear I may lose you to them."

"You have nothing to fear. You will not lose me." She smiled. "Our souls are destined to find each other even if we are separated for a time. The Good Christians will explain it to you. I will listen to Guilhabert de Castres preach this afternoon. Will you come with me?" Her eyes lit up. She smiled hopefully.

I could not refuse her. "I will come. Providing other matters do not detain me."

"Wonderful! I will look for you. Now I must go to help at the infirmary."

"What is our status?" I asked Pierre-Roger.

"Unchanged, sire. The French seem content to wait us out in hopes we will run out of food or water. There is no sign they are preparing to attack us. Thankfully, our wells did not dry up in the summer, and the winter rains will replenish them."

"How are we for provisions?"

"We are well furnished with food. Isarn has had few problems bringing supplies through the French lines up the hidden trails. Fortunately, the French did not have enough troops for an effective siege, so they were forced to supplement their number with Occitan soldiers from Count Raymond and other Occitan lords. Many are sympathetic to our cause."

"I am ill at ease with this waiting game. I long to know their next move. What do you estimate is their strength?"

"Probably around two thousand, no more."

"And what of their commander, Hugues des Arcis? He is said to be cautious and level headed. A popular man with his troops."

Pierre-Roger nodded. "That is also what I hear from the Occitan troops who serve under him. He is certainly no Simon de Montfort. He will not risk his men on foolhardy missions as we have already seen these many months."

"True. He has besieged us for four months but has not launched a serious attack. Simon de Montfort could not have held himself back for so long even if he risked defeat. He has merely sent sorties against us to probe our defenses. I am glad to say we swiftly repulsed them each time. As long as the projectiles from his arbalettes and trebuchets cannot reach the castle, our position is safe."

"We must thank those who constructed the castle on this mountain," Pierre-Roger said. "for the site was well chosen. There is no ground high enough for him to fire at us. In desperation, his troops tried ascending the path up the eastern side of the pog, but it was a hopeless attempt. Our arbalettes behind the barbican hailed them with stones. They retreated in panic."

"It seems we have reached a stalemate."

"It would seem so, my Lord."

A stalemate? The idea did not sit well with me, nor, I feared, with Hugues des Arcis. "He is clearly a patient man, which worries me. We should all pray hard for him to withdraw when winter sets in, just as the crusaders always did. However, I am troubled that he may have been forged on a different anvil."

1243, Early December – Castle of Montsegúr

December's harsh weather increased the suffering of all on the pog. In the castle, life was difficult. We were very cramped in the drafty castle. However, we had the consolation of fires and blankets and a plentiful supply of bread, food, and wine.

In comparison, there were few comforts for those trying to cling to their meager existences in the dwellings outside our walls. Their living conditions were abysmal. Their shelters of mud and straw did little to protect them from the fierce winds, snow, and ice. Built as they were on steep terraces, it is a wonder many of their dwellings did not blow off the mountain. Most slept on straw on top of rock with only thin blankets to cover themselves.

In the village, the Good Christian men and women lived apart, as was required by their vows. Once they had given their souls to God, they could not share them with another mortal. I was in awe that despite the horrendous conditions, the faithful were sustained by their unshakable belief that worldly comforts were of little importance compared to the rewards awaiting them in heaven.

While the soldiers occupied themselves with our defenses, the Good Men and Women kept our community functioning. They were millers, weavers, bakers, blacksmiths, and cobblers. They prepared all our food and made our clothes, shoes, and coverings. They mended whatever was broken and helped soldiers chop trees or move rocks.

The Good Christians also took care of our spiritual needs. Every day, they came into the castle to instruct the soldiers and their families in how to lead good lives. As conditions worsened, the Good Christians and their fellow believers became increasingly occupied with caring for and consoling the sick. Corba, who had always been one to empathize with those who were suffering, assisted them. She was spending most of her waking hours in the house of the sick. This was especially so after the bishop of Toulouse, Guilhabert de Castres, whom she revered so much, was confined there with illness.

After Guilhabert's confinement, the Good Christian Bernard Marty assumed his responsibilities and preached daily to the garrison and to the many visitors who despite the siege were still able to go and come relatively freely from and to the pog. The visitors were usually escorted up or down the mountain at night by those who knew the many secret trails and difficult climbs plus the hidden trails through the forest and the French lines.

As the siege continued, there was widespread hope among many that we would not be abandoned by Count Raymond. I did not share their optimism, but as lord de Péreille and overlord of Montségur, my duty was to explore all avenues of hope. To that end, I sent an emissary to the count to plead with him to use his good counsels with the pope or the king of France to lift the siege. His reply came back within a few days.

He would not intervene. His excuse was that if he showed sympathy to our cause, his excommunication would never be lifted. He argued he could help us more by continuing to support us covertly by ensuring we received arms and supplies.

In hindsight, I see his behavior was duplicitous. He was giving our people the illusion of hope while actually serving those who were persecuting them. He had made a pact with the Devil in Meaux to save his title and had surrendered his soul in payment.

I thought it best not to let Count Raymond's response be known to most of our inhabitants. They did not need to know they had been deserted by their lord. Only a few others shared my burden in that matter. Maintaining the morale of the garrison and defending us against the onslaught of the Catholic forces became my priority.

When on occasion, some poor soul would run through the village declaring he had seen a beacon fire on a neighboring mountain to tell us Count Raymond and his forces were coming to relieve us, I would simply nod and reply, "If God wills it."

It was a cold day a week or so before Christmas as Pierre-Roger and I walked on patrol around the pog. The ground was white, and it was very quiet as a dense fog clung to the sides of the pog below us and cut us off completely from the sight and sounds of the valley.

"I wish it were as it seems today that we were alone on this mountain floating on a soft sea of clouds with no danger below." I was dreaming aloud.

"Aye, would that it were so," Raymond-Roger said. "I have talked to many whose spirits are uplifted by not having to look down on the French troops. They pray that when the fog blows away, the troops will melt away with it."

"I am glad they still dream that things will be better, for it shows they have not lost hope. Unfortunately, I cannot afford that luxury. Hugues des Arcis is dug in for the winter?"

"I am afraid that is what our contacts tell us," Raymond-Roger said. "But they also say there is widespread discontentment in the French camp. Many want to go home. They see nothing to be gained by waiting out the winter and freezing to death."

"That is some reason for hope. See what you can do to encourage that sentiment. If we can remove the noose from around our necks, I will breathe much easier," I said.

We were interrupted by the sound of cracking twigs from below. "What was that? A goat perhaps?" I asked. We drew our swords and lay down in the snow, as the noises grew louder. We heard voices. They were speaking Occitan. My heart stopped pounding so heavily.

A party of four appeared from the forest. Leading them was one of Isarn de Fanjeaux's men. The others—a man, a woman, and a young boy—I did not know. We stood, swords still in hand.

"My Lord, I am Raymond de Belvis, a carpenter. This is my family. We are all true Christians and believers and ask permission to join you. We should like to learn from the Good Christians how we might dedicate our lives to God."

"You are of course welcome," I said. "Unfortunately, our conditions are poor at best, and our rations meager. However, you will find the hearts of those you seek to be warmer than any fire in the French camp below, and you will not lack instruction."

The man bowed, as did his wife and child. I sent them to the village outside our walls, where I was confident a warm welcome would be given them.

1243, December 20 – French Camp at the Base of Montsegúr

The sergeant at arms rubbed his hands together briskly to ward off frostbite. It was dark. The night was especially cold. "Commander, we have lost more men today. I fear we will not be able to keep many of the mercenaries even if we pay them what they are owed. Our own men are demanding we break camp and return in the spring. In the eight months we have been here, we have made little progress against the heretics."

Hugues des Arcis shrugged at hearing what he already knew. "The men are demoralized, understandably. I am as unhappy with our lack of progress as they are, but I will not yield. We have not yet had a successful assault against the pog or managed to maneuver our catapults within range, but we will succeed. I am determined to do so. I have vowed not to leave this place until I have crushed the evil before us. If we give up the siege now, those eight months will have been for naught. The enemy will restock and improve its defenses. If we were to return in the spring, our task would be even more difficult."

"That may well be, my Lord, but I do not know how long we can keep the men from rebelling. They will not endure it much longer."

Hugues shot him a glance with a hint of self-satisfaction. "They may not have to. I have a plan to turn the balance in our favor. I will not reveal it to anyone beyond those involved in its execution, for the enemy has many ears. The endeavor is risky. It will require the element of surprise."

The sergeant looked unhappy but resigned. "I will probe no further except to ask when we might know our profit from this endeavor."

"We will know by morning. It is in motion as we speak."

To avoid attention, the seven men had come separately to meet outside the French camp. Charles and Henri, who had recently arrived from Gascony, were expert mountain climbers. It was upon their skills that the lives of the others would depend that night. Two other men, Guiraud and Bernard, were local Catholic sympathizers with a good knowledge of the area and the mountain. They were to act as guides. The remaining three were French soldiers who were lightly armed. They had been chosen for their youth and agility. All were carrying backpacks with equipment. The climbers had long ropes slung over their shoulders.

"We will talk here," said Charles. "But once we begin the climb, no man is to utter a word. We will try to keep you all safe, but if one of you loses his footing, he should not cry out in his fall. It will not save him, and it will certainly doom the rest of us."

Henri stepped into the light with a map in his hand. "Our plan is to take the Roc de la Tour on the eastern end of the pog, the lowest point on the plateau. We cannot take the trail up to the Roc for there is a tower that commands it and is garrisoned at all times. Before we could even get close to it, we would be stoned. We will go around the eastern edge of the pog and climb up the rocky precipice on the northern side. Guiraud and Bernard have scouted out an ascent route, but it will be very difficult in places."

"Especially in this weather with the ice and at night. You must take great care," warned Charles. "But the darkness will be our ally, as will the difficulty of the climb. No one in the tower will be looking this direction for an attack. It will be a long and arduous climb, but we must make it up the mountain before first light."

"Each man take care. May God watch over us," said Guiraud, making the sign of the cross. The others did likewise before moving off along the trail.

When they reached the base of the mountain, the two Gascony climbers looked up and pointed at various features as they planned their ascent. They debated quietly in Gascon and moved toward the intimidating rock face. They beckoned the others to follow. Even in the darkness, they could sense their companions' fear.

"Keep your eyes on us and the rock immediately beneath your feet," ordered Charles. "On no account look down. That will only disorient you and weaken your resolve."

"Once you commit to the mountain, the only path to safety will be up," Henri said.

The soldiers nodded reluctantly.

The climb challenged even Charles and Henri in places. Several times, they had to change direction when ice or snow made the path too treacherous. The soldiers were inexperienced at climbing and slipped several times on the icy rocks. Fortunately, they were saved by the ropes Charles and Henri had secured to the rocky outcroppings above them. Fierce gusts of wind came close to blowing them off at times or peppered their faces with grains of ice that scoured them like sandpaper.

About half an hour before sunrise, they made it to the plateau. They sat for a moment to catch their breath. They looked at the valley below. A few clasped their hands in prayer and thanks they had made it.

Lying on the snow-covered ground, they looked across the plateau at the tower, their target. They saw light from the window slits and two inattentive guards out front. The French slipped off their backpacks and silently took out their swords and knives. They motioned to each other where each was to go. They ran low toward the tower, crouching each time the guards turned their way. When they were close to the tower, they lay down on the ground.

The guards moved in opposite directions to walk around the tower. The French troops, seizing the opportunity, split up to stalk their prey. It was all over quickly. Out of the darkness, the French soldiers came up from behind each guard and slit his throat. They had no time to call out. They crumbled to the ground; their blood flowing out and melting the snow.

The soldiers turned to the tower entrance. Swords drawn, they moved swiftly inside. Before long, one emerged and waved to the Gascony climbers and the local guides.

In the tower, the handful of soldiers who had constituted the garrison lay dead in pools of blood. Most had simply been run through where they slept. Others had clearly been caught off guard.

"We will stay here to hold the position," said the leader. "Go down the trail and inform Hugues des Arcis the tower is ours," he declared triumphantly.

Pierre-Roger woke me early to break the news the tower on the Roc had been taken. The news stunned me. I tried to convince myself I was having a terrible nightmare, but Pierre's presence was too real.

"I ordered a counterattack as soon as I was informed," he reported. "But we failed to retake the tower. The French had already managed to install a small garrison, and a hail of arrows drove back our soldiers."

"This is dark news indeed. With control of the tower, Hugues des Arcis will construct his war machines on the plateau."

"I am well aware of the danger, my Lord. The wooden barbican still stands between us and the tower, but we will not be able to hold it for long against a bombardment."

"We must try to hold it for as long as we can to give us time to strengthen our walls. Strengthen the garrison on the barbican."

"I have already done that. I anticipate we will be able to hold it until spring, for the French will not be able to do much until then. However, after that, I do not believe our position will be defensible for long against the French artillery."

"Nonetheless, we must hold the barbican as long as possible. It will help our cause if we can harass the French as much as possible as they endeavor to build their war machines."

"I have ordered some of our trebuchets to the barbican. We will pound them with rocks whenever they are in range."

"Let us get with the stonemasons as soon as possible to see how we might strengthen the castle and better protect the village on the terraces."

CHAPTER 50

Blessed Are the Meek, for They Will Be Burned

1243, Christmas Day – Castle of Montsegúr

It was a crisp morning. The sky was the deepest shade of blue. At a prayer service, one Good Christian preached it was a sure sign the Good God would protect us.

Bertrand Marty, the bishop of Toulouse, had organized an outdoor service for all on the mountaintop. Such was the power of his sermons that many believers from the French camp and the villages around had risked the journey up the mountain to attend. As the people gathered for the service, the mountain was eerily quiet, for none would work on that day in our camp and the French outside the barbican had ceased their daily bombardment.

Guilhabert de Castres was there, though his health was failing rapidly and he had to be carried on a litter. Despite that, his spirit remained unshaken. He was confident he had led a good life and would have a good end. No one doubted that when he died, his soul would quickly be reunited with his spirit in heaven.

Bertrand Marty gave a long and rousing sermon aided by the bishop of Razès, Raymond Agulher. Their message was that only those who had been tricked by the Devil would risk salvation for the sake of transitory pleasures. The Catholic Church was not the Church of Christ; it had lost its way and had betrayed Christ's message of poverty, love, and tolerance.

By seeking power and earthly riches, the pope clearly served the Bad God, not the Good God who is the source of eternal salvation.

All were moved by the powerful sermons. Even several of the soldiers I knew to be practicing Catholics were affected by the words; some were in tears. Corba stood by Guilhabert's litter. She had been attending to him in the infirmary in recent days. I had long known she admired him greatly, but I could see she held Bertrand Marty in near-equal awe. As our existence had become more precarious, I had observed her increasingly seeking strength from her faith in the teachings of the Good Christians. When we were alone, she confessed it was all that had kept her going in the face of the terrible brutality she witnessed daily in the infirmary as skirmishes with the French increased.

It was around that time I realized I might lose her.

Bertrand Marty summoned the deacon of Toulouse, Pierre Bonnet, and a fellow Good Christian, Mathieu, to visit him in his quarters after the sermon. They came alone and without fanfare, as he had instructed. The room was dim. The bishop stood with his hands clasped as if in prayer. "Good Christians, the times are dark. The evil one is strong and cunning. He has deceived those who would follow the Good God into following him. Even as they do his vile deeds, they believe they are following the path of Christ and are blinded from seeing the truth. As true Christians, it is our responsibility to return people to the worship and love of the Good God in the manner of the early Christians."

Pierre Bonnet and Mathieu nodded.

"Our situation here is increasingly precarious. The Devil has sent his servants to obliterate us. If he succeeds, his victory over the Good God will be complete, for we are the last refuge of opposition to his enslavement of men's souls. It is my responsibility as a bishop of the church to ensure the true message of Christ is not lost even if Montségur were to fall. It is that responsibility I entrust to you this day, but your task is not without risk."

"You do us a great honor, brother," said Pierre Bonnet. "Our souls are already given over to God, so we will do whatever he requires of us."

Mathieu nodded. "We will risk our lives to carry it out in silence and humility."

Bertrand Marty smiled. "I expected no less." He walked to a darkened corner of the room and returned with a small chest. "I ask you to take this chest off the mountain. You are to take it unseen through the French lines to Queille. There, you are to seek Guillame de Mirepoix, the deacon of Mirepoix. He will provide you with a guide for the final stage of your journey to the caves of Sabarthès. The chest is to be hidden there until the darkness has passed. Your guide will know the location but will not reveal it to you or anyone. You will entrust the chest to him at the caves. At that point, your mission will be complete. You may go where you wish."

"What is in the chest, brother?" asked Mathieu.

"The foundation of our church. There is no greater treasure than what you will carry. Come here to pick up the chest after the sun has set. A servant of Isarn de Fanjeaux will be here to show you a path off the mountain. Speak to no one of this."

1244, January – Castle of Montsegúr

Until the French took the tower on the Roc, the spirits of the soldiers at the castle had remained relatively high despite the adversity of our position. They had been confident that the castle could not be taken and that the French would be forced to lift the siege. In the past few days, though, all that had changed. The French had gained a foothold on the plateau, and we did not have the strength to dislodge them. Their attacks on the barbican were increasing daily, and all in the castle were coming to realize we could not hold it for long. Once the enemy overran the barbican, nothing would prevent Hugues from assembling his war machines before the castle and bombarding us mercilessly. It would only be a question of time before our submission.

To counter the increasing despair, Pierre-Roger did his best to rouse the spirits of his men and give them hope of victory. He organized several daring raids on the French positions to slow down their efforts, but he was unable to do any lasting damage.

In January, the weather was on our side. The bitter cold, biting winds, and ice made the steep mountain trails treacherous, and heavy snows thwarted the French preparations.

But even the Good Christians could not prevent spring from arriving. The experienced soldiers in the garrison grew increasingly apprehensive that the French would soon become stronger and organized enough to overwhelm us. They would have an abundant supply on the plateau of all the materials they needed to build their war machines, wood and projectiles for trebuchets and mangonels were in abundance.

As the threat increased, our community grew closer spiritually. The daily sermons given by the Good Christian men and women drew ever increasing attendance. For many of the soldiers and their families who were Catholic, their message of a tolerant, accepting, and loving God was in stark contrast to the vengeful, murderous, and intolerant God they had been threatened with by the priests of the Church of Rome. Inevitably, many became believers and submitted themselves to the oath of the *Convenensa*. In that ceremony, they promised to assist and honor the Good Christians. In return, the Good Christians promised to come to them if they were close to death and administer the Consolamentum to ensure them a good death even if they were too incapacitated to request it.

As the winter receded, the French brought more troops and engineers up the mountain. By the end of the month, the barbican was being subjected to continuous bombardment. At first, the defensive wall held up, but after weeks of ferocious pounding, the great timbers weakened and began to split.

Despite the perils faced by those manning and repairing our defenses, we never lacked volunteers for even the most forward positions. The terrifying sight, which was becoming all too commonplace, of people being crushed and killed or having limbs torn off by projectiles did not deter others from stepping in. I marveled at this, but by then, our community had become one extended family. Each of the injured or killed was known by all.

Though the Good Christians would not participate in the fighting, they risked their lives in our defense. Those skilled in carpentry and metalwork labored alongside our soldiers under heavy fire to repair the damage done to the barbican. But day by day, it became obvious they were steadily losing the battle.

One day, Pierre-Roger strode into the room, interrupting Corba and Esclarmonde as they were enthusiastically recounting to me the content of a recent sermon of Bertrand Marty. It had been a welcome distraction from the worry that was beginning to obsess my waking hours. Pierre-Roger's manner filled me with foreboding. I dismissed Corba and Esclarmonde, not wanting to burden them. "It is clear you have urgent news. Are the French ready to sue for peace?" I said in jest. It did not have the desired effect. Pierre-Roger looked confused for a moment before his previous serious demeanor returned.

"My Lord, I have just inspected the barbican and find it breached in several places. It cannot be held much longer."

"But can it not be repaired? We have ample wood and stone."

Pierre-Roger grimaced. "We have the materials to repair it, but we cannot. It is much too dangerous. The barbican is under constant bombardment."

I had known for some time we would have to abandon the barbican, but like death, I had hoped that day would always be in the future. Now it was before me. "What do you advise?"

"We must abandon the barbican and fall back to our defenses in front of the castle."

"But without the barbican," I said, "the French will bring their siege engines up to our walls. We shall be in constant danger of being crushed by their large rocks, especially those in the village on the terraces."

"My Lord, we have no choice," he said as if the failure was his alone.

"If we have no choice, there is no decision to make. I do not doubt your judgment in matters of warfare, but this will put us all in grave danger. And what of the castles defenses? How long do you predict we will be able to hold out?"

"One or two months, perhaps, my Lord. It will depend on the effectiveness of our artillery and of theirs. I have sent for Bernard de Capdenac to aid us. He is an expert at constructing war machines. With his help, we should be able to inflict a heavy toll on the French and at least slow them down."

"The time will be welcome, but I am not sure it will avail us of much. Our options are few. The only acceptable option is to find a way to drive these accursed French and their priests off the mountain. The consequences of all other options tear heavily at my heart."

Pierre-Roger shared my anguish. His expression lightened slightly as if he had found new cause for hope. "What about the count? Maybe he will finally acknowledge the duty he has to defend his people. Maybe he can petition the pope or the king of France to end the siege."

I shook my head sorrowfully. "I am afraid there is little hope of that, for he does not have the fighting spirit of his father. He believes he can regain his power by appeasing his masters in Paris and Rome. However, at this point, I am obliged to exhaust all options that might save our people. I shall appeal to him for help, but I expect little to come of it."

"I will have Isarn deliver it to him. I will also ask him to plead with the count on our behalf," Pierre-Roger said.

"Very good. I will see it is done this day. But do not allow any hope of salvation by the count to distract you from your duties. For now, we have only ourselves to depend on."

"I am only too aware of that, and you know I will give it my all. No one has fought against the Church of Rome and its French allies more than I. As commander of the garrison, however, it is my duty to advise you that our position is extremely precarious. I have absolute confidence in my men. They are valiant and will readily give their lives to defend the castle, but they are too few in number, and our armaments are limited. We will likely not be able to hold off a sustained attack."

"I agree. You and your men have demonstrated countless times great courage. All here owe their lives to those knights and soldiers who came voluntarily to defend us. I would not seek their sacrifice any more than I would seek the sacrifice of the true Christians who came to us for protection. My challenge is to find a way all will be saved."

"I will try to think again of how we might drive the French off the plateau. Before they captured the tower, we were relatively secure. But now they are well entrenched and close. Even on the plateau itself, we are greatly outnumbered. I will commune with my knights to consider our options, but whatever we decide, it will take time to organize."

"See that Bernard de Capdenac comes as soon as possible. It is imperative that we hold the barbican as long as we can. Its loss will weigh heavily on all our spirits."

1244, February – Castle of Montsegúr

Despite all our efforts and much loss of life, the barbican's timbers were destroyed by a constant hail of heavy rocks from the French trebuchets. What remained was pulverized by the mighty French ramming machines. In the end, I had no choice but to give the order to abandon it. Our losses had become unsustainable.

Once inside the barbican, Hugues des Arcis ordered his forces to move their war machines up to the timber-framed defenses outside the castle gates. In short time, he demolished those as well, leaving the castle and much of our community living on the rocky terraces fully exposed to the rain of death from French artillery.

In the middle of the month, we had a bloody day indeed. I was wounded but fortunately not seriously.

"Come," cried Corba. "Let me tend to your wounds."

"Go tend to others who need you more," I urged her. "I have little more than cuts. Most of the blood on me is not mine."

"Esclarmonde is at the infirmary. She is tending the wounded and together with the Good Christians is consoling the dying."

"Hugues des Arcis thought that we were broken and that he could take us by storm, but he found much to his cost the morale of our defenders is still strong and that the walls of Montsegúr stand firm. We fight for all Occitanians. I wager that he will not try to attack us again for a while. With the Good God's help, we may yet overcome them."

"I am glad you are safe, my love, but the Good God does not take sides in warfare, according to the Good Christians. He eschews all violence. The God of the Old Testament leads men to violence. Yet all killing is for naught. Our physical existence is but a short breath in the scale of time. We must use what time we have to purify our souls in preparation for the eternal life with God, not to kill others over physical pleasures."

"These are high ideals you speak of, and undoubtedly the world would be a much better place if all thought as do the Friends of God. But they do not, and as overlord of Montsegúr, I have a sworn duty to protect those in my care in the world as it is. In this, I hope the Good God will look favorably upon me."

Corba smiled. "Of course he will, but killing is still not his way. Go to the infirmary and look at the torn limbs, the gaping wounds, the terrible suffering, and the death everywhere. No one can claim to see the hand of the Good God in that. Only the Bad God can rejoice in such a sight."

"My Lord," announced Pierre-Roger, "the French have brought their ballista close to our ramparts. It can hurl rocks into the castle."

"Yes, and onto the terraces," I said. "Corba told me several Good Christians were killed this morning by a projectile that crashed through their roof."

"I also lost two men on the ramparts to crossbow fire," said Pierre-Roger.

"Is there anything we can do about it?" I implored him.

"We are trying. Bernard de Capdenac is targeting our improved trebuchets on the French war machines and those operating them. His devices are very effective and have done heavy damage to the French on several occasions, putting them out of action. We have also killed many of the French, but each time, our relief has been only temporary. They have repaired the machines very quickly and brought in fresh crews."

"Will these French never tire of this siege? Are they not ready to return to France?"

"They tire just as we do, my Lord, but we reap no benefit from it. In the French camp those who tire are quickly replaced. My contacts inform me Hugues has recently received fresh troops and has been reprovisioned with food and supplies."

The news could not have been more dispiriting. One of my last vestiges of hope seemed dashed. But I was not yet ready to accept defeat and pay the ultimate price. "We must assume Hugues des Arcis will press his advantage until he has taken Montségur."

"I fear so, my Lord."

"We must do all we can to prevent it."

"Without more men, I fear our cause is lost. My men are prepared to fight to the end, but I cannot in good conscience ask that of them if it will avail nothing. As much as it pains me to suggest it, I believe we must consider terms of surrender."

"No! I will not consider surrender. Not until all hope is beyond us. Did we hear from Count Raymond?"

"My Lord, the Good Christian Mathieu returned only this morning with news of the count. I have not spoken to him yet."

"Send for him immediately."

Mathieu was accompanied by the two knights of Isarn de Fanjeaux, Guillaume Mir and Raymond Dejean. "My Lord de Péreille, Count Raymond sends his greetings."

"I am more in need of his sword than of his greetings," I said impatiently.

"My Lord, my master Isarn de Fanjeaux has spoken with Count Raymond," responded Guillaume Mir. "He is in Italy with him at this moment meeting with the Holy Roman Emperor, Frederick II, King of Germany, Italy, and Burgundy."

"I have heard good things of this emperor, this 'astonishment of the world' who defies the pope and like us has been excommunicated. What seeks he of Frederick?" I asked.

"There is no love lost between Innocent IV and the emperor, my Lord. Count Raymond hopes to raise an army to drive the French and papal forces from our lands."

"What is the chance he will succeed?"

"The count informed us that negotiations are going well," answered Raymond Dejean. "But it will take time."

"Time is the one thing we do not have! Did you speak to him of our plight?"

"We did, my Lord. The count says that he supports your cause and that if you can hold out until Easter, he hopes to return with an imperial army."

"Idle promises," cursed Pierre-Roger. "The count seeks the emperor's help to recover his lands from the French. He cares little for us or his Occitan subjects. Do not forget that only recently he handed Good Christians over to the Catholic priests for burning to try to help his cause. I have lost faith in his promises."

"He is most certainly no longer a worthy leader of his people. I believe it is very unlikely the emperor will risk warfare with the pope to save the count or a few Occitanians. Count Raymond sees us as mere pawns in his struggle for power. Yet the people are in need of even the smallest glimmer of hope. It could help morale if we let it be known the count has offered to come with an army to lift the siege."

Pierre-Roger shrugged. "As long as we do not believe the lie ourselves, I suppose there is little harm in encouraging such a rumor."

"There is little danger we will be deceived into such complacency, but it could be a support for many. The challenge before us is that while our people are being consoled, we must find a way to bring them true hope."

"Without more troops, I see no way to do that," Pierre-Roger said.

"I will try again to find some. I have heard that two Occitan lords, Arnaud d' Usson and Bernard d' Alion, have men available who are willing to fight in return for gold. I shall send for twenty-five of them without delay."

"I am surely desperate for them, but can they be brought here? Isarn sent word to me that the French noose around the pog draws tighter each day. It may no longer be possible for them to slip through the siege lines."

"Nonetheless, I will try. While I do, plan an attack on the French lines."

"But—"

"I know. We do not have the strength. It will be a desperate action. However, if we surrender, many here will die. We owe it to them to try everything possible to save them."

Pierre-Roger shook his head. He was torn between the loyalty to the men who served under him and those he had taken an oath to protect. But he acquiesced.

"I will prepare a plan of attack. May the Good God show us mercy."

From that point, from one day to the next, our situation grew increasingly desperate.

"Raymond, I have just come from the storerooms," announced Corba. "Our food is running dangerously low and will have to be rationed."

"If they are rationed, how long will they last?"

Corba clearly did not wish to answer. "It is hard to say. Many have already cut back drastically."

"I have heard many Good Christians give most of their food to the soldiers. Even in good times, they eat neither meat, milk, nor eggs, and they fast more days than not. I wonder how they can survive by giving away the little they accept."

"They are nourished by their faith. They are no longer of this earth and do not seek what they can take but rather what they can give."

"If they do not eat, they will truly be no longer of this earth."

"That is of little concern to them. They would welcome the release of their souls from their physical confines. You would find relief from much of your anxiety by talking to them. They will help you see what is truly important in this life. I learned so much from talking to Guilhabert in the infirmary during the few weeks before he died. His words transformed how I look at the world. I no longer live in fear but in tranquility, as he did. I do not fear what the Catholics or the French might do to us, for they have no power over my soul. The only person with power over my soul is me. To return it to heaven, I must strive to lead a pure life without lying or harming others. That will assure me of a good death."

"You are truly fortunate to have found that strength," I said. "I have seen it also in our mothers. Unfortunately, it is difficult for me to detach myself from the physical world and counter the French attempts to terminate our worldly existence."

"You must find time for yourself. It will help you, my love. I promise you."

Pierre-Roger strode into my chamber. "My Lord, we shall launch an attack on the French in the morning as you have commanded."

"What are our chances of success?"

He breathed deeply. "Slim to none, my Lord. The French are well dug in and have an overwhelming artillery advantage."

"Then you would advise against the mission?"

"No, my Lord. I do as you command. You are the overlord of Montségur."

"But you are co-lord since you married Philippa and commander of the garrison."

"I accept that this action is probably our last hope of survival. Nonetheless, it will be a foolhardy and desperate venture. I just pray our losses will not be too great."

"In normal times, I would have never countenanced such an action. However, these are desperate times. Each day we hold out, we lose more men to French projectiles and crossbow bolts. Our losses are becoming unsustainable. If we do nothing, it is only a question of time before the French overrun us."

"I am only too aware of our losses. I know every man who serves under me, and their lives are as dear to me as my own. I did not feel I could command them to go on this mission. However, they all volunteered. They would rather die fighting than be crushed by rocks while cowering behind ramparts. As long as there is even the slightest chance of success, they will fight no matter how great the risk."

"I will go with you. I would ask no man to risk his life for a cause I did not think was worthy of my own."

"My men will draw both comfort and strength from your presence," Pierre-Roger said. "But I ask you to hold back. The castle must have a lord. If we both were to fall, all those within its walls would immediately fall prey to the attackers. We saw such tragedy many times with the sieges of Simon de Montfort. It must not be repeated in Montségur."

"Fear not. I shall take care."

We launched our attack at dawn, but it did not take long to realize its futility.

"Our men are being cut down by the French artillery and crossbows before they even reach the French lines!" yelled Pierre-Roger.

"Can we not blast our way through with our artillery?" I cried back.

"We are trying, but des Arcis has brought up many more troops recently on the eastern end of the plateau. They have installed themselves in heavily defensive positions."

In spite of the heavy losses, our soldiers continued to pour out of the castle to press the attack. Wherever our troops did manage to break through the French lines, they fought ferociously. However, we knew it would not be long before a swarm of French reinforcements would arrive and fall upon them.

Having no more stomach for seeing our men butchered to no avail, I sought out Pierre-Roger again and found him fighting fiercely in hand-to-hand combat. I joined in the mêlée to help him. In the rest of the field, it was clear our attack was lost.

"Sound the retreat," I commanded. "There is nothing further to be gained by this slaughter."

Pierre-Roger gazed intently at me to gauge the sincerity of my command. Sensing my resolve, he blew his horn. Our men fell back.

As we retreated, the French poured out from their lines after us. They tried to turn our retreat into a rout and enter the castle behind us. Our men fought hard and slowed their advance. It was very close, but we managed to close the gates just before a wave of French arrived at our walls.

A couple of days later, Pierre-Roger and I had a painful meeting to discuss the only option now open to us, surrender. It was with a heavy heart I opened our discussion with an assessment of our current situation. "Life is now intolerable for all here. The terraces have been abandoned. As a result, the castle is greatly overcrowded. Everyone cowers in fear of death raining down upon them. Sanitation is a problem. We are running short of food."

"The situation is dire," Pierre-Roger said. "Hugues des Arcis has now pulled the noose so tightly around the pog that we can no longer bring in anything through the siege lines. I have lost many loyal knights I cannot now replace. Those we do have are running low on supplies and ammunition. It is now too dangerous to go into the forest for timber or to quarry rocks outside the castle."

"Given our plight, and though it tears my heart out to say so, I think we both know we have only one option."

Pierre-Roger nodded in sorrow. "We must sue for peace."

"I hear he is not an unreasonable man, a soldier rather than a 'man of God'," I said to partially assuage our guilt. "Nonetheless, the church will insist on a high price for our surrender. Before we go, I must speak to Bertrand Marty to inform him of our decision. I must ask him the terms on which he and the other Good Christians would agree to surrender to the French."

"Understood. I will send envoys to the French camp today to inform des Arcis we intend to negotiate surrender tomorrow," Pierre-Roger said.

My talk with Bertrand Marty was long and difficult for me, though surprisingly it seemed much less so for him. The man had a captivating, charismatic personality that commanded respect and left me with the feeling, as Corba had said, he was no longer of this world, no longer a mere mortal. As I talked to him, his mind seemed to dwell on a higher plane, leaving all I had come to discuss as being little more than an inconvenient triviality.

This leader of the Friends of God was aloof but at the same time personable. It was impossible not to feel humbled in his presence and yet not to like and respect him. His mind was very sharp. He frequently anticipated what I was about to say before I even knew myself. His understanding of the human condition was profound.

"You are planning to surrender?" he asked before I even offered him a greeting.

"Yes," I stammered. "We did not see any other way."

"No. There is none. You have no choice."

"The Catholic priests will demand that all renew their vows to the Church of Rome."

"And those committed to the Good God will refuse."

"Then you will—"

"Be killed. We are prepared. We shall surely not betray our souls to the satanic Church of Rome merely to keep them bound to this physical world for a few more years."

I was in disbelief of his detachment. "I am deeply troubled, Bishop, that I have betrayed your trust in me. You and your congregation came to Montségur seeking my protection. I extended it to you but have let you down. I ask for your forgiveness."

"I cannot grant you forgiveness any more than can any man. The Catholic priests in their arrogance claim to speak for God, but no man can claim that presumption. Only the Good God can grant forgiveness, and no man can intercede for you on his behalf. In this case, however, there is no need of forgiveness. You kept your vow to the fullness of your ability. You betrayed no trust."

"Your words offer me consolation but little comfort. I will always blame myself for not having served you better."

"Guilt and sin are the tools for the slavery of men's souls woven by the Catholics in the service of the Bad God. The true, loving God, the God of the gospel of John, cares nothing for such things. All that matters is that in the time allotted you on earth, you lead a good life. Do that, and you will have a good end. You have served us well in our time of struggle and may yet be called upon to do an even greater service for us before this is over."

His comment took me by surprise. "I would gladly do whatever you might want of me, but after our surrender, I will have little power to help anyone. What is this service you speak of?"

"The time is not ripe for this discussion, but it will come soon enough," he replied enigmatically. "Now, to the surrender terms. I have had discussions with my fellow Good Christians, and we do have one request. We will surrender freely to the French and to their Catholic priests, but we ask to be allowed to remain in the citadel until the sixteenth of March. We wish to observe the Manichaean rite that marks the vernal equinox and welcomes the coming of the New Year. It will help us prepare for our sacrifice. Just as the year is renewing itself, we will we also be renewing our own journey back to the Creator."

His use of the word *sacrifice* made me shudder. "Will all abjure the oath to the Catholic priests?" I asked.

"That will be left to the conscience of each individual. However, none of those who have received the Consolamentum and have committed their souls to God can bear false witness or swear to any oath of man. Our souls no longer belong to us, so to do so would break our covenant with God."

"Then all the Good Christians will be burned as heretics!"

"The inevitable outcome," he acknowledged without emotion. "The Church of Rome is but a bloody vehicle for carrying out the commands of Satan. But we shall not yield before him, and there are many more ready to take our places."

"You do not fear the conflagration?" I asked incredulously.

"I do not fear it. Quite the contrary, I welcome it. Fire is the absolute purification. It will cleanse whatever impurities remain in our souls for the everlasting life."

"And what of the believers?"

"They have not yet received the Consolamentum and are thus not bound by it. They are free to swear any oath if they wish since their souls are still their own, but I believe many will follow our example."

1244, March 1 – Montsegúr

The first of March 1244 was a sad day for all who treasured the freedom and great culture of Occitania. The mood in the castle was sullen and silent as I set out with my son-in-law Pierre-Roger to negotiate our surrender. A horn sounded. The castle gate opened. Waiting outside was a French detail to give us safe escort to the French camp.

During the long walk down the mountain, I went over what I might have done differently to avoid this outcome. How I might still salvage the situation and save the lives of all who had put their trust in me, but I could come up with no answers.

To my surprise, we were received by the seneschal with great courtesy. He treated us as knights of rank equal to himself and ensured that all others in his camp showed us similar deference. After encountering many of the churlish French knights who had accompanied Simon de Montfort in his campaigns, it was not at all what I had been expecting.

Hugues des Arcis was clearly a man of honor who shared the Occitan tradition of chivalry. Negotiations, therefore, proceeded more amicably than I had anticipated given the circumstances. The seneschal acceded to all our major conditions. It was agreed there would be an immediate cessation of hostilities guaranteed by hostages from among our community. The fortress of Montségur would surrender to the French forces without resistance on the sixteenth of March. The defenders of the citadel would be given pardons for all past events, including participation in the murder of the inquisitors at Avignonet. The defenders would be permitted to leave with their lives and possessions provided they agreed to appear before the Inquisition, which would demand only a light penitence. Others in Montségur would also be spared if they agreed to renounce the heresy and accept the Church of Rome. They too would have to appear before the inquisitors but likewise would be liable to only light penitence. Those who refused to renounce the heresy would be burned.

As we left the camp, I had mixed emotions. Most of the terms were more lenient than I had dared hope for. However, many I had lived alongside would shortly die a horrible death for holding steadfast to their principles of tolerance and nonviolence that had characterized the spirit of Occitania until the crusades of Innocent III. After countless years of brutality, the Church of Rome had its victory.

1244, March 1 – French Camp at the Base of Montsegúr

No sooner had Raymond de Péreille and Pierre-Roger de Mirepoix left the seneschal's tent than the archbishop of Narbonne, Pierre Amiel strode in, gloating. "We have them! At last, the synagogue of Satan will fall along with all its perfects and dignitaries of the Cathar Church. We shall burn each one of them. It shall be a glorious occasion. You have truly done God's work here today, seneschal."

"No. I have done the king's work. It is you who claim to do God's work."

The archbishop was taken aback by the criticism. "We all do God's work!"

"Even those in the citadel?"

"No! They are heretics. They have no right to live among God's flock. They are a diseased part of humanity that must be excised."

"I am but a simple military man, Father. Such things are not for me to judge. My job is but to wage war and win battles for the king. However, to that end, I do try to weigh up my adversaries as best I can and to get inside their minds so I can think as they do and anticipate how they will react to my moves on the battlefield. The defenders in Montsegúr put up a valiant struggle for nine months against overwhelming odds. For that, they have earned my respect."

The archbishop fumed. "Have a care, seneschal, or the inquisitor will be visiting you to inquire into your support of the heretics. You gave in readily to most of their demands. Some might construe that as showing sympathy to the heresy, a heresy in itself."

"Do not threaten me, priest. I can defend my actions without fear of retribution," exploded the seneschal. "The enemy's offer to surrender in two weeks was music to my ears. A major assault on the castle would have been costly, bloody, and not without risk. The defenders and the community within the walls had already demonstrated they can endure much hardship. If they were to continue to put up a strong resistance, it might have taken many more than two weeks to overwhelm them. That would have been very expensive to the king's purse and more important to me. Many of my men would have been wounded or killed. My army is weary after nine months of siege. My men desire to go home. You shall have your heretics, Father. You can wait two weeks!"

The seneschal stormed out of the tent.

The archbishop was annoyed at his snub but decided it was of little import since he had brought them victory. He turned to the monks with him. "The seneschal is right. We can wait two weeks. It will change nothing. The perfects will refuse to abjure their heresy and will all burn. They will all burn and go to hell!" he thundered.

"There are said to be two hundred perfects in Montsegúr," a monk said excitedly.

"We shall have to build a big fire," replied the archbishop with enthusiasm. "Send woodsmen to the forest. We shall be in need of much wood for this pyre. Come, let us hold a special Mass to celebrate this joyous occasion."

1244, March – Castle of Montsegúr

The news of our negotiations spread quickly through our community. The terms of the treaty had been widely anticipated, so outward reaction was muted. There were no protests or calls to continue the struggle. No calls for celebration or of mourning, just quiet acceptance of the inevitable.

The passive reaction of those who called themselves the Friends of God was expected. Faithful to the example of Jesus, a holy spirit they believed the Good God had sent to enlighten man, they would not attempt to flee from or even condemn those who were to crucify them. However, the lack of any public display of anguish by the remainder of our community unnerved me. It caused me to reflect on how greatly the Occitan people had changed since the first crusaders had invaded our lands. Before their coming, we had never hidden our emotions but rather rejoiced freely and openly in the pleasures of life. This attitude had been typified by our beloved troubadours, the envy of all Europe. In contrast, after thirty years of war and suffering, Occitanians were so beaten down that they would stand by without protest while their friends, neighbors, and family were torn away and burned. It was a sad commentary on what had become of us.

The two weeks passed slowly in Montségur. I spent as much time as I could with my mother, who, like Corba's mother, had received the Consolamentum. I knew my time with her was short. I talked with my mother about my father, dead for thirty-seven years. She told me he too had rejected the Church of Rome because of its decadence and corruption. Unfortunately, he had not received the Consolamentum before his untimely death, but she was confident that he had led a good life and that his soul would quickly rejoin hers in heaven.

Much as I loved my mother, I made no attempt to persuade her to abjure her beliefs. I had too much respect for her. Besides, I knew any such attempt would have been futile.

Bertrand Marty and the other spiritual leaders moved tirelessly throughout our community preaching frequently and spontaneously wherever they were asked. They counseled those who were about to die or those who were about to lose loved ones.

In the early days after we had signed the treaty, the faith of some of the younger or more recently committed Good Christians wavered at the prospect of their upcoming deaths by fire. In response, Bertrand Marty and the other elders reminded them that as Good Christians committed to God, their souls were foremost in line to rejoin their spirits at the side of God. If they renounced their contract with God, their souls would lose their privileged places and would have to suffer earthly existence many more times.

By the end of the first week, all the Good Christians who had wavered had renewed their faith and had accepted or even welcomed their upcoming ordeal. Never once during this trying period did I see anyone coerced to keep their faith or commitment to their beliefs. Each person was left to make his or her own decision.

The Good Christians prepared themselves for martyrdom. They distributed the few earthly possessions that had sustained them in this world to others; candles, lamp oil, flour, belts, shoes, and tools of their trades were given to those in need. They spent much of the time in prayer and reading the Gospels. Much as they wanted to, the Good Christians did not give away their Bibles in the Occitan tongue. To give one to someone would mark that person for death.

As the second week began, there was a startling resurgence of faith across our community. The example set by the Good Christians in affirming their faith in the face of death was an inspiration to believers and Catholics alike. Fearing the ascetics would not be around long to teach them how to lead good lives, people flocked to hear their sermons. Many renounced their Catholicism and became believers. More surprisingly, given the consequences, four people opted to receive the Consolamentum.

The greatest shock of all, however, came to me three days before I was due to surrender the castle to Hugues des Arcis. Corba and Esclarmonde came to see me.

"Raymond, my love, we have something to tell you, something that makes us very happy but might bring you pain."

I was scared by her serious tone. "What is it you wish to tell me?"

My daughter replied. "Father, Mother and I have decided to receive the Consolamentum today with nineteen others. Archbishop Marty has declared our souls are pure enough to be received by God. I pray you will be happy for us."

My jaw dropped in horror. "You will be thrown onto a pyre and burned alive! Tell me this is not true."

"We all die, my love," Corba said calmly. "Death is unimportant. It is what we do with the brief time on earth that is important. Just as your mother and my mother did, Esclarmonde and I have decided we will dedicate our lives to the service of the Good God. There has been so much killing and wickedness in the world. We must take a stand against it and set an example to others that a good, loving God exists."

I wanted to scream but could not. I wanted to wake from a nightmare.

"Father, we shall not be parted for long. You have led a good life, so you too will join us shortly," Esclarmonde said in an attempt to console me.

"Please wait to receive the Consolamentum until we have surrendered the castle," I implored them. "Then you will not have to die so soon. You will have more time to show others how to lead a good life. Surely a few more weeks would make little difference to the salvation of your souls?"

Corba shook her head. She took my hand. "My dear, our souls already belong to God. We have promised them to him. If we were to turn away from our promises simply for worldly gain, he would know we were not yet pure enough to join him in heaven. We love you very much and will be waiting for you."

"It was enough to have to face losing my mother. Now you tell me I must also lose my wife and a daughter. You will leave me little to live for."

"Each person must live for the salvation of his or her soul, not through others. When we are gone, it will be for you to find your path to a good ending so your soul too will be liberated from earthly torment."

"I am not sure I can find the way."

"Look to others to guide you. Bertrand Marty would speak to you of this. Will you agree to meet with him?" Corba asked.

"If that is your wish, I will not refuse you. But his time is short and very precious. Are you sure he can find time for such a meeting?"

"He would meet with you tonight if you are agreeable," she said.

"If he can find the time, for your sake, I will hear him out, but I am not sure what will come of it."

"Thank you," she said. She squeezed my hand and kissed me.

Later that day, Corba and Esclarmonde joined nineteen others to receive the Consolamentum from Bishops Bertrand Marty and Aguilber in the presence of many believers. The supplicants came from all walks of life. Four were knights, and six were soldiers, two with their wives. Two were messengers, one was a squire, one a crossbowman, one a peasant woman, and another, like Corba, a lady of high birth. After the Consolamentum, they were all equal, humble servants of the Good God. They found consolation in the belief they had exchanged the riches of the flesh for the riches of the soul.

I found myself lost in grief. It was an effort to force myself to concentrate on even the simplest tasks I had to complete before handing the castle to the French in a few days.

During the afternoon, Pierre-Roger came for the final wages the soldiers were due. I did not begrudge them a penny. They had fought bravely and uncomplainingly. Many had suffered horrendous wounds and would never be whole again. The blame was not theirs that we had been forced to surrender the castle.

After giving Pierre-Roger the four hundred pennies owed his men, I entrusted him with a chest of money and valuables that had been consigned to me by the Good Christians who were winding up their affairs. The wealth was not theirs; it belonged to others who had entrusted them with its safekeeping. The Good Christians could own nothing of the physical world, nor could they lie. Such qualities were rare and in stark contrast to the Catholic priests whose honesty was regarded by many as being lower than that of most common criminals. In consequence, and as a service to the community, the Good Christians were widely entrusted as bankers. In return for this service, they were typically rewarded only with food and shelter. A list in the chest named the rightful owners of its contents.

The most valuable treasure Pierre-Roger was to take from me was not of gold, however, but of the flesh. "Go now and take care of Philippa," I beseeched him. "You will have to help her through the upcoming ordeal. She is even more precious to me now that I am to lose her sister and mother."

Pierre-Roger sighed. He put a hand on my shoulder. "I have heard the news. Philippa grieves for them as deeply as you do. They told her she should be happy for them, but all she feels is grief and a sense of deep loss that they would no longer be there for her. She tried to get them to change their minds."

"I have known Corba long enough not to try," I confessed despairingly.

That evening, I visited Bertrand Marty, as I had promised Corba. Contrary to my expectation, I found him very anxious to meet with me. Some time into the meeting, I learned the reason. He had a proposition to make to me that took me by as much surprise as Corba's revelation had done earlier in the day. It is the reason I wrote the account you are reading, and I shall get to an account of it later.

1244, March 16 – Montségúr

The sun rose too early on the morning appointed for our surrender. I had lain awake all night hoping the morning would never come. But night yielded to day, regardless of the consequences. I arose and dressed quickly to make my rounds of the castle one last time.

The castle was unusually quiet. The blacksmith's forge was unlit, as were the baker's ovens. There was no one chopping wood to prepare for the day's cooking or grinding wheat to make the day's flour. Many people were still in their shelters praying or gathering their belongings.

On the terraces below the castle walls, Bertrand Marty was leading a religious service, almost certain to be his last. He was accompanied by all the Good Christians in our midst, including sadly for myself, many in my family. They were wearing thin, coarse robes emblematic of their vow of poverty. Many believers thronged around the gathering, anxious to listen to the guidance of the venerated preacher while he was still among them.

On the ramparts, there was only a scant garrison, just sufficient to alert us of the arrival of the French. Pierre-Roger was among them. I climbed up to greet him. He seemed to be lost in a trance, staring over the valley below.

"This is such a beautiful land. I shall miss it," he confided to me.

"Where shall you go?"

"To Aragón, probably. If I stay here, I would not be able to resist slitting French throats and murdering their wretched priests. They have despoiled all we held of value. I shall never forgive them for it."

"It is best that you leave. Take my daughter to safety. There is nothing more you can do here. The struggle is over for now."

"For now? Is there hope then for the future?" he asked disbelievingly.

"There is always hope," I promised him.

As I had expected, we did not have long to wait until the enemy was outside our gates demanding entry to claim their spoils. Hugues des Arcis was in command of the contingent that had been sent to accept our surrender. He was accompanied by a large number of his knights, men-at-arms, and an equal or greater number of Catholic clergy.

After meeting the seneschal earlier in the month, I had acquired at least a modicum of respect for him. As I surrendered the castle to him and he accepted it in the name of King Louis IX of France, I felt a deep sadness but no revulsion in the act.

The same could not be said when Archbishop Pierre Amiel of Narbonne accepted the surrender of the castle in the name of Pope Innocent IV. The brutal crusades of Simon de Montfort launched by the Church of Rome had slaughtered so many Occitanians that it made me wretch to have him gloat in front of me at his triumph.

Pierre-Roger and I escorted Hugues des Arcis and some of his knights around the castle to acquaint them with its layout and armaments. As he shouted orders to his men about how the castle was to be garrisoned, I was glad to be away from the scene in front of the castle where the clergy were already aggressively interrogating our population.

Archbishop Amiel, assisted by Bishop Durand of Albi, set about their work with great enthusiasm. Brother inquisitor Ferrier, of the Dominican order, and his assessors were assigned the responsibility for interrogations. The names of everyone who had been in the citadel were to be recorded for the inquisitional records. Nobles and their families were allowed to leave first, followed by the mercenaries who were allowed to leave with their arms, the tools of their livelihood. The remaining soldiers, servants, and craftsmen were likewise allowed to depart.

The procedure to be followed before each person was permitted to leave was the same. Everyone had to abjure the Cathar heresy and sign the record that they had accepted the Church of Rome as the one true church of Christ.

Having completed their first task and freeing those who were not regarded as a significant danger to the church, the inquisitors addressed those accused of having Cathar sympathies. They were divided into two groups, believers and perfects. The division required little effort on the part of the inquisitors as the garments worn by the Good Christians set them apart. Besides, they voluntarily segregated themselves.

Inquisitor Ferrier, anxious to waste as little time as possible on these 'Devil worshippers,' elected not to question them individually. Instead, he asked them as a group to abjure the heresy and swear allegiance to the Church of Rome. Those who agreed to do so were allowed to go after being given light penance. It grieved him to let them off so easily, but he was forced to abide by the terms of the treaty agreed by Hugues des Arcis. His consolation was that he expected many of them to continue in the heresy and that he would therefore have another opportunity to interrogate them more thoroughly.

For those who would not abjure the heresy, he ordered that their hands be bound by leather straps and then bound to one another by a long rope.

As the believers who were to be spared set off down the mountain, many wept as they looked back at their friends and family members they were leaving.

When all was prepared, Archbishop Amiel led the procession down the mountainside, his hands clasped in prayer. In front of him, a monk carried a large cross with an effigy of the tortured Savior. Beside him was Bishop Durand, and behind him walked Inquisitor Ferrier with his team of assessors. Their faces made it look as though they were celebrating a Saint's day; each smiled with contentment.

In stark contrast, the procession behind them told a different story. Soldiers with pikes led the long line of prisoners in single file, tied together. They were a sorrowful sight. Young and old, men and women, they had little in common other than the strength of their faith and their refusal to submit to the authority of the church. They numbered over two hundred souls.

The prisoners had given away all items of value to others before beginning their march down the mountain, which included even their shoes. As they walked and were prodded down the trail by their captors, many stumbled. They were in pain as sharp rocks cut their bare feet. At the top of the mountain, patches of snow and ice still covered the trail.

To maintain their spirits and unite them in the face of their upcoming ordeal, the prisoners began singing. Near the bottom, the trail was lined by rejoicing monks and clergy who had come to witness God's work being done. They tried to drown out the singing of the heretics by chanting loudly "Te Deum." They also struck the heretics with their staffs as they passed, threw rocks, and spat on them. Many in the procession were bleeding. Their thin robes were torn to shreds by the time they made it to the bottom of the mountain.

At the base of the pog, on the southwestern side of the mountain, a large enclosure had been erected. At its center was a huge pile of wood and sticks surrounded by dry straw that had been soaked in resin. The prisoners were herded into the enclosure as if they were no more than wild animals.

Once inside the enclosure, the prisoners were made to climb ladders onto the wooden pile. Those that were injured or too weak to climb were thrown up by the monks and soldiers. Several were even impaled on pikes and lances and simply thrown onto the pile like discarded carcasses.

As the heretics mounted the pile, monks began to clamber up after them and sort them into groups, which they tied to a line of stakes driven into the pile. They performed the task with such enthusiasm that it did not take long before all the heretics who could stand were bound. Satisfied their job was complete, the monks climbed down, removed the ladders, and exited the enclosure.

Satisfied that the preparations were completed, Archbishop Amiel held a short prayer service praising God for his beneficence. The clergy joined in to drown out the singing of the heretics.

When the prayers were finished, the monks resumed their chanting while several picked up resin-soaked torches of brush wood. They lit them from a fire in front of the archbishop and encircled the enclosure.

On a sign from the archbishop, each monk threw his torch upon the tinder around the pile. The tinder caught fire and crackled loudly as angry flames roared up from it. The flames spread among the dry branches to seek out the humanity within. The Catholics stopped their chant as the singing of the heretics could no longer be heard over the angry hissing and spitting of the fire. As they looked through the smoke, they saw the glorious sight of the heretics writhing and struggling for breath as the flames consumed them. However, the pleasure of watching their enemies burn was quickly stolen from them by the fire itself. In no time, it became simply an inferno of reds, yellow, and orange licking high into the sky without distinguishable form. The searing heat forced the onlookers back. The sky dimmed from the billowing black smoke.

Late in the evening, when the sun dropped below the horizon, there came the close of one of the most sorrowful days in the history of Occitania. The field at the base of the mountain still glowed red with the embers of our loved ones. The French, along with their priests, had returned to their camp, abandoning the site to those who mourned their losses.

Meanwhile, high on top of the pog, something stirred in the darkness. A heavy slab of stone on the floor of the keep moved and was lifted upward. It gradually slid across the floor, scraping gently on the other slabs. Moonlight shining through an arrow slit revealed a dark hole in the floor. Moments later, hands appeared. A human form emerged from the blackness. This person was followed by three others.

Together, the men carefully moved the stone back into place. They made their way to the door of the keep. Each was carrying a bag. One had a long rope over his shoulder. Once outside the castle, they walked stealthily toward one edge of the pog, crouching as they went and making every effort to remain in the shadows.

At the edge of the pog, the four looked down and observed the cliff drop near vertically for thirty feet or more. The man with the rope secured one end to a tree and threw the other into the void. It swung to-and-fro below them.

Each man grabbed the rope and clambered over the edge. At the bottom of the rope, they loosed their hold and fell safely into some bushes not far below. When they had confirmed that each of them was fine and their bags still secure, four Good Christians, Aicart, Hugon, Peytavi, and Sabatier, followed a path into the forest.

CHAPTER 51

Revelation

My account to you of the darkness that came upon us from outside our borders and then swept so cruelly across our lands is now complete. I grow weary. I have not eaten since entering this cave nearly three weeks ago. I shall soon lie on the bed on which you will find me. I shall let the oil in my lamp burn down until I am alone in the darkness with my thoughts and death takes me. I swore an oath to God I would complete this task and then end this cycle of my existence, as its purpose would have been fulfilled. The Endura is an honorable way to release one's soul when it can no longer serve the Good God's purpose in its current physical entrapment.

In the short time remaining me, and as I promised at the beginning, I will impart to you the most important part of my task. That is to reveal to you your role in these events and what brought you to my cave, where I awaited your coming. For that is the purpose of this whole account. That is why much was done to prepare for it, and that is why you are the hope for us all. To explain your part, I must give you an account of the meeting I had with Bertrand Marty three nights before his murder.

1244, March 13 – Castle of Montsegúr

It was dark as I left the keep to go to the house of Bertrand Marty. I had promised Corba I would hear what he had to say, although I knew nothing of what that might be. The night was cold. The year was young. I walked briskly. The moon was bright, so I had little difficulty finding my way. The dwelling of Bishop Marty was on the terraces among the other members of the community of the Friends of God. Though he was their spiritual leader, there was nothing remarkable about his dwelling. It was functional, simple, inside and out. I reached his house. An oil lamp flickered in the window, indicating I was expected.

"My Lord de Péreille, we have been expecting you," he said.

The furnishings in the room were extremely Spartan. The roof had clearly been patched in several places where it had suffered damage from the French projectiles. Bishop Durand was at a table where it appeared the two had been talking and sharing a few slices of dried bread.

"I came at the request of my good wife, Corba. Since I am still in shock at what she and my daughter Esclarmonde told me today, I was hoping it might help me comprehend their actions."

"I think you will find it will, my Lord," replied Bertrand Marty.

"That and much more," added Bishop Durand.

"My Lord, you are a true Occitanian. Like your good wife, you have endeavored to live a good life, though unlike her, you have not yet committed it to God," Bertrand said.

"We understand this. As Lord of Mirepoix, of Péreille, of Montsegúr, and more, you bear a great burden of responsibility to many. You put their needs ahead of yours. This is only to be admired, and your soul will be rewarded for it," proclaimed Bishop Durand.

"Indeed," said Bertrand. "And it is your soul we wish to speak of this night."

"What importance can my wretched soul have in these troubled times when so many in our community have already dedicated their souls to God?"

"That is precisely why it is important!" exclaimed Bishop Durand. "Your soul is not yet dedicated to God, and there is no time to prepare it for such a commitment before the day of our surrender, but we know your soul is far along the path to salvation, for you risked all to protect God's servants from evil."

"You talk in riddles. What do you want of me?"

Bertrand Marty exchanged glances with Bishop Durand before sitting across the table from me. He closed his eyes. "My Lord de Péreille, the

Devil sent his servants bearing crosses of blood into our land to exterminate those who worship the loving God. Since their coming, our people have suffered in the name of the false church."

Bishop Durand leaned forward and looked at me intently. "In worshipping the Good God, we have remained faithful to the teachings of the earliest Christians, we have labored tirelessly to teach people how to lead good lives that will bring them to good ends and their souls closer to heaven. We have led by examples of piety and poverty to show all that those who follow Christ's path must reject worldly possessions created by the Devil."

"Yet we have failed. The Devil has triumphed," Bertrand said.

"You have not failed," I said. "You have brought light and hope to many in Occitania. Your preachers are greatly loved while the Catholic priests are universally hated."

Bertrand shook his head. "It is for that very reason we failed. The people's rejection of the Devil's testament has brought his wrath down upon them. It is because we showed them the truth that he sent his servants to destroy them. We failed to protect them by allowing the Church of Rome to become his instrument while pretending to follow Christ."

"It is hard to see what more you could have done," I said. "The church is a powerful enemy. When you challenged the legitimacy of the church, you challenged not only the authority of the pope but also the authority of the kings of Europe. They viewed our Occitan experiment as a poison that had to be neutralized."

Bishop Durand nodded. "What you say is true, but it was a consequence of our mission, not our purpose. Our purpose was always to reform man's spiritual world, not his physical one. We sought to do this by revealing the hidden meaning in Christ's parables to all men. The Good God sent the spirit of Christ to earth to show us how to lead a good life that would free our souls to return to him. Tragically, the Devil has succeeded in exploiting the greed and brutality of man to suppress his truth, for he would see us trapped in the physical world that is his creation."

"And now you would abandon us and leave us to fight him alone?" I asked. "If you surrender to the French, you will be sacrificed. How can it help to have your strength and guidance taken from us?"

"You will never be alone. The Good God will always be watching over you even if it is the Devil who shows his face," countered Bishop Durand.

Bertrand seemed to enter a state of deep contemplation. He snapped out of it. "Since the arrival of the crusaders, and even before, we have debated among ourselves how we might best turn mankind back to loving the Good God and themselves. We have devoted much time in prayer and contemplation to the problem and tried many ways to show people the true path. An inestimable number of Good Christians have given their lives for this cause, and all of us would gladly do so. Sadly, we have seen that despite our efforts over these last thirty years in Occitania, our enemies have overwhelmed us and our message has been drowned out by those of Satan."

Bishop Durand continued in a somber tone. "In consequence, we have reached the conclusion that man is not yet prepared for enlightenment and that the darkness that has descended upon us may endure for many generations. However, we remain unshaken in our faith that the darkness will eventually be lifted and that people will be ready again to seek out the word of the Good God."

"When will that be?" I asked.

"We do not know," replied Bishop Durand. "God is eternal. Time has little meaning to him. But when mankind is finally prepared to seek him again, someone must be there to guide them."

"If it is not to be for generations, none of us can fulfill that role," I said.

Bertrand shook his head. "That is not what we have foreseen. It is our vision that it will be you who leads mankind out of the darkness."

"Your soul will not be trapped in the body it is today," explained Bishop Durand excitedly. "It will have passed through many cycles of reincarnation, awaiting the moment for its final rebirth."

I found myself completely without words as I tried to absorb what they were saying. They looked at me, appearing kind and patient, and anxious to hear my response.

"You will have nothing to fear," promised Bertrand Marty. "The Good God will know when mankind is ready to be brought out of the darkness and will guide your rebirth. It will be for you to show man again how to lead good lives, to be selfless, to kill neither man nor beast, to help others, to be honest, and to follow Christ's divine revelations. Only when man has lost his obsession with the material world can his life truly have a good end."

"I do not know I am up to this burden," I stuttered.

"The Good God will prepare your soul for the task. You will be ready when he needs you," proclaimed Bertrand.

"But I do not even have the knowledge to lead the good life you speak of. How could I lead others down that path?"

"The knowledge will be given to you," explained Bishop Durand. "On the day of the surrender of Montsegúr, Pierre-Roger will conceal four of our brothers in a passageway beneath the castle. When all is clear, they will make their way unseen down the mountain to Queille, taking paths known only to our brethren. There they will wait for your arrival. They will instruct you in the Gnostic teachings of Christ, a holy spirit, not a man, the Good God sent to guide us back to him. He spoke in parables to hide his meaning from those who served the vengeful God of the Old Testament."

"It is only by seeking out the hidden truths in Christ's message that one can become a true Christian," declared Bishop Durand.

"The four Good Christians we have chosen to prepare you for your journey will instruct you in these matters. You have led a good life, so we do not anticipate it will be a lengthy task. Once their instruction is complete, they will administer to you the Consolamentum and your soul will become God's to use for his purpose."

"Why not administer the Consolamentum to me before our surrender?"

"There is not enough time to prepare your soul for its long journey. If you take the Consolamentum before our surrender, you would also have to answer all the questions of the inquisitors truthfully, and you would not be able to swear the oath they will demand of you. The inquisitors would burn you, and your soul would be released prematurely, ill-prepared for the transmigration through time that would serve mankind better."

"There must be others more suited to this task than I. My soul is far from pure. I have done much in the service of my people that the Good God would surely look ill upon. Bishop Marty, no man's soul is more pure than yours. It has long been given to God. Why would your soul not be better entrusted with such a task?"

"I would gladly volunteer my soul if it were mine to command to wander outside of heaven until it could lead mankind back to the true path. But that is not what we have foreseen. It is your soul that we have seen chosen for this mission. Even I cannot change God's will."

"Perhaps Bishop Marty's soul has been too long given to God that it has already escaped many of the bondages trapping it in the physical world," Bishop Durand said. "It would be more difficult to keep it from rejoining its spirit in heaven through the many regenerations that may be necessary to accomplish this task."

"And my spirit is so far from heaven that it can wander for an eternity before God is ready to receive it?" I asked, jesting.

Bishop Marty seemed to take some offence at my comment. "Your soul is not yet ready to find its way back to the Good God, for you have not devoted enough time to understanding Christ's Gnostic teachings. However, he longs to receive it or he would not have sought it for this important mission. It is an honor to be chosen to do his work."

I collected my thoughts. My head was spinning. I had never thought myself a pious man, and yet in front of me, two of the most devout people in all Occitania were telling me I had been chosen by God to serve him in a critical task that might endure generations. I was disbelieving and at the same time flattered.

I had sworn allegiance to the Church of Rome when I assumed my titles of lord of Mirepoix and Péreille. Was I then to betray that oath by swearing to aid those the church declared heretical? But the church had betrayed me. The tragedy of the Occitan people over the previous thirty-five years at the hands of that church had destroyed all faith I once had in the Church of Rome. I could feel nothing but revulsion for their actions. I saw only the hand of the Devil in everything it had done. It was about to burn my mother, my beloved Corba, and my dearest daughter alive for simply defying them.

All the Good Christians I had encountered lived closer to the example set by Jesus than any Catholics I knew. Like Christ, they eschewed all forms of violence, even against their enemies, treated each man and woman as equals, and led lives of purity and chastity. I had to believe that was the life Christ had meant for us.

I could make only one decision. In a few days, I was to lose most everything I cared about to a murderous body that saw someone as kind and caring as Corba as a threat. The consequences of any decision I made could not bring me more pain than that. Besides, I did not see how my decision either way could be of much import.

"I am unsure that I am up to the task, but I will do as you require of me," I said. "When I have lost most of those I love, this life will have little meaning for me. Do with it as you will."

"Do not mourn for your loved ones when they are taken from you. Rather rejoice in it, for they will go straight to God. You will see them again," Bishop Marty assured me.

"When your soul has completed its task, it will be ready to rejoin your spirit in heaven, where Corba and your loved ones will be waiting for you," promised Bishop Marty.

"Until then, however, your soul will be as a chrysalis that awaits the coming of spring and the return of the sun before it is reborn for its last glorious existence."

CHAPTER 52

A New Resolve

You hold the history of our people in your hands. You must accept the Good God guided you to the cave in which you found my earthly remains. He returned you to the place from which you began your journey so you might finally complete your mission. If the prophecy is to be believed, you are the last worldly abode for the soul that dwelled in me. You are Raymond de Péreille reborn for one last time, before our shared soul will be released to return to our spirit in heaven and be reunited with those we have loved.

Archbishop Bertrand Marty predicted that at the time of your coming, the world would be ready to leave the darkness behind it and begin anew along the path to God. I have no way of knowing how many years will pass between us or of the reality of your world. It is likely you will also have suffered through a great darkness as I did. Be consoled by the knowledge of the Good Christians that the time of darkness for you is nearing its end. With your guidance, and the Good God's help, the world can be born anew in peace, spirituality, and tolerance, rejecting the obsession with worldly wealth and power the Devil created to keep man from fulfilling his destiny.

After the tragedy at Montségur and a brief hearing before the Inquisition, I journeyed to Queille as agreed. The four Good Christians Bertrand Marty had chosen for the task were waiting to begin my instruction. I urged them to saturate me with the hidden knowledge they had to impart. It was my way of escape, for I found that if my mind remained unoccupied for too long, it would quickly fill with horrendous images of recent events that would come close to overwhelming me.

While my lessons helped me through the daylight hours, finding a safe haven for my thoughts during the night proved more challenging. I had great trouble sleeping. On the fortunate occasions when I did manage to escape the conscious world, I would frequently wake up sweating and in a panic, desperately reaching out for something to extinguish the flames that consumed my thoughts. I therefore resolved to focus on filling my mind with as much information as possible that I could learn from the four Good Christians.

I spent several weeks with my mentors deep in the caves outside Queille, where we were alone and as devoid of worldly distractions as possible. My lessons lasted from early light until usually very late into the night. If my fair wife had been alive, she would have been greatly envious of me. The Good Christians guided me to an understanding of the meaning in the Gnostic teachings of Christ and of other true Christian teachers such as John and Thomas. Their common message was the importance in focusing on the needs of the soul within rather than the needs of the flesh.

In that, as the Good Christians emphasized, the Church of Rome has lost its way. In its lust for earthly power and wealth, it had long ago betrayed the tenets of the early Christians, and strayed to follow the evil God, Jehovah. To hide this deception, the church sought to eradicate all true Christians who remained to challenge its authority.

The original Christian church, dominant until the Council of Nicaea, believed as do the Good Christians that Christ taught of the duality of a Good God and a Bad God. The creation of an all-powerful, infallible God and church was the creation of the pagan emperor Constantine and a few avaricious priests. It was forced upon the world at the point of the sword. Thus, the dogma and the Bible of the Catholic Church are illegitimate in their claim to represent Christianity.

Principal among the grievances of the Good Christians against the Catholic Church is the false teaching that only their priests, not the individual, may talk to God. It is the very foundation of the wealth and power of the Church of Rome. Yet this untruth is totally against the teachings of Christ and not supported by any of the gospels. Countless Good Christians have been burned for daring to challenge this blasphemy or for translating the Bible into Occitan so people may learn to talk to God on their own.

No man can save another's soul or talk to God on his behalf since all souls are equal. Killing is forbidden by God in his commandments, for each living being houses a soul that will one day return to God. Similarly, procreation is forbidden to those who have taken the Consolamentum, for birth traps another soul in the physical world.

The physical world is where all souls are trapped by Satan, the bad or evil God, until they are pure enough to escape and return to heaven. There is no hell save the physical world. Hell was a creation of the Catholics to threaten people into obeying their edicts and enriching them in return by selling indulgences to escape the fictitious threat of eternal suffering.

As the instruction progressed, my mind gradually started to clear. They helped me understand what truly mattered in our short earthly existence and what we must do to purify our souls to escape the physical world forever. All this knowledge was transcribed for you and placed with this account in the chest to guide you on your journey, and through you, the rest of humanity. It will be for you to lead them out of the darkness and back to the path of lightness and ultimately back to heaven.

In the chest, you will also find original copies of the gospels. In compiling the Catholic Bible, they were deliberately mistranslated and then destroyed by Bishop Irénée de Lyon to serve the purposes of the Roman Church. In addition, there are the gospels of Thomas, Philip, and others. Bishop Marty sent these documents from the castle of Montségur around Christmas time so they would not fall into the hands of the Catholics, who would certainly destroy them.

At the end of my instruction, when I was fully prepared, I was administered the Consolamentum. When you removed the ring from my finger, you touched my hand and thereby continued the unbroken touch that has been passed down from one Good Christian to another originating with the touch of the Holy Spirit. It is now left for you to read and swear the Consolamentum yourself before God, and your commitment to him to serve as a Good Christian will be fulfilled.

Your task will be to reestablish the Church of the Friends of God in your world as a source of tolerance, hope, love, freedom, equality, and nonviolence. We tried and gave our lives to do this in our time, but alas, the forces of Satan were too strong. If Archbishop Bertrand Marty has seen truly, you now have the chance to succeed where we have failed. May the Good God help you to finally vanquish the forces of darkness and set man again on the path to spiritual rather than worldly riches.

As Lord of Mirepoix and of Péreille, I inherited and accumulated a great deal of physical wealth during my lifetime. Though it is of no value to the soul, I tremble at the thought of it falling into the hands of the Church of Rome. I know it would use it only to advance its Satanic cause and bring more suffering upon the Occitan people. Therefore, I commanded that it too be concealed in a cave not far from the one you found me in. You will find directions to its hiding place in one of the papers in the chest.

As a Good Christian, you must eschew all worldly possessions, for they will not serve you, only the Devil. You will find fulfillment in rejecting such transitory riches. Regarding the wealth in the cave, it is for you to decide if any good might come from it. If it can be used in the service of the Good God and his people, so be it. If not, it should be left where it is, lest it corrupt those who touch it. It will be for you to decide.

I grow weary. My quill fights my hand. But my work is complete. I have given you a full accounting of what befell us in these fair lands and the part you must now play. The future of mankind is in your hands.

I go to lie down now for the sleep I have yearned for these many weeks since that terrible, tragic day at Montségur. In the deep sleep that beckons me, my soul will be released from this body, which has fulfilled its purpose, to begin its journey. I pray your coming is swift, for I long to be restored to those whom I love and who were taken so cruelly from me.

May the Good God bless you! Let him show you how to become a Good Christian, and let him grant you to a good end.

Raymond de Péreille.

Friday, July 14, 1944 – County of Foix

Emile dropped the manuscript on the table. The task of reading the journal had drained him. His mind was in deep confusion. When he threw open the cellar door, he wondered whether he would find himself in the Occitania in the year 1244 or the Languedoc in 1944. *Which enemy will I have to face? The French and the Catholic crusaders with their crosses or the Germans with their swastikas?* Both worlds seemed to melt into one in his mind.

Emile tried hard to concentrate on who he was and how he had come to be there. His first recollection was of the Limousin and his wife. However, the pleasant memories were quickly swept away by angry flames that leaped out to take her and his daughters in a terrible conflagration. One moment, he saw them in a church, the next he saw them tied to stakes on an enormous pyre at the base of the pog. As he looked at his wife, he became confused as to what to call her, Monique or Corba? The two faces had become indistinguishable in his mind. He began to fear he was going crazy.

As the figures burned in Emile's imagination, his eyes seemed to float out from his head. Through them, he saw what looked like himself amid the terrible scene at Montségur. The likeness was unmistakable, yet it was an older version of himself with a long beard and dressed in the dark-blue robe he had found in the cave. Slowly, the figure turned and looked at him. He realized he was gazing into the face of Raymond de Péreille. Or was it he Raymond de Péreille gazing at Emile Garnier? He didn't know.

Feeling disoriented, Emile lay down and rested. Despite his best efforts, however, his mind denied him sleep. He could not stop a collage of confusing images from racing through his mind. He decided to return to the outside world and find what awaited him.

As he pushed up the heavy cellar door, rays of bright light blinded him. He paused between the two worlds, uncertain which way to go. Then a familiar voice called to him to emerge from his hiding place. It was Maurina, the kindly peasant woman. That meant it must be 1944 and that he was indeed Emile Garnier fleeing the invading armies of the Third Reich, not the crusading armies of the pope.

Maurina helped Emile with the door and reached down to help him up the ladder.

"Welcome, my Lord. Did you finish reading the journal?" she asked excitedly.

"I did, and it has quite exhausted me."

"That is only to be expected. I am sure he had much wisdom to convey to you. He was a great support to our people long ago, and we are in need of his help again. We know it was not by chance that you came upon his resting place."

Emile felt embarrassed by the faith she had in him. He feared it could lead only to disappointment. "His account was lengthy, and he directed it to a purpose. But I am not sure I am the one it was intended for. If so, I fear I am not up to the task he set for me."

Maurina clasped his hand in hers. "Do not doubt yourself. If the Good God has chosen you for his task, you will accomplish it. He will guide you."

"I wish I shared your confidence. I have neither the knowledge nor the experience of a lord of Occitania. I am a schoolteacher no one could confuse with Raymond de Péreille."

"You are wrong, my Lord, for many already do. We saw him in you the day you appeared to us in the cave. For seven hundred years, we have awaited the rebirth of one who would guide us out of the darkness and set mankind back on the path of the Good God."

Maurina knelt. Her eyes watered. Hers was an expectant look as she clasped his hands tightly. Emile was embarrassed by her show of humility. He wanted to tell her to get up but could not for fear of trivializing her emotions.

"My Lord, you have brought hope to us in these dark times. You have brought us hope that the world will have a new chance. We believe you have returned to us to show us the way, and we are ready to follow."

Emile had no idea how to respond. His only leadership experience had been heading the small resistance group, but its aims had been limited to driving the German occupiers from their lands. He was being asked to save humanity from itself with a mandate that had been written seven hundred years before his birth. "You expect me to be more than I am. I owe you much, and I am willing to repay you, but I will not mislead you into thinking I am something I am not."

Maurina became only more determined. "When you read the account of Raymond de Péreille, did some of it not seem familiar? Did you not feel a closeness to him that reached deep into your soul? Did it not seem to you that the centuries separating you were but a mist that would evaporate and allow you to be united?" she asked, almost knowingly.

Emile was reluctant to answer. He had hung on every word the ancient lord had written. He felt a great admiration for the man who had sacrificed so much to write his journal of the terrible injustices that had befallen his world. Emile reflected how the tragic reality of his own world in 1944 had much in common with that of Raymond de Péreille in 1244. Yet, he was not ready to accept that his life was meant to fulfill a preordained destiny. "Maurina, I will gladly do whatever I can to help you and Guillème. I will stay as long as you need me, but I cannot promise anything else until my mind is clear"

"That is all we ask! If you are truly the one we have waited for, the Good God will make his purpose known to you."

"What news of Guillème?" I asked.

Maurina's expression turned sullen. She raised her apron to her face to dry her eyes. "You must not concern yourself with Guillème or with me. The world has waited so long for your return that all that is important is for you to complete the Good God's task."

"No one can truly know the will of God," Emile replied. "It may be that it was part of his purpose that I help you. Now tell me, what news of Guillème and the others?"

"It is too late," she sobbed, shaking her head. "Guillème and all the others will be shot in the castle tonight at sunset if the treasure of the Cathars is not surrendered to them."

"No! I can give them nothing today. I must have more time!"

"Do not blame yourself, my Lord. Guillème and the other believers have prepared themselves for a good death. They are ready for their souls to be released from their flesh."

"They must not die because of me! Is there a way to get a message into the city?"

Maurina sat quietly for a moment, wiping her tears. She looked at him as if she was going to answer him, but instead shook her head.

Emile grabbed her arms. "Maurina, tell me how I can get a message safely into the city. It is the will of the Good God that I know."

Maurina looked up with surprise. He had invoked the name of the Good God. If it was truly his will, she could not refuse him. Emile was determined to have an answer. He continued to glare at her.

She squeezed her handkerchief tightly. "Maybe there is a way. Gilles Garreau is the local resistance leader. It is said he sends messages to Carcassonne by carrier pigeons."

"Where can I find him?"

"My Lord, you must not put yourself in danger. It is too late for Guillème and the others. "They will die a good death knowing you are safe."

"Tell me, Maurina. Where can I find this Gilles Garreau?" insisted Emile. "I will not let Guillème and the others die for me."

Maurina struggled to decide what to do. She was sobbing and shaking her head. She looked at Emile's piercing gaze. "He has a farm in the valley just at the base of the mountain. Follow the path down and you will see it. He has a mill on the side of the river with a big waterwheel."

"Thank you," cried Emile as he flew out the door.

"What have I done?" Maurina buried her head in her hands.

Emile ran down the mountain. After a while, his knees and his calves began to tire, and he had to check himself to keep from falling. Blisters began forming on his ankles where his poorly fitting shoes rubbed his flesh, but he refused to lessen his pace.

Slowly, the rough, rocky, mountain terrain sparsely dotted with scrubby alpine vegetation began to soften. The grey-white rocks yielded to patches of green that had been grazed down by goats, which jumped between them with no apparent fear.

As Emile felt close to collapse, he saw the rough trail transitioning into a smooth, red dusty path of beaten earth between row upon row of grapevines. His spirits lifted. He realized it should not be much farther to the farm.

He took a few deep breaths. The sun was high in a deep-blue sky, and he was sweating. Emile focused on the cool water in the river that should not be far ahead.

As he emerged from the seemingly endless vineyards, the land flattened into a small pasture. Ahead of him was the farmhouse, just as Maurina had described it, nestled beside a large waterwheel. Emile slowed his pace so as not to startle its occupants. The farmhouse appeared deserted, but then a voice cried out from an uncertain direction.

"Halt! What is your business here? You are trespassing. Declare your purpose or you will be shot."

Emile stopped in his tracks and raised his arms over his head.

"I am a friend of Guillème and Maurina," he cried nervously. "I am looking for Gilles Garreau. Maurina told me he could help me save the life of Guillème and many others. But we must act quickly or they will be shot this evening."

"Are you the preacher I have heard about? The ancient lord come back to save his Cathar brethren?" cried the voice in a mocking tone.

"I am Emile Garnier from the Limousin. My family was killed by the Germans. I am on my way to Spain to join the Free French in North Africa."

A solidly built man with red cheeks and a large moustache opened the door to the farmhouse. An old shotgun was couched in his arm. "Come in quickly. It is not safe to be so public with such intentions in these parts. The Germans are paranoid since the invasion in Normandy. They need little excuse to shoot anyone."

Emile lowered his arms and walked into the dark house. The man scanned the fields warily before shutting the door and securing it with two heavy bolts. "It is best to keep prying eyes out and trust no one. I have found caution to be conducive to a longer life. The Germans patrol these mountains frequently with field glasses. The less they see the better. I am prepared to risk my life for France, but I do not welcome death as your Cathar friends seem to," he said sternly. "What do you want of me?" he demanded impatiently as he banged a bottle of wine and glasses on a table.

Emile picked up a glass of wine. "To France! Long may it be free!"

Gilles looked at him coldly and mistrustfully before deciding to join him. With a fierce determination in his expression, he raised his glass. "Vive la France!" he shouted before downing a mouthful of his homemade elixir.

Having survived the introductory formalities, Emile was anxious to present his case. "Gilles, the Germans will shoot Guillème and his friends tonight in Carcassonne unless I can stop them. I need your help and that of the resistance to save them."

Gilles leaned back in his chair and laughed. "My friend, you must be from the past, as they claim. Maybe in the thirteenth century, you could ride into Carcassonne on a horse and in a suit of armor to rescue your friends, but today, I regret that is no longer possible. The Germans would cut us down like dogs."

"No. I am not asking you to attack the castle."

"That is good because I have no intention of doing so," declared Gilles. "At most, I can muster maybe thirty men armed with a few old shotguns and rifles. They would be more than sufficient if Carcassonne were still defended by a few knights with swords and crossbows, but alas it is not. The Das Reich Division has made the castle their headquarters. They have machine guns, mortars, and tanks they would be pleased to demonstrate to us."

Emile shuddered at the mention of the name Das Reich. Memories of his day in hell in Oradour-sur-Glane came flooding back to him again and sickened him. The Limousin seemed like an eternity away, and yet there he was again up against the same enemy.

"I am not asking you to storm the castle. I am not asking you to risk your life."

"Then what do you want me to do? Simply bang on the castle gate and ask them nicely to set your friends free?"

Emile allowed himself some small amusement at the suggestion, a welcome distraction. "No. Maurina tells me you have carrier pigeons that can take messages to the city."

Gilles sighed. "Ah, you are interested in my friends the pigeons. I used them to send messages into the city, but no longer. The Germans discovered what we were doing, and they shoot them to intercept our messages. I'm sorry, but I cannot help you." He shrugged.

Emile was not deterred. "You can help me! If the Germans intercept all the messages, so much the better, for it is to the Germans I want to send a message."

"What can you have to say to them that might save the life of Guillème?"

"I have what they are looking for. They will do as I ask."

Gilles put his glass down and stared at him with intrigue. "Whatever you might have, you will be playing a dangerous game. If, as you say, it is worth enough for them to consider exchanging it for the lives of your friends, they will not hesitate to kill you to get it. You cannot expect to barter with the Devil and not end up in hell."

"I am aware of the danger but am prepared to risk it. I have crossed paths with this particular devil before, and this time, it will be on my terms. Do you still have pigeons?"

"I do, in the barn. I can fetch one. But what is this message of yours to say?"

"It is to propose an exchange of all the Cathar prisoners they have taken for the Cathar treasure. The exchange is to take place at Montségur at noon on Wednesday next."

Gilles sat up in his chair. His eyes widened in disbelief. "You have found the fabled treasure of the Cathars? I thought it only a myth."

Emile saw no reason to disclose to Gilles the existence of the treasure of Raymond de Péreille. It would only have complicated his task. "I have found what the Cathars treasured, though it may not be what the Germans will be expecting. It is knowledge, not gold. What was valuable to them were the holy texts and Gnostic teachings. That is what they hid."

"Your plan is crazy! When they see what you have brought them, they will most certainly be disappointed. They will shoot you and all your friends together." He laughed.

"We will have to come up with a plan to prevent that. Maybe we can create a distraction long enough to get everyone away. At least we will have a better chance if we can get them out of Carcassonne. I need time to think of something. In the meantime, I am open to suggestions if you have any. What is important is that we do something today or they will all be shot tonight."

"Yours is a rotten plan, but I have none better. I will go along with it on one condition. The Germans are holding two of my men in the dungeons in Carcassonne. One is a close friend of mine. I owe him much. He saved my life on more than one occasion. This may be my chance to repay the debt. The other I do not know, but I have been ordered to do everything to effect the release of this agent. He is needed to assist with the allied invasion of southern France. You must add these two to your list of those to be released."

Emile shook his head disapprovingly. "I sympathize with you. I too have lost many good friends to the Germans." His voice choked up with sadness. "But it is a risk we all knew we were taking when we took up arms against the Nazis. I would like to save your people, but I worry this additional demand might scuttle any deal with the Germans. They do not fear the Cathars. They know they will not take up arms against them. They may even be glad to be rid of them, but resistance fighters are a different story. They are a direct threat, and they will set a much higher price on their release."

"Let us hope what they believe you have to offer them is worth that price, for that is my condition."

Emile growled in frustration. "You are putting the lives of Guillème and his companions in great danger. What if the SS commander is ambivalent about the Cathars and their treasure and is interested only in winning the war? If so, he will never agree to release two resistance fighters. He may decide to save himself further trouble by shooting them all."

"If it were the commander's decision, I would share your concern," Gilles said. "But fortunately for us, I do not believe it will be."

Emile did not understand what he was implying. "Then who will decide?"

"The Reichsführer Heinrich Himmler. He and his Ancestral Heritage Research and Teaching Society, the Ahnenerbe-SS, have long been obsessed with the Cathars. They believe the Cathars possessed the Holy Grail and are part of the Aryan heritage. It would be a personal triumph for him if he could claim the treasures of the Cathars for the Third Reich. Many in the Ahnenerbe-SS even promise that such treasures could be imbued with mystical powers that could help the Nazis win. For over ten years, Himmler and Hitler have been sending agents in a desperate search to find the treasure."

"Maybe you are right then. Maybe they will accept your terms. We will have to hope so. After their fruitless search, hopefully they have not yet given up looking for the treasure."

"I know for a fact they have not. I have contacts in the city who tell me Dr. Herrman Reischle, deputy curator of the Ahnenerbe-SS, just arrived in the Carcassonne. We believe he received word of the apparition of an ancient Cathar lord and came to investigate the occurrence, very probably on orders from the Reichsführer. He will be in no hurry to dismiss your demands."

"For all our sakes, I pray you are right."

"If it is agreed then, I will fetch the pigeon."

"It is agreed," replied Emile with some reluctance. "But do it quickly."

"It will not take long. My birds fly fast and straight. Your message will be in the hands of the SS within the hour."

Emile shuddered and felt pity for the fate that awaited the bird in the castle.

"If they accept our terms, I will demand they release Yves immediately to show their sincerity. I think a white dove will be appropriate to deliver a message of the Cathars," he added with a chuckle.

CHAPTER 53

Resurrection

Monday, July 17, 1944 – County of Foix

To Emile and Maurina's relief, Gilles Garreau's gamble had paid off. The Germans released the resistance fighter as a show of good faith. Guillème and his fellow believers were still alive in the dungeons. The responsibility fell heavily on Emile to assure their lives would also be spared.

Yves had returned to Gilles with the Germans' terms. The prisoners would be exchanged for the Cathar treasure at the base of the pog of Montségur at the time proposed. However, as an assurance against treachery, the SS demanded a large pyre of brush and small logs be built in the *prat des cramats,* the "field of the burned," where the Friends of God had been martyred in 1244. If anything were to go wrong with the exchange, the SS threatened that all the prisoners would be burned on the pyre just as their ancient brethren had been.

Emile knew that the Cathar "treasure" he had to offer the Germans would not satisfy them. He could search for the family treasure of Raymond de Péreille, but even that would probably not be enough. Besides, to give any of it to the modern purveyors of darkness would be a total betrayal of the intentions of the ancient lord.

There was no Holy Grail, no Ark of the Covenant, nothing to convey to the Nazis the mystical powers they were seeking. They had become so obsessed with the legend of the Cathar treasure that Emile knew anything he would offer them would be seen as insufficient or worse still, as a deception.

Emile knew from personal experience that the Das Reich SS did not make idle threats. If they were not satisfied with the exchange, they would certainly not hesitate to kill all the prisoners. He also knew that even if they were satisfied, they would still see no reason to keep any of them alive. As he had learned in Oradour-sur-Glane, the Das Reich SS preferred to clean up its loose ends before moving on.

For the next few days, Emile racked his brains for a plan. He knew only too well what the Germans were capable of. He could not underestimate them. Emile paced, barely eating or sleeping.

His nervousness made Maurina even more on edge. "My Lord, maybe you are looking in the wrong place for guidance," she suggested. "The Good God brought you to us and led you to the ancient chest of Raymond de Péreille. Maybe the answer lies there."

Emile shook his head. "I have read everything in the chest. I cannot think of how any of it might help us."

"Look again. If the answer is there, the Good God will help you find it."

Emile looked at her in disbelief. He could remember nothing that might help him, but to placate his faithful friend, he agreed to review the papers again.

Maurina waited two hours before Emile emerged from the cellar. He was smiling. Maurina knew her prayers had been answered.

Emile shut the cellar door and hugged her. "I have it! The secret is right here," he said, gleefully holding up a parchment. "You were right. Thank you!"

"It is not to me that you owe your thanks," she said.

"Maybe not, but you sent me back to the chest. I must act quickly. There is much to do in the little time we have left before the exchange on Wednesday."

Emile hugged Maurina again and kissed her on the cheek. "I must visit Gilles. I will need his help and that of many others in the community if this plan is to succeed."

"My Lord de Péreille! Remember that as Friends of God, we are opposed to killing. However much you hate the Germans, Guillème and the others would not condone your killing anyone to save their lives."

"If my plan works, no one need die. We must hope the Good God is truly watching over us."

Emile spent the rest of the day and all of Tuesday with Gilles frantically trying to organize the effort needed to put his plan into action. He had last faced the Waffen SS in Oradour-sur-Glane and had been ill prepared for that encounter. That had devastated his life. He vowed the outcome this time would be very different.

Emile spent most of the two days working frantically in Montségur alongside many of the villagers. After five years of murderous occupation by the Nazis, there was no shortage of volunteers willing to do whatever they could and even risk their lives to free their Cathar neighbors. In truth, they would probably have agreed to help free anyone from the clutches of the hated Das Reich SS, but Emile also sensed the Cathars were special to them. Everyone he met spoke of them with unveiled reverence and pride. They were admired for their honesty, meekness, charity, and their message of the inherent good in everyone that would eventually triumph and free every soul to return to the side of the Good God. They continued to exemplify hope to the people in a world where many had lost theirs.

As Emile gathered brush and wood for the pyre as the Nazis had demanded, he thought of what had occurred there seven hundred years earlier. The images of it had seemed vivid enough when he was reading the journal, but in the very location where those horrible events took place, they took on a life of their own. He could see flames licking the deep-blue sky as captives tethered to stakes cried out to him to save them.

Eventually, Emile could take no more. He had to leave the place of death. It was haunting him like a terrible memory of something he had actually witnessed. He tried to remind himself that his wife and daughter had perished in Oradour-sur-Glane, not in this green field they had never seen. But the more he tried, the more confused he became about who he really was.

Emile ran from the field and started up the trail to the top of the pog. He climbed the sometimes steep trail with determination. At first, he simply wanted to put the prat des cramats as far behind as possible, but then another drive overtook him—the desire to get on the plateau. Something about it was pulling him up like a magnet, a force he could not resist.

Emile had important preparations to make in the castle to prepare him for the exchange. He told himself that was the real reason he had to reach the plateau, but he knew there was more to it than that. He wanted to see for himself where everything Raymond de Péreille had described in such detail had taken place. He wanted to stand where Raymond's wife, mother, and daughter along with Corba's mother and more than two hundred other innocent souls had said their good-byes to their loved ones before walking to their terrible fate. He could picture the scene so vividly in his mind that it haunted him.

As Emile climbed out of the forest, he looked out at a breathtaking panorama that seemed eerily familiar. When Emile reached the castle, he took the ancient map he had found in the chest of Raymond de Péreille from his backpack and tried to get his bearings. At first, he was very confused. The building in which he was standing bore little resemblance to that on the map. Emile realized that the castle must have undergone extensive modifications and renovations since Raymond de Péreille and his ilk had committed it to the hands of the papist and royalist forces in 1244.

Emile looked for features on the map that may have not changed. Rocky outcroppings, a steep falloff in the terrain, the forest, and the lay of the plateau itself allowed him to orient the map correctly. When he was confident he had his bearings, he left the castle and carefully followed the map. He walked to the edge of the pog and looked down to confirm it was the place he sought. It was. Overjoyed, he reached into his backpack, buoyed by a new optimism that his plan might work.

When Emile had completed the necessary tasks on the plateau, he retraced his steps down the winding, uneven trail to the valley. When he arrived, it was still buzzing with activity. Emile looked for Gilles. He found him surrounded by many of his resistance compatriots. Emile was grateful to have their help; they had taken over much of the supervision of what needed to be done. Fired up by their hatred of the SS, and wanting to do something to avenge their fallen comrades, they had all volunteered to help in any way they could.

Emile took another map from his backpack and rolled it out carefully on a large boulder before Gilles. He pointed out the features of the pog that would be essential to his plan. After some discussion, Gilles screamed orders to his men, and they set off together across the prat des cramats, which was brimming with firewood, toward the base of the pog.

Reassured that all was well in hand, Emile set out for the long steep hike back to the house of Guillème and Maurina. He would spend the evening with Maurina before retiring early. He wanted a good night's sleep so he would have all his wits about him in the morning. It was a dangerous game he was about to play with an unforgiving adversary. Emile's life and that of many others would depend on everything he had planned working flawlessly. One slip, and he would risk visiting a similar tragedy to Oradour-sur-Glane down upon the equally innocent citizens of this ancient land of Occitania.

Wednesday, July 19, 1944 – Montségur

Emile awoke with the dependable Midi sun as its rays crept over the horizon. Anticipation of the day and his increasing and confusing nightmares had robbed him of much of his night's rest. As he entered the kitchen, Emile observed that, as always, Maurina had risen before him. He was not sure if she ever slept.

"I have gathered some fresh berries for your breakfast and made you a herbal infusion to calm your nerves."

Emile thanked her. "Maurina, I do not want you to come to Montségur today," he said calmly. "It will be too dangerous."

"But I must come! It may be my last chance to say good-bye to Guillème."

Emile feared she could be right, but he did not want to have to worry about her safety in addition to those that would already be depending on him. "Maurina, I have seen what the SS can do to a town if they are angered. I do not want to risk having any more of those I love slaughtered in front of me. There is nothing you could do in Montségur to help

Guillème. I am sure he too would not want you in danger. Stay home. I will do everything I can to return him to you safely. I give you my word."

The woman looked at him for a moment and smiled as a mother does to her child. "I do not doubt your word, but I must go. I have prayed to the Good God for a good end. If today is when my soul is to be set free again, then I am ready to die. If that is what the Good God has planned for me, I accept it. But I must be there for Guillème."

Emile sighed. He knew any further discussion on the topic would be fruitless. "If you must go, please take care."

"I will. But Emile, you promised you would not kill anyone to set Guillème and the others free. They would not want it. It is against our beliefs."

"Maurina, it is not my intention to kill anyone today. I will try to save lives, not take them. However, this is war, and sometimes unfortunately, events can spiral out of control. There is always a risk that someone will get killed when one side is heavily armed."

"That is all I ask," she said, touching his hand tenderly.

After Emile had eaten breakfast, he returned to the cellar and dressed in the dark-blue robe of Raymond de Péreille. He took the ancient lord's ring from the heavy leather bag and put it on his finger. If the Nazis were expecting a Cathar Lord to deliver his treasure and secrets to them, he would play along with the subterfuge as best he could. After reclosing the leather bag bearing the crest of the house of Mirepoix, Emile slung it over his shoulder and set off toward Montségur. He had much to do.

As the sun reached its zenith, the din of army trucks, people shouting, and doors slamming broke the peace on the outskirts of the village of Montségur. The Germans had arrived punctually as usual.

The sound of soldiers marching on the gravel road could be heard long before anything could be seen in the village. As people looked nervously down the road in anticipation, the first thing they saw was the dust kicked up from the dry road. Not long after, however, they could see the chilling sight of a column of armed storm troopers in black uniforms emerging through the dust and marching toward them. As the soldiers came closer, they could see the lightning flashes on their collars that identified them as belonging to the dreaded Das Reich Division. Many people ran terrified into their houses.

For those who remained on the street, a more bizarre sight gradually came into view. In startling contrast to the impeccably attired soldiers, they were followed by a bedraggled line of shoddily dressed men and women of various ages, their hands tied together by a long rope. They were barefoot, and their clothes that looked as they were from the Middle Ages were torn and ragged. The faces and exposed flesh of several of the captives showed clear signs of bruising and abuse.

As the sad procession got closer, Emile managed to pick out Guillème. They were clearly the prisoners the SS had arrested on suspicion of being Cathars and whom the SS had agreed to exchange in return for the fabled treasure they hoped would contribute to the greater glory of the Third Reich. Emile was under no illusion. His plan had to assume that whatever the exchange, the Germans planned to kill him and all the prisoners after the exchange no matter the outcome.

The line of prisoners advanced toward the village, accompanied by a droning sound that was at first unintelligible but became recognizable as some form of liturgical chant. Its origins were revealed only when the procession came close to entering the village. The line of Cathar prisoners was followed by twenty or so monks in habits and cowls. Emile was aghast at the ghoulish sight. It brought to life for him the tragic last day of the Cathars who had been burned on the same spot seven hundred years earlier. *What kind of sick mind would conjure up such a sight?* he wondered. He did not have long to wait for his answer.

The German armored car at the end of the procession pulled up beside Emile. In the back were two officers. They descended from the vehicle and approached Emile.

"Heil Hitler!" cried the first man, who gave a stiff salute. "I am Oberführer Schiffner of the Second SS Panzer Division, Das Reich."

The second man was much less formal. He tipped his head to Emile and looked him over with obvious curiosity. "I am Wolfram Sievers, Standartenführer of the Ahnenerbe-SS," he announced proudly. "I am charged by Heinrich Himmler, the SS Reichsführer, with restoring the cultural heritage of the Germanic people to advance the new world order."

Emile tipped his head in acknowledgement but did not salute. "I am Raymond de Péreille," he heard himself saying. "Welcome to Montségur."

"So you are the one that they speak of." Wolfram Sievers smiled. "They say you have come back to save the world. Can this be true? If so, your timing is most appropriate, for we too seek to cleanse the world. Hopefully, we can work together on the task."

"One man cannot save the world by himself," answered Emile. "But perhaps he can set an example to others that will show them how to save themselves. I would gladly work with anyone who seeks to change the world by peaceful means."

"Ah, peace. Yes, that is something we all crave, but sometimes, violence is necessary to restore peace. In our new world, there will be no violence, for there will be no need for it. The natural order will be restored and each person will be content in assuming their appropriate place in the hierarchy."

"Being a historian, you must know the Friends of God believe the souls of all men and women are equal. There is no natural order that values one above another," Emile said.

Commander Schiffner looked infuriated. "Only the inferior would seek to console themselves with such nonsense! The triumph of the Third Reich in this war has shown that there is truly a master race intended to rule others for their own good."

"The war is not over, Herr Oberführer," said Emile to the commander's displeasure.

Wolfram Sievers raised his hand to discourage any further angry retort from the commander. "What you preach is anarchy, or worse still, communism. That is reason enough to get you killed. Have you not learned the lessons of the past? That is why the Cathars were ruthlessly hunted down by the Church of Rome seven hundred years ago. Would you see that repeated? Would it not be better to become part of the new order? The purity of your beliefs could blend well with the purity of fascism. We share a common enemy, the Church of Rome, and we could do well to work together."

Emile had never contemplated how he might respond to an offer of cooperation from the Germans. The historian was clearly more sophisticated in his methods than was the SS. He also appeared very knowledgeable, but if so, he would know the Cathars would give their lives rather than sign a pact with the Devil. "We seek to make enemies of no one," Emile said. "We seek only to lead good lives and to show others how to do likewise."

"Enough of this nonsense!" interrupted the commander. "I have more important matters to attend to. We have brought the prisoners. Where is the treasure?"

"You shall have it," Emile said. "It is in the castle of Montségur, from whence it came."

"I have no time for games," screamed the commander. "Captain, shoot the prisoners!"

Wolfram Sievers raised his arm again. "Halt! That will not be necessary! At least not yet. We shall go up to the castle. The Ahnenerbe has searched for it long enough that I am prepared to show a little more patience."

He turned to Commander Schiffner and lowered his voice. "Besides, Oberführer, we agreed the prisoners would not be shot," he reminded him in an absolute tone of authority.

The commander fumed but said nothing.

Wolfram Sievers appeared dissatisfied by his attitude. "I remind you, Oberführer, that this is Montségur and that the prisoners you hold are Cathars. Herr Himmler was most anxious that we use any opportunity to reeducate the people about their history. We have the perfect opportunity here to remind people of the barbarism of Christianity so they will understand why it must be replaced by a new Germanic purity."

The commander grunted. "Very well." He lit a cigarette to calm his frustration. "Captain, take all the prisoners to the enclosure and bind them to the stakes!"

Wolfram Sievers smiled disingenuously. "You see, my Lord de Péreille, if you try to deceive us or the treasure is not there, I will see history is repeated."

Emile shivered at the thought. "I will take you to the treasure of the Cathars. No one need die here today."

The Germans herded the prisoners into the enclosure around the enormous pyre. The mound rose toward the back, up against the pog, where a line of stakes had been erected. The Germans untied the prisoners before forcing them to climb the pile. Some were too weak and had to be helped up by their fellows. Others were thrown up by the soldiers.

A few soldiers mounted the pile and tied groups of prisoners together to the stakes. When they had completed the task, they exited the enclosure and secured the gate. Wolfram Sievers nodded to a soldier, who shouted a command to the monks who surrounded the enclosure. The monks began to chant a litanic dirge.

Wolfram Sievers smiled contently at Emile. "I believe everything is in order. I thought it would be a nice touch of authenticity to bring the monks along with us. We rounded up some 'volunteers' at the monastery. I trust you of all people appreciate the effort we have gone to?"

Emile tried to hide his revulsion. "I would have expected no less from the SS. You have a reputation for thoroughness."

"It is well deserved, I assure you," boasted Oberführer Schiffner, who had missed the irony in Emile's tone.

"Ah! Before I forget. One last thing," Sievers said. He snapped his fingers to a soldier, who ran to the armored car. Emile saw him reach inside. He returned with a long stick with a twisted mass of fibrous material on one end covered in some type of resin. Emile recognized it immediately as a torch and had no doubt of its purpose.

"Beautiful, isn't it?" declared Sievers as he caressed it lovingly. "It is quite authentic, I assure you. I had our researchers create a torch that resembled as closely as possible the torches likely used here seven hundred years ago. The Ahnenerbe is always anxious when opportunities such as this arise to ensure that any reenactment is as historically authentic as possible. It is critical to preserving our national heritage."

"What do you propose doing with that?" asked Emile, knowing full well the answer.

"Why, a torch is for lighting," replied Sievers as he held it out menacingly.

Sievers nodded. The soldier lit the torch with a cigarette lighter. It caught fire immediately and gave off a bilious, black smoke. "If you give us cause, I will have one of the monks cast this torch on the pyre, and history will be repeated."

"I trust this wood will catch fire readily," remarked Oberführer Schiffner. "I do not trust these French to do anything properly. We should have built the pyre ourselves."

Overhearing them, a man stepped from the crowd. The soldiers pointed their guns at him. The commander bade them not to shoot.

"Herr Schiffner, we built the wood pile per your orders," the man exclaimed proudly. "The wood is dry, as is everything here in June. For good measure, we also poured some paraffin on the tinder around the pile. I assure you it will burn fast and hot."

Emile fidgeted nervously while Oberführer Schiffner looked at the man disdainfully. Emile knew only too well the man who had been so audacious as to approach them. Gilles Garreau. Fortunately, the Germans had no idea they were face-to-face with the head of the local resistance.

As the Germans prepared for their hike up to the castle and gave orders to the soldiers who would remain, Emile looked at the sad sight of Guillème and his fellow believers tied to the stakes. He noticed one woman who was more noticeably abused than the others. Her face was swollen and badly bruised. Her lip was cut. Despite the injuries, Emile thought there was something familiar about her. Emile walked to Gilles. "Gilles, who is that woman over there? The one with the bruises all over her face."

"I do not know her." He shrugged.

"But I thought you knew everyone in these parts."

"I do, but she is not from around here."

"Where is she from?"

"I do not know. Turns out she is the one the maquis were anxious to save. They didn't tell me it was a woman. Like most of the maquis in this area, she is Spanish."

"Spanish? Do you know her name?"

"Yes. It is easy to remember because I had never heard it before. She calls herself Azeri. They say that she is Basque."

Emile almost dropped to his knees. "Azeri! I know this woman. She saved my life! How was she taken? The woman I know would have fought to the death."

"I have heard she was found unconscious after some kind of accident outside Limoux. The Germans gave her medical treatment until she was well enough to be interrogated. Apparently, they were not very successful in extracting any information from her in Carcassonne, so they planned to send her to Germany, where they have more-aggressive methods of questioning. I probably should not tell you this, but there are members of the maquis in the crowd here. Their orders are to shoot her rather than let the Germans take her back alive."

Emile grimaced. "We must save her from the Germans and from the maquis."

"For all our sakes then, pray this plan of yours works," Gilles said.

Emile realized it was too late to turn back. "Has everything been prepared?"

"It has," Gilles nodded discreetly. "Now it is up to you."

The trail up the side of the pog to the castle was steep and rough going. The sun beat down relentlessly. By the time Emile, Schiffner, and Sievers reached the top, they were exhausted. Emile was depending on that. *So far so good.*

As they walked along the plateau toward the ruins of the castle, a warm breeze was blowing.

"I can hear the voices of the ancient Cathars as we walk through this place," uttered Sievers, looking around himself as if he were in a trance. "It will make an excellent pilgrimage site for all Germans after the war to remind them of the corrupt brutality of Christianity and why it was necessary to replace it with the purity of the Nazi ideal."

Emile observed that Schiffner did not seem in the slightest to share his colleague's enthusiasm. His expression was showing annoyance that he had been forced to leave his men behind to go on a treasure hunt.

"I hope it is not much farther," the Oberführer said. "My men will be growing impatient."

"It is just a little distance ahead," Emile reassured him.

They entered the ruined castle of Montségur through a small arch in the walls and walked among the fallen stones. Wolfram Sievers breathed the sacred air deeply into his lungs. The high walls about them cast long shadows, making it difficult to see into many of the corners and crevices of the ruins after the bright light outside.

"Where is the treasure?" demanded Oberführer Schiffner impatiently.

"Over there," said Emile. He pointed to a rock bathed in shadows.

Wolfram Sievers walked briskly in the direction Emile was pointing. Once there, he shouted, "There is nothing but an old satchel here! What sort of treasure could it contain?"

"The treasure of the Cathars," replied Emile. "They did not value gold and silver, for they were put here by the Devil to tempt us. They valued knowledge. Open it. You will see."

Sievers frantically tore open the satchel and began reading some of the papers. "They appear to be authentic," he cried excitedly. "But there must be more. It is well documented that Bernard Marty sent two perfects out of the castle during the siege to hide the treasure in the caves of Sabarthès."

"This is that treasure, Herr Sievers," Emile said. "It was not worldly riches but spiritual riches they wished to preserve."

Sievers glared at him with deep suspicion.

"That is all there is here?" asked Oberführer Schiffner angrily.

"Yes, that is all they left," responded Emile.

"Then we are done here? Standartenführer Sievers, I must return to my men. They must prepare for our move north. This has been an unwelcome distraction for them, and it would seem an unprofitable one. Let us take the prisoner to the village and conclude this affair."

Emile observed an exchange of glances between the two men that seemed to acknowledge some unspoken agreement.

"Very well," nodded Sievers reluctantly. "But Oberführer, I believe we should take this man with us to confirm his story. I am not convinced he has told us all he knows."

The Oberführer looked annoyed. "So be it, but he will be in your charge. I do not have time to pursue this matter further while our brothers are dying in the north."

"I shall take him and these papers to Berlin."

Oberführer Schiffner left the castle impatiently.

Sievers stuffed the papers into the satchel and handed it to Emile. "Here. Carry this down. It was you who caused us the inconvenience of this climb."

Once outside the castle, they saw the village below them and the Cathar prisoners tied to stakes.

"We can take care of one of the loose ends right now," Oberführer Schiffner declared enthusiastically, a malign expression across his face. "We have what we came for, so we can now bestow upon your Cathar friends the martyrdom they seek. They claim to welcome the day when their souls will be freed from their worldly bodies. I shall oblige them by ending their wait. In doing so, I will be carrying out the will of the Catholic Church, so I will make everyone happy." He drew his pistol and held it above his head.

"No! You cannot!" screamed Emile, rushing forward. "They are innocent. They are no threat to you or your fatherland. Let them live!"

The Oberführer pointed his pistol at Emile. "Come any closer and I shall kill you first. I grow tired of all this Cathar nonsense. The Catholic Church was right to exterminate them. They will no more swear an oath of loyalty to the Third Reich than they would to the Church of Rome. They are anarchists and as such a threat to all society."

Emile stopped dead in his tracks. Oberführer Schiffner studied him for a moment to ascertain his intentions. When he was confident Emile would advance no farther, he raised his pistol and fired it.

Down below them in the valley, the shot had its intended consequences. With a gun at his back, one of the monks threw the lighted torch on the tinder surrounding the pile of wood. The fire caught hold. Flames spread rapidly through the pile. Black smoke rose from the paraffin-soaked wood. Soon, people were coughing and choking. The smoke and the intense heat forced everyone back from the enclosure.

As the fire reached the larger timbers, the heat and smoke intensified. It was impossible to see the heart of the fire or the fate of those being consumed by it. Many around fell to their knees and prayed for them, Maurina among them.

For a while, the soldiers forced the monks to continue chanting. Finally, when they were satisfied by the size of the conflagration, when the smell of burning flesh let them know their job was done, they lowered their guns and allowed the monks to leave. They had only to wait for their commanders to return with the treasure they had come for.

As Oberführer Schiffner and Wolfram Sievers looked down with satisfaction over the edge of the pog upon their handiwork below, Emile slipped quietly away behind them. He ran back into the castle and out an exit on the opposite side. Keeping low and moving as fast as he could, he made his way to a small group of trees at the top of a near-vertical drop over the edge of the pog. Reaching between the rocks, he found what he was looking for. The rope he had placed there the day before.

Hurriedly, he grabbed firmly onto the rope and launched himself over the edge. He lowered himself slowly, being careful not to look at the dizzying fall beneath him. As he descended, he thought of the two Cathar perfects who had escaped from the castle by the same route and with the same documents he was carrying.

When he reached the bottom of the rope, he alighted onto a narrow ridge that descended into the forest. Emile pulled sharply down on the rope to cause it to come crashing down toward him from where he had lodged it in the rocks above. He threw the rope into the forest and started his long hike down the mountain, following a trail he had committed to memory from the map of Raymond de Péreille.

Emile would wait in the forest until nightfall before returning to the village. He judged it would not be safe before then. As he walked slowly among the trees, he dared not think what he might find when he got there.

At dusk, Emile wound his way around the pog to the prat des cramats. He had left it only a few hours earlier piled high with wood, which he knew only too well would by now be little more than smoldering embers. As he drew closer to the field, each gust of wind brought with it the strong smell of burning and destruction, smells that ever since Oradour-sur-Glane, Emile would always associate with horror and death.

As the sun sank, Emile could see an eerie, orange glow in the forest coming from the prat des cramats just ahead of him. As he came out from behind the trees, he saw that such had been the intensity of the fire that the ground itself was still smoldering and many embers were still glowing. There was no sign of any Germans, so Emile left the shelter of the forest and approached a group of women praying and talking quietly.

When the women saw Emile approaching, they fell to the ground as if they had seen a ghost. Several fell to their knees and placed their palms to the ground. They bowed deeply and beseeched him with the plea, "Bless me, Good Christian, and deliver me from an evil death, and lead me to a good end."

Emile was greatly surprised and embarrassed by their reaction until he remembered he was still wearing the blue robe.

"My Lord de Péreille, we were told you had been taken from us again, but you have returned to us. It is another miracle!" cried one women.

"The Good God answered our prayers," sobbed another.

"Please show us how to lead a good life. We will follow you," begged another.

"What happened today?" asked Emile calmly.

"The Germans burned the Cathars." She wept. "Some say that their souls were set free to go on to their next lives, and that it was a happy event, but it was so terrible a sight to witness that I had to turn away."

"Did none survive?" asked Emile with concern.

"No, none," replied a woman. "How could they? I have never seen such a fire. We could not help them." She cried.

"There was nothing you could do," Emile said. "And there is nothing you can do for them now. Go home. Remember them as they were. Pray for their souls."

Pained by self-doubt, blame, and uncertainty for his part in the day's events, Emile wandered around the area. He was anxious to find anyone who might give him more information of the day's events, but he found no one. At one time, he thought he saw Maurina, but on approaching the woman, he realized she was someone else. He imagined her at home with her grief.

After a fruitless search, and feeling very alone, Emile walked to Gilles' farm. It was a difficult path lit only by moonlight. When Emile reached the farmhouse, it was completely dark. Given the late hour, and Gilles' obsession with privacy, Emile had expected no less.

Cautiously, Emile knocked quietly. For a few tense moments, he wondered whether Gilles was inside, or whether he too had died in Montségur that afternoon, or whether he had been taken by the Germans. His heart rate slowed when he heard the sounds of activity behind the door.

"Who is there?" demanded the familiar voice.

"Emile," he whispered.

Emile heard the crack of the large bolts as Gilles slid them back. The door opened just enough to allow him in.

Gilles locked the door behind him before coming over to Emile and giving him a forceful hug that took his breath away. "I was beginning to worry about you, my friend. The hour is late. But it seems you and the satchel have evaded those Nazi swine."

"Everything on the mountain went according to plan, but what happened down here? What happened to the prisoners?"

"Ah! What happened down here? Well that is the question." He rubbed his chin.

"Gilles, tell me. I must know. What happened to the prisoners?"

"The plan worked well." He smiled broadly, putting his arm around Emile. "As we had anticipated, the Germans gave the order to set fire to the pyre. They threw the torch on to the tinder that we had placed around the pile and had soaked in paraffin. It did its job. It created enough thick black, acrid smoke within a few minutes to obscure the center of the pile we had doused in water. My men, who had been hiding in the tunnels we had concealed within the pile, emerged and quickly cut the prisoners free from the stakes. The flames started to advance upon them rapidly, but fortunately, they managed to get everyone into the tunnels before they were overwhelmed."

Emile breathed a sigh of relief. "But what then? Did you manage to get everyone safely out?"

"We had also soaked the walls of the tunnels with water, and we threw water over everyone as they entered. It gave us just enough time to lead everyone into the main tunnel that led to the side of the pog. Under the cover of the smoke, we guided them the short distance to the caves you had shown us on Raymond de Péreille's map. The caves were cool inside, so they simply waited for the fire to die down and for the Germans to leave."

"Then everyone is safe?"

"A few people were burned, but nothing serious. Yes, my friend, thanks to you, everyone is safe!" he exclaimed joyfully. "The dead goats we hid in the pile were a nice touch too. The Germans thought they were smelling burning flesh. Let us have a drink. It has been a thirsty day's work but a very rewarding one."

Emile grinned. "Where is everyone?"

"I told them to go home and to lie low for a few days. The Germans will be leaving Carcassonne soon.

"And that resistance fighter? The Basque? Where did she go?"

"Ah, the Basque. I thought I had detected some special concern for her when you asked about her, so I brought her here."

Emile's heart pounded.

With a big smile, Gilles went to one of the bedrooms and knocked on the door. "Azeri, someone here wants to meet you," he bellowed.

A short while later, a bleary-eyed young woman came into the room looking extremely tired and dazed. Her face was very swollen and bruised, but for Emile, there was no mistaking her. She was the woman who had saved his life, the enigmatic Basque from the camp of the White Mouse he had fought alongside and had traveled south with.

She focused her tired eyes on Emile. Her expression changed from confusion to realization. "Zori!" She ran to him to hug him. "I thought you were dead!"

"I thought you were dead too!"

"Where have you been? You have come a long way since we first met. And how did you do what you did today?"

"A lot has happened since we parted. I have much to tell you, but it can wait. You will need several days to recover. We will have plenty of time to talk."

"I look forward to it," beamed Azeri. "After that, we will continue our journey to Spain. I owe you at least that much."

Emile looked at Gilles and at Azeri. "No. I have decided to stay here. The war will be over soon, and our challenge will be to build a better world. I have learned much here that might help with that. I was hoping you might join me."

ಎ ... ... ಡ

At the end of seven hundred years, the laurel will be green once more.
  —Anonymous troubadour, thirteenth century

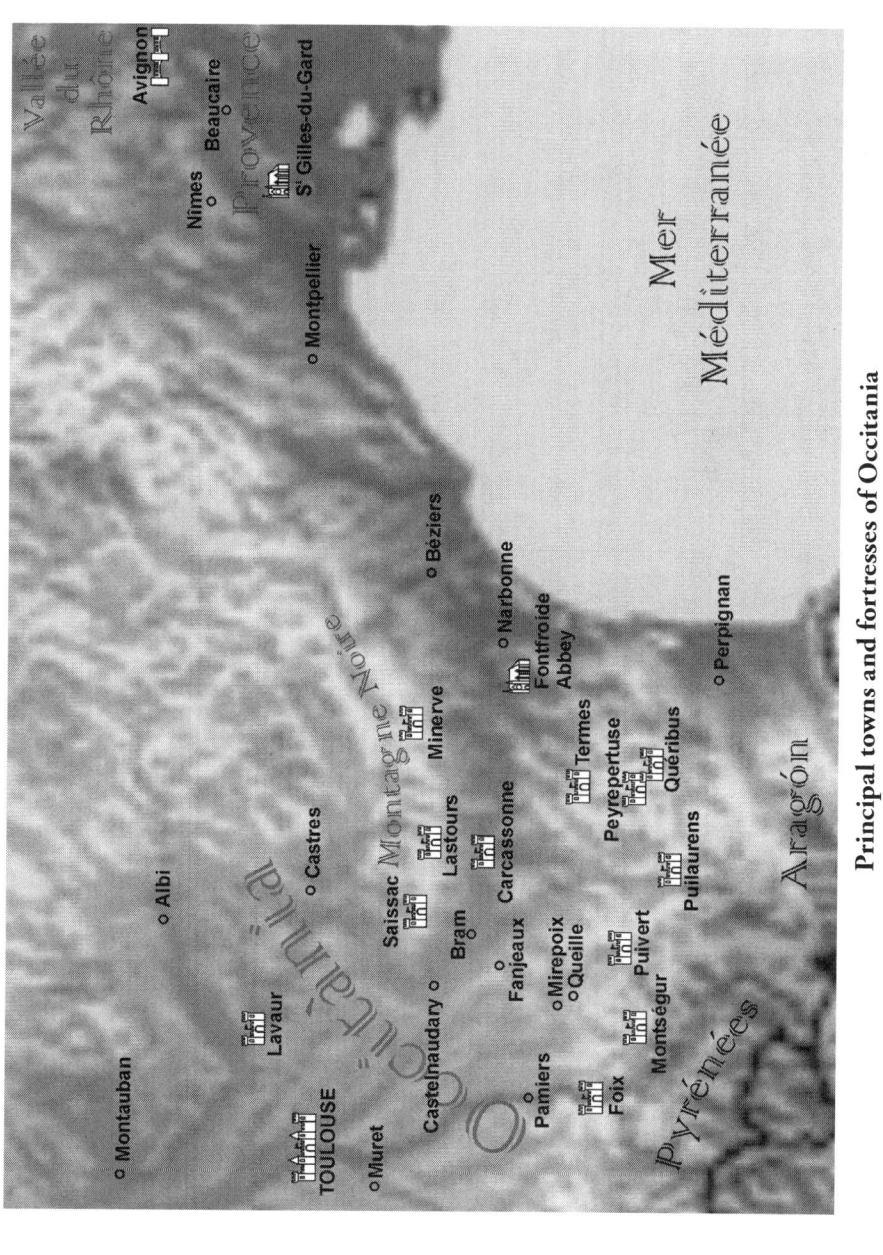

Principal towns and fortresses of Occitania

Timeline of the Feudal Oligarchy

Year	1198	1200	1202	1204	1206	1208	1210	1212	1214	1216	1218	1220	1222	1224	1226	1228	1230	1232	1234	1236	1238	1240	1242	1244

Papacy: Innocent III | Honorius III | Gregoire IX | Innocent IV

French Monarch: Philippe Auguste II | Louis VIII (le Lion) | Blanche de Castille | Louis IX (St. Louis)

English Monarch: Richard I | John Lackland (Prince John) | Henry III

Count de Toulouse: Raymond VI | Raymond VII

Crusade Leader: Arnaud Amaury | Simon IV de Montfort | Amaury VI de Montfort | Blanche de Castille

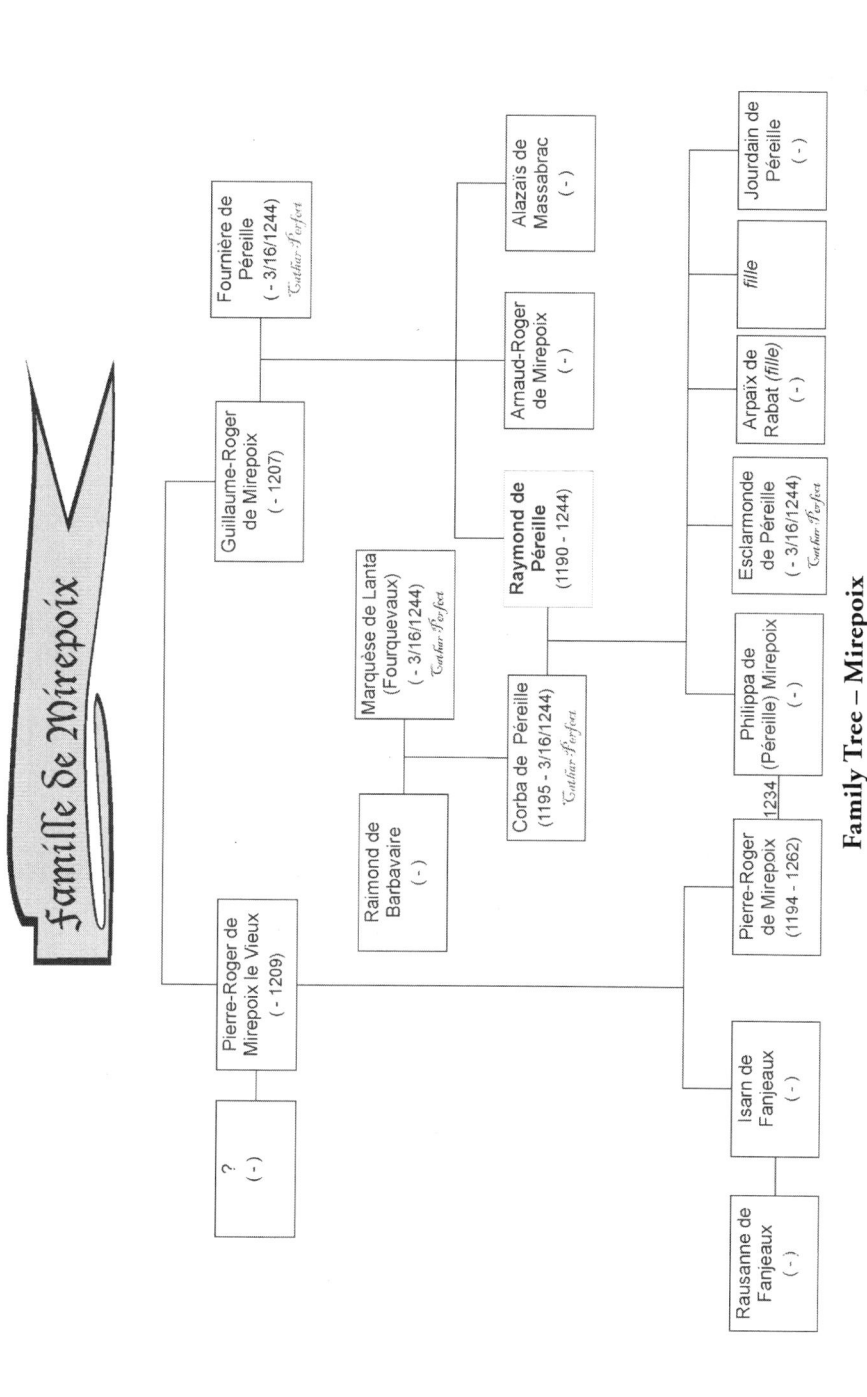

Family Tree – Mirepoix

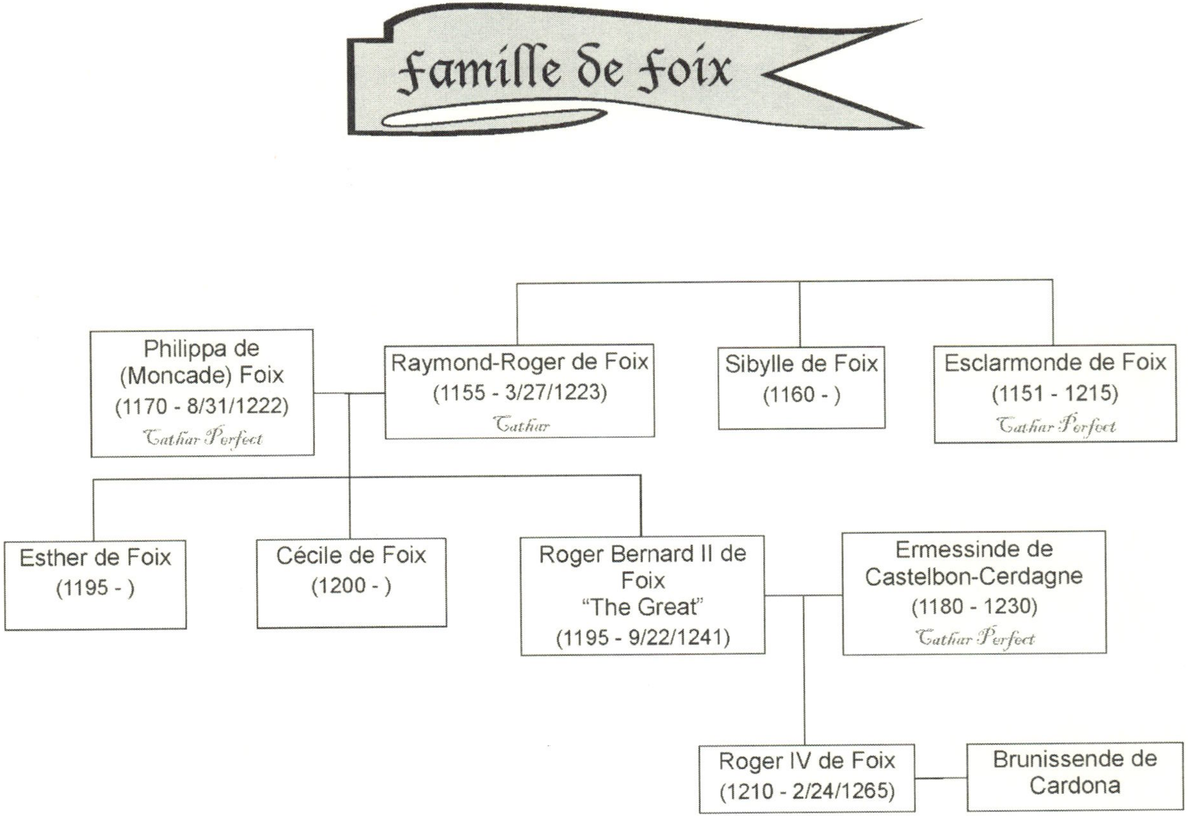

Famille de Foix

```
                    ┌─────────────────────┬──────────────────┐
                    │                     │                  │
          Raymond-Roger de Foix      Sibylle de Foix    Esclarmonde de Foix
            (1155 - 3/27/1223)         (1160 - )          (1151 - 1215)
                 Cathar                                    Cathar Perfect
                    │
                    │
        ┌───────────┴───────────┐
        │                       │
  Philippa de            Roger Bernard II de         Ermessinde de
  (Moncade) Foix               Foix                Castelbon-Cerdagne
  (1170 - 8/31/1222)         "The Great"             (1180 - 1230)
   Cathar Perfect          (1195 - 9/22/1241)        Cathar Perfect
        │                                                   │
   Cécile de Foix                                    Roger IV de Foix    ─── Brunissende de
     (1200 - )                                      (1210 - 2/24/1265)        Cardona
        │
   Esther de Foix
     (1195 - )
```

Family Tree – Foix

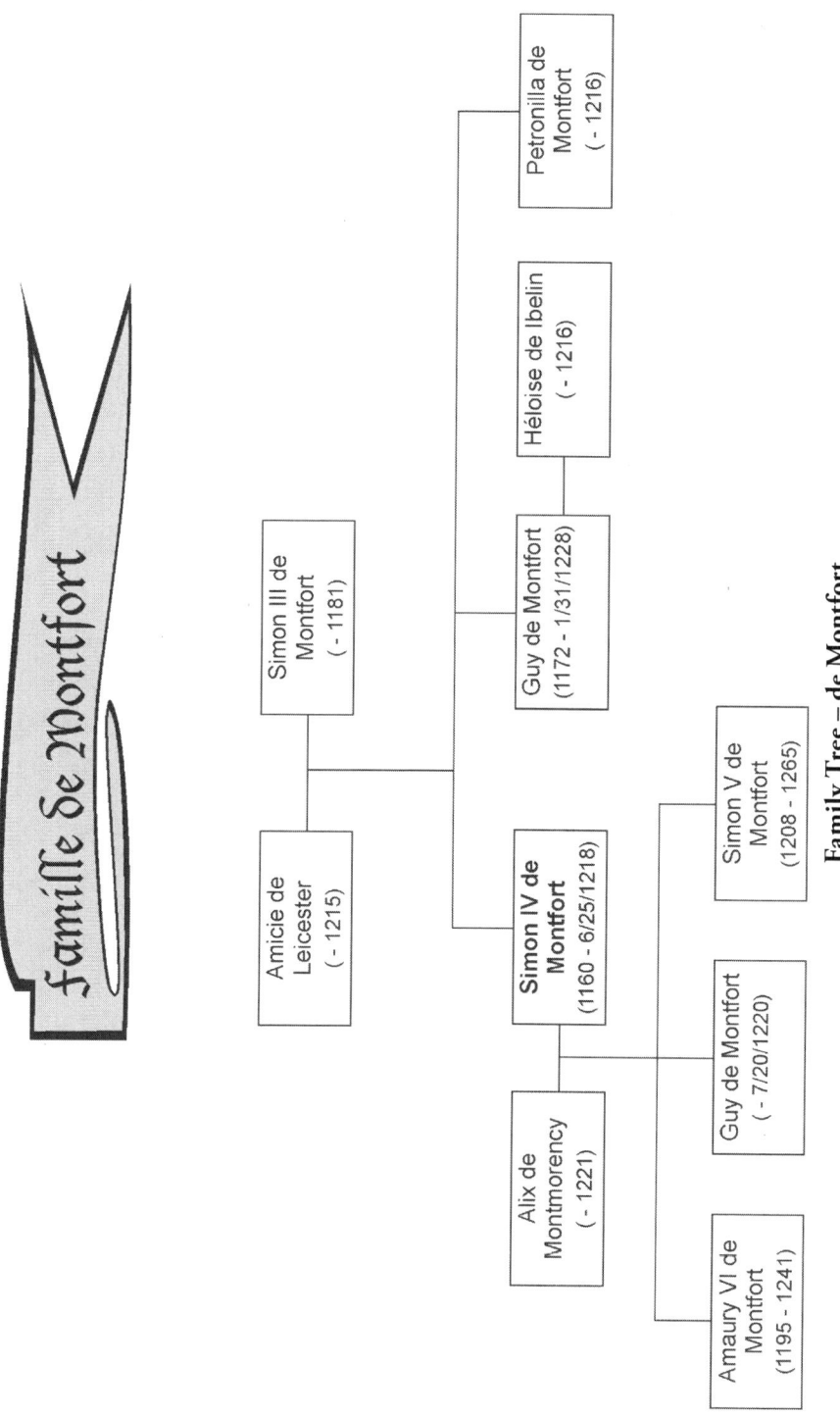

Family Tree – de Montfort

Epilogue

As was stated in the preface, the vast majority of people and events in this tale are as close to the historical record as the author could make them. Emile, Azeri, and a few of their contemporaries were created to help guide the reader through the historical events.

The burning of the contemporary Cathars at Montségur was fictional, created to try to give the real-life events some closure and some hope for the future. Nonetheless, there are indeed modern-day Cathars both in Europe and the U.S. and the movement has been seeing a re-birth in recent times.

The interest, verging on obsession, of the Ahnenerbe-SS and Heinrich Himmler in finding the treasure of the Cathars is entirely factual.

A memorial stands today about four kilometers east of St. Léonard de Noblat on N141, commemorating the spot where Major Kämpfe was kidnapped on 9 June 1944 by the French resistance. He was taken to the nearby town of Cheissoux and was eventually executed.

General Eisenhower recognized that the abduction of Major Kämpfe by the resistance had delayed the march of the SS armored Division Das Reich toward the Normandy by forty-eight hours and thereby saved the allied bridgehead. There is no evidence Major Kämpfe was ever taken to Oradour-sur-Glane.

It is common practice to recount to young, impressionable minds in Sunday school how the Romans cruelly persecuted and murdered early Christians for their beliefs. However, the persecution of the Christians by the Romans was as a drop of dew before a hurricane. Down the ages, the overwhelming majority of Christians who were brutalized and killed for their faith were persecuted not by Romans but by fellow Christians. Also,

Christians have killed a vastly greater number of people for refusing to accept their beliefs than was ever the reverse.

The Albigensian Crusades launched by the Church of Rome brutally destroyed one of the most peaceful, cultivated, and prosperous areas of thirteenth-century Europe. It is estimated that close to a million people, much of the population of southern France, were murdered by the church's henchmen. Among them were men, women, children, and babies of all faiths, including Catholic. For comparison, the Romans are estimated to have killed about two thousand Christians.

In recognition of his enthusiastic efforts to seek out and burn alive any who spoke out against his will, or that of the church, and in whose name the the pogrom against the Algigensians was initiated, Pierre de Castelnau was beatified by Pope Innocent III.

After eight hundred years, the Church of Rome finally expressed its regret at the brutal sacking and pillaging of Constantinople by the Fourth Crusade of 1204. In 2004, Pope John Paul II accepted responsibility and offered a formal apology to the patriarch of Constantinople. However, the majority of valuable articles, religious relics, statues, paintings, and other riches taken by the crusaders have yet to be returned.

To this day, the Church of Rome has never apologized for its instigation of, and zealous participation in, the genocide against the Albigensians.

The youngest son of the crusader Simon de Montfort, brother of Amaury, bore his father's name Simon V de Montfort. He led a rebellion against King Henry II of England in 1263, which stripped the king of much of his authoritarian power. In acknowledgement of this, he is regarded as one of the fathers of modern democracy and as such was rewarded with a relief of his likeness on the wall of the chambers of the US House of Representatives.

Despite this honor, however, he was far from enlightened; he shared his family's hatred of those who challenged the teachings of the church. As Earl of Leicester, he banished all Jews from the town, in his words "to the end of the world."

The Good Christians, or Cathars, were pacifists. Yet they were brutally exterminated, in the name of religion, in an attempt to eradicate progressive ideas that terrified those in power. The Albigensian crusade largely succeeded in eliminating the heretical religion and its followers, but not its ideals. Many of the Cathar beliefs, which they valued above their lives, are today taken for granted in most modern pluralistic societies. Tolerance for other races and religions; the right to speak freely; the right of women to own property, inherit, or become priests; the belief that arts such as music and poetry enrich life more than warfare; acceptance that vegetarians are not evil; the right to read scriptures alone; that none has special powers entitling them to sell eternal forgiveness to another; the belief that materialism should not be the ultimate goal of humanity.

We shall never know if these foundations of modern civilization might have taken hold much earlier if the Albigensian crusade had not taken place.